UNDERMONEY

A NOVEL

JAY NEWMAN

SCRIBNER

NEW YORK LONDON TORONTO SYDNEY NEW DELHI

SCRIBNER
An Imprint of Simon & Schuster, Inc.
1230 Avenue of the Americas
New York, NY 10020

First Scribner hardcover edition January 2022

SCRIBNER and design are registered trademarks of The Gale Group, Inc., used under license by Simon & Schuster, Inc., the publisher of this work.

For information about special discounts for bulk purchases, please contact Simon & Schuster Special Sales at 1-866-506-1949 or business@simonandschuster.com.

The Simon & Schuster Speakers Bureau can bring authors to your live event. For more information or to book an event, contact the Simon & Schuster Speakers Bureau at 1-866-248-3049 or visit our website at www.simonspeakers.com.

Manufactured in the United States of America

10 9 8 7 6 5 4 3 2 1

Library of Congress Cataloging-in-Publication Data

Names: Newman, Jay Hartley, author.
Title: Undermoney : a novel / Jay Newman.
Description: First Scribner hardcover edition. | New York : Scribner, 2022.
Identifiers: LCCN 2021022976 (print) | LCCN 2021022977 (ebook) | ISBN 9781982156022 (hardcover) | ISBN 9781982156046 (ebook)
Subjects: LCSH: International finance—Corrupt practices—Fiction. | Black market in foreign exchange—Fiction. | LCGFT: Political fiction. | Action and adventure fiction.
Classification: LCC PS3614.E62616 U53 2022 (print) | LCC PS3614.E62616 (ebook) | DDC 813/.6—dc23
LC record available at https://lccn.loc.gov/2021022976
LC ebook record available at https://lccn.loc.gov/2021022977

ISBN 978-1-9821-5602-2
ISBN 978-1-9821-5604-6 (ebook)

For Elissa, Freddie, and Zach

undermoney [əndər mənē]

> noun, obscure, trans. from the Japanese (アンダーマネー)
> wasei-eigo (和製英語, Japanese-made English)
>
> 1: money which is unknown publicly but that controls individuals
> and events
>
> 2: the currency of corruption
>
> 3: bribery (賄賂)
>
> See also *blood money.*

Prelude

Rwaished District, Jordan

Five hours out from al-Tanf, Syria, a military base controlled for the moment by the U.S. Army, Staff Sergeant Chappie James walked into the cockpit and handed the copilot a printout. New orders, new coordinates: a change of plans.

Moments later, his superior officer, Major Hank Arnold slipped into his pilot's chair and pulled on his headset. "This had better be good."

Capped-out on promotion, relegated to flying transport and biding his time until his pension kicked in, Major Hank could not control much in his life. But nap time, that was sacrosanct. He snatched the printout. When he looked up, his face was red.

"They want us to make the drop and fly straight back to Andrews. We're not going on to Incirlik."

Arnold had been looking forward to overnighting at the massive U.S. base in Turkey, sleeping in a bed. Now he'd have to stay in the air for another night and another round of air-to-air refueling.

His day had started fifteen hours earlier when Staff Sergeant James arrived at Andrews Air Force Base in Maryland trailed by two unmarked 18-wheelers belonging to the Federal Reserve Bank of New York, each carrying half of a $2.4 billion withdrawal from a Fed warehouse in East Rutherford, New Jersey—a million square feet, the world's largest repository of American currency, hidden in plain sight in the Jersey Meadowlands, just across the highway from a Home Depot. Now it would be another fifteen hours before he would see an actual bed. He hated it when stupid people—all people, really—made him do stupid things. Like dumping twelve 463L master pallets of perfectly good American dollars, each weighing almost four thousand pounds, out the back end of his C-17's massive hold and into a patch of the world's ugliest desert. He knew exactly where all that money would end up: in the hands of some of the world's worst people who would use it to buy weapons that would destroy nations that had not attacked the United States and posed no threat to American national security.

Ever since the Coalition Provisional Authority—the legally dubious governmental body that oversaw the festival of chaos, blood, and greed that was post-invasion Iraq—had pioneered the risible strategy of using U.S. dollars as a prime engine of U.S. foreign policy and military strategy, billions of greenbacks, measured by the ton and delivered by long-haul aircraft, had poured out over the Middle East, *"Al-mutar lakhdar,"* the Arabs called it. Green rain. The equation was simple: cash from above or death from above. A bribe or a drone strike. *Take the money and we'll pretend to be friends. Don't and we'll be enemies. And we won't be pretending.*

Major Arnold's copilot directed his attention to the display on which she had plotted new coordinates for the drop: fifty-five miles south of al-Tanf, a flat patch of sand in the Rwaished District, Jordan. Three miles west of the Iraqi border and a mile north of the Baghdad International Highway, the region's only major artery, stretching across mostly empty desert from the Iraqi capital, through Jordan, and all the way to the Mediterranean.

Arnold hadn't seen one of these last-minute diversions in years, not since the cowboy days of looting and shooting after Baghdad fell. No explanation then either. Whoever gave the order had to have some serious stroke.

"Where's this coming from?" Arnold tapped his fingers.

"Army two-star, Major General Thomas Taylor."

"Never heard of him." Arnold crumpled the printout into a ball and tossed it aside. "Reason they're having us drop our load in the middle of nowhere is they don't want anyone to see who picks up all that dough. Us included."

"The guy's very low profile. Delta Force. Ran JSOC in Iraq and Afghanistan," James said. "He just moved into some big new Pentagon job."

Typical, thought Arnold as he settled deeper into his seat, probably more of a politician than a soldier. The cargo manifest identified the source of their shipment as frozen Syrian accounts traceable right back to leaders of the Syrian army, Syrian military intelligence—the al-*Mukhabarat*—and Asma al-Assad, the stunning, cold-hearted wife of Syria's dictator.

"Just to be sure, ask for confirmation."

"Already have," replied the copilot. "It's Taylor's call sign. Looks like it's his operation."

Arnold stared out the window, resigned. The new kind of war. Someone else's country, someone else's money. But, always, American lives. *My last tour.*

"Okay then, punch it in. We're heading for Jordan."

Three hours later, Arnold took a wide turn over the sprawling refugee camp outside of Rwaished, a small city grown fat on smuggling in the years since the Assad family and the American army had turned the neighborhood into a permanent war zone. He brought the plane down to fifteen hundred feet to take a look: nothing for miles except a few dusty buildings at the Al Karamah border crossing, some camels, and corduroy dunes. And God only knew how many stinger missiles, AK-47s, IEDs, and roving bands of Syrian regular army, Islamic State bandits, Syrian rebels, and local tribes playing all sides against one another.

At the drop point, six Humvees, two semitrailers, and several heavy-duty forklifts. Half a dozen people in the lee of the trucks. A few hundred yards off from the cluster of semis and Humvees, Arnold spotted three GAZ-2330 Tigrs, the Russian equivalent of a Humvee, just sitting there. That made no sense. Russians and Americans kept their distance in Syria, engaging only through deconfliction lines and through proxies. He'd been making these runs for years, and this was a first. So many shadows in a land with so little shade.

Arnold tipped his wings, acknowledging the crew on the ground, and took a wide turn as he descended. At one thousand feet, James opened the rear cargo door. Even after hundreds of drops, it was still a rush—the roar of air, the light flooding into the plane's dark cabin, the heat rising from the desert, and the earth unrolling beneath them, all framed by the jagged maw of the cargo door.

At five hundred feet, two miles from the target, Arnold gave the all clear and James released the floor brakes. Slowly at first, and then *thwack, thwack, thwack* twelve times, a pallet every second, followed by a parachute blooming in the desert sky.

Arnold took the C-17 up and turned to catch the view. A lovely, crazy, breathtaking sight. Twenty-four million one-hundred-dollar bills, floating gently toward the hard sand.

———

Below, standing on the desert floor next to her Humvee, Greta Webb fixed her binoculars on the first pallet drifting down toward her. The landscape shimmered, but she barely registered the vicious heat. Just another day, she told herself, another test, another mission. But one that might divert the course of history—or land them all in Leavenworth for the rest of their lives.

"Beautiful sight." Don Carter, standing next to her, looked up from his phone and squinted at the merciless blue sky. "Hope we know what the fuck we're doing."

Was it only twenty-nine hours ago they had been shredding the sheets at his Georgetown house, falling back into a hole it had taken them both years to crawl out of. Greta lowered her desert goggles and watched Don survey his team, ex–Special Forces, now under contract to Carter Logistics, all of them standing crisply in line, field glasses locked on the descending pallets. The only one she knew was Chip Beekman, a top lieutenant in Don's old Delta team. Aloof, an Ivy Leaguer who looked and acted it. But you didn't go to war these days without an IT guy, and Don said there was no one better than Chip at protecting their own cyber networks and penetrating others.

She elbowed Don and tilted her head toward the drop zone. The pilot knew his business; the pallets were landing in a tight cluster. Success would not be measured by what went right, but how they reacted to things that went wrong. She needed both trucks loaded and the whole convoy rolling out across the sand in six minutes. It was two hundred miles to the crossing at Beit She'an. Once they got to Israel, she'd be able to breathe again. Israelis were expensive, but consistent. Until then, no margin for error.

"I was just looking at Ben's latest tweets," Don mused, while his team scrambled into action. He spoke calmly, almost distractedly, as if reading a newspaper over morning coffee. "He's gonna blow his political career if he keeps on about decimating the Pentagon budget." The last pallet hit the desert floor. Don hardly seemed to notice. "As usual, we're out here risking our asses for him, and he's off on his own looking for a burning building to run into. You'd think the junior senator from Nebraska could keep his mouth shut for a few minutes."

Greta didn't bother to answer. Eyes forward, she pulled on her helmet and jumped into the Humvee, barely giving Don time to scramble into his seat.

"Forklifts!" she barked into her microphone and hit the gas. Suddenly, every piece was moving: the Humvees, the lifts, the 18-wheelers. They had planned everything down to the second, but were always ready to veer sharply from the playbook and improvise. Without hesitation or mercy, as Tommy Taylor liked to say.

The semis, flanked by the forklifts, moved into the drop zone, while Greta and Don joined the other five Humvees to establish a tight perimeter around the twelve large wood crates. Two hundred yards out, in Greta's peripheral vision, three Tigrs raced into position to form a second perimeter. Two defensive rings: one manned by Don's guys, the other by their Russian contractors. Don had no choice but to trust them, but he brought a massive arsenal just in case. The essence of Don, Greta thought, defended to the point of overkill, yet somehow vulnerable to his own explosive nature.

Four minutes later, a forklift loaded the last of the pallets into the first semitrailer, and their men began loading the forklifts themselves into the second. Ahead of schedule. Too good to be true. Then the radio crackled in her ear.

"Squad leader." It was Tommy. That voice, threatening and reassuring at once, part drill sergeant, part priest. Of course he had an eye on them. Where was he? Langley? The Pentagon? Had to be Langley, since she was the only one on the team still on active duty. Her case officer's blue badge provided agency cover. She worried that it was the only reason Tommy wanted her on the team.

"You have two Kamaz Typhoons approaching. Six miles northeast. Doing about fifty." Tommy was speaking a little more slowly than usual, laconic but also urgent, as if he was trying to relax into the chaos he saw coming. She knew that cadence: time to go off book.

"Typhoons are Russian armored personnel carriers." Chip chimed in over the radio. "Heavy, but fast. Probably Syrian army. Assad buys them by the boatload."

"How many men on board?" Greta asked curtly. She didn't need Chip demonstrating how much he knew about Russian military hardware right now.

"Two up front, sixteen in the back. AGS-30 grenade launchers on the roof. Thirty rounds each—range of two thousand meters." Don leaned into his mic and glared at Greta.

"Weren't your Russians supposed to keep the flies away?"

Tommy cut in.

"We've identified the markings. Presidential Guard."

Greta took a deep breath. They'd run dozens of scenarios. The Syrian dictator throwing his special forces into the fray might have been the one she dreaded the most.

"Don, your take?" Tommy asked.

Of course he doesn't ask me, Greta thought.

"Either Greta's Russian friends are fucking with us, or an enterprising Syrian army commander smelled burgers and invited himself to our barbecue."

Or both, Greta thought. The levels of greed people were capable of still astonished her. She had promised the Russians $50 million to protect their operation from any surprises. Now they were sending local thugs out to shake her down for more. "They'll be up your asses in five minutes." Tommy, again, impatient. "Don, what's your plan?"

"Can't outrun them. Our semis aren't nearly fast enough."

"I didn't ask what's *not* your plan," Tommy said coldly. "If you can't light these guys up, I will."

Before Greta could bring the Humvee to a complete stop, Don was out the door, dragging an FGM-148 Javelin antitank missile and launcher behind him, and plugging his ever-present camera into the sight. A sharp whistle brought the rest of his team out onto the sand, readying their own missile launchers. A drone strike was the last thing they wanted, especially one ordered from inside CIA headquarters by a two-star general. The electronic signature of American Hellfire missiles, launched from a Predator drone cruising over a patch of sand where American and Russian military deployments intersected, hitting a target inside Jordan—an American ally—would light up half of the world's intelligence services. Tommy had taken enough risks. They had to keep him off the field. Which gave Don two choices: Erase a couple of trucks full of al-Assad all-stars and blame it on the fog of war. Or incinerate the semis they'd just loaded, get the hell out of there, and wait for another clean shot at a jumbo jet loaded with cash streaking over the desert. Like that would ever happen. Don and four of his men readied their Javelins. All it took was a tap on the trigger and the fire-and-forget infrared guidance system would do the rest. The Syrian carriers would be in range in less than three minutes.

From the start, Don thought it was a mistake to bring in the Russian security contractors. That had been Greta's idea. She had convinced them, a year earlier in Ben's Senate office, when they first started talking about the heist. Everyone agreed that the logic of grabbing the money was unassailable: Why let it disappear into the Syrian desert, where it would only be fuel for more corruption, more killing, when they could use it to actually help their own country? They would keep it somewhere safe for a few years, until Ben decided he was ready to run for the presidency. The strategy was to use the money to prime the pump, dominate the first round of primaries, and become the front-runner, not beholden to anyone: the people's candidate. And then to march steadily to the nomination, laying waste to anyone who stood in the way, a political campaign conceived with the failure-is-not-an-option discipline of a military offensive. These days, that took billions.

Greta had insisted that they would need help getting the cargo out of Syria and Jordan. Quiet soundings had led her to the Parsifal Group, one of a new, entrepreneurial breed of Russian private military companies that sold what they termed "in-theater services" to almost anyone, as long as the price was right. Off-budget and out-of-sight, and offering lethality, reliability, and deniability. The three most valuable and expensive commodities in modern warfare.

She had argued that no one navigated Syria's unstable political landscape more surely. If anyone could provide safe passage through the gauntlet of al-Assad's forces, tribal militias, Al Qaeda, and ISIS, they could. The cost was high, but it would be much higher if they got sideways with Parsifal.

But can we trust them? Ben had asked. Greta wouldn't guarantee success; she said the risks were manageable. Parsifal had done a couple of jobs for the Agency. They knew that there would be more business to come. Why would they mess that up? Think of it as insurance.

Whatever doubts Don had, Chip dispelled them. She hadn't expected that. Her ideas usually elicited only patronizing lectures from Chip, but he seemed more enthusiastic about the Russians than she was. Parsifal was the best, he had said. They were Russian, but as solid as they come. His old friend from Princeton, Vadim Ivanov, was the number-two there. Chip could make the introduction. Parsifal would provide all the insurance they'd need. Ben and Tommy were convinced.

As Don and his team assembled their weapons, Greta knew exactly what he was thinking: that the only insurance policy he trusted was one that could pierce tank armor. Don, already on autopilot, knelt into position and hoisted the heavy Javelin launcher onto his shoulder.

"*Wait*," she shouted, hoping he was still able to hear another voice besides the one in his head. "I need to talk to Ivanov first."

"Vadim, tell me again how you got your American girlfriend to pay so much?" Fyodor Volk, the Parsifal Group's charismatic founder, was sitting in the passenger seat of one of the Tigrs.

Ensuring safe passage for a high-value convoy through a war zone was Parsifal's bread and butter. A job that involved only escorting a few trucks through the desert wasn't usually enough to draw Fyodor Volk from the sixty-meter, carbon fiber sloop he called home, docked these days for reasons of location and legality, in the barely tolerable Cypriot port of Limassol.

Volk had flown in that morning because he was curious about the American client Ivanov had landed, this woman Greta Webb who had presented herself as a war-theater contractor for an undisclosed government, and then had agreed to pay $50 million for what seemed like a simple job. He also worried that Vadim, who was getting more and more comfortable in Brioni suits, might be out of his depth. Vadim wouldn't like the intrusion, but if problems arose, he might benefit from his presence.

They had been baking for hours in the hot sun, air-conditioning on full blast, to no effect.

"Once she said that it was an airdrop—and so close to their base at al-Tanf—I figured the cargo was something special. I named what I thought was a stupid number. She just nodded."

Through binoculars, they picked up two large dust clouds on the flat horizon: the Syrians.

"Looks like *mademoiselle* has discovered this might be more difficult than she thought."

Volk put down his field glasses and fixed his cold blue eyes on his number two.

"What *are* you up to, Vadim?"

"Just my job, sir." Ivanov shifted in his seat. The boss's standing orders were clear. No freelancing. Vadim may have learned how to work the corridors of power in Moscow and Washington, but he didn't think like a soldier anymore. Out here, his job was to play it straight. Provide the escort. Gather intelligence. Get paid.

"Don't bullshit me, Vadim. Who's out there in the Typhoons?"

Ivanov tried to maintain his composure.

"We've spread a lot of money around to create a bubble for the Americans out here. Maybe Suleimani couldn't resist having a look."

Qassem Suleimani, the diminutive and enigmatic leader of Iran's Quds Force, a man who could make trouble—or stop it—anywhere in the Middle East, but who cast a particularly long shadow in Syria. Not likely, Volk thought. Suleimani would never be so obvious.

He drew his binoculars back up to his eyes and let silence linger. One beat. Two beats. Long enough for Vadim to get the message. And then, matter-of-factly, he asked, "Why would my friend Qassem get between me and one of our clients?"

Ivanov turned to Volk.

"It was an opportunity—create a little noise. See what these Americans are made of. Shake them down, take whatever we can get. Maybe even hijack the whole cargo."

Without warning, Volk's hand—with the weight of his arm behind it—shot out and struck Ivanov beneath his left eye. In the confines of the Tigr cab, the slap across Ivanov's face sounded like a thunder clap. A welt began to rise where Volk's heavy, gold Federal Security Service—FSB—ring had caught Ivanov's cheekbone. Volk's thin upper lip disappeared into a tight saurian smile.

"I don't know exactly what you're up to, but this is not how we do business—it's dumb. Makes us look incompetent—not to mention dishonest."

Ivanov accepted his punishment without reacting. Impressive, thought Volk, and well trained. The young man was not easily rattled.

"Sir, I'm almost positive they are operating without official sanction. The girl's name is Greta Webb. I don't know much about her, except that her father was Iranian and she works for the CIA—"

Volk cut him off.

"Who are the guys with her?"

"You'd expect an active-duty team. That's how the Americans do these things. But those guys were rented. Very expensive—former Delta, Green Berets. *Kontraktniki.* The way *we* do it."

"So you decided that, if they're going off the books, you would too?"

"I wanted to find out what was being dropped. I thought if I tipped off a couple of Syrians—"

"Vadim, they've been dropping pallets like these all over the Middle East for more than a decade. How many did you count?"

"Twelve, sir."

"Yes. And do you know what's inside each one? Two hundred million dollars. That's more than two billion in American dollars over there."

Ivanov did a double take. It hadn't occurred to him the boxes were full of cash.

"And we're going to let them drive away with it?"

"Exactly."

"That's crazy. It's free money. I made a deal with the Syrians to split whatever we found in the trucks down the middle."

"Vadim, if you take the money, all you get is money. Smarter, I think, to watch where it's going, figure out who these people are. If they can execute an operation like this, there's no telling what else they are capable of. It would be a shame not to be part of their project, no?"

"*Ivanov,*" Greta interrupted sharply over the radio, speaking Russian. "Tell me what those Typhoons are doing here."

Volk hit the mute button on Vadim's microphone. "Tell your girlfriend we'll handle the Syrians." Volk's voice was much softer. Volk drew his hand back.

"I was just about to alert you," Ivanov said into the mic. "We're heading out to intercept them now."

"Don't bother."

They saw jets of flame and, even from their distance, felt the pulse of heat as five Javelins emerged from the Americans' shoulder-mounted launching tubes. The inelegant rockets, which had the contours of stubby pencils with flippers stuck to their back ends, hovered momentarily in midair, blunt noses dipping slightly, before their rocket motors ignited and they shot upward parabolically: the "curveball" shot. At five hundred feet, the missiles paused again while their infrared seekers searched for a heat signature. Once the five missiles locked onto the Syrian army vehicles below, now just three miles away, they pivoted and plunged downward in tight formation, piercing the lids of the troop carriers. Seconds later, angry black plumes erupted on the horizon, sending geysers of smoke and flame a thousand feet high, pulverizing metal, ceramic armor, and rubber. Vaporizing the souls of a few dozen men.

"We're heading out." Greta, speaking to Ivanov, all business. No mention of the mayhem she had just ordered up. "I want one of your trucks out in front. The rest bringing up the rear. We'll settle up when we get to the Israeli border."

Ivanov noticed the tension drain from Volk's body. "I like that girl. No hesitation."

The convoy fell into line, with Russian Tigrs leading and following. Ivanov took up the rear.

Volk settled back into his seat. "Whoever these Americans are, they're enterprising. Good job connecting with them. But they will learn, I am sure, that that much money, acquired through such means, can quickly become a burden. An albatross. Perhaps even a noose."

Part One:

Spring, Three Years Later

1

The Pierre Hotel, New York City

In a world of excess, nothing exceeded expectations like Elias Vicker's Fire Rites of Beltane, the legendary stag party he held every year on the first Tuesday of May, just as spring buds were bursting into the brightness of just-opened leaves, lending midtown streets a transitory illusion of innocence. For years, the hedge fund centibillionaire, dubbed by *Forbes* New York's richest man and by the *New York Post* its most odious clown, had taken over The Pierre Hotel on Fifth Avenue to cultivate a couple hundred carefully curated denizens of the hedge fund, finance, and political elite. To avoid an uproar, Vicker went to extraordinary lengths to make sure that the details of the party, as well as its guest list, remained closely guarded secrets. It was the perfect Elias Vicker event: no expense spared, perhaps defiant of the prevailing mood, but, really, just tone deaf. If someone took offense, Vicker seemed incapable of understanding why he should care. Nonetheless, grandees who should have known better showed up every year. Not simply to be part of the bacchanal, but, particularly after memories of the pandemic had faded, to be seen, to be chosen, to be part of the elect. They knew better, but, somehow, when the summons came, they couldn't help themselves. Not being there seemed a greater risk.

The fifteen public rooms of the hotel had been transformed to make them feel like deep woods, part of a Celtic ritual, celebrating life, fertility, and the power—and danger—of fire. Hundreds of trees had been trucked in to cover every wall and ceiling. The rooms, the halls, even the elevators, felt like clearings in a dense forest. Embedded in the foliage were dozens of forest nymphs wearing nothing but body paint. Only their eyes moved. The whites of their scleras—in sharp contrast to the sylvan tones of the brown and green body paint that covered their skin—followed the flow of millionaires, billionaires, and covetous politicians, promising, posturing, and pandering.

Under the sure hand of his majordomo, Pete Stryker, Vicker quietly invited the finalists from international beauty pageants that consistently attracted the most alluring women on earth: Slovenian Beauties, Magyar Stars, Miss Teen Poland, Miss Ukraine, Caucausus Debs, Girls of the Russian Steppes. The girls were treated to two weeks of theater, fashion shows, ballet, educational programs, and dinners with men that Vicker sought to cultivate and compromise. Given that the girls were housed at a Times Square tourist hotel, packed five to a room, and given a measly five hundred dollars a day, they soon figured out that, if they wanted to eat at Le Bilboquet and shop at Bergdorf's, they needed friends.

The hungry beauty queens roamed the hotel, scantily clad, each wearing a gold Cartier bracelet discreetly engraved with a number. Nothing spoken or required, and, well, there was not much to be said about what happened between consenting adults. The fantasy that Vicker created was so compelling that it was almost as if a fog had settled over them all, the minds of his guests clouded not so much by tequila as by a more toxic brew. The combination of otherwise unattainable beauty, proximity to Vicker's enormous wealth and power, and a distorted sense of community with other aggressive men caused them to swat away any moral impulse. Succumbing to a collective delusion, his guests became willing to indulge the inexcusable, to thumb their noses at behavior that could easily immolate them on a pyre of public humiliation and well-deserved damnation.

Within that miasma, Pete worked the room, placing an arm around socially inhibited quant geniuses, whispering morsels of gossip in the ears of influential senators, and smoothing the feathers of hedge fund guys whom Vicker had pissed off. At every step, he introduced his sometimes charming, sometimes reticent boss casually, but purposefully. Senior bankers, political pundits, and erstwhile competitors were, none too subtly, encouraged to join forces with Elias Vicker rather than pick a fight. To a man, they knew full well that Vicker's fund—Industrial Strategies—dwarfed the $500 billion sovereign wealth funds generally considered to be the lions of the money jungle. And he liked nothing better than to unleash the dogs of law on anyone who got in his way. In the face of Vicker's legion of combative attorneys, only the very richest and most ruthless adversaries could hope for a fair fight.

"Senator Conway." Pete sidled up to Senate Majority Leader Frank Conway of Tennessee, a jowly potentate who ruled the center-right with an iron hand. "Do you have everything you need?"

Conway looked around as lissome elves slid through the crowd ferrying flutes of champagne and trays of blinis topped with Beluga caviar. "You've really stocked the pond this year, son," Conway purred, in his soft drawl.

Pete registered the barest reaction. He prided himself on knowing what made people tick, particularly powerful men like Conway who required elaborate care and feeding. Considering the range of perversions that he made it his business to know, the majority leader was plain vanilla: stock tips, sweetheart real estate deals, and pretty girls. Pete handed the senator a key card for the Presidential Suite, more than five thousand square feet, comprising the entire thirty-ninth floor.

"You have the best room in the house." Pete held out a small bag containing numbered poker chips, each one matching the number on a bracelet. Conway gave Pete his famously lascivious grin. "It's always fun matching the chip to the girl. But, listen up, Pete. Come see me real soon. We've got a real problem. Rachel can't hold off those pinkos in her cabinet much longer. They want to tax you hedge fund boys out of existence, and they're convinced they have the votes."

There was no greater proof of the strides women had made over the decades than the fact that a reassuring nonentity like Rachel Bridges had ascended to the White House. Nothing in the energetic seventy-five-year-old's biography said "first woman president." She'd burned no bras, broken no barriers, shattered no glass ceilings. Her appeal was that, in a time of turmoil, she liked to keep things just as they were. Or as close to it as possible. She wore bright headbands and approached politics as if her main responsibility was to make sure everyone was comfortable and well-behaved. Even though she'd been in the Senate for more than forty years, no one had a clear idea what she stood for, and no one much minded. She was kind and calm. In the moment, that was what mattered. As the country hovered on the edge of chaos, culture war grievances regularly erupting into spasms of violence and lunacy, she projected the comforting illusion that there were no differences that couldn't be resolved with a gin and tonic and a handwritten thank-you note. The right didn't completely hate her. The left viewed her with suspicion, obsessively parsing her every word and gesture for proof she was about to sell them out. The millions in the middle clung to the anxious hope that she could keep things from spinning out of control. It seemed like the best that anyone could hope for.

As president, she'd proven to be adept at delivering difficult news to the

American people with empathy and a certain resigned good sense, whether it was downplaying the impact of strict new pronoun regulations that had passed Congress after a bitter fight, or apologizing for the FBI's botched raid on the Baker County Oathkeepers compound in Eastern Oregon, where thirty-eight people died, half of them children and young mothers. As president, Bridges didn't actually want to soak the rich, but, shrugging her shoulders almost apologetically, claimed she didn't have much choice. Her increasingly restive party demanded it, as much for retribution as for revenue.

"Don't worry, we'll get her. My oppo guys are on her twenty-four/seven."

Conway looked disappointed.

"I keep telling you. It's that son of hers. That funny business with the Indian casinos. You nail that down, and we've got both of 'em. But it'll be expensive. Vicker and his buddies are going to have to dig deep."

As Pete tried to break away, Conway bore down on him, raising an index finger, poking him in the chest. "I've been looking for your buddy Ben Corn. I thought I told you to make sure he showed up tonight. Cost me a lot to get that boy on the finance committee. He needs to be out here bowing and scraping. Pretty boy thinks he's above it all."

Notwithstanding the efforts that Pete made to build a veil of secrecy around Vicker's annual bacchanal, there was no way Ben Corn would risk showing up—or that Pete would let him.

"His daughter had a dance recital, Senator. You know he *wanted* to be here."

Conway snorted. "I *don't* know that, Pete. But what I do know is that he's making mistakes all over. This business about canceling aircraft carriers is bad enough. You know what else he did? Just the other day, he went out to the Pentagon and told a roomful of admirals the entire U.S. Navy is obsolete. You think they like hearing that? From an army guy?" He wagged a long pink finger in front of Pete's face. "You better rein your boy in."

Conway shook his white mane. "Dance recital my ass."

He gave Pete's arm a friendly squeeze. "You know what I always say, son. Can't trust a man who won't commit at least two of the deadly sins right before your very eyes."

It was no secret to Pete that Ben's carefully cultivated public image of piety—his Boy Scout act—rubbed Conway the wrong way. Just as Conway was gearing up for another rant, an elf approached. "Oh hello, little lady." The senior senator grabbed a glass from her tray, and then turned back to Pete. "We can talk about this later, I've got to attend to some business."

To his relief, the senator drifted off. Chances are, Pete thought, he won't even remember the conversation. As he headed to the bar to get himself another glass of Badoit, he bumped into a bear of a man in a chalk-stripe suit and looked up to see the flushed, rubbery face of Jason Renton, the Wall Street columnist for *Roundelay* magazine, a venerable glossy that had been reinvented as a purveyor of high-end gossip and score-settling hatchet jobs masquerading as investigative journalism. A one-time high-flying bond trader whose career had spun out in a tornado of cocaine, six-figure bills at Scores, and a misguided bet, shorting puts on gold futures, Renton had gone through rehab; written a best-selling memoir, *Snorting Bull: Confessions of a Wall Street Wildman*; and reinvented himself as a droll truth-teller spilling the secrets of the temple. He had brought down venerable brokerage firms and exposed all manner of insider trading and Ponzi schemes. But he was hardly the fearless journalistic predator he made himself out to be. In fact, Pete thought of Renton as one of the most useful people in his bulging contact list. Because as much as Renton wanted to strike back at the world that had written him off, what he really wanted was its attention. Whenever Pete needed to bring someone down a notch or two, all he had to do was wind Renton up, point him in the right direction, and, a few times a year, fly a courier down to Panama City to deposit a cashier's check into his numbered bank account.

"Thanks for the invite, Pete."

"You know this evening is closed to the 'press.'" Pete said with mock seriousness.

"No worries. I left my notebook at home. I'm here to observe these strange creatures in their natural habitat—and maybe live like them for a few hours. Helps me understand them better."

"Well, I'm sure they'll appreciate your sacrifice." Pete craned his neck, checking the room. "I noticed that you called this afternoon. Sorry I didn't get back."

"It was nothing really. The column I'm working on just crashed and burned in fact-checking. These young kids. So serious. They're now telling me I have to record everything—is it my fault that I get my best stuff on private jets? It's a real problem. All you get is engine noise."

"Remind me never to invite you on Elias's plane again." Pete enjoyed sparring with Renton. He was one of the few people he dealt with who knew their place.

"Anyway, I have a deadline in two days and no column. I'm collecting the private newsletters that guys like Elias send to investors. I want to write about them. I know that I can't quote from them without permission, yada, yada, yada, but all the guys I've approached so far—Citadel, Two Sigma, Baupost, Pershing Square—have given me the go-ahead. Think the E-man would be okay with it? His *are* really interesting."

"Yeah, I don't see why not. Elias is really proud of those letters."

Right then, Pete noticed a striking young man—early thirties he guessed, European, blond, model handsome—emerge from a copse of spotlit birch trees and knife his way through the pillowy buzz. Every year, a few crashers managed to slip past security, and were quickly evicted. But this guy was ignoring the elves and the champagne, and heading straight for Pete. Probably best for a reporter, even one Pete owned, not to see this. Pete fished a numbered poker chip from his pocket.

"You've been a good boy this year, pal." Pete slapped it into Renton's hand. "Don't tell anyone where you got this."

———

"Can I help you?" Pete gently took the man by the elbow and maneuvered him behind a table that held an ice sculpture of a satyr mounting a forest nymph from behind. Whatever this man was doing here, he dressed the part: Anderson & Sheppard suit, Belgian shoes, Charvet tie. Pete used to think the obsession with high-end tailoring was just a foppish affectation of the very wealthy. But after being around Elias Vicker for a few years, he realized it was the opposite. A $20,000 bespoke suit was not clothing. It was armor. It sent a message that you were ready for things to get bloody.

"Mr. Stryker, apologies for the intrusion. Sven Rask." The young man extended a hand.

Stuck-up British accent, thought Pete, reeks of entitlement. Eurotrash probably. But there was a hardness to his eyes that Pete found disconcerting.

"Mr. Rask. This is a very private party. May I ask how you got in?"

The man ignored his question while maintaining eye contact. "I do not intend to stay, Mr. Stryker, but I represent one of Mr. Vicker's largest investors. My principal has a matter of some urgency to discuss with him."

"Here's my card." Pete reached into his pocket. "Call anytime. Feel free to grab a glass of champagne on your way out."

Rask, acting as if he did not even notice the proffered card, impatiently scanned the room. Whoever this asshole is, thought Pete, the last thing we need is a scene.

"Is that him?" The stranger pointed to an elegantly dressed man, late fifties, fit, six feet tall, with a thick, precisely styled mane, standing against the far wall, hunched over an iPhone, oblivious to the hubbub.

"Yes, it is, but Mr. Vicker appears to be attending to some important business."

"I understand that you are doing your job, but I must insist." As Rask strode off, Pete rushed nervously behind him.

Elias Vicker looked up as they approached and gave the intruder his trademark look, a blank, only slightly aggressive scowl that, in the lexicon of Vicker's body language, passed for friendly. Or, at least, not openly hostile. "Elias, I'd like to introduce you to Sven Rask. He says he represents one of our investors."

"Oh, now they're *our* investors." He looked up. "Who's this?"

Rask gave Vicker the barest nod and handed him a small calling card that read, simply: STICHTING ESKANDARFOND. Vicker tried to pocket it before Pete could see it, but, with years of experience in reading upside down on other peoples' desks, he managed a glimpse. Vicker raised his hand to crack a few knuckles, then shooed Pete away.

"Mr. Vicker." Rask spoke through his stiff upper lip. "We have a matter of some urgency. Wennerström sent me."

"Rask? Don't recognize the name. Have we met somewhere?" Vicker, spooked, tried his best to sound curt and imperious.

"No, sir, and please, call me Sven. I really cannot apologize enough for dropping in without an appointment." Rask enunciated, as if explaining something complicated to a tourist. "But, given the time pressure, Wennerström asked me to approach you soonest."

"Then please come by my office tomorrow."

Vicker stepped away brusquely. Whoever this Rask was, he was out of line. For years, there had been wild speculation about how Vicker had gotten his start—about who his original investors had been, and who his biggest investors were now. The answer, then and now, was Stichting Eskandarfond, SEF, a secretive, stateless investment fund that had been collecting assets since its founding in the 1600s by Amsterdam traders who pioneered the use of opaque legal structures to hide fortunes made moving slaves from Africa and tea from Ceylon. Even within Vicker's own firm, the relationship was treated like a state secret. Any dealings with SEF were shrouded by complex offshore corporate structures and trusts—no meetings, no calls, no emails, no memos. All communication with his silent investors came through his mentor, Lorenzo Gonzaga, vice chairman at Allard Frères et Cie and the man who had made the original introduction decades before. Until that moment, Vicker had never met anyone from SEF. Nor had he been terribly curious. Lorenzo saw to whatever caretaking they required.

Before Vicker could turn his back, the interloper wrapped a large hand around his forearm. Rask squeezed tightly. "I thought it more discreet to avoid your office. We are partners in a little project in the Berlin office with your nephew Oscar, and Oscar has become . . . shall we say . . . *difficult.*"

Partners? Oscar? Vicker willed himself to think hard, and fast.

"You have me at a disadvantage. If I knew more, I could speak with Oscar. Then we could have a constructive meeting." Vicker knew he shouldn't, but he couldn't help cracking his knuckles methodically. He tried to pull away, but Rask held on. Vicker looked around to see if anyone had noticed.

"Mr. Vicker, there is time *pressure.*" Rask squeezed even tighter. Vicker's hand was now numb. "Your nephew committed to open a letter of credit in support of a transaction in which my principals are investors. Unersättlich Vereinsbank—UVB—has still not issued the letter."

"But there's nothing we can do tonight is there? It's three in the morning in Berlin."

"With respect, my principal insists. He's outside. He does not like to be kept waiting."

Vicker hesitated.

"Perhaps we should call Wennerström." Rask reached for his phone. Vicker was stunned. Wennerström ran SEF. Gonzaga had always told him to be happy that he didn't have to deal with Wennerström's people directly.

"Fine." Vicker felt tightness in his chest. He needed space and air, and would say anything to get out from under Rask's grip. "Let me speak to a couple of people. I'll be with you shortly."

"Perhaps I did not make myself clear." Rask, holding on to Vicker's arm just as tightly, turned Vicker's wrist sharply enough that he almost lost his balance. "Shall we?"

Vicker, not wanting to risk an awkward scene, complied. Rask led him to a blacked-out Suburban parked directly in front of the hotel on East Sixty-First Street. He opened the back-seat door for Vicker and climbed in after him. The limo had been kitted out with four facing swivel chairs. Inside, an elegantly dressed, wizened man, with a nose that seemed as if it had been honed to a sharp edge, waited for him. In the front sat two silent hulks, ex-Israeli commandos, Vicker guessed. Top of the line, not your average pudgy ex-cops.

"Mr. Vicker, may I introduce Dottore Ferdinando."

Ferdinando extended the firm, slightly calloused hand of a sportsman, making Vicker self-conscious about his own doughy palm. The Suburban began to move.

"But before we start. Mr. Vicker, may I have your phone please?"

One of the front-seat bodyguards turned around, eyeing Vicker like a lazy pachyderm. Vicker reached into his jacket pocket and handed over his phone. Rask dropped the phone into a Faraday bag, which blocked all signals, including GPS tracking.

"Forgive what must seem a rather abrupt introduction," Ferdinando began, speaking softly in the stiff-lipped RP accent characteristic of English royals, public school boys, bad American actors, and almost no one else.

"Dottore," Vicker advanced, giving the man his honorific. "As I suggested to your colleague, I have no idea—meaning no disrespect—who you are and whether you are an investor in my fund, much less whether we are partners in some project involving my nephew. I agreed to step into your . . . parlor because Mr. Rask invoked the name of one of my largest investors, but shouldn't we simply schedule a daylight meeting?"

Ferdinando sank back into his chair, elbows on the armrests, fingertips together and drawn to his lips. "Fair points, Mr. Vicker. Very fair points, but Eskandarfond has its own way of doing things."

Vicker receded into himself, trying to make sense of the turn his night had taken. He was embarrassed to think how little he knew about SEF, even though SEF's investment in Industrial Strategies amounted to more than half of the firm's total value. SEF was rumored to control a couple of trillion dollars. Some said even more. Gonzaga had told Vicker never to ask: to simply be grateful that SEF had put him in business—and kept him in business. What he *did* know was that he alone managed almost $300 billion of their money—so their total assets were probably much, much greater. There was, by design, no way to find out. A stichting was an ancient legal fiction—neither a company nor a trust, nor a foundation, nor a partnership, neither visible nor completely invisible. Very like a church—an entity with no obvious owner, self-perpetuating, unregulated, with no public management structure. A giant cloud of money that seeped into everything, financing everything, controlling vast industrial empires, and, for all he knew, entire countries. Nearly the stuff of myth or legend, but with the capacity, as Vicker was discovering, to materialize from the abstract miasma of finance into corporeal form, malevolent when provoked.

"Ah. Judging from your expression, you have understood how unusual SEF is."

"Of course, Dottore Ferdinando, I'm quite aware that SEF has its own ways of doing things. This is just . . . well, completely unorthodox."

Vicker tried to imagine what it sounded like to be accommodating and contrite, while feeling frightened, sick, deflated, his anger rising—but with no place to vent it. Inside the safety of the elaborate bubble he'd constructed around his daily life, he reveled in what he saw as his toughness, his capacity for brutality, and his penchant for humiliating others. The briefest sneer flickered across Ferdinando's upper lip. The Suburban continued moving slowly south and west on dark Manhattan streets.

"We are not constrained by the social mores or the orthodoxies of others, Mr. Vicker. However, what *is* unorthodox is that a board member such as myself would find it necessary to meet one of our managers."

"What can I do?" Vicker capitulated.

Ferdinando nodded toward his younger associate.

"Your nephew, Oscar, has been financing an operation, a European used-car business." Rask consulted a tablet on his lap. "Providing trade finance through a letter of credit intended to be issued by UVB and guaranteed by your firm."

"I've never even heard about this, and I'm certain that I've never heard of this Unersättlich Vereinsbank." Vicker frowned, truly perplexed. "What's the problem?"

"The problem is that we have sixty-eight acres of used cars—seventeen thousand five hundred of them—sitting at the docks in Durres, the port outside Tirana, Albania. Nippon Yusen Kabushiki Kaisha—NYK—has a six-hundred-fifty-eight-foot Panamax car carrier anchored in the harbor waiting to load. Oscar pulled the credit support yesterday, and he won't answer our calls." Rask looked up, squarely at Vicker. "The demurrage runs two million dollars a day. That's the problem." Delaying a ship cost money, demurrage was the penalty rate.

"Financing car shipments? We're not in that business."

"Mr. Vicker," Ferdinando interrupted, irritated, "this is the sixth cargo that Oscar has financed for us. Each one worth three hundred million dollars. It's been very lucrative for him."

"The sixth shipment? What are you paying us?"

Ferdinando looked at Rask.

"Thirty million per letter of credit?"

"Give or take."

"No one pays that kind of money for a ninety-day loan," Vicker snapped. Rask raised a cautionary hand. "Mr. Vicker, I am certain that you did not mean to impugn Dottore Ferdinando's veracity. Perhaps the simplest idea is to get Oscar on the phone."

"Gentlemen." Vicker, snide now, eyed the door release, even as the truck kept moving. "It's three a.m. in Berlin. Let's get together again tomorrow morning. It's been real." He reached for the door latch and pulled. Nothing happened. Trapped. Vicker couldn't resist cracking his knuckles. Was that a smirk on Ferdinando's face?

Silence in the car, which Rask broke.

"Oscar is enjoying himself at The KitKatKlub right now. My people tell me that his nose has been getting quite the workout."

Jesus Christ, thought Vicker. *Who are these people?*

Rask retrieved Vicker's phone, and five rings later, Oscar's voice boomed from the van's speakers over the sounds of thumping bass, clinking glasses, and women laughing in the background.

"Uncle Elias, it's the middle of the night here, what's up?"

"Oscar, I'm visiting with a few—four—gentlemen who seem a bit miffed about a trade that seems to have gone sideways. Something to do with a Unersättlich Vereinsbank letter of credit and a guarantee from Industrial Strategies?"

The background noise receded a bit. Oscar must have moved out of the fray.

"Oscar. I need you to tell me a story, and use all these words: Unersättlich Vereinsbank, letter of credit, seventeen thousand used cars, Albania, our partners in the trade."

"Uncle Elias—"

"Oscar, don't *fucking* 'Uncle Elias' me."

"Am I on a speakerphone? Is someone there with you?"

"Oscar, the goddamn story. *Now.*"

"Okay. *Okay.* About eighteen months ago, a British banker, a friend of my friend, Percy Kirkham, approached me at my club. He told me that our investor, SEF, suggested he be in touch. Said he had a Russian client, some guy named Volk, engaged in sourcing used cars in Europe for export to Tunisia, Jordan, Vietnam, South Africa—all over. They needed someone to guarantee an evergreen letter of credit so that Unersättlich Vereinsbank could advance funds to the seller while the ships were in transit. We would provide the guarantee with the cars as collateral, and UVB would issue the LC. Our partners were offering to pay ten percent of the nominal amount— thirty million dollars—for paper that would only be outstanding for sixty to ninety days. Unbelievable rate of return on an annualized basis."

"Unbelievable. Exactly. In other words, too good to be true! You never asked where's the hair on this? You never thought that it couldn't be that simple? And, Oscar, I don't recall ever hearing about this trade. Where is it booked?"

Silence on the line.

"Oscar?"

"This is the sixth revolver. The first three shipments are closed, two are on the water. They're booked as short-term overcollateralized corporate commercial paper in our Emerging Markets ledger."

"Last I looked, you can't sign for more than ten million dollars without me."

"I booked them as back-to-back transactions with UVB, so the risk-weighted exposure was only three percent of the nominal amount of the letter of credit."

"So, you lent three hundred million against used cars, but booked it as a loan of nine million. Do I have that right?" Vicker snarled. "And if two ships are still in transit, that means we're exposed for six hundred million. Before this 'sixth' transaction?"

"Uncle Elias, all three earlier trades went fine. We made ninety million bucks. With no risk."

"No risk? Really, Oscar? Then why am I sitting in the back of a black SUV, missing my own party, with a kindly old gentleman telling me there *is* a problem?"

"It's just this new compliance guy at UVB. He wanted to make a due diligence trip with me to look at the collateral. I figured he just wanted a boondoggle, so I rented a jet and flew him to Albania—like Albania is anything close to a boondoggle. I figured that compliance stooges don't get out much and take what they can get, especially a couple of legs on a private jet."

"Why would the bank start due diligence now, if you've done this trade five times?"

"I booked this one in my personal account," Oscar answered, sheepish, nearly inaudible. Ferdinando barely blinked. The Suburban turned onto the West Side Highway.

"And?"

"When we got to Tirana, we were met by this guy Turhan Krasniqi, a tatted Albanian in a leather jacket."

"Tatted?"

"Covered in tattoos—knuckles, face, neck. Anyway, he was nice enough, spoke decent English, showed us the cars—all late models, BMW, Audi, Mercedes, Ferrari mostly. Barely used by the look of them. But the UVB guy got freaked because most still had their license plates—Dutch, German, French, Italian. He sent scans of random plates to his head office, they all came back as stolen. Then he googled the name 'Krasniqi,' and it turned out Turhan is a brother of Saimir and Bruno Krasniqi, who are in jail in the U.S. for robbery, arson, kidnapping, murder, trafficking narcotics, weapons possession—"

"More to the point, the bank discontinued the trade."

"Yes," Oscar whispered.

"Allow me to summarize: Some guy comes up to you in a bar, offers a deal that's too good to be true, and neither you nor the bank do any due diligence. You use *my* cash to backstop the trade, then you decide to cheat me and Industrial Strategies by trying to make it a personal trade involving this criminal mafia, and I get accosted by some folks who, from the sound of it, have a right to be angry, even if they are crooks."

Rask muted Vicker's phone.

"Mr. Vicker," he said softly. "We need the transaction funded by ten a.m. GMT."

Vicker nodded, grim, and motioned for Rask to open the mic.

"Oscar, you need to fund the damn trade with cash, in full, ASAP. By ten a.m. your time."

"Uncle E, it's not so simple, UVB is freaked."

"I don't care if we have to write a check for the whole three hundred million. If this isn't done by ten a.m. GMT, I will personally call the Bundespolizei and BaFin and tell them that you and Unersättlich Vereinsbank were complicit in financing a gang of Albanian thieves and that *you*, you piece of shit, and your piece of shit banker buddy tried to defraud me and IS. Got it?"

"Yessir," replied Oscar, sarcastic.

Rask clicked off. The Suburban had come to a stop at the West Thirtieth Street heliport. The rotor of a Sikorsky S-92 turned slowly.

"Gentlemen, are we now square?" Vicker asked.

"Progress, Mr. Vicker, progress," Ferdinando replied.

"Sven and I will be leaving you now. Our colleagues will keep you company, until the funds are released. Feel free to select drinks and snacks from the mini-fridge. *Arrivederci*, Mr. Vicker." Ferdinando and Rask climbed out onto the tarmac and boarded the chopper without a backward glance.

As the bird spun away, the Suburban started to move, beginning what would be a long nighttime crawl down I-95. For hours, as the van moved steadily south, Vicker alternately berated Oscar and cajoled bankers in New York and Berlin he roused from their beds. By the time dawn broke the funds had been moved. A depleted Vicker nodded off in his seat, but, just to be sure, one of the minders injected a chemical assist. When Vicker finally awakened from that deep, nearly comatose sleep, he found that he had been deposited, indecorously, on the National Mall in Washington, D.C., two hundred twenty-five miles south of New York City.

2

Kalorama, Washington, D.C.

Wearing nothing but an old pair of shorts, Ben Corn was pounding the treadmill that faced his rear garden in Kalorama. He'd been running for nearly an hour when the rays of the sun poked through the hedge. Wiry, just shy of six feet, solid enough not to be skinny but too lean to be thick, he ran barefoot—the same way he had trained for high school football, in all seasons, all weather. Maybe a little slower, but just as strong. And tougher. The army and politics did that to you. Sweat poured off him, drenching his hair, which he wore a little longer since moving to D.C. A slightly hipper, sexier, L.A. version of his former hayseed self. Custom suits, five-hundred-dollar haircuts so perfect and precise that from one angle he looked like a small-town high school principal, from another, a French banker.

Ben had long since discovered that, at the sixty-minute mark, when he kicked up his heart rate to 150 beats per minute, the dopamine hit and his mind soared. Natural endocannabinoids were the closest thing to what he felt from the Hindu Kush he had discovered on his first tour in Afghanistan, though in some ways the high was deeper and richer. Since being elected the junior senator from Nebraska just shy of two years earlier, he had given up weed, but its aftereffects had served him well. During his campaign, when his opponent leaked a picture of him in uniform smoking a joint, the only impact was to give him a bump with younger voters.

Morning Joe played on the flat-screen, sound turned down—Washington wallpaper. He thought of it more like recon. If an ambush lay in store on a given day, hints generally surfaced during Joe and Mika's amped-up Punch-and-Judy act.

He looked up as they flashed a photo of him walking on a beach in Malibu, bathing trunks low around his waist, surfboard tucked under his arm. Okay, he thought, incoming snark. That was the photo Kimmel and Colbert always used when they wanted to mock him. Serious news shows usually had him in a suit. He put in his earbuds and turned up the volume.

So, Mika, doesn't Senator Six-Pack know that first-termers are supposed to be seen and not heard? Especially after that thing with the Legos.

He was referring to a video Ben had posted on his YouTube channel during his campaign in which the then-candidate had used Lego warships to explain how the navy was blowing over half a trillion dollars on a fleet that would be useless in confronting America's looming adversary, an expansionist China with unstoppable DF-26 hypersonic missiles. Eight million views later—half of them churned by Chinese bots—Corn had found himself as the nation's most visible critic of a Pentagon procurement system that was more about corruption and pork than national defense.

I don't know, Joe, Mika chimed in. *That* Mr. Smith Goes to Washington *act gets me every time. I just hope he knows what he's doing.*

As he was making a mental note to email a thank-you note to Mika, he heard the crack of breaking glass on the other side of the room and watched in confusion as Elias Vicker stuck his hand through a shattered pane of the French door that led to Corn's garden and let himself in. Like he owned the place.

"Jesus, Ben, someone leans on your doorbell, breaks your window, and you don't even notice until they're already in your house? Delta no less. No wonder we can't win a fucking war."

Vicker shook his head, in seeming disbelief. Ben pointed to a chair and kept running, his feet slapping the wet track, slick with sweat.

"Gimme a sec to cool down, Elias. Take a seat."

As Ben dismounted the treadmill, wiped his face, toweled his hair, and pulled on a Cornhuskers T-shirt, Vicker jabbed impatiently at his phone. He grabbed a bottle of Perrier from a nearby wine fridge, took a long pull, and tossed another bottle to Vicker, who bobbled it before salvaging the catch.

"What would happen if the cousin-fuckers back home caught you drinking fancy French water—*au revoir*, Spamboy." Vicker sneered. As his heart settled back to its resting rate, Ben quietly let out a deep breath.

"Good morning to you too, Elias."

Spamboy. If that's how Vicker chose to underestimate him, Ben was fine with it. It had been a steep ascent—and an even steeper learning curve—for a boy from Fremont, Nebraska, population 25,024. The home of the factory where Hormel turned pigs into Spam. A steady, seemingly preordained path had taken Ben Corn, the charming and ambitious quarterback and valedictorian of Fremont Senior High, to an Odyssey Scholarship at the University of Chicago, a Rhodes at Oxford, and then a young-man-in-a-hurry gig at McKinsey in New York. The road ahead was clear: a C-suite-level job, beautiful wife, even more beautiful children, the Maidstone Club every summer, and a couple of weeks heli-skiing in the Canadian Rockies every February. Seats on boards—both corporate and presidential advisory. Endless money and the kind of quiet influence that not even endless money can buy. But when Ben looked ahead, those lush fairways looked like a dead-end.

So he quit and joined the army, no one's idea of a slick career move back then. That was the late nineties army of peacekeeping missions and no-fly zones, a lone-superpower afterthought that handed out fat pensions and chests full of meaningless ribbons while America's real alpha dogs were engineering math-geek financial instruments on Wall Street or scaling up virtual empires on the West Coast. But Ben had sensed—hoped—that for those with the right instincts and qualities, and the right rabbis to guide them, another army existed deep within that status quo–defending bureaucracy, a true meritocracy based on character, skill, and courage, not family legacy, test scores, or the whims of administrators. The men who learned the secret handshakes of that other army were the ones who shaped history. He was determined to be among them.

Captain Ben Corn had just been coming into his own when the Towers fell and the call came from General Tommy Taylor, a JSOC up-and-comer with a reputation for surrounding himself with the best of the best. Over the course of deployments under his aegis, Tommy gathered a small, disciplined, cohesive band, with Ben at its center, and ensured that the bonds they formed went well beyond the camaraderie of eating the same dust, and depending on one another as they risked their lives. With Tommy as their tutor in stoicism, they built a furious case against the senseless waste of lives that defined the American war machine—a rage that turned messianic after their friend Teddy Buckfire was blown to pieces by an eight-year-old suicide bomber in Afghanistan. As they waited for the chopper to retrieve what was left of Teddy, Tommy was consumed by a rage as pure and deep as they had ever seen. He was bone-weary of seeing American soldiers die for all the wrong reasons, in ill-conceived wars launched without forethought, compelling national interest, or clear definition of victory. And he was even more tired of bitching about it. As the chopper came over the ridge to take away the remains of yet another young man of great promise, Tommy looked at Ben Corn and said: *You, sir, are going to become the president of the United States, and we are going to get you there.* Almost like it was an order. At least that's how Don, Ben, and Chip took it. From then on, Tommy had never let them lose sight of that vision. He would get them there; they just had to trust him.

Ever since, Tommy had made certain that Ben's ticket got punched, first in a series of elite combat roles—Special Forces in Iraq, Ground Branch in Afghanistan and Pakistan—before graduating him into the institutional ranks of the army's war machine. He served as a liaison to the Israelis, the Saudis, and the Indians and earned plum gigs briefing influential elected officials. As Ben excelled in each of these roles, and as Tommy climbed the Pentagon ranks, the feelers began coming in. From kingmakers at home, from bigwigs in the party, from Tommy's seriously rich and clandestinely conservative colleagues at MIT, from McKinsey partners offering introductions to the corporate money circuit. Tommy had predicted it all. Ben was irresistible, the perfect package. A man of proven integrity, grit, and courage, not to mention movie-star looks. The urban and coastal elites saw him as a man of rare intellect. Heartland voters connected with him as a minister's son and a decorated vet.

To donors he seemed a breath of fresh air, too good to be true: a man of eloquence and idealism, but also eager and deferential. Someone who could be counted on to listen patiently and not to move too fast. But there was something else about him. A quality of mystery that allowed those who did not know him well to project onto him their own thoughts and hopes.

Ben looked closely at Vicker. They had met many times at political events large and small, but had only rarely been alone together, which made the seven a.m. visit even more perplexing. Why him? Why now? But more to the point, how could he make use of whatever stress had brought Vicker to his back door, because the Vicker sitting five feet from him was not a Vicker he had ever seen before: nervous, off-balance, vulnerable.

"You missed a great party, Ben. Really should've been there, bunch of guys I wanted you to meet. Great food, great crowd. Sexy party favors." Vicker shifted about in his chair, knee jiggling. He almost seemed to be vibrating.

"Aren't you going to offer me some coffee?"

"Sure thing. In the kitchen. Come on up."

Vicker followed him upstairs, uncharacteristically docile. Ben poured two mugs and gestured for Vicker to take an overstuffed chair in a sunroom drenched with morning light.

At first, he could not remember how Vicker knew his address, but recalled that they had met there once before, when Vicker had asked him to arrange a discreet get-together with the head of the Committee on Foreign Investment in the United States (CFIUS). Vicker wanted to know if the committee, an obscure unit in the Treasury Department with power to kill any foreign investment that might compromise national security, would allow the Chinese to purchase a Silicon Valley start-up that was developing 6G chipsets. The meeting had been a disaster, Corn had been surprised at Vicker's ham-handedness. Instead of posing subtle inquiries and knowing how to parse a convoluted, bureaucratic answer, Vicker asked his questions directly, like he was soliciting an inside stock tip in a golf club locker room. The director had been polite but had spoken around his question with so much evasive policy talk that she might as well have been laughing in Vicker's face.

"You owe me two hundred bucks for the broken window," said Ben, with a laugh.

"Put it on my tab. Or just call Alison." Alison Winger, his long-suffering assistant. "She'll take care of it."

He doesn't even get that I was kidding, Ben thought.

"Listen, Ben, I really need your help."

"Anything, Elias, name it."

"I've had a little incident. And I've decided that I need to upgrade my security. It's got to be industrial grade. Like what the Secret Service does for the president. I figured with your background, you'd know some people."

That's it? Ben thought. That's why he barged into my house at dawn? "I'm sure that Pete can help you with that, he runs in those circles."

"Pete's a little soft for this kind of work—might get his manicure chipped. I'm looking for Special Forces types. Guys you used to run with—just not one of those PTSD psychos. I don't want to scare Piper." He paused, thinking about his trophy wife, Bronte "Piper" Thornton, a Daughter of the American Revolution and lineal descendant of Matthew Thornton, signer of the Declaration of Independence. Then he smiled. "Also, they need to have the good sense to say no when she wants them to fuck her."

Fueled with a bit of coffee, the Vicker that Ben knew snapped back into focus. Imperious and ingratiating at the same time. Trashing his wife and his best guy. Drawing you into his circle of spite, Ben thought, that's what passes for intimacy with Elias Vicker. Thank God his own wife, Peggy, and the kids were traveling. She would have thrown Vicker out in a second.

"Of course, I'll do whatever I can. I know lots of guys in that business." Ben probed.

"Anything in particular you want protection from?"

"I had a little problem last night." Vicker rubbed the back of his neck with his hand, breaking eye contact. He showed up here impulsively, thought Ben, and now he's trying to decide how much to trust me. "Some people ambushed me during my party in New York, drugged me, and dumped me by the Washington Monument."

"Come again?"

"Kind of spooky, but . . . well . . . here I am having breakfast with you."

Vicker had been kidnapped from his own party? The event that Pete planned all year? And now he was making light of it, at the same time that he wanted to be protected like he was the president?

"Not a big deal. I just . . . I just don't want anything like that to happen again. Ever."

"Do you know who they are? The kidnappers?"

Vicker was silent, which Ben took as a yes.

"Not exactly. Look, Ben, it's not about these people. I just don't want anything like that happening again. That's all."

"Elias, I can have the FBI here in five minutes." Ben feigned outrage. "These people need to be apprehended."

"Ben, stop." Vicker held up his hand, palm out. "We are absolutely not, no way, calling the cops."

Vicker had regained control over most of his body. His face reset into the benign mask that he usually wore. The superrich *are* different, Ben thought, or at least they become different. Arrogant even when they were pretending to be nice.

"Can you do this? Or not?"

Before Ben could answer, an enormous smile broke across Vicker's face. Ben felt a soft hand on his shoulder.

"Well, well, well. I guess it's true, they literally are in bed together—politics and the media."

Five years earlier, Maggie had been an intern on the *Washington Post*'s suburban news desk. Now, in her late twenties, she wrote an obsessively parsed Politico column that half of Washington fought to stay out of, and the other half fought to get into. Simply the way she mentioned your name on her weekly *Morning Joe* appearance could determine if you were a hero or a punch line that news cycle. The daughter of a D.C. cop, she'd gone to Sidwell Friends on a free ride, where she studied her well-heeled classmates—and their mothers and fathers who had turned dealings with the federal government into lucrative careers—with anthropological obsessiveness. Ben would have thought she knew better than to insert herself into his business, much less to reveal their relationship. But here she was. In her bare feet, wearing Peggy Corn's favorite pink *jeté de fleurs* D. Porthault robe, which hung half open. It had been years since Peggy walked around the house like that.

"What an unexpected pleasure," Vicker exclaimed. "Two of my favorite people. Well done. Both of you." Vicker reached out and gave Ben an attaboy nudge. "You're officially forgiven for snubbing me last night. Guess there's one part of your life you don't need Pete's help with."

Vicker patted the armrest of the chair next to his. "Maggie, come sit."

She closed her robe, but just slightly, and gave Vicker a peck on the cheek before taking a seat across from him, drawing her signature mane of strawberry-blond hair behind her neck.

"Now here's a story," she began. "New York's most ethically challenged billionaire stopping by for a predawn chat with Washington's straightest arrow." Maggie took a delicate sip of green tea from an Amari cup. "A girl would do anything for access like this." She adjusted the lapel of her robe to show a flash of cleavage, turned to Ben, and giggled. "But it looks like I already have it."

Maggie smiled, faux-demure. "Oh, did you think this is off the record? You're supposed to tell me that *before* the interview begins. But don't worry, I'll let it slide this time."

Ben didn't say a word, and Maggie took the hint. Once she left, Vicker visibly relaxed, as if the thrill of discovering another man's peccadillo centered him.

"So, Ben. Where were we? Are you going to help me? Or not?"

"Count on it, Elias. I have just the guy, if he'll take you on. Ex-Delta. He's handled some of the hairiest shit you can imagine. I'm sure you read about the family that got kidnapped in the Red Sea. By Eritrean pirates?"

"The hedge fund guy from Miami? Konstantinidis?"

Ben figured that Vicker would know Tasos Konstantinidis. The incident had spooked all the big Wall Street money guys. For years, marauders had been operating out of a seaside Eritrean village—everyone living there was in on the business, getting rich attacking and hijacking passing ships—most of them freighters but also the occasional superyacht cruising in the Indian Ocean.

"Don handled the extraction. It was a lot worse than what you read about. They nabbed his daughters too. Ten and twelve. That made Don angry. He got a little, I guess you could say, emotional." When Don was done, nothing—no one—was left. Men, women, children: Don brought in his own air force to take the village out.

"He's your best bet for physical security. Digital too. His people are all former Army Cyber Institute—and Ground Branch." Ben paused. "But he doesn't just play defense. He can go on offense as well."

Vicker tugged an ear. Ben knew he had taken that in: offense always interested Vicker.

"Trustworthy?"

"Don Carter? Wouldn't be here without him. I've put my life in his hands. In rougher places than this."

"Good, set it up. And call me a cab." The old Vicker, dismissive, peremptory. For the next few minutes, waiting for a car, Vicker hunched over his phone, typing furiously. He ignored Ben so completely that it was as if Ben, not he, was the uninvited guest.

———

Moments after Vicker left, Maggie sashayed back into the room—hair wet, stark naked—and expertly knelt between his legs. A few moments later, as Ben approached climax, she pulled away.

"So, aren't you going to tell me what Elias Vicker was doing here?"

Ben, eyes closed, leaning back on the chair, his body tense, shook his head. "Ah, nothing really. We just have coffee from time to time."

"At dawn, with him wearing last night's party clothes?"

"What can I say, he's a weird guy," Ben said weakly. "Don't stop."

Maggie raised her arm, as if looking at her watch.

"Well, in that case, I'd better get to the office and find a story for today." She pulled up Ben's shorts and snapped the waistband against his throbbing penis. "Time to put that thing away."

After she left the room, Ben picked up his phone to call Pete. "Hey. Did you lose your boss?"

"Why? You find him? Some Swedish guy crashed the party last night. When I turned around, they were gone."

"Let's say he found me. How quickly can you get your ass down here? We need an all-hands meeting. I think I may have found a way in."

3

Jūrmala, Latvia

I love this job, thought Greta Webb, as she half sat up in bed, elbow on a down pillow, head resting in the palm of her hand. Bright, late-afternoon Latvian sun filtered through voile curtains. Reflecting off the water, the light drew fuzzy shadows on Persian rugs and played across rare antiques. The entire villa, at the edge of the Baltic Sea in Jūrmala's best neighborhood, was furnished with the sort of objects—sideboards, mirrors, sconces, tables, credenzas, couches, chairs, and ottomans—that came up for sale only when a European royal died and the heirs needed cash. But it was the art that surprised her more. Someone had an eye. Money too. But it was the eye that interested her. Math and economics had come easily, but art had been her passion since she was a child. A gift from her father, who whispered Ruskin's words in her ear: "Great nations write their autobiographies in three manuscripts: the book of their deeds, the book of their words and the book of their art." Art as a way to see reality and illusion, and to see how others understood the world. And here, on every wall, at every turn, was another Netherlandish master—Frans Hals, Jacob van Ruisdael, Frans Snyders, Osias Beert, Rogier van der Weyden. Drawings by Rembrandt and Dürer. And that haunting, finely rendered portrait in graphite, perhaps by Ilya Repin. Not flashy, just . . . perfect. A scholar's collection: each one exquisite.

An empty champagne bottle sat, upended, in a silver bucket, its butt end pointing toward the fourteen-foot ceiling like a toy cannon. Their other empties—too many—lay on the floor. Clothes everywhere. She remembered tearing at the buttons of Mara's black silk Yves Saint Laurent shirt, but was a little foggy as to how it had ended up hanging from the ballroom-size Baccarat chandelier like a leftover New Year's Eve decoration. She looked down at her sleeping lover, and at the bruise on her own shoulder from where Mara had thrown a shoe. Making love to Mara was a narcissistic fantasy, like making love to herself—svelte, strong, long black hair. Mara knew how to push it; she had a sense of danger and a willingness to take risks that matched

Greta's own. What had begun as a purposeful, professional seduction had become something else. Fun, for sure, but also a connection of sorts, not easy to find—or allow—in her line of work.

It was just as well that Mara had been asleep when Tommy called a couple of hours ago. Typically cryptic and imperious, he told her he was bringing her back home, effective immediately. He was on his way to Ben's office and didn't have time to talk; just pack your bags and he'd explain Sunday afternoon at that place you like in the Loire Valley. What she had thought would be just another weekend of roughhouse sex in some mysterious oligarch's weekend house was now suddenly a farewell fling, maybe the perfect way to end things.

Mara was not her first central banker, but the first one that she had actually enjoyed getting into bed with. Even asleep, Mara looked like she was plotting something. Or maybe it was just the way her lips relaxed into a delicate half smile in repose. The girl had the skills and training for her job, but seemed improbably young and high-spirited to be the governor of Latvia's central bank. Greta had watched her stride down corridors across the continent, heels clicking along expanses of polished marble from Zagreb to Düsseldorf, trailed by gray men with grabby hands, surrounded by the ever-present clatter and stench of stale, fearful, endlessly corrupt European Union economic power. Until six months ago, that was as close as Mara let Greta get. But then, after the last quarterly public meeting of the bank's board, in its grand conference room, Mara greeted her as if they were actually friends. By the next day, they were already talking about places they could meet without being seen.

Greta drew the sheet back gently, slowly uncovering Mara's lovely full breasts, her stomach, bite marks along her inner thigh. Greta did not give much thought to her sexuality. Men. Women. She used them both, as needed. Sex was an itch, a drive, an instinct. An adventure. Goose bumps rose on Mara's skin as Greta traced small circles around her nipples with an index finger. She leaned in to flick one with her tongue. When Mara didn't react, she clamped down with her teeth. Still nothing, so she bit down harder. Mara purred, arched her back, stretched, and opened her eyes slowly, not quite waking, not seeing. Closing them again.

"Don't stop."

Greta stopped.

"Presumptuous of you."

"*Please,* don't stop." Mara arched her neck, reaching up, drawing Greta's lips to her own, kissing her dreamily, eyes still closed, running her fingers through Greta's hair. "More . . . *please.*"

Greta put her hand around Mara's throat and applied gentle but un-mistakable pressure. Just how they taught at the Farm: what to do when you wanted to be absolutely certain that you had someone's attention. She squeezed a little harder. Mara's face flushed red and she started to writhe, but not hard enough to free herself. She pushed her hips into the air, trying to rub up against Greta, who released her grip.

"Tell me about your friend. The one who owns this place."

Over the two years Greta had been based in Riga, officially seconded by the U.S. Treasury to help the central bank combat money laundering, she had actually been working for Tommy and the Agency. She had the back-ground for the Treasury job—she'd studied economics and finance and had worked at a Wall Street investment bank and in management consulting. But she knew that her cover fooled no one, least of all Mara. Their dalliance had been defined by the secrets they sensed in each other but were forbid-den to reveal. She and Mara shared wild abandon when no one was look-ing, but little else in the way of intimacy. In public and, for the most part, in private, they stuck to their scripts. The pursuer and the pursued, their roles ever shifting, never stable or clear which was which. Greta played the part of serious analyst intent upon helping the Latvian government clean up its act by combating organized crime. Mara, swimming in the fishbowl of Latvian politics, projected the image of a stylish, but tamped-down, technocrat. Composed, unflappable, and, to all appearances, earnest in her attempt to help her homeland become a modern, rule-abiding European nation.

Initially, Greta bridled at the assignment as boring and bureaucratic, and it had been, until her seduction of Mara. But, through Mara, Greta had been able to develop a much deeper understanding of how klepto-crats and oligarchs in Russia and its client states looted their national treasuries and concealed the proceeds. The former Soviet republics, ruled for decades by strong men who preferred weak institutions, had become petri dishes for criminal experimentation. Had Tommy called her back six months earlier, she would have been elated. Now his order hit her harder than she would have expected. Only a few hours left. She had to make them count.

"You mean Fyodor?" It was the first time Mara had volunteered a name. But Mara had dropped enough clues for her to understand that, whatever his name was, this—Fyodor—was more than a friend. A lover? Perhaps. But likely more: a mentor, a force, a presence in Mara's life. Clearly a man of taste and a good person to know: normal Latvians did not hoard old masters or own massive villas in backwater resort towns.

"You'll meet him later, at the party."

Spring and summer in Jūrmala were an endless party, revolving around Laima Rendezvous, the annual music festival staged by Laima Vaikule, Latvia's timeless platinum-haired pop diva, which would be getting under way in a few hours. The weekend had become an excuse for overlapping elites to mingle, neutral ground for the bosses of every faction: FSB, Russia's powerful spy agency, successor to the KGB; luminaries from Russian military intelligence—the GRU; oligarchs; cabinet ministers; members of parliament; and, above all, organized crime. The takeover of the Jūrmala festival had occurred organically, as friends invited friends—and as American and, to some extent, European economic sanctions limited the number of venues where the elites of the Russian kleptocracy could meet and speak in relative privacy.

Mara drew Greta's hand down toward her crotch, but Greta simply allowed it to rest there. Feeling oddly restless, a little reckless. Her last night in-country.

"You're torturing me, Greta Webb. Is this what they taught you at Abu Ghraib? How to make poor innocent bankers miserable?" It was Mara's perennial joke, poking at Greta's cover story. *"Of course, you're CIA, Greta Webb. Real Treasury analysts are four-eyed cows with tunnel vision."* Greta began to thrust her hand, gently. Mara responded, moving her hips to meet Greta's fingers.

"Promise that I'll get to meet him?"

"Yes, yes, *yes* I promise. Just . . . *don't* . . . *stop*."

Mara took a deep, shuddering breath, releasing a deep moan as she came and rolled over to fold herself into Greta's arms. She dozed fitfully, her way: so intimate, and so distant. Neither of them knew much of each other's lives. She wondered what Mara had been like as a teenager. Greta—like half the world—had seen the pictures of Mara, the chess prodigy. Tournament after tournament—in Helsinki, Madrid, Singapore. The skinny sixteen-year-old, with pigtails and a grin full of braces, slaying chess masters, men two or three times her age. And not just winning, but destroying them with a game that was almost cruel in its relentless precision. Clever little Mara Bērziņš, darling of the international press. And then, retiring from the game board to study at Oxford and Princeton, math and economics. A prodigy in whatever she took up. Somehow, out of nowhere, she had become Latvia's top banker, welcomed without obvious protest by a cadre of gray men who had been waiting years for their own turns. It was clear to Greta that the Kremlin had deemed it essential that every lever of power in Latvia be held by hands that were just as pliable as they were glamorous or competent. As a member of the European Union, the European Central Bank, NATO, and a participant in the euro, Latvia had become Russia's useful backdoor to the West, an unofficial portal into the international financial system, and, some said, a thin blade of Putin's wedge. Despite its announced goals of breaking free of Russia's orbit, Latvia instead became the perfect vehicle to move Russian money—and, really, dirty money from anywhere in the world—in and out of the EU. Which meant, as the CIA had long suspected, that Mara had to be nothing less than a committed apparatchik, approving, from her perch atop the central bank, every significant foreign currency transaction and privy to the full detail on the flow of funds into and out of the nation: the source bank, the ultimate beneficiaries, the destination. Sanctions be damned.

In a good year, half a trillion dollars, mostly in cash, skated into the country. Control of Latvia's central bank offered the Kremlin a solution for the most difficult form of money laundering of all: channeling large amounts of cash, either stolen or acquired, through large-scale criminal activity, into the financial system. Few Western banks would accept suitcases of money; fewer still could convert oddball currencies like Mexican pesos and Turkish lira, flown in on cargo planes, into euros and dollars. But for certain Russian banks, and for a favored few in Latvia, truckloads of bills presented no difficulty. Just an opportunity to be of service.

Greta was unsure exactly how Mara's friend Fyodor was wired into all that. Mara, perhaps proud of her connection to so powerful a man or, in a more sinister interpretation, leading Greta on, had dropped a trail of bread crumbs suggesting that the previously unnamed Fyodor was someone who made things happen.

Greta nudged Mara.

"Let's go, Mara. Getting late."

Mara stretched languorously.

"They'll wait for us. I told Fyodor you're coming. He's very excited. He loves meeting mid-level bureaucrats."

"Why?" Greta sat up. "What have you told him?" She leaned in until her face was just inches from Mara's.

"I didn't have to tell him anything. Riga is a small town. People talk. Fyodor has his fingers in everything—he owns the best hotel in town, one of the biggest banks, and thousands of acres of timber. You know damn well he's heard about the Russian-speaking supermodel the U.S. Treasury sent to help us clean up our filthy banking system." Mara opened her eyes wide in feigned surprise. "And you haven't exactly kept a low profile. Especially once you started palling around with me."

Greta got out of bed, tugged Mara into the bathroom, and turned on the shower. "Did Fyodor help you get your job?"

Mara just laughed. "You don't think I got to where I am by being the better chess player? You two will have a lot to talk about. You're always so curious about how cash moves, and no one knows more about moving large amounts of cash than he does."

Surprising to the very end, thought Greta. For months, they had danced around how much Mara—and how much the central bank—knew about money laundering and movements of the proceeds of organized crime. Now, suddenly, she seemed willing to pull back the curtain. They stepped into the stream of water, kissing, washing each other. Mara took Greta's face in her hands and ran them through her wet hair. In the end, just part of my job, thought Greta. But why not enjoy it?

As they dressed in the bedroom, there was a discreet tap on the door. Sometimes Greta almost forgot that they were never alone. Mara grabbed a robe and jogged into the suite's living room while Greta watched Mara open the door to a smiling pillar of muscle with a shaved head with three prison tattoos. Greta recognized the two eight-pointed stars on the man's collarbones, signifying high rank in Russia's criminal hierarchy. The dagger-tattoo on his neck oozed drops of blood: one for every person he had killed, an advertisement that he was for hire. Mara chatted with him briefly and skipped back into the bedroom.

"That was Yuri, Fyodor's valet, bodyguard, chauffeur. He's so sweet. He offered us a ride to Dzintari, but I said we'd walk. It's a straight shot along the beach."

"And the light is lovely. I'd much prefer that." Greta pulled on a demure flowered-print Chanel dress, black with camellias, that fell just two inches above her knees, and slipped into black Ferragamo ballet flats. She and Mara were almost twins, in simple dresses, damp hair pulled back into ponytails.

Mara took Greta's hand and led her down to the beach, where they took off their shoes to walk in the warm sand. The beach and cafés along the strand were thronged with Rigans, lounging, sipping wine, swimming, sunning, just happily watching the light the long winter months would soon take from them. After a few minutes, the bustle gave way to grand weekend homes belonging to some of Latvia's most successful—most politically connected—entrepreneurs.

"Lots of stories on this stretch." Mara pointed to two of Jūrmala's most coveted villas, Villa Adlera and Villa Marta.

"Valery Kargin owns Adlera. The other is owned by his partner, Viktor Krasovitsky." The Russian duo had parachuted into the city, in 1991, after managing to obtain the first foreign exchange trading license issued by the Kremlin. While their monopoly lasted, people from all over the former Soviet Union made pilgrimages to their storefront in Riga, desperate to swap useless rubles for precious dollars. Soon they were rich enough to start their own bank, Parex Bank, and they never looked back. "I'm still cleaning up the mess that they made when depositors and creditors staged a run on Parex. If the government hadn't bailed it out, the entire Latvian economy might have collapsed. Scary times."

Mara squeezed Greta's hand tightly and stopped walking, drew her close, and frowned, giving Greta an intense look, something she did frequently, but mostly when she thought that Greta wasn't looking.

"This is where Nikolai Kirillov, a Russian *biznesman*, was shot dead a few years ago. Right here, in broad daylight. With his twenty-four-year-old girlfriend of the moment." The theory was that Kirillov had been involved in smuggling—no one knew what, exactly: guns, girls, cars, drugs, cash. Probably cheating his partners. "Nobody was caught, because no one even both-ered to look." *Biznes* as usual.

"But that's not why I wanted to walk." Mara seemed nervous. "I need to ask you something. Were you serious when you talked about the two of us disappearing to that beach town in Brazil—Búzios?"

Greta looked at Mara in mild confusion.

"Yeah, you were pretty drunk." Mara's eyes softened into the beginning of disappointment. "You asked if I'd ever thought about disappearing. I as-sumed that you meant with me. You said you were afraid of turning into someone you wouldn't recognize."

It started coming back to Greta, not so much what she'd said, but how it had felt to share a private thought with someone she cared about, or at least thought she did in that drunken moment. By the time Greta had fled Tehran by herself at the age of seventeen, first by car, then on horseback, and finally on foot to the Iraqi border, where she'd applied for asylum, she had mastered her two core competencies: the inner strength to never rely on another hu-man being and an uncanny ability to turn any door into an exit. What other people thought of as loneliness, to her was safety. Letting Mara in like that was sloppy, and sloppy was dangerous.

"Oh, I was just thinking out loud. I never saw myself making a career at Treasury."

Greta dropped her flats in the sand and reached up, cradling Mara's head in her hands, stretching her fingers under her hair.

"Well, I'm completely serious," Mara said. "I don't know who you really are, and I wonder if you do either. But I'd like to find out." Mara shook Greta's hands loose. "And I have a feeling it would be easier to figure out in a coun-try with no extradition."

"But . . ."

"You see all this." She gestured at the narrow road that ran back toward the center of town, jammed with Ferraris and Bugattis. "When I was a little girl everyone was poor. Now most of us are still poor, because these people steal everything. It's not what I signed up for. I wanted to make a difference in my country. But now all I want is to get out. And I think you do too."

Greta felt weary. The woman Mara was reaching for, perhaps was in love with, did not exist. She was a fiction, dreamed up in a small room in Langley and in the cold, plotting imagination of Tommy Taylor. And now she was about to disappear without saying goodbye.

"We could do it. New names. Brazilian passports. My 'friends' here, they'd never find me."

Poor Mara. That could never happen. Greta knew it. Mara had to know it too. Mara had joined a mob and risen to a position high enough to have learned its secrets. The closest thing to a way out would never be a clean break. Maybe following some soft, respectable path, to an endowed chair at the Harvard Kennedy School or a sinecure at the Johns Hopkins School of Advanced International Studies. But she'd still have to report to the FSB, the GRU, or whichever Russians handled her, and she'd continue to be seen as a threat to them for many years, until she aged out of her real-time knowledge. Mara would be an old woman by the time she was free.

Getting no response, Mara looked away, making an effort to smooth out her dress. "That's where we're headed." She pointed at a contemporary open-air structure, Jūrmala's largest venue, the Dzintaru Koncertzāle. "Paid for with donations by our permanent 'guests.' Not just Russians, but anyone who needs a European Union passport—in their own name." Greta reached for her hand, but Mara pulled it away. "I'll wait, Greta. But not forever." She wiped her eyes.

Mara stole one last tender glance at Greta. Now it was back to business. Fyodor had been adamant that she bring Greta along this evening and equally adamant that she not mention his full name. She wondered if Greta had any idea what the night held in store. Mara hoped it wasn't something she'd have trouble forgiving herself for as their game played out.

4

Hart Senate Office Building, Washington, D.C.

Don Carter punched the accelerator on his brand-new electric Porsche Taycan Turbo S—his only concession to success—and merged with a silent blast of torque and power onto the traffic-swelled Memorial Parkway. He was headed out to the Pentagon for an eleven a.m. meeting to finalize a multimillion-dollar, multiyear contract to handle protection for a fleet of liquified natural gas carriers. In the real world, it would be a ten-minute Zoom call. But DoD officials didn't care about your time. He'd probably be stuck out there all day.

As he settled back into the caterpillar-paced traffic, a snippet of the Police's "Every Breath You Take," the song he'd chosen as Tommy's ringtone when he was annoyed with his former CO's constant hovering presence, burst from the speakers. Don braced himself. Tommy, now a three-star general in charge of coordinating covert activities between the three branches of the intelligence community, had not reached out in months. He knew Tommy had quietly pushed behind the scenes for Carter Logistics to land the LNG contract, but that wouldn't be why he was calling. Tommy kept things like that at arm's length.

Don waved his hand to answer.

"How soon can you be in Ben's office?" Even in the Porsche's 3D surround sound system, Tommy's noteless monotone was as unreadable as ever.

"I'm heading out to the Penta—"

"Good. See you in half an hour."

Not even a hello or some gentle teasing about Don's new $185,000 ride. Don knew this day would be coming. But so soon? Questions began to flood his mind—timing, logistics, finances. As he began to sort through them, they resolved into the dark pit of his real issue: Greta. Would she be there too? He hadn't seen her since Paris, after they stashed the pallets. That had been three years ago. Last he heard, Tommy had her bouncing around the Baltics, tracking Russian criminal financial networks. If the campaign was launching in earnest, she'd have to be there. He got off at the next exit and circled back toward Capitol Hill.

As he parked his car across the street from the Hart Senate Office Building, he had to suppress the urge to bolt. Don had promised himself that after that last operation in the sands of Jordan, he was done. Did he really need this now?

Just across from the entrance, he saw an old friend, his former staff sergeant Jack Kunze, sitting in a small grove of trees near the entrance, surrounded by old newspapers and a ring of bodega candles Jack burned in memory of the thousands of lives lost in America's forever wars. Jack's dog, Freddie, lay in his lap. A few feet away, uniformed soldiers milled about, each outfitted in combat gear and carrying an M-16 and an arsenal of lethal and non-lethal weapons hanging from their belts. Jack inhaled deeply on a joint, and as, as he exhaled, extended a fist to Don.

"Capitol Hill. Greatest concentration of active-duty military personnel anywhere in the world. Can you fucking believe it?" Jack asked, military patrols having become an everyday sight, not just in DC, but in tinderbox cities across the country. "Course, if Rummy had flooded the zone in Baghdad like this, we would have been out of there in six months."

Don felt the burn of rage. And shame. Not toward Jack, a brave, kind man, but at the raw deal the army had given Jack—and thousands of other vets. Jack had more deployments than just about anyone Don knew. After the last one, where he miraculously survived a blast outside Kabul that took out the other two members of his unit, the army just spit him out, told him he was fine—see, look how nicely the leg healed—and sent him on his way. But all the fighting, the noise, the killing, the fear, and the deaths of men he had been responsible for had eaten away at the foundations of Jack Kunze's psyche. We're no different, Don thought. We just hide the damage better.

"How goes, Major?"

Don sat down next to him in the dirt and crisscrossed his legs, not thinking about the $300 jeans and Hermès loafers a recent girlfriend had convinced him to buy. Jack passed him the joint.

"Never better, Jack. You?"

Jack motioned for him to take another toke, which he did. "This week? Not bad. The new meds are better. Ben hooked me up with a private doc, not another VA hack. She's nice." Jack touched his right temple. "Still there, but not screaming. At least not all the time."

"Anything you need?"

"They're out to get Ben."

"Who's out to get Ben, Jack?" Some days Jack's hold on reality was tenuous.

"Major, I read the funny papers." Jack gestured at a pile by his side—the *FT*, the *Washington Post*, the *New York Times*. The trash cans were full of them every morning.

"You mean this thing with the carrier?"

Jack nodded. "The generals. Lockheed. Electric Boat. Boeing. They own Frank Conway. Ben has to be very, very careful."

"I'll tell him. Anything else?"

"I could use a new jacket."

Don peeled off his bright orange Norrøna fleece and handed it to him, along with all the cash he had in his pocket. Jack took off his tattered camo, folded it carefully, and reached up to reclaim the joint as Don took one more hit before turning to head up the stairs.

"Make sure you tell him."

———

An aide ushered General Tommy Taylor into a sitting room adjacent to Ben's Senate office. Tommy was struck, not for the first time, by the opulence: twelve-foot ceilings, burnished walnut paneling, crown molding, antique Persian rugs, leather sofas, a huge flat-screen, MSNBC on mute. He picked up a remote from a two-hundred-year-old Duncan Phyfe table, on loan from the Smithsonian, and turned up the sound. Maggie Hoguet was interviewing Senator Robbie Plumptre, a slick Virginian from a well-known political family who, eighteen months ahead of New Hampshire, posed Ben's most serious threat to the party's nomination. Tommy stared up at the senator. White collar and French cuffs on a blue shirt, the swamp uniform. He wasn't worried.

Just outside, in the main office, Tommy could hear Ben joshing with his staff, quietly asking questions. And then, with an athletic lunge, Ben bounded into the room and dropped into the chair next to Tommy.

"Hadn't expected you to be early, sir. All good?"

Tommy stood up and pointed to the screen. Maggie was biting her lip while Senator Plumptre, making a call for military sacrifice, teared up while talking about his newly married son, deployed overseas, separated from his gorgeous young wife.

Ben pointed at the screen. "Military sacrifice my ass," Ben said. "That guy's basically an arms dealer, except I think he takes a bigger cut. Grosses me out."

A soft knock on the door, and Ben's chief of staff poked her head in. "Major Carter is here, are you ready for him?"

Tommy held up his hand.

"We need a minute, Audrey."

The door shut. Tommy stood up, drawing himself close to Ben. He gestured toward the screen. Maggie was finishing up her segment. "If you want to just hand it to Plumptre now, let me know. Save me a lot of time and effort."

Ben flashed a leave-me-alone grin.

"And *no*, Mr. Senator, it's not just a matter of being more careful. When you sit down for your interview with Maggie Hoguet, I need her looking at you like she wants to fuck you, not like she's already fucked you and wonders what the hell she was thinking. We're about to enter the no-mistakes zone. Knock it off."

"Oh, come on, General," Ben said, miffed. "And stop spying on me. It's just recon."

"You may have nine lives. I don't have that luxury."

Tommy had grown up in the notorious Robert Taylor Homes on the South Side of Chicago, one of America's least-promising addresses. Arrested for dealing crack when he was fourteen, holding his own on streets ruled by real criminals twice his age, the judge saw a kid with grit and brains and offered Tommy a deal: if he maintained an A average and committed to going to college, he could avoid juvie. Tommy took the admonition—and the copy of Marcus Aurelius's *Meditations* the judge gave him—to heart. He barely looked up from a book until he proudly said yes to a full-ride from Yale three years later.

The door flew open and Don strode in, followed by Chip Beekman. Audrey followed, apologetic. "I'm sorry, sir, I couldn't stop them."

Don looked around in wonder, relieved—at least he thought so—that Greta wasn't there. "Jesus, Ben, who let you in this place?" Don rummaged in the trash and pulled out an empty water bottle to use as a spit cup. "Pretty nice for a dirtbag who didn't take a shower the three whole months we were in Banyam."

"I thought you were too stoned to notice." Ben jumped up, took Don by the shoulder, and pumped his hand. Chip hovered behind them, business-like. "Or maybe *I* was." He shook his head. "Black Afghan kush."

"You sure smelled like shit back then," Don sank into the couch. "But at least that weed made you more fun to be around." He wondered if Ben and Tommy noticed the odor on his breath. He must reek.

"Man, I loved it there. Sometimes, when I can't take this place, I fly back home to Fremont to go hiking in the Wildcat Hills and pretend I'm in the Koh-i-Baba."

"Natural beauty, living off the land, friends, fresh mountain air, calling in airstrikes," said Don.

"Wasting bad guys at a thousand yards." Ben sighed.

In their reveries, they had all been superheroes. But recently, Don had begun to question that. They had been anything but heroic. More like feral, frightened animals—jacked up on adrenaline, hash, and uppers—getting by on firepower, cunning, and ruthlessness. Killing without thought, surviving. Making mistakes, sometimes pushing much too far.

"Afghanistan was simple compared to this cesspool. Out there, we got up, got out of bed. Blew shit up. Capitol Hill is a hundred times more dangerous."

They had a lot of theories about politicians: how they had no core beliefs, catered to big donors, and sent young people to die on foreign battlefields because they didn't have the brains or balls to manage disputes peacefully. But Ben had discovered that in Washington the rot was deeper and more advanced when you saw it from the inside. The typical lobbyist was vastly richer, better organized, more venal—and more dangerous—than any Afghan warlord.

"We didn't know the half of it." Ben looked at Tommy. "The arrogance, the narcissism, and the self-aggrandizement defy description. Everything we trust them to care about, the big things—our lives, our security, our financial well-being—are just chips that get traded for campaign donations. Our *real* enemies are here—and we don't have the right weapons to fight them."

"I thought it would take you a few more years to become this cynical," said Don.

Ben eyed Don's spit cup. "I don't want to steal Tommy's thunder, but we're accelerating the timeline."

Don looked to Tommy. "Didn't we agree on next year? I'm just about to sign that tanker security deal you lined up for me."

Audrey appeared at the door again. She was smiling and holding a small box of Teuscher truffles with a drawing of a forest nymph on top.

"Excuse me, Senator, Mr. Stryker is here." She shook her head. "At least I think he is. He might need a Bloody Mary to prop himself up." She shot a look at Don, who was dribbling tobacco-stained saliva into the bottle he'd fished from the trash. "But at least he's house-trained."

Pete gave Audrey a friendly peck on the cheek and collapsed on Ben's leather couch, suit wrinkled, tie loose. He had bags under his eyes and his face was ashen.

"You look like shit, Pete," said Ben.

"It was a long night, and a whoremaster's work is never done. Have to keep the customers happy." Pete turned to Ben. "What's so urgent that I couldn't go home and change my clothes before getting on the shuttle?"

"Just that Elias Vicker crashed through my patio door at sunrise this morning."

Tommy signaled for a time-out. "I don't have a lot of time."

"I've never been in a meeting where that wasn't the first thing Tommy said." Pete laughed.

Tommy nodded at him, smiling but impatient. Tommy's attention span was calibrated to the fifteen- and thirty-minute intervals of a man who lived his life giving or receiving briefings. "I'm flying to Brussels later this afternoon for the North Atlantic Council meeting."

The council was the top of the NATO food chain, the primary decision-making body for the alliance. For more than seventy years, its weekly lunch meetings had been the place where the real business got done.

"What's President Bridges giving away this week?" Ben asked.

"Rachel has decided to let the Europeans count the money they spend on refugee assistance as meeting their military spending requirements. In return, she wants them to withdraw their warning radars from Poland, our one truly solid ally in Eastern Europe, because the Polish president doesn't share her views on abortion." Tommy drummed his fingers. "Her kind of grand bargain. Two lousy ideas in one. I'm trying to salvage what I can."

Tommy glanced at Don. "At least it's not far from the Loire Valley. I'm swinging down there to meet Greta for a day." He paused just long enough after mentioning Greta's name to let Don squirm for a moment. "I'm bringing her back in. After France, she'll be based here—or New York. Depending on what we decide today."

They all snuck uneasy glances at Don. Don didn't flinch.

"Let's get on with it, before we lose Tommy," said Ben.

Ben related the story of his strange encounter with Elias Vicker that morning—leaving aside any mention of Maggie Hoguet.

"It's not Elias's style to slide off by himself," Pete said. "He can barely cross the street without an entourage."

Ben picked up a football that sat on top of a stack of papers on his desk, a gift from a Cornhusker QB who'd stopped by the day before. The visit was supposed to last fifteen minutes. Ben had spent all afternoon with the kid, pointedly blowing off a meeting in Conway's office, to talk about triple option offensive schemes. Ben ripped a tight little spiral to Pete's left, trying to catch him off guard. Pete pulled it in as if he'd been waiting for Ben's pass all along. "That tall Swedish guy you told me about this morning. The one who dragged Vicker out of his big wingding. What do we know?"

"He introduced himself as Sven Rask. Said he represents a big investor and handed Vicker his card. Vicker looked like someone had punched him. He tried to keep me from seeing it."

"But that didn't stop you, did it?" Don said.

"Does Stichting Eskandarfond ring a bell with anyone? That's what the card said."

"Greta will know," said Don. "What's it got to do with us? Shouldn't you be talking to the FBI right now?"

"Like I said, Vicker was adamant. Some crap story about not worrying his investors. All he wanted was an introduction to the best security guys I know. He says he needs better protection than the president—'industrial' level."

"That's his fixation," said Pete. "Everything has to be 'industrial,' the absolute best, perfect, inhuman. The toilets at IS, they talk to you."

Don leaned forward, elbows on knees.

"He says he was kidnapped. Won't say by whom. Won't go to law enforcement. I don't get it."

"Elias Vicker's idea of law enforcement isn't cops and FBI agents," Pete said. "It's armies of lawyers and walls of money. His law. His enforcement. He needs to be in control."

"By the way, before I forget this, I saw Jack Kunze downstairs. He thinks you're going to get crushed if you don't back off on this carrier thing."

"When have you ever seen me make a mistake?"

Ben had the most natural smile he'd ever seen. But Don knew him well enough to tell that Tommy had gotten under his skin, and Ben was faking it. It was subtle, his eyes got a little bit tighter, like he was telling you to mind your own business. Aw-shucks, no problem, was Ben's default. But nice didn't mean simple, predictable, or soft. There was a kind of impulsive, improvisational, self-righteousness to Ben Corn. He was always going to go his own way. He expected you to keep up and not ask a lot of questions.

Tommy looked at his watch. "Back on track. Ben?"

"I told Vicker that if he was serious about security, I had the guy he was looking for."

"You want the billionaire prick who funds your political ambitions, and asks for God knows what in return, to hire me to infiltrate his operation? After you've already sent Pete in to run his political operations? Would I be out of line in suggesting that Elias Vicker's security is not your main concern?"

"I'm just trying to help out a friend." Ben showed them his open hands, empty.

"What Ben is trying to say"—Tommy weighed in—"is that, as Marcus Aurelius said, the secret of all victory lies in the organization of the non-obvious."

Oddly, they all knew exactly what Tommy meant.

"Let's turn it around. Why would this Vicker trust you, some junior senator he barely knows?" Don always led with the pointed, sometimes aggressive, question. If his boots were going to be on the ground, he needed to see it. "And why would he trust me, or any team I put together?"

Pete jumped in. "It's a macho, overcompensating Wall Street thing. These guys love soldiers and spooks. It's why Vicker is so obsessed with Ben. He thinks they're fellow warriors. When Vicker looks in the mirror, Ben is the guy he wishes was looking back at him."

"And he thinks Ben believes in chain of command, secrecy, and discretion?" Don asked.

"Mostly he thinks he owns me," Ben said, in a way that was both self-deprecating and an astute read of the man who had underwritten his political career. "The way he thinks he owns Pete, and the way he's going to think he owns you, buddy boy. We're all just shiny toys." Ben paused. "You mind if I tell a story?"

Don sank back into the couch. Count on it: Ben always had a story.

"It starts with Frank Conway. When I first thought about running, before I had any idea what I was getting myself into, the senior senator from the great state of Jack Daniel's decided to adopt me—I mean to co-opt me."

Conway had been a force in the upper chamber for more than thirty years and majority leader for a decade. A large man with a snow-white mane, an easy drawl, and vicious instincts, Conway could make a man. Or break him. He boasted to friends—to the extent he had them—that he did not much care which it was, as long as he got his way.

"Frank put his fat paw on my shoulder and said, 'Son, you ever heard of Elias Vicker? You're gonna be his new best friend. And if you do the job right, that could make you *my* best friend. And *if* you're my best friend and that pretty hair don't fall out, well, I'm not promising anything, but . . .'"

"That's what we risked our asses for?"

Ben pretended to be annoyed and pointed a thumb at Don. "This guy—he can be a little touchy. He'd ask what we all risked our asses for if we broke into an outhouse and there was only one-ply tissue." He turned back to the group. "I told Conway I'd think about it. He didn't like that: 'It's not your place to tell me who you do and don't want to be friends with,' was what he said."

"Most freshman senators would drop a nuclear bomb on their own state for an assignment like that from Frank Conway," Pete said. "Conway gave it to Ben anyway. He had to. I knew Vicker would love Ben, so I arranged a meeting."

Ben interrupted.

"After I did the yes-sir, no-sir thing and told him some war stories, Vicker took me into his office to show me his heli-skiing photos. There's one where he's in powder up to his waist. He was really proud of it. I told him his form was off. He was holding his hands too high. He loved that. Know what he said? 'You can be a prick. I like that.'"

"Ben is all Vicker talks about," said Pete. "He's already got me working on the endorsement he wants to publish. The 'grand wizard' anoints our next leader."

Pete was the only member of the team who had never been in uniform. Ben, Chip, and Don all looked like first-round draft picks—bright eyes, athletic, always ready to kick ass. Pete looked like the guy who wrote their papers for them. He was Ben's guy. Pete and Ben went back to freshman year at the University of Chicago, when Pete, a local boy who'd grown up in the fishbowl of Chicago politics, his father the bulldog negotiator who mayors sent into stare downs with the labor unions, befriended the too-good-to-be-true small-town BMOC. They were an unlikely pair, so much so that it was almost a cliché: the big-city operator and the guileless country boy. Many found Pete Stryker unctuous, a Machiavellian jock sniffer always looking for an alpha male to kiss up to. But Pete saw Ben's promise—and, more crucially, because it wasn't as obvious, Ben saw Pete's. If Pete hadn't been part of their team, they would have hated him—though Don not so privately worried that one day Pete might yet give them a reason to. But Pete quickly earned Tommy's respect. He was tougher than he looked, a creative problem solver, and he had faultlessly guided Ben's political career. Not even halfway through his first term in the senate, Ben Corn was already one of the most talked about figures in American politics. If Don had any issues with Pete, that was his problem. Tommy wanted him on the team.

Pete brought an unusual level of subtlety to the game of collecting power and influence. He had written Vicker a playbook, and ran the plays using Vicker's money, long and short. Pete would find pliable candidates for Vicker to back, spend heavily to support them, and then fund opposition research and political action committees to anonymously destroy any challengers. Over the years, Vicker had assembled a stable of elected officials to do his bidding, mostly killing financial regulation or pushing through special-interest riders to legislation in the interests of boosting or destroying the futures of companies that caught his attention.

For those who proved themselves especially useful, Pete and Vicker had made an art of showing their favored electeds how to become very rich. Though congressional rules forbade members from trading on information acquired in the course of their duties, the guidelines were so conveniently vague as to be unenforceable. Subtle investment ideas, perhaps a nugget of actionable dark information were much cleaner than outright bribes. That was how Pete maintained his inventory of compromise-able electeds. The lawmakers who showed a willingness to bend, if not break, the law could always be counted on to deliver when Pete or Vicker needed a favor.

"Selling my soul to Vicker made me uneasy, but Tommy convinced me. He was right." Ben's tone was now earnest, tinged with anxiety. "Before we go any further, I need to say that not all of us are going to like everything about what's about to happen. There'll be a lot of trade-offs. Hard choices. But necessary ones." He looked each of them in the eye as if he were about to put a brand on their foreheads. "I didn't come here to be the guy who loses."

He turned to Tommy. "What have you got?"

Tommy took a manila folder from his briefcase and passed copies of a single sheet of paper around the table. "I asked my people to search for red flags around Vicker. This guy skates on the edge—and makes a lot of enemies."

In a series of bullet points, Tommy's memo summarized some of Vicker's most notorious exploits: collecting bad debts from Russian oligarchs, aggressive attacks on foreign currencies, and, most often, buying stakes in solid companies, attacking management, and then hollowing them out by paying out big dividends and exporting good-paying American jobs.

Don shifted uncomfortably, making no attempt to hide his distaste. Tommy reached over, placing his hand on Don's forearm, not forcefully, not unkindly, but firmly. "You're free to walk. If that's what you want, be my guest. Go enjoy your life. You've earned it. Make that fortune. Marry a model. Fill your garage with Lambos. I won't judge you. You'll still be my brother. But I have a lot of brothers."

He looked at Pete.

"That goes for you as well. Ben and I are moving forward. It starts today."

Pete raised a finger. "One small thing, General Taylor. Where do we start?"

"We're going to take over Elias Vicker's hedge fund."

Don almost swallowed his dip. "Did you smoke a bowl with Jack Kunze on the way in this morning?"

Ben reclined in his swivel chair.

"One thing we didn't quite think through before we helped ourselves to that Syrian blood money was how we'd feed it back into the system," he explained. "We had no idea how difficult it would be. That's why Greta's been in Latvia, to learn how the oligarchs do it. Unfortunately, we can't force another nation to launder two tons of stolen cash through its central bank like Vladimir Putin can. Which leads to the next thing we didn't think through. Two billion dollars isn't nearly enough. It's just the buy-in. These are big problems. I was getting worried. But then, this morning, Elias Vicker wrapped a silk pocket square around his fist and punched a hole in my glass door—"

"The answer to our prayers," Tommy said, and then, sarcastically to Ben, "and Ben hadn't even put his trousers on yet."

Don grimaced. "So we're going to give all our money to Elias Vicker? Does he throw in a toaster?"

"Vickers makes his investors double-digit returns every year," Tommy said. "No one knows how. Seems that his investors are all offshore. We need to be inside that operation. There is too much money in there and too many secrets. Five hundred billion dollars. Do you know how much that is? Bigger than the GDP of Sweden. And the American government can barely see into it. Frankly, I see this as a national security issue. A dark pool of money that big is a weapon of mass destruction. Imagine if it fell into the wrong hands."

"Which also gives us a predicate to put Greta on your team with a company jacket," Ben said. "Far as Vicker knows, she'll be part of the Carter Logistics crew. And yes, it is a national security issue. All that money rolling around out there in the shadows, it's a financial dirty bomb."

Tommy stood and buckled his satchel.

"We've been talking about this since Baghdad. I always assumed everyone was on board. Never occurred to me otherwise. But If I've misread any of you, now is the time to speak up. We could just leave the money in the piggy bank. Forget about it forever, decide it was just too crazy an idea. If that's what you think, there's the door."

Without thinking, or perhaps because he realized that if he thought it through he would have said no, Don nodded.

"In," said Don softly. "All in."

"Me too," said Pete.

Failure hung over them like a shroud, not just over their own careers, but over the entire military, the enterprise to which they had dedicated their adult lives. More than two decades of endless, useless war—fought with bravery and discipline by the best soldiers, but, tragically, waged by leaders without a clue. They shuddered at the near-criminal negligence that would someday be laid at the feet of three generations of military brass and vowed that, when they were in positions of leadership, they would do everything they could to reverse those failures. The numbers were stomach-turning. Nearly a million men and women put in harm's way, thousands of them killed. Over two trillion dollars gone. Half of it virtually unaccounted for, aerosolized into clouds of waste, mismanagement, and corruption. Osama bin Laden must be laughing in his grave at how many lives, how much treasure, how much psychic damage, and how much political division and social distraction he had cost America. Bin Laden had won.

They were finally going to do something about it.

"Never forget how the weak win wars," Tommy said. He taught a course at the National War College based on Ivan Arreguín-Toft's book of the same name. "Strategy matters more than power, strategy combined with unrelenting pressure and focus."

"And never forget how the weak lose wars," Ben said. "Very quickly and brutally. If we lose, they'll string us up in the town square, entrails leaking all over the sidewalk. We're not going to fuck this up."

5

Riga, Latvia

The Great Hall at Dzintaru had been cordoned off by a hundred or more broad-backed soldiers in green shirts and Kevlar vests, carrying PP-2000 submachine guns with Zenit-4TK laser sights, the weapon of choice for Russia's Ministry of Internal Affairs. "Mr. Putin's Little Green Men," Mara said. "They light up a party, don't you think?"

When they got closer, several soldiers were frog-marching an enraged gate-crasher from the tent. "I am an officer of the United States government," the man shouted, "you have no right to treat me this way. You'll be hearing from the ambassador."

Mara flashed Greta an angry look: Cletus Truax, a lifer in the U.S. Treasury who had been seconded to Latvia at the same time as Greta. With a difference: he was hell-bent on becoming a financial crime superhero, stopping bad guys in their tracks by shutting down their networks. Greta shrugged. Disrupting the Latvian networks made no sense. Better to watch the fish through the walls of the tank rather than drain it.

"That asshole should have stayed in Riga," Mara griped. "This is the wrong crowd to cross." She squeezed Greta's forearm anxiously. "I can't stand to be around these guys. They terrify me. If you ever decide to go after one of them, make sure they don't see you coming."

Members of the Russian elite were impatient and easily moved to violence. Noisy busybodies did not last long, whether they were unreliable business partners, local journalists, fallen oligarchs living in London, or finicky U.S. Treasury lifers. Greta had explained the Truax problem to Tommy more than once, but someone was intent on keeping him just where he was. Or just happy to have him and his sharp elbows out of their own way.

Far from letting go of Greta's arm, Mara held her grip, hard enough that it almost hurt, and steered her away from the fracas, past the ring of armed guards. Inside the auditorium, the concert seats had been replaced with fifty round tables covered with white linen tablecloths. Tall candles shed a warm light. A jazz band tootled pointlessly onstage. A bevy of women in short togas glided from table to table, offering platters of *zakuski*—radishes, salads, dumplings, caviar, blinis—and bottles of vodka. Scores of other women, fashionably and expensively dressed—some very young—clustered everywhere, balancing on their Manolos, nursing flutes of champagne, watching expectantly to see if they were needed by their sponsors.

"Recognize anybody?" Mara seemed to have recovered her composure; she carefully scanned the tables. Greta tried not to stare. She had heard the stories, but the reality—being in the presence of so many legendary villains—still came as a surprise. Like some fractured version of Davos, a collection of the bad, the very bad, and the even worse gathered under the big tent. Mara leaned over, whispering in Greta's ear. "I'll brief you," she said tenderly. "It's how I flirt."

She jutted her chin in the direction of a young, fit, blond man who was making his way from table to table. Smiling easily, shaking hands, eyes sparkling through Zero G aviators, and wearing Gucci loafers. "You know him, right?" Voldemārs Ozols, the former mayor of Riga and a regional superconnector: in Latvia, in Russia, and, more recently, in Europe generally.

"Who is he talking to?"

"Mikhail Rebo, allegedly the main money-mover for the Tambovskaya prestupnaya gruppirovka." The Tambov Gang, a persistent, resilient, and powerful tribe of Russian mafiosi long rumored to have been extremely close to Vladimir Putin ever since his days as deputy mayor of Saint Petersburg. The Tambovs specialized in contract killing, extortion, loan sharking, prostitution, bootlegging, sex-slave trafficking, construction shakedowns, money laundering, robbery, theft, and, increasingly, like criminal cartels everywhere, moving relentlessly into legal businesses, even if most were acquired through illegal means.

Greta tried to remain discreet but was hungry to take it all in, to commit the faces to memory.

"Don't stare," Mara said. "Act like you don't care. There, in the plaid shirt. Used to run Rosneft. Two tables down, two minor oligarchs who founded Russia's most successful bank. That's Symon Petliura with them." Ukraine's richest man.

"Who's that with Gennady Bogdanov?"

"I'm surprised that you don't recognize him, Greta. One of your opposites: Vladimir Pronichev." General of the Russian army, deputy director of the FSB. "Want to meet him?"

Greta became distracted by a man making a beeline for them across the room, swiveling his slim hips to slide between the tables, like an athlete, parting a sea of jowly, gray, corpulent blobs. He had short-cropped blond hair, blue eyes, regular features, thin lips. Fiftysomething, sure-footed, confident. *I know you,* thought Greta, *but from where?*

"That's Fyodor."

"You didn't tell me he was . . . gorgeous."

"And spoil your first impression?"

Coming upon them, Fyodor kissed Mara on each cheek, but grasped her shoulders just a bit too firmly—and held on just a bit too long. To Greta, he extended a hand.

"Miss Webb, I'm Fyodor Repin, and I'm jealous. Mara is besotted with you."

"Repin? Like the painter?" Greta asked, almost before she became aware of how much it meant to her to impress Mara's friend. "In the nineteenth century, he dragged Russian painting out of its academic past into the European tradition."

"My patronymic. Yes, a distant, very, very, very great-grandfather. You surprise me. No one has heard of Repin."

Repin led them to a table near the center of the room. Yuri held chairs for them, with surprising agility and grace for such a large man. Mara began chatting in rapid-fire Russian with the array of oligarchs already seated, waiting for her. Valery Kargin and Viktor Krasovitsky, the founders of Parex Bank. Viktor Kaluzhny, the former Russian ambassador to Latvia. Arkady Rotenberg, who had had the good fortune to join the same judo club as Vladimir Putin—when they were both twelve years old. In recent years, Rotenberg had received contracts from Gazprom to build a 1,500-mile-long pipeline to the Arctic Circle, even while under sanctions, along with his brother Boris, from the U.S. government as a Specially Designated National—a person with whom U.S. citizens were prohibited from doing business.

And then it hit her. She hadn't met him—not exactly, but felt as if she knew the man well from many grainy photos she'd seen, and numerous briefings where his name came up. Fyodor Volk, founder of the Parsifal Group—

Fyodor Repinovitch Volk. The same Fyodor Volk whose company had sold them protection for transit across Syria. Did he really think she wouldn't see through the fake name? Maybe he didn't care. If she was confused, so be it. He probably liked that. She sensed he felt no obligation to explain himself to anyone.

Volk held forth on power politics in the Middle East and Russia's advantage in military hardware, subjects that sailed over the heads of his wealthy but unpolished guests, who nonetheless nodded in agreement with everything he said, fearful of getting sideways with such an important personage. As the sycophants droned on, Greta surveyed the room. There had to be five hundred oligarchs in attendance, none of them worth less than $1 billion—most with fortunes many times that amount. Conservatively, she pegged the room's aggregate wealth at $2 trillion, give or take a few hundred billion. The wealth of nations, drained through corruption and brute force into the coffers of predators, and then funneled here to Latvia, where wolves like her new friend Fyodor injected it into the arteries of international finance—no doubt stealing as much as they could for themselves.

A stream of supplicants came by to pay obeisance to Volk. He made a show of deferring to Mara, as if it were the central banker herself, not the Russian visitor who controlled her, whose ring had to be kissed. The message was clear: if you wanted access to this delightful, brilliant, beautiful banker, you went through Fyodor Volk.

After an hour, Volk grasped the edge of the table and whispered in Mara's ear. The audience had ended. He stood up from the table and bid Mara and Greta to follow. Yuri led them through the security cordon to Volk's Maybach Pullman and ushered them into a cabin trimmed in African blackwood. Greta and Mara took the two rear seats. Fyodor sat across from them in a custom-mounted swivel chair.

Greta sank into the soft leather, allowing her dress to creep up a few inches. She caught Volk's eyes resting on her exposed thighs.

"I thought we'd have dinner at my hotel. You don't mind going back to Riga, do you? I took the liberty of having Yuri pack for you both. Your bags are in the trunk."

Mara nudged Greta. "The Grand Palace. The first time Fyodor stayed there, he thought the sheets were too scratchy. So he bought it."

Volk stared out the window. "If one has the opportunity to address life's small indignities," he said, with ostensible levity but no smile, "I believe one owes it to his fellow man."

Greta waited for a droll laugh to punctuate the witticism she assumed Volk must be proud of. It never came. "And I enjoy taking care of my friends, being able to anticipate their needs. It means getting to know them"—he paused, as if distracted by a distasteful thought—"as people." She didn't need him to spell it out. Before her time, back when bolder spirits ruled Langley, the Agency had operated hotels across the world, good places to capture the comings, goings, and intimate activities of anyone you might need to keep an eye on.

"Mara tells me you're interested in how money moves." He shifted in his seat and stared meaningfully into Greta's eyes. Just as unashamedly, she stared back. The game was on.

Well-timed, to her very last day, and she was ready to let go. Did Mara and Volk somehow know she'd been recalled? Was this introduction Mara's parting gift? Or something more complicated?

Greta nodded.

"Academic curiosity, Miss Webb? Or something . . . actionable?" That mildly scoffing tone.

"Certainly you know that already."

"Academic, then. Okay. Let's pretend that we are at the Council on Foreign Relations, a panel discussion between tut-tutting policy wonks and government officials with maybe a senator thrown in for excitement, about your country's sanctions against some of my fellow businessmen." She saw the hardness, not far below the polished surface. "It's all very high-minded. Everyone in the audience nodding along. Seriously? I can barely keep myself from laughing. I raise my hand to ask them how it's possible they don't realize they are wasting everyone's time. Or do they just get off on beating up on Russian oligarchs—making fun of their hairy knuckles, and their blond girlfriends in tight red dresses—while not actually doing anything about it. Because, as you well know, they will never shut us down. They can't afford to.

"Large-scale criminal enterprises account for about twelve percent of the world's GDP. That's one dollar out of every eight. Many governments are mere fronts for criminal interests—think about Mexico, where every president for the past five decades has essentially served at the will of the drug cartels."

He tapped Mara's knee. Greta noticed Mara's eyes dart away uncomfortably, before she laughed uneasily.

"Moralists might call it blood money. They are not wrong. Bankers have a more utilitarian word for it: liquidity." He grinned, looking pleased with himself. "There's actually a Japanese term that describes it best— *wasei-eigo*—money that changes hands under the table: 'undermoney.' Undermoney is the glue that binds whatever passes for a world order these days. It lubricates the gears of the global economy; it's the rainy-day fund that keeps 'too big to fail' from failing. If your rather impolite colleague who tried to make a scene earlier this evening, Mr. Truax, were to have his way and stanch the flow of undermoney, it would hardly be worse than handing the nuclear codes to a chimpanzee. What do you think kept your nation from sinking into a decade-long depression after your financiers blew up the world's economy in 2008? How do you think the U.S. government was able to sell ten trillion dollars of bonds to raise money to fight the coronavirus? Do you think liquidity grows on trees?"

Volk tented his tensile fingers, nails buffed to an industrial sheen, before his chest. "Of course, undermoney must be handled very gingerly, lest the illusion that the American and European finance ministries oversee a squeaky-clean system be disrupted."

With a professorial air, and somewhat less detached body language, he described for Greta the elements of the skills he'd purposefully acquired in anticipation of needing to manage—and hide from the FSB's hyenas—his own hedge fund once the Kremlin was through with him. Step one: create layers of shell companies in multiple jurisdictions worldwide, paying special attention to ones in which regulators don't ask too many questions. Step two: open accounts at pliable banks in still other jurisdictions. Step three: mainstream the funds by filtering them through apparently legitimate transactions—stocks and bonds, real estate—to disguise their illicit origin. That was the theory. Then, he explained, there was the reality: get the cash to Riga and deliver it to a certain central banker who might be expecting your call for further credit to a friendly private bank. Maybe his bank.

"And what makes all this work—I mean *really* work?" He looked squarely at Mara, a teacher calling on a prize pupil.

"A friendly central banker gently swings her censer, creating a cloud of smoke, blessing the sanctified cash as it oozes back into the system." She smiled and interlaced her fingers with Volk's. "A few clicks on my keyboard and everything is kosher. Some other clicks?" Mara gave a little shrug. "Well, let's just say that large amounts of cash need a rabbi. Someone to guide it."

"Then the final step—I call it the button." Volk raised both hands, snapped his fingers, and then spread them, pointing at the sky. "Kaboom. Your money explodes. Every account vaporized into thousands of subaccounts: transferred, retransferred, bounced here, moved there, through investment banks, brokerage firms, financial advisers—in Hong Kong, Paris, Morocco, Cape Town, Zurich, Limassol, Beirut, Jersey, Malta, Thailand, Singapore. Those droplets shower down, precipitating into new vessels in, ostensibly, more upstanding jurisdictions."

"Sounds complicated," Greta said. "How are you compensated for these efforts?"

Volk pulled a bottle of sparkling water from the armrest and offered them each a glass as the car kept rolling. "Complicated is the whole point. As to cost? Every client has different needs, requires different thresholds of discretion." His tone was sympathetic, suggesting that he was not unfamiliar with the need of foreign spies to hide money. "It's rare I discuss these matters with someone who hasn't agreed to utilize my services."

"Even if she's already a satisfied customer?" Greta looked at Volk coyly.

"Brava, Miss Webb!"

Volk grinned at Mara and back at Greta. "Mara and I had a little wager. She wasn't sure you'd make the connection. I said you'd figure out who I was before we got back to Riga."

He leaned toward Greta. "I've been in your shoes. It's no fun. You have all this cash. You think you're home free. Then you discover that unless you can account for it, it's just paper. You've hidden it somewhere. How do you unhide it?"

As Volk turned to face Greta directly, his leg slid against hers, thigh to ankle. He didn't acknowledge it or pull it back. He left it there, not pressing into her, just touching hers, a fact, not a suggestion. If she wanted to withdraw, the choice was hers. She left her leg where it was.

"When clients come to us with large numbers of bills that have sequential serial numbers, we do field work around the world, buying up old, used currency and swapping it with the original central bank. We transport the new bills across the globe to multiple geographies—cash economies in Africa, the

Middle East, Southeast Asia—where they'll remain in circulation locally and rarely reenter the formal banking system. Labor intensive, but safe."

"Intentionally messy, but elegant at the same time, isn't it?" Mara reached over, putting a hand on Greta's knee, with a gentle, but arousing, scrape of her fingernail on Greta's skin. "But important not to lose sight of the fact that the work doesn't end, even once the money is back in the system, attached, however tenuously, to its web of shell companies. It still requires tending—management. Wire transfers to wherever you want it. Proper investment to make it grow."

"We handle that as well," said Volk. "With Mara at the helm, day-to-day. In fact, you might find us to be good partners. Suggesting investments, joint ventures, let's say."

He looked at her expectantly, but without telegraphing that he'd made an offer, a threat, or really, anything at all, the expression of no expression, a subtle trick that forced his interlocutors to project their own fears and neuroses onto his impassive countenance, to reveal what they were thinking without his ever having to probe directly. In other words, your move.

Greta responded with her own version of stone face, pulling back, giving the impression she'd taken in all she needed to know. But she was sold. She only wondered why it had taken so long for Volk to show his face.

"One last thing, not small: you'll have to trust someone. *That's* the leap. That's where the risk is, the one you can't quantify. There is nothing easier to steal than stolen money. It's a temptation few can resist."

He laid his hand on hers. "But enough of this tedium." As it lingered there, she sensed a sharp change in his demeanor, his entire body quickening to an energy coiled within his taut frame. "Let's have fun—talk about art, and life, and ask the gods what they do to distract themselves."

As if he'd timed it to the second, they pulled up to the Grand Palace. Yuri sprang out to open the car door. Out of nowhere, a trio of young security guards materialized: two young men and a young woman—a line of six perfect cheekbones—wearing pigtailed earpieces, with slight bulges under their jackets. They ushered them into a private elevator to the left of the hotel's main entrance. Five floors up, the elevator doors opened into Volk's home, an entire floor. The formal entry gallery displayed his collection—paintings everywhere, filling four walls—most from the Dutch Golden Age: Pieter Claesz, Jacob van Ruisdael, Frans Hals, Jan de Bray, Rembrandt, Jacob van Loo. Greta hardly knew where to look first; Mara bit her lower lip with pleasure at seeing Greta's response.

"My favorite period, such precision—so demanding. I love the light. It was a time when the Dutch could afford the best of everything—they led the world, not just in art, but in trade, science. An object lesson in the fragility of empires."

He ushered them into the living room, where he conferred, briefly, with a formally dressed butler. A table in front of plush sofas had been laid with a simple but extravagant feast. Blueberries, strawberries, pistachios from Iran, chocolate truffles from Belgium, bowls of caviar, blinis. Several bottles of Cristal on ice. Volk dismissed the butler, who backed out of the room. He poured champagne into crystal flutes and brought them over to Mara and Greta, who were discussing a group of framed drawings, sketches that seemed to have been intended as studies for Ilya Repin's most famous painting, *Barge Haulers on the Volga*, which depicted eleven men in a harness, barefoot, filthy, in rags, struggling to haul a barge along a riverbank. Volk pointed at one of the studies, a portrait, in pencil, of a wizened man.

"That's a sketch of Kanin, the former monk my forebear befriended." Ilya Repin had lived in Samara, on the Volga River, for an entire summer, getting to know the haulers, sketching them. "Strange that it was Grand Duke Vladimir Alexandrovich who bought the painting in 1873. An advanced sensibility for that time. Now, of course, it's in the Russian Museum. The property of the people. But, who knows, maybe that one is a copy." He paused, his expression suggesting he knew exactly where the original was.

Greta looked up at him, studying him as he studied the drawing, flushed with curiosity, uneasy with what might lay beyond it. She might just have to drink enough wine tonight to find out. An unusual man, if only because most Russians—men and women—made no effort or pretense of projecting charm. It was more important for those of his generation and stature to project an uncompromising core. She felt a familiar rush—opportunity, attraction, physical proximity, but, most of all, a challenge. As she watched him with Mara, she decided that she would have them both: to see how that would work and what chemistry it might produce. Greta did not spend much time worrying about her sexual identity. If "interesting combinations" was an orientation, she would check that box. As if reading her mind, Volk laid his hand on Mara's ass and moved it slowly up her back, drawing it up to her shoulders, her neck, threading his fingers into her hair. Cradling her head, gently, he drew her toward him. Not resisting, or surprised, Mara raised her lips to meet his. As they kissed, Greta placed her hands on his hips from behind, shifting them to give herself an opening. He was all muscle. Lean, hard.

She inserted herself between them, first kissing Mara, and then turning to Volk. Suddenly, four hands were all over her body. She closed her eyes, giving into it, kissing him as he cupped her breasts beneath her dress, feeling Mara's fingers probing her thighs. In return, she drew them both toward her, reaching for the hem to Mara's dress to lift it over her head. Mara extracted Volk from his shirt and tugged at his belt; she took them both in hand, dragging them across the flat to a bedroom. An enormous bed. Fresh, crisp white linen. Someone had already removed the bedspread, folded it carefully, and laid it on a chair. Greta stripped off her clothing, and she and Mara pushed Volk onto the bed, where Mara greedily straddled him, taking him inside her, moving her hips slowly up and down as Greta kissed her, kissed him, and caressed his chest. Suddenly he leapt up, flipping Mara over onto her back. Greta was surprised at his speed, and, then, at the animal force of his thrusts into Mara. He leaned forward, one hand pinning her shoulders to the bed, the other on her neck, pushing her down into the mattress as he drove deeper inside her. Quickly, rhythmically. At first, she moaned with pleasure, but then she began crying. Shrieking.

"Stop. STOP. You're hurting me. You're KILLING me." She began to sob, trying to pull his hand off her neck. Volk responded by covering her mouth and nose with his hand. She writhed beneath him, begging in Russian for him to stop, but, if anything, her muffled cries only seemed to excite him more. Removing one hand from her mouth, he slapped her face hard, once, and then again. Mara screamed louder, tears running down her cheeks.

In an instant, Greta felt a surge of all-too-familiar emotions. Trauma and tragedy. She hated the feeling of being overtaken by that uncontrollable urge to violence. Without hesitation she flipped back onto the bed, drew her knees toward her chest, and extended her legs with full force, catching Volk squarely in the sternum—flinging him across the room and into a Chippendale side table, which splintered under his weight. But he tumbled expertly—a judo move—and was on his feet in an instant, even if his erection seemed to have lost some of its enthusiasm. He faced Greta, who stood, in a slight crouch, at the edge of the bed. His speed had surprised her. He was fast—perhaps she was faster—but he was also stronger. As she braced herself for an attack, he rose and stood naked before her, defenseless and grinning. A surrender? Or a tactical retreat? In either event, she admired his confidence. The man was a risk-taker. He had to know how easily she could put him down: two lightning kicks and he would be writhing on the carpet, balls swelling and knee shattered. But in her peripheral vision there was Mara, watching. She held out her arms, reaching for both of them.

"Fighting over . . . *me*? I'm flattered." Mara was smiling, jubilant, as she daubed tears from her eyes. "I should have warned you. It's how we play; it was his turn to get rough. Join us?"

———

Hours later, Volk slipped out of bed, careful not to disturb Mara and Greta, who lay sleeping, curled into each other, lips almost touching, hair splayed on the pillows, bodies glistening with drying sweat, saliva, and semen. Angelic, he thought. At least from appearances.

He pulled on a plush robe, tied it snugly, and poured himself a tumbler of scotch before settling into a leather club chair. He took a sip of the whiskey and held up the glass to the light. Lagavulin, sixteen years old. On one of his first assignments, the FSB sent him to Norilsk, a grim, flat, frozen hellhole one hundred miles north of the Arctic Circle to have a cup of special tea with a pesky British investor who was loudly alleging that some Putin cronies had cheated him out of his stake in a palladium mine. The poison did not work quickly. As he watched the corpulent sod succumb to paralysis, and then grow cold and stiffen, Volk had helped himself to the bottle his host had left behind. Ever since, his signature drink.

He raised his glass. A silent toast to serendipity: Greta's decision to engage Parsifal as backup for her audacious money caper, his own decision to show up that day in the Jordanian desert, unannounced, and to keep Ivanov from blowing it up. He had recognized then that she was extraordinary, and several years of discreet inquiries since had taught him how much so. It was not just her stunning package of skills and beauty, but also the company she kept: Tommy Taylor and his Delta protégés, chief among them Ben Corn, the ambitious young politician who had been Taylor's dogsbody. A bigger game was surely afoot.

Best of all, this talented agent had, unwittingly, come to him. He'd guessed she would, once she and her crew realized they didn't have the skills, or the right collection of crooked bankers, to move that much money by themselves. Going into business with the Parsifal Group, a company not exactly known to be friendly to American interests, might be a crime in itself, but to launder money they had stolen from their own government was many degrees of recklessness beyond that. Or the exact opposite. He was content, for the moment, that her motives remained murky. He would learn, soon enough, what she and her colleagues intended to do with their desert cargo. He could afford to wait. He already had all the leverage over them he needed. When he was ready, they would discover how he intended to use it.

6

Chinon, France

Tommy tossed his duffel into the trunk of the Citroën DS 7 waiting for him in front of the Gare de Tours. It had taken most of the four-hour trip from Brussels to clear his head after two days at NATO headquarters. A once noble idea—defending Europe from Soviet aggression—had devolved into a self-sustaining quagmire of bureaucratic fiefdoms and privilege. A farce played by a small army of international military officers, in dress regalia, strutting the halls of NATO's billion-dollar headquarters, attended by national delegations, diplomatic liaison officers, and hundreds of staff.

The waste and pretension disgusted him. Like the International Monetary Fund, the World Bank, and the European Bank for Reconstruction and Development, NATO lurched along, because member state politicians had neither the stomach nor, perhaps, the aptitude to pick a fight. But its original premise, an ironclad promise of American might and manpower, sheltered by a nuclear umbrella, was all but obsolete. Did anyone believe that an American president would push the red button to rescue Europe from Russian aggression? Or, for that matter, that the Europeans would even ask? Gazprom, Russia's state-controlled energy giant, supplied 40 percent of Europe's natural gas and more than 75 percent of the gas used by Estonia, Poland, Finland, and Slovakia. By controlling the flow, Russia determined whether Europeans had heat in winter, air-conditioning in summer, and electricity all year long. A stranglehold. For Tommy—and for Ben—NATO was just one more problem that needed fixing in order to rationalize how the United States deployed its military and spent its treasure.

Tommy's destination was Sazilly, a village commune of 250 people nestled amid some of France's most pristine vineyards, an hour southwest of Tours along D751 through the lush Loire Valley. It was not easy for a three-star to simply disappear for a day, but far from impossible, especially if one wore a black turtleneck and a brown tweed jacket—and the right guy was watching your back.

As he walked through the door of the Auberge du Val de Vienne, the aroma of freshly baked bread and simmering stock wafted from the kitchen. The hostess greeted him with a warm smile. As well as he thought he knew Greta, she continually surprised him: her ability to find things, places, people, to figure things out. "*Tu dois être l'ami de Greta*," the hostess said, and, without waiting for an answer, motioned for him to follow her.

Seeing him, Greta jumped up from a corner table and fairly ran, arms outstretched, to wrap him in an enormous hug. It had been a while, and he'd forgotten how much strength she held in her delicate frame.

"Urky, let me look at you." It was Tommy who had bestowed her nom de guerre—*urkraft*, the German word for an elemental, primitive, sometimes savage force of nature. The moniker amused her. It fit how he saw her—and how she saw herself.

"No sir! Let me look at *you*. No one to talk to for months," she said, giving him a fake pout. "I've missed *you*."

Grabbing his hand, she led him to the table and sat him down, nodding to the hostess, who poured them glasses of 2014 Clos de la Dioterie, Greta's favorite, from a local winemaker, Charles Joguet. The sandy, flinty, chalky soils of Chinon and Saumur were ideal for cabernet franc.

"I thought we'd have a light lunch first. Jean-Marie is a genius, you won't find better food anywhere. Shall I order for you?"

"Why change now?" She always made him laugh.

Tommy had a knack for drawing the sharpest and most unusual minds in the various clandestine services into his orbit, but he had never met anyone who combined as many disparate talents as Greta Webb. She had worked for Tommy, in one capacity or another, even while she juggled a succession of ever higher-powered jobs. Under the cover of running a proprietary trading portfolio at Goldman Sachs, she had penetrated a money-laundering network involving a string of banks and shell companies that undulated through Iraq, Jordan, Qatar, Cyprus, the Seychelles, Greece, Morocco, France, and the U.K. Before Tommy sent her to Latvia, Greta had immersed herself in another of his pet projects, determining just how deeply the Chinese army had infiltrated Scandinavian tech companies.

Greta had emerged from a sandstorm in Basra twenty years earlier, a near-starving twig of a teenage girl, with a letter addressed to Tommy from her father, a scientist and inventor who could have lived and worked anywhere in the world, but who had chosen, as a patriot, to return to Iran. He owed that man a great deal, but even without that sense of obligation, Tommy would have done what he could for the man's emaciated, brave, and brilliant daughter. Tommy had taken Greta under his wing, seen to her education, and, eventually, placed her at the Agency. Over time, with kindness and patience, he broke through her defenses, until she began to share her fears and reveal the vulnerabilities that she could show to no one else. He had read her, early on, as *his* perfect spy. Supremely able, secretive, naturally suspicious, and willing to do whatever he asked.

"In that case, the langoustine with mango and the monkfish with Espelette pepper. And a little cheese."

"Can we speak here?"

Greta blinked. "They've adopted me. But I have a better place. We'll take a little drive after lunch."

"In that case, I'll keep it clean. I've got a lot to tell you, and it had to be in person. We have an opening at a major hedge fund. That's why we pulled you out of Riga. You're moving to New York." As he scanned the room, his eyes fixed on the wall behind her, on a pencil drawing of the nearby Château du Clos Lucé, a mansion that had belonged to King Francis I, where Leonardo da Vinci had spent the last years of his life. He added: "I almost forgot, sorry about the short notice."

"Just as I was getting used to an all-potato diet."

The food had been one of her running complaints. Latvian fare was disgusting: cabbage and pork, washed down with cloyingly sweet birch sap drinks. Gray food, in a gray country, in a gray area between Russia and the West. Things had gotten better when she discovered a taste for Latvian women—or, at least, the particular one who'd made her job so interesting during the last few months. Tommy had not exactly ordered Greta to seduce Mara, but he had made it clear he expected Greta to get close to the glamorous central banker. You might even get to like her, he said. As usual, he was right. Now Greta feared she would miss Mara, or even worse, that on lonely nights, she'd go to sleep tormented and tantalized by the fantasy of escaping with Mara to that beach in Brazil. But that door had closed once Fyodor Volk had insinuated himself into their idyll.

She saw no reason to debrief Tommy on the details of her dalliance with the powerful Russian. Not that Tommy would be unhappy—or surprised—

to learn that she'd seduced a potentially dangerous adversary. She had no doubt that Volk would angle back into her vision before too long. That was fine with her. Against all expectations, he thrilled her, and it would give her an opportunity to learn more about him.

"When do I start?"

"I hope immediately." Tommy took a breath. "It'll start as Don's show. That's our way in. Physical and digital security. He thinks he'll need a few months."

Greta stiffened. "That'll give him plenty of time to just up and disappear. Again."

"I know this is tough for you, but I can't be in the middle—"

Greta cut him off, suddenly unexpectedly emotional.

"He hurt my feelings. My very best feelings. And sorry won't help." English was not her first language. Or even her third one. Her diction became awkward when she was upset. Embarrassment rose in her chest, even as the words came tumbling out. Maybe Tommy knew the whole history between her and Don. Maybe he barely knew a thing. You never knew. What never changed was his constant acute understanding—the way he could be so tuned into you while at the same time not seeming especially curious about you, as if he always had a better source of information, as if he knew you better than you knew yourself. Was it extraordinary emotional intelligence? Or, she wondered, the other kind of intelligence, data gathered and organized from many different sources, sifted and analyzed by experts toward ends he never fully shared. Whatever it was, she had to admit that it felt good to be watched over by General Taylor. She'd gotten good at putting the more troubling questions out of her mind.

She wondered what Tommy would say if she told him about the other side of Don, the one he kept hidden, that she had discovered in the weeks they'd spent planning the Syrian job, in the tiny berth she and Don had shared while crossing the Mediterranean, and during the weeks they'd spent in Paris, holed up in a suite at Le Bristol, once the pallets were safely hidden. She had not been surprised at the vigor with which Don made love—his dial was generally set to overkill in all pursuits—but she didn't expect the boundary-pushing playfulness of his sexual imagination. Or how comfortable and unguarded he'd seemed. He'd shown her photos taken the summer before he left California for West Point—a lanky surfer laughing with his buddies on a beach in Mexico, with long hair and a gentle smile, like he didn't have a care in the world beyond the next wave and a solid weed connection. But as fast as the walls between them had fallen, they went back up. Whatever furies drove Don away six months later, with no explanation or precipitating event—a fight, an argument, or even a pained conversation—it was hard to square that sun-kissed kid with the enigmatic loner who was always running in the other direction.

Tommy sat silently, allowing her to vent. She was expecting some anodyne piece of wisdom culled from his precious *Meditations*—maybe that line he loved about the foolishness of trying to escape other people's faults. But by the time Tommy spoke, his expression had darkened.

"I won't defend Don, but I do try to understand him. That man can handle any situation except for the one that might make him happy. So he runs away, off to find yet another way to punish himself. You have to let it go. It failed. Move on. Do better next time."

He took another sip of wine and went quiet again. *Oh, so it's that simple*, Greta wanted to say, but held her tongue, worried that Tommy actually did think it was that simple.

Warmth crept back into Tommy's eyes. "He's made a lot of progress in the last two years. Built a big business—and seems to be on an even keel." What Tommy didn't say was that he'd actually been far more worried about Greta than Don. Don's disappearance had shaken loose an elemental trauma buried deep in Greta's psyche, a fear of impending loss, of abandonment perhaps, dating back to the formative upheaval of her youth—the kidnapping, torture, and imprisonment of her father, at the hands of Supreme Leader Ali Khamenei's Ministry of Intelligence and Security.

After Don left, there'd been that incident while she was on assignment. One night, at a bar in Valletta, she maimed the playboy son of a local power broker after he'd suggested what he thought a woman as beautiful as Greta was good for. One punch. The best surgeons in the world were unable to reconstruct his eye socket. It took all of Tommy's power to pull her out of jail and onto a private plane before the sun rose. After that, he put her on ice and under the care of an Agency psych team led by Dr. Elizabeth Leonard. Six months later, she announced that she was over Don and ready to go back into the field. Whether Greta had come to terms with her pain or just pushed it further into the burrows of her psyche, Tommy had little idea.

"I'm glad he's doing better," Greta said. "It will be a lousy day for all of us if he decides to fade again. Now, can we please change the subject?

"Tell me about this hedge fund."

"Industrial Strategies."

Greta brightened.

"I gather you've heard of it."

"Elias Vicker? How'd that happen?"

"Ben has been cultivating Vicker for years—he placed Pete there, but this fell into our laps. Vicker had a weird incident and went running to Ben for help. Vicker has funneled millions into Ben's political career and thinks he owns Ben."

"Well, that's what Ben does."

She tentatively raised her glass, not quite sure how the line played. It always worried her slightly—the way the men were so unquestioningly dedicated to Ben Corn. Thinking she was going up for a toast, Tommy returned the gesture, Russian style: clinking glasses while looking her in the eye.

"Don still has to nail a contract. I can't believe I'm saying this, but the man's a closer. He barely knows how to have a real conversation with a civilian. But clients love him."

Greta swirled the wine in her glass. "The grunt, you mean? Me Tarzan, you fool?" They both laughed, relieved that the subject of Don had found a natural stopping point.

"So, what do you need me to do?"

"Start reading up on Industrial Strategies. You'll be Don's number two, and Chip will lead cybersecurity."

"And how are you so sure Vicker will want me and Chip?"

"That's the only deal on offer."

———

After lunch, Tommy pretzeled himself into Greta's impossibly small Peugeot. They drove west out of Sazilly for three miles before turning left onto a dirt farm road that meandered between carefully tended vineyards. At a barely noticeable break in the vegetation, Greta slowed to a crawl and edged the car into a ditch that bottomed out six feet below grade. She turned off the ignition.

"We're home."

Tommy followed as Greta scrambled through ten feet of dense brush before reaching a massive stainless-steel door bolted with a SimonsVoss key-fob padlock. She clicked the MobileKey on her phone, held the camera to her eye for iris recognition, and the door swung inward. She closed it behind them and grabbed Tommy's arm to guide him through the darkness. "Careful, there are steps here."

Greta used the light from her phone and reached out for the railing of a steep staircase that led down another ten feet. She ran her hand along a rough wall of rock, feeling for a switch. Overhead, floodlights illuminated a vast limestone cavern, the obverse of a cathedral, circles of light giving way to depthless shadows. In medieval times, the plain had been mined for the creamy, lustrous *tuffeau* used to build the hundreds of châteaus that dotted the landscape, leaving behind elaborate networks of caves and tunnels, invisible and undetectable beneath the fertile farmland above.

"Whoa!" Tommy yelled, quickened by awe and delight, his voice echoing across the cavern.

"You like?"

"I'd expect nothing less," said Tommy.

"During World War Two, the French hid everything they could from the Nazis in caves like this one. Wine, silver, jewelry, art, furniture. Then they plowed dirt over the entrances, scattered some seed, and left them alone. This one is self-contained, but some of them extend for hundreds of miles."

Motioning for him to follow her, Greta moved farther into the cavern, past galleries carved into the rock and massive stalactites hanging from the roof of the cave, twenty feet above. After three hundred yards, she turned left into a room completely filled with wooden cases of wine—thousands of them.

"All this yours?"

"Around here, they know me as an eccentric wine collector. Makes me popular. Especially because I pay cash. We have a thirty-year lease, set up by a young Parisian lawyer who is very good at not asking questions."

She kept walking. A hundred yards farther on lay dozens of wooden crates the size of larger steamer trunks labeled לארשי לש רצות / רב יחרפ שבד.

"My Hebrew is a little rusty," said Tommy.

"Wildflower honey, product of Israel," said Greta. "Crates marked 'Federal Reserve Bank of New York' tend to get noticed."

Tommy walked over to one, gave it a shove, and knocked on the top.

"So that's what 2.4 billion dollars looks like."

"Minus costs. Took a lot of bribes to get here—five hundred thousand dollars to a harbormaster in Haifa to sign off on a shipment of 'honey,' one million dollars for a Sardinian freighter to move it across the Mediterranean, half a million to ship it from Valras-Plage up the Orb, two hundred thousand dollars for the truck that Don and I drove from Béziers to here. And then there were some personal expenses."

"Like?"

"Ask Don," she said coyly.

Tommy looked at the pallets, awe-struck. He'd been imagining this since his crazy final days in Iraq, wearing his first star, running Green Zone security, supervising the distribution of the vast sums flown from Andrews to Baghdad every week, sending out teams to spread around the cash. A sick joke, but a mere footnote to Donald Rumsfeld's misguided strategy of using Saddam's plundered billions to buy the peace and order that George Bush had promised the Iraqi people—when what was really needed was détente with the Republican Guard. Or, even better, for mighty America to have stayed out of Iraq altogether. Instead, money that was meant to serve as a down payment on democracy and civil society ended up being used to fuel a Sunni insurgency that soon turned Iraq into a deadly quagmire.

A decade later, Tommy's civilian betters in the national security establishment, despite claiming they'd learned the lessons of Iraq, became hellbent on repeating the same strategy in Syria, handing out withdrawals from Bashar al-Assad's frozen accounts to any opposition crook who was able to sell gullible American diplomats on their ability to foster representative democracy—and offer sweetheart deals to U.S. oil companies. Since Tommy had handled dozens of money drops in Iraq, he was drafted to manage the same kind of operation in Syria. But this time, he was ready. He knew full well that, once the parachutes burst open, no one would be able to know exactly what happened to the cargo. Nor would they care. If the money didn't end up at its intended destination, who was going to raise a fuss?

Tommy had seen it with his own eyes. In his final days in Saddam's palace, someone ordered a C-130, loaded with more than $2 billion in cash and bound for Baghdad International, to change course at the last minute and make its drop out over the desert. Not only had the cash never been accounted for, the incident had been forgotten in a way that Tommy could only conclude was deliberate. That's when he realized that for the perfect heist, you had to make what you stole disappear twice. First when you took it. Then when you made sure no one could tell it was gone.

He jumped up to sit on one of the crates.

"Smells nice in here. But as long as these crates sit in this cave, it's just Monopoly money. How much have you actually been able to move?"

He gave her the look that had taken him to the highest reaches of the Pentagon, an unyielding stare that said "Give me an answer, not an explanation."

"About three hundred fifty million is in our vault in Geneva. And I have diversified another fifty million into a small portfolio of Old Master paintings and select antiquities. They represent high value and can be moved easily and liquidated quickly."

"Thank you for not making excuses. I'm assuming you have a plan for moving the rest of it."

Greta had anticipated this moment and had used her time in Riga well. "I've become quite close with the head of the Latvian central bank."

Tommy smiled approvingly. "The chess prodigy? Nice work. I was wondering how you got that little bruise. You thought I wouldn't notice?"

She touched the tender spot on her cheekbone that had collided with Mara's signet ring, hoping Tommy wouldn't notice how flustered she was, but also taking comfort that he'd noticed.

"Yesterday, she introduced me to one of her Russian friends who owns a bank in Riga that handles a lot of money coming out of Moscow . . . and elsewhere. He has offered to manage the process of mainstreaming our money."

"Mainstreaming? That's a nice word for it. Who's the friend?"

"Someone we know from Syria. Fyodor Volk."

"Your buddy." Tommy looked into the distance. "How did that work out?"

"In the end? Fine. This much money is a logistical nightmare. I didn't fully anticipate that. We need experts. Not just to wash it back into the financial system safely, but to invest it, to move it afterward. To wherever we need it."

Tommy nodded. "I get that, and sorry for the time pressure, but it's real. Let me know what you decide." In other words, get that money moving, don't screw it up, and don't tell me anything that could get me into trouble. He gave her a milder look. "Strange bedfellows, eh, Urky?"

An odd choice of words, thought Greta, wondering if there was any way Tommy could have known about what she, Mara, and Volk had gotten up to the night before. As she regained her composure, she gave Tommy the detailed tutorial in advanced money-laundering techniques Volk had shared with her, including his vague offer of partnership—whatever that meant. What it came down to, she explained, was that, for a price, they'd need help from the central bank of a corrupt foreign nation to launder their ill-gotten gains. But it wasn't as simple as making a deposit and waiting for the bank to dribble the funds into circulation. That was too risky. An overeager meddler like Cletis Truax might pick up on the sudden influx of greenbacks into the Latvian economy and trace the serial numbers, which would lead him right to the airdrop in Jordan. No, first they'd have to swap the new bills for old by physically moving them around the world in small enough chunks that no one could say where they came from. Perhaps using the Vatican Bank—with "branches" in 189 countries—as their currency trader.

"That's why it's taken me so long. You and I are both completely exposed if anyone ever decides to follow that money."

"I can't second guess whether your Russian is the right guy to handle this. He might be. He better be. We don't have any more time to futz around. Three hundred fifty million dollars *maybe* gets us to Super Tuesday. That's what we get for playing it safe. Every day this money sits there, it's worth less to us. We need to let the dogs out of their crates and put them to work."

7

The Imperial Tower, New York City

The offices of Industrial Securities occupied the top three floors of The Imperial Tower in the West Fifties, a 1,750-foot-tall spire, financed by a consortium of Asian banks, that had shot up out of a narrow lot where an elegant historic mansion had stood for more than a century. It was just a short stroll across town from Vicker's apartment on the ninety-ninth floor of 432 Park Avenue. Aerie to aerie, Vicker could make the trip in eleven minutes. He usually enjoyed the walk, but when it was cold or rainy he liked to imagine building a personal cable car that could zip him right to the office from his bedroom or, better yet, in the personal electric air vehicle that he had on order from Opener—the Blackfly—to hop from roof to roof—his feet never touching the ground.

He tried never to vary his routine: his seventeen-hour daily fast, half an hour of training with an orthopedist who specialized in dynamic neuromuscular stabilization, a palmful of supplements prescribed by Clinique La Prairie, the life extension spa in Switzerland where he spent two weeks every year undergoing embryonic cell therapy treatments, and, most important, his hour with Vinnie.

Vinnie Pantangelo. Vicker had erased all outward traces of his lonely Queens boyhood except for his friendship with Vinnie, his only friend then, now, and, perhaps, ever. A bulldog of a boy and a sweetheart of a man. They had been a couple of oddballs: obsessed with the Mets, *Star Trek*, and the stack of *Playboy*s Vinnie's dad left in the garage after Vinnie's mom kicked him out. Vinnie, who was much bigger than Elias, had looked out for him from P.S. 89 all the way through Monsignor McClancy Memorial High School. In return, Elias made sure that Vinnie never failed a math test. Later in life, Vicker spent years seeing a shrink, but there was one shameful secret he had never revealed. When they were twelve, Vinnie's mom bought Vinnie a portable AM/FM radio you built yourself. A Heathkit GR-151RS. When Vicker asked his parents to get him one just like Vinnie's, his father had angrily said no. One day after school, Vinnie, who was always leaving things everywhere, left the radio at Vicker's house. When Vinnie asked Elias if he knew where it was, Elias said no. It seemed so unfair that Vinnie had one and he didn't. Vicker still had that radio. In a drawer next to his bed. The shame still burned within him even though Vinnie had never cared.

Every workday began with a visit to Vinnie. For public consumption, Vinnie was his personal barber, ensconced in a man's lair designed after London's Pankhurst Barbers: beveled glass mirrors, burnished mahogany paneling, an elaborate coffered ceiling, two leather club chairs, and his personal barber chair, custom-made for him in tufted maroon leather by Bentley. Vinnie had no angle. He didn't know or care much about Industrial Strategies; he hardly seemed to understand what the business was. But he was a shrewd judge of people. When Vicker was puzzling over whether to hire someone, he'd often send them down to Vinnie for a read.

Vinnie looked up from the *Post* as Vicker walked in at eight a.m., like clockwork. "Hey, Elvis, I was just reading about you." He held up the paper for Vicker to see. "Not a bad photo, but your left side is better."

"Let me see that." Vicker snatched the paper Vinnie was holding, not caring that he hadn't offered it.

"Good on you, Pete Stryker." He chortled.

The front page of the *Post* had a story about a #MeToo scandal that had forced the sudden resignation of a high-flying biotech entrepreneur who'd been in a bitter fight with Industrial Strategies for control of his company. The story suggested that the timing of the revelations was not a coincidence.

Vinnie started to lather up Vicker's face.

"You seem a little on edge today."

When something was on his mind, Vinnie always picked it up.

"I'm thinking of making some changes—overhauling our security. You remember last week when I was in Washington, right?"

"The last-minute trip? That must be exciting, calling those important senators and getting meetings like that."

"When I was there, my friend Ben Corn told me about a very impressive guy he wants me to meet. Don Carter. Former member of Delta Force. Supposed to be the best. He's been working on a proposal for a week, and he's coming up today. Should be in my office by the time we're done. It's a big decision."

"You need me to meet with him?"

"Please."

———

Dressed in a white shirt and a black tie under a gray Armani suit, Don followed a cowering young woman to an internal conference room at Industrial Strategies. An extraordinary turn of events, he thought. The army had been a cold place after he had taken on a senior officer—beating a full bird colonel to a pulp after discovering him trying to rape a nineteen-year-old corporal behind the mess tent. Too bad that the guy lost an eye, but, really, thought Don, the colonel was a prick, and someone needed to teach him a lesson. That was just how he was wired. But it was thanks to Tommy—and only Tommy—that the court-martial had acquitted him. And now, here he was. Thanks to Tommy.

He found Elias Vicker sitting at one end of a long glass table, with his tools carefully arrayed before him: three pencils, a pad of ruled white paper, two coasters—one supporting a Baccarat tumbler of Badoit—reading glasses, his phone, and a remote control wand with a few buttons. Not my cup of tea, thought Don. Neurotic, a control freak. He had promised Tommy and Ben that he would give it a go, suck it up. But he doubted that his initial, visceral dislike would fade.

Without rising or offering his hand, Vicker picked up the remote and pressed a button. As if he had conjured a rain cloud from a clear blue sky, the room's four walls turned to fog, lending the large almost empty room a weightlessness that was at once ominous and peaceful. With a flick of his head, Vicker motioned for Don to sit next to him on the long side of the table. Even sitting down, Don judged Vicker to be five-eleven, rail thin, fit but not muscular. Late fifties, with a full head of dark hair combed straight back, fashionably long, trailing over his collar. That kind of haircut—and the dye job—probably set him back a thousand bucks. Watery blue eyes flanked a long sharp nose. A flat, tight, controlled expression. Decent-looking guy, thought Don. Cares about how he looks. Then he noticed the rapid-fire knuckle-cracking, making Don thankful that Vicker had not bothered to extend a hand.

"You've had seven days, Mr. Carter. So, what have you got?"

Don drew two inch-thick manila file folders from a well-used leather portfolio and placed them on the table.

"May I speak freely, sir?"

Vicker nodded, impatient. But Don made no effort to adjust his deliberate pacing. "You have enemies. And what you have now in terms of physical and digital security is worthless."

Vicker appeared not to react, except for the left corner of his mouth, which drew back ever so slightly. "Tell me something I don't know, Mr. Carter. I make omelets, I break eggs. You've read Page Six, so what?"

"If you please, sir, allow me to run you through this file."

Don pushed one of the folders across the table. Opening the file, Vicker looked down at a glossy photo, date- and time-stamped as of 7:45 a.m. three days earlier, of himself leaving his apartment building.

"So what, Mr. Carter, you know where I live. So do fifty shitty little paparazzi."

"Of course, sir, merely for sequencing. The second photo may be more helpful." Don flipped to it in his file.

Turning the page in his own file, Vicker found another photo of himself, date-stamped the same day, but an hour earlier, sitting in his home office, hunched forward at his desk holding his favorite souvenir coffee mug—with the name of a now defunct company that he had looted a few years earlier. It took him a few seconds to absorb.

"My computer is looking at me. I'm looking at my own computer."

"Correct, sir. Now turn to the next two photos. Number three is a screenshot of what you were reading, a report from Gerson Lehrman Group on United States oil refining capacity. Number four is a screenshot of the email you were writing to GLG, requesting a meeting with one of their experts."

Vicker paused, stared straight ahead, then flicked his eyes in Don's direction. "You've hacked my computer, commandeered the camera—whatever you call it."

"Please have a look at the next few photos."

Vicker flipped through a series of supersharp full-color 8 x 10 photos of the trading room at Industrial Strategies. In one, the camera appeared to be peering over the shoulder of his head trader. Another, from his own screen, showed an open Excel spreadsheet, detailing Industrial Strategies positions in a wide range of investments. Another screen showed a memo about trading strategies that had yet to be implemented. Don could see over the shoulders of every single trader.

"You've hacked my video security system."

Feigning nervousness, Don fingered the last manila folder in his stack. He and his team had debated whether to use the next part of their presentation. The content made Don uncomfortable, and there was no telling how Vicker would react. But Tommy had insisted. He wanted Vicker to understand how vulnerable he was.

"This is a little delicate, screenshots of a WhatsApp conversation between you and your wife, but—"

As Don hesitated, Vicker shot a hand across the table and snatched the folder impulsively, almost violently, and glared at Don. He opened the folder greedily, scanned the pages quickly, and then settled back into his chair to read them slowly for a second time, with concentration. Don watched his face carefully, unable to discern any reaction.

Waiting for Vicker, he too turned his eyes to the pages, still amazed, even though he'd read the chat transcript many times.

[Piper] Darling, we'll take a four-bedroom suite at the St. Regis. A different scene in each room. And you'll be down the hall, in front of your bank of monitors.

[Vicker] Who are you casting?

[Piper] The MOST beautiful boys and girls. The ones you picked from that ballet company playbill and the catalog of that modeling agency that casts your annual spring party. An even dozen.

[Vicker] Plus you.

[Piper] Of course. BTW, I deserve a bonus for this one, Ellie.

[Vicker] Bonuses are earned, Piper dear. Performance based. Is there a theme?

[Piper] Always, darling! Venice Carnival. I had a case of those wonderful masks shipped from Ca' Macana—you know it. That sweet shop on Calle delle Botteghe. We'll have the bauta, the colombina, the moretta and all the boys will wear the medico della peste. I love that—it's the one with a big nose shaped like a beak—looks like a long cock. Yum.

[Vicker] You're so crude, Piper. LOL. Part of your charm.

[Piper] That is how you like your sluts, right sweetie? Reverse oreo—pure on the outside, dark in the middle? Anyway, it will be a blast.

[Vicker] Can you make one room a dungeon? I might want to play a bit.

[Piper] Consider it done . . . Sir!

[Vicker] You need anything from me?

[Piper] I've promised each one 50K. A bargain given how hot these kids are—and that includes confidentiality agreements. We'll need a suitcase of cash.

[Vicker] Got it.

[Piper] And, honey?

[Vicker] Yes?

[Piper] You can settle my honorarium by wire transfer? The Goldman account?

After what seemed like an impossibly long time, Vicker looked up and gave Don a wolfish, unabashed grin. Apparently, the man could not be embarrassed. He did what he did. That was his entitlement, and, in the ever-changing tableau of their relationship, his tanned, toned, sylphlike, socially prominent wife, Piper, had found her niche in organizing risqué performances for an audience of one. He had married her thinking that he was simply buying a hood ornament for his extravagant lifestyle, but she had turned out to be so much more. Not a love match, their relationship was too transactional for that, but, to Vicker, something even better.

"Our birthday present to each other last year. She's the actress. I'm the director."

Still smiling, as if at his own private joke, Vicker put the papers back in the folder and slid it toward Don.

"If you behave, I'll show you the video someday."

Don couldn't imagine anything he'd be less interested in seeing.

"With respect, sir, there's no reason you would know the mechanics of computer science or the details of physical and digital security. Right now, we are merely probing weaknesses in your digital infrastructure."

"You seem to have found a couple."

"Your systems are no match for an even moderately sustained effort. In technical terms, sir: they suck."

Vicker paid a fortune every year to hire people from all the right schools—CalTech, MIT, Carnegie Mellon. Beyond the personnel, he spent a king's ransom on machines and purportedly hardened facilities. In the face of the team that Don had fielded, Vicker might as well have left his passwords hanging on the wall outside the front door. What Vicker did not know was that only a few nation-states could have withstood, much less detected, the incursions Don had organized. Tommy had asked S35, the division of the National Security Agency that collects data from major fiber-optic cables and switches, to have a go. That might have been overkill, but Tommy wanted to make sure that Don made a good impression. The pummeling of the Industrial Strategies systems had been, in fact, a massive display of brute computing force, designed to completely shatter any confidence that Vicker might have had that his systems were secure.

Vicker focused into the distance, his facial expression blank.

"I've obviously hired the wrong people if you can just burrow into my house, my office, my computer systems. Now I have you nosing around my business."

"Sir, I took the liberty of seeing what I could find—and of being brutally honest with you because of your relationship with Senator Corn. Ben told me to pull no punches."

"A cool one, that Corn. One of the few guys in D.C. I trust." Vicker paused. "We'll have to fix all of this. How?"

"Depends on your goals. The digital may be the simplest, but that requires a deep dive by a red team—that will give us an inventory of all the weaknesses in your systems. People, software, hardware. Followed by a complete systems audit."

"Red team?"

"A shadow. The guys who watched you eat breakfast. They would need free rein—working from outside of Industrial Strategies—to determine what holes a dedicated adversary could exploit. Then we map out a plan to plug them. My guess is that hackers are stealing your data every day, and most of the time your guys don't even know they're there. Whether they're sophisticated or not, they're trying to take your stuff and they won't go away. You're a target and always will be."

"And after you know who they are?"

Don stared directly into Vicker's eyes. "Case by case. We always shut the door. Sometimes we go after them digitally. Sometimes . . . we snap their necks."

Vicker nodded approval.

"And physical security?"

"Senator Corn mentioned an abduction."

"That cannot happen again." Vicker shuddered involuntarily.

"I've been there, sir."

"Ben told me. It's part of why he recommended you. Said that you'd get it."

Don's mind wandered to the bleakest ninety-two days of his own life. Snatched from Kabul, moved like chattel to a tribal area just over the Pakistani border, and held for ransom. Starved, beaten, isolated. Forced to listen to endless chatter from naive Afghani teenagers about the global Christian and Jewish conspiracy to control their country and obliterate Islam. And the moment that Ben showed up with the cavalry to break him out of his Taliban jail.

"Mr. Carter, I never want to experience that again. New York just isn't a safe place any more. It's a lot worse lately, and going downhill from here. I need to be able to get out of the city and disappear at a moment's notice."

"Any particular reason?"

Vicker seemed to drift off. His mind somewhere else.

"My job is to assess risk, Mr. Carter. It's my passion—my brand. I've industrialized it. I spend every waking minute thinking about what can go wrong in the world. Unintended consequences, natural disasters, currency crises, incompetent auditors, corrupt management. It's what I do."

Don nodded approvingly, warming to his solipsistic riff.

"There are pockets of danger everywhere, Mr. Carter. Some physical, some financial—some both. Ferreting them out is the key to making money. Failure to focus on every last detail can destroy capital. That's how I make money." Vicker sat back in his chair, self-satisfied.

Smug bastard, thought Don.

"I can afford to protect against risks real and unreal, high probabilities and fat tails." Vicker paused. "You never know what can happen in New York. After 9/11 this town was locked down. Boarded up during COVID-19. When things like that happen again, I want out. No matter what."

Don held a deep breath, seeking the stillness that all snipers need to make the shot—or, in this case, the sale. He wasn't exactly nervous, but a lot was riding on his ability to draw Vicker in. He began to feel the same sick rush he once got from watching a head explode at a thousand yards.

"You're asking for a major commitment, Mr. Vicker," Don began. "None of this comes cheap. Especially the physical security. To give you what you want, we'll need places to stage escape vehicles, personnel, resources. Around-the-clock protection requires twenty-five men, full-time—six or seven men on a shift, times three, plus some swing seats."

Vicker stared at Don, as if he just was not getting it.

"It's my money, Mr. Carter. I don't need a reason. Last month Piper dragged me to some sappy event, raising money for the kids of murdered cops. Only good thing was she put me next to the police commissioner. You know what he told me? They have a detailed plan to seal off the island in the event that something crazy like 9/11 happens again. Complete containment. No one gets in or out. For as long as they deem necessary. That doesn't work for me. I need an industrial-strength plan. Industrial-strength protection, industrial-strength freedom of movement. Under any and all conditions. Can you do that?"

Don began thinking through the logistics of running an exfiltration protocol in a Manhattan with no power, maybe no running water. Roving marauders, intensely suspicious New York City cops, trigger-happy nineteen-year-old National Guardsmen toting M4s, and miscellaneous Feds commandeering the very resources Don would need in order to move Vicker. His kind of fun. Especially with an unlimited budget.

"Do we need an extraction plan for anyone besides you? Family, friends, associates?"

"Yes and no. Just me, but I expect you'll have to build a significant team."

Don nodded.

"You tell me what kind of financial safety net we will need to keep a team like that motivated. They'll be worried for themselves, their families, at a time when I will need everyone to focus on . . . me. I survive, they'll be rich men, their families taken care of, safe."

"Budget?"

"Just work it out, and tell me what you need. Anticipate problems, show me roadblocks, build me solutions."

"Can do. But I need to be crystal clear with you, sir."

Vicker sat back in his chair.

"Ben Corn and I have planned and led dozens of missions. Maybe a few you've read about, but mostly not. We've never launched anything without the right resources—men, matériel, bases, support—in place. We're not suicidal. We're realistic. We know we may lose friends, but we don't want to lose them because we tried to save a few bucks."

"Then we're cut from the same cloth."

Don mulled that over. Not likely, considering that Vicker had just given a standing order to leave employees, friends, and family by the side of the road while they whisked him to safety.

"Happy to hear, sir. I'll draw up a plan, but, just so we are on the same page"—Don went in for the kill—"I won't field a team unless I've got responsibility for physical and digital security. In this world, there's no longer any separation; try to compartmentalize those and it all falls apart."

"And what does that look like, Mr. Carter?"

"At your level of success and visibility, we assume that our adversaries could be state actors or world-class hacktivists, basically, best of breed."

"Steps?"

"We can start this week with a full-bore red team to develop a baseline."

"Done."

Vicker closed the notebook that lay open on his desk, even though he hadn't written anything in it, and looked up at Don. "One more thing: you look like you could use a little cleanup. Why don't you stop and see Vinnie on the way out?"

Don was confused.

"Sir?"

"Vinnie. He's my barber. Just let Alison know. She'll show you."

Vicker hit the button on his intercom. "Alison, get Pete in here."

When Pete trotted in, Vicker reached into his briefcase and pulled out a large envelope with the *Roundelay* magazine logo on which someone had scrawled: "Rush/By Hand: Elias Vicker."

"Remind me, Pete, who is this Jason Renton again?" Vicker did not bother to look at Pete, but began unsealing the envelope with so much care and concentration that Pete almost wondered if he had ever opened an envelope himself.

"He's their Wall Street reporter—"

"Oh him, yeah. He's ours, right?"

"Well, we . . . have an arrangement."

By now Vicker had wrested the magazine from its envelope and was carefully paging through it, staring at each page intently as he spoke. "I have a deal with the editor—whenever I'm in the magazine, I get a copy in advance. She told me I'm in Renton's column this month and I'm going to love it. But I don't remember talking to him."

"There it is." Pete leaned over the conference table. "'Money and Power'—that's Renton's column."

"What's this drawing?"

A cartoonist had attached Vicker's head to a bird of prey, with hundred-dollar bills as feathers, and wings extended, soaring over New York City wearing a maniacal grin. The caption quoted from one of his quarterly letters to investors: "Money has wings. It flies to where it is loved."

"Well, sir, I think it's actually meant to be satirical—*lightly* satirical. That's not a bad thing. It humanizes you. In politics, there's a rule: if no one's making fun of you, it means no one likes you."

"Pete, are you aware of the fact that I am not a politician?"

Vicker leaned back in his chair, put his feet on the table, right in front of Pete's face, and started to read the article. A few moments later he looked up; his dyspepsia had stiffened into a cold rage. Oh shit, Pete thought, he's not even going to yell. Don picked a good day to meet the boss.

"Peter, my newsletters. We have a policy here. They are not to be quoted from. That's a first principle."

"Sir, I have to apologize," Pete said. "I told Renton it was okay. He told me he had letters from Citadel, Pershing Square, Baupost, and Two Sigma. I thought it would look bad if you weren't there."

"Renton should have known better," Vicker snarled. "Of course a flack's going to say yes. That's why he asked you. We need to teach that guy a lesson. Call Max Carmody—I love the way he includes a copy of the Bankruptcy Code when he serves legal complaints. Tell him Renton has stepped way out of line. He needs to hit him, and hit him hard. I don't care what it costs."

As they left, Don and Pete exchanged glances: this man is insane.

8

The Pentagon

"A bit melodramatic, isn't it?" Don asked as he and Chip were shown into Tommy's SCIF.

"Smart thing to do," Chip said. "Now that Tommy's got this big job, he has to be just as worried about our side—NSA, Agency, whoever the hell else—listening in on him as any adversary."

Pentagon sensitive compartmented information facilities—SCIFs—like their counterparts in secure facilities maintained by governments and businesses around the world—conformed to both Intelligence Community Directive Number 503 (ICD 503) and TEMPEST requirements for shielding, filtering, and masking the facilities from a wide range of threats—state actors, rogue case officers, or just teenagers hungry for a challenge.

"Thanks for coming down," said Tommy. "So, what do you make of Ben's buddy?"

"Decisive. He signed off on everything, including the most elaborate exfiltration program we can invent, with safe houses, transport, armory. Didn't even ask the cost."

"Safe houses—plural?" Tommy placed his hands on the conference table and tilted back in his chair.

"We've found two that could work: one in the Village, and another in the West Fifties."

Chip pulled up photos on his laptop: building facades, floor plans, zoning rules. "A town house and a small commercial building. Central locations, curb cuts, perfect for what we need, and Vicker hit the bid without haggling: thirty-five million clams just to buy them. The structural work is already under way."

"Budget?"

"Open checkbook. To kit it out we'll need another forty, fifty million. Vehicles, sea-air support, ammo, hardened comms. And that's before the operating costs: I've convinced Vicker he needs his own small army—

twenty-five soldiers for the physical security and a half-dozen or so pencil-necks for cyber. All former Delta and army cybercom alums. He's crazy for the idea."

"What do you get the guy who has everything?" Chip laughed. "His own personal special ops team."

"And one fetching lady spy," Tommy said.

A heavy look flashed across Don's face, liked he'd just absorbed a blow and was trying not to show it. "Of course, sir, we can't do this without Greta. There's no way," he said, somehow managing to speak with even less emotion than usual.

"Thanks for understanding." Tommy's tone was gentle, but Don thought he heard a note of sarcasm.

"It's not just that this is up her alley, but we have to keep this in the family," said Tommy. "None of us knows where this might lead, and I'm moving forward only with the people I trust."

He turned to Chip. "What's your timing?"

"Our red team is working full throttle. Vicker's computer systems aren't exactly a joke, but pretty close."

"You mean they suck compared to USCYBERCOM."

Chip looked up from his laptop. "Right. It's not a fair fight."

Information technology had become the blind spot—and the black hole—of the financial services industry. Those at the top of the food chain knew how to make money, but they were clueless about the software, hardware, and information technology that protected their businesses and their clients from fraud and identity theft. Beyond hiring dweeby, nice guys with fancy degrees, thinking that one Ivy League engineer was much like another, they barely thought about it.

"For the money he is spending now," said Chip, "Vicker will get as close to weapons-grade as legally possible."

"So you think Industrial Strategies is everything we want it to be?"

"Looking good so far," said Don. "I just can't believe these things exist. I mean, this company manages five hundred billion dollars, and, as far as I can tell, it doesn't do anything but solve really complicated math problems."

During the last decades of the twentieth century, hedge funds seemed to have sprung from the earth and begun dividing and multiplying like cells undergoing mitosis. But not only did hedge funds manage and earn a lot of money, they were completely unconstrained, subject to few rules and fewer norms of behavior. An entity like IS could provide cover for all manner of covert activities, moving people and money as it liked, earning the kind of profits it would need.

In search of *alpha*, the holy grail of finance, that elusive excess return over the broad market, hedge fund managers had created the perfect black box. They bought and sold stocks, bonds, farms, Chinese ceramics, mines, wines, factories, rare cars, airlines, railcars, jumbo jets, paintings, gold, diamonds, and people. No one questioned the right—or asked for a reason—when a hedge fund sent its people anywhere and everywhere, to meet anyone, anytime. No one blinked if some hedge fund guy showed up at a copper mine in Mongolia or in the antechamber of the finance minister of Burkina Faso. Or in the Oval Office.

In the history of investing, really in the jungle of business, there had never been a breed of cat like the hedge fund. Individually—and especially in concert, when they smelled blood and ran, like spotted hyenas, in packs— hedge funds had become the apex predators of the global financial system, often more powerful than even a sovereign government that stood between them and whatever prize they coveted. Hedge funds processed vast amounts of information—who knows how much of it proprietary—in search of the "black edge," the hidden market insights that turned millions into billions. But exactly what was a hedge fund? At its core, nothing more—or less— than a collection of powerful and unusual brains that often fell pretty far out along the Asperger's spectrum. Minds uniquely attuned to making nonobvious connections, spotting patterns, inconsistencies, and correlations where others saw only noise. In another time, those minds might have found their way into less worldly callings: physics, pure mathematics, medicine, music, or art.

But, beginning in the 1980s, as Wall Street became more central to the American economy and earning vast fortunes there more central to the American idea of success, the raw power of those Asperger's brains got plugged into financial machinery that connected IQ to testosterone and spat out money. The whizzes discovered that they didn't have to spend their lives quietly seething while the jocks got ahead. Wall Street was desperate for them. The quirks of their atypically ordered intelligence enabled them to spot anomalies that might produce only a fraction of a fraction of a cent per trade, but which could be repeated, instantaneously, a billion, or even trillions of times. To the naked eye, they appeared to make money from nothing. Forget splitting the atom. All you had to do was to visualize a minute inefficiency.

Some of those brains were housed in the skulls of perfectly well-ordered and sociable people: who as kids might have played baseball, run cross-country, or strummed a guitar. But, more often, hedge fund brains belonged to the socially awkward, the slightly odd and obsessive. The boys—and they were mostly boys—who sat in the back row not to mock, disrupt, or distract, but because they were absorbed by their own thoughts or reciting *Dr. Who and the Daleks* in their heads, from memory. They might have gotten straight A's, or, just as likely, flunked out of high school. They were the kids who spent Saturday nights by themselves, fiddling with antique slide rules, building their own computers, relating to other humans only electronically, and obsessively watching *Star Trek*.

The Wall Street ecosystem gave these brains new outlets for aggression and entrée into a world even more remote and virtual than Dungeons and Dragons or *Lord of the Rings*: the world of money and the exploding universe of incredibly cool things to spend and waste it on. In a Pavlovian loop, their brains responded—as most would—to a seemingly endless stream of positive reinforcement. Their natural, if somewhat unsociable, capacity for intense and unrelenting focus produced streams, then rivers of nickels, dimes, dollars, and then hundreds of millions of dollars that filled their electronic buckets, and, which, in turn, rapidly escalated their sense of self-worth. But, rather than producing contentment, the feedback loop spun them up to pursue more. More money, to be sure, but, more than money; the winning, beating the odds, surpassing what others of their ilk might achieve.

Such was the potential for profit, that the hedge fund brain began to widen its scope. The world outside wasn't made up of people and cultures, of oceans, cities, and lakes. It was just information, infinitely more of it every second, expanding chaotically, impossibly. Hedge funds needed all of it because that's where the money was hiding, secrets locked away inside of all that, seemingly, senseless data. Hedge funds became the bleeding edge of both data science and, then, even human intelligence. The data were scraped, absorbed, shaped, scrubbed, and analyzed. On a scale rivaled only by Abu Dhabi's G42 and state security actors like the NSA, the hedge fund brain devised ways to find, refine, and accelerate the task of finding tradeable signals—and converting those signals into money. Perhaps counterintuitively, they also did well in the world of human intelligence—HUMINT. Those big brains applied themselves to social anthropology, applying game theory to working out solutions to the problem of understanding and influencing corporate managements, central banks, bureaucracies, and, not least, the political class.

"Does that mean that you've figured out exactly what 'hedge fund' means?" Tommy asked.

"Doesn't mean anything, actually." Don shook his head. "People use the term indiscriminately to describe outfits that do lots of different things—and most of those things are full of risk and not hedged at all. The main thing is that it's a cutthroat meritocracy that attracts very smart, and often very weird, people. Take Vicker. We don't know exactly how much money he runs, but the low estimate is five hundred billion dollars. He collects two percent of that every year just to manage his investors' money."

"Jesus." Tommy worked the sums in his head. "Ten billion a year just for showing up? That's twenty-seven million dollars every single day."

"On top of that, he keeps twenty percent of the profits. If he makes investors one hundred billion dollars, he keeps twenty of it. Adds up to thirty billion a year."

"In a good year, even more," Chip added. "Plus, most of these guys have figured out how to avoid paying taxes—or at least to defer them more or less indefinitely."

"What happens if he has a bad year?" Tommy asked.

"He's never had a bad year," said Chip.

"Sounds sketchy," Tommy said.

Statistically, unless you had perfect information, it was impossible to never lose money. No one could get it right all the time, year in and year out.

"But he doesn't appear to be an outright crook like Bernie Madoff. The assets actually exist."

"I'll reserve judgment on whether this guy or his 'industrial strategy' is who and what we are looking for. But we've been hamstrung operationally for too long. Elias Vicker could create a lot of opportunity for us." Tommy began thinking about what those kinds of resources—or simply the ability to generate those kinds of returns—could mean for their project: for getting Ben elected and, as important, beyond.

Over the years, the CIA and dozens of other intelligence agencies had operated behind the cloak of businesses created solely to house and camouflage foreign intelligence gathering operations, enabling case officers to move freely, providing cover for injections of cash where they needed it. Those fronts—airlines, hotels, freighters, commodities traders, trendy restaurants—were often the only way to put people on the ground for extended periods without attracting undue attention. But, at least in the case of the CIA, nothing had really worked in decades. The reasons were complicated. Case officers inhabited and reflected the societies in which they lived. The culture of risk aversion that had infected the Western world, particularly since 9/11—and even more so after Abu Ghraib—had insinuated itself even deeper into the fabric of Western intelligence directorates. Fear and second-guessing corroded the capacity of intelligence officers—and, ultimately, the entire national security establishment—to analyze threats dispassionately, to take risks when needed, and to muster the courage to take risks even when failure was likely. Deploying case officers, undercover and often in unfriendly places, had given way to reliance on remote data analysis. Historically, the best risk-takers operated outside of a conventional chain of command, with the ability to speak freely without fear of reprisal, but fear had corrupted even that tradition. As Tommy liked to say, "They used to tell us to go out and kick ass. Now they just tell us to make sure we cover our asses."

Even more pernicious was the fact that fear caused Western democracies to turn inward, making them dangerously vulnerable, not just to adventurers like Osama bin Laden, but also to traditional adversaries who saw retrenchment as an opportunity to strike at the foundations of Western democracy. The Russians, the Chinese, the Iranians, and the North Koreans had become more effective than ever: infiltrating sleepers, mounting elaborate false flag operations to create social disruption, poking daily, even hourly, at the nation's cyber infrastructure, stealing trade secrets from American corporations. And with morale and courage at historic lows, treachery within the intelligence services had become rampant, leaving only the Israelis with effective special activities divisions. The coup de grâce came from supposed friendlies, witless congressmen intent upon playing to the human rights cabal by cutting back on the freedom of action that spies needed to function. Not to be outdone, statists in the European Parliament further clipped

American wings by banning rendition flights and forcing European Union states to clamp down on American agents and assets. In all, where there had once been a will to cultivate and maintain human sources, the nerve and the infrastructure of the CIA's once world-beating HUMINT capabilities were history. But the biggest gap had always been the inability to self-fund. The need to keep going back to Langley, and Congress, for money. Scrambling for dollars, month after month, and year after year, meant that sooner or later even elegant setups that had taken years to fund and build would be trimmed or abandoned.

Tommy drifted, thinking about what they were embarking upon. For years their small group had been talking about—and planning for—the fielding of their own—private—intelligence service. It was an audacious plan that required not only dedicated officers who were disaffected with the status quo, but also money and a strategy for developing and supporting operators whom they could trust. With those elements in place, a president— their president—would have tools for projecting American power, and defending American interests, that had not existed for half a century. In place of reliance on endless, constipated diplomatic missions to convince coalitions of the willing to topple recalcitrant tyrants and corrupt dictators, the American president would be able to direct long-term strategies—or order immediate action, as needed. And, if they did their jobs well, without leaving fingerprints or suffering recrimination.

There would be a clean reporting structure: Ben to Tommy. Tommy to the team. Sabotage, espionage, and targeted assassination—traditional tools, too long neglected—offered a vast range of options, exempt from oversight or bureaucratic constraints. Instead of trying to make overtures to North Korea through endless, futile diplomatic forays, a president could gain leverage on Pyongyang by quietly disappearing North Korean diplomats and members of the ruling class as they traveled abroad. Expanded operational capacities might also help rein in the chaos on the Mexican border. For the moment, the only way to handle the Mexican generals who ran drugs and facilitated the transit of illegals was to indict them and drag them through the U.S. courts, a cumbersome, endless process that invariably failed. Under Tommy's plan, they would have a free hand to simply eliminate the troublemakers. As for the Chinese, it was beyond time to begin hacking away at China's Belt and Road Initiative by co-opting the same corrupt third-world autocrats that China suborned to buy ports, mines, forests, and farmland on the cheap.

They modeled their ambitions on Iran's Quds Force. No matter what anyone might think of the mullahs, the Quds structure was unsurpassable. Lean and nimble, it functioned like the CIA's Ground Branch and the Joint Special Operations Command rolled into one. But better, because Quds was organized for flexibility and structured to be self-financing. Quds owned businesses, mines, and oil fields; dealt arms; and sold protection. But true beauty lay in a remit that extended well beyond conventional intelligence and special operations. Quds units handled networks of agents with critical language skills and could deploy specialized teams skilled at sowing political mayhem and, as needed, sabotage.

"I just don't want to end up a cliché," said Don. "Rogue ex-agent, government within—or outside—government, charismatic leader with a god complex. And I certainly don't want to go through all this and we end up making the same dumb decisions as a McNamara or a Rumsfeld."

"Me least of all," said Tommy. "But Industrial Strategies gives us everything we need. It's just a matter of planning and execution. How much more time do you need?"

"Four to six months for phase one. Our proposal is for me to deal with physical security, Chip on systems, and Greta, under the guise of data protection, will dig through Vicker's entire trading history, balance sheets, money flows, and people. Once she's on board, we can be fully operational in a couple of months. But I have one more concern. A big one: Vicker."

"Go on," said Tommy.

"If he's simply a nasty piece of work and lots of people hate him, we're fine. But there's a strangeness to the man, and it's not just that weird kidnapping. I wonder if we're missing something about him or about his business."

"I get it," said Tommy. "And I agree. But given the time pressure, I don't see a better option."

Don stood and gathered his papers.

"There was one other thing. At the end of the interview he looked up at me. The first time he made eye contact. This guy does not make small talk or tell you about the birdie he hit on thirteen last weekend. All business. So he looked up and said, 'You need a haircut,' and sent me to his barber."

"Let me guess," said Chip. "A guy in Queens who's been cutting his hair since forever."

"Almost—but odder. He's got this guy, Vinnie, from Elmhurst, where he grew up, who has a full barbershop setup inside Industrial Strategies. Vicker stops in every morning for a trim and a shave. The rest of the time, Vinnie just sits around reading the *New York Post*. I walked in and he started fussing over me. 'You must be very important. Elvis'—that's what he calls Vicker— 'doesn't send just anyone to me. He likes you.' A real character—asked me way more questions than Vicker did."

"Vicker is a busy guy, so what?" Tommy asked.

"So it almost felt like Vinnie was interviewing me. And then at the end, he got all quiet and said, 'There's something I want to tell you about Elvis. Coming up, he didn't have things easy. I know, he acts tough. But all he's looking for is somebody to be nice to him. Just try to be nice to him.' Weird."

Don hoisted his bag over his shoulder.

"I've got to run. Chip can take you through the details. It's a big contract, and we'll need your help getting to vendors who are restricted in selling certain tech to private companies."

Don was gone so quickly, Chip didn't have time to react. He hadn't expected to be alone with Tommy.

"How is Don doing these days? He seems a little skittish. What happened to the gung-ho Don of old?"

Chip tried to think of a careful answer.

"The security business is going really well. Turns out, Don can really, really sell. Rich guys love him. And he likes palling around with them too. I think he's actually enjoying life these days."

Tommy nodded approvingly. *Keep going.*

"He's away a lot though. Puts a big load on me."

Tommy's expression narrowed into impatience. "I didn't ask how you were doing."

"You told me to keep Don on the rails. This is what I'm noticing."

"Noted."

The tension between Chip and Don went way back, to Wardak, maybe even earlier. Tommy had finally told them both he didn't want to hear any more. Whatever it was, they had to work it out between themselves. Tommy wasn't interested in rehashing ancient history. He was looking ahead.

But he didn't let go.

"Is Don up for this? I need you to be completely straight with me. We are talking about infiltrating an American company, on American soil, which we will then use to launder a huge sum of money. That we stole, right? We need the original Don, steady, icy. Bamyan Don. You spend more time with him than any of us. If he's not up to it, I need to know."

If Chip were being honest, he'd tell Tommy that it was time to let Don take it easy. Too many bodies, all his nerves fried. Don finally seemed to be at peace, or on the way there. Why not just leave him be? Frankly, it would be better for all of them.

But that's not what Tommy wanted to hear. Or Ben—especially, Ben. To Tommy, Don was a weapon—not an easy one to handle but reliably lethal, and always at hand. Ben's attachment to Don was more emotional. When Don was behind him, Ben felt invincible. Don was afraid of nothing, impossible to bring down, a one-man force multiplier. But Don's prowess on the battlefield only fed the dangerous fantasies of these two terrifyingly competent men: Ben's that there was no raid too dangerous, and Tommy's that with enough intel and manpower he could manage any threat.

Of course, he couldn't say that. If Don was out, he was out too. There was no way he was going to let that happen. He wanted, desperately, to hang around long enough to get his piece. He had a life to live, a big one—and every intention of being able to afford it.

"General, Don is good to go. Ready for the hunt. We all are."

9

Syria

Fyodor Volk was in a foul mood as he drove across the tarmac at Paphos International Airport on Cyprus, threading his way around more than a dozen sleek, shiny private jets parked at the far eastern edge of the airfield, where a Gulfstream G650ER, painted the icy white of a thin winter cloud, awaited him, engines idling, ready to be airborne in a matter of minutes, if not seconds. The plane belonged to one of the few men in the world Volk could not say no to: Alexei Smeshko, otherwise known as Putin's Butler—not merely for his elegant wardrobe and the veneer of aristocratic refinement that masked his past as an enforcer on the tough streets of Saint Petersburg, but also for the obsequiousness with which he catered to the Russian autocrat's every whim—whether it be whipping up an *île flottante* for a light dessert or mounting a disinformation campaign large enough to sway an American election. Volk had been trying to meet with the Butler for weeks. Then, this morning, barely an hour ago, he had gotten the call. The Butler needed him. Now. Laying his eyes on the monochrome Gulfstream in front of him, so garish in its attempt to be understated, Volk wondered if his Kremlin patron just wanted to show off his new toy.

He grabbed his bag and bounded up the stairs. Inside, Smeshko had tarted up the main cabin to look like a starving Soviet teenager's fantasy of a Romanov-era bordello. The walls were covered in 24-karat gold leaf applied by the craftsmen who had restored the domes of Moscow's Cathedral of the Annunciation. The seats were upholstered in crimson-colored crushed mohair velvet, multicolored Murano-glass chandeliers hung from the ceiling, and a two-million-dollar solid-gold toilet designed by Maurizio Cattelan squatted in the bathroom, awaiting Smeshko's skinny ass. And then there were those pathetic paintings of that blue dog.

Smeshko, like so many of his ilk—a shifting, shiftless, ruthless band of pirates and primitives who seemed to have crawled out of Russia's sewers— had laid claim to a massive share of the Russian patrimony. While giving lip service to the glories of Russian history and culture, but with no sincere concern for the future of the motherland, they had managed, under the malign leadership of Vladimir Vladimirovich Putin, to commandeer and control the wealth of the nation and to funnel a large share of it—hundreds of billions of dollars, an amount believed to be multiples of the nation's declared financial reserves—into well-concealed international financial networks. Volk had no illusion that, at least for the moment, he was any better than his thuggish masters. Volk was a hired hand, a highly sought after contractor, expert at building an army, projecting force, and extracting plunder. But, in the end, a tradesman.

In this case, he'd been brought on to manage—but not to question—the very risky and very hostile takeover of an oil-rich chunk of northeast Syria.

Volk had no doubts about VVP's strategic vision. Syria is the critical land-bridge link between the Persian Gulf, which sits atop the world's largest natural gas reserves, and the Mediterranean Sea. Putin's strategy—to disrupt the world's energy markets by partnering with Syrian president Assad and the Iranian mullahs, to snatch control of those Gulf reserves from the Saudis, Qataris, Turks, and Americans, and to feed that production into the European market through pipelines across Syria—would achieve an ever tighter stranglehold over the continent's energy supplies. But on the ground, where Volk lived, he was concerned they were moving too fast. Success would depend too much on other people doing what they were supposed to do, in real time: the Russian military, al-Assad, and, for that matter, the Americans. But he was in no position to argue.

As Volk folded himself into a seat directly across from Smeshko, the face that he showed his host admitted no sign of discontent or uncertainty. His was the flat, jejune countenance cultivated by senior Russian soldiers and spies. It was an expression Volk could maintain almost indefinitely if he was sober, although he might relax it a bit to indulge in a tight smile, sneering at someone else's discomfort or misfortune.

The artistic son of apparatchik intellectuals—a high-spirited, warm, but volatile mother and a charming, voluble nuclear physicist father—at age sixteen Volk had given up the piano and paintbrush for the sword and the judo mat. Without much more to guide him than a hunger for immediacy and relevance, he studied math and joined what was then the KGB. His parents chided him only mildly for wasting his talents. They were greedy opportunists at heart and, not so secretly, saw value in having their talented and ambitious son join the nation's all-powerful security services.

For most of their adult lives, Volk and his cohort had been buffeted by forces of change—glasnost, perestroika, *demokratizatsiya*, the dissolution of the USSR and, now, a poisonous brand of authoritarian rule best described as Putinism. For the moment, at least, he was joined inextricably to the Butler. Smeshko had seen an opportunity in military contracting and had plucked the young Volk from the ranks of the FSB. With Putin's support and silent participation in the profits, Volk and Smeshko had built the foremost private military company in Russia—perhaps the premier mercenary force in the world: the Parsifal Group. No matter which theater of conflict VVP chose to enter—and no matter what the mission—there was always a role for Parsifal: Crimea, Georgia, Turkmenistan, Chechnya, Ossetia, Transnistria, the Central African Republic. And now Syria.

In Syria, it was Parsifal—not the Russian regular army—that VVP had directed to deploy matériel, ships, planes, missile launchers, tanks, armored vehicles, and, of course, men. That was, after all, Parsifal's real business: buying broken men and lost boys—convicts, petty criminals, Siberian serfs— molding them into efficient killers, and then reselling them to the Russian state as deniable, expendable fodder. Volk had emptied out prisons, mental hospitals, and entire insane asylums. As mercenaries, Parsifal's seemingly disparate mélange of human dross found fraternity. War brought them together. It calmed their minds. He saw them as living proof of Durkheim's observation that war gave even the psychotic and depressed purpose. And, in the event they fell in battle, they were worth more dead than alive—much more. Volk made certain that their families received fat checks along with their death certificates.

From the exasperated look on his face, Volk surmised the Butler had spent the entire flight from Moscow to Limassol on his satellite phone, wheeling, dealing, wheedling, promising, threatening. In modern Russia, everything was for sale, but prices and the sharing of spoils required intense negotiation. And the noneconomic terms demanded the most careful consideration of all, particularly in cases like this, where Parsifal was being asked to achieve very specific, very sensitive military—and financial— objectives in the quicksands of Syria.

For its troubles, Parsifal would be well rewarded. With his share of the spoils, Volk saw the chance to vault himself from his current position of fabulous wealth into the world-shaping ranks of the oligarchy, expanding his empire from mere kinetic exploits and banking into oil and gas exploration and production, pipelines, heavy construction, refining.

But with so many long arms stretching out for a piece of the Syrian geopolitical pie, there were endless opportunities to get crosswise with the wrong people—or with those who had been the right people until they changed sides without warning. Volk made it his business to keep track of them all. He sidled up to Bashar al-Assad, of course, and also managed to develop ties to the CIA, doing them occasional favors, and the American army, and their proxy, the Syrian Democratic Forces. The SDF, in turn, gave him access to the Kurds, Arabs, Assyrians, Turkmen, Armenians, the al-Sanadid Forces, the Deir al-Zour Military Council, and even random Chechens who, generally speaking, preferred to pick Russians off, rather than to share a bowl of *jijig-chorpa*, their mutton stew. The Syrian soup was thickened even more by a shifting cast of well-funded and well-armed troublemakers, all claiming national interests: the Iranians, the Islamic State of Iraq and Syria, sundry Al Qaeda factions, and, never least, the Turks, projecting Erdogan's narcissistic brand of mayhem. Volk managed, as best he could, to have eyes and ears on them all.

Beyond that, Smeshko and Volk spent just as much time worrying about the risk of friendly fire. Conventional, declared adversaries and battlefield friends could be mapped, but the range of possible enemies within could not. Factions within the army, the FSB, the GRU, and other oligarchs competing for their own kickbacks and payoffs were the unknown unknowns. The regular army eyed the private military companies—PMCs—jealously as competitors for Putin's favor and government largesse. The generals, running their own schemes to skim millions here and tens of millions there, wanted control: of the contracts, of the money—and of the decisions when, where, and how to strike. Parsifal and their cohort of private companies disrupted that cozy ecosystem, and the Butler's direct line to VVP fed all their insecurities.

As the Gulfstream lifted off, heading for the Russian-controlled Khmeimim air base just outside the Syrian coastal city of Latakia, Smeshko placed his phone on the table and switched it to speaker so that Volk could listen in as he hammered out an understanding with Anton Vavilov, VVP's chief of staff and second-generation Communist Party royalty.

"Anton, it's not an issue of trust between us—you and I both know what the Boss wants, but we need to be certain that the generals won't get in the way."

What VVP wanted, what he always wanted, was nothing less than a share—the lion's share—of whatever was at stake. In this case, Syrian oil and gas fields, the Deir al-Zour and, beyond that, the bragging rights attached to capturing—confiscating—massive refining and transmission facilities that had, not long before, been built by Conoco, an American national champion.

"Help me out here, Alexei," said Vavilov. "Maybe you should talk to General Gerasimov yourself. As I recall, you can be extremely charming. When you want to be."

Smeshko muted the phone.

"Fucking bureaucrat," he said to Volk. "He knows it's a race. If we don't take these fields soon, the army will, and the generals will claim them for themselves." Smeshko switched the microphone back on.

"Anton, we're talking about sending five hundred men to support al-Assad in re-taking Deir al-Zour from the SDF," the Butler said, a note of pleading in his voice. The territory around Deir al-Zour was one of the Middle East's last great prizes in terms of both territory and oil—and one of the last redoubts of American forces. Even though the White House had announced it was pulling troops from Syria, no one knew if the Americans would defend the oil fields U.S. oil companies had until recently considered their own.

"We can handle the SDF, but we can't take the risk that American Green Berets are babysitting those guys and looking out for Conoco's stuff," said Smeshko. "Someone has to give them the heads-up so that they can back away and let the SDF take the heat."

Vavilov said nothing. Volk was becoming even more worried they were moving too quickly, and that he would shoulder the blame if it went sideways. Still, he could not be the one to say no to the Butler.

"This has been agreed to for weeks—that we would make the final push against the rebels and you would run interference with the Americans. I wouldn't have promised Assad a 'good surprise'—something fast and strong—unless VVP had asked me to. It's the Boss's name on this too, not just mine."

They could hear Vavilov exhale, blowing smoke from his ever-present Marlboro. "What do you need?"

"We need to know that the deconfliction channel will be open," said Smeshko, referring to the formal line of communication that often existed, even in wartime, between opposing forces—with verification protocols and authorization codes. Russian and American forces had created one in Syria to prevent them from killing each other's soldiers and risking an international incident. Of course, neither power cared if their Arab proxies fought and died, but both wanted to make sure that the Americans did not accidentally kill Russian soldiers, and vice versa. As for his own men, Volk was well aware that no one in the Kremlin saw them as anything but expendable.

"I need to know that some fucking general will be on that line, in real time, talking with his American counterparts *every single minute* that we are on the move, telling the Americans that Russian *uniformed* forces are active in the area."

"Agreed. I'll make sure it's in hand," said Vavilov. "Anything else?"

"Thank you, Anton. That's all we need."

Smeshko clicked off.

"Do you believe him?"

Smeshko paused. "I've had this discussion with the Boss, directly. Speaking with Vavilov is added insurance. Are you ready to move out?"

"We're already in position. Two units. Vadim is leading one," said Volk. "Anatoly is leading the other."

Anatoly, thought Volk, his accidental son, his unearned gift, his beautiful boy. A pity that his mother turned out to be such an intolerable bitch; she had forced his hand and paid the price. Anatoly was better off without her, being raised by his aunt, Volk's unmarried older sister. A pity, he thought, that I neglected the boy for so many years, but that was probably good for him. Gave him some grit. Something to prove. Top of his class at M. V. Frunze, Russia's West Point: brilliant and fierce. He had earned the right to join the family business, and what better way to mold him and to keep him safe than to keep him close.

"Fast and strong, Fyodor. That's what I promised al-Assad."

As if I did not know that, thought Volk, annoyed. I was in the fucking room with you, jackass.

"You should be able to drive the SDF off without even getting close. As it is, they're nearly cut off. Assad has left them a narrow path to retreat—and he'll cut them down as they run. Wouldn't want to be them."

Volk could put up with almost anything from Smeshko, except his lectures on military tactics. To hear him talk, you would imagine that he had served in every war since the revolution, but his hands told the real story. Look at those fat paws, thought Volk. The closest they had ever come to blood was deboning a chicken—or picking up his phone to have someone killed.

Volk shifted in the plush leather chair and gazed out the window. The plane had begun its descent into Khmeimim, the massive air base Assad had ceded to Russia sovereignty in perpetuity, a convenient outpost in the Eastern Mediterranean. Parsifal, seeking some distance from the regular army, kept its matériel and barracks in a hulking warehouse and two hangars at the edge of the base. The Gulfstream taxied into one of their hangars, where they were met by two men in fatigues bearing the Parsifal insignia on their left shoulders: a black Maltese cross with a silver five-pointed star at its center. At the foot of the airstair, the four men embraced.

"Where do we stand?" Volk directed his question to Ivanov.

"We have five hundred men and another fifteen hundred Syrian regulars massed just east of the Euphrates. A dozen tanks, fifty-odd armored troop carriers—and a full battery of artillery. All in place."

"And there's no question that the SDF—and the Americans—can see all this?" asked Volk, wanting to be certain that there would be no accidents.

"No question. In plain sight."

"And the reaction?" asked Smeshko.

Anatoly Volk, their intelligence officer, gave a single, tight nod. The same mannerisms as his father, same chin, same eyes. Volk felt a flush of pride. It was frightening what nature and nurture could produce. He felt what all proud fathers of sons feel, that this young man, flesh of his flesh, was redemption incarnate, the only secret solace in the face of the indifferential void, more important and fulfilling than sex or power or money. "A steady stream of SDF forces is leaving Deir al-Zour, heading east."

"And the Americans?" asked Volk.

"Not much sign of them at the facility, but, based on reports from SDF deserters, we think about thirty Delta, alongside some Syrians, Kurds, and Arabs. We're pretty sure Nasser Haj Mansour is still running things," said Anatoly, referring to the SDF commander who had snatched the Conoco fields from ISIS the year before. It had been a bloody battle, with sixty-five ISIS fighters dead, while a hundred surrendered.

"But the bigger worry is the American mission support site, twenty miles southeast. They've got a platoon of marines and a bunch more Green Berets. Those guys could deploy in a heartbeat, and rain holy hell on us if they decide to stay and fight."

Volk considered the pieces on the field. With his help, and Russian military support, Syrian government forces had driven the rebels—as al-Assad called them—steadily east, cornering them and gradually pushing them all, including the Americans, toward Iraq—and out of Syria. There was no way that the SDF could defend Deir al-Zour on their own, and, provided that VVP kept his word, Vavilov did his job, and the generals did what they were told, a big chunk of those massive oil and gas fields would soon belong to Parsifal. And VVP.

"Then what are we waiting for?" asked Volk.

Leaving Smeshko behind to manage Moscow, if needed, Volk, Anatoly, and Ivanov climbed into an Mi-35M Hind, Russia's premier assault helicopter for the short flight to the staging zone. Capable of cruising at two hundred miles per hour, mounted with eight 122 mm anti-tank guided missiles and twin-barreled 23mm cannon, the Mi-35M was an army in itself. If the massing troops and columns of tanks and heavy armor did not cause the SDF to turn and run, the sight of the gunship should.

From a thousand feet, they surveyed the wreckage of what, before the Arab Spring and meddling by Americans, Turks, and Iranians, had been a perfectly peaceful police state, ruled without remit by al-Assad and his enforcers, the ruthlessly efficient Mukhabarat. But so many years of incessant fighting had left Syria a wasteland. Hundreds of plumes of acrid smoke—burning oil—billowed across the flat desert plain. Every time territory had changed hands, the retreating forces—whether ISIS, SDF, or the Syrian army—smashed pipelines, destroyed well heads, and did their best to sabotage and booby-trap the refineries and wells. Rivers of crude flowed through the landscape. In some cases, resourceful locals had created massive open pits—lakes of raw crude—which they used to store oil while they tried to refine it themselves using primitive pot stills. From what looked like prehistoric encampments centered around oil seeps, they produced fuel for local consumption, while spewing sulfur and ash into the atmosphere and pouring tens of thousands of gallons of waste, the remnant crude that they could not crack, into the ground. An irremediable environmental night-

mare, al-Assad's legacy to future generations. A poisoned landscape in a be-
nighted country.

Volk gestured toward the scurrying figures on the plain. "What's happening down there?"

"The Syrian army controls most of it, and extracts rent from the informal
refining industry," said Ivanov. "Those people are ingenious. Industrious. It's
an oil rush, people staking claims—probably like what Ontario or Pennsylvania were in the 1800s when people were just figuring out what oil was
and how to capture and release that energy. Instead of making moonshine,
they're producing gasoline."

"It was a beautiful country." Volk sighed. "And not so long ago."

Anatoly raised his arm to point toward the east.

"You can just see the Euphrates now. There. And, just beyond it, the back
of our column."

Volk thought about the Euphrates, coursing over more than a thousand
miles from Turkey to the Persian Gulf, and what it had meant to human
civilization. Russian kids, like American kids, studied the Fertile Crescent,
Mesopotamia, and the civilizations that had emerged there: the Sumerians,
Babylonians, Assyrians, Egyptians, Phoenicians. The earthly location of the
Garden of Eden, and the birthplace of agriculture, urbanization, writing,
trade, science, history, and organized religion. Those early peoples—the not-
so-distant ancestors of the blackened wraiths scurrying across the plain—
had been the world's first astronomers, scientists, mathematicians, writers,
and doctors. And now? Desecrated. A holy place that had become a desolate
playpen for him, and others like him.

Parsifal's war machine stretched for several miles. An undulating, coiled
kinetic ribbon of T-72 tanks, armored personnel carriers, and mobile rocket
launchers, pointing, like a lance, at the prize of Deir al-Zour. Volk called
Smeshko on the satellite phone.

"We're about to land. Anything new at your end?"

"All good. Vavilov is on it."

Volk turned to Ivanov.

"What's our timetable?"

"In two hours, at 1500 hours we'll begin edging toward the Conoco plant.
Spreading the column out. We want to give the Americans plenty of time to
see what's happening. At 2030, when it's fully dark, we'll send in the T-72s.

Move up to within a mile and wait. They'll see us with thermal imaging, but we'll give them more time. The attack begins at 2230."

"The Syrians will take the middle," said Anatoly. "I've got the southern flank, and Vadim will take the north."

As agreed, Volk himself would stay in the rear to deal with communications, direct traffic, and to decide on when—or if at all—to cease firing and allow any remaining defenders to pull back. To his mind, it made no sense for the SDF and the Americans to do anything but withdraw. Not least because the refinery was barely functional, half of it a bombed-out shell. Not worth the fight.

Parsifal and the Syrian force began their assault at precisely 22:30. They barraged the Conoco complex from tanks, with large artillery and mortars. Someone, likely the Americans, began to respond, with anti-tank missiles, machine guns, and a howitzer. Volk was stunned. This was not the deal. The Americans should not be responding at all. Why were they shelling troops that might well be Russian regulars? Parsifal and the Syrian troops continued to advance, but the American barrage only intensified. It took fifteen minutes before Smeshko reached Volk, who could barely hear over the din.

"The Americans are on the deconfliction line, urging us to stop," said Smeshko. "Maybe we should pull back?"

"Why would we do that?" asked Volk.

"Because somebody is making Vavilov nervous. Maybe the generals are saying we can't handle it. Maybe the Boss doesn't like getting in the middle of internecine battles," said Smeshko. "Maybe you should back off. There's no need for a massacre. Let them back away in daylight."

"Are you telling me the Kremlin isn't backing us?"

"Not saying that," Smeshko replied, clearly nervous. "Just saying that I'm not completely sure what's going on."

"Give me two minutes." Volk hung up. He was almost certain that they could prevail—even against the Americans—and if Smeshko wasn't giving an order . . . well . . . he could do what he wanted. But he needed to be certain. Anatoly and Vadim were leading the advance. It was barely two miles away, but, still, that was the front line.

"Anatoly. Vadim." Volk shouted into his mouthpiece. "What are you seeing? Someone upstairs is suggesting we sit tight and let it go until morning."

"No way," Anatoly responded. "We just took out their howitzer. They're not even scratching us, we're moving in steadily. We should have them surrounded soon."

"Vadim?"

"I agree with Anatoly. No reason to wait. Let's go."

Volk released himself into the rush of adrenaline, the thrill of conquering land and space, and an enemy, the feeling of absolute power, of conviction. He called Smeshko.

"Alexei, we've got this." Volk clicked off.

In that moment, he heard a roar of American planes, the whistle of drones. General Atomics MQ-9 Reaper drones, Lockheed F-22 stealth tactical fighters, McDonnell Douglas F-15E Strike Eagles, Lockheed AC-130 gunships.

Something had gone very wrong. He'd been promised the generals would signal the Americans that the attacking column was regular Russian army.

Rattled by the vibration, buffeted by the deafening sound waves, Volk suddenly realized that someone had sold them out—and he understood how high that decision must have gone. Somewhere, a Russian general, either for his own purposes or at the behest of another oligarch, had assured his American opposite number that there were no Russian soldiers on the field. So have a go. We don't care. And, somewhere, an American secretary of defense had unleashed the chairman of the Joint Chiefs of Staff to issue the order: whoever was out there, annihilate them. Maybe the Americans felt they had little choice, that if they could not defend Deir al-Zour, they might as well slink away, admit defeat, and accept that Syria had been lost.

For three hours, sortie after sortie, wave after wave, American warplanes kept coming. Volk maintained constant contact with Ivanov and Anatoly, trying to make sense of the battle. He admired the Americans for their skill and the raw power of their war machine. He could hate them for standing in his way, but not for their courage and resourcefulness as warriors. They would make better friends than adversaries. For another day, he thought, when he had time to work through it.

From their base, twenty miles away, the Americans began to take their aerial bombardment to a new level, dropping missile after missile using the Lockheed/BAE High Mobility Artillery Rocket System (HIMARS). Watching those missiles hit through a field scope, he felt a chill. *There would be no American retreat.*

Anatoly's voice broke in.

"Papa, we're fucked," Anatoly shouted into his headset. "The Americans are sending in advance recon teams, right up to the line."

They all knew what that meant. Marine commando teams would be able to give air force combat controllers precise target coordinates, down to the inch. They were sitting ducks.

═══════

Four hours later, Volk numbly picked his way across the battlefield, avoiding bomb craters, burning trucks, and mangled, crisp bodies. Searching. Then he saw Ivanov, kneeling in the blackened sand. As he approached, Ivanov stood. Seeing his face, Volk felt a dread that he had never experienced before.

"Fyodor, please. You don't need to see this. He died a brave death." Ivanov stood, as if to shield him from whatever lay behind.

But Volk pushed past him and fell to his knees beside Anatoly's body. How strange, he thought, his boy's face seemed nearly untouched, his uniform barely singed. He reached out to stroke Anatoly's cheeks, only to realize that he was holding his son's head. That wonderful, beautiful, brilliant head had been severed from his body. He held Anatoly's head up toward the sky, looking into bright glassy blue eyes that reflected the light of a hundred fires burning around them. He screamed until he could no longer breathe, and then lay down in the sand, cradling his son's head in his arms.

Part Two:

Winter

10

The Imperial Tower, New York City

Don had to admit that he was liking the job. For eight months he'd been building a private cyber and kinetic army with a blank-check budget and almost no oversight. Hanging out with a great team, sleeping in his own bed every night. He'd been alone for the holidays, with the perfect excuse—big job, can't tell you what or where, and, yes, it's safe. Just the way he liked it. He'd wanted to ask Greta how she'd spent her Christmas, but it seemed better not to go down that road, which would lead inevitably to Paris, and to what happened after he left her for that six-week job he couldn't tell her about—and then just disappeared. She would want to know why. He sometimes felt he wanted an answer as badly as she did. His excuse, to himself, was that he got busy, found it difficult to focus on more than one thing at a time. But that was a lie. Paris had been perfect. Maybe it was best to just ride the memory. What he did know was that he loved seeing Greta every day; just being near her made him feel more like the man he'd been before the war. But that guy didn't exist anymore.

It was an unusually warm January evening, under a weak midwinter full moon. Don had just hauled two large duffels up to the roof of the IS office building, one hundred stories above the street, so high up that Central Park looked like a moonlit painting. Not that he paid much attention to the view: his focus was on tonight's mission.

BASE jumping was his new obsession. He'd begun experimenting with it over the summer, when he was brainstorming creative ways to exfiltrate a billionaire from his aerie in the middle of a clogged and teeming city. Tonight would be his fourteenth jump, but every jump still felt like that first one. The act of hurling oneself into oblivion was not something that would ever become second nature. He still had to calm his mind, and bury that never-changing cauldron of deepest fears.

As Don was laying out his gear, he heard someone cough. Odd, he thought, no one comes up here at night. Then another cough. A familiar one.

"I hate it when you do that," Don said, without looking up. "And don't say you were just in the neighborhood."

"Well, I was. Just finished dinner at Smith and Wollensky. Feeling out a donor for Ben. I haven't been doing this long, but one thing I've figured out. If they bring the wife along, that means they'll write a check."

"Was she the second or third wife?"

"Given the age difference, I'd say third." Tommy walked right up to the edge of the building and looked down calmly.

"What is this?"

Don gave him a huge grin. "Just a state-of-the-art wingsuit with a chest-mounted electric jetpack that Peter Salzmann has cooked up with BMW." Built on BMW's iEV technology, the wingsuit was powered by a chest-mounted rig: 15 kW of grunt split between two 7.5 kW carbon impellers.

"Right now it has only five minutes of charge, but at one hundred miles per hour, it's all I need, and once I pop the canopy, I can drop to within a few feet of the target."

"Which is?"

"A zodiac. Gunner's out there waiting. You want to come? I have another suit downstairs."

"So you and Vicker can glide down holding hands?"

"Vicker demands full redundancy—says it's 'industrial.'"

"I'll pass."

"Then I'll meet you in the lobby downstairs. About an hour. I can show you what we've been doing."

It was not the usual field trip for an active-duty three-star, especially one assigned to the National Security Council, but it was well-known that Tommy could be elusive. He thought his own thoughts and made his own schedule. In many ways, he fit the mold of a typical general officer: extensive combat experience, including leading Delta units, a stint teaching at the War College and two tours of duty at the Pentagon. In other ways, he broke that mold. His BS in electrical engineering was from Yale, not West Point, and he had earned a PhD in computer science from MIT, on army time. But there was nothing close to a script for this unorthodox, semi-off-the-books foray, running Don, Chip, Pete, and Greta Webb in an infiltration and assessment of one of the world's largest hedge funds.

He had received periodic reports, but from a distance. Now it was time to reengage, particularly since other pieces of the broad strategy were falling into place. Thanks in no small part to Tommy's efforts behind the scenes with political figures, tech and corporate types, and money people, Ben was emerging as a leading contender for the presidency and, as far as Tommy could tell, keeping a safe distance from Maggie Hoguet. Crisscrossing the country with Ben, ostensibly to keep him current on matters of national security, Tommy had managed to smooth the way with elites on both sides of the ideological divide. What had begun as a pipe dream was taking shape, and the marathon had begun: endless fundraisers, speeches, scoping possible competitors, currying favor with the national committee.

At Tommy's direction, Don thought he'd shot the moon in proposing a program that would provide Vicker and Industrial Strategies with world-class security, physical and cyber, but, at every step, Vicker had even more grandiose ideas and an endless appetite to dig deeply into every aspect of Carter Logistics' risk assessment. He barraged Don and Chip, at all hours, with calls and texts, an endless stream of what-ifs. What if the U.S. government was watching him? How could they tell? What if a foreign state tried to hack them? How exactly would they extract him if New York was under martial law? And what if, for some reason, they could not get off the island, how would they survive until a measure of normalcy was restored?

As the mission expanded, so had the need for men, for facilities, and for matériel. In short order, Don realized that nothing was too aggressive, outlandish, or expensive. As sour and imperious as Vicker could be, Don was strangely impressed at the inordinate glee his client took in building his own kinetic and cyber armies of Special Ops veterans and world-class hackers.

Once his suit was in place, Don unzipped the second duffel, gesturing for Tommy to have a look.

"Sweet little armory you've got there." Tommy pulled out an M600.

"Ballast—and protection," Don said. "If I ever do this for real, I'll have Vicker strapped to my back."

The pack held forty pounds of firearms, ammunition, and accessories, all bagged for a water landing: a suppressed SIG Sauer 9mm, four clips, a hundred rounds of ammo and a TrackingPoint M600 service rifle with a Wi-Fi trigger and a detachable sight that allowed a sniper to shoot around corners. All legal, or mostly legal, somewhere, Tommy thought, but definitely not in New York City. Tommy held the pack so that Don could slip into it.

Don had made a thousand jumps, from choppers, from Cessnas, from gliders, from Boeing 747s, dropping off rock faces from the Altai Mountains in Kazakhstan to the Swiss Alps and in every kind of weather. It's what Deltas do. But BASE jumping was a different beast. It wasn't legal in New York City, for one thing. He'd undoubtedly spend the night in jail if they caught him. BASE jumping also required inordinate skill and a keen understanding of how air moves around a city: one miscalculation and you'd be a red smudge on the side of a building or a broken jar of raspberry jam on the sidewalk. Don stepped onto the parapet and flipped on the camera attached to his helmet, telling Tommy how to follow his jump remotely. He would drop fast, flex his wings to create some lift, and then the jetpack would kick in, taking him uptown to Riverside Park or out over the Hudson.

"I'm off. See you in an hour. Prepare to be blown away."

"I'm looking forward to it." Tommy looked down for a moment. When he raised his head again, any trace of playfulness had drained out of his expression. He drew his face close to Don's. "Greta is more fragile than she looks. She's also not replaceable."

Tommy left unsaid who could be replaced. He reached out and tightened Don's shoulder strap.

"You really want to jump with a loose strap like that?" he asked coldly, as if to remind Don not to be careless. "I don't know what went on between the two of you, but whatever it was, it should not have happened. I knew it all along, but I didn't say anything, because I thought it wasn't my place."

He checked Don's other straps. "I was wrong. It is my place. After you pulled your disappearing act, I lost Greta for the better part of a year. There's too much riding on this job for me to have to start worrying about my best officer again. Do I make myself clear?"

"Permission to speak freely, sir?"

"Go ahead."

"Mind your own fucking business."

Don stepped off the parapet and glided into the darkness.

11

New York, New York

An hour later and 120 stories closer to sea level, Don met Tommy at the service door of the building. Any trace of the tension between the two men had been shelved. Tommy knew his message had gotten across. There was no reason to push it. They clambered into a blacked-out Mercedes Sprinter van the size of a New York City studio apartment and fitted out like the library of an English country house. Inside were Chip, and two more men. Seeing Tommy, they snapped to and barked in unison: "General Taylor, sir."

Don raised his hand to stand them down.

"No rank in this project, boys."

If anyone got close enough to ask, Tommy was not General Taylor, but just another ex-army guy doing private security for a paranoid billionaire. Brawn, perhaps with some brains, collecting a military pension, and double dipping into the private sector.

As Tommy belted himself into a leather club chair upholstered in Simmental hides—nothing too good for Vicker's money—the van started moving, heading west across Fifty-Seventh Street toward the West Side Highway, where it took a left to head downtown.

Tommy looked through the tinted glass, thinking about money: the immense amounts Vicker had amassed and, now, was spending on Don's project. He knew more than a bit about the financial elite, and how wealth, and the pursuit of wealth, changed people. He had seen it too often. Money somehow reformatted their brains, freeing their consciences from the tether of societal constraints—amplifying their worst proclivities. Half of his Yale class had gone to Wall Street, and it seemed like most of them now ran hedge funds. Brilliant men and women who could have done anything—but who decided to do money. His decision to join the army, and then to study computer science at MIT, seemed oddball choices at the time—at least to the Goldman Sachs partners who tried to ensnare him in their web. The joke was that Tommy had done the bankers one better, staking out patents and intellectual property that powered every technology on the planet: microwave ovens, transhuman chips, 3D printers, drones, cell phones, robots, computers, autonomous cars. Few people in military intelligence—other than Ben, Don, Greta, and Chip—knew that at least a dozen of those patents, and tens of thousands of shares in some of the unicorns that exploited them, were in the name of Thomas T. Taylor. For Tommy Taylor, royalties meant that he could keep doing the things he loved most: reading, thinking, trying to shape the world. He was, to his mind, a rare exception: a modern-day Stoic, able to control his feelings, and accept whatever happened. It was true enough that he had become wealthy, and that he sought power, but, at least so far, he thought, his soul remained intact, his core beliefs unchanged. After so many years, still an itinerant, no home of his own. No wife. No kids. His library in special crates that moved with him from one military base to another or, more often than not, an empty mansion owned by one billionaire friend or another.

The Sprinter took them south on Eleventh Avenue, turning left onto Fifty-Second Street. They stopped in front of a nondescript, windowless three-story building on the south side of the street with a steel garage door. The ex-Delta driving the van doused the headlights and punched a code in his smartphone; his copilot, Ed "Gunner" Nuzine jumped out. As the door swung up, the Sprinter pulled in, and the door noiselessly folded down behind them. It took all of six seconds. The bay was spotless: a room with cement walls, floor, and ceiling, smooth except for nozzles poking out of the walls. To Tommy's eye, it looked like the walls hid an array of rifle barrels or flamethrowers. Seconds later, another hardened steel door opened in front of them.

"Cool, right?" asked Don. "This is a vault, an incinerator, and a gas chamber. Just in case someone gets through door number one."

The Sprinter drove through the far opening and into a second vault. As the door clicked shut behind them, Tommy rubbed his thumb against his index and middle fingers, the universal money sign.

"Yep, twelve million dollars for the build-out, and that doesn't include the real estate—or the contents. Thanks to the call you made, our very discreet Canadian friends at WSP/Parsons Brinckerhoff designed and built it, in record time."

As Don and Tommy exited the Sprinter, the floor—actually a vehicle turntable on a hydraulic elevator—began to descend rapidly. One story down, it came to a soft stop. Level Negative 1 ran the full footprint of the building, forty feet wide and a hundred deep. It housed a complete machine shop and a panoply of transport. A slick, armored Bentley limousine. A tricked-out Oshkosh MRAP, a mine-resistant, ambush-protected, tactical vehicle, generations removed from the Humvees in which so many American soldiers had been incinerated. A squadron of powerful motorcycles and a maze of bicycles strung from the ceiling, all customized for weapons.

"I think you boys are having way too much fun, Don." Tommy pursed his lips. "No limits?"

Don spit a wad of Copenhagen fine-cut into his cup. "The guy pockets twenty-seven million dollars *a day.* Every day. If anything, I should be spending more."

Nuzine drove the Sprinter off the turntable, on the garage level, and Don used a hand signal to take the turntable elevator down another fifteen feet. Level Negative 2 housed an arsenal and shooting range. Racks of ordnance, side arms, sniper rifles. A bomb squad in reverse. Chest after chest of lord knew what. And a walk-in safe.

"This stuff may be legal for some people, and maybe for you—but only because I have your back. Does Vicker have any idea that he'd be looking at at least ten years if the wrong person got wind of this?"

"It's a strange thing. When it comes to things that affect him directly, Vicker seems to have major blind spots."

"You know why that is, don't you? If there's trouble, he thinks you'll take the fall—that he can buy his way out of anything. What's in the safe?"

Don spun the dial on a Chubb Sovereign safe—straight out of Harry Winston. As the door beeped open, Tommy peered over his shoulder.

"We call this the money museum—dollars, euros—enough to live comfortably at the Ritz for a year, or two if you stick to nonvintage champagne. And this—"

Don picked up one of a half dozen small leather boxes and passed it to Tommy. Tommy opened the box. There were a number of capsules inside.

"What's this, cold medicine?"

"Nope. A hundred perfect two-and-a-half-carat diamonds. Each one hand-packed into an indigestible gel-cap. In one end and out the other. Worth fifty thousand each. Five million dollars that can fit in your pocket.

Or thirty million dollars in a small backpack." Tommy poured a few into his palm, pretending to pop them into his mouth.

"There are two more levels below this." Don led Tommy back to the elevator. "N3 is the comms center built by CACI to military specifications, fully manned."

"Seen one, seen 'em all, what's below that?"

The door to N4 opened onto a festive living room, and Don ushered Tommy into a salon that might have been decorated by Sister Parish, Jackie Kennedy's decorator and the doyenne of grand, luxurious style, the only concession to the twenty-first century being floor-to-ceiling OLED arrays programmed to create the illusion of perching on a cliff high above crashing surf. As they settled, incongruously, into man-size chintz-covered armchairs, Tommy glanced around.

"Good thing I'm not afraid of heights."

"If you'd prefer the view from East Hampton or the Amalfi Coast," said Don, "let me know."

"What does Vicker plan to do down here, host cocktail parties?"

Don started to laugh. "When I told him we needed to build a SCIF, he said he didn't want to be stuck in one of those depressing gray rooms you always see in spy movies and told me to call his wife's decorator."

"I spend half my goddamn day bored silly in depressing gray rooms. Maybe I should get her number."

Chip, sitting across from Tommy, fiddled with his laptop. The lights dimmed. A grainy image of Elias Vicker flashed on the screen.

"Here's a security camera video of Vicker leaving The Pierre at ten forty-four p.m., on the evening of the abduction. Watch his face."

Vicker, blank and watchful, with only a hint of tension, climbed into the back of a black Suburban. Voluntarily. No struggle, no hesitation.

"That area is infested with security cameras. But the guy who was with Vicker, the tall Swede Pete saw, doesn't show up on any of them. Impressive tradecraft. Much harder than it looks; I'm terrible at it."

Don laughed. Tommy didn't.

"The plates on the Suburban were counterfeit. Not stolen. Someone went to a lot of trouble. You see what I'm getting at?"

"Ben's hunch was correct. Vicker's story about how he didn't know who nabbed him is bullshit."

"Exactly. He's not confused. He's not resisting. We've been with the guy for a while now. He's never wondered out loud about who might have grabbed him, never asked us to run any names."

"I can understand him not wanting to call the FBI," Tommy said. "Mysterious kidnappings are never good for business. But I would have expected him to ask you to discreetly investigate."

"He knows exactly who muscled him out of his own party," said Chip. "And he doesn't want us—or anyone else—to know."

"Because he's scared," said Tommy. "Comforting to know you can be one of the richest people in the world and there's still someone you're afraid of. But you have no idea who grabbed him?" He let the question hang.

"Don't worry, General. We've been busy," Chip said. "Did Don tell you we're putting on a little show tomorrow?"

12

Industrial Strategies, New York City

The next morning, at precisely 10:01 a.m., Vicker slid into his seat in the conference room where he'd first met Don months earlier and pressed a button on a remote to instantly fog every window and wall. The forty-odd seats around a thirty-foot-long Gorilla Glass conference table—the same diamond-hard surface used for iPhone screens—were all taken, as were another forty seats on banquettes around the perimeter. The room was utterly silent. Showing up less than five minutes early to one of Vicker's meetings was considered late, and making small talk in his presence was strongly discouraged.

After Vicker sat down, he took a few moments to shift in his chair. Despite its thick leather padding, Don noticed he always found it difficult to get comfortable. Vicker scanned the room, as if unaware that all eyes were focused on him alone, pausing to smile, awkwardly, at Don and Chip, who were sitting at the other end, as far across from Vicker as possible. Chip nudged Don and whispered: "Do you get the feeling that whatever's about to happen, it's all for our benefit?"

A young woman placed a cup of coffee on the coaster in front of Vicker. He touched the cup with one delicate finger.

"Alison." Vicker spoke in a whisper the entire room strained to hear. The woman stopped in her tracks, twitching as if she had been stuck with a cattle prod.

"Alison," Vicker repeated, without even glancing at her. "Is it really so difficult for you to remember? Coffee at one hundred eighty degrees Fahrenheit. Not one sixty-five, not one ninety-five. One hundred eighty."

Alison scanned the room, looking for sympathy. Few met her gaze, and she scurried to remove the offending cup, closing the door behind her. Vicker shook his head and smiled.

"Great girl," he said, more to himself than to anyone in the room. "One in a million. I'd be lost without her, but you've got to keep them on their toes."

Vicker tilted his head and turned deliberately to a slight, bespectacled Punjabi man to his left.

"Shankar, how long have you been running IT?"

"Very good, Mr. Vicker, sir. Eight years, sir."

"Have I ever denied you anything you've asked for in terms of hiring people, spending money on PhDs, MBAs, servers, software, services, consultants?" Vicker spoke in a mild tone—cool, detached.

Shankar Srinivasan squirmed, as did the five deputies who flanked him.

"No, sir. No, sir, Mr. Vicker, sir, never. You've always been very generous, very supportive." Srinivasan rocked slightly, as if in prayer.

"And, Shankar, what was your goal? What did you and I agree would be the standard for our global computer, accounting, informatics, and trading systems?"

"Very clear, sir, you've always been very clear. I-I-Industrial-strength protection, i-i-industrial-strength controls, i-i-industrial-strength analytical capabilities, i-i-industrial-strength secrecy." Srinivasan stammered nervously. Everyone in the room—including Srinivasan—had seen the show before. A town-square flogging, at a minimum. Something far bloodier more likely.

"Shankar, what did I pay you last year? Just a ballpark number, please."

"Three point five million dollars, sir." Someone sitting along the wall gasped audibly. An IT guy? Three and a half *million* dollars? So what if he had a PhD from Carnegie Mellon?

"And, Shankar, what was your total budget last year? Just a zip code, please."

Srinivasan cracked his neck so hard it sounded like his head might snap off.

"Sir, fifty-three million dollars," he whispered.

"Shankar, I can't hear you. Louder please."

"Fifty-three million dollars, sir." Srinivasan croaked.

"Very good, Shankar, very good. I'd appreciate it if you and your team would look at the little slide show Mr. Carter has prepared. You all know Mr. Carter? He's spent the last few months assessing our security needs. I wanted all of you to hear from him how we might do better."

Don entered a few clicks on the laptop in front of him. Lights dimmed. Screens lowered from the ceiling on all four sides of the room.

"The firm has experienced a spike in attempted firewall breaches over the last six months. One you all know about, the one that made it into the press." Don displayed a string of articles from the *New York Post*, the *Wall Street Journal*, and Business Insider, and continued.

"Before my team was able to scrub most of the stolen data from the web, some investors were reading about their own accounts online. We went down a lot of rabbit holes before one of our friends in the hacktivist community tipped us to a site on the dark web, where it was all just sitting there. Trade blotters, employee profiles, emails, annual reports, medical bills, correspondence with lawyers and the SEC. Some old, some fresh."

Don flashed through unindexed pages of IS files, spreadsheets, legal documents. Each click brought up more and more IS data for sale, redeemable in cryptocurrencies that most people had never heard of. Vicker sat, stone-faced. Don took that to mean Vicker was enjoying himself. He had not been in the business world long, but he'd quickly learned that there was no surer way to gain the trust of a founder or CEO than to demonstrate that their current guys were either incompetent or ripping them off.

"Shankar. Any thoughts? Ideas? Questions?" Anyone who did not know Vicker might have mistaken his tone as friendly.

The IT guy blanched. His hands began to shake and nystagmus overtook him, eyes darting, near tears.

"What about the rest of your sidekicks? Ravi? Suketu? Can you help your buddy?"

Ravi jumped in. "Shocking, sir, absolutely shocking. We just need a bit of time, we will find the problem. We can solve the problem."

"How about if you let me help," replied Vicker. "Company IDs and credit cards, on the table."

No one moved.

"Now." Vicker nodded at them.

A public execution. Rustles of discomfort echoed around the room. Gratuitous humiliation—industrial-strength humiliation—was a Vicker trademark. They remained frozen.

"Mr. Carter?" Vicker signaled.

Three of Don's physical security team stood cautiously, and edged, almost gently, behind the shocked IT team. Slowly, they all brought out their wallets, placing credit cards, IDs—life as they knew it, the American dream—on the table in front of them.

"Bye bye, guys." Vicker gave them a little wave. Don's men showed them out. Right out, in fact. Onto the street. The Vicker way. Coats, family photos, souvenirs to follow by U.S. mail.

"For now, IT reports to Mr. Beekman." Vicker gestured toward Chip. "Mr. Beekman—Lieutenant Colonel Beekman—was part of the Army Cyber Institute at West Point until his recent retirement."

13

The Plaza, New York City

For Vicker, a public execution of the leaders of his IT team was merely the opening act, a good way to get in a groove for the event of the day: a carefully planned and scripted appearance onstage as the featured speaker on the final panel of Woody Hamilton's annual investment conference. Hamilton, author of a dozen books on finance, economics, and history, had been publishing an eponymous weekly newsletter for almost forty years. Everybody in finance, economics, hedge funds, and finance ministries around the world read *Hamilton's Market Observer*, and everyone who could pay the steep admission fee showed up for his annual winter conference at The Plaza. Year after year Hamilton drew the best minds and biggest names in business and finance both as speakers and as attendees. He always saved the final slot of the two-day event for someone who would be a big draw for his otherwise jaded audience. It had been a coup that Pete was able to get Hamilton to agree, since Hamilton hated Vicker's guts. But, ever the showman, Hamilton appreciated the novelty of providing his loyal subscribers with the rare opportunity of seeing Elias Vicker in person.

The prestigious booking was the capstone of Pete's elaborate campaign to reshape Vicker's brand image, to buff off the last traces of the boiler room, and position Elias Vicker as matured and mellow, even if still mercurial. Not merely the richest man on Wall Street, but a creative genius, an oracle of finance. An important personage, even if you took the money away. Except that it was impossible to imagine Vicker beyond his money. Pete was not sure that, without money, there even was an Elias Vicker. The Hamilton appearance, on center stage, in New York was meant to convince a tough hometown crowd that Elias Vicker, reciting monologues that Pete had written, was that man.

Operation Soros, Pete called it. After George Soros broke the Bank of England by speculating against the British pound, the Hungarian émigré could barely get a table at Michael's. But once he started dropping seven- and eight-figure donations on organizations like the Sierra Club and National Public Radio, everything changed. Soros generously funded campaigns to legalize drugs and gay marriage and advocated for steep tax hikes on the wealthy, safe in the knowledge that his brethren in the 1 percent owned too many elected officials in both parties for that to ever happen. Before long, the same limousine liberals who'd denounced Soros as a greedy sociopath began treating him as an oracle of the modern age, a man whose wisdom dwarfed his wealth. Underwriting left-wing causes was a bridge too far for Vicker, but he respected Soros's contrarian instincts. You got a lot more bang for your buck with the so-called progressives; at his end of the spectrum, there were so many conservative billionaires that it was hard to stand out, no matter how big a check you wrote.

Feet up, drinking cappuccinos in Don's office, Greta, Pete, and Chip waited as Vicker readied himself to be escorted to The Plaza.

"Maybe you should lay off the caffeine for now." Greta gently nudged Pete's cup toward the center of the table. "You're vibrating. Breathe."

Pete smiled at her. "Sorry, it's a big day."

"Right," Greta said dismissively. "Shareholder activism as a moral crusade."

That, Pete was secretly embarrassed to admit, was the message: When Elias Vicker buys a big stake in a company and forces management to make changes that juice its share price, he's not just lining his pockets. He's fighting for retired cops and firefighters living on their pensions, he's protecting the 401(k) Grandma's been living on since the coronavirus took Gramps.

"The only problem is that the people who sit on the boards of the companies Vicker goes after also run the big charities, the fancy clubs. Every time he forces out a socially prominent CEO or blows up a do-nothing board of directors, he pisses those people off, and they end up blackballing him. Two steps forward. One back. But if Elias eats enough crow today, they might be willing to give him another chance."

Don's phone pinged. "Time to move."

———

Vicker appeared calm, as Don, with Pete and Chip in tow, led him to the elevator and through the basement to the Sprinter van. But his eyes were hooded, as if he was bored or needed sleep.

As they crawled east across Fifty-Seventh Street, the sky a dull winter gray, Pete, anxious, filled the space with words. "They had to move your session to the grand ballroom—seven hundred people have signed up to see you and Woody onstage."

"How big was the crowd for Bill Ackman this morning?" Vicker asked, not looking up from his phone.

"Less than half that."

"I won't say that this makes me nervous, but it doesn't make me not nervous." Vicker looked out the window, his world, New York City, rolling by. "Let's go over my lines one more time. No hassles from Woody, right?"

Pete and Vicker had spent hours shadowboxing the event. Pete had tried to anticipate every question Hamilton might ask, joke he might make, or curveball he'd throw, and prepared Vicker with scripted answers and comebacks.

"Just remember, boss, he needs you more than you need him. This is huge for him, publicly burying the hatchet with *the* Elias Vicker."

It had taken months of back-and-forth to negotiate the terms of engagement: two armchairs on a low, softly lit stage, old friends chatting, as if sipping brandy in front of the fire—no "gotcha" questions.

"Okay, okay. Then you're completely sure bygones will be bygones?"

A few years earlier, after Hamilton had questioned Vicker's ethics—and mental acuity—for trying to force a major oil company to pay dividends and buy back its stock rather than making acquisitions. Vicker sued him for defamation. Ultimately, Hamilton won, but not before wasting hundreds of hours and nearly half a million dollars on lawyers.

Suing *Hamilton's*—and Woody Hamilton personally—had been vintage Vicker, except that it ended with a rare, humiliating public loss. The courtroom festivities—both he and Hamilton had taken the stand—were standing room only, performance art for both Page Six and the financial press, and HBO turned the saga into a miniseries with John Krasinski playing Vicker as a hapless, overbearing dolt. The biting tone of the legal ruling cut deep, beginning with the chief judge's withering observation that "sometimes civil litigation is far from civil," and going on to flay Vicker for bringing a frivolous suit.

"Jesus, what a fucking mistake that was. Fuck, fuck, fuck. I should never have let you talk me into that idiotic lawsuit. Fuck, fuck, fuck."

Pete had begged Vicker to back off. Suing Woody Hamilton would blow up in his face. But he held his tongue. "I told you so's" did not go over well with the boss.

"Tell me again," said Vicker. "The format."

"As we've rehearsed." Pete launched. "For the first forty-five minutes, Hamilton will run through your career—the history of Industrial Strategies, your investment philosophy, your management style, your charitable giving, plus your views on social activism, politics, political activism, and investor activism."

"Elias Vicker: investment superstar, guru of finance, social philosopher." Vicker seemed to perk up. "I like that. Then we ride off into the sunset."

"Actually," said Pete, "we had to make one concession. Woody insisted on a Q and A, his ticket-buyers demand it. He wanted twenty minutes. I got him down to eight. It'll be nothing. Everyone in the audience makes half their money latching onto your trades after the brokers leak them the details. All they'll want to know is how you got to be such a genius."

━━━━━━

The grand ballroom at The Plaza glittered under the soft light of twenty Baccarat crystal chandeliers. The room itself, one of the most coveted in the city for important business and social events, was a masterpiece of subdued elegance. A domed ceiling rose to fifteen feet, framed by ornate plaster moldings, and small balconies in the Renaissance style ringed the room. The plush taupe-colored Italian carpet was barely visible under the dozens of tables that had been packed into the room.

Woody Hamilton leapt onto the stage. An ebullient, athletic WASP with a signature crew cut, he was so vigorous and slyly aggressive that he could annihilate men half his age on the squash court, hardly moving off the T. For the occasion, he wore his signature outfit: a simple but expensive blue suit, a black tie, and a bemused expression behind round wire-rimmed glasses.

"Because you've all been such a lovely, attentive, low-key crowd," said Hamilton, to some tittering in the room, "we've got a special treat. A man seen by all, but known by few. A man who really put me on the map—by suing my ass."

A roar of guffaws from the crowd.

"I am pleased to welcome the founder and general partner of the re-nowned hedge fund Industrial Strategies: Mr. Elias Vicker."

The crowd erupted with raucous, enthusiastic applause, wolf whistles, catcalls, and shouts. Vicker emerged from a corner of the room and took the stage confidently, like a movie star making a talk-show entrance. He and Hamilton settled into armchairs. As a tech pinned a mic to his lapel, Vicker gazed off into the distance with the bemused, above-the-fray expression of a guru enveloped in his own aura of genius, though anyone who looked at him closely would have noticed the tension pulling at the corners of his mouth.

"Elias, it is beyond fabulous to have you here." Hamilton gushed. "Let me set the stage. You've had one of the greatest runs in the history of American finance. Decades at the helm of Industrial Strategies and, if I've got this right, you've made your investors money—often a lot of money—in all but a few of those years. Industrial Strategies now runs—and I know the actual num-ber is a state secret—something like, what—five hundred *billion* dollars?" Hamilton paused to let the number sink in. A significant hedge fund might manage $5 billion. A large fund might manage $20 billion. But *$500* billion? "When you began, no one even knew what a hedge fund was, so you've not only built a firm, you've pioneered an entire industry. But you're famously secretive, no one seems to know how you do it. You're the Tommy—the pin-ball wizard—of the hedge fund world."

In an aside to the audience, Hamilton asked in a singsongy Pete Townsh-end voice: "How do you think he does it?" Always alert to a good ad-lib, the crowd shouted back: "We don't know!"

Vicker appeared to be unruffled, but Pete reacted as if he had been prod-ded with a stun gun. Not a good start. He knew too well that Vicker had a thin skin, remarkably sensitive to any whiff of disrespect. He glanced at Piper, sitting next to him, looking perfect: thin, toned, blown-out, her brow unfurrowed—but that was the Botox.

Motioning with outstretched hands, palms down, Hamilton quieted the room.

"What got you started investing?" Hamilton asked.

"My family lived in Queens. But my dad owned a little grocery store on the Upper East Side. My job was to stock the shelves, tote up purchases, post to customer charge accounts, and make deliveries."

Vicker had been telling the same story forever. How he used to chat up the customers, how he saw early on that the Wall Street guys and their wives were the best dressed, never asked what anything cost, always seemed to have plenty of dough. How he really had no idea what they did, but wanted to be like them, not a stock boy in an apron.

"I asked one of my customers how to get started, and he told me to read *Barron's* and the *Wall Street Journal*, so I did. Eventually, I started investing a little here, a little there, with my and my family's tiny bits of money."

"And after that?"

"I studied accounting, became a CPA, went to law school at night, joined one of the Big Eight—when there still were eight—worked on audits for financial service companies, trust companies, and banks, like Citi and J.P. Morgan. I kept investing, on the side. A little here, a little there."

"When did you become a full-time investor?"

"After about five years I set up a little broker-dealer to manage money for myself, family, and friends." Vicker settled into the rhythm he had practiced with Pete.

"I recall reading somewhere that you said that stage was difficult. That it didn't go well at first."

The Vicker fairy tale: He wasn't perfect, but he was hardworking. Smart. That he had figured out the secrets of finance, broken the code and rewritten it.

"That's true, Woody." Vicker chuckled, a small, tight laugh. "For a while, I managed to find every possible way to lose the little money I had. And my family's too. I lost money in stocks, in bonds, in options, in convertible bonds, in gold, oil, real estate. I was practically broke. My dad was practically broke. My mom was about to start cleaning houses. Public accounting started to look really good. But then I had my epiphany."

Vicker launched into what had become his own personal superhero origin story. How he began to read—a lot—about John D. Rockefeller and Henry Ford. How he realized that industrial methods could and should be applied to investing. How, if he broke every decision down to its component parts and then reassembled them, knowing everything about the parts, the decision-making machine, and the competitive environment—like Rockefeller did for oil and Ford did for cars—he could industrialize his investment decision-making process. How by applying back-breaking labor to investment decisions he could reduce risk and make better investments. How he lowered risk by being more industrial and industrious. Everything was connected to everything. "Industrial" meant having the right resources, paying attention to tolerances for error, using the right tools—people, money, information—for the right jobs. Once he got going, he could barely contain himself. Waxing almost poetic, riffing off the words "industrial," "industry," and "industriousness."

Piper reached over, placed her hand on top of Pete's, and squeezed. A squeeze of concern, worry. Whatever her relationship with Vicker had been or might become, the last thing she wanted was for him to be unhappy. Or, perhaps, the squeeze communicated that unhappy was better for her, since she could play the sympathetic wife and organize some entertainments that would distract him. No one knew better than she did how tough this crowd was. She had grown up with half of them. Snide, sarcastic, critical, backstabbing, competitive private school boys. Dalton, Trinity, Buckley, Browning. And a few equally sharp-eyed girls, her posse, who'd gone to Spence, Brearley, Chapin. They'd all make a pretense of sympathizing with her about how Hamilton beat up on her husband, but she knew there was nothing they enjoyed more than watching a sharp-elbowed newcomer like Elias Vicker stumble into a booby trap set by someone as supremely clubbable as Woody Hamilton.

A few rows ahead of Don, someone snickered. There were murmurings, restlessness, in the room. Perhaps the Vicker story—which had been reported and repeated more or less verbatim over the years—made more sense on paper or in a cool medium like television. But uttered out loud, by Vicker himself, under hot lights and before an audience of his peers in the banking and hedge fund elite, it seemed almost childish, like something he'd read in a comic book as a kid.

That's his foundation myth? Don thought. *"I lost all of Mommy and Daddy's money, and then, suddenly, I figured out how to not lose money." Really?*

"Elias, how does that work, day to day? How do you train your people to be 'industrial'?"

Pete, already wondering how he was going to spin this, cringed. Vicker was going off-piste, venturing into a storyline that they had not rehearsed. Piper squeezed even harder. Odd, he thought, usually she didn't show much interest, much less indicate that she cared what Vicker did or said. But he knew that Piper hated it when Vicker was mocked or attacked publicly. It rubbed off on her. People would start talking. Jacques-Alexandre at Bilbo-quet might start seating her closer to the back of the room.

"Well, Woody, maybe the best way to explain it is by analogy to an actual machine. A machine that must be built to a very high standard. A precision machine, like—let's say—a pistol." Don and Tommy both noticed Vicker making restless, micropostural adjustments in his chair, feeling the pressure of the handgun he liked to carry around the city. "Take the Glock 17. It has thirty-four parts. I like to give my people firearms training, teach them how a machine works. Learn how to take it apart, learn the parts—the barrel, slide, frame, magazine, recoil-spring assembly, and learn how to put it back together. Blindfolded, hands behind your back."

"That must make for an interesting morning meeting," said Hamilton. "But I'm not sure I follow the analogy."

Even though it was pointless and explained nothing about running an investment firm or how to make money, Vicker loved the pistol analogy and defaulted to it when he started to lose his footing before an audience. He thought it showed his toughness and burnished his self-image as a man of daring and danger. And, anyway, who was Hamilton to question his meta-phor, however inapposite? Hadn't he agreed to only throw meatballs?

"Woody, investments are like guns, or like cars or any other machine. If the parts don't fit together properly, if one part is missing, if the frame is crooked, or if the barrel bent, the machine won't function."

Hamilton looked up, elbow on the armrest. Holding his chin in his hand, he tilted his head, began to say something, but then changed direction.

"Elias, you're famous for a couple of things, and one of them is your rev-erence for the rule of law and respect for property rights. Would you care to comment on that?"

Pete took a deep breath, drew his hand back from Piper, and gave her the barest nod. This should be Vicker's strong suit. He was a fierce, and in-formed, advocate for property rights, routinely providing financial backing for little-guy plaintiffs fighting what he saw as government violations of the Takings Clause of the Fifth Amendment.

"Woody, I'd be happy to. You know, I've written about this in my notes to investors, for many years. Capital goes where it is welcome, and money stays where it is well treated. I treat money very well—kindly, respectfully, like a good friend. I listen to money, my money, my investors' money. Money is not inanimate, it is animated by the people who earn it, care for it, take care of it; money talks to other money, there's a money grapevine, money will flee if it is treated badly."

Piper glanced at Pete, but then looked directly at Vicker, hoping he would see her mouthing the word "no."

"So, money is . . . alive? That's a lot to chew on."

Vicker looked away, staring at the back of the room, which, Pete knew, sitting up close, was not a good thing.

"Well, Woody, of course, we should take the point metaphorically." He adopted an avuncular tone. "But to the extent that money is an abstract symbol of man's hopes and dreams, a store of value, the manifestation of the sweat of a man's labor, I suppose it is not unreasonable to think of money as a living thing."

"Elias, I don't think I've ever seen you so animated as when you speak of money. You're so passionate, and the way you describe your approach to it, it's almost as if you treat money like a . . . well . . . ah . . . you treat money like a . . . lover."

Piper began to shake her head.

"Woody, thank you, that's not a bad way to describe how I think about money. Some people say money isn't human, but money is not *not* human."

The crowd rustled, whispers rippling through the room, some open snickering.

"That's a fascinating way to put it, Elias." Hamilton shuffled his note cards. "Another topic that many people here are curious about is the magnificent—some might say otherworldly—consistency of your returns. You've experienced only a few down months in decades of investing. Would you share your secret?"

Pete knew that question was coming. It had to be, and he knew that Vicker didn't have a good answer for it. "Consistency," in financial parlance, was a polite way of implying that someone was lying—that they were somehow managing, massaging, or manipulating their results. Every year, the SEC barred some people from the investment management business for life because of it. Some went to jail.

"Industrial approaches apply to vision, Woody. I don't mean X-ray vision. I mean paying attention to your peripheral vision, seeing what is going on not only in your immediate field of sight, but at the edges, behind you. I call it equine vision. Horses have big eyes, and a three-hundred-fifty-degree range of sight. Turn their heads just a little: that's three hundred sixty degrees. Horses are prey animals, they need to absorb as much of their environment as they can. Constantly. Investors are prey animals too. Big cats with sharp teeth and claws are always after them, looking to tear them apart, mislead them, trick them, defraud them, anything to separate them from their cash."

Given the wide-eyed, slightly crazy look that Vicker had directed at him, Hamilton was pretty sure that Vicker was looking at him as prey. He was about to ask another question, but, before he could, Vicker cracked a few knuckles and held up a long skinny finger to make it clear that he was not done.

"Perhaps one last question before I open it to the floor," Hamilton said. "I know from personal experience that you don't mind suing people, that's kind of your trademark isn't it? Industrial-strength litigation? What's the idea behind that?" Hamilton got in a dig, and tried to move the conversation somewhere closer to a main track.

"The rule of law is the flip side of money going where it is welcome. Rule of law makes civilization possible. If there is no rule of law, it's the law of the jungle. Money doesn't *not* love the law of the jungle. But money loves civilization more. Some folks make money in the jungle—trappers, hunters, African dictators, French banks, Brazilian politicians, Panamanian lawyers—but that's a different game, a very dangerous one."

"Elias, thank you for giving us so much of your time. Okay if we take a few questions?"

"I'd be happy to," said Vicker, looking anything but. Pete, uneasy in the front row, watched him retreat behind a look that most read as somber, but Pete knew to be icy, dangerous.

"Ma'am, you there, in the middle, please identify yourself and your firm. What's your question?"

"My name, Fatima Abubakar, Datalitique Advisors, we mine big data." A statuesque African woman held up a card. "Perhaps I am just following up on the point Mr. Hamilton raised about your returns. One of your investors asked me to analyze monthly returns of your funds since inception. I found them to be statistically impossible. Over history, ninety-six percent of all months you make returns one point five percent per annum, plus-or-minus twenty basis points. Lots of words for results like this, but, for polite company, maybe we say, strangely smooth."

The room grew quiet. It was a dirty secret of the industry that some hedge funds used sophisticated tricks to make their returns seem more consistent. Big companies—like General Electric—played the same game, trying to comfort investors by avoiding big spikes in either direction as much as possible, managing their earnings to make them seem steady, even though in real life earnings tended to be anything but consistent. But investors did not like volatility. Less fluctuation in performance attracted more money, even if investors had to suspend belief—and ignore basic probability theory—to believe the results.

Vicker ever so briefly flashed the look of a cornered rat, a mixture of fury and contempt, before starting to speak, in his mildest, most measured tone.

"Ms. . . . er . . . Abubakar was it? You're Nigerian perhaps?"

Abubakar gave nothing away and remained standing.

"I don't recall that we've met, but perhaps you'd like to stop by sometime for a longer chat. I will say that, as a student of math, I'd commend you to think about how mathematics and industry form a whole. Industrial-strength analysis, data-driven analysis. Industrial strength is the key."

Abubakar retook her seat. Vicker's absurdly evasive nonanswer elicited a collective groan from the crowd. Necks craned to see who had asked the question. More than a few wondered how Hamilton had decided—when faced with a sea of hands—to call on someone who would ask something neatly tailored to enrage a notoriously prickly target. With the question having clearly hit a nerve and destroyed whatever, limited, bonhomie he and Vicker had achieved, Hamilton surveyed the room with his characteristic crooked half-smile.

"A lively bunch today! Elias, perhaps another question? You, sir." Hamilton pointed at an older man near the back of the room.

"Thank you, Woody. Mr. Vicker, my name is Nandor Gyongyosi. I'm a private investor from Budapest, but my background is in people operations—human resources. You run a large amount of money, and if I understand it right, you've got several hundred people working for you—front, middle, and back office."

"Three hundred and seventy-two souls, as of this morning." Vicker adopted a reductionist tsarist shorthand for serf.

"Mr. Vicker, finding good investments is one talent, but when a fund gets big, it's quite another talent to hire and manage top-flight employees. It is said that you pay people very well but don't delegate any responsibility. And that you shackle them with contracts that sharply limit what they're allowed to say about your firm and its operations, even after they no longer work for you. Could I ask you to comment on your human resource philosophy?"

Tittering from the audience. Two questions, two kill shots. One at his ethics and the other at his management style.

"Mr. . . . Gyongyosi. Hungarian . . . indeed. As we say, this is a free country. Everything is connected to everything, and people are free to work where they want to, no?"

Signaling Hamilton with a dismissive wave of his hand, Vicker made it clear that the session was over.

"Elias, thank you for joining us, it has been a privilege to have you here, and to introduce you to the Hamilton clan. We can be a fractious bunch, but, hey, it's all in the family."

Standing, barely able to manage a civil handshake, Vicker turned and strode off, stage right, to applause that he knew was meant more for Hamilton than for him. Hamilton stood erect, in front of the room. A twinkle in his eye containing what? Glee? Revenge?

"Friends, Romans, Nigerians, Hungarians, thank you for joining. That wraps the festivities, except to answer the one question that I know is on everyone's mind. The answer is yes, the bar downstairs is open, and drinks are on me."

To wild applause, Woody Hamilton cast his very long arm toward the door, and led a boisterous crowd down the grand staircase.

14

West Tenth Street, New York City

"Fuck, fuck, fuck. Where's my nearest bomb shelter?"

Outside The Plaza, the weather had turned from gray to freezing rain, which seemed only to make Vicker angrier. The Sprinter was parked right by the hotel entrance. The door slid open and Vicker barreled in. A hurried lunge landed him on one of the van's four facing leather club chairs. Don and Pete trundled in behind him, neither man instantly noticing that the large Black man in the third row wasn't one of Don's off-the-shelf Green Berets. It was Tommy Taylor himself.

For a moment, Don was almost paralyzed with rage at his meddlesome former CO. It was absolutely crucial that Tommy stay as far away from Elias Vicker as possible. If anyone connected any of them to the Pentagon official who oversaw a vast archipelago of secret operations, not only would it blow their mission, it would expose all of them to the wrath of both the criminal and military justice systems, where they'd no doubt be charged with violating the kind of laws you never know exist until you break them. Don had been in untold life-or-death situations. He needed to be able to control whatever variables he could and to have a plan for every foreseeable contingency. His boss popping in for a pointless joyride in the middle of an epic Elias Vicker meltdown was not one of them. They would talk about it later. For now, he had to focus on calming the lunatic in front of him.

"Jesus fucking Christ. You walked me into a total fucking ambush." Vicker, as tight-lipped and as ferociously calm as Don had ever seen him, trained a murderous eye on Pete.

"Guru. Social philosopher." Vicker hissed. "Nice work, Pete. What the fuck?"

"A couple of the questions weren't so great, but you fielded them perfectly." Pete knew how to play this. Shift into flack mode. Let Vicker rough him up a little. Vicker turned away, stared out the window, and smiled to himself. Pete stared at the floor, preparing himself for whatever was about to happen.

"Tell the driver to pull over." Vicker murmured to no one in particular. Before the van stopped, he touched a button on his armrest. As the door whooshed open, he grabbed Pete by the shirtfront and tossed him out of the van into a storm drain torrent of chicken bones and used coffee cups. Not waiting to see if Pete was okay, Vicker sat down and calmly flicked a button to close the door. Looking out the back window, Don saw that Pete had done a shoulder roll and was already on his feet. Pete knew how to take a fall. Who knew?

Speaking softly, almost to himself, Vicker began running down his own differential diagnosis of what had happened at the conference.

"No peace pipe. Tomahawk job. Hamilton is 'his own man'? Held a grudge. How'd those guys get in? A check? Credit card? Security cameras. Fucking Hamilton singled them out—two for two—picked from a crowd? Rat-a-tat. Planted. Why those questions? Why'd he pick *them*? No other answer. Worth that much to humiliate me . . . *me*? Make a permanent enemy . . . of *me*? Pete. Goddamn Pete."

As they inched down Park Avenue through angry rain and snarled traffic, Vicker's rage abruptly slackened and his face went blank, as if an inner switch had flipped and his cognitive gears snapped back to their default setting. Tommy sat silently in the back row, across from Vicker, watchful but not appearing to take anything in, the blank stare of a large man who has learned to make himself inconspicuous. He was glad he'd come. He knew it was a risk, maybe even the kind of stupid one he always cautioned the team against. Before Tommy went all in on an operation, he needed to get up close with the principals. Ben had once asked him why. "I don't know," said Tommy, "I just need to watch them breathe."

Tommy studied Vicker's face for any sign of the rage that had boiled beneath his skin just moments ago. There was no trace of it. But Vicker didn't look relaxed either. Tommy had a theory that in order to read an expression properly, you had to know if the person thinks anyone is looking at them. Vicker definitely acted as if he did. His composure seemed like a performance. But maybe his tantrum was too. He believed that once you understood a person's patterns, whether they were friends or adversaries, you could be reasonably sure how they would behave in a given situation. With a borderline personality like Elias Vicker's, the job was much more difficult. Vicker was a volatile element, fiery and convulsively unstable. Definitely dangerous, but everyone in this line of work was dangerous. Before he gave the final okay to the assault on Industrial Strategies, Tommy needed to know the degree of this man's volatility, his capacity to unleash havoc. He'd already seen enough to know that he was going to need help.

Luckily, Dr. Karl Beck, a protégé of Paul Ekman, owed him a favor. Dr. Paul Ekman, the University of California psychology professor had done groundbreaking work on cataloging human facial expressions, and Beck was his most talented disciple. After Ekman himself, there was no one better at reaching into the bubbling cauldron of a psyche, even one as explosive as Elias Vicker's, and mapping its hidden drives and concealed emotions. He'd need Beck to provide a workup on Vicker as soon as possible.

"So, where are we going?" Vickers asked, suddenly chummy, one of the guys. "The safe house you built me in Greenwich Village? What's it again? Campari? God that swill is disgusting. And pretentious. Boy the Italians must be laughing at us . . . Never trust a woman who drinks Campari—they're the ones who are just out to take your money."

Don remained silent. As annoyed as he was at Tommy for dropping in, he was glad Tommy got to witness Vicker in full. He'd picked a good day.

"Oh, you don't think you have to worry about that?" Vicker needled Don. "With the contract I just gave you?" Vicker looked pensively out the window. "Just be careful, son. You're not married, right? My advice, find a girl who doesn't pretend she's in it for anything but the diamonds. Then at least you can have some fun." Vicker flashed Don his version of a friendly smile and his expression faded back into impatient blankness, as if he was waiting for Don to change the subject.

"Negroni, sir. Negroni is what we call the house on West Tenth. We bought it from the heir to an Italian liquor fortune. Greenwich Village charm on the outside, military-grade fortress on the inside."

"This is the one where we beat out that Facebook fucker, right?" Vicker asked, almost distractedly. "Nice job. That cat lost. Never enough that the dogs win, the cats must lose." Every time he brags about a deal, Don thought, he drops that aphorism as if he had just thought it up.

Ten minutes later, they turned left onto West Tenth Street from Seventh Avenue. Vicker's mouth had not stopped moving the entire time.

"Greenwich Village." Vicker dragged out the words in an exaggerated drawl. "Suddenly everyone wants to live down here. You know what I think?

They don't want to be grown-ups. They're so rich they don't think they have to get old. They lived down here when they were twenty-three and they want to relive their bohemian days, except not crammed into a tiny apartment with roommates who never flush the toilet. I didn't have bohemian days. I worked."

The car came to a stop alongside a forty-yard dumpster filled with construction debris.

"I know the guy who bought that place." Vickers pointed out a five-story town house shrouded behind elaborate scaffolding. "He gave me a ride on his plane to Aspen last year—I'd lent mine to Conway for a fundraising trip." Vicker wagged his finger theatrically. "I'm only telling you guys that because you're my friends. Don't you go blabbing—Conway wouldn't last a week in prison, even at a club fed. Anyway, my friend is putting in a full-size NBA court, three stories down. He bought the parquet floor from Boston Garden that Larry Bird played on. Now he and his wife are splitting. She's getting the house, she insisted on it—even though she hates basketball."

The garage door to the safe house snapped open, the van slipped inside, and the door snapped shut again. Seven seconds.

"But I'd rather have my own shooting range. Take me there now."

Vicker leapt out of the van, Don following. Tommy remained in his seat, intending to slip away.

"What about the goon?" Vicker said in passing, as if he'd just noticed Tommy for the first time.

"Back-up," said Don. Tommy looked down at his feet, like he was just another serf, unworthy of eye contact with the monarch.

═══════════

The layout inside was much the same as the Eleventh Avenue safe house. As the elevator plunged downward, Don waited for Vicker to remark on the house, but he didn't. Vicker simply stared ahead at the carbon-fiber-paneled doors. Seconds later the elevator came to a barely noticeable stop. The doors opened onto a vast room illuminated by a ceiling that seamlessly bathed the space with a diaphanous light precisely calibrated to feel like the East Hampton beach on a bright late-summer afternoon. Three live ammunition target range lanes ran the thirty-yard depth of the building. An iron table stood at the end of each lane, covered with green baize to protect the guns and prevent ammunition from rolling.

Don led Vicker to the left, where a portion of the floor had been walled off, and dialed the combination to a vault door. An electronic beep sounded. He swung the wheel, and they found themselves inside an armory sufficient to stage a coup on a small island nation. One wall racked weapons ranging from handguns to sniper rifles: SIG Sauer pistols; an assortment of Heckler & Koch MP5s, a G36K, HK169s; a few Knight's Armament SR-16s (a NATO favorite); and the latest in high-tech laser-guided, thermal-tracking hunting and combat sniper gear, TrackingPoint M1400s—with suppressors and night vision—accurate to over a mile. Vicker gasped, his ears flattened against his skull.

"Any of this legal?" Vicker asked.

Don had been expecting the question and responded with a well-rehearsed mistruth. He was behind enemy lines. The usual rules didn't apply. "All of it, sir. Properly documented, all accounted for, in my name. With my rank and reserve status, no issues." Truth stretched to the breaking point. Vicker nodded, seeming to not miss a beat.

Active-duty military might be allowed to maintain an arsenal like this in New York City, provided the right people in D.C. and the NYPD had signed off on it. But those courtesies did not extend to civilians, no matter how expensive their lawyers. If law enforcement learned about the cache, Tommy could protect Don, but Vicker would be on his own. He would be lucky if the U.S. Attorney offered eight years on a plea.

Don followed Vicker out to the range. "Sir, what would you like to try first? You might like the SIG—"

"I like to roll my own." Vicker reached a hand behind his back, drew a pistol from a holster clipped to his belt, and thrust it into the air right in front of Don's face. A paper torso target hung thirty yards away at the end of each lane. Vicker slipped on a pair of electronic ear muffs, and, not waiting for the others, began shooting. He braced himself and emptied his clip with five rhythmic double-taps, cutting a neat five-inch hole in the torso's heart before placing his gun on a padded table.

"Something bigger." He snapped at the marksman on duty. The marksman handed him a tricked-out M1911, .45 caliber, the sidearm of choice for Delta. Vicker gave him a savage grin and stepped into the next lane. This time aiming for the head, Vicker snapped off the clip, surgically obliterating the left eye socket. He turned around and stared, gloating, at Don, who tried to hide his surprise.

"Nice. You eased the trigger pull—to what? Two pounds?"

Don nodded. "Standard Delta Force modifications: lighter pull, flared magazine well, extended slide lock—to make reloading faster. Where'd you learn to shoot like that?"

"Israeli special forces." Vicker looked around for effect. "They invite me to the Negev to train with the Sayeret Matkal every year—a thank-you for my support. They told me I was pretty good for a goy."

An hour and a half and almost a thousand rounds later, Vicker could barely hold up his arms, having completely annihilated dozens of targets. All the time muttering his mantra: *"Not enough for the cats to win . . . the dogs must lose."*

15

Langley, Virginia

A week later, Don and Greta joined Tommy in a SCIF at Langley, to accommodate Tommy's day job. In Don's experience, little worthwhile happened in these nameless, windowless bunkers: mostly, bad ideas were hatched or good ones killed. When they walked in, Tommy was already there. As was Dr. Elizabeth Leonard, which did not improve Don's mood. She was undeniably brilliant, but he worried that Tommy was a little snowed by her. If Tommy had a weakness, it was for experts and their theories. Especially if they worked for the CIA. Elizabeth was a psychiatrist with the CIA's Office of Medical Services' Behavioral Science Consultation Team and, like Greta, a former nonofficial cover operative. Her primary job was to counsel CIA officers who were having a hard time coping with the unique stresses of clandestine work. But BSCT doctors, and Elizabeth in particular, often participated in interrogations and frequently analyzed interrogations performed by others.

The moment everyone took their seats, Tommy started the meeting. "Don, Greta—I hear you're doing an amazing job digging through Vicker's financial history. My friend at Virtualitics says you're setting new benchmarks in terms of what can be done with forensic financial analysis." Tommy paused. "But just a few minutes face-to-face with Vicker last week convinced me that's not going to be enough."

"What have I been telling you?" Don asked. "The guy is human plutonium."

"Correct. And we are going to learn how to contain him. I want to build what amounts to a 3D model of this man's psyche. That's why I asked Elizabeth here today. She is in charge of the project. We're going to keep adding data points until we know so much about this man that we can predict how he'll react to any stimuli. No guesswork. No margin for error."

He leaned back and pressed a button on a remote.

Karl Beck's larger-than-life face appeared on a screen across the room. For more than thirty years, Beck had been a pioneer in the study of human emotions and their associated facial expressions. Working with his mentor, Paul Ekman, they had cataloged more than ten thousand discrete facial expressions, all reflecting one of seven basic human emotions: disgust, anger, fear, sadness, happiness, surprise, and contempt. Beyond the basic emotions, they had detected a range of subsets: amusement, embarrassment, anxiety, guilt, pride, relief, contentment, pleasure, and shame. And then there were the compound expressions: anger/disgust, sadness/surprise.

For most people, microexpressions are very difficult to hide, disguise, or fake. They come in three flavors: simulated or false, neutralized, and masked. A person we consider normal—someone without a major personality disorder, that is—reveals simulated microexpressions almost continually, the kind that switch on and off in an instant. The classic example being the Miss America runner-up, a girl who seems to smile her way through disappointment, but, in reality, flashes a look of anguish for one twenty-fifth of a second before regaining her smile.

"Let's get right to it. This guy gives me the creeps." He pressed a remote and began playing a video of Vicker onstage at the Hamilton conference, parrying questions with his host, seeming relaxed and engaged. Then, when Beck replayed the tape in super slow motion, microexpressions evidencing fear, anger, contempt, and disgust rattled across Vicker's face. In one clip, there were so many micros in competition with one another that, at slow speed, his face seemed to vibrate. But viewed at normal speed, they were all but imperceptible.

"These are the money shots," Beck said. "And I mean that quite literally. Every time Vicker mentions money, his baseline expression is flat, but his micro? Clear as a bell: happiness, pleasure, pride. 'I treat money very well': pleasure. 'I listen to money': contentment/happiness. 'Money is not inanimate': happiness/pleasure.

"Now look at the micros when he talks about his father. 'Lived in Queens': contempt. 'Little grocery store': disgust. Off the charts. We see the same thing when he mentions his investors. Watch this—that same compound micro of disgust and contempt."

Beck flashed three shots of Vicker on the screen, one after the other.

"Vicker experiences a lot of fear too. When he mentions 'Mommy,' when the moderator asks him about the consistency of his returns, and when this woman from the audience asks him a question. Look at those faces. Fear. A man at sea with no lifeboat in sight. And he's not happy about it. This is a violent—potentially a very violent—man."

Beck flashed one more portrait: furrowed brow, tightly compressed lips, clenched jaw. Next to it, Beck posted a grainy photo of another, much younger man. Their expressions were nearly identical. "Compare this shot of Vicker with John Hinckley's face just before he shot President Reagan."

He put up a photo of a young man, with a demonic grimace.

"I've never seen a more definite warning micro. We've standardized this expression across a dozen countries, Western and non-Western. We're training law enforcement and the military to look for it. I might not have much direct history with this guy, but I know enough to tell you to stay away."

"This might interest you," Don said. "Right after that event, Vicker became so furious that he shoved the guy who organized it out of a moving Sprinter van."

"My hypothesis is that he is capable of far worse."

"When we researched his history, we learned that he once attacked a maid at the Jefferson," said Don. "Beat her bloody. Big financial settlement, nondisclosure, the whole deal."

"That fits. I'll continue."

Beck replaced the first set of micros with a dozen more in which none of the words were consistent with the expressions on Vicker's face.

"Concealed emotions," Greta observed.

"Precisely."

Concealed emotions were those that did not fit the words being spoken, or suggested that the speaker was thinking well ahead of what was happening in the moment. In this case, there were so many that Beck suspected that either Vicker had significant training in concealing his emotions or had been so traumatized in his childhood that masking emotion had become a central element of his psyche.

"He presents the way some of your people do after we've taught them to control micros." Beck eyed Greta, alluding to the courses that he and his colleagues regularly led for CIA field operatives.

"Only when I need to, Dr. Beck," Greta responded blithely.

"In this one, Vicker has just mentioned his mother. Look at the oblique eyebrows on this one. That's sadness. It is almost impossible to make this movement voluntarily, that's why it is rarely faked, and why we believe it can't be suppressed."

"Dr. Beck, can you venture any sort of a diagnosis?" Greta asked tentatively. "I know it's a lot to ask based on what little you've seen."

"First. I need to ask a question. What *is* your interest in this severely damaged creature?"

Don and Greta looked to Tommy.

"Without telling you things you don't want to know, we're trying to figure out if we can work with this guy."

Beck massaged the back of his neck, thinking.

"You've asked me to analyze lots of faces over the years." Beck frowned. "This outwardly handsome man has one of the ugliest. The hard edge, the control, and the capacity to suppress micros suggest a diagnosis, but there are a lot to choose from. I'm thinking high-functioning psychopath."

"No remorse, no empathy, no attachments. A grand tradition on Wall Street: Bernie Madoff, Carlo Ponzi, Roberto Calvi, Allen Stanford," Greta observed.

Beck paused.

"You're the last people I would warn to be careful, but this guy will always be a hazard to whoever gets near him, especially if he feels humiliated."

Greta, Don, and Tommy exchanged looks. Elizabeth took notes on a secure tablet.

"Roger that," said Don.

"Never forget it." Beck looked at Greta.

16

Saint Petersburg, Russia

Volk asked Smeshko's pilot to make a wide circle over Saint Petersburg before landing at Pulkovo Airport on its southern edge. Nestled at the eastern end of the Gulf of Finland, Saint Petersburg's bridges, canals, palaces, and the mosaic domes of its cathedrals glittered. With its fine, if down-at-the-heels, baroque buildings, museums, and theaters, Saint Petersburg manifested bittersweet, nagging collective memories of times when the world had looked to Russian artists, composers, musicians, writers, and dancers for inspiration and Europe saw Russia as she wished to be seen, a nation, no, a civilization on the march, ready to take its seat at the table, respected. Saint Petersburg embodied those ideals and transmitted them across generations, memories embedded deep in the Russian psyche of what Russia had been, might have been, and Volk had often hoped, against admittedly bleak odds, what she might become. But in the dark months since Anatoly had been killed, Volk hoped for little.

The previous day, he had been sitting on the deck of the *Better Place*, comfortably reviewing Ivanov's projections for the coming quarter, when the Butler summoned him here to meet a mysterious new client. Volk hated these dog and pony shows. When he tried to beg off, the Butler insisted, even offering to send his Gulfstream—an almost unheard-of act of generosity. As a rule, the Butler did not lend his plane to anyone, even his own children. Volk could have pushed back, out of sheer stubbornness. But he'd been saying no a lot recently. Not a good idea, because for all the Butler's threats and bluster, the older man's feelings were easily hurt and he never forgot a slight.

When Volk left Saint Petersburg, eighteen years old and already attached to an elite military unit, he'd vowed never to return. Saint Petersburg was a lie; its pretensions were a lie. Peter the Great had built the city to be an intellectual capital to rival Vienna and Berlin, maybe even Paris. But a century of trauma—almost three decades of Stalinism, and decades more trying to recover from it—haunted Saint Petersburg, as if its dangers and deprivations were not just conditional but fated, if not deserved. When he was seven, Volk asked Ded Moroz—Grandfather Frost, Russia's equivalent to Santa Claus—to skip his neighborhood; the thieves might try to steal his sled. He appreciated the Mariinsky Ballet as much as anyone—in fact, he had become its biggest patron—but, as a boy, he would have preferred a tongue sandwich, or a second helping of borscht.

It had been Anatoly who brought him back to the city. As Anatoly grew and provided Fyodor with reasons to be proud of him—citywide wrestling trophies, academic honors at the city's most rigorous schools—Volk had started spending more time there, forging a relationship with the boy he had virtually abandoned. Since Anatoly's death, Volk had started visiting Saint Petersburg for no other reason than to wander through its grubby splendor, communing with the memory of his fallen son.

A deep blue Aurus Senat limousine, Russia's answer to Rolls-Royce, was waiting for him at the foot of the jet stair. Yuri, looking like an over-muscled bear stuffed into a gray suit, stood beside the car, waiting with an enveloping hug. Flying in Yuri, thought Volk, nice touch. The Butler's really going all out.

"Hello, Yuri. What a pleasure, I had no idea."

Yuri grunted and opened the back door for Volk.

"The Butler has us staying at the Hotel Astoria. That's all I've got right now. No one's telling me who sent for you. But they seem to be making a pretty big fuss."

Volk was momentarily confused. Yuri was there alone, no police escort. Didn't seem like much of a fuss. Yuri closed the door, hopped into the driver's seat, and sped off with menacing efficiency, blue and red lights flashing rapidly behind the Senat's massive square grill. The highway was strangely free of traffic, but it wasn't until they hit the city streets that Volk realized what was happening. Broad thoroughfares that should have been crowded with pedestrians, buses, cars, trucks, and scooters were empty except for discreet, unmarked SUVs. Only one man could command that a busy city center be virtually shut down on a summer evening: Vladimir Vladimirovich Putin. No wonder the Butler had said nothing. Fyodor Volk was about to take a very big step up.

Why now? Volk wondered. During his months of grief, Smeshko had been empathetic and, unusually for him, solicitous. The Butler's advice had been fatherly, but harsh: A man digests his grief quietly, for as long as it takes, never losing track of it but not succumbing to it. It takes strength to bear grief, the kind of strength that makes a strong man stronger. But if you make a show of your pain, the jackals will rip your heart out even as they wrap their other arm around your shoulder in sympathy. Volk appreciated the straight talk, but the Butler's advice went only so far and missed the mark. Volk did not wallow; he was in no risk of drowning in a puddle of self-pity. He moved in only one direction: forward. His engine ran on logic, control, and rigor. And rage, of course, efficiently sublimated, a constant reliable power source. But grief had unchained his demons. Every waking moment, he was consumed by a thirst for revenge. At times, he feared that in the mania of desolation he might lose control of the compulsions and obsessions he kept at bay through sheer discipline: the two hundred push-ups every morning before breakfast, the hours he spent at the archery range, firing off arrows until his fingers bled, the miles he burned on his treadmill deep into the evening. His furious, dangerous, sometimes murderous daydreams about lashing out at the Butler, and others around him.

Perhaps Smeshko was right. Focusing on matters at hand might be the cure. After all, they had a business to run and all the indicators were pointing up. A debacle like the one in Syria would have destroyed a lesser courtier than Alexei Smeshko, but the perfectly tailored kleptocrat, who spent his young manhood in a Soviet prison for petty theft and pimping teenage girls, had impeccable survival skills. Over the fierce objections of Kremlin military advisers, VVP took the Butler's side. The problem, the president decided, wasn't Parsifal. It was the army. The Kremlin needed tighter control of its foreign policy adventures, which meant a bigger role for Parsifal and, just as important, a vow to exempt certain Parsifal operations from the military chain of command, which meant that the Parsifal Group, in addition to managing billions of dollars of sensitive contracts all over the world, was now effectively Vladimir Putin's personal army. This was never published in a newspaper, or even written down, but word got around and Parsifal was busier than ever, as fat contracts for easy jobs began rolling in: security at twenty embassies, protection for a North Sea pipeline terminal, work that paid whatever the boss wanted and put no lives at risk. These jobs didn't just provide easy money, they also signaled VVP's approval, which led to more and more of the oligarch-class hiring Parsifal for their personal and corporate security needs. This is how they lure you in, Volk thought. You get better jobs, charge a lot more for the same work. You get a taste of the life. The yachts get bigger, the women younger and more beautiful. You think you're in the room. But soon you find out that there's always another room. No one gets invited into that room. You have to force your way in.

It was a bright, unusually mild winter day. They followed the embankment east, past Saint Michael's Castle, where Yuri turned left to follow the Moyka River past the Mikhailovsky Garden, then left again onto the Griboyedov Canal. When they passed in front of the Church of the Savior on Spilled Blood, Volk asked Yuri to stop. The car that had been following them at a distance stopped a hundred yards behind them. He got out of the car to take a better look at the massive confection of towers capped by elaborately tiled and gilded Moorish domes.

Right where he stood, a cabal of nihilists had assassinated Tsar Alexander II in 1881, spilling royal blood onto the foundations of a church built with slave labor. We've always been a violent country, thought Volk, ruled by successive bands of ruthless autocrats, each crew more oppressive than the one they supplanted: three hundred years of pillaging by Romanovs, eighty-odd years of totalitarian terror under Marxists, Leninists, Stalinists, Bolsheviks, and Communists, and, for the past three decades, first under Yeltsin, then Putin, a return to something like a monarchy, now rebranded as "democracy," but in reality a criminal organization masquerading as a government, or, maybe, a government masquerading as a criminal organization; historians would debate it for years. (And what does that make me? Volk asked himself, night after sleepless night, in the depths of grief, clawing my way to wealth and power by commanding a private army for the man who thoughtlessly allowed my son's life to be extinguished?) In historical terms, Putin was an anomaly. President? No, that was a title that could always be taken away. Tsar? Closer, but without the family drama and imbecile-filled royal bloodlines. Godfather? Tyrant? Dictator? King? Nothing really fit. Except, perhaps, Volk thought, Survivor: a man who coolly did what it took to gain and hold power because to lose it was to face oblivion.

Volk got back into the car, unable to stop thinking about the risks he faced. He could not afford to fall into one of his fugues right now. He needed to eat. One of his cardinal rules was to never go into a meeting hungry. Hunger warped your decision-making.

"A blini, Yuri? Let's stop."

"The usual place?"

"Yes, the Stolovaya Lozhka, right near the Mariinsky Theatre." His mother had dragged him to the Mariinsky hundreds of times: opera, ballet, music. Some of it stuck. He knew that Yuri had no such memories, only scars. They had grown up in the same grim housing block. Yuri had joined a gang and ended up in a prison camp up north, which is where Volk had rediscovered—and recruited—him.

"Yuri, take a right on Gorokhovaya. Blinis and coffee. Then the hotel." Fast food blinis, the Russian answer to McDonald's. Volk sipped his coffee from a plastic cup as they pulled up to the Astoria.

The manager showed him to the Tsar Suite overlooking Saint Isaac's Cathedral. Volk sat on a plush sofa trying to recall what he knew about who had stayed at the hotel. Putin, of course. But so many others: Lenin, Madonna, Margaret Thatcher, Jack Nicholson, Tony Blair. And, very nearly, Adolf Hitler, who had been so certain of succeeding in his siege of Leningrad that he had invitations printed in advance for a victory banquet in the hotel's Winter Garden.

But we didn't fall, thought Volk. We suffered at the hands of the Germans—and the Finns—for 872 days, through blockade, shelling, bombing. A genocide—1.5 million men, women, children, and soldiers killed. Or died of starvation. The stories of his childhood, how his parents and grandparents ate sawdust or— how did that old doggerel he'd read in Dmitri Lazarev's diary go? *In a basket he carried a corpse's arse. / I'm having human flesh for lunch, / And for supper, clearly / I'll need a little baby.* He had never asked his parents directly: What do people taste like? How do you cook them? Were those family meals? Every child knew that there were secret histories. They had all grown up whispering the awful words that rendered fine distinctions between the *trupoyedstvo*, the corpse-eaters, the foragers, and the *lyudoyedstvo*, the people-eaters, the hunters. Legend had it that Putin's mother had nearly been buried alive, carted off for dead after she had collapsed by the road and loaded onto a wheelbarrow for cremation, waking just in time to avoid the fire.

That's who we are, Volk thought. We feel fierce pride, even pleasure, in our capacity to endure physical and psychic torment. It's been that way for a thousand years. We are proud of everything. Of our elegant, cultured, beautiful, romantic, brutal Romanovs—and our ability to take the abuse that they dished out. Even, perversely, of our ostensibly righteous but equally cruel Stalinists and Communists with their gulags and fiendish brilliance in devising institutions that pulverized the human spirit, turned friend against friend, parents against children, and crushed any bond of trust that might have propelled human creativity and a civilized society. We failed ourselves, but we didn't break. Saint Petersburg did not fall. And Hitler never slept here.

There was a knock at the door, and Volk opened it to find Yuri, standing stiffly, looking like Yuri never looked: uncertain and—what?—afraid.

"You're wanted in the lobby." The words tumbled from Yuri's mouth. "Sorry, sir. Now."

Volk grabbed a light blue cashmere V-neck sweater and a down jacket and followed Yuri into the wide hotel corridor, empty but for a matched pair of extremely fit thirtysomething men—buzz cuts, pigtail earpieces, dark blue suits, white shirts, black ties—who flanked his doorway. He knew the type, because he had a few hundred on the Parsifal payroll. More important, he recognized their lapel pins: Presidential Security Service. He held out his arms and they gave him a desultory frisk. Not their usual rough handling: someone must have told them to keep it light.

Two more SBP officers held the elevator doors and brusquely motioned Yuri back as they ushered Volk inside. Moments later, the doors opened on an empty and eerily quiet lobby. Two men in khakis, open-necked shirts, and sweaters sat at a low table drinking espressos. There was the Butler, with his full head of silver-gray hair combed straight back, looking as well turned out as ever. The other was extremely fit, ramrod straight, blond hair and watery blue eyes. Stiff, but somehow also relaxed. Not big, not small. Not friendly, but not not.

Volk had once heard an old KGB general describe Vladimir Putin as a perfectly ordinary man who resembled no one else you had ever met. But even so, face-to-face with his nation's most powerful leader since Joseph Stalin, Volk felt a shiver down his spine. What lies would they tell him? What truths? Russians have made such a fine art of lying that it isn't just a matter of whether we lie to each other, but how we lie. There were the lies to make things better: *vranyó*. Not outright deception, Boris Pasternak had written, more of an embellishment. The lies politicians utter every time they open their mouths, because the exercise of power requires deceit. *Lozh* are the lies that do real harm, create injustice, cause mayhem. Lies intended to deceive, to disable, to destroy. And there was the vast gray area between the two.

As Volk approached, the Butler wrapped a bony arm around his shoulders, and Putin extended a hand, giving him his signature look: direct, flinty, with that slight tightening at the corners of his lips that passed for a smile.

"Fyodor Repinovich Volk."

Volk stood a little straighter and bowed slightly from his shoulders.

"Let's walk." The Butler gave Volk's arm a gentle squeeze, like a proud father sending his boy off to war.

Putin led Volk out of the lobby onto the corner of Saint Isaac's Square. Volk looked around in amazement. He had seen some strange sights in his life, but the only times he had seen an entire city emptied of its people had been in war zones. So this is what it's like, Volk thought, to be, quite plausibly, the richest man on earth, with single-handed control over a more-or-less modern, industrialized nation. It meant being able to make tens of thousands of people simply disappear. People like my parents, who might otherwise be out for dinner or strolling through a park. Just so he could walk freely. What kind of disordered personality, Volk wondered, feeds on disrupting lives, commerce, and industry like this, subduing people who offered no threat and whose presence wouldn't have inconvenienced him at all? Just because he could?

Putin retrieved a pair of Persol sunglasses from the neck of his sweater, put them on, and zipped himself into a long down coat as they walked across the usually teeming square, expecting Volk to follow along at his side.

"I wanted to quit," Putin said flatly. "In my first term. I was tired of fighting with Yeltsin's people, all of them thieves. One of my mentors told me I had to rule for thirty years, like Catherine the Great. It was the only way to restore order. A very intimidating thing to hear. It scared me, a boy from Saint Petersburg, just like you. I didn't know if I could even handle one more year. My life was no longer my own. I just wanted to be able to do this, stroll through Saint Isaac's Square and down along the river on a perfect summer evening if I wanted to."

Kremlin lore. Volk was never sure whether to believe it.

"It's all your fault." Putin seemed to be joking. But he didn't smile. "Did you think I'd remember?"

After completing his KGB training, Volk joined a secret military detachment that "monitored" events in Chechnya and reported directly to the highest levels in the Kremlin. At the time, Putin was seen by voters as a lifeless but competent technocrat better suited to a dull European country. Russian voters wanted swagger, a real-life tough guy who would ruthlessly face down any threats to Russia's sovereignty and honor. Someone not squeamish about things like putting down a simmering terrorist rebellion in Chechnya. Putin was game, but he needed a reason to send an armored battalion into Grozny, a pretext, and, to achieve that, he needed operatives who knew how to make pretexts happen. Volk's team staged apartment bombings in Moscow, which they then blamed on Chechyan separatists, and eliminated nosy activists and journalists who got too close to the truth. One October night in 2002, those exploits backfired horribly at Moscow's Dubrovka theater when 170 members of an opening-night audience died in a horribly botched hostage rescue after purported terrorists stormed the theater and placed explosives throughout the building. Volk had been in-volved in the early planning, when the bombs placed were meant to be fake, creating an opportunity for Putin to claim he defused a terrorist act without resorting to bloodshed.

"I signed off on your plan. Brilliant. If they'd followed it, no one would remember that night. But there was a miscommunication." Putin shuddered, the memory fresh. "I was angry." Volk, of course, remembered. He'd been sidelined by a commander jealous of the attention-grabbing junior officer and kicked off the team. "I was terrified. Heartsick. I felt responsible." Putin continued. "How does a man live with that on his conscience? I wrote my resignation, I was ready to crawl away, never be heard from again. But the generals wouldn't let me. If I wasn't out in front, blame would have fallen on the security services. It would have torn them apart. We could not afford that. The country would have spun out of control. They gave me an order. I might have been elected president of the Federation, but to them, I was still a colonel in the KGB and I'd given my oath. I didn't like it. But they were right. I didn't have a choice. It was my duty."

"Or?" Volk asked, trying to keep the story going without seeming too interested. He'd heard the rumor: that General Patrushev had delivered the news while Putin was sitting on the gold-plated toilet he'd installed in the presidential throne room.

"Go north. Not a difficult decision."

"You're a pragmatic man."

"I made some adjustments. When I took this job, I thought I had to be smarter than everyone else, all the time. I was always doubting myself. I was not happy. Then I had my epiphany: you don't always have to outthink everyone. It's not about being a genius. You can just be a ruthless bastard. It's a lot easier. Just throw the guy—or a couple of thousand guys—in jail and decide why later." The guy, Volk assumed, was Mikhail Khodorkovsky, who had been the richest man in Russia at the time Putin took over. After years of trying to bring Khodorkovsky to heel, Putin simply packed him off to a Siberian penal camp for ten years on trumped up embezzlement charges.

"Made me so much calmer. Then I figured, if I have to serve like a tsar, I might as well live like one. A few more years. Then I should be able to fade away and enjoy life."

He stopped and lifted his eyes, taking in Saint Isaac's imposing Romanesque facade. He nodded his head, ever so slightly. "We all make sacrifices, don't we, Mr. Volk?"

Putin began walking again, toward the cathedral, clearly intending to leave Volk wondering what he meant, the *vranyó*. Reeling me in, thought Volk, treating me as an equal. The flattery, if one were to take it that way, a lie that paved the way for something. Every Russian knew the Putin mythology: growing up poor, often hungry, roaming the streets of what was then known as Leningrad. Living in a communal apartment, picking fights.

When they reached to the cathedral's top step, the bronze doors swung open for them, by what mechanism, Volk was unable to detect. Putin led him to the transept, directly beneath the great dome. "How can a man not be awed by this?" He bowed his head and dropped his shoulders slightly. Volk couldn't tell if prostration was Putin's idea or if he was mocking the very idea.

"So much of what was brilliant about Russia," Putin continued, "what *is* brilliant—was gifted to us by the Romanovs."

"Peter the Great, most of all." Volk was curious to see how Putin would react at the mention of the legendary eighteenth-century tsar, credited with the creation of modern Russia.

"Probably the most productive period in our history. Peter made us Europeans; we were part of the scientific revolution. Leaders in math, chemistry, biology. We were relevant. The world finally needed us. It's right here. This building. One of the first cast-iron structures anywhere." Putin pointed at the statues of twelve angels that ringed the base of the dome. "Volk, do you believe in angels?"

Ordinarily, Volk would have shut down a question like that without thinking. But he was genuinely moved, rendered nearly speechless, standing in the vastness of Saint Isaac's, not another supplicant in sight, no throng of tourists to interrupt the stillness. It wasn't just the bold colors, detailed ornamentation or the shafts of light and shadow that affected him, but the sheer, stunning quiet that filled the space beneath the frescoed dome. If Volk was a believer, he was quite sure he would have taken that magisterial hush for the voice of God.

After looking up briefly, Putin seemed impatient, ready to move on. "Of course, you don't."

Volk snapped himself out of his reverie. "We're all brought up to love the Church. The pomp. The priests in bizarre hats and fancy dresses. Harmless fairy tales. Good for tourism and a comfort to lonely widows, but not much else."

Putin pursed his lips slightly.

"I am trying to become less cynical in my old age. Properly managed, the Church is very useful, especially one like ours that emphasizes orthodoxy. The tsars understood that. People need *something*. We eat people. Use them up. Like cattle and potatoes. It's only fair that they receive something in return. They can walk in here and think they're in heaven. Even you. Do you think I didn't notice? Your mouth was hanging open when you were looking up into the dome."

Putin placed a hand on Volk's shoulder. His touch was surprisingly tender.

"I brought you here because I needed the right setting to express the depths of my condolences. I am profoundly sorry about Anatoly. I did not know him, but Smeshko has told me he was a young man of extraordinary promise. There's simply no way to make sense of our loss. You've been in my thoughts every day since."

Our loss, thought Volk. He turned away, bitterness settling in his chest, as his mind spiraled in an endless loop, replaying the events of that day. Always ending with the same poisonous unanswered question: Who exactly had ordered the annihilation of his son? And what did the man now trying to soothe his rage and grief have to do with it?

"Thank you, sir. Not a day goes by—" Volk coughed, the words caught in his throat.

"No words needed. I can only imagine your pain. Let's walk. The light is beautiful this time of day."

Putin led the way out of the back of the cathedral, doors once again opening magically. They crossed into the Alexandrovsky Sad, an English garden, and strolled toward the embankment of the Neva River. He stopped at the base of a monumental bronze statue of Peter the Great on horseback. Looming nearly fifty feet high, Peter straddled a horse that reared as it stepped on a serpent. *The Bronze Horseman* was, at once, the most popular work of art in Russia and the subject of one of the most influential works of Russian literature, a narrative poem by Alexander Pushkin.

Putin placed a hand on the Thunder Stone—the massive pedestal on which *The Bronze Horseman* stood. "This is the largest piece of stone ever moved by men. No machines. No animals. Just four hundred strong backs. Nine months. Five hundred feet a day over frozen ground. Actually, more like a thousand men, because so many died during the move. It weighs more than *three million* pounds." With that, he walked up the back of the granite rock, grabbing the horse's tail, to stand beside Peter, towering above him.

"From time to time, we produce leaders with vision. Men who are fearless, willing to take on the world. I make fun of the Communists—which they richly deserve. Those buffoons squandered our patrimony. Dissipated our influence. Demoralized our people. That's my cross. Fixing the fucking mess they left behind." He puffed his cheeks out, contemptuous. "But they changed the course of history. I give them that."

Putin led him along the Neva embankment, past the Hermitage Museum, building after building. He waved his arm at the massive buildings that were home to one of most extensive art collections ever assembled. Almost all of it confiscated from tsars, boyars, and capitalists.

"This is what eluded the Communists. Sure, they filled the museum with priceless treasures they expropriated. But to them, it was just property. What did they know about the miracle of the individual creative impulse? What did Stalin leave behind that ennobled the Russian soul? Or Brezhnev?" He scoffed. He kept walking but turned his head to look at Volk. "No need for men of action to be philistines. You're not. I'm not." He paused and then continued matter-of-factly, "You must come to my dacha sometime. I've got a couple of Repins that I'm sure you've never seen."

A vainer man might be flattered by the invitation. Volk tensed. It had to be a trap.

They turned left and walked across the Trotsky Bridge, right down the center lane, usually jammed with cars, buses, and people. "This is going to sound funny," Putin said. "I miss traffic. The fumes. Running across the street against the light. Jumping out of the car and yelling at a cabdriver when he nicks your fender. Little things you never think of until they're gone." He glanced at Volk's watch, a steel Blancpain Aqua Lung Grande Date on a well-worn deployant rubber band, very expensive, but not flashy.

"Mind if I have a look?" Putin asked, extending his hand.

Volk flipped the catch open and handed it to him, reluctantly.

"I gave this to Anatoly for his nineteenth birthday. He was wearing it when he was killed."

Putin examined it closely before slipping it onto his own wrist, snapping the band closed. An almost perfect fit. He gave his wrist a shake. "It has a nice weight to it."

Volk waited for Putin to hand the watch back to him.

"I'm getting hungry. Alexei is arranging something special. But let's stop by Peter's cabin first. I visit whenever I'm here, usually by myself, but I'd like you to see it as I do."

In just three days during 1703, Peter the Great, returning victorious from the Great Northern War with Sweden, had soldiers from the Semyonovs-kiy Regiment build him a small log cabin using masts and doors plundered from Swedish ships, the first building in the great imperial capital of Peter's vision. He lived in those rough quarters for five years, three small rooms, barely six hundred square feet, overseeing construction. Volk had visited the cabin many times, as a boy with his father and then, just a few years ago, with Anatoly—but he had never been inside. It was strictly off-limits to visitors. Putin simply turned the doorknob to enter. The table—the very table that Peter supped at—had been set for two: embroidered linen, a plate of radishes, a dish of butter, a shaker of salt, two glasses, and a bottle of vodka on ice. Next to their picnic sat an iron cast of Peter's own hand, his pipe, tobacco, and a box of matches. Putin sat in a pearwood chair that Peter had made with his own hands, gesturing toward another chair for Volk.

"I don't mean to seem immodest, but, well, Peter's become like a brother to me. It seems like I spend half my time talking to him."

"It must be wonderful having an older brother like that," Volk said. He wondered if he'd gone too far. What if Putin thought he was being sarcastic?

Putin laughed gently. "The problem is, sometimes, I see him more like a kid brother—headstrong, but sheltered, a little immature." Putin sprinkled tobacco into Peter the Great's three-hundred-year-old boxwood pipe, tamped it down, and lit it, thoughtful. "But he made Russia into a great European power. At a time when the Americans were . . . what? English serfs?"

Volk slathered a radish with butter, salted it, and popped it into his mouth.

"And he built this city. But those battles with the Swedes went on for twenty years." Putin downed his vodka, continued to puff. "Hundreds of thousands of Russian lives. "I would never fight a war that way today. Too crude. Sometimes it's best not to let your opponent even know you're at war. Much better that, when they figure it out, it's too late."

Volk watched him, warily. Putin examined the pipe carefully, perhaps imagining Peter doing the same, holding the same pipe, more than three hundred years ago, as he made decisions that sacrificed so many lives on the altar of Romanov glory.

Putin was less rehearsed than most of the very powerful men Volk had studied. The man's friendliness seemed genuine, but whatever warmth he projected was overshadowed by a sense that you could slip off the knife edge of his favor in an instant. Volk understood it perfectly. The same wolves had chased him down these same streets. Everyone you met was a blood threat. You always had to know where the exits were.

It must be exhausting, Volk thought, to maintain that unbreakable facade, to radiate, at every waking moment, that refusal to be intimidated. It was rumored that Putin was in the early stages of a neurological affliction, perhaps Parkinson's disease. Putin was rarely seen in public anymore, and when he was, only under tightly controlled conditions. The man still had presence and energy, but, here, sitting before this rustic table with no grand audience, he looked slightly drained, diminished. Perhaps it was the illness. Or maybe the job of running the world's biggest country—stretching across eleven time zones—and appropriating a nontrivial percentage of its wealth was simply wearing the man out.

"Sometimes I wonder if Peter felt trapped," Putin said. "Only able to move forward, needing to feed the beasts that surrounded him—factions, obligations—when all he wanted to do was be off by himself. Do you ever feel trapped, Volk?"

"We're all captives of our place and our time, aren't we, sir?"

"I suppose you could say that. But we make do."

Putin gave him an inquiring, challenging look. Rushing to fill the silence, Volk spoke without thinking.

"At your service, sir."

Putin narrowed his eyes, as if what Volk had just said was so obvious he wondered why Volk felt the need to state it.

"It took me a while to figure out how to handle the Americans," Putin said, with no explanation as to why he was changing the topic. "Yeltsin played into their savior fantasies, he led Clinton and his people to think they could redeem us. You could argue it made sense at the time. We were broke, everything in chaos. But it sickened me. What did that tell our people about the sacrifices they'd made, their parents, their grandparents? Generations of suffering. At first, I wasn't sure how to talk to the Americans. They weren't my friends. But they weren't my enemies either. Then I realized they could become something far more useful: adversaries. We didn't have to bring them to heel. That's what the communists got wrong. We didn't have to beat them. We just had to keep them off-balance."

He stopped abruptly.

"You are probably wondering why I'm telling you this. Don't think about that too much for now. I'm going to need you around."

Putin tapped the tobacco out of the pipe and stood. "Alexei and I have a proposition for you. We'll discuss it over dinner."

Outside, the sun still hung high in the sky. An official car, another Senat, waited outside. Ignoring Volk, Putin reclined his seat and fell fast asleep as the big car headed south, speeding along empty roads, heading for Podvor'ye, his favorite restaurant, in Pavlovsk, a nineteenth-century village where the tsar had maintained his summer residence, twenty miles from Saint Petersburg.

Volk was grateful for the break. Almost two hours walking beside Putin—trying not to take a false step or hit a flat note—had left him on edge. The Butler had once told him that, as close as they had become, Putin's true inner circle remained the small crew he had grown up with: the Fursenko brothers, Vladimir Yakunin, Nikolay Shamalov, Yuriy Koval'chuk, and a few others. Childhood chums and, later, founding members of two secretive investment firms with tentacles that reached into every sector of the Russian economy: Quark and the Ozero cooperative. And, not least of those old friends, his childhood judo sparring partner, the cellist Sergei Roldugin, godfather to Volodya's eldest daughter, and rumored to be his most trusted front man, perhaps the only person who understood the full scope of Putin's fortune. With that loyal crew behind him, Putin's true genius blossomed. The key to his ability to amass and retain great wealth and power had been his mastery of *sistema*—of *blat,* the informal personal networks of influence and favor-trading that permeated every aspect of Russian life. By the time he consolidated power in the Kremlin, the forces that shaped Russian life— the criminal gangs, the security directorates, the courts, and the nominally democratic parliament were all under his control. Putin had organized all of Russia, the entire country, to respond to just one man. A reign of *bespredel*: unconstrained power and a complete absence of accountability. Now napping, peacefully, blissfully unconcerned, head flopping onto his chest, mouth slightly ajar, a bit of saliva dripping out of the corner of his mouth. If he was concerned, he never showed it. Volk looked, wistfully, at the watch, realizing that he'd never see it again anywhere other than on Putin's wrist.

Putin woke, almost on cue, as they arrived at Podvor'ye. Local legend had it that the restaurant set a table for him every night, just in case he decided to show up for dinner. The Butler trotted out of the kitchen wearing a white apron and led them to a rustic open-air pavilion built of pine logs, warmed by a massive stone fireplace. Tossing the apron onto a sideboard, he gestured for them to sit at a large table set for three, piled with Russian delicacies: pickled herring, a salad of sheep's tongue and grilled onions, boiled sturgeon, smoked bacon, wild mushroom fricassee, potato salad with peas and carrots, veal liver shish kebab, sorrel soup, grilled rabbit legs, beef stroganoff.

Putin smiled, popping a pickled pepper into his mouth.

"Alexei, you spoil me." Smeshko had started off as Putin's official taster. "Your chef might not be trying to poison you," Smeshko had told the boss, "but his cooking, it's torture." Soon, the chef was gone and Smeshko was on his way.

"How have you two made out?" Smeshko asked. Putin simply nodded.

"We'd like to bring you inside the tent, Fyodor." Smeshko tasted the sorrel soup and stuffed a piece of bread into his mouth. "Everything Vladimir Vladimirovich has done—everything in his entire career—has been driven by a single goal: to restore Russia to its rightful place among nations. To restore its respect. Its greatness."

Right, thought Volk, what do you get the man who has everything? Revanche: the resurrection of a proud, now second-rate, power, to make Russia great enough to equal the greatness of the man. I have to give them credit. They've gone to a lot of trouble to make it seem like I have a choice.

"I'm flattered. What do you need me to do?" He'd been elevated from being a mid-level government contractor running a band of mercenaries, to a puppet of the tsar himself. A fairy tale.

"Help us cut America down to size," said Putin. "You've earned the right. For what they did to Anatoly." Volk fought to control a surge of bitterness: That was the price of admission—a blood sacrifice?

The Butler jumped in, speaking through a mouth full of potato salad, Putin gnawed intently on the rabbit legs he'd piled on his plate. "Not that we're not making good progress," Smeshko said. "We've outmaneuvered them in the Middle East and gotten far deeper into their computer networks than they'll ever know. Even Reddit, that's our playpen. And their hold on Europe is slipping thanks to the continent's bottomless appetite for the cheap natural gas. When they have to choose between NATO and a hot shower in January, they'll side with us."

Smeshko took a sip of wine and smiled.

"Best of all, we've sowed so much internal dissension through Facebook and Twitter that the biggest story on CNN is America's coming civil war, if you can believe it. Labor against capital. Black against white. Suburb versus city versus country. Poor against rich—the democratic virtue of 'equality' versus the unattainable communist illusion of 'equity.' We had no idea how easy it would be."

Putin had suddenly become animated. He held up a pinkie.

"This is all I need to knock them over. Or at least scare the crap out of them. A nudge. A very delicate operation. No freelancing. We think you're the man to make it happen. Alexei will take it from here. You and I won't speak of this again."

Putin tossed his napkin over the mound of picked-over rabbit bones on his plate, stood up, and, then, he was gone.

17

Doyers Street, New York City

A week later, on a bitter cold, gray, and hopeless February afternoon, Don and Greta found themselves in another hardened, featureless bunker, this time behind an empty storefront on Doyers Street, a narrow alley in Chinatown, with Chip and Pete in tow. Tommy had summoned them, as usual, on short notice. He was in town only for a few hours, just back from Vail, where he'd been back-country skiing with an old acquaintance, a data-mining entrepreneur who wanted to offer Ben's nascent campaign access to a suite of predictive algorithms that were so powerful, he promised, that using them would be like stealing the election.

When they walked in, Tommy was slouched in a conference table chair, wearing a bright red ski sweater with a giant black spider on the shoulder and ridiculous furry after-ski boots. For a second, Greta was almost embarrassed, as if she'd walked in on him naked. He looked up at Greta and smiled warmly. "Urky, thanks for coming down." He turned to Don. His voice dropped. "This guy giving you any trouble?"

"Not recently," she said, smiling. Don looked uncomfortable.

"Good."

For the last ten days or so, since Tommy had last been in town, Don had been even less communicative than usual. If she tried to talk about anything outside of the job, he just shut down. A wisecrack, maybe, but more likely pained silence. The whole ride downtown, he'd just stared out the window. It was beginning to annoy her. Does he think I'm so fragile that I'll take it the wrong way if he even talks to me? I'll tell you who the fragile one is—the guy who ran away three years ago, never stopped running, and now has to soothe himself by spending almost $200,000 on a car.

"Shall we start?" Tommy said. "I don't have much time."

What else is new? Greta thought. Tommy looked drained. Not just because he'd been skiing, it was deeper than that, in the slope of his shoulders and the way the light just seemed to lie on his skin instead of bouncing off it. She laid out her materials and plugged in her laptop. Tommy straightened up in his seat.

Greta jumped right in. "Industrial Strategies is the most opaque institution I've ever studied. Vicker may operate out of New York, but all his corporate structures are offshore—and the identity of his investors is guarded like a state secret. In the age of know-your-client and government compliance rules, that kind of secrecy requires a huge effort. The norm these days is to communicate frequently with all investors. He doesn't. It's as if he's protecting something. Or someone."

Greta flashed the first slide of her deck, a complicated schematic of the IS corporate networks, onto a large flat-screen. Tommy studied the document, with total concentration, as if every pore of his linebacker-size body had been optimized for the absorption of raw data.

"I've been pawing through forty years of the Vicker sock drawer. IRS, SEC, CFTC filings, parking tickets, school transcripts, *all* of the IS files from inception, Vicker's medical bills, financial records from before he started IS. And a *very* interesting series of CIA reports on some of Vicker's offshore transactions. He and his nephew have done business with some naughty boys. We've uploaded hundreds of thousands of pieces of paper. Everything you can imagine."

Hedge funds generate massive volumes of documents: trade blotters, prime brokerage statements, regulatory filings in twenty jurisdictions, contracts, emails, payables, receivables, wire transfers, credit card statements, health insurance claims, travel records, consultant contracts, client communications, employment records. The IS physical archives—paper documents—lived in a secure warehouse. They went back more than twenty years, and every single one had needed to be scanned and OCR'd. She had hired a team from Palantir to mirror all the live IS systems—essentially a full backup—just in case their team lost access. Terabyte upon terabyte of data. But without Virtualitics' AI-driven data analytics and 3D visualization platform, she would have been flying blind into a blizzard of information, unable to discern patterns, much less to analyze the data. Still, for those tools to be useful to Greta, she needed the complete data set and the ability to manipulate it offline, on the mirrored servers. Even with the level of security and clearances that Virtualitics and Palantir offered, she added a layer of complexity by insisting that the data be sufficiently anonymized so that no one would know the source.

"Impressive," Tommy said, life now back in his face. "What kind of tools are you using?"

"Primarily my own adaptation of XKeyscore. And we're using Palantir's data fusion and analytical tools, but it's a bespoke system, and our Israeli friend Ari babysits the data." XKeyscore, a formerly secret NSA computer program, enables a user to tag an individual and create a comprehensive digital fingerprint: to read their email in real time, watch any computer they use, track their online associations, and follow their network activity.

"We've really just begun the analysis; our focus has been on creating a real-time shadow of the IS computer systems. I never want to be shut out in the event that the volatile Mr. V changes his mind."

"Anything of interest so far?"

"Where do we even start? Come by our war room sometime. One or another of our analysts jumps up and does a jig every six minutes with some other vein of interest or tocsin."

"Urky, please, most of us didn't learn English by memorizing Webster's while walking across Dasht-e Kavir. Tocsin?"

"From the Latin. From *toccare* and *signum*, ringing a bell to warn villagers of danger."

"What bells are ringing?" Tommy asked.

"Informally, our colleagues in the agency's financial interests section have flagged Vicker's relationships with some particularly unsavory people—mob types, convicted felons. And—this is a bit weird—he's also tight with a *very* senior guy at Allard Frères who seems to also have a lot of the same friends, as well as some good friends in Langley."

"I'm not following," said Tommy. "The Agency has friendlies with whom Vicker does business?"

"Exactly. 'A well-informed private individual,' in Agency parlance. In the Venn diagram of Industrial Strategies' many interests—both legitimate and less so—this one banker, Lorenzo Gonzaga, is right in the center. From the earliest days of the firm. He has visited Industrial Strategies' offices more than any single person who doesn't work there."

"That explains a lot," said Pete. "I've noticed that there's definitely someone who pulls Vicker's chain. Sometimes his schedule, which is usually broken down in precise fifteen-minute segments, just has these grayed-out hours. Last year, in the middle of a meeting in Senator Conway's office in

D.C., Vicker got a call and asked me and Conway to leave the room. It was incredible—Conway sitting in his own reception area. That's who it must have been."

"Whatever Gonzaga does for him, Vicker appears to compensate him by allocating fund shares. Gonzaga's IS account runs to eleven digits. You wouldn't believe how hard it was to figure that out. His interests are camouflaged through layers of offshore companies submerged in a swamp of foundations and trusts. Most sophisticated I've ever seen. If Al Qaeda knew as much about concealing assets as this guy, the world would be a more dangerous place—"

"Name again?"

"Gonzaga. Lorenzo Gonzaga. Unlike most people who style themselves Italian counts, he actually is one. Very elegant, old world, about seventy, but the girls don't seem to mind." Greta batted her eyes, theatrically.

Tommy perked up. "Wait. I know this guy . . . Allard Frères. He touched down in Iraq for six hours when I was running security, protecting the jackasses who ran the place. Don? Remember him?"

"I had completely forgotten. The story was that Dubya sent him in to discuss sensitive financial matters—something to do with funneling money to former Saddam cronies. Which they turned around and used to outfit the insurgency."

"Yup. Gonzaga is *that* guy, the human back channel." Tommy added. "Every president has them, the ones they call on to smooth feathers or to send a message quietly. Wherever a guy like Gonzaga shows up, one thing you know: money starts shifting around in the background, most likely into untraceable offshore bank accounts."

Tommy placed his palms on the table and closed his eyes. The war and reconstruction of Iraq embodied everything he hated about politics. The narcissistic electeds and predatory financiers who bought and sold them, the self-important State Department sherpas and Pentagon posers. Glorified bureaucrats, steering no-bid contracts to cronies and Green Zone vultures. All while American soldiers—boys and girls barely out of high school, young mothers and fathers forced into second and third deployments—getting ripped apart by IEDs outside the wire. He broke the silence, looking at Greta.

"All this before you've really even begun to dig, Greta. What else?"

"There's another thread we've been pulling." Don leaned forward, on his forearms. "Something that got flagged at the Hamilton conference. The idea that Vicker's investment returns are statistically improbable, and even more unlikely given that, as he tells it, he found every possible way to lose money before he had an epiphany and magically turned into the greatest investor of all time."

"The first part is true," Greta began. "He did manage his family's money—and he did indeed lose it. The second part's a little more complicated."

Greta displayed several graphs on the wall screens.

"In addition to IS, he ran a broker-dealer called Backwater Securities out of the same office. Lots of cross-trading between the two—which was noneconomic given that he owned all of Backwater and controlled IS. But what's interesting is that it looks like IS, from the start, has made almost all—maybe ninety percent—of its profits from very chunky low-probability trades."

"Like what?" asked Chip.

"Like IS shorts Cameroonian sovereign bonds, and two weeks later, Ambazonian separatists happen to blow up a pipeline, and the bonds lose more than half their value overnight. Like a low-odds patent infringement lawsuit against a biotech company going in the plaintiff's favor and sending the company's stock up five hundred percent in a single day, making a fortune for its biggest investor. Like an eerie ability to predict unexpected actions by central banks around the world. Like a very aggressive enforcement action by the European Union against a U.S. pharmaceutical company that, seemingly, came out of nowhere. Should I go on?"

Tommy nodded.

"It is not just that the outcomes were always significantly against the odds, but that the investments were profoundly disparate. Vicker's interest in the subject matter of the trades surfaced out of nowhere. In the early years, Vicker did not trade often, but, every time he did, he bet the ranch on outcomes that seemed impossible to predict—and his timing was usually perfect. He would get in, an event would occur, and he would get right back out again. All in narrow time frames—weeks, months, sometimes even days."

"So why does Vicker have all these high-priced traders working for him?" Don asked. "If the firm makes investments only here and there?"

"My guess is camouflage. There's a lot of trading going on, but just to generate noise. Basically, he is paying several hundred people to look busy, while he makes big bets on exogenous fat-tail events, which, somehow, he always foresees."

"Why hasn't the SEC, or someone else, nailed him?" Tommy asked.

"They might yet. But maybe he's careful and hasn't broken any laws. And IS is structured so that it's totally offshore. No U.S. investors, except Vicker himself, and the biggest profits may not be coming from information or knowledge that emanates from inside the United States or U.S. companies."

"Can anyone guess what this sounds like to me?" Don said with mock seriousness. Don had written his War College thesis on the subject of foundation myths and the need to understand the ways that the stories that countries, tribes, corporations, and even people tell about themselves amplify some truths and distort others. Origin stories.

"I accept that he was a shitty investor before founding IS. But what about after that. How did he 'miraculously' spring forth as a modern Midas?" asked Don.

"You mean a radioactive spider didn't just bite him?" said Chip.

"We all project our own creation myths, don't we?" said Tommy. "To amplify, obscure, and enhance how the world sees us. I've got my own ex nihilo story, poor little Black boy who springs from the ghetto unscarred, fully formed, a creation of his own mind."

"You all know mine." Greta clasped her hands in her lap, prim. "A fragile, idealistic waif fleeing corruption, injustice, and oppression, seeking freedom. Walking alone through an Iranian desert, aided by kind strangers at every turn."

They all looked at Chip, who rarely talked about his past. He shrugged.

"Since we're in a sharing mood," said Chip. "My legend is my reality. Two hundred years of good family fortune terminated by a daddy who gambled it away. And then blew his head off with an antique Purdey shotgun he told me I'd inherit one day."

Greta, taken by surprise, glanced at Tommy. Don sat back in his chair, constitutionally discomfited by emotional intimacy, and particularly unsettled by Chip's sudden willingness to begin sharing.

Finally, Tommy broke the silence.

"Well done, Chip."

"Are we through?" Don asked. "I mean, what else do we need to know about Elias Vicker—which hand he jerks off with? He's a psycho and a crook. Everyone hates him. But he's our psycho."

"Speaking of psycho, there is one more thing," said Greta. "Starting three years before he formed IS, and extending for years after, Vicker had huge medical bills from New York-Episcopal Hospital."

Tommy tensed. "That's a long time. For what?"

"A serious neurological condition—Guillain-Barré syndrome. It looks like he was in intensive care for over a year, and then in extensive rehab for a year after that. An extreme case. But the bills went on for a few years more. Psych consults. If you can believe it, he was in psychoanalysis. The real kind—four, five times a week. And his shrink, a Dr. Thaddeus Kerry, was one of the earliest investors in IS—through an offshore company."

"And you're just telling us this now?" Tommy stared at her, incredulous.

"I meant to flag it sooner." Greta looked chagrined. "Kerry specialized in treating patients recovering from paralyzing neurological conditions. He was controversial because he filmed his patients extensively. He called it putting them 'outside the frame,' enabling his patients to see themselves as others see them."

"*Damn.* We need to figure out how to approach him." Tommy slapped the table. "Maybe Elizabeth can find a way in."

"Not happening. He was killed in a hit-and-run, years ago, corner of First Avenue and Sixty-Eighth Street. He left fifty million dollars, his entire estate, to a foundation for the advancement of the psychiatric treatment of GBS patients and their families."

"And who runs that?" Don asked.

"The sole trustee is Lorenzo Gonzaga, and it's all invested in IS."

"If there are tapes of his sessions with Vicker, or practice notes, we need to see them. Fantasies, fears, hatreds, loves, origin story . . . everything." Tommy spoke almost to himself, but they all got the message. "I want to meet back here in two weeks."

As the others filed out, Greta shut the door behind them, and turned to Tommy.

"I hired Volk. He'll move our crates out of France—to Riga."

"When can we tap it? I'd like to start funding some political action committees stat."

"It won't be long. Send me wire instructions via Signal."

18

Industrial Strategies, New York City

Lorenzo Gonzaga's chauffeur-driven black Mercedes, courtesy of Allard Frères, pulled into the underground garage at Vicker's Manhattan spire, where an elevator reserved for the building's most important tenants awaited him. Gonzaga felt he deserved a Bentley, but the government-relations folks at the bank had nixed it as unseemly. The big Mercedes was quite enough. Not by accident, Greta happened to be chatting with the receptionist as the elevator doors opened and Gonzaga walked into the austere marble and glass lobby. Seeing him, the receptionist hustled from behind her desk.

"Miss Carina, lovelier than ever," Gonzaga purred in his crisp RP. Taking her hand, he raised it to his lips, the refined Italian courtier. Carina, an ebullient, fiftysomething, second-generation Italian woman from Staten Island, beamed and blushed.

"Oh, Dottore, please, let me take your coat."

He shrugged off his cashmere Cucinelli topcoat and dropped it in Carina's arms without looking at her. Carina touched it to her cheek, murmuring, *"Morbido come il sedere di un bambino."*

"Che espressione affascinante, Carina. So lovely to hear the mother tongue."

He turned to Greta, no longer feigning interest in the receptionist.

"Who might you be, my dear?"

That's your best move? thought Greta. No, more likely he was such an arrogant prick that it did not occur to him that he needed a move. She knew the type: a snap of his fingers should have sufficed. Another time, in another place, she thought, he would be writhing in pain.

"Greta Webb, sir. I'm a senior software engineer, recently joined as co-head of the IT security department." Greta cast her eyes down modestly.

"My pleasure to meet you, Ms. Webb. You must be good at keeping secrets." Gonzaga extended a hand. "Perhaps I could introduce you to some of our men—I am told that they are among the very best—at Allard, compare notes." *All men?* His best suave charm, no incisors visible.

"That is up to my boss and Mr. Vicker, of course. But I would appreciate it."

"In my hands, then." Gonzaga gave her a slight bow. Turning, he followed Carina to Vicker's office.

———

An hour later, Vicker strutted into his secure, hardened, internal conference room for a hastily convened meeting with his sovereign bond, energy, and currency trading teams. Don and Greta sat in the outside ring. Pete sat by himself at the far end of the table, just beginning to emerge from his post–Hamilton conference purdah.

"Mr. Vicker, would you like me to get Oscar on the conference line?" Alison asked, referring to Vicker's nephew, based in the Berlin office.

Vicker fluttered his eyelashes and mouthed an exaggerated no. Sitting at the head of the long table, he pressed a button to fog the glass walls.

"I assume you all saw the story in the *Wall Street Journal* today about this very public spat between the Saudis and the Russians?"

No one said a word. "The Saudis want to cut production to bolster prices, but the Russians want to keep pumping so that prices stay low and American shale producers go bust. Maybe it's just shadowboxing. Everyone thinks they know how it ends: Mohammed bin Salman does the rational thing and cuts production. After all, the Saudi economy is sucking wind these days. They need those high prices."

Vicker methodically cracked every knuckle on his left hand.

"It's only logical, right? The whole purpose of OPEC is to manipulate prices, keep oil prices high—and fuck the West."

He began working on the knuckles of his right hand: *snap, snap, snap, snap.*

"Isn't that right?" He looked at Doug, his head trader.

"Yeah, that's how the entire market is positioned. People have been betting that the Russians and the Saudis will cut a deal, and they've been bidding up everything in the energy space. The stock prices of all the shale producers are at all-time highs. WTI and Brent futures have been rocketing." WTI—West Texas Intermediate—the most actively traded contract for crude oil and, along with Brent and Dubai crude, one of the three main international benchmarks for pricing crude oil.

"So the entire market is a one way bet at the moment?" Vicker asked.

Doug nodded. "Pretty much. People think that they've seen this show before and that, at the end of the day, the crown prince and Putin won't leave that much money on the table. Oil's at sixty-five dollars a barrel now. The market is predicting it'll be at eighty dollars once VVP and MBS kiss and make up."

Vicker's eyes sparkled, he broke into a wide grin.

"What if I don't buy it?" He paused, deliberately.

Doug looked stunned. "You want to bet against the oil producers *and* the stock market? No one in the world thinks the entire oil market is mispriced."

Vicker stopped smiling.

"What if it turned out that MBS and Putin want oil prices to hit new lows? What if this whole game of chicken they're playing is just an act?"

"But, that would be crazy—"

Vicker cut him off.

"Doug, treat this as a thought experiment."

Doug swallowed hard, he had seen the show before. Vicker knew more than he was letting on. Likely much, much more.

"Depends on how much oil they pump, and for how long. But, at a minimum, WTI would crater, maybe drop forty, fifty percent."

"And the shale producers—like Continental Resources, Whiting Petroleum, and Chesapeake Energy?"

"Also depends how long they keep pumping. If it goes on long enough, most of those guys go belly up, bankrupt . . ." Doug looked at his tablet, connected to the Bloomberg terminal at his desk. "There are two hundred fracking outfits producing oil and gas in North America. If a barrel of oil goes below twenty-five dollars, their equity would be wiped out. Their costs of production are high—they need high oil prices to survive. On top of that, they've got over one hundred and fifty billion dollars in debt outstanding."

Vicker picked up a pen and began jotting numbers down on a pad.

"Okay, I'm penciling in a short of—let's say—two hundred billion of oil futures . . . down forty percent . . . we make eighty billion. And let's just say we short another one hundred billion of debt and equity in . . . those frackers. Eighty plus a hundred . . . that's one hundred and eighty billion."

He looked up. "Not a bad day's work. And what about the sovereigns—the Norways, the Nigerias, the Russias? What happens to their debt? And their currencies?"

"Boss, before we go down that road, Saudi Arabia runs a welfare state—they need an oil price of one hundred dollars a barrel to balance their budget. They'd be fucking themselves."

Vicker shook his head. "Doug, it's so helpful to hear you spouting conventional wisdom. But why put so much trust in the market view of what's rational and what isn't? Maybe MBS and Putin have other agendas. Go on."

"The Norwegian kroner would be crushed. Ditto the Nigerian naira. But if we're really thinking big, the U.S. stock markets would be shredded. You could get picky and just short the big banks, but . . . might be simpler to just bet against the S&P index."

Vicker jotted down more numbers on his pad. "So . . . let's say . . . we can pick up another fifty, sixty, a hundred billion being short crappy currencies, the S&P, the DJIA, the FTSE. Okay, okay . . . good."

Pete squirmed. He could not help entering the fray.

"Holy shit, boss. Betting against the guys that have made America not just self-sufficient in oil, but an energy exporter for the first time in our history? That's going to make us a lot of enemies."

"Pete, really? Why? Just because I might be right, and they might be wrong? It's my money against theirs. And what can they do?" Vicker gave him one of his mildest stares, more withering for that.

"Soros was right when he broke the Bank of England. Didn't stop people from hating him. He still hasn't lived it down."

"And?"

"If we make this kind of money while the oil industry tanks, it won't be just the bankruptcies. Tens of thousands of people will lose their jobs. If people figure out that we're the ones who profited, it doesn't matter that we're right and they're stupid. And there'll be no way to keep something this big quiet—they'll try to crucify you."

Vicker was more still and controlled than ever, his face nearly void of expression. Then, his mirthless grin. And a shrug.

"Why do I even need to explain this to you? The whole international political establishment is going to get caught with its pants down. Of course, they'll lash out. But they're the ones who'll have fucked up by not preparing for the possibility that the Saudis and Putin have a more complicated agenda. Frankly, I can't understand how anyone could miss it: Putin gets to kick America in the balls, the only thing that makes him happy these days, and the Saudis wipe out their biggest competitor. How many times do we need to be taught the same lesson? OPEC has been taking us to school since the 1973 oil embargo."

Pete opened his mouth to speak, then thought better of it.

"And, Pete? Pete—look at me. This is your job, right? Payola? You've asked me to fill the bucket so you can line campaign coffers down there in Washington and over in Brussels. Now's the time to make sure I get a return on my investment. Call in some chits, run some interference."

Vicker turned back to his trader.

"Doug, draw me a picture. By this time tomorrow, I want to see a masterpiece. A whole package of trades on the blotter. Short WTI, Brent, and Dubai. See how much borrow you can get on shale company shares—most of those are going to zero. And think big on currency shorts. There may not be good liquidity in some, but the kroner is going to crash and burn, and the Russian ruble? Rubble." Vicker chuckled at his own attempt at a joke.

"Size? Price limit?" Doug asked.

"I think there is an orchestrated plan here. Oil prices even could go negative. So, see how much storage capacity you can lock up—both onshore and off, in the form of empty tankers." The possibility that, in a crash scenario, traders would actually pay someone else to take their oil had been a market fantasy for years. It took time to turn off the spigot. Producers kept producing, and oil didn't stop moving through pipelines and over the seas. If storage was tight, there would be no where to put it.

"How long can this go on, sir?" Doug had gone white, excited, but also frightened, by the prospect of what Vicker had laid out.

Vicker leaned back in his chair. "The Saudis have five hundred billion in reserves. The Russians have over six hundred billion. They don't need marginal cash flow for a month, or two, or three. The game goes on until they say it's over."

Doug pressed as far as he dared: "Any limits?"

Vicker waved a hand, dismissive. "It should be cheap to build this position—no one is expecting it. So . . . no . . . no limits. Just keep me updated."

Pete exhaled softly, not quite sure why he should be cautioning Vicker, but, after their meeting with Greta, wanting to hear a reaction.

"Boss, if we're wrong, we could drop billions. Isn't this a lot of conviction for a new trade? Word will get out. Someone will leak it to the press."

The room grew quiet.

Vicker's expression didn't change.

"Right . . . Pete. Then let's make sure that word gets out. As soon as we've built our position, call Blackrock, Blackstone. Call JPMorgan, give them all a heads-up. Tell 'em it's a fundamental view, based on research by Industrial Strategies. Fuck it. We'd be doing them a favor, so better that they hear it from us first, rather than read about it in the *Wall Street Journal*."

With that, Vicker reversed the glass, the fog cleared, and he loped out of the room.

Greta turned to Don.

"You understand what just happened?"

"Only sort of, but I'm still trying to figure out how oil is a negative. Isn't it better for a lot of people to be able to buy it at lower prices?"

"Cute but dumb." Greta smiled. "Oil and gas production is a three trillion dollar industry, five percent of the world economy. But there's not much spare capacity in the system. It is built on the assumption that oil and gas will keep flowing. The upstream part of the oil and gas business—the people who find it and produce it—depends on predictable flows, moving it into tankers, pipelines, and refineries. But because storage and transport capacity is limited, if supplies suddenly spike, and create a glut, there's nowhere to put all that filthy stuff. So they might have to pay people to take it off their hands. That's the 'negative.'

"But that's beside the point right now. Focus on Gonzaga. He dropped by for an unannounced chat and the minute he's gone, Vicker charges out of his office and commits one hundred billion dollars—maybe more—on one trade. No analysis. No debate. Kinda makes you wonder."

Don grinned.

"After he got rid of the old IT team, I had my guys put eyes everywhere—including Vicker's office. We can see exactly what Gonzaga told him."

———————

They almost ran to Don's command center, an interior office carved out of the IS server farm. The data pipes, a dozen gleaming six-inch-diameter conduits, passed right behind his desk, ported for direct access from the servers lining one wall. The entire room had been hardened, secured, and was swept continually for electronic intrusion.

Don pulled up a video of Vicker's meeting with Gonzaga. The man that he and Greta saw, sitting at a small table with Gonzaga, was vastly different from the image that Vicker presented publicly. He was relaxed and looked at Gonzaga with an openness, almost admiration.

"Elias, I have a little—maybe not so little—play for us," said Gonzaga. *"You've been following the very public spat between OPEC—really driven by the Saudis—and Putin? From outside, it looks like a cat fight?"*

"Not like them to let people see how the sausage is being made."

"Your instincts are spot on. It's complete misdirection, a scheme to make the world think that it's just another raucous family squabble among OPEC and the OPEC-plus countries."

"Go on."

"Putin has been telling MBS for years that they're cutting their own throats. High prices are the only thing that enables the American frackers to thrive. As long as they keep prices high, the Russians and Saudis are essentially subsidizing their American rivals."

Vicker started bouncing his knee. *"I'm smelling so much blood there I can't even think straight,"* he said.

"But there are even bigger prizes here: revenge, pure power. Putin actively detests America and its meddling in what he considers his own affairs. It's personal. American financial sanctions are not just aimed at Russia, they target some of his best friends. As for the Saudis, from time to time, they like to show the Americans whose foot is on whose throat."

"So, what's our play?"

"Essentially the same as theirs. Putin and MBS may have their faults, but they are superb strategic thinkers. Both of them have personal trading teams, and they like taking advantage of the market dislocations their own actions cause. When the Saudis cut prices and the Russians start pumping at peak capacity, everyone will think they'll make peace quickly, before their economies are destroyed. But if you tote up how much the Saudis and the Russians will earn from short-term trading and how much they have in their international reserves—nearly a trillion dollars between them—they can keep on pushing prices down almost indefinitely."

"But they won't. Will they?"

Gonzaga smiled. *"No, of course not. It will go on just long enough that the markets decide it's the new normal. Then—suddenly, unexpectedly—they'll make peace and send prices rocketing right back up. They'll unload their short positions and take their profits. By then, of course they will have snapped up cheap energy assets around the globe."*

"Stunning, Lorenzo. And your level of conviction?"

"One hundred percent. I'm helping them design the trading strategies. We will know what their plans are in real time."

"That's all I need to know. How big should we get?"

"What is your quaint expression? Back up the truck?"

Vicker punched the button on his intercom. *"Alison, get the entire equities, energy, sovereign, and currency desks into my conference room. Now."*

"Do you want Mr. Carter and Ms. Webb too?"

"Sure. They might learn something."

Don hit pause. "Well, now we know." Greta, riveted by what was unfolding onscreen, reached over him and restarted the video.

Vicker got up to leave, as if he could hardly wait to tell his staff about his amazing new idea. Then, he caught himself at the door.

"Remember my asshole nephew?" Vicker said. *"Not only did we end up having to cash fund that stolen car deal he financed with your Scandinavian 'friends,' now they've refused to repay the money Oscar lent them. But I'm writing it off. I don't ever want those SEF goons sneaking up on me again."*

"Whoa. Stop right there." Greta shivered involuntarily and shot out her hand to pause the video. "Did you hear that? SEF! I cannot believe it. The ghost. We have been trying to find a way into SEF for years."

"Who's we, and what's SEF?"

"The Agency. More and more, when a really big and really dirty piece of business requires financing—drugs, arms, counterfeit gold bars, stolen matériel—we see the fingerprints of a massive, completely opaque financial entity. We think it's SEF. Stichting Eskandarfond. We know it exists but every time we think we've found it, there's nothing there, not a trace. It's a Dutch thing. There's nothing in American law that really compares to a stichting."

"Stichting?"

"It's an obscure legal structure that allows you to own things without really owning them. Lawyers in Amsterdam have been building these financial black boxes for centuries. We believe they collectively hold hundreds of billions of dollars in assets. Is SEF the biggest? The dirtiest? We have no way of knowing. But now we at least know it exists."

The possibility of being at the table with the legendary Stichting Eskandarfond, a thing of mist and rumor, made the drudgery of the last few months worth it to Greta. This stateless, formless, and ageless pool of capital had remained nearly invisible for centuries. Most likely, it had influenced the course of history—financing wars, toppling kingdoms, electing popes—in ways that might never be known: as enduring a monument to avarice as great cathedrals were calls to a higher purpose. Among those who pretended to know, it was said that you did not find them. They found you, particularly in situations that required size, speed, and secrecy, and when the high cost of assistance would not be an issue. If you were a major company with an acquisition opportunity that required fast action—or anyone with a sudden problem that required a capital injection—chances were that they would send an emissary, someone like Gonzaga, to feel you out. Even among aficionados, like Greta, for whom an understanding of the ecosystem of the world's largest pools of capital was a matter of professional pride, SEF was a shadow that swept across the periphery of the landscape. A presence sensed, because suddenly billions of dollars of financing appeared out of nowhere. In the gossipy world of finance, in which no one kept secrets, it protected its privacy religiously.

"Let's keep watching." She started the video.

"There's a reason I've kept Ferdinando away from you all these years. After your journey to Washington, D.C., I think you can understand why. He can play a little rough—as I warned you, when we accepted their money. But I do have great admiration for his tailor."

Vicker waved a hand, as if to tell Gonzaga not to worry.

"It's just my mother. I'm sure she'll somehow blame me, like it's my fault that her idiot grandchild is an incompetent crook. I've been looking to get rid of that worthless prick for years. Even if it costs me three hundred million, it'll be worth it."

Gonzaga, looking slightly alarmed, began collecting himself to leave, *"Families can be difficult. I'm glad to help out if that makes it easier for you."*

"Thank you, Lorenzo. I'll let you know."

Greta paused the video.

"He wouldn't need help to just fire the guy."

Greta restarted the video.

"Elias, that new girl, Greta," Gonzaga said. *"She interests me. Strong legs. Do you know if she likes to ride horses?"*

Greta got up to leave, to Don's relief. Neither of them wanted to have that conversation. As Greta made for the door, Don reached out his hand, motioning for her to sit down again. A window had popped open on his computer monitor.

"Well, well. What have we here? Incoming from the PP in Berlin."

"PP?" Greta asked.

"The *petit Prince,* that's what they call Oscar around the office. Apparently he's a complete asshole. Take a seat."

Don tapped his speakerphone: Oscar was shouting at Vicker.

"Uncle Eliassssssssss! What the fuck? I just heard from the trading desk that you authorized them to trade *billions* of dollars of oil contracts. What the fuck? What the actual fucking *fuck?* The guys working that trade report to *me*—the *sovereign* traders, the *currency* traders. They sit outside my office. They kiss my ass. It's humiliating. You should have brought me in."

Silence from Vicker. Then, in a low tone of controlled rage: "*Your* traders? *Your* office? I gave you a chance to play in *my* playpen. All I asked was that you make money. So far, how long is it? Seven years? Seven useless years of constantly filling holes you keep digging," Vicker paused. "Oscar, what's the first rule of holes?"

No answer.

"Oscar?"

"Stop digging," Oscar muttered.

"If I didn't love my brother and Mommy, you would have been gone a long time ago. Not . . . a . . . fucking . . . dime. In seven years. Not . . . a . . . dime. And let's not forget what you exposed me to by financing car thieves. Have you ever been kidnapped, Oscar?"

Nothing.

"Have you ever been picked up off the street, driven around for eight hours with a hood over your head, drugged, and dropped in the dirt two hundred and twenty miles away?" Vicker demanded, getting quieter and quieter as he went along.

Nothing.

"You *are* a fool. Shut up and get to work or whatever it is you do with my time and money. I pay you a goddamn fortune to buy familial peace. Now start earning it."

"Hey, Uncle Elias, you're really hurting my feelings," Oscar purred, sounding strangely smug. "I get that we're family, and we stick together. And I do know how things work around here."

"Meaning what?"

"Meaning I know that what you do is basically impossible. Whatever it is, you've basically split the atom of never-fail trading. Clue me in, Uncle Genius. What's your secret?"

"Secret, Oscar? What are you getting at?"

"You know, the family jewels, that kind of thing—Gonzaga, SEF. I have my own connections to SEF. Give me another chance. I might have screwed up that car thing. But I learned a lot too. I mean, you know all about second chances. What if Grandpa never gave you one?"

Vicker started to speak—but caught himself. Threatened? By Oscar? This call was over. He disconnected without saying anything and made another call, as Don and Greta continued to eavesdrop.

"Lorenzo, the problem in Berlin that we discussed?"

Gonzaga paused, thinking, then said: "Yes?"

"It's gotten worse."

19

Doyers Street, New York City

"I know it seems super weird to you, but there was a vogue." Elizabeth, tablet in her lap, feet in flip-flops propped up on the table, blew an enormous pink bubble with her gum, exhaling until it popped in her face. Feigning delicacy, she peeled it off her nose and chin, stuffed it back into her mouth, and loudly chewed it down into a malleable wad.

"Why do two of my best friends have such disgusting habits?" Greta asked. "I'm getting signs made: 'No gum, No dip, Nohow.'"

"Hey, as long as you're making SCIF rules to live by, let's add 'No knuckle-cracking.' That habit of Vicker's drives *me* nuts."

Notwithstanding the fact that Dr. Kerry's videos and notes had been placed in secure storage and embargoed for thirty years, Tommy had been able to work his magic. Elizabeth managed a frantic effort: ten CIA-trained psych PhD/MDs worked around the clock, for a week, sifting through two thousand hours of videos, hundreds of pages of Dr. Kerry's contemporaneous longhand notes, and his treatment plan for Vicker, culling the most significant elements for Liz and Greta to study more deeply.

Liz pulled up a video of a much, much younger Elias Vicker, sitting in a chair in front of a wall of books. "I've cobbled together a little movie. It starts just before Vicker met your *inamorato*—and confirms a lot of your suspicions about Vicker and Gonzaga."

The Vicker videos, as Liz had dubbed them, spanned more than seven years, almost every weekday during the two years of his treatment and recovery, and continuing for five more years following the founding of Industrial Strategies. A period that coincided with the start of his meteoric rise. Elizabeth pressed play, and a younger, thinner, Vicker began moving, speaking, shifting uncomfortably in his chair.

"Here, at the beginning, you see a weak, physically sick, dependent, depressed, and uncertain Elias Vicker. Easy to feel sorry for him. He is anguished because he has just lost most of his own and his family's money, nearly destroyed the family's business, is out of a job. Thinks of himself as a complete loser—a dying loser."

Intent, they both watched several minutes of clips, without sound. The unspoken message was clear, Vicker the aggrieved. Tearful, uncomprehending.

"I'll play some parts with sound in a minute, but I like watching without sound, just watching his face." Slouched in his chair, a young Vicker was wan, almost lifeless. His lips quivered. He bobbed his head, wrung his hands, and yanked on his knuckles with self-flagellating intensity. "I think the neurologists cured Vicker physically, but Dr. Kerry saved Vicker's life, by giving him the hope of emerging from his illness a better and more successful person."

"In other words, it's all Dr. Kerry's fault."

Liz turned up the sound.

"Why me? Why me? Why me? I have all the fucking bad luck. I am cursed. Who else eats one little fucking diseased piece of chicken and is paralyzed for an entire year. Fucking campylobacter. I'm a worthless piece of shit."

"My god, that voice? I can't bear it," Greta said. "The whining. How did Kerry handle it? I would have smacked the guy."

Dr. Kerry's voice, soothing, mellifluous, almost unctuous, chimed in from offscreen.

"Close your eyes, Elias. Tell me: when you say you feel worthless, how does it feel? What do you think about?"

As Vicker complied, tears began rolling down his cheeks. He wiped his nose on his sleeve.

"I'm looking up at the ceiling. I'm crying, I'm lying on a blanket, on the floor. I can't turn over. The floor is cold. I'm cold, no one is holding me. Mommy is on the other side of the room."

"Elias, is there anyone else in the room? Can you see anyone else?"

"My brother. He's running around. Throwing a ball. My mother picks him up and kisses him, smiles at him."

"Open your eyes now. What would you say to your mother now? About what you felt then."

"What are you talking about? Mommy is in Queens. I'm going home after this, and on the subway everyone will look at the skinny pale freak who can barely walk and think, 'He must have AIDS and he deserved it.'"

"Elias, focus on the memory. Speak to your mother. What would that infant lying on the rug say to her today?"

Vicker swallowed hard.

"Mommy why did you ignore me? Didn't you care that I was cold?"

"What does your mother say?"

"Mommy says, 'Elias, leave me alone. It was a long time ago. I had so much to do, I had your brother, I had you, and your father was always working. You think only about yourself. No one ever thought about what I wanted.'"

"And you reply?"

"But you never hold me, you never love me, no one loves me."

"And your mother says?"

"'I don't have time to love you, Elias, I have no love left.' And then I ask her, I finally get up the nerve to ask her, 'Do you love me now? Do you love me now?'"

Vicker paused. *"'After you lost all our money? After you got sick and I had to take care of you all over again? After that you ask me if I love you? Is anything ever enough for you?'"*

A soft chime struck in the background, signaling the end of the session.

"Elias, I'm proud of you. This is work, hard work, excavating these painful memories. Your neurologists tell me that you are responding extremely well to treatment."

"I'm already dead, Doctor. Ruined. I live? I'm still dead," Vicker replied, an involuntary shudder racked his emaciated body.

"You're going to make it through all of this. See you tomorrow."

Elizabeth stopped the video. "See what I mean? That's one messed-up little puppy."

Elizabeth carefully took the pink wad out of her mouth and set it on a saucer, for later use. "Looking at the early clips, I'm guessing growing up in that house exacerbated some latent sociopathic tendencies and Mom seems to have destroyed whatever native potential Vicker had for intimacy, empathy, compassion. My hypothesis is that from earliest childhood, his psyche was built around survival and, secondarily, recognition."

She began playing another video, time-stamped nearly two years later than the first. Vicker, no longer emaciated, hair growing back, stubble darkening his features, a hint of fierceness in his eyes.

"I'm in a weird spot, a very senior guy from Allard Frères—Lorenzo

Gonzaga—wants me to help him start a new investment fund." Vicker fidgeted, but wore an open expression. No longer hunched over, he looked more like a younger version of his present-day self.

"The same Allard that you're suing for misrepresentation, fraud, and racketeering because of how their brokers bankrupted you and your family?" Dr. Kerry asked.

Vicker nodded.

"I know—too good to be true, but the guy is some sort of heavy-duty problem-solver at the bank. He says he needs someone he can work with because he just lost his protégé, some guy named Tony Brandt who is doing jail time for cheating bank clients—including me. The top brass want me to drop my suit. It's bad for business if the scale of Brandt's fraud comes out at trial."

Dr. Kerry didn't respond.

"Elias, what does it mean 'needs someone he can work with?'"

"That's why I said that it seems too good to be true," Vicker snapped. *"But we'll be real partners. Me out front, him in the shadows. He's putting up all the capital. Plus, in return for me dropping my suit, Allard will handle all the costs of setup and administration—"*

"Pause for a sec," Greta said. "This is interesting. Vicker is admitting he's just a cutout, a front man. He's at his absolute nadir, he's still not even sure he wants to remain alive, but he somehow sees himself as an equal partner with Gonzaga, one of the most feared and respected executives at a major bank. Start it up again."

"I've got to make money. I've got to prove that I am not a complete loser."

"Sorry, pause it again," Greta said. "Prove to whom?"

"Dr. Kerry's notes are very instructive. As Vicker gets his physical health back, his dormant obsessions—money and proving himself to his 'Mommy'—resurface with a vengeance. Kerry doesn't seem to like Vicker, but can't tear his eyes away from this disaster of a human being."

"Did Kerry make a formal diagnosis?"

"He was considering reactive attachment and borderline personality disorders, tending toward psychopathy. We shrinks don't throw that term around lightly. True psychopathy is an infrequent diagnosis. Not because there aren't many of them but because psychopaths don't often go into therapy. They don't tend to think they need it, but the opportunity to try to manipulate someone like Kerry was probably seductive to Vicker."

"More, please?"

Elizabeth restarted the video.

"Gonzaga wants this new venture to break the mold. He thinks we can start a fund that will never lose money, because it will use his knowledge of foreign governments, bond markets, currency markets, how the big banks are positioned, and his friendships with central bankers. He wants to stay offshore, away from stuff that the SEC follows."

She paused the tape.

"Dr. Kerry's notes on this session are revealing. 'Insider trading? Why Vicker? Damaged goods? Easy mark?' Anyway, here's more."

"Elias, I understand how seductive this Mr. Gonzaga must be, but how do you know that you can trust him? After all, he works for the same bank that ruined you in the past."

"Doctor, do you know the old Wall Street saying? If you want a friend, get a dog? I'm not in a mood to trust Lorenzo, but he is opening my eyes to how business is really done on Wall Street and in the hedge fund world. More importantly, my family isn't about to trust me with any more of their burger money and he's putting up a lot of cash."

"That does seem attractive—this all sounds, well . . . amazing. But surprising to those of us who have known finance types over the years. Allow me to play devil's advocate: he is choosing you to confide in, to bankroll, because . . ." Dr. Kerry asked, sounding disbelief.

"Okay, okay. I left out something important about this guy Brandt. He was Gonzaga's go-to guy for these 'special' trades, which Gonzaga and Brandt funded with client money that would later be returned to the client accounts. They made a fortune, never got caught. Until Brandt decided he didn't need Gonzaga anymore. He could find his own can't-miss ideas. But his ideas were all losers and he chased the losses by stealing even more money from customer accounts. And now he's in jail."

"And why isn't Gonzaga in jail, if he was part of Brandt's game?" Dr. Kerry asked, worried.

"Because he's not an idiot. Since he wasn't the one who 'borrowed' from the bank's customers, the bosses saw no reason to call attention to it. And the Feds didn't mind. They don't like going after senior executives at the big banks. So the IRS got millions in back taxes, the SEC raked in big fines, and Brandt took the fall."

Vicker made a faux-sad face.

"Oh, c'mon, Dr. K. Feel good for me! This is how it's done in the big leagues. This is my shot."

Greta couldn't believe what she was hearing. "Did it bother Kerry that his patient is talking about launching a large-scale, likely criminal, enterprise?"

Elizabeth paused the video.

"Dr. Kerry wrestled with that." She posted a scan of a handwritten page on the screen.

"After a lot of tortured ruminations, he decided that since his patient wasn't talking about a specific crime, only potential future crimes, his obligation to respect patient confidentiality takes precedence. But there seems to be something weirder going on. I think he's jealous of Gonzaga. Look at this."

She cued up another clip and hit play.

"Elias, I am pleased for you. Extremely pleased. I have never seen you more positive, more optimistic. Please don't take this the wrong way—you know that I am your staunchest advocate—but why has Gonzaga singled you out, Elias? How much do you really know about him?"

"I know some," Vicker said, seeming less certain. *"I've now spent twenty, thirty hours with him. I've also asked around a bit. He's Italian royalty. Machiavelli wrote The Prince for his great, great, great, great granddaddy—Lorenzo de' Medici. Lorenzo's namesake."*

"Anything else?" Dr. Kerry asked.

Vicker sat back, sat a little straighter. *"He says I have ice in my veins. Admires how I stood up to the pressure of being bankrupted by bad eggs at the bank. How I've handled the arbitration with the bank so far."* Vicker paused. *"He knows about my medical history, and about you."*

Dr. Kerry seemed surprised. *"How so?"*

"It's strange, but we have really hit it off. We're kind of an odd couple, maybe even kindred spirits."

Elizabeth flashed another page of Kerry's notes on the screen and started reading.

"'Is V making transference to Gonzaga? Moving from me, to a new support system? How do I feel about that? Grown attached to this broken, narcissistic husk of a human being.'"

She blew another bubble and popped it.

"As a psychiatrist, I appreciate that Dr. Kerry is in touch with his own emotions, but it's hard to understand how he made this connection to Vicker. 'Broken' doesn't begin to describe Vicker's psyche."

"I can't wait to see what happens next."

Elizabeth resumed the video.

"Dr. Kerry," Vicker began, *"would you consider meeting Lorenzo? I need your opinion. Besides Vinnie, you're the only one who has ever taken my side, my whole life. It would mean a great deal to me, and if I end up working with Gonzaga, I want to give you a part of my new fund. If I succeed, I'd really like to repay you for giving me . . . a life."*

Elizabeth plopped the hardened pink wad back into her mouth. "This part ought to be really easy for an ethical therapist. Patients often attempt to cross the line between patient and friend, it's natural. They're vulnerable, they want to be special. It shouldn't have taken a nanosecond of thought on Dr. Kerry's part to shoot down that offer. There is no way you should ever get involved financially with a patient."

"What did he do?"

"Glad you asked. Watch."

"Elias, I'm willing to meet Mr. Gonzaga. In fact, I am extremely curious about him. So . . . yes. Regarding your offer to include me in your next project, that's a bit unusual, allow me to think about that for a week. Of course, no matter what, I am open to continuing to work with you for as long as you like."

"We know what Dr. Kerry decided," said Greta. "He took Vicker up on his offer and made tens of millions of dollars. Anything in the notes?"

"You would think that someone straying from ethical practice wouldn't keep a record, but Dr. Kerry did. Fascinating. 'V offered me a shot at making some money with them. A bit . . . unusual. Would solve a lot of my problems . . . divorce . . . tuition.'"

"Wow. Even after documenting Vicker's narcissism, speculating about his potential for psychopathy and hearing Vicker describe the kind of sketchy business Gonzaga proposed—even then Kerry was willing to violate his own ethical canon?"

Elizabeth frowned. "The man is a legend in psychiatry. He pioneered so many diagnoses, revolutionized the treatment of patients suffering from neurological diseases. As a shrink, as a doctor, I'm hugely disappointed, but am I surprised the idol had feet of clay? No."

Elizabeth inflated another bubble and popped it. "I want you to see one more thing, and then you're going to buy me a drink. Because I need one. Look at the time stamp on the video; it's dated just a few months before Dr. Kerry died in that hit-and-run. So, more or less five years after Vicker started therapy."

Dr. Kerry had changed his video format, adding a camera that showed him in a small box at the top right. He and Vicker appeared in the same frame, like two pals sitting in someone's living room, chatting. Dr. Kerry, legs crossed, bounced his foot slightly, taking notes. Vicker was pale, but seemed robust, animated. "This is some crazy shit," Elizabeth said. "Watch."

"Elias, I wanted to let you know that I am working on a book, completely anonymized of course, about my experiences treating patients from the realm of finance."

Elizabeth froze the frame. "I'm going to play some of this in real time and then slow it down so we can watch it at one fifteenth of a second. Look at Vicker's face."

In real time, Vicker seemed to register the barest shudder when Dr. Kerry described his book project. In slow-motion increments, an avalanche of emotions coursed through Vicker's features. Panic. Anger. Hatred. Contempt. Rage.

"You'll rarely see such a panel of microexpressions," Greta remarked. "The sort of guy you would not want to cross."

Elizabeth began toggling through more stills. "Look at that face. No shame, no fear, just outwardly directed aggression." She began playing the video again.

"Dr. Kerry," Vicker began, speaking slowly, in the controlled tone now familiar to them both. *"This feels like a breach of our trust."*

"Elias, I can assure you that I am going to extraordinary lengths to obscure the identities of my patients. Many of them have high profiles. I have assured them all that I am taking extreme security measures."

"Still, your book will likely be something of a sensation. How long did it take for people to figure out the names of Dr. Freud's patients? Given your connection to New York-Episcopal, some people might even be interested in discovering what I was being treated for—the diagnoses and treatments. I, for one, have told very few people—and certainly not my investors. Investors would freak out."

"I'm not sure I see your point. There is no shame in having been sick. You've recovered completely, and we cannot live our lives on the assumption that criminals will break into the hospital's vaults to steal information. Can we?"

Elizabeth froze one last frame, Vicker's face filled the screen.

"You're now looking at one of the most frightening faces I've ever seen in all my studies of our interrogations. Pure resolve. Vicker had just made up his mind about something."

20

432 Park Avenue, New York City

Lorenzo Gonzaga stared into the distance from Vicker's apartment: the entire ninety-ninth floor of 432 Park Avenue. At that height, he thought to himself, problems, like the microscopic pedestrians and cars rolling through winter slush fourteen hundred feet below, seem picayune. Even problems like keeping the insatiable Wennerström content, which required finding new ways to ensure that Industrial Strategies continued to earn tens of billions of dollars a year, year after year. Though the oil trade had turned out to be bigger and more lucrative than they had ever imagined possible, it was getting harder—much harder—to keep pulling those rabbits out of his hat.

Gazing at New York's bridges, lifelines of freedom and commerce, memories of postwar Florence captured his mind. From the time he was five years old, little Enzo had made a game of scrambling up an ancient iron ladder to the roof of the Pitti Palace, imagining that he had been on that same roof on August 3, 1944, the day of the Nazis' retreat from Florence when they ordered the city's entire population to huddle in their basements while they blew up five of the city's six bridges across the Arno. He would sit on the parapets for hours at a time, gazing out over the razed cityscape, imagining the deafening explosions that took out one stately Arno crossing after another. Only the Ponte Vecchio, a favorite of the Führer, had been spared. The Nazis pulverized half the city into chaotic, smoking piles of rubble, ash, and dust, many of which remained, the playground of his youth. In their year-long occupation of his native city, the Nazis killed over half his family, and mostly obliterated their fortune. But the Gonzagas were Medicis. Across half a millennium, his cruel, resourceful—and timeless—clan had won and lost many fortunes. In Enzo's generation, the task of rebuilding had fallen to him.

Life, that strange concatenation of events, had led him from a ruined—but now pristine—Florentine palazzo to a leather armchair in Rafael Viñoly's brutalist glass and steel monstrosity. A barbarous blight on the skyline, inspired by a trash can. And, like all the oligarchitecture that had reconfigured the midtown Manhattan skyline in the first decades of the twenty-first century, it was not so much an apartment building as a stack of safe deposit boxes with an underground garage where corrupt foreigners could hide millions of dollars of flight capital in plain sight.

Vicker, in his man cave, sat directly across from Gonzaga, his feet in velvet slippers, propped up on an ottoman, the wall behind him covered with framed Mets jerseys and covers from *New York* magazine celebrating his status as New York's politically incorrect bad-boy billionaire. No books in sight. A creature of my own invention, Gonzaga thought: callous, sapient, but barely human. Handsome and well-tended in the way of wealthy New Yorkers, but, if you peeled back the veneer and attempted to discuss anything that did not involve making or spending money, Vicker had little to add to a conversation. It had been several decades since he had plucked the man from his ruined life. Vicker, Gonzaga thought, would serve as an empty vessel and solve a knotty problem: how to continue rebuilding a fortune on a scale needed to support the next five hundred years of Medici supremacy. He couldn't do it alone. He needed someone smart and loyal to help. His first attempt, his first creation—a devious, gregarious, solipsistic Romanian refugee—had double-crossed him. Gonzaga could still picture the slight, deathly pale mongrel in his only suit and worn shoes, who, like so many refugees from the ruins of Europe, radiated a desperate, excruciating hunger to succeed. After he'd schooled that *golan* in the conduct of discreet international business, the little *vulg* shut him out. For no good reason. Or for all the standard reasons: envy, pride, anger, arrogance, greed.

For his next protege, Gonzaga chose his sharpest disciple, a poor but well-bred Venezuelan dandy named Antonio Brandt, a Sorbonne graduate, fluent in Spanish, Portuguese, Italian, French, Russian, and German. Long before Gonzaga brought the young man into his inner circle, he carefully tested and groomed him. The younger man responded with such obeisance that his fawning devotion became a running joke in the bank. But, thanks to Gonzaga, Tony also became the youngest partner in the long history of Allard Frères.

Gonzaga put him in charge of a gold mine: Latin America. Long before the days of know-your-client rules and compliance departments populated by ranks of pencil pushers hired away from the Federal Reserve, international banks had a license to steal. On a sea of government

corruption that spanned an entire continent, the bankers were the cap-
tains. Buying guns? Running drugs? Stealing oil concessions? Trafficking
girls? *Someone* had to form the layers of shell companies, manage the accountants and lawyers, move the money around, invest it, buy apartments
in Paris and New York, issue credit cards to the mistresses, wives, and
kids—and to sort them out when they got wild, or find them someplace
discreet to sober up. Brandt had been just about perfect. Until, that is, he
started dipping into customer accounts to keep up with his jet-set clients,
pela bolas. Years of methodical work, destroyed—and a mess to clean up.
The Feds sent Brandt off to jail for four years, but Rudy Giuliani, then the
U.S. Attorney, did not poke his finely tuned nose any further up the food
chain. Giuliani, wildly ambitious even then, knew better than to take on
the financial elite. He might—for show—take down a few outliers, but, in
the end, he would need support and money to fuel his political ambitions,
and he knew where the money was.

After the Brandt debacle, Gonzaga decided it was time for a different approach. Instead of investing directly, Gonzaga would recruit what his agency
friends referred to as a cutout. It would be a long play: not years, but decades.
He knew the exact profile he was looking for, a type common on Wall Street:
young and driven, insecure, and unformed, someone who feared being on
the wrong side of a deal like it was the very definition of eternal damnation,
but also enough of a bullshit artist to pull off a genius investor act.

He'd first met Elias Vicker under inauspicious circumstances. After er-
rant brokers had emptied what little remained of the Vicker family trading
account, which Vicker had already churned down to almost nothing, Gonzaga had been given the unpleasant task of placating the poor fool. Vicker,
barely thirty, had just survived a nearly fatal bout of Guillain-Barré syndrome. He'd been completely paralyzed for nearly a year, and had then un-
dergone months of excruciating rehab therapy, re-learning how to breathe,
to move, to walk. Gonzaga expected to spend a few minutes offering apologies to a sad young man, charming him deeply and obsequiously enough
to get him to withdraw his legal claims, and then never thinking about him
again. But Vicker was neither broken nor abashed. He showed up, using a
cane, in a slightly too-tight-fitting suit and a bright yellow tie, like he'd just
waltzed into Barneys and told the salesman he wanted to look like Gordon
Gekko. He proceeded to try to sell Gonzaga on a close to nonsensical idea

of taking an "industrial" approach to investing. As Gonzaga nodded along politely, he realized he'd found his man.

From the start of Industrial Strategies, Stichting Eskandarfond had been the perfect partner, providing both ideas and money. As a child, Gonzaga spent some of the happiest summers of his life on the Wennerström family island in the Stockholm archipelago, the first place he had fallen in love. Fiercely competitive, the Wennerströms could trace their lineage even farther back than the Gonzagas. Warriors, with tentacles everywhere, they rode a voracious leviathan of cash, in need of constant care and feeding. Stable capital. Great ideas. But, even as their wealth multiplied, the Wennerströms—far from being satiated—kept reaching for more, developing some risky appetites, and volatile friends, as each generation sought to make its mark. Gonzaga had no scruples about working with them or any of the Mafia tribes—the 'Ndrangheta, the Turatello Crew, the Sacra Colona Unita. All part of the ecosystem, they had their uses, but had to be managed carefully.

Gonzaga drew on his Behike. His visits to Vicker's vast, tasteless, fish tank had become increasingly rare. He had come to detest the man Vicker had grown into. And to detest the fact that, whenever a new approach to their business became necessary, Gonzaga had to come before Vicker as a supplicant, needing to placate, wheedle, and manipulate—when a straightforward conversation, if not a brusque order, should have sufficed. Wealth affected people in different ways, but, in his experience, nature won out. Wealth exaggerated inherent tendencies bred in the bone. In Vicker's case, nearly immeasurable wealth had made him indifferent to the idea that life might—should—be animated by an idea beyond amassing lucre.

Gonzaga began carefully. "It's getting more and more challenging to find the kind of large, riskless trades we've come to rely on."

"I'm not seeing it, Lorenzo. That oil play was *amazing*—one of your best ever—we made tens of billions."

"Yes, it worked out, because you and I were flexible—congrats to us for playing the game so brilliantly. But we need to diversify."

Vicker looked past Gonzaga into the distance. For years SEF had been a passive investor—albeit a very large one—happy making money on information Gonzaga generated, or that they generated and fed to Gonzaga. But, over time, they had begun proposing more and more of their own transactions, pushing Vicker to generate even higher returns—and insisting on the right to coinvest, sometimes dwarfing investments made by IS itself. In the year since Vicker's kidnapping, they had become assertive in new ways; the favors they asked felt more like orders: just move the money for us—out of the Caymans into a bank in the Cook Islands or Singapore, say, with no consideration of the risk that some regulator, somewhere, might start asking questions.

"So, diversify how? What do you have in mind?"

Gonzaga offered a half smile, ghoulish.

"SEF is beginning to demand services that could put Industrial Strategies in jeopardy—they want us to take too much risk. That transaction of Oscar's—financing a massive stolen car operation that was, ultimately, on behalf of Hezbollah—was imprudent. We need to rebalance the relationship."

"Great idea," snapped Vicker. "We'll announce a pro rata redemption of all investors—across the board. Just to send a message."

After so many years, how could the man be so naive? Gonzaga wasn't surprised that Vicker had been happy to leave the SEF relationship completely in his hands, but he marveled that Vicker had made no effort to understand the insatiable hunger that motivated Wennerström and SEF. He chalked it up to Vicker's simplistic, unidimensional worldview: that everything was always—and only—about money. "Elias, that would be much too aggressive. You've seen how they behave. We might think of them as investors, but they view us as partners. A redemption like you suggest would infuriate them. More important, we still need the ideas they generate. Even if we were to consider severing this relationship, we'd first have to line up another partner who could supply a reliable flow of trading opportunities. Not an easy thing to find." Gonzaga took another pull on his cigar, staring affectionately at the long ash forming on its end.

Vicker said nothing, but felt the stirrings of contempt. Why now? Why the mystery? What if Gonzaga wasn't the wizard of finance who'd dazzled Vicker all those years ago, but just the well-dressed lackey of these mysterious Swedes—a hanger-on, a middleman, who, like all middlemen, exaggerated his worth and demanded more than his share? Vicker had always thought he'd be nothing without Gonzaga. In a flash, he began to ask himself, what if it were the other way around?

Gonzaga continued, "That leads me to my next point. *Knowing* that things will happen is lovely and SEF, with its many investments in such a broad range of industries and markets, knows a lot. We've made a fortune trading that way. But, at our size, I'm beginning to worry that there simply aren't enough 'conventional' trades out there that will generate the returns we need to keep growing. We need to start thinking about *making* things happen—not just trying to spot the black swan before anyone else but giving birth to black swans of our own."

Fat-tail events were both fascinating and frightening—unpredictable, rare, often catastrophic. Nassim Taleb popularized the notion in his book *The Black Swan,* named after the fact that, until Willem de Vlamingh discovered the existence of black swans in Australia in 1697, people in the West thought them to be an impossibility. Metaphorically, black swans were the statistical phenomenon known as large leptokurtosis—the likelihood that extreme events would occur, or not. Some leptokurtic events, like the emergence of ISIS from the chaos of Iraq and Syria, had widespread geopolitical significance. Others, like the September 1982 murders caused by cyanide-laced capsules of Extra-Strength Tylenol, resulted in specific and contained impacts: Johnson & Johnson stock dropped almost 20 percent in a single day—and then rebounded 30 percent higher within a few weeks. The 1918 flu pandemic; COVID-19; Adolf Hitler's rise to power; Chernobyl; the release of methyl isocyanate gas at Union Carbide's pesticide factory in Bhopal, India; World War I; the sinking of the *Titanic*: black swans all. Impossible to predict. But highly lucrative for anyone who did.

"I like where this is going. What do you propose?"

"We have a friend who knows how to make things happen."

"We?"

"Yes, he helped us out with Dr. Kerry."

Vicker jerked his head to look around, thinking about whether his aerie was safe from electronic intrusion, eavesdropping.

"Is this the friend you want Oscar to meet?"

Gonzaga nodded.

The phone next to Vicker's chair rang. Seeing the caller's name, Vicker pursed his lips in apprehension and shook his head. Not for the first time, Vicker pondered the fact that so many fashionable upper-crust New York women went by nicknames better suited for stuffed animals—Buffy, Pepper, Skipper, Poppy, Zippy—that belied their brutal, transactional cores. Piper's crowd of New York women were the latest in a long line of genetically modified organisms, their DNA buffed and manipulated over hundreds of years, bred to be smart and beautiful and schooled in the martial arts of marrying and unmarrying money—while keeping the money. His glamorous—tall, blond, svelte, and charming when she needed to be—wife of six years had seemed a sensible acquisition at the time. Brearley, debutante of the year, Princeton. When they first met, Piper had been the perfect cutthroat Christie's art hustler. Deploying low-cut blouses and her own social standing, she inveigled men with more money than taste to buy garish, hideously ugly, soulless paintings with the promise that—having won a false competition to pay millions for nothing—they would acquire a social status that, as she put it, money alone couldn't buy.

Had he thought about it, Vicker would have considered Piper to be out of his league. But, in short order, she slid into the role she'd been born to play: Jackie O to Vicker's not-so-gnarly, not-so-contorted Aristotle Onassis. She—not he—made it clear from the start that there would be a prenup and a budget far in excess of what it would take to reel in, say, a B-list Slovenian model. She would keep her own place and there would *probably* be no babies, having already curated two with the scion of another Mayflower dynasty—who she turfed after he turned gay on her. And she had offered no guarantees as to how long Vicker would suit her.

"Piper!" Vicker tried to sound upbeat.

Gonzaga motioned to leave, but Vicker shook his head and gestured for him to stay.

"This won't take long, it never does."

Vicker flipped on the speaker phone.

"Piper, to what do I owe this pleasure?"

"That prick Hamilton. I'm going to kick his bony ass down a flight of stairs the next time I see him at the Century." Vicker had always loved the fact that you never knew what was going to come out of that gutter mouth.

"Thanks for that, Piper. I'm glad you were there but sorry you had to witness it. Anyway, all in the past."

"For you maybe, but that fucker is part of my crowd, and I *will* get even."

Rare, he thought, for Piper to show any interest beyond the transactional, much less to come to his defense. He wondered if she was up to something.

"I'm just in the middle of a meeting, dear. Can I ring you back?"

"Oh, Ellie, just give me a sec. I'm calling about the Met Ball. I'm afraid I just can't go this year. I've heard that Anna is planning to sit us next to that ghastly Cardinal what's-his-name . . . Fogerty, Duggan, O'Dwyer . . . whatever."

"Well, I did pay extra for that. I thought you'd be thrilled. Besides, I need you there, love."

"Ellie, please don't take this the wrong way but no can do. I hate that fat, phony asshole. The creep dragged Bippy into a closet and tried to stick his tongue down her throat at Maidstone last summer. If he was a poof like all the rest of them, maybe. But a girl has limits."

Vicker shook his head. Limits. Piper wouldn't know a limit if it came inside a Birkin bag.

"Piper . . . honey . . . I really need you there, I even took an extra table for your pals. Temple of Dendur, it will be fun . . . as *usual*."

In their own cryptic language, "usual" was a euphemism for Piper's "usual" appearance fee. Although it would be much too crass to refer to their relationship as purely pay to play, Piper did have her rules, and she observed them strictly. Allowance: $4,000,000 a year. Birthdays: $500,000 in cash or in kind, preferably Graff. Stepkids' birthdays: $1,000,000 each, in trust. Anniversaries: strictly cash, a sliding scale starting at $800,000 for year one, $1,000,000 for year two and rising from there. Special events: $150,000 per, not including a dress, hair, and makeup. But that was only if it did not run too late, was not going to be *too* dreadfully boring, and he bought an extra table for her posse. And when he wanted to watch her get gang-banged by some of the Argentinian polo players who showed up in the Hamptons every summer, he paid for that too. If Piper decided that one of her rules was about to be broken, negotiations began, and she was relentless and effective.

"Ellie, darling," she said, to all outward appearances affectionately. "I'm sorry. My mind's made up. But you go. I'm sure you'll have a great time."

Vicker grimaced. He never got the better of Piper, because she really just did not care.

A heavy silence hung between them.

"Oh, honey, I think I've hurt your feelings. I didn't think you'd mind. Now I feel terrible. Just awful. Come to think of it, there are maybe, um, *five* ways you could convince me to go with you." Of course, Vicker thought. Five being her shameless but delicate genteelism for five times her usual appearance fee: a cool $750,000. At times like this, he was glad he was only married to Piper, not sitting across a conference table from her, negotiating a deal.

"I can take care of my own hair and nails. You do the gown, of course."

Gonzaga put his finger to his lips and gestured toward Vicker to cut the call short.

"Piper, honey, let me get back to you on that."

"Okay, hon. *Ciao.*" Vicker rang off.

Vicker cracked a knuckle.

"Sometimes, I'd like to make *her* happen."

"Elias, you cannot bump people off just because they irritate you. Piper is no threat. You can make her go away any time just by writing a check."

Vicker often thought about the idea of buying Piper out of their marriage, but, somehow, he could not bear to do it. She was a cunning and manipulative bitch, but what would he be without her? A trophy wife is something you simply, easily acquire. With Piper it was more like she—her world, her lineage—had acquired *him*. His money was fungible. What she offered was not for sale. Only for rent, on exorbitant terms. He hated to admit it, but in the cold-hearted calculus of their relationship, she held the upper hand. Piper could always—or at least for the next decade or so—find another obscenely rich man looking for a status upgrade. Another Piper would be much harder to come by. She was the scarce commodity.

"Why did you tell me to hang up on her?"

"Two things. First, we need to finish our conversation. Second, why not ask Greta Webb to join you? That will certainly get Piper's attention."

"You want me to pimp for you?" Vicker snickered.

"Just an idea," Gonzaga replied, with a noncommittal but lecherous grin.

"Does your friend who makes things happen have a name?"

Gonzaga acted as if he had not heard the question—an aspect of the hauteur he projected so skillfully, as if any question he preferred not to answer was posed in a frequency he couldn't hear. Staring at his cigar ash, Gonzaga worried that he was about to make a huge mistake. There was a danger in mixing volatile elements. But he didn't think there was a choice. They needed to balance Stichting Eskandarfond, add a counterweight to its brilliant but mercurial leader, Wennerström.

"Lorenzo?"

"Indeed. His name is Fyodor. For now, he doesn't have a surname. When we go to Geneva next week, I'd like to take you on a little side trip to meet him. He doesn't live too far from there."

Vicker nodded. Though he tried to hide his excitement, his face flushed red. "One more thing." Gonzaga steepled his fingers. "Please leave your security professionals at home. There is no place safer than Switzerland, and, to someone like Fyodor, showing up with a squadron of armed protectors only signals fear."

21

Berlin, Germany

Oscar shielded his eyes with a hand to filter out the midafternoon sun streaming into the bedroom on the top floor of his penthouse at Eisenzahnstrasse 1. The light made his head ache as he peeked out through two fingers, spread wide enough to check the time on a yellow-gold Cartier alarm clock. Just two thirty, he thought, before collapsing back into a pillow and pulling another over his face. What day was it? Monday, he decided. Not that it mattered much whether it was one day or another. Particularly in Berlin, a continuous, wanton party. Percy had showed up Thursday afternoon. They had ended up at Berghain sometime after midnight on Friday and, fueled by drugs, techno, and sex, they had stayed there for nearly forty-eight hours, until the early-morning hours on Monday. That was one of the many great things about being Oscar Vicker: he did what he wanted, whenever he wanted—to whomever he wanted.

Gradually, some of the events of previous three days and four nights came back into focus. Percy Kirkham, a ne'er-do-well, impoverished viscount, was the only person who could keep up with him in sport or in life: dissolute and thrill-seeking. He recalled the long, late dinner on Thursday at Tim Raue. Then, memorable massages performed by that Czech girl, followed by some steam. Then drinks at Soho House, before finding their way to the KitKatKlub, and, finally, to Berghain twenty-four hours later. Oscar couldn't even begin to calculate how many martinis he'd sucked down over dinner or how much 2C-B he'd ingested—he had to hand it to Percy and his chemist friend from Oxford; it did the same job as MDMA with no hangover. Strange, really, he thought, 2C-B was the only thing that made him feel warm and loving. Even if he had little patience, or use, for love or empathy when he was sober, he did love the way the designer compound caused the music to envelop him, making him feel one with the crowd of gyrating dancers. And then Percy kept dripping a tincture of something onto his tongue—a secret potion distilled from a Mexican mushroom. Finally, Mexicans were useful for *something*. What a trip.

Sliding his hand under the bedsheet, he felt heat. And then skin. And who would you be? he thought. I must have really been wasted if I didn't pack you off in a taxi after fucking you. Lifting the pillow, he saw an avalanche of blond hair, and, drawing back the sheet, a magnificent ass. Whoever she was, she grabbed the sheet, covering herself, just barely, and turned around, smiling.

"About time." She gave him a more than merely friendly peck on the lips. "Been up for an hour, tried not to wake you."

Posh accent. He knew that face, but struggled to attach a name—until it hit him: Lily Plimpton, described in *Private Eye* alternately as this year's Paris Hilton or Kate Middleton, but with a profitable OnlyFans account. He'd seen her from a distance in London, and, this month, looking out from the cover of *Vogue*. But how had she ended up *here*, in his bed? In *Berlin*? Nice score, Oscar thought, even if he couldn't remember if he *had* scored. She reached under the sheet, gently stroking his balls. Oscar felt himself getting hard under her practiced hand. *Maybe, I'll make an exception and give this one a replay.*

"Lily, I've got to be somewhere. How about a shower, and lunch later?"

"Yes, to lunch, but I need *this* first, Oscar." Not to be denied, she climbed on top of him, taking advantage of his erection. Feels great, Lily, and thanks for doing all the work.

"Nicely done. Now, I've got to get a move on."

Oscar padded into his bathroom, passing through a dressing room the size of a train car, lined with immaculate rows of rods and shelves. Everything custom, and only the best: more shirts than Gatsby, and shoes, boots, suits, jackets, jeans, and gear for every sport and occasion.

He showered and toweled off before squaring up to take a good look at the magnificent creature before his eyes. Mirror, mirror . . . what have we here? Oscar inspected himself carefully. Hair fashionably long, crawling down the nape of his neck, just short of a ponytail. Eyes only slightly yellow: not too bad, he thought, considering what he must have imbibed and swallowed. He turned sideways, flexed his pecs, and slowly ran a hand along the dimpled corrugation of the six-pack one of his friends had described as the only thing he'd ever worked hard for. Peering at his face he had a decision to make: just the right amount of stubble? Or too much? Lily walked in, hugging him from behind, rubbing her breasts across his back, and her crotch against his ass.

"Pretty sexy for a rich boy, O.V." She smiled, but Oscar thought he could see behind it: the sign. This one might get clingy. Maybe lunch wasn't such a good idea. Next thing, she'd leave a toothbrush and underwear. And *that* wasn't happening. So much pussy, too little time.

"Thanks, Lily. Help me dress. But you . . . take your time."

Oscar slipped into his work uniform. A suit in featherweight dark gray wool from Henry Poole, Winston Churchill's tailor, not too form fitting: strong. A white shirt, spread collar, top two buttons undone, a maroon silk pocket square, no tie, shoes by Lobb.

Downstairs, in his breakfast room, everything was as he liked it. His housekeeper had prepared poached eggs on toast, *fraises des bois*, a soy cappuccino, and the day's papers arranged just so. Best of all: no conversation. *Thank you, Fraulein Schmidt, for knowing your place.*

For all the trappings, it was the first time in years that Oscar felt as if he was actually getting somewhere. No thanks to his uncle. That asshole. There had been plenty of money—the penthouse alone had cost twelve million euros—but no respect. Then, seemingly serendipitously, Percy had connected him with Sven Rask. Even after the issues with the Albanian cargoes, Rask had been solicitous, flattering. There was so much more they could do together. Rask hadn't said it in so many words, but, well, he intimated that maybe SEF was interested in seeing a transition in management—that it might be time for the old man to step aside. Rask had promised to help him get out from under Elias Vicker's thumb. At least *someone* appreciated him; he was so much better than that.

Stepping outside onto Eisenzahnstrasse, Oscar watched his driver, Mirko, square his cap and move to open the rear door of his latest indulgence: a Rolls-Royce Phantom. Six hundred thousand dollars of pure magnificence. Heavy, quiet, fast. Oscar waved him away. *I need some air.*

"Fetch me from the office at six. I feel like walking." It was twenty minutes to the Industrial Strategies office in the Upper West Tower on Kantstrasse. Turning left, he ambled up to Kurfürstendamm. *What a day . . . I could own this town.* Enveloped in his own world, daydreaming: How would it feel to be a billionaire in his own right? A great-looking thirtysomething *billionaire.* With all the money in the world, and the keys to a kingdom that would allow him to coin even more. There was no reason for him to register the Mercedes parked a few doors down from his house, or the two athletic, fashionably dressed young guys who seemed to shadow him, trailing along casually as he made his way.

Oscar crossed Konstanzer Strasse and stopped for a minute to look in the windows at Louis Vuitton before continuing along Kurfürstendamm. No hurry. Too many pleasant thoughts. Like banging Lily Plimpton in the bathroom of Eins44 at lunch—and turning the tables on that arrogant prick, Uncle Elias. Both delicious fantasies. Two blocks farther east, Oscar stopped at the corner of Knesebeck Strasse, waiting for the light to change—watchful of a gunmetal gray Mercedes S-class barreling toward the intersection. *Too fucking fast, asshole.*

Valery and Kirill, the men who had been tailing him, stepped up behind him. In two quick motions, too deft to be captured even by the cameras trained on them, Valery reached under Oscar's jacket and grabbed the waistband of his trousers as Kirill pivoted ever so slightly, one foot in front of Oscar's. Kirill gave Oscar a solid shove, planting him flat, facedown in the crosswalk. Stunned, but conscious, time seemed to slow down as Oscar watched the speeding Mercedes, doing at least fifty, bear down on him, the intricate pattern of an oncoming zigzag tire tread filling his field of vision. Two seconds later, the world went black as first the front tires, then, a beat later, the rear ones, rolled over his face and his legs. Concerned, or just professional, the driver backed up—fast—and then sped forward again. Kneading, pummeling, and flipping Oscar's rag doll body. Four seconds, twelve tire hits. Gut-wrenching sounds: the thump of impact, pops and cracks as Oscar's body bore the weight of 4,700 pounds of rubber and metal. His skull not broken, but steamrolled flat, a pudding of brain, bone, and carefully gelled hair. Three seconds later, the car was out of sight, turning left onto Mommsen Strasse. Long gone.

The two men slowly backed away from the curb, seemingly stunned, as other pedestrians began to crowd forward, taking photos, calling 999. Within a minute, the Twitter-verse was awash in images of a mangled corpse—arms and legs at impossible angles—as if it had been put through a massive pasta machine, lying in a pool of blood.

"A pity," Valery whispered to Kirill, as they faded into the pedestrian traffic. "Yes. It was a beautiful suit."

22

432 Park Avenue, New York City

At dawn, Vicker—in a tightly belted trench coat, fedora pulled low—took the service elevator down to the underground garage at 432 Park and folded his lanky frame into Gonzaga's Mercedes. The dim dawn light and heavily tinted glass obscured them both. Don's crew, on twenty-four-hour duty outside the building, had never considered the prospect that their liege might want to slip away. After all, he was the one paying for the cocoon.

Lowering the glass partition, Gonzaga uttered a single command to his driver. "The heliport," he said, before raising it again.

"True confession, Lorenzo." Vicker struggled to mask his excitement. Far from his signature bored, stony expression, he seemed almost gleeful. "I might just piss myself. Maiden voyage today on the new plane."

"Another? Didn't you buy one last year?"

"Yes, the Airbus A340-300. I gave Bekzod a ride last year, and he loved it so much he demanded I sell it to him—one of those macho 'what's your price' Russian things where they insist on ridiculously overpaying and then act like you owe them something. I didn't care. I was about to take delivery on this baby. My latest . . . um, achievement, a Boeing 747-8. Right now, I'm the only private guy in the country who has one. Other than the president."

Predictable, thought Gonzaga. First hundred million, a Bugatti Chiron. First five hundred million, a "starter" Gulfstream. First billion, a Gulfstream G550. Second billion, an Airbus. Five billion and up? That's when the real arms race started. Airplanes and yachts were how the world's wealthy kept score. And right now, Vicker was winning. Bekzod Kodirov, one of Russia's richest men flying someone else's cast-off jumbo jet. At least Kodirov was trying harder than those Google dweebs, Page, Brin, and Schmidt. Cheapskates, with their "pre-owned" G5s and rehabbed 767s they bought for themselves and then leased back to Google. The only real competition came from Al Waleed Bin Talal, the Saudi prince who traveled the world in a double-decker Airbus A380 with a prayer room that rotated toward Mecca and an on-board garage big enough for two Rolls-Royces and stables for his horses and camels.

The chopper dropped them at a private terminal, nestled in the freight hub at Newark airport, the enormous unmarked airship, 250 feet long, loomed before them. Vicker practically sprinted from his helicopter to the foot of a truck-mounted escalator. He'd bought the flying palace off-the-shelf from Boeing, a snip at $380 million, then poured in another $90 million for six months of interior work—the "head of state" upgrade. Gonzaga, a man who had arguably been on as many private jets as anyone alive, had to admit he was impressed, but not pleasantly so. As he floated up toward the plane, he shuddered at the sheer scale of the massive object before him, so large he had to lean over to take in the whole, and what he could only imagine were the infinite and terrifying wellsprings of insecurity and ego compensation it personified.

Gonzaga paused at the top of the jetway to take a very short call: two words, while Vicker rushed into the plane. When Gonzaga caught up to him, Vicker was staring in wonder at his new airliner's vast cabin. When Vicker was making plans for the interior, he'd had what he described to anyone who asked as a "vision." *I told my decorator, when people fly on my plane, I want them to feel like they are in my living room.* The decorator ran with the idea and had outfitted the interior to look like the library of an English country house, with faded leather couches, antique overlapping Anatolian carpets, and a taxidermied polar bear in one corner, the suggestion being that Vicker was the lord of a celestial manor, the man who owned the heavens.

He turned to Gonzaga. "The poof says it's ironic. I love it. Piper calls this Vicker Abbey." Vicker laughed at a thought he wasn't sharing. "She's got all sorts of ideas about who she wants draped over these couches."

At the front of the cabin were a pair of swivel leather club chairs—Vicker's spot. He sat and gestured for Gonzaga to take the seat next to him. As they settled in, Gonzaga looked around, making certain that no one could overhear.

"I just got word. Oscar's dead."

Vicker looked at him, expressionless, and then motioned to a steward. "Champagne, please."

Seven hours later, Vicker's flying ocean liner set down gently at Cointrin Airport, two miles from the center of Geneva, and taxied inside the securely fenced perimeter of a vast warehouse complex at the airport's northern edge. Rather than deplaning and joining queues of weary travelers to present their passports to Swiss border guards, Vicker and Gonzaga took leisurely showers while a team of chefs from Il Lago arrived to prepare their dinner and a team of housekeepers freshened two onboard staterooms. No Swiss hotel, perhaps no hotel anywhere, could match the comfort and privacy the jet offered, but, more to the point, these warehouses and their immediate environs were not *exactly* in Switzerland.

Founded in 1888, the Ports Francs et Entrepôts de Genève SA, better known as the Geneva Freeport, functioned like a sovereign state within a state: no customs duties, no taxes, and, until the Swiss government hastily enacted measures—perhaps intentionally feeble—to increase transparency, negligible law enforcement. Originally created to facilitate trading in commodities and, then, to accommodate manufacturing plants that straddled national borders, freeports had evolved over the years to become storage vaults for the international elite. Hundreds of billions of dollars of the world's wealth—in cash, proprietary digital data, gold, guns, wine, cars, antiquities, and art—sat in hardened rooms tucked away in corners of the world's busiest international airports. Repositories of millions of objects, whether Etruscan bronzes, Michelangelo drawings, van Gogh landscapes, rare Ferraris, pallets of hundred-dollar bills, and who knew what else.

Any nation that flight capital escapes from or flees to has a freeport. The United States alone has several hundred. Among them all, Geneva's is legendary for being the least regulated and the most opaque: a one-stop safe room qua shopping mall for money launderers, terrorists, kleptocrats, tax dodgers, oligarchs, drug dealers, and run-of-the-mill billionaires looking to stash a nest egg, just in case of a change in regime, divorce, or death taxes.

But what really set Geneva apart was art. If the Geneva Freeport were a museum, it would rival the Louvre. It offered an entire ecosystem—from fire-fighting systems that released inert gas to displace oxygen to biometric security, state-of-the-art temperature and humidity control, conservators, restorers, appraisers, and frame makers. But its biggest draw was the presence of the world's premier art dealers, who discreetly maintained their own vaults as showrooms. When an anonymous bidder snared a masterpiece at

Christie's and the painting or sculpture seemed to vanish into thin air, more likely than not a circumspect art mover had delivered it on a private plane to a vault at Cointrin. Art moved from one dealer to another, from dealers to investors, and back, paid for in cash or in kind—a few gold bars bearing the mark of the Federal Reserve of New York in exchange for a John Singer Sargent sketch. A nondescript wooden crate labeled "Family Photos" might really contain van Gogh's *Poppy Flowers*, Vermeer's *The Concert*, or Rembrandt's *Storm on the Sea of Galilee*.

"I do cherish our little sojourns here." Gonzaga sipped a '62 Madeira as the waiters cleared.

"It's as good a way as any to settle up," Vicker said, draining his glass in one gulp, as if he were worried someone might swipe it if he left any.

A trip to Geneva was an annual event, part of an ongoing ritual established by Gonzaga at the inception of their relationship. In addition to his silent partnership in Industrial Strategies, Gonzaga got his pick of the collection Vicker had assembled under his tutelage.

"Yes, Elias, I know you see it all as currency—bullion, art, a bag of emeralds, a van Dyck etching."

"You don't give me enough credit, Lorenzo," Vicker replied, with a sly grimace. "Let me propose a trade. You can judge for yourself if I know what I'm doing."

Gonzaga nodded, in a manner so courtly that it was difficult to determine if he was expressing contempt or respect.

"Two Warhols—a *Triple Elvis* and a *Last Supper* study—for a Rothko? Or maybe a Duchamp urinal for that Lucian Freud drawing—the one of that disgusting fat guy with a huge cock? Oh no, I have it: four Banksys for a . . . what? A Damien Hirst?"

In one go, Vicker managed to name five artists that Gonzaga detested. Was he tweaking him on purpose? Gonzaga wondered. Probably. More and more, he'd noticed, Vicker was taking subtle little digs at him.

"Shall we visit Charlier? It is rather late, but he said he would keep the shop open for us."

23

Port Authority Bus Terminal, New York City

Greta was at her computer, running the Virtualitics Immersive Platform, sorting and resorting Vicker's trading data, looking for patterns, oblivious to the housefly picking its way across the uneaten turkey sandwich on her desk and to the former boyfriend—a now distant, but polite, work colleague—who was sitting across from her. She looked up with a start. She'd barely seen Don in the two weeks since he'd stiff-armed her at the meeting in Tommy's SCIF, when Elizabeth guided them through the lower circles of Elias Vicker's rabid psyche. She was just starting to get used to not having him around.

"Some people knock," she said, looking back at her screen. When she made eye contact, Don met her gaze with a tight frown.

"What's wrong?" she said. "What happened?"

Don leaned back and pushed the door shut.

"Vicker just called me. Oscar had an accident. Face-planted into a busy intersection in Berlin. Splat. He wants me to handle it."

"Did you tell him your job is to put the bodies in bags, not pick them up?"

Even as Greta tried to crack a joke, her stomach dropped. Russians. That was how they did it: A nondescript couple ambles down a busy sidewalk. Natasha subtly trips the target; Boris rolls the poor sap into the path of a stolen delivery van. Semion, behind the wheel, rolls hard and fast, zips back into the rushing traffic, and heads straight for Heathrow or Orly, leaving behind a grim statistic and barely more than a wisp of suspicion.

She had no facts, but couldn't escape the feeling that Oscar's murder somehow contained a message intended for her. That it wasn't just Russians, but one very specific Russian, reaching out to her, bouncing bodies off pavement and signals off satellites, reminding her that when you acquired Fyodor Volk's services, his dark shadow inevitably tagged along. But, if Volk was behind it, what was he trying to tell her? He had more direct ways of making contact—either through Mara or even directly. Some men send chocolates, but not Fyodor Volk.

"Let me guess, no surveillance camera on that corner?"

"Actually, tons of them," Don said. "And none of them caught anything suspicious. What are the chances?"

"Not an easy thing to pull off," Greta said. "Has to be FSB."

"Goes back to the glory days. They have Berlin mapped down to the millimeter. Point of pride for them, since before the cold war even started, that they can do whatever they want right under the nose of the West."

"As I always say, the job doesn't really start until someone gets killed," she said blankly. "I need to go for a walk."

"You okay?"

She smiled tightly. "Thanks for letting me know about Oscar."

Greta turned and made for the door without even looking at him.

"Don't do anything I wouldn't do," Don said to the empty doorframe.

━━━━━━━━

Her walks always started the same way, with no conscious agenda other than a growing sense of powerlessness and the urge to fix something. Volk clearly wanted her to know that he had her surrounded. All the live wires in her psyche—the burning fires of rage and risk, her need for control, and her compulsion to seek chaos—were suddenly fused, dangerous currents running together in ways that were terrifying and, even more terrifying, liberating.

She set off down Seventh Avenue wearing flats and her trademark outfit—black skirt, white shirt, and a lightweight black jacket, all custom-tailored by Armani to hide a Glock 42 holstered at her back and an ultralight gravity knife inside the waistband.

By training and force of habit, Greta had developed an uncanny ability to make herself seen or unseen, to blend in or stand out, depending on the circumstances. Some of it was tradecraft but mostly it was a survival skill honed over a lifetime of danger and privation. Using the Hungarian glide, a languid way of walking taught at NOC school, she had perfected the art of cutting through bustling crowds without attracting attention, sometimes covering ground quickly, sometimes barely at all. Even a professional observer would have found her difficult to follow. She also excelled at another skill honed during her NOC training: the ability to project specific emotional states. In one moment, she could give off the aura of a formidable business executive and, in the next, a flustered out-of-towner. Not always admirably, she experimented endlessly on the streets and subways of New York City just to see what kind of attention she could attract or deflect. After slipping through Times Square, she emerged at the Port Authority Bus Terminal, Ninth Avenue and Forty-First Street: a predators' lair and the perfect spot for a woman to attract unwanted attention. In an instant, she shifted her affect: lost, afraid, a bit confused, a perfect victim.

"Excuse me, miss." Greta gave the man who had addressed her a profiler's once-over: white, mid-thirties, short brown hair, clean-shaven, five-eleven, solid, but not a bodybuilder, pin-striped suit, polyester tie, decently put together but off-the-rack, cheap shoes, dirty nails. A new breed of pimp? Greta thought, feeling the tip of an adrenaline rush. Trafficker? Mugger? She looked up, doe-eyed.

"You look like you need some help, may I be of assistance?" Accent slightly rough, English not his first language. Greta could relate. Bosnia? Croatia?

"No, no. I'm fine, just waiting for a friend. She's late. We have a bus to catch to Des Moines, and she's not answering her phone."

"That's New York for you. People can get overwhelmed, lose track of time."

"Gee, I hope not, we've got to be back at work in two days."

"Might be better to head up to the platform inside the terminal and wait there. Maybe she's already up there."

"Oh, wow, now I *am* confused." Greta fretted. "Did we decide to meet at the bus? Darn it."

"It's a better bet. I'd be happy to walk you up there. Bags left with Greyhound?"

"Yes, we checked them this morning so we wouldn't have to lug them around town. Thank you, I *am* a bit frazzled." Shy smile, she flicked her ponytail.

Greta walked into the building, her new friend at her elbow, heading toward the escalators leading to the baggage check.

"Hang on, miss, I know a shortcut, come with me."

Greta followed him through an unmarked door into a service hall for the bus station's custodial staff, cleaners. He led the way through another door, and they were outside again, but this time in an alley next to the building, below the ramps that the buses took to reach the passenger platforms.

"Where are we?" Greta feigned confusion.

"Miss, forgive me. I just thought, when I saw how pretty you are, maybe we could spend a bit of time together." His benign smile had become a leer.

Greta glanced around. She was trapped, a door behind, a metal security gate ahead. He began to move toward her, an arm extended. Greta's krav maga training kicked in, second nature: react with force, aim for soft spots—groin, eyes, nose, jaw, ears, throat, knees, Achilles tendon. She stepped back slightly to stagger her stance. Then, moving forward quickly, she placed her weight on her right leg and kicked with her left, full-force, between his legs. Her shin bone connected to his groin, crushing his balls. He shrieked in pain, gasped for breath, and began to double over. As he did, Greta tightened her core, mobilizing the weight of her upper body to power her forearm and elbow, swinging them into his temple. From the sharp snapping sounds, she was satisfied that both the zygomatic and frontal bone had shattered, likely forcing bone chips into his right eyeball. For good measure, she crushed his ankle with the heel of her foot, shredding his Achilles tendon. He felt nothing, having already passed out from pain and shock.

Not bad, she thought, seven seconds, start to finish. For a fraction of a second a thought flashed through her mind: what kind of person would inflict such ruin and feel . . . nothing? No, and feel better. But, then, she thought, what kind of society enabled creeps like this to roam freely, certain that she was not his first intended victim. Smoothing her skirt, instinctively checking for her Glock and knife, Greta walked back through the door to the main hall. Another itch scratched. She set off again, walking south on Ninth Avenue. Not much exertion, the adrenaline rush fading, her heart rate back to normal. A mile later, on Twentieth Street, she turned left and walked east toward Fifth Avenue and headed downtown. As she passed 20 West Twentieth Street, she looked into the stairwell, toying with the idea of ducking into the Westside Rifle & Pistol Range to destroy some targets. But then she had a better idea. It was Tuesday night. Camille's shift would be ending soon. She needed a friendly face, an uncomplicated evening with someone who had no idea about her. Or her life.

24

Geneva, Switzerland

An introduction to Hervé Charlier, the owner of Martial-Laurent, was yet
another element of the liberal education Vicker had received from Gonzaga. They walked thirty yards from the gangway to a plain, gray, metal-
clad building shell, under the mindful stares of guards carrying Heckler &
Koch MP5s. A formidable steel door framed by foot-thick walls of fireproof
concrete opened just enough to permit them to enter an austere but gra-
cious and brightly lit foyer. It snapped shut after them. Seeing them, Charlier whispered into a landline before ringing off. A trim, stylish man with
close-cropped gray hair, hooded green eyes, and a cautious mien, Charlier
wore his signature double-breasted blue blazer, dark gray slacks, and crisp
white shirt, top two buttons undone. He rose smoothly from a plush couch
upholstered in mauve mohair velvet, extending his hand to offer a cordial, if
reserved, welcome.

"*Mon ami,*" Gonzaga murmured. "Kind of you to meet us so late."

"Really nothing, Lorenzo. I am on Panama time these days."

Charlier released Gonzaga's hand and turned to Vicker. "Sir, it is my
pleasure to welcome you back to Martial-Laurent. I have been admiring the
audacity of your recent investments. You are the David of finance, a slayer of
giants. My hat comes off to you." Charlier, the archetype of a courtier.

Vicker graced Charlier with his version of a smile reserved for someone
who did not matter. "Thank you, Hervé. How is our investment in Panama
doing?"

Gonzaga was taken aback. Of late, all sorts of relationships seemed to be
sprouting from the seeds that he, himself, had planted. It disturbed him that
Vicker, who remained his stooge when it came to coming up with money-
making ideas, freelanced on other stages, like, apparently, investing in Charlier's Panama freeport.

"I keep reading about it, how is Jacques doing?"

Jacques Genet, their French-born partner, had been parachuted into

Panama to take advantage of Switzerland's hasty and ignominious retreat from bank secrecy—as if the wealthy wouldn't seek protection elsewhere. Genet had taken Panamanian citizenship, married a well-born *rabiblanca*, and had helped the government there create a passel of laws that made bank secrecy sacrosanct and trusts inviolable. The result: a boom in offshore banking, as banks, particularly Swiss, flocked to the isthmus-state. Many of their clients, and especially the newly rich Chinese who had already invested heavily in the country, also took advantage of the storage and curatorial services that Martial-Laurent's spanking new freeport offered.

Charlier sighed.

"It has been a boon, because people who get nervous about Switzerland can still use our services here or in Panama. We keep them in the family."

"And Sokolov?" Vicker probed.

"Ah, yes, Sokolov."

Oleg Sokolov, the Russian potash billionaire, had had Charlier arrested in Monaco allegedly for defrauding him of a cool billion dollars. Over ten years, Charlier sold Sokolov thirty-seven paintings: Picassos; Dutch landscapes; French impressionists; a handful of Rothkos; a Modigliani; newly discovered Vermeers; and a putative da Vinci. But, in the course of Sokolov's ill-chosen battles within Russia, Charlier had found himself in the middle. A rogue's gallery of litigants showed up, claiming rights to everything he had built—not merely the art he had acquired for Sokolov.

"All settled, then?" Vicker asked.

"Nearly. My assets are mine again. Oleg and his friends have retreated to their corners, settling their internecine battles without killing each other. At least so far."

Gonzaga laughed, gently shaking his head in bemusement. What Charlier said was true, on some level, though he had always suspected that Charlier's involvement in Sokolov's business ran much deeper than he let on—and that he had become much too deeply enmeshed in the dealings of sharp-elbowed Russians than was prudent for an outsider. But the collection had been magnificent. Rarely had so many jewels been assembled under one roof, in a specially constructed room at Martial-Laurent. A pity to see it dismantled.

"What happened to Sokolov's gallery?" Gonzaga inquired.

"I'm renting it to a Dutch gentleman who deals in old masters—Luuk de

Jong. Come have a look. Didn't you mention you're shopping for a house-warming gift?"

Charlier led them down a long hall that bisected the building, softly lit by warm LEDs, footfalls absorbed by plush taupe wool carpet. Burnished steel doors with biometric readers flanked them, running the entire length at thirty-foot intervals. Two hundred feet from the entry foyer, Charlier stopped at a door identified by a four-digit number. He placed his hand on a reader recessed into the wall. With a mechanical click and a hydraulic hiss, the door swung inward. Vicker and Gonzaga followed him inside. A box fifty feet square had been divided into a series of rooms paneled in antique walnut buffed to a soft sheen. The intimate scale of the rooms suited the art. De Jong displayed particularly fine examples of works by Dutch old masters from the sixteenth and seventeenth centuries: Bruegel the Elder, Jan Steen, Hieronymus Bosch, Lucas van Leyden, Hendrick ter Brugghen, Willem Kalf. Gonzaga paused in front of two still lifes by Rachel Ruysch, both asymmetrical, energetic arrangements of drooping roses, convolvulus, wild stems, and poppies. Charlier sidled up to him.

"You have always had an eye for the ladies," Charlier quipped.

Gonzaga stood quietly: Rachel. That was how he thought of her. Mother of ten, a career spanning sixty years. He stood quietly, absorbing her compositions, sensing her arranging each flower, the fineness of her brush strokes, every petal rendered in painstaking detail and the vibrance and subtlety of her palette. In her day, her work commanded higher prices than Rembrandt's.

"You know me too well, Hervé."

"I told de Jong how you admire her work. Are you really going to give her away? Or is this one for you?"

"When we leave you, we will be going to visit a very dear, old friend. He will treat her well. How much is de Jong asking?"

"Seven hundred fifty thousand dollars, but a gold bar might do the trick."

Gonzaga did some quick math: a Good Delivery gold bar, 400 troy ounces, 438 avoirdupois ounces, roughly 25 pounds, close enough to $750,000. Not a bad price for a Rachel, and, in any event, they could not show up in Cyprus empty-handed.

"And what about the other one?"

"One of my newer clients bought it sight unseen just last week. A young woman with impeccable taste," said Charlier. "And, like you, an eye for the ladies."

"Do you think she might consider turning a quick profit?"

"Not likely. I've never seen Greta sell anything. But I can ask."

Gonzaga sighed. The best pieces moved quickly and often disappeared for generations. Greta? Not a rare name, but not common either. Gonzaga dismissed the thought that this Greta could be that Greta; he'd learned over the decades not to confuse hopes with intuition.

"In that case, I'll take the one that de Jong has on offer. Can you crate her for me?"

Charlier whispered into his phone and, a few minutes later, two serious-looking young men with closely cropped beards arrived in an electric cart, placed the Ruysch on a blanket, and drove off to the conservation studio to build a secure crate that would be delivered to Vicker's plane. Leaving de Jong's gallery, Charlier led them farther along the center hall to two adjacent safe rooms, one belonging to Vicker, one to Gonzaga.

The contents of Vicker's safe room echoed the cache houses Don Carter had set up for him in New York. Industrial-grade racks held dozens of four-hundred-ounce Good Delivery gold bars, specially designed briefcases held exactly $1 million each, and a single cabinet held Vicker's favorite form of portable, divisible wealth: diamonds. A five-carat diamond worth $100,000 at wholesale weighs just one gram: one pound of diamonds is worth $45 million. The ten pounds of two-carat, three-carat, and five-carat stones—worth almost half a billion dollars—would fit into a carry-on, with room to spare for a change of clothes. And an extra passport.

Vicker had long ago decided—with Gonzaga's encouragement—that he needed at least a billion in portable assets, in the event that he needed to change venues quickly and start over. Gonzaga had been more than willing to aggravate those anxieties. The world, in Gonzaga's experience, was a volatile, unpredictable place. Top of the Pitti Palace one day, foraging through rubble the next.

Gonzaga was more interested in the other half of Vicker's doomsday collection of precious portable assets, the half—easily worth a billion—stored in neat racks on the far wall. Over more than a decade, Gonzaga had helped Vicker acquire an enviable collection of master works, some old and some contemporary, each carefully chosen for its longevity, marketability, and provenance. Money alone would buy admission and temporary safety in some parts of the world—Paraguay, Ecuador, Russia, Cuba, Brazil, Morocco, but perhaps only for a time. It was often harder to keep the decision-makers in those havens bought than to buy them in the first place. Once they had money, something that appealed to their vanity was a better bet—the occasional Rembrandt drawing or Klee watercolor was an effective way to stay on the good side of, say, the Paraguayan interior minister. Even though Vicker's taste ran to the Toulouse-Lautrec posters that hung on the few walls at 432 Park that were not glass, the collection stored at Le Coultre connoted a man of exemplary taste and erudition, thanks to Gonzaga.

"Lorenzo." Vicker managed a courtly bow. "What will it be? We have had another good year—a very good year." Gonzaga raised his eyes. Notwithstanding Vicker's midnight road trip and the need to deal with Oscar.

"Hervé, please pull that Bastien-Lepage."

"A variation on *L'Amour au Village*," Hervé observed. A scene typical for Bastien-Lepage, a young couple lost in their conversation, lost in each other.

"And the Sargent, the one in which the woman holds a parasol."

"*Midday Walk*." Hervé stepped back to admire it.

Gonzaga studied them, each in turn, from near, from far. Vicker became impatient, tapping his foot.

"There's always next year, Lorenzo."

Gonzaga smiled.

"True enough. The Bastien-Lepage, then. Will you lend me one of your gold bars? I have to pay Hervé for the Ruysch, and I am fresh out. Imagine that."

25

SoHo, New York City

Greta took her time walking down through Greenwich Village and SoHo, cooling down, meandering toward Canal Street. At the corner of Broadway and Canal, she turned right and found herself at Clandestino: her favorite bar, a hole-in-the-wall saloon run by a hip French girl. Greta took a stool at the bar, and was surprised, but not, to find Don sitting next to her. He knew her too well, she thought. Of course. Sidling up to him, Greta felt a familiar pang. Camille, who knew most of her guests, glanced over at Greta, who nodded at Don's bottle of Badoit. Unlike most people, when Don didn't drink it meant something was bothering him.

"You that broken up about Oscar?" she asked.

"I'm not the one who stormed out of the office like a moody teenager."

For a second, she wanted to storm out of there too. Don had been so distant and, when she tried to break through to him, condescending. And now here he was, suddenly looking for comfort. But then again, he had shown up. Clandestino was a refuge for both of them, one of the few places anywhere where they felt comfortable being themselves. They'd spent so many long nights there, just talking about the things they never told other people, surrounded by Clandestino's eclectic band of young, hip, urban strivers who had moved to New York so they could gather in just such comfortable, swanky, hidden spots. For the price of a dirty martini, Don and Greta could imagine they belonged among these archetypal Manhattanites—grounded, settled, maybe even content, if not happy.

"It always pays to monitor the police radio when you disappear on one of your walkabouts. You shredded that guy."

"Trying to keep the world safe for defenseless girls from . . . Iowa." Just comfortably bantering with Don calmed her down and allowed her to push Volk from her mind, back into the darkness, where, she prayed, he would remain until she was ready to face him.

"So, I guess our friend must be getting to you?" Don said quietly.

For a second she thought he meant Volk and felt a momentary panic until she realized Don was talking about Elias Vicker.

"What worries me is that he isn't getting to you." Greta paused. "He's a stone-cold psycho."

"I thought you told me everyone on Wall Street is a psycho."

"There's your run-of-the-mill prick with a Learjet. And then there is Elias Vicker."

"What makes him so special?" Don asked dismissively. "Richer? More arrogant? Greedier?"

Greta could feel the old tensions between them rising. She wondered why he was picking a fight when there was nothing to argue about.

"Has it ever occurred to you that there might be people that you cannot handle?"

"Has it ever occurred to you that when an opportunity presents itself," Don shot back, "you have to grab it and sort out whatever problems arise on the fly. Isn't that the point of all our training?"

"We are also trained to distinguish between necessary and unnecessary risks. Tommy and Ben—all you *boys*—have a hard-on for this idea of taking over Vicker's fund. But it's our job—yours and mine—to tell them if we have doubts. Besides, weren't you the one saying you didn't want to do this anymore?"

"Once I said I was in, I was in. Ambivalence gets people killed."

Realizing she wasn't getting anywhere, Greta changed the subject. "You still haven't told me why you're not drinking."

"We lost them, G." Don's bravado started to falter.

"Lost who?"

"Vicker and Gonzaga."

Greta stared at Don's impassive mien, reflected through the mirror behind the bar, well aware of what microexpressions Liz might uncover. Shame. Guilt. Anger. Frustration. All the feelings that a lifetime in the army—and in an emotionally distant family—had taught him to suppress. Here she was, again, trying to draw back Don's curtains. She had promised herself when she took the assignment that she was done with that. But if she did not take on the job, who would?

"Camille"—Greta gestured to the owner—"I think my friend needs a Jameson. A double."

"And she'll have, what was it you liked, Pernod?"

"I thought you only ever noticed what kind of gun I was carrying."

"I was always more interested in relieving you of the knife strapped to your thigh."

"Clearly it wasn't big enough. Now, tell me what's going on."

"They slipped our noose early this morning, 0600." Don slid back into briefing mode.

"As near as we can figure, Vee snuck down to the garage. The Count picked him up and they headed out to Newark, where he hangars his brand-new 747-8. We tracked it to the northern edge of Cointrin."

"Obsessed with security, then he scampers off without it. What does that tell you?"

"That there is something he really doesn't want us to see."

She pulled out her phone. "Let's see if they're on their way back yet."

In seconds, they were viewing live footage from airport security cameras showing the 747 taxiing away from Martial-Laurent. Greta scrunched her eyebrows. As a client, she knew Hervé Charlier well. To her, he was a shrewd, well-connected, and useful scamp. Every NOC had escape plans, and hers, including a vault at Martial-Laurent, were more elaborate than most. Although Don's put hers to shame.

"Okay, let's see where they're headed," she said, more to herself than to Don.

Using the call sign for the plane's transponder, Greta accessed the flight plans on her iPhone. After Geneva, they had flown to Tunisia.

"It doesn't look like they'll be home in time for dinner. After landing in Tunis, the plane went dark. The pilot must have disabled the transponders. No flight plan. Pretty unusual for a plane that size."

"Where do you think they're headed?"

"More important, have you told Tommy yet?"

26

Tunis, Tunisia

The landing in Tunis, soft as it was, jolted Gonzaga awake. Though they were aloft again minutes later, staying at Tunis-Carthage just long enough to turn off the transponders, Gonzaga had lost any chance at sleep. The man they were going to visit, Lieutenant Colonel Fyodor Volk, most recently of the FSB and now principal of the Parsifal Group, viewed himself as a direct descendant of the early soldiers of fortune. For thousands of years, mercenaries, proxies, contractors—however named—have been alluring to state actors. Available, deniable, expendable instruments in the pursuit of national interests without the direct participation of the state. Easily written off as whores and zealots, their lethal behavior lessened the risk of escalation with an enemy. And dead mercenaries drew far less of the bad press and scrutiny that came with young recruits arriving home in body bags.

Gonzaga amused himself with the thought that modern-day mercenaries, like Volk, had gone corporate. They had rebranded themselves as Chastnye Voenniye Companiye, private military companies. PMCs sported all the trappings of international business consultancies: dramatic websites, and glitzy advisory boards packed with retired generals, buttoned-down compliance officers, and hyperaggressive lawyers, mercenaries in their own right. They still excelled at the traditional jobs: assassination, kidnapping, killing, and not being killed. But, like the state actors that contracted for their services, they were prepared to mount aggression on any front: on battlefields, in cyberspace, in the boardroom, and in the social media feeds of countries where clients wanted to sow dissent and disruption. Hybrid war. Kinetic and violent, as required, but, ideally, violence leavened by active and passive cyberattacks, legal forays, *kompromat,* and disinformation to maximize disorder.

Looking up, Gonzaga saw Vicker padding into the lounge wearing a bathrobe and slippers embroidered with a skull and crossbones, custom made by George Cleverley. The pilot poked his head in to let them know that they would arrive in Cyprus in an hour, and that the transponders would stay off until they left the island the following day.

"This 'mysterious' Fyodor, is he going to try and kidnap me too?"

Gonzaga thought about the fuse he was about to light. He had done Volk many favors over the years: bypassing know-your-customer rules, vouching for him at the reliably opaque Vatican Bank, channeling Volk acolytes into jobs with influential Wall Street firms. With Volk, favors bought no loyalty, only continued access. To many, the man defined psychopathy, but Gonzaga enjoyed the man's natural charm and impeccable manners. At his core, the diagnosis was apt: Volk was, indeed, violent, manipulative, lacking any shred of empathy, grandiose, narcissistic, and, on occasion, impulsive. Of course, those characteristics also described his traveling companion perfectly. Gonzaga mused that, had he been asked to isolate the key to his success, he would say that he had a rare capacity to insinuate himself into the lives of difficult people and to manipulate them to his own ends.

"He can be charming." Gonzaga measured his words. "Cerebral. Lettered. An accomplished pianist. An intellectual. Studied history and philosophy in Russia, and then at Oxford. Admires the aesthetics and ideology of the Third Reich. He adopted 'Parsifal' as his nom de guerre, after an opera by Hitler's favorite composer. It's an epic story of an Arthurian knight and his quest for the Holy Grail. Fyodor named his PMC in Wagner's honor, the Parsifal Group."

"PMC?"

"And, now, dear friend," Gonzaga began, at his manipulative best, "I will draw the curtain back on how things really work."

What a supercilious asshole, thought Vicker, wondering how much longer he would have to put up with Gonzaga's airs and condescension. Had he—Elias Vicker—not built Industrial Strategies into the biggest hedge fund in history? In fucking *history*. Had Gonzaga ever gotten his hands dirty running an actual business: hiring, firing, dealing with lawyers, regulators, accountants? No. The old man held himself above all that. Vicker couldn't believe the presumption, and felt a surge of annoyance at being dragged halfway around the world. But at least now he would have a direct relationship with one of Gonzaga's people. Without being intermediated by the puppeteer. And Fyodor, well, from the problems that the guy had solved so far, he clearly had abilities.

"Private military company."

"Got it. Like Executive Outcomes and Blackwater."

Not bad, thought Gonzaga. Executive Outcomes, founded by ex–South African commandos who made their bones defending apartheid, disbanded after doing dirty work in Angola and Sierra Leone. Blackwater, the brainchild of Erik Prince, a former Navy SEAL, had been a prime contractor for the U.S. Government in Iraq and after that had been renamed a couple of times, first as Xe Services, then Academi. Every major power has PMCs, or access to them as needed. For the Brits: WatchGuard, Sandline, Keeni Meeni Services, and Defence Systems. For the Americans: DynCorp and Engility/ MPRI.

"Exactly, but with Russian state cover. Volk is one of Putin's golden boys. Parsifal contractors 'liberated' Eastern Ukraine from what Putin called the 'fascist junta' in Kiev. Then they shipped out to Syria. But do not mention Syria unless he does. Fyodor makes a huge amount of money there. He and his partner, Alexei Smeshko, own a big chunk of the oil business, but the Americans killed two hundred of his men. Including his son, Anatoly."

Vicker looked puzzled. "He's a mercenary. People die."

Gonzaga ignored the comment. It was no surprise to him that Vicker, a man devoid of empathy, completely missed the impact that the death of a son could have on a man.

"Fyodor is a remarkable man. But at the risk of repeating myself, be cautious. Russian DNA tends toward the tetchy, irritable, and sensitive. They are quick to take offense and unforgiving."

Good advice. But when Gonzaga turned to look, Vicker was fast asleep.

27

Limassol, Cyprus

The pilot circled low and slow, giving Vicker and Gonzaga an aerial tour of sunny Limassol, a tiny strip of beachfront on Cyprus's southern coast. Conveniently located just two hours from Moscow, Limassol had long surpassed Monte Carlo as the destination of choice for crooked Russian money. Flexible banking rules, greedy banks, compliant locals, and a biddable government made Limassol—and Cyprus generally—a safe zone for Eastern European and Middle Eastern outlaws and their loot.

Nestled at the eastern end of the Mediterranean Sea, fewer than 150 miles from the Syrian coast and a mere skip to Europe, Cyprus occupied its own netherworld of geopolitical intrigue and contradictions. Having been ruled variously by Assyrians, the Egyptians, the Byzantines, and the Romans, Cypriots marked the peaceful twentieth-century invasion of Russians as just another chapter in their long history as a refuge. As a member of the EU, it grants the Brits sovereignty over military bases comprising ninety-eight square miles, replete with airfields, radar stations, ports, and eight thousand troops. But, at the same time, it cozied up to Lebanon, Syria, and Israel. Ever commercial, Cypriot bakers, bankers, and real estate brokers loved Russian money.

"If we actually meet any Limassolinos, you'll like them," said Gonzaga. "Charming, solicitous, fun loving, unless you get in the way of their tribal feuds."

As the plane banked to land at Paphos International Airport a few miles west of Limassol, Gonzaga pointed out the window toward a sensuous, sleek 180-foot-long carbon fiber sailboat anchored offshore.

"Oh, that must be Fyodor's latest Wally," Gonzaga said. "He told me when I saw it, I'd be jealous."

Vicker glanced out the window. He did not acknowledge boats, or anything else for that matter, as things of beauty. The physical world—whether animate or inanimate—only made sense to him as an extension of his ego and as a manifestation of his wealth. Beyond that, objects and people held no thrall, but those boats did reek of money. Perhaps, he thought, he needed to have a couple of them bobbing in New York Harbor.

A swarthy fireplug of a man, wearing a sweat-stained shirt that identified him as an immigration officer, boarded and waited obsequiously at the doorway to the lounge. With a short bow and a furtive look, he glanced at their passports without bothering to stamp them and scuttled away. Behind him stood a very fit-looking man, six feet tall, blond, late-thirties, with military bearing, wearing navy Orlebar Brown khakis and a white polo. Gonzaga's face blossomed into a broad grin. Vadim Ivanov: Parsifal's factotum. He motioned for the younger man to enter and rose to give him a handshake and then grabbed him in a bear hug.

"Vadim! I had no idea you would be back from . . ." Gonzaga caught himself before he gestured eastward, in the direction of Syria.

"Rough duty." Ivanov gave Gonzaga a look: do not ask.

"I present Vadim Ivanov," Gonzaga said. "*Major* Ivanov, FSB, retired. Fyodor's right-hand man." Ivanov extended his hand cordially.

"My great pleasure, Mr. Vicker. You won't remember, but we met several years ago, after your lecture at the Knickerbocker Club. I very much enjoyed hearing you describe your approach to corporate activism and your techniques for motivating spineless and entrenched chief executives to take steps to enhance shareholder value."

Vicker turned his head, surprised. That was more than ten years ago, he recalled. He also noted that Ivanov spoke English with a neutral, almost preppy, mid-Atlantic accent. Not like any Russian he'd ever met.

"The boss sent me to fetch you," Ivanov said. "You have suites at the Four Seasons, but he is anxious to get started, and hopes that you will find it convenient to join him on the boat straightaway. Some lunch, take a cruise. We will send your things to the hotel and head out for the *Better Place*."

"Fyodor's new Wally?"

"He just took delivery and wanted you to be his first guest."

"The absolute pinnacle of Italian design and engineering," Gonzaga said. "A rare privilege."

"It's a boat, I guess," Vicker said. "How much does one of those things cost?"

"The question, Elias, is whether Luca is willing to accept you as a customer."

Designed and built by Luca Bassani, Wallys had the lines and performance of stealth bombers: carbon fiber hulls and sails made them exceptionally fast. At the bottom of the stairs, two young women, dressed like Ivanov, but wearing sunglasses and carrying sidearms, scanned the environs through wary eyes. A single-lane driveway descended from the tarmac to a floating dock a few hundred feet away, where another Wally, this one a fifty-eight-foot power cruiser, waited for them. "The *Better Place* is ten miles out," said one of the women. "Travel time is approximately twenty minutes. May I get you something?"

Gonzaga gave her an appraising look. One of the joys of visiting Fyodor—or Parsifal, as he preferred to be known—was his commitment to equal opportunity. His girls were at least as lethal as his boys, but a lot more fun. She met his gaze coolly.

"It is good to see you, Vesna. I would love a glass of water."

Vicker raised an index finger to add to the order as Gonzaga turned toward Ivanov.

"If you are not in the field, Vadim," said Gonzaga, gesturing eastward, "what has he got you doing?"

"I'm on finance and investment, working with Parsifal and the Butler."

"Have U.S. sanctions on Alexei been a problem?" Gonzaga asked.

"Brutal."

"You're making progress?" Gonzaga asked.

"Inch by inch, not easy."

"What kind of deals are you financing?" Vicker asked.

"I don't want to jump the gun here, but Parsifal Group has acquired exploration and production rights for important Syrian oil fields and refineries. Right now we're trying to put a funding package together."

"And the obstacles?" Gonzaga asked.

"The sanctions really bite. We need to finance oil shipments and guarantee drilling rig contracts. We're swimming in money and can put up cash for guarantees, but we need someone of repute to vouch to the bankers—or to stand in the middle. We also need to invest our money."

Ivanov made it sound so antiseptic. They all knew reality loomed larger. The Butler, their various corporate fronts—Parsifal Group, Harmony—and, of course, Bashar al-Assad, and most of his ministers, were subject to international sanctions that prohibited providing financial assistance to the regime. That did not make the kinds of transactions Ivanov described difficult or impossible. It made them expensive. They needed to find investors with decent reputations to front for them, and that bearding cost money. But since the Syrian people would, ultimately, end up footing the bill, no one would complain. Vicker made some mental calculations about how he might stick his fingers into that pie. Probably part of the reason he was there. When al-Assad won, Putin would win. With Volk and the Butler as proxies, Putin would be in the perfect spot to guarantee al-Assad's security and to join in plundering the carcass. The Russian might be a bridge to the ultimate prize: a stable but irascible Syrian client state squarely in the middle of the Middle East.

"Vadim, are you able to travel these days?" Gonzaga inquired, wondering if Ivanov had also made the U.S. Treasury sanctions list. Ivanov nodded.

"Under my own name, and a few others," he laughed. "Cyprus prints lovely passports, and, until recently, they didn't mind revising a few personal details here and there."

Most countries sell passports, some more blatantly than others. The United States requires an investment of half a million dollars, but the cognoscenti know better than to make that mistake: American taxes are sky-high and its regulators are nosy. Until the EU decided to clamp down, the Republic of Cyprus, with its low taxes and a laissez-faire view of private business, had raked in more than a billion dollars a year selling passports at $2 million a pop. Cyprus, as a member of the European Union, could offer its "citizens" entry into 147 countries, including the United States, without visas. Little wonder that parts of Limassol sported more signs in Cyrillic than in Greek. Shrewd observers guessed that the Cypriots would find a way to resume the trade in passports before long.

With the cruiser making forty knots, the *Better Place*, Volk's yacht, came into view quickly. An ocean-going sloop, she could sleep ten guests and ten crew comfortably, but, for Volk, she wasn't so much a party boat as a completely private floating office. Clients could sail from Tartus, Beirut, or Latakia or fly from Aleppo or Damascus to join him, unnoticed. As the cruiser cuddled up to the stern of the *Better Place*, Volk made his way down the stairs from the upper deck. An ensemble of sleek, bronzed young women, scattered like dolls on chaises, rose to follow him, curious. He fairly pulled Gonzaga onto the boat, embracing him in a ferocious bear hug, kisses on both cheeks. But Gonzaga thought he sensed something new, something had changed. Just as charming, outwardly, but a reserve. He might be projecting, but losing your only son could change a man.

"Too long, old friend."

"Fyodor Volk. Elias Vicker."

Vicker and Volk gave each other quick, cool appraisals. Vicker saw a fit, wiry, tanned, fiftysomething bantam of a man. Crewcut, even features, pale blue eyes. Superficially calm, but coiled like a cobra at rest, watchful. What Vicker could not discern was Volk's raw brain power: schooled as an electrical engineer, widely read, fluent in English, French, and Arabic.

Volk had been extensively briefed on Vicker. He knew how awkward the man was, how cold-blooded. But here, face-to-face with him, he sensed something in Vicker's watery eyes that hadn't surfaced in his briefing papers: an instability that suggested not only a capacity for cruelty but also an inability to control that impulse to inflict harm. Vicker was a strange one, but likely useful.

"My dear Elias—if I may call you Elias—a privilege to meet you. Lorenzo speaks of you often. I have a deep admiration for your approach to business. It is much like my own: take no prisoners. Please call me Parsifal, a bit droll to use my nom de guerre, but it pleases me." Volk smirked and extended his hand.

"Mr. Volk—Parsifal—I am at a disadvantage. Lorenzo has been so circumspect about you, yet you have done me . . . favors. I very much appreciate that."

Volk waved a hand, brushing away Vicker's thank-you.

"Nothing. Forget it. I enjoy helping my friends."

"Good, good, there's a lot more you can do," Vicker said awkwardly. "I don't know how much Lorenzo told you about me, but I think you'll find I'm a good person to know."

"I shudder to think where I'd be without the doors Lorenzo opens for me."

As Volk led them to the upper deck, Vicker looked around for Gonzaga, who was engrossed in a tête-à-tête with a young woman in a bikini, her hand resting gently on his chest, his on the small patch of fabric that suggested how a proper bathing suit might cover her derriere.

"Lorenzo and Svetlana are old friends," Volk observed as he watched

Vicker take in the scene. "A little holiday from the Mariinsky for my ballerinas. They are amazing athletes. They work so hard. Later, they will dance
for us."

On the top deck, a feast of summer salads covered a table set for five.
Ivanov chatted with a trim older man. Once again, Gonzaga found himself
in a full-body hug.

"Sasha!"

Releasing Gonzaga, Smeshko turned to Vicker.

"And you, Mr. Vicker. We have been waiting for you, please sit, eat. There
is so much to discuss."

Putin's Butler, the consummate showman, directed them to their seats.

"Cyprus is nothing but joy for me. Such a long season, everything grows
all year. Look at these lovelies—chioggia beets, green zebra tomatoes, kyoto
red carrots. Mr. Vicker, any allergies?"

Vicker shook his head. Not what he expected from Russians at the top of
the food chain, men who ranked high on Forbes's most-reviled list. But, he
thought, oligarchs are people too. What did it matter that Volk and Smeshko
were engines of al-Assad's war on his own people and agents of Putin's brutal
adventurism in the near-abroad? Maybe they were his kind of mass murder-
ers. The Butler made plates for everyone.

"You must try everything. Then take what you like."

Smeshko pulled a bottle of vodka from a block of ice, pouring shots
all around. Ivanov turned his glass upside down, not drinking while on
duty. Vicker, not a teetotaler but with no tolerance for alcohol, attempted
to demur.

"You must toast with us," Volk chided him. "*Za nashu druzjbu*, to friendship. The Russian way, look each other in the eyes and, as you say, 'down the
hatch.'"

Gonzaga watched as the scene that he had orchestrated so meticulously
unfolded. A magnificent day on the water, a beautiful Italian boat, spectacular Russian women, and both Volk and Smeshko at their most cordial. But
he knew the frightening speed at which a clear and bright day among such
combustible elements could turn dark. He glanced at Ivanov and received
the barest flick of an eyebrow in response. Vicker was conspicuously quiet,
overwhelmed and out of his bubble. Time to move things along.

"Fyodor, for years I have thought you and Elias could accomplish a lot together. He is really quite talented at trading events. You are brilliant at creating events."

"You know me too well, Lorenzo." He pulled a book from the pile next to his chair and held it up: *Making Things Happen* by Scott Berkun. "This book had such a profound effect on me, I held a seminar for my people. This was the textbook."

He turned to face Vicker. "Are you familiar with Berkun? He managed some of the biggest projects at Microsoft—Internet Explorer, Windows. Microsoft Office, Skype. His methodology for examining management processes helped us to organize our thinking and helped us develop our philosophy. We make things happen all the time—big events, little things. Scott taught me to think less about the individual parts and more how they fit together. How do our different skills complement one another? How do we network events, scale them, optimize them?"

Vicker had been pensive, but Volk's monologue stunned him. Soldiers talking about business philosophy? Networked events? He considered the sorts of events that, he already knew, they had made happen: hit-and-run accidents in foreign countries, extermination of Syrian rebels, occupation of countries like the Ukraine, the takeover of oil fields and refineries. And who knew what kind of cyber-mischief Parsifal's geek army, with dozens of advanced degrees in math and computer science, could pull off? They carried laptops, wrote code, and provided state actors with deniability in a different sphere of aggression. Lots of potential.

"What kinds of events have you been thinking about?" Vicker asked.

The Butler looked thoughtful "Fat tails. Black swans. With the right ingredients, I can cook anything." The Butler laughed so hard his entire body shook. Moments later, he regained his composure and turned to Volk. "Fyodor, explain it to them."

"Human beings have always been buffeted by unpredictable, random events."

"And always will be," Ivanov added.

"You are not, I take it, interested in occasional random events caused by the irrational exuberance of investors," Gonzaga observed.

Volk nodded and reached for another book from his pile—a dog-eared first edition of *Normal Accidents* by Charles Perrow, the Yale sociologist.

"Perrow took our thinking to the next level."

"A man of genius!" The Butler slapped the table, rattling the china. The girls on the lower deck looked up for a second and then went back to stretching at the barre and working on their tans.

Berkun and Taleb had not told Volk and the Butler anything they did not already feel in their bones. The Butler had made a food empire happen from nothing—from jail to hot dog truck to feeding millions of Russians on no-bid government contracts. Volk had made entire countries happen, like bringing Crimea and half of Ukraine back into Russia's orbit. But it was Perrow who enabled their epiphany: they didn't have to wait around for normal accidents. They could make them happen.

"Until Fyodor brought this man to my attention, I never realized how simple it could be."

Volk riffled the pages of the book. "Perrow was the first guy to visualize the modern world as a spider's web of increasingly complex technological systems: electrical grids, air traffic control systems, bridges, highways, oil refineries, undersea cables, the internet, chemical plants, dams, nuclear power plants, pipelines, marine traffic."

He opened it to a dog-eared page.

"Here it is. I'll paraphrase: society depends on complex systems, but— this is the point—those systems are so tightly coupled, so interdependent, that when a piece of one system fails, many others fail. Combine that with the fact that human beings make mistakes all the time, big accidents arise from small beginnings. Sometimes trivial events—or seemingly trivial—can cascade into catastrophe. Chernobyl is an obvious one. But there are really so many of them."

"And so rarely," the Butler added, "are they appreciated as, shall we say, creators of value."

Volk looked at the Butler, and then at Vicker. "I really must show gratitude to my patron," he said. "He is always receptive to new ideas. When I explained that a lot of what we do for clients could very easily be made to look like an accident, Alexei immediately saw the opportunity."

"What is downstream from a disaster?" he asked, his smile revealing a mouth full of perfect, expensive, teeth. "Money!"

"Remember Bhopal? A few valves failed, two thousand people died immediately," Vicker said. "Union Carbide stock fell sixty percent the next day and stayed there for a couple of years, until the company settled with the

Indian government—for a pittance. Then it shot right back up. Two juicy trades. I could have turned fifty million dollars into a couple of billion overnight."

Vicker sat deeper into his chair, tented his hands in front of his face, deep in thought. When he looked up, color had flushed out the jet-lag pallor on his face. "Gentleman," he said. "You have my undivided attention."

Finally, Volk thought, a sign of life from Lorenzo's strange friend. "Let's talk about the petroleum industry, one of our areas of interest. As you know, oil and gas production is an expensive, complicated, and dangerous activity. From finding it, to producing it, to transporting and refining it. Lots of accidents, lots of unintended consequences as the effect of those accidents ripple outward," Volk remarked. "Let me show you something."

He raised a hand and snapped his fingers with tightly controlled vigor. "My iPad please."

A steward appeared by his side and handed it to him. He walked around the table and sat next to Vicker. The picture on the screen looked like it was being taken from a boat bobbing in choppy waves. A legend at the bottom of the screen said "Vodrone1," a contraction of the Russian word for water, "vody," and drone, "waterdrone." The upper left corner displayed GPS coordinates corresponding to the North Sea, more precisely, the Statfjord oil field operated by Nordsjoen Navigasjon ASA, a company listed on the Oslo Stock Exchange and fifty-five percent owned by the Norwegian government. Volk carefully dragged a finger along the bottom of the screen. Three sleek watercraft resembling dark gray-green surfboards emerged from the gentle chop of the slate-gray northern ocean. Solar cells covered their topsides and small domes bristling with antennae sat on their noses. As he maneuvered the drones, a colossal oil production platform loomed in the background, larger than two football fields, rising 250 feet above the water, perched on four massive, submerged tubular legs. What looked like a small apartment building, big enough to house a hundred-odd workers, squatted on one corner, a heliport on its roof. One helicopter landed as another took off. Barely visible, several dozen men moved purposefully around the decks, up and down staircases, across the roof of the building.

"Is this live?" Gonzaga asked, peering over Volk's shoulder, to which he nodded.

"Some kids I know in Saint Petersburg made these. Brilliant marine engineers," Ivanov said proudly. "Vodrones are mostly used for scientific research, like measuring ocean currents, temperature, and weather conditions. We asked them to modify a few for us."

"They are not intended to be fast, but steady. In normal use, they can sail indefinitely. We launched from a freighter a hundred miles away," said Volk. "The batteries charge from solar panels and wave energy converters supply power from the motion of the waves."

The drones cruised closer to the platform, which came into clearer focus.

"Elias, would you like to drive?" Volk asked. "These three, in the center of the screen, are tethered together. Steer toward one of the legs of that monstrosity."

Gonzaga worried that the entire scene was getting a little crazy, but Vicker accepted the tablet eagerly, recalling what it was like, as a kid, to sail his first boat on a pond in Central Park. He moved his fingers gently, weaving the drones toward the platform's southernmost leg.

"Okay," said Volk, "when you are about fifty yards away, slow it down. Dead slow, throttle is on the left. Just inch forward so the drones encircle that leg."

Vicker carefully guided the gray-green surfboards until they snuggled up against the massive stanchion. Gonzaga looked on nervously. The drones were so close that the only thing visible from their cameras was orange paint.

"Very nice, Mr. Vicker, very nice!" The Butler popped a fresh olive into his mouth.

Volk leaned over the tablet to input a password. A virtual bright red button popped up on the lower left-hand corner of the screen.

"Whenever you're ready, push the button."

Vicker looked up to see Gonzaga, Volk, the Butler, and Ivanov watching him closely. With a flourish, Vicker cracked a few knuckles, loudly, before making circle in the air with his long right index finger and bringing it down squarely on the virtual button. In an instant, an electronic instruction flashed invisibly into space and bounced back down to Earth. It registered with the three drones, and a blinding flash filled the screen.

Ivanov had used another tablet to maintain the camera-equipped Vodrone1 at a distance of two miles from the platform. He passed it across the table to Volk and Vicker, as Gonzaga watched over their shoulders. A sunny day in the North Sea became the scene of an inferno. With one of its legs severed, the entire platform listed precariously into the sea and boiling clouds of black smoke billowed from its superstructure as secondary explosions fueled by gas and crude oil erupted. Seemingly in slow motion the entire structure began to tilt farther. Volk drove Vodrone1 closer, steering it through an obstacle course of flotsam and smoking debris. Vicker reached over to turn the drone for a 360-degree view. Bodies floated by; some people swam, looking for purchase on anything that floated, while others tried to launch lifeboats from the sinking rig. A helicopter toppled into the roiling water, while another chopper, probably from another rig, moved into view. Vicker looked up, ignoring the human tragedy unfolding in the icy waters 2,500 miles away.

"Vadim, would you please check how NSNA is trading?" asked Volk.

NSNA, the ticker symbol for Nordsjoen Navigasjon, which owned and operated the production platform, was already live on his screen. With a market capitalization of more than $60 billion, the loss of a single E&P platform might not have much of an impact on the stock price, but as a test case for making things happen it might provide useful data. Within minutes, video of the explosion was streaming live over the internet, going viral, hitting the newswires.

"NSNA is getting crushed. Down twelve percent as we speak. Seven billion in market cap, gone. Poof." Ivanov snapped his fingers, looking at Volk. "Do you want me to cover our short?"

Volk gave his crooked grin and asked Vicker: "What do you think, boss? We cover? Or wait for the stock to sink more?"

"How much are you up?"

"Let's see . . . we bought puts at different strike prices . . . we sold calls . . . borrowed and sold short almost two billion dollars worth of stock . . . we're up about five hundred million dollars."

Volk turned to Vicker. "Elias, what do you think? It's tempting."

"Let it ride for another couple of hours. Wish I had known."

A phalanx of waiters appeared, placing a plate before each guest.

"I hope you brought your appetites with you." Volk unfolded a linen napkin and placed it, fastidiously, in his lap. "It's lunchtime, and the Butler has outdone himself."

"Skate in brown butter," the Butler announced. "And fresh raspberries with zabaglione for after."

———————

Later that afternoon, Vicker and Gonzaga lounged at a table on the roof of the Four Seasons in Limassol, overlooking an island of secrets. As Cypriot society paraded around them, drinking French rosé and Greek ouzo, they spoke, episodically, trying to process their meeting with Parsifal and the Butler. Cypriots, like their Mediterranean cousins in Sicily, Corsica, Malta, and Sardinia, have made their ways in the world for thousands of years by being useful to potential threats and invaders. Seemingly pliable and accepting, Cypriots keep their thoughts and their closed, dark world of intermarried clans to themselves. It was no surprise to Gonzaga that Cyprus welcomed Russians—selling passports, accepting billions of dollars of bank deposits, and tolerating Cyrillic signs and menus. Extracting tolls for safe harbor and keeping confidences was good business. In a world in which the Swiss could no longer be fully trusted and even the money-grubbing Panamanians occasionally rolled over for Uncle Sam, Cyprus filled a void.

A few yards away, a dozen ballerinas sashayed in, stretching and warming up, using a handrail as a barre, while waiters moved tables to clear space on the terrace. Vicker noticed all heads turning as a hushed murmur filled the air.

"Oh look, some bigwig's about to show up," Vicker said. "Who do you think? Like the biggest rug dealer on this fucking island?"

"Rug dealers don't usually travel with bodyguards," Gonzaga snapped, pointing to a detail of armed men who had suddenly materialized.

Moments later, Volk, Ivanov, and the Butler took a table on the far side of the terrace, opposite Vicker and Gonzaga.

"Shouldn't they be sitting with us?" Vicker asked. "I thought this whole thing was about your friend sucking up to you and me."

All manner of what passed for local royalty offered fealty to the Russians. Cypriot, Greek, and Turkish politicians, local businessmen hoping for oil field service contracts, and visiting *vory*—mobsters—stopped by to pay respects. A few were invited to sit and chat for a few minutes, most received nods and were led to nearby tables.

"With Parsifal, everything is a message, and everything is theater. I suggest you sit back and pay attention."

"To what—"

"Well, you see who's approaching Fyodor?" Gonzaga pointed to a woman of a certain age dressed in a conservative suit, very fit, with curly red hair.

"Hardly seems his type," Vicker said dismissively.

"Just watch."

All three men rose, briefly, to shake hands before sitting again. Their visitor remained standing, even though there was an empty chair at their table. She spoke at Volk, nonstop, for fully five minutes. Neither Volk nor the Butler showed any reaction, until Volk stood up, abruptly, and glared at her, saying nothing, until she walked away.

"Looks like that didn't go too well," Gonzaga said. "I know this might be a lot to ask, but Elias, I'm going to need you to be charming."

Moments later, the woman had made her way across the terrace.

"*Come stai vecchio amico?*" she asked Gonzaga in melodious Italian, "How are you, old friend?"

Gonzaga gave her his most dazzling grin and a kiss on both cheeks. Part of the strangeness of this place, he thought: its capacity for an unpleasant surprise. Kathleen Harper, career foreign service, the U.S. ambassador to Cyprus. Fluent in five languages, including Russian. Not strange that she would be at the Four Seasons, but nearly beyond comprehension that she would publicly impose herself on Volk and the Butler. So much for keeping their little sojourn quiet. There was little chance of that anyway, but now the ambassador would be cabling Washington: *Gonzaga, Vicker, Volk, and the Butler. In Cyprus. Together.*

"Kathy, what an absolute delight! Allow me to introduce my friend Elias Vicker."

Harper offered Vicker a firm handshake.

"Mr. Vicker, I've read so much about you. A pleasure."

"Interesting company you keep, Kathy." Gonzaga laughed.

"A diplomat's life, Lorenzo. What brings *you* to sunny Limassol?" She looked around at the motley crew that Volk had assembled.

"We have investments on the island. Every now and again I stop in for a visit."

"And you, Mr. Vicker? Any tempting carcasses?"

"Time will tell, Ambassador, time will tell," Vicker replied, annoyed. What was it with bureaucrats that they couldn't help but disparage hedge fund guys as vultures? It wasn't as if every last one of them didn't suck blood out of taxpayers.

"If you have time for coffee while you're here, let me know." Harper handed them calling cards as she left.

"What was that about?"

"That, in the diplomatic world, is as close as you come to an ambush," said Gonzaga.

"Volk had been avoiding her, but she knew exactly how to get in front of him to deliver a message he clearly did not want to hear."

"And look, here they come."

Volk's face was a picture of barely masked rage. He helped himself to an empty seat next to Vicker.

"Mr. Vicker, do not get me wrong, I have no problem doing business with Americans. But your government—more than two hundred of my men, slaughtered by American missiles." Volk took a deep breath and clenched and unclenched his fists. "My son was murdered by the American government. And Mrs. Doubtfire here tells me to just suck it up, fog of war, mistakes were made. Fucking bitch."

"Fyodor, what happened to Anatoly and to your men was tragic, completely inexcusable—"

"Lorenzo, I suppose you are going to remind me that we are playing the long game here," said Volk, vibrating with fury. "But that was my *son*. Those were my men. Their lives were sacrificed to the naive American idea that 'democracy' will make everything better. What you people don't want to admit is that we are fighting for the same thing—to keep a mob of brutal fascistic religious crazies from controlling Syrian oil—and from controlling the Middle East. We deal in interests. Not fantasies. Your leaders have these childish notions that the Free Syrian Army or the Syrian Kurds or the Kumbaya Front will build a huge campfire and everyone will hold hands and overthrow the evil al-Assad. Fools. You have no idea of the hell that would be unleashed if al-Assad were to fall. Didn't you people learn your lesson from your misadventures in Iraq? Two hundred men. My men. *My boy.* Incinerated. Why? So your president looks like she's as tough as any man? And now this ambassador, this functionary, warning *me* off? Telling *me* not to retaliate?"

"Fyodor, can I give you a little advice?" said Vicker. "Governments are weak. And you know why? People who choose to work in government are weak—most of them wouldn't last a month in the real world. Here's how I deal with them: I nod my head, say yes, and then I do what I need to."

Volk looked at Vicker as if seeing him afresh, his rage coalescing into a hard glint of recognition and purpose.

"Exactly. Excuse my outburst. I couldn't help myself. I'm sure ours will be a fruitful partnership and we will help each other do great things."

A small orchestra appeared, seemingly out of nowhere. After playing the overture to Tchaikovsky's *Swan Lake*, a dozen ballerinas, Parsifal's personal company, sashayed into the open area in front of the bar and began to dance the lake scene, one of the most romantic and beloved pieces of choreography in history. The first act of their dance ended with a stunning performance of the famous thirty-two *fouettés en tournant*—one of the most difficult and beautiful turns in all ballet, in which the dancer turns on one toe while making fast outward and inward thrusts of her working leg at each revolution. Volk watched, entranced.

It was their second act, however, that brought him to tears. The Parsifal company's prima ballerina, in a role choreographed in 1877 by Julius Reisinger for Polina Karpakova at the Bolshoi in Moscow, danced the part of Odette, a princess who had been turned into a swan by a sorcerer. No one had any doubt that she was performing for one man alone: Volk. Who was that girl? Gonzaga wondered. Vicker merely stared at his phone, replaying the vodrone video, over and over. He could not get enough of the fact that he, Elias Vicker, had pressed the button that sent billions of dollars of value crashing into the wild seas of the North Atlantic. It was a thing of beauty: a quick, clean, way to make half a billion dollars, except that, if they had involved him from the start they could have made more. Much, much more. Quite a transformation, he thought, for a boy from the boroughs of New York. If only Dr. Kerry could see him now.

28

Hart Senate Office Building, Washington, D.C.

Greta, Don, and Tommy, in full uniform, sat in Ben's private conference room looking out at the Capitol. Greta scanned the dozens of photos on Ben's wall: Ben with Amal Clooney and Salman Rushdie; Tony Bennett with a fatherly arm around Ben; Ben flashing his megawatt professional grin with Jack Nicklaus, Elon Musk, and Franklin Graham; Ben in a Team USA jersey mugging with Kobe Bryant and LeBron James. On a corner table was a framed snapshot of the team, taken at Quam, in Afghanistan, one of the first times Greta had met them all, when Tommy brought her in to help figure out how the Taliban coordinated fighters across different insurgent groups. In the past, that photo had made her cringe. The men all looked at the camera with serious, soldierly mugs while she flashed a cheerleader's grin. But when she looked at it today, she saw something else: a lost young woman beaming with the relief that she had, maybe, finally found a family.

"You have our attention." No cornpone small talk from Ben this time.

Don had told them only that he and Greta had some urgent business to discuss.

"We lost them."

"Say what?" Tommy barked.

"Vicker and his pal Lorenzo Gonzaga slipped our net. Snuck out of Vicker's building through the garage early yesterday morning, took Vicker's plane to Geneva."

Tommy glanced at Don, then at Greta, then back. Both remained quiet.

"And how did that happen? With all the tools and manpower at your disposal, you *lost* him?" Tommy snapped.

Don could have offered an explanation. He did not. It should have occurred to him that Vicker might scoot. Ben shifted in his chair, but he looked calm. A good sign. Ben didn't seem to be sweating it.

"What does Pete say?" Ben asked.

"That Vicker just vanishes from time to time, without warning. Always with Gonzaga. Hadn't occurred to Pete that he would scamper off without minders, given his security obsession. Otherwise, Pete said he would have mentioned it. He says he takes full responsibility."

"If that's what he needs to feel important," Tommy said impatiently. "That's his prerogative. What's your last sighting."

"They stayed in Geneva for only a few hours before taking off for Tunis. The transponder went dark as soon as they touched down. That was twelve hours ago."

"A 747 flying blind . . ." said Ben.

"Not exactly," said Greta. "The pilot can see just fine, but no one can see them. A risky move, but manageable if they were not flying far—and had help from air traffic controllers at their destination."

Tommy broke the silence. "We learn more about our friend Mr. Vicker every day, don't we?"

"Like that he thinks we're all a bunch of idiots," Don said.

"I doubt he's thinking of us at all, we're the hired help," Tommy said. "Besides, you can't hide a 747 for long. We'll find out where he is soon enough."

With that, the tension in the room dissipated. Greta marveled at the way military guys could not only take bad news in stride but convince themselves it was good news. At the CIA, every little mistake would be the subject of reports and analysis, memos in personnel files, blame and recrimination. But once these guys made a decision, they didn't question their fundamental assumptions. They simply adjusted. It was all game theory: applying rigorous logic to decision-making, being realistic, choosing their best moves. They were never wrong: the battlefield just kept evolving. Was it arrogance? Self-confidence? She liked to think it was the latter. She had never met anyone with as finely calibrated a sense of risk as Tommy Taylor. Something either mattered or it didn't. It was that simple. In her experience, impossible didn't faze him. Stupid did. Tommy knew the risks. She didn't have to keep harping on them. He wasn't going to turn back. She could threaten to walk. But he would never let her. She had to trust him. There was no other way.

"Now, Don, Greta, since we're all together, I believe you owe us a briefing," Tommy said, "which is as close as I get to any real action these days. Tell me what you've been learning about Mr. Vicker and his Industrial Strategies."

"There's another thing. Did you see Drudge this morning?"

Ben winced. "About Vicker's nephew? Awful."

"It wasn't an accident," said Greta.

"He couldn't have just fired him?" Ben asked. "Damn. I didn't think Wall Street guys had the stomach for that kind of rough."

"Oscar threatened to blackmail his uncle a couple of days ago," Don said. "We overheard the call."

"What worries me," said Ben, "isn't so much that he had the desire to have his nephew knocked off, but that he knows how to find the real professionals who can do those jobs."

"Or Gonzaga does. I've been digging into Agency files to see if anything comes up," Greta continued. "He keeps a very low public profile, but he's been on various watch lists—ours, FBI, Treasury—for years. Whenever the Vatican Bank is accused of money laundering, which is pretty much continuously, Lorenzo Gonzaga pops up to run interference. The most attention he ever drew to himself was when he was allegedly the kingpin behind major frauds at Allard Frères, but set up his protégé to take the fall."

Greta flashed a larger than life-size photograph of Lorenzo Gonzaga on a screen that nearly filled one wall: a long, slightly weary face, deeply lined, tanned, his thinning gray hair combed straight back, curling slightly around his ears. She then overlaid an infographic showing Gonzaga's connections to international nodes of money and power.

"I know that guy. Lorenzo, or Enzo, as he asked me to call him," Ben said, excited. "My grandmother had a phrase for guys like him, 'made of silk.' Knows everyone—here, Europe, Latin America, everywhere. Throws around an awful lot of money. If he considers that you're worthy, there's no favor he won't do for you."

"In the geometry of Industrial Strategies, Gonzaga is our Euclid," said Greta. "If you want to know how a damaged loser like Vicker ends up sitting on half a trillion dollars, there's your answer . . . and here, gents, is my presentation."

Greta added a graph showing monthly returns from an investment in Industrial Strategies, very nearly a straight line of profits reported over several decades. Precious few months registered even a small loss.

"The way I see it, Gonzaga uses his connections, particularly inside central banks, governments around the world, and securities regulators, to obtain information. He and Vicker almost always trade offshore, going to great lengths to avoid regulators getting wind of what they are doing. But I wanted to show you one of their earliest schemes, so you have an idea how . . . creative Gonzaga is."

She replaced the graph on Ben's wall with a flow chart. Dozens of boxes contained company names, all connected by solid lines, dotted lines, and arrows. Using a laser pointer, Greta drew circles around the names of the first two companies Vicker created after meeting Gonzaga: Industrial Strategies, which he registered in the Cayman Islands, and Eastern Plate Capital Ltd., a Delaware-incorporated broker-dealer. Broker-dealers can trade directly on U.S. stock and commodities exchanges. As "dealers," they can trade discreetly with other broker-dealers and with banks. As "brokers," they can stand between customers and the exchanges, charging brokerage commissions to customers. They can also share those commissions with big banks, other brokerage firms, and middlemen, and refund commissions to their own customers, if it suits them. Operating together, Industrial Strategies and Eastern Plate would be able to trade directly and indirectly with each other, seamlessly moving money and commission dollars from one entity to the other—and back. "Domiciling Industrial Strategies offshore allows Vicker to accept money from non-U.S. investors—and to remain one step removed from the U.S. regulatory net. We think that at first—and until Vicker built up a track record—the only investor was Gonzaga."

She wrote Gonzaga's name across the top of the board, sketched a box around it, and drew a solid line with an arrow from his name to a box below it labelled "IS." She placed a dollar sign next to the line. She then drew another box to the right of Gonzaga's name and labelled it "Mr. X," drawing a dotted line from Mr. X to Gonzaga's box.

"Vicker and Gonzaga play lots of games. I'll take you through one that they've used time and again in different forms. Let's say that Gonzaga has a 'friend' who is a trader on the NYMEX. The 'friend' just happens to get all his financing from Gonzaga via his bank." She pointed to the board. "Call him Mr. X."

The New York Mercantile Exchange, or NYMEX, is where companies and investors buy and sell all manner of commodities—coal, crude oil, heating oil, gasoline, palladium, silver, chromium, platinum, and uranium.

"As Mr. X's banker, Gonzaga has access to all kinds of information about Mr. X's business. The dotted line represents a flow of information from

Mr. X to Gonzaga. But let's just say Mr. X is only too happy to let Gonzaga know when he has a large order from an industrial company or a major fleet operator—like United Parcel Service—to buy gasoline.

"If Mr. X executes a large order well—which is what his clients pay him to do—market prices will not move. In that case, the client saves money. But, if a large order is executed poorly, or if Mr. X fills it in an intentionally clumsy way, the price might move higher. Perhaps a lot higher—at least temporarily. In a classic front-running scheme, if Gonzaga tips off Vicker before Mr. X starts buying gas, Eastern Plate could load up on gas—on behalf of IS—before Mr. X starts buying for his corporate customer. When Mr. X starts buying enough gas for his customer, prices go up, Vicker reverses the trade and sells the gasoline at a profit. In the process, Eastern Plate makes money because IS pays it commissions for buying and selling the gas, and IS makes money because the price of gas goes up. UPS loses money because it has to pay more for gas, but maybe not enough to notice and stop working with Mr. X."

"How does Mr. X get duked for tipping off Gonzaga?" Ben asked.

"Vicker shares half of East Plate's commissions for buying and selling the gas with Mr. X's brother-in-law—who just happens to own another broker-dealer, but based offshore, in London, and domiciled in Malta."

"Exactly how terrorists do it," said Don. "Multiple chains of companies, apparently unconnected, but with common, informal, links."

"True enough. Sad thing is that none of these techniques are new. Most of these schemes for moving money were invented by our very own best and brightest," Tommy remarked.

The source DNA—the *Australopithecus*—of contemporary insider trading, money laundering, and hedge fund technology could be traced back to pre–WWII spooks working for the Office of Strategic Services. Wild Bill Donovan hired Ivy League–educated Wall Street bankers and white-shoe lawyers to concoct elaborate subterfuges for making, hiding, and moving money in support of clandestine networks. They used tools at hand, tools they well understood: companies domiciled in multiple jurisdictions; purchases and sales of stocks, bonds, and commodities; obscure banks—some of them invented just for their use. None of the individual elements were terribly complicated or secret in themselves, but, in various arcane combinations, virtually impenetrable.

"Terrorist groups, Bulgarian hackers, Russians trolls, Chinese girls with PhDs from Georgetown, they've all picked up where our spooks left off, creating networks and structures built on these rather antique and primitive constructs."

"I don't want to oversell what we've unearthed so far in Vicker's trading history. There are a lot of different versions of trading on information. Not all of them are illegal per se, and Vicker seems to have tried to steer clear of the most obviously criminal. One of his persistent gambits has been mis-marking his portfolio, to make his results very, very consistent. Less volatile."

Investment funds reported the value of their portfolios to investors on a regular basis, usually every month, but no less frequently than every quarter. "Marking" means putting a value on every individual asset or security in the portfolio. Mis-marking involved assigning a market value that was either higher or lower than the actual value, to manipulate how much profit or loss is reported.

"How can people get away with that? Aren't prices published every second of every day?" asked Ben.

"Depends on the asset, and, for example, whether they can claim a liquidity discount or a control premium. Hedge funds rely on an entire industry of consultants that helps them 'massage' the value of the assets in their portfolios—always looking for the happy ending."

"What about the public accounting firms that audit hedge funds? Aren't auditors paid to ferret out this kind of soft fraud and misdirection?" Ben asked.

"Who do you think pays the accounting firms and the valuation 'consultants'?" Don interjected.

"And I'd just like to point out that the little gimmick I described a few minutes ago—using a broker-dealer to launder commission dollars—no longer works in exactly the same way. The regulators got wise to it. But using offshore companies to do the same thing works just fine."

Being domiciled offshore also made it easier for Vicker to deal with foreign companies owned by friends—like Gonzaga. Sometimes he would sell a small piece of an investment to a friendly fund at the "wrong" price just before the end of the month to be able to use that price as a "mark." Vicker also paid finder's fees, and consulting fees and set up an offshore brokerage firm to build up a slush fund that could be used to rebate money directly to IS in order to offset a bad month.

Ben made the time-out sign with his hands.

"I see the potential for manipulation and obfuscation, and I understand the desire to pay people for useful information. But why go to such lengths just to show that returns don't vary much from month to month? What's wrong with making five percent one month and losing two percent the next? If the returns are good, who cares if you make twelve percent per year by earning one percent a month or twelve percent a year by earning two percent in one month and losing one percent the next? The money still spends the same."

Ben, of course, was right as a matter of arithmetic, but a different logic governed the decisions of big investors, Greta thought, especially sovereign wealth funds and university endowments. Financial markets were, by their very nature, volatile. Prices could move dramatically, hour-by-hour, day-by-day. Investors loved volatility when it made them money, but losing money made people crazy. Chief investment officers *hated* volatility, because, sooner or later, it meant a frantic call from the board of trustees or the politicians at the top of the public pension fund food chain. Nobody wanted that call. Investors paid a lot for the illusion of steady, consistent profits.

Tommy's phone pinged. His expression barely changed, but the tone of his voice brought them all up short. "Lost . . . and found. A flare from our ambassador in Cyprus." Deadpan, he held it up for them all to see: photos of Vicker and Gonzaga, with Fyodor Volk in the background, on the terrace at the Four Seasons, just a few hours earlier.

Greta did the sums: so she *had* been right about Oscar. And now, Vicker, IS, and Gonzaga, all connected to Volk. And Volk connected, inextricably, to all of them.

"*Great.*" Don spat into a plastic bottle. "Just fucking *great.*"

Tommy held up a hand. "Does this change anything?" He looked to Greta. "Seems like a lot of coincidence—the way Volk keeps popping up in our lives. Syria. Latvia. Now palling around with our target. Think hard before you answer."

Greta didn't say anything for a moment. She couldn't help thinking that it was one thing to infiltrate a hedge fund that made its fortune from seemingly victimless crimes like money laundering and insider trading, but that the introduction of the Parsifal Group changed the game from checkers to Go. Or, perhaps, it had been Go all along and they had misread it. This would be a good time, she thought, to be more like Tommy and attempt to reframe potentially bad news not as disaster, but as opportunity. "Greta?"

"No, sir, I don't think it changes anything for us. In fact, it might even make it easier for us to move our funds into Industrial Strategies."

"Damn right it does. It might not be our first choice, but when a Russian businessman who's only a few Treasury Department red flags away from ending up on a sanctions list takes a major position in the world's largest hedge fund, that's a table we need to be at. Nice work, Greta. If you told me you meant to make this happen, I'd put you up for a medal."

Tommy's approval always made Greta feel good. But this time, she found it hard to share his enthusiasm. Volk had snuck up on them from behind. If Tommy thought he could still back out, Volk's sudden appearance changed that. The predator was inside their house. They'd left themselves exposed. Tommy would counter that and say no, they had flushed Volk out. That's what a successful operation does: it creates enough chaos to draw out adversaries and opportunities.

Until she met Elias Vicker, she'd assumed, without giving it much thought, that she would never meet anyone richer than Tommy. Or someone who cared less about money. He worked harder than anyone she had ever met, but that's not why he was worth somewhere in the high nine figures. A generation of tech entrepreneurs had cut in Tommy on their financing early rounds. In return, he offered advice and mentorship, but, mostly, they wanted his occasional presence and attention, ascribing to him near-mystical powers as a summoner of unicorns. Tommy had money. But she wondered if he really understood what people will do to get as rich as Tommy had become without really trying.

Greta had not debriefed Tommy as thoroughly on Volk as she would have liked to. But she couldn't. Tommy needed to be blind to a certain spectrum of Volk's activities. But Greta could never say she didn't know what she was getting into. That night in Jūrmala, she'd run one of her standard routines on Volk: *Tell me a story about yourself.* In spycraft, it's called elicitation: get them talking about themselves while revealing as little as possible about yourself. You need to build trust, acting interested in them in a way that makes them interested in you. The first thing a person decides to tell you about themselves says a lot about who they are. Volk told her about the day his dreams froze.

As a young man, Volk had entered the service of his nation with a sense of privilege and idealism. The Communist Party, which controlled and degraded every aspect of Russian life, had evaporated. The future was unwritten. Russians were hopeful. For the first time in generations, a bright young man could look forward to an exciting future. Volk had excelled at High School #281, where Saint Petersburg's smartest boys received elite educations and were funneled into the management caste of the state bureaucracies, which, though crumbling, still controlled the vast wealth of the nation. But Volk craved a different life. One with purpose and adventure. When a recruiter from the Soviet Committee for State Security—the KGB, later reconstituted as the Federal Security Service—approached him, he jumped at the chance, though his classmates and teachers thought he was crazy. Why would this man with so much potential want to attach himself to the reviled organ of a dying state?

But Volk saw something else. In his hometown, the KGB was as powerful as ever, though less visible than in the terrifying days of midnight raids and forced confessions, when every Russian lived in fear of unannounced visits from men with no names. As Volk came of age, democracy seemed within reach and a folk song army strummed guitars in front of city hall and poets ran for office talking about freedom and dignity, but behind the scenes, the secret policemen made common cause with the criminal mobs that had grown fat and powerful through the Soviet collapse. The parasites had invaded their host. Now they were looting the hospital.

The alliance was inevitable. There was no instruction manual for throwing out Karl Marx and replacing him with Adam Smith overnight. The only two groups that actually understood capitalism, and had the expertise to quickly adapt to a free-enterprise—free-for-all—system were the spymasters and Mafia dons. The KGB had been studying Western financial markets for decades and had moles in banking and financial circles throughout Europe and America. Since at least 1987, when Mikhail Gorbachev waved the white flag of glasnost, the well-organized, well-informed men who managed the Kremlin's secrets had been preparing for a post-Soviet future. The system might be dying but there was no reason they should suffer. They knew where all the bodies were buried—and, more important, where the money was. As the empire entered its terminal stage, they stole the nation blind and built a well-concealed secret worldwide banking network to hide their spoils. As ever, Gonzaga, and his cohort, were there to guide and enable. As for the criminals, as the old system crumbled, the Mafia dons had filled the vacuum with a violent, homegrown capitalism, enforced by their own vicious, and very effective, forms of social and economic control. Even if there had been a functioning legal system, it wouldn't have stood a chance.

Volk did not, exactly, understand all this at the time, but he had the sense to make the contrarian bet and accept the offer of the KGB recruiters, in part because he was familiar with the legend of a local boy made good: Vladimir Putin, a mid-level KGB officer who'd grown up in Saint Petersburg, and who had come back home from his posting in East Germany after the Berlin Wall fell. Putin quickly became one of the most powerful men in Saint Petersburg, consigliere to Anatoly Sobchak, the city's charismatic mayor, who gained power by co-opting the idealists while quietly allowing Putin to "manage" organized crime's takeover of city hall. Barely a decade later, Putin was on the verge of succeeding Boris Yeltsin.

After completing his training, Volk joined a secret military detachment that "monitored" events in Chechnya and reported directly to the highest levels in the Kremlin. Many careers had been destroyed by the botched operation at the Dubrovna, but that was when Volk's took off. Once Putin won his second term and consolidated his power and he began to systematically plunder the nation's wealth, Volk was tapped to serve as a sort of advance man for Kremlin interests, traveling Russia's vast footprint to ensure that the Kremlin got its way in matters involving money and politics: removing political irritants and any other obstacles blocking the way of favored candidates and businessmen. To that point, his career had gone exactly as he had hoped. He was not proud of everything he'd done, but he felt he was serving the general cause of greater Russia: that he was on the right side of history. The nation needed an enlightened strongman, a leader who would push the nation into the future, by whatever means necessary. And an enlightened strongman needed a corps of strong, equally enlightened officers—fierce, loyal, and lethal. Men like Fyodor Volk.

That illusion served him well until he got to Norilsk, an arctic wasteland where the seasons broke down to nine months of frigid gloom and three months of late evening sun and horseflies. Until the early 1930s, the only permanent residents of Norilsk were prisoners sent to the labor camps there and the poor souls who guarded them. The prisoners, at least, had a chance of leaving. Then Stalin, eyeing the region's endless mineral deposits, decided to rebrand the sorry outpost as a worker's paradise. The new Soviet man himself would be mined and refined in those icy reaches. Thousands of families were lured north with the promise of jobs and a life of dignity and purpose. What they got instead was one of the most toxic environments yet created by mankind, where eating the mushrooms locals loved to forage from hillside forests was forbidden on account of the toxins that had leached from the mines into the region's earth, air, and water. As if to mock anyone who bought into the lie, Norilsk had a way to remind the transplants of their tragic gullibility on a daily basis: There was no escape. The only roads out of town led to factories and smelters that belched toxic smoke, before dead-ending into grim mining colonies that teetered at the edge of the open pits slashed into endless tundra.

The KGB had sent Volk to Norilsk to meet a British businessman who owned a controlling stake in a nearby palladium mine, making him a local hero in both Norilsk and Davos. The capital came from a respected London syndicate and carried with it the promise of Western standards, not just of professional management, transparency, and creditworthiness, but also worker safety and fairness. *The Economist* hailed it as a new model of foreign investment in Russia—a harbinger of greater freedoms and rapid economic development. But the deal offended local sensibilities, at least those having to do with property rights and the rule of law. When the investor tried to withdraw a portion of his profits, he was told no. When the investor sued, his case disappeared into the morass of the Russian courts. It wasn't until he traveled to Norilsk and announced a press conference for the next day that he finally got results. An official, ostensibly from the Kremlin's foreign investment office, would stop by his hotel suite for a quiet talk. Perhaps something could be worked out.

Volk had no qualms about killing the man. That was part of his training. It was not up to him to decide whether an extrajudicial killing was justified. Some were. Some weren't. The dissonance came from what he learned about money. In the new Russia, as in the old, money itself was virtually worthless. What mattered was access and influence. Someone could always decide that you had no right to your own property; if they had enough influence, they could always get a court to agree with them. Now that this new world had revealed itself to Volk, he vowed to behave accordingly. The only way to make anything yours in Putin's Russia was to steal it. And the only way to hang on to what you'd stolen was to keep stealing it. That, he explained to Greta, was really what money laundering was, stealing stolen proceeds from anyone who might attempt to put the capital to legitimate use, a victimless crime in which every citizen, if not the entirety of civil society itself, was the victim. Once you were in the game, you had to keep stealing. Stealing the money you had already stolen, so you could steal more money and use that money to buy more power, and use that power to steal more money. You could never rest. Survival mode.

Tommy leaned back in his chair. The issue of Volk was closed. Greta was relieved Tommy was changing the subject, but she was hardly off the hook. She understood Tommy's implicit directive: *Don't tell me anything more about your dealings with Volk, but make sure he is contained. I'm trusting you.*

"How are things working out in Latvia? Any problems there?" Another curveball. She clamped down on her rising anxiety and shut off the impulse to hit the streets and hunt for emotional release. The pallets were still in the caves. She'd hoped Tommy wouldn't ask for details. "Just a few more weeks. A lot of red tape. It's taking a while."

"Get it moving," Tommy said impatiently. "We'll need to start making some big withdrawals. Even before Ben formally declares this fall, we're launching a couple of super PACs—a lot of policy stuff, white papers no one will ever read, but we have to do it. We pay the wonks who write it very well—by wonk standards, that is—which means no academic or intellectual wants to get crosswise with us. And we have to start on the infrastructure: seeding grassroots organizations, building our databases, constructing geo-targeting algorithms for fifty states. And new tech for oppo research. It's a big ticket."

"Oppo is Pete's baby," Ben chimed in. "I told him that we need to build our own NSA. Tommy said he'd help."

Tommy's friend in Vail was developing a program that would go far beyond the capabilities of any previous presidential campaign: state grade, maybe better. Superior even to the Israeli Pegasus-3 software that was so simple that Mohammed bin Salman himself was said to have used it to gain access to his friend Jeff Bezos's cell phone by attaching a malware-infested video to an innocuous WhatsApp message. When MBS met Bezos in the spring of 2018, he'd been on a goodwill tour of the United States, dining with actors, politicians, and power brokers in New York, Washington, Silicon Valley, and Hollywood. The young leader had presumably swapped phone numbers with them all, opening a swath of the richest and most powerful Americans to extortion scams similar to the one the Saudis were said to have run on Bezos, which included leaking stolen text messages to influence the outcome of an important business negotiation to bring Amazon to Saudi Arabia.

Tommy wanted to go even further, mounting a similar operation in the political world. Opposition research was generally understood to be about collecting *kompromat* to embarrass a rival. Tommy framed a more expansive approach: It was also about shaping the central battlefield of a political campaign, the information space. It was psychological warfare. On the most basic level, in a close race, a leak about a campaign manager's crushing gambling debt a week before election day would degrade a campaign's operating abilities at a crucial moment, throwing it into disarray as the campaign scrambled to react.

For Tommy, such serendipitous one-offs weren't nearly enough. Starting immediately, Tommy's team would build a secret tech unit to target family, friends, and all known associates of Ben's potential adversaries, as well as anyone who might work for their campaigns—from volunteer envelope lickers all the way up to the most trusted advisers. Tommy's digital tools would provide a fully stocked and regularly replenished arsenal of weapons-grade dirt. Not just cancel-worthy bunker busters like sexting chains with teenage girls, but a constant supply of one-day stories, mortars lobbed over the fortress walls: a spouse's extravagant Amex bills; travel manifests revealing rides on private planes belonging to oil executives; an anti-Semitic joke the wunderkind policy wonk posted on a long-archived frat house message board; security cam photos of a sanctimonious evangelical power broker loading up on edibles at a Nevada cannabis dispensary. Once the leaks started, they would never stop. Wave after wave. The goal was to heighten the mistrust and dysfunction that were endemic to all political campaigns, but raise them to intolerable levels, keeping everyone on the other side off-balance, frightened, and demoralized. And claiming as many scalps as possible along the way.

"I'd just like to make it clear that I have no idea what Tommy's talking about," Ben said.

Don looked disgusted. "All this makes me want to vomit. In a civilized country, a presidential campaign would take three months and involve nothing more than candidates telling voters what they plan to do—and voters deciding which plan they prefer. Anything more is just a personality cult."

"You think I like it?" Ben said, surprisingly snappish. He paused for a moment and continued, turning from Don, focusing on Greta.

"Just so you're aware of the timeline," said Ben. "Six months from today, I'll be officially announcing that I'm *un*officially running. Pete is arranging for Vicker to host an event for us—someplace in Greenwich Village. The Striped Pony, I think it's called, sixty-five bucks for a bowl of mac and cheese. I told the chef she should add some fried Spam. She loved the idea."

"A bowl of Spam and roomful of billionaires," Don cracked. "Ben Corn's recipe for world domination. What if everyone's sick of you by the time the primaries start?"

"We've thought about that. But waiting means losing control of the key variables. It's the kind of fancy thinking I hate—thinking we can catch a falling knife. But I want to get out there first and stake my claim to the nomination. Make the money guys think that they've got to jump onboard or be left behind."

While Ben talked, Don sat stiffly in his chair, and Greta uneasily looked out the window.

"Are we just going to skip over what just happened?" Don asked. "You're saying this is good news? We already knew Vicker and Gonzaga have people killed and are somehow tied up in financing terrorists. And now we find they go on beach vacations with one of Putin's top henchmen?"

Tommy understood their apprehension, but cut Don off. "We all deal with bad people every day," he said flatly. "That's our job."

"Except that here we are not just dealing. We are contemplating a hostile takeover of a criminal enterprise, and this Putin henchman, by the way, is also laundering the money we stole from our own government. A bit different, no?"

"In the interest of national security? What's criminal?" Ben looked at

Tommy. "General Taylor puts his magic cape over it, mutters the right in-cantations, and tells the busybodies to look the other way. We crack a couple of bad eggs. So what?"

Tommy gestured, a throat slash, to bring the conversation to a close.

"If you think I'm deterred by any of this, I'm not," Tommy said, without a hint of threat or aggression. He'd made up his mind and was just stating his position, like it was any other data point in his decision matrix. To his mind, what had begun as an extremely speculative foray that involved lots of moving parts, was going well, better than he had expected. They had infiltrated IS and knew how it ran. Don had, against all odds, managed to create cache houses with enough ordnance to fight a small war, and they had mounting—damning—evidence of dozens of crimes for when-ever they needed to exert leverage over their quarry. Money laundering alone offered prosecutors two hundred predicates. Weapons charges cre-ated even more vulnerability. Thinking ahead, toward a point at which they might decide to take IS over completely, neither Vicker nor Gon-zaga would have much choice but to take whatever deal was on offer. Of course, there would be loose ends. There always were. Vicker had proved himself unpredictable, and Tommy felt some unease at Gonzaga's ambigu-ous, complicated role. The emergence of Fyodor Volk could be seen as troubling. Or as a rare opportunity. It was too early to tell. But, overall, Tommy's concerns were minor in comparison to the prize, and he felt an urgency. They needed an operating base, and they didn't have time to build one from scratch.

Don was about to speak. Ben stopped him.

"Every time we've ever contemplated something ambitious, there's been a moment like this, when one of us wanted to pull the plug. Always for a good reason, which is why I like these conversations. Keeps us thinking about the risks. But either way, I think we've played out the line on this conversation. We're past the point of second-guessing or even thinking we can walk away. Greta's friend Volk decided that for us when he crashed our party. He's not going to leave until he sees what's in the goody bag."

He bored in on Don and Greta.

"So here's what I'm going to say. You know how you're always complain-ing Tommy never leaves you alone? Here's your chance. I need you guys to handle Volk. Any way you see fit. Just keep me and Tommy out of it."

His face snapped back to its regular countenance of sunny competence, and he turned to Tommy for the final word.

"And one more thing," Tommy said, "I shouldn't have to say this . . ."

"But you will . . ."

"Don't lose track of Vicker, or Gonzaga, again."

29

Limassol, Cyprus

After the ballet, Volk whisked them back to the *Better Place*. Vicker and Gonzaga watched as the Butler ladled his own variation of bouillabaisse into warm bowls. Ivanov poured ice-cold vodka.

"Mr. Vicker, I am interested to know your reaction to what we discussed at lunch. How can we work together?" Volk asked.

"Lorenzo and I have been talking about nothing else. You got me thinking about how Perrow includes 'tightly coupled' systems in his definition of 'normal accidents.' So I spent the afternoon reading up on some related ideas. One is 'network effect' and the other is 'disaster creep.' The 'normal accident' idea is neat, but we may as well work on accidents that ripple, causing potentially catastrophic effects. Let's call them normal, networked catastrophes."

Volk nodded: his pupil was catching on. Network effect and disaster creep were the logical extrapolations of Perrow's insights. In the decades since 1984, when he first published his research, every man-made system on earth had become infinitely more complex and ever more tightly coupled to other systems. Back then, for instance, local electric utilities were still controlled by human beings who looked at dials and gauges, turned knobs and flipped breakers and switches. Thirty-five years later, human operators were pretty much along for the ride. In the name of efficiency, utilities relied more and more on "smart"—tightly coupled—computer programs that talked to one another and taught themselves by employing artificial intelligence algorithms. But that was just the system effect. The network effect arose from the fact that each utility's "smart" software talked—or tried to talk—directly to the software of other utilities, educating and learning from one another. American utilities might be legally separate, but, as a practical matter, they operate as one huge network. Every country had organized the same way, and, in Europe, transnationally. Those interconnections mean that, when accidents happen and disasters occur, they tend to be bigger. In academic lingo: disaster creep.

"For the sake of conversation, in the U.S., most electric and gas utilities are public companies," said Vicker, fairly vibrating with excitement, his left eye twitching involuntarily, cracking his knuckles unconsciously. "People can buy and sell their stocks and bonds. What if it's a hot summer and a transformer explodes? Maybe it is no big deal. Happens all the time. What if three explode? Or five? What if major transmission lines are damaged? What if, at the same time, one of the power lines overheats and fuses and an LNG tanker on 'shore' power loses the juice it needs to keep the gas cool? What if it explodes and takes out a nearby generating station? What if all that prevents the utility from supplying power to major industrial companies—so that factories have to shut down?"

Vicker, on a roll, stopped for a breath. In thirty seconds, he had drawn a roadmap for the guys who could make all those things happen. A series of improbable, fat-tail events occurring in quick succession—all "normal accidents"—equipment failures, human errors, one thing building on the next, rippling through the electrical grid and the economy.

"The utilities would face huge losses, industrial customers would lose sales, cities and states would lose tax revenue. Someone insures the LNG tanker, we can make money there too. Stock prices will drop. We can short every company connected to that . . . catastrophe," Ivanov volunteered.

"Well, done, Vadim," said Vicker.

"Ah, Elias," said Volk. "We have so much to talk about. The more that you can explain to us how you will make money under different conditions, the more effective we can be. Also, we need to understand how *we* will make money. Vadim, pour please." Volk chugged a shot. "But, even more important. I want to invest in Industrial Strategies, and maybe bring along a few friends. Also . . . how do you call it? Coinvestment rights if we want to supersize a trade."

"What size were you thinking?" asked Vicker.

"One point five billion from Parsifal, another two billion for some good friends. Let's say we need twenty-five billion dollars of capacity to start. But we could be much, much bigger."

"One thing we don't want to do is to dilute your—and our—returns," said Ivanov. "Depending on how things go, it might make sense to redeem some of your current investors."

The bear hug. Did Vicker have any idea what was happening? Gonzaga wondered. They do you a couple of favors, start with smallish investments, and then move in for a full takeover. For now, though, he felt relaxed for the first time since touching down in Cyprus. Vicker seemed to have passed the first test. Vicker may not have been the genius investor that the world imagined, but he did understand financial instruments, how to trade stocks, bonds, options, futures, commodities, ETFs, foreign exchange, CBOs, CDOs. All part of his tool kit. What he could not do well was to sort good investments from bad, but that was where Gonzaga, and now Volk, came in.

"I'd be cautious about kicking out other investors too quickly," Gonzaga said carefully, thinking about how Wennerström might react to being booted: not well. But Vicker waved him off.

"We can handle that," said Vicker. He picked up where they had left off earlier, discussing Union Carbide and the gas leak at Bhopal. How hard could it be to get toxic gas to leak, particularly in a hopelessly corrupt country like India? What other factories? What other countries? He compiled a quick mental list of other events that would have created opportunities for tidy little trades: Tesco's "beef" burgers made of horse meat. Cancer-causing bromate in Coca-Cola's Dasani water. The *Exxon Valdez* running aground on the Alaskan coast. All of those happened in the ordinary course of human invention and error, but they could also be made to happen systematically. Large industrial, energy, food, and drug companies would be particularly vulnerable because of their size and the dispersion of their operations around the globe. In companies with tens of thousands of employees, the likelihood was high that, at any given moment, somebody, somewhere was doing something really stupid.

"Elias, the Parsifal Group has many developing countries as satisfied customers. Sasha and Fyodor only operate at the highest levels—presidents, finance ministers, military brass," observed Gonzaga.

Vicker was nearly drooling with excitement. Countries were the last frontier of opacity; anyone who could penetrate the deliberations of presidents, central bankers, and finance ministers would have the field to themselves. He and Gonzaga had already dabbled, successfully, in currency manipulation, but no major plays as yet. Certainly not like the clever guy who had shorted more New Zealand dollars—kiwis—than the entire money supply of the country, causing a massive crash. The trick would be knowing how a country, a central bank, would respond if its currency was attacked. But there were so many other ways to make money if you "knew" how a government would react to a crisis. If an Italian bank got into trouble, would it be allowed to fail or would the government pump money in to save it? When Greece was on the verge of bankruptcy, would the all-powerful bureaucrats who run the European Union let it go under or bail it out? And how about that Argentine nut job, Cristina Kirchner? Would she pay off pesky creditors who were suing Argentina's ass or keep digging the country in deeper by telling them to pound sand? Or, if you had the ear of a Mexican president, perhaps you'd be massively short bonds of the state-owned oil company, Pemex, just before an unanticipated default.

While Volk and the Butler were taking in Vicker's monologue, listening carefully and watching him closely, Ivanov looked at cross-referenced lists: countries in which they did business, countries with which Russia had particularly close relationships, countries where the political class was so completely venal that anyone and anything could be had for a price. They were not short lists. He looked up from his tablet.

"Transparency International ranks one hundred eighty countries from high to low on a corruption scale. We can deliver whatever you want in one hundred forty-six of the one hundred eighty. The other thirty-four are possible to a greater or lesser degree," said Ivanov, playing to his boss. "Even America."

Gonzaga, who had been largely silent, chimed in. "A surprise devaluation of a currency—particularly in a country that did not really need to do it—could be hugely profitable. The best victim would be a country with a large, liquid foreign exchange market, because our trading would be less visible. Not a complete basket case like Nicaragua or El Salvador. A pretty big economy, like Colombia or Brazil."

"Nice thing about bad stuff happening in third world countries is that no one will be surprised, and no one cares," said Vicker. "Business as usual. The Securities and Exchange Commission doesn't give a rat's ass if the Mexican peso crashes and burns."

"What about network effects after a currency event?" asked Volk.

"Plenty," responded Vicker.

The whole point of a devaluation, particularly a large—or "maxi"—devaluation is to cause the value of the local currency to drop precipitously. Usually it is for a good reason, like making local exporters more competitive.

If someone knew in advance, not only could they make money by shorting the currency, but much of, say, the Mexican economy would be affected. Because Mexican imports would immediately become more expensive and exports cheaper in terms of U.S. dollars and euros, some companies would suffer, and others profit. People would lose their jobs, there would be social unrest and rioting. Maybe the market for their hard currency debt would crap out, so they could make money by shorting bonds as well.

"We can be short and long the stock of different Mexican and Western companies that will be affected," said Vicker, eyes opened wide. "Some of the Mexican banks will be totally fucked by a devaluation, might go belly-up."

With no small surprise, Vicker found himself laughing, smiling broadly, gesticulating vigorously, and the tone of his voice rose as he built to a point. He didn't have to fake it, to suppress the glee he took in this conversation about creating mayhem and profiting from chaos. He dropped his efforts to control his face, his body. He became aware that, suddenly, he felt strangely free. Like he was finally among people with whom he could communicate on a deep level. People who embraced aggressive tactics. People not bound by bourgeois morality. People who could blow an oil platform out of the water, killing dozens of people, and go on enjoying their meal. His kind of guys. Even better: now, finally, after years of taking direction from a supercilious Gonzaga and an invisible Wennerström, he was in the driver's seat.

"Fyodor, before this lovely vodka goes to our heads, Elias and I brought you a boat-warming gift." Gonzaga gestured to one of the boatswains, who brought over the small crate that he and Vicker had brought from Geneva. Volk popped the brass clasps on the sides of the box to reveal the Rachel Ruysch still life, the Butler peering over his shoulder. Volk gasped.

"Gentlemen, I will not pretend that you shouldn't have—of course you shouldn't have, but thank you. This is beyond beautiful. Exquisite. A gem. Ruysch, correct? One of your many women." Volk beamed at Gonzaga, then turned toward Vicker. "I have learned so much about art from Lorenzo. It saddens me that my current circumstances, sanctions and what not," he said, with a casual flick of his hand, "prevent me from traveling as much as I would like. All the more precious that you bring such beauty to me. Here."

He lifted the painting, lovingly, and propped it up so that they could all see it better. Gonzaga had spent hour after hour with Volk touring the Hermitage in Saint Petersburg, and, returning the favor, giving him private tours of the Berninis at the Galleria Borghese, meditating under the Pantheon's dome, and meandering through the Uffizi. Now, against the glow of Rachel Ruysch's luminous flowers, they plotted cunning schemes to rupture the fabric of civilization. Over several hours, with Ivanov at his tablet maintaining a spreadsheet detailing their plans, five conspirators ranged widely over the means, merits, and risks of creating opportunities for profit, sorting and refining by geography, scale, and network effects to achieve the most efficient allocations of capital—and to minimize the probability of piquing the curiosity of regulators and law enforcement.

As they were winding down, pleased with themselves after a solid evening of effort, Volk yawned and stretched. Gonzaga recognized the tell: here it comes, he thought. What he's really after.

"Elias, there is one particular project we would like your help with." He nodded toward Ivanov. "We have developed expertise in demolition and bought up a handful of small and midsize contractors in the Middle East, Eastern Europe, South America, and Asia. Vadim thinks that with the right firm heading the charge, we can 'roll up' the demo business. Become the dominant international player, the Waste Management of demolition."

In the lingo of investors, a "roll-up" meant buying many smaller companies in the same industry and merging them into a single, much larger enterprise. The goal was to focus on a fragmented industry and to make the business more efficient by achieving economies of scale, but also, ultimately, to be able to charge higher prices because there would be fewer competitors. Waste Management, one of the most successful roll-ups in business history, started when a couple of garbagemen began buying hundreds of small-time garbage collectors in the 1970s and 1980s, eventually becoming a $50 billion business.

"We got interested because our military engineers have developed fantastic technology in various war zones," Ivanov explained. "We bought out a Bulgarian demo company with fifty million dollars in revenue and replaced management, we took over the assets of a Syrian outfit, then a Hungarian firm. We are already up to five hundred million in annual sales, but it could be six, seven billion in revenue very quickly. Then we would have real pricing power."

"Demolition also fits well with the primary business of the Parsifal Group," the Butler added. "Government contracts, cleaning up ruined cities." And, of course, what he did not mention was that owning an international demolition business would provide a convenient, legitimate front for Parsifal, enabling it to move men, machines—and money—anywhere in the world at a moment's notice.

The hair on the back of Gonzaga's neck bristled. Where, he wondered, did this idea *really* come from? It made sense that the Parsifal Group, with its massive cash flow from private military operations and, now, exploration and production of oil, would want to invest and diversify. But the combination of Fyodor Volk and demolition made him nervous. Vicker, not sensing trouble, seemed happy to oblige his new friends.

"Why not?" said Vicker. "We have to put our profits somewhere, and I have one last question for this evening. How do we coordinate? Making things happen and profiting from them will require a lot of communication."

"By secure means only," offered Ivanov. "We cannot rely on electronic or telephonic means. Not even Signal, or Silent. Certainly not WhatsApp."

Vicker snickered. "I've learned that lesson."

"Major Ivanov will be your point of contact. One-on-one. You tell him what you want. He tells me. And vice versa. No need to write anything down. He is a clean skin, can go anywhere. A Princeton boy," said Volk, not without pride. His second son, and, now, his only son.

Volk rose.

"Gentlemen, it has been a long day. Vadim, please ferry Elias to the hotel. I need a few minutes with Lorenzo and Sasha, old business." He gave Vicker a bear hug, slapping him on the back affectionately with both hands.

———————

Twenty minutes later, unsteady from the vodka, Vicker found a surprise behind the door to his suite. Six of the dancers who had been performing on the terrace a few hours earlier were now cavorting in his living room. From the look of it, they had been at it for some time. Champagne bottles littered every surface, a tray held remnants of a caviar feast. His first thought was to wonder how such tiny girls could put away so much wine. His second was that they must be high on more than alcohol. A silver dish brimming with cocaine sat on the coffee table, a few untapped lines ready to go, and next to it, a few tightly rolled two-dollar bills. Anatole Fistoulari's recording of *Swan*

Lake played at full volume, but at twice the normal speed. Three girls, wearing nothing at all, danced languidly, making their own rhythm to the hyperspeed Tchaikovsky. Almost anyone else would have been moved deeply not merely by their physical beauty, but by the grace of these magnificent athletes, some of the finest dancers who had ever lived, taking joy from music, and from their capacity to feel it and lose themselves to it so absolutely.

Vicker was more interested in what the other three dancers were up to on the couch. Flowing hair, arms, legs, breasts, lips, tongues, vulvas, and buttocks undulating in a contorted Bosch-like pile of angles and skin. He stood, transfixed, excited, drawn to it all. The girls on the couch remained oblivious to his frozen stare, but the dancers finally noticed him. They approached him, gently, caressing his back, his chest, his cheek. Svetlana, the dancer Volk had identified as his favorite, rubbed her naked crotch on his leg and tilted her head up to kiss him. His body jerked as if he had been shocked with a Taser. He took a step back, leaving them swaying to the music in a surprised semicircle around him.

"You don't like?" asked one dancer, in lilting, lightly accented English, holding her breasts in her elegant hands.

"I-I do," Vicker stammered, flustered. "I like to watch," he said, gesturing toward the couch and then to the women in front of him.

The girls studied him as he sank into a chair, watching. They began to kiss and stroke and scratch one another, moaning loudly, putting on a show, and as they did, the girls on the couch finally noticed that they had company. One knelt in front of the coffee table to snort a line, the other two flanked Vicker's chair, undoing the buttons on his shirt and starting to undo his belt and zipper. The harder he tried to push their hands away, the harder the girls, thinking it was his game, tried to hold him down and undress him. In an instant, Vicker snapped. He kicked one of the dancers to the floor, slapped Svetlana with the palm of his hand, and then backhanded a third girl, knocking them all to the floor as he rocked to his feet. The coked-up dancers started laughing and moved to join the fun that their girlfriends were having with their guest. But, for Vicker, their intrusion, their unbidden touching, triggered every anxiety he had ever known. In a rage, he struck out at whoever was in reach, and then dragged them, by their hair, arms, and necks, tossing them like so many mannequins into the hall. Naked.

On the deck of the *Better Place*, smoking Cohibas and sipping bourbon,

Volk, Gonzaga, and the Butler watched the entire scene unfold on video streaming from every angle in Vicker's room. It was, after all, Volk's hotel and nothing that happened inside escaped his electronic gaze. Volk raised Ivanov on his cell. Without speaking, they watched over a security feed from the hotel hallway as Ivanov showed up with blankets to bundle up the ballerinas and, as gently as he could, spirit them away.

"I had a bad feeling about him, but this is unexpected. He likes to beat little girls," Volk observed, with distaste.

"I warned you. He's an odd one." Gonzaga seemed unconcerned, and drew on his cigar, watching the ash grow precariously long. "But . . . useful?"

Volk scrunched up his nose, as if he smelled something rotten. "Useful, yes. For now."

Part Three:
April–May

30

Giorgio Armani, New York City

"Ellie, darling, you've been soooo hard to reach."

"Traveling, Piper. Making a living."

Vicker had avoided his wife for weeks, since Cyprus, accepting Gonzaga's suggestion to let her stew for a bit. She could be fun, but he was tired of being held up. No way he was going to pay extortionate rates just to get her to show up for a party that would do more for her social standing than for his. He went quiet to see what she would say, hoping that, for the first time ever, he might win one.

"Just checking to see if you still want me at the Met Ball next week."

Vicker broke into his broadest grin. Turnabout felt really good.

"Piper, so sorry, after our last call I made other plans."

On the other end of the line, Piper tossed her head and stamped a perfectly manicured foot, looking every bit like a thoroughbred that had been annoyed by her rider. Shit, she thought to herself. Finally overplayed it. She looked around her bedroom, wondering where she had filed the prenup. Probably in the lawyer's safe.

Except that Vicker hadn't made plans: he'd forgotten all about it. Clicking off, but without putting down the phone, Vicker barked at Alison to get Greta into his office.

Moments later she walked in. "Miss Webb, I'm just letting you know that I need you to be my date for a charity gala next week."

"Excuse me, sir?"

"I am not hitting on you. There's a party at the Temple of Dendur. My wife can't make it. Honoring Archbishop so-and-so, Catholic priest dresses or something. He's a buffoon, but this is a big New York thing. Trot yourself over to Bergdorf's and find yourself something to wear. Okay?"

"Happy to join you, sir. But I'm an Armani girl if you don't mind," replied Greta, surprised but not missing a beat.

Vicker hit the button on his intercom and shouted, "Tell Mr. Carter that

I've changed his plans for the afternoon. I need him down in the lobby right now. Ms. Webb will explain."

———————

In the weeks since they lost Vicker and Gonzaga, and made that tense trip down to D.C., to inform Ben and Tommy, she hadn't seen Don outside of the office. They were so deep into the minutiae of their respective and very different jobs, they had little reason to speak. Even when they did, Don made it clear he didn't want to know anything more than he had to. The viability of Carter Logistics depended on Don maintaining his security clearance, which he might lose if he was discovered to have as much as Fyodor Volk's email address in his contacts. Beyond that, if anyone made a more substantive connection between Don and Volk, Tommy might not be able to protect Don. Greta understood the logic, but it did not make her feel less alone. It had been a nerve-racking interval.

Even though she had left Vicker's office straightaway, Don was waiting for her in the lobby, in front of a twenty-foot-tall, shiny, almost obscenely pink Jeff Koons bunny, recently acquired by Vicker to make the building's cathedral-like marble and steel entryway even less inviting. His lean body was sheathed in a tight-fitting jet-black mountaineering shell, and he was staring at his phone, completely detached, as if he was trying to dissociate from an alien environment. Greta laughed to herself when she thought of where she was taking Don next.

As Greta approached, he looked surprised.

"Okay, so you're here. That answers one of my questions. Where are we going?"

She told him about Vicker's demand that he escort her to the Armani boutique.

"Not the first job I'd give to the decorated combat vet who I hired to protect me from high-grade threats, but sure," Don said. "Is there something fucked-up going on here that I need to know about?"

"Probably, sure. Who knows?" Greta said. "I don't think Vicker really differentiates between us. If it doesn't concern making money or keeping people out of his bubble, he doesn't seem to focus. He just assumes where I go you go."

"Mind if I take a pass? I hate the way those places smell—"

"Yeah, perfume and flowers. Pretty rough," Greta said, starting to walk away. "Up to you. But I've got lots to fill you in on."

As they strolled up Madison Avenue toward Armani's flagship at Sixty-Fifth, Greta called her friend Yuki Minagawa. Yuki would know exactly what Greta should be wearing, what everyone else would be wearing—and what could be tailored to hide a handgun and a knife.

Once inside, Yuki ushered them into the most elaborate of the six private fitting rooms Armani reserved for their best clients. Decorated in soothing shades of beige and furnished with elegant chairs, a chaise, a couch, a makeup table, and a private bath, most New Yorkers would have found it more spacious and comfortable than their cramped apartments. For Armani's clientele, Yuki's soothing, quiet elegance and the offer of comfort made perfect sense. On a bad day, she might find herself commiserating with a pop star over boy problems, dispensing fashion advice to the wife of an African dictator, kitting out a social x-ray with a nine-figure trust fund for summer in the Hamptons, or dressing a self-made investment banker pulling down eight figures. Spending a few hours with Yuki building out a wardrobe for a single season might run to a quarter of a million dollars. Four seasons a year, plus winter at the beach. A gaggle of Russian debutantes could drop a cool million in an afternoon, each trying to outdo the others. Frocks, skirts, shirts, sweaters, coats, bags, shoes, jewelry: it all added up.

Yuki gave Greta a demure smile as she led her by the hand upstairs, all the while casting a professionally appraising glance at Don. So, *that* is Don, she thought. No wonder they had never been introduced. Catching the direction of Yuki's look, Greta gently grabbed her upper arm to turn her around.

"So, the Met, Temple of Dendur? Very big deal," Yuki crooned. "Of course, lots of rubbernecking because of this churchy thing. Vatican lending the pope's dresses. Everyone excited, especially because of all the nasty little boy and girl stuff the Church is being sued for. And who knows how far up the food chain that goes." Yuki raised a perfectly tweezed eyebrow. "Did he or didn't he? Boys, girls? Boys and girls? Priests and priests? Nuns and nuns? Priests and nuns?"

Greta kicked off her shoes and began to strip down to her underwear even before the door was closed. Don made a motion to leave, but she put a hand on his chest and pushed him down onto a chair, handing him her Glock for safekeeping.

"Nothing you haven't seen before, and, anyway, this may take a while. It is a perfect place to talk."

A barista came in to take their orders, and Yuki bustled in with several possible gowns over her arm.

"Any budget, girlfriend?" For Greta, Yuki squirreled away lots of her best stuff, pulling it out of hiding at sale time and marking it down. Greta shook her head.

"Just send the bill to Elias Vicker. He's my date."

"Piper's going to be pissed," said Yuki, giving Greta a happy clap before running off. Greta sat on the couch across from Don, legs crossed, completely unselfconscious in lacy underwear, sipping an espresso, clearly enjoying the impression she was making.

"I have more to tell you about the way Vicker's trading has changed recently, since Cyprus," said Greta. "Almost all of it is now driven by specific events affecting specific companies or countries. Very, very targeted."

Since Vicker returned from Cyprus, Industrial Strategies had been on a roll, trading in a very different, even bolder style. The fund had begun taking enormous short positions in different companies, in different industries, in different stock markets, and in different countries. In every case, Vicker had been able to build those positions well in advance of unforeseen events that caused asset prices to move quickly, to crash.

Just before a Brazilian aircraft manufacturer was about to get approval from the Federal Aviation Administration for a breakthrough design of a midsize business jet, not one, but two, prototypes exploded in midair. Test pilots and a dozen visiting dignitaries were incinerated, viewers on the ground were strafed with debris. The stock price plunged over 50 percent in an hour.

In the Norwegian sector of the North Sea, the Sleipner A platform collapsed, severing Langeled, an underwater pipeline running 725 miles on the seabed from Nyhamna, Norway, to the Easington Gas Terminal in England. In an instant, the source of 20 percent of England's natural gas disappeared. Vicker made hundreds of millions of euros when prices for U.K. electricity and European natural gas spiked. Playing for a network effect, he made another billion shorting the stock and bonds of Nordsjoen Navigasjon, the Norwegian energy giant. The price of NSNA had largely recovered from the loss of the platform that had exploded while he was in Cyprus. But losing another platform so soon after the first scared off investors, raising concerns that there were bigger problems at the company.

"These things are all within the realm of normal," said Greta. "They look like the typical sorts of random events and accidents that happen all the time. But because they have fat tails—unpredictable and very low probability— the economic effects are dramatic. And Vicker just happens to—"

"Know ahead of time."

"No question, and doesn't seem to care if people die."

Yuki walked in with a few floor-length dresses, followed by the barista holding a tray with sparkling water and more coffee. Greta slipped into a sheer, body hugging sheath in a pearl-gray silk twill that hung off one shoulder. Don could not help recalling the emaciated waif he met in Iraq, gravity blade at her side.

"Funny, right? Sexier in that dress than in her underwear." Yuki laughed. Not exactly, thought Don, as Greta strapped a holster to her thigh. Yuki took note, caught Don staring at Greta's ass, and shook her head, less in judgment than in sympathy, he was pretty sure. Yuki went off, humming to herself.

Greta stripped down again, took a sip of espresso, took out her phone, sat down on the pillowy couch, and started hungrily scrolling through her notifications.

"Oh, so now you do it," Don said, sitting at the other end of the couch.

"But I don't dive into a screen every time I'm alone with my thoughts," Greta said. "Now give me a minute, I need to check on something." Moments later, a wide smile broke across her face.

"It's moving. I can't believe it."

Without thinking, she showed Don her phone: a map of Central Europe, with two red dots in the northeastern corner of France, not far from the German border. Their money. Two trucks, on the move—finally—to Riga, where it would be given a good scrubbing and placed under the care of Mara Bērziņš and the protection of Fyodor Volk. Hiring Volk to reintroduce their crates of stolen money to the world's financial system had not been a difficult decision. In fact, it had not been a decision at all. She had no better choice. Until Tommy gave her the stare down in Ben's office, she'd been ready to turn in her badge and walk away in shame. Once she got over herself, she finally realized what Tommy had been trying to tell her. She was looking at it all wrong. If she saw Volk as a threat, then she was obligated to respond in kind. But why pick that fight? It wouldn't end well for anyone. She could turn her threat map on its side, so that the line pointed in a new direction: straight up, a vector to a new reality. Like what Ben was saying to his donors as he prepared his campaign: get on board or you'll be sorry. The threat was in saying no to Volk. Without Volk, they would not even be here; their money would have evaporated into the Syrian desert, leaving nothing more than bloodstains in the sand. Without Volk, it would be gathering dust in a limestone cave in the Loire Valley.

In less than twenty-four hours, the convoy would arrive in Riga, where Mara's people would load the pallets into a vault near the airport. Mara had arranged everything, so there would be no questions. If the central bank of a sovereign nation—an EU signatory, no less—says your money is legitimate, there's no better stamp of approval. She'd simply credit the funds to Volk's bank, and, then, to be safe, Volk would ship those crisp, new, traceable notes from Latvia to a dozen or so developing countries whose underground economies ran on U.S. dollars. His teams would blitz banks and currency exchanges in those nations, exchanging the crisp new notes for well-used ones in local circulation that Volk would then ship back to Latvia and return to Mara's vault. Having Mara as a go-between had been an unexpected delight. They were in constant touch. Whatever started between them in Riga had softened into something that felt almost as alien to Greta as love: friendship. Mara was coming to New York soon, whether as a friend or more, Greta wasn't sure.

She didn't know how much of this she could share with Don. She decided to throw out a line, see how he reacted.

"I think we can work with Volk," she said bluntly.

"You've told me that before."

"Okay, let me rephrase that. I've decided not to be afraid of him."

"That's more like it."

"And I think we can trust him."

"Really?"

"Everything's been businesslike. They've delivered everything they promised."

"Is there going to be anything left for us after Volk takes his cut?"

"Good question. He's charging seven and a half points. I told Mara that seemed low. She said it's a sign of serious respect. The only other person he gives that rate to is the Butler."

"That doesn't worry you?" Don scowled.

"Why?"

"A friend of mine had an uncle who sold used Rolexes. Very dirty business. The guy was a total crook, but upfront about it. I asked him how he found a mark. He said that if he sensed a customer was really interested in watches and had some money to spend, he'd start the guy off with a deal that sounded too good to be true. Tell him everyone else was a snake, but that he was about 'building relationships.' The minute the mark began to trust him, that's when he started selling *him* fakes and marking everything up."

"Aren't you the life of the party," Greta said.

"Sorry, I didn't mean to snipe. It's just that there's no line with these guys. I look at Volk, and I just see chaos, like monkeys and baboons with chainsaws and a hurricane about to hit."

"A high compliment, coming from you. Does it scare you?"

"It doesn't 'not scare me,' in the words of the infamous Elias Vicker."

"Not 'not scared' is when you do your best work, *aziz-aram*."

She paused for a second, waiting for Don to recoil. *Aziz-aram*, an all-purpose Iranian endearment, was one of her pet names for him. He didn't flinch.

"You're not mad at me, right?"

"Why would I be?"

"You do know about me and Fyodor?"

"More or less."

"Not my finest hour. The optics, I mean. I'm sorry if that bothered you. I could tell it did. But of course you never said anything, so I had to drive myself crazy thinking I'd somehow let you down." It was all coming out; Greta almost couldn't believe it. She just wished her timing was better.

She decided to keep going. "So, yes. I'm sorry if you're mad at me, but also not sorry because I don't owe you an explanation. But, now that I am being totally honest, it hurts me that you don't seem to want one. You pretend like nothing ever happened between us. Or maybe it's that too much happened, and you can't handle it so you walk around like a zombie."

She stopped. She'd given Don a lot to chew on. It would take him a while to process it. "You know, maybe this isn't the best time for this conversation. We have work to do. But before I go on, are you angry with me?"

"'Angry' isn't the word I'd use," Don said, so quietly he was barely audible. "I don't know what the word is."

"Cowardly? Immature?"

"You got me," Don said. "All of the above. I ran. And I'm ashamed of myself. It's not you. I promise you that. The opposite. I'm sorry. I thought I was doing the right thing. It was too dangerous. I didn't want anyone to get hurt."

"We're not going to talk about this now," Greta said. "But thank you for the apology. I shouldn't have brought up Volk. In the end, that night didn't make a difference. We'd be in this position either way. But there was a point I wanted to make. It was an instructive evening."

"From an intelligence-gathering perspective, you mean?"

She nodded.

"He likes to get rough. Likes to push it. At one point, he had his hands around Mara's neck. She could barely breathe. She was flailing, arms and legs everywhere, trying to pull his hands away. Sheer panic. I had to put Fyodor down. Hard. I was not polite. I thought maybe I overdid it. But he loved it. You've never seen someone so happy. You know why? You know what he's looking for?"

"Someone who can hit back harder?"

"Yes! That's why I miss talking to you. We see the same things."

Don raised his wrist to look at his watch. Greta pushed it down.

"I'm not done. Volk is using his IS account—"

"What account?"

"I thought you didn't want to know these things. I've been keeping you out of the loop on purpose—we can't do anything that might put a ding on the shiny new fender of Carter Logistics, can we?"

Don let the comment pass.

"What say—did Volk put his own money into IS after Cyprus?"

"Yes. And If Mara hadn't told me—she manages Volk's accounts like she'll manage ours—there's no way I would have been able to figure out the identity of the big new investor. You've never seen anything spun through so many shells and jurisdictions, so many layers."

"Winner of the pastry contest."

"Very funny. But here's the oddest thing: Fyodor uses IS like it's a checking account, always taking money out. Not the way Vicker's other investors behave—once they get their money in, they leave it there."

"And you think he's that using the money to fund the improbable events he's staging?"

"Right again," she said. "But why? Those events should never be connected, even indirectly, to money coming from Industrial Strategies. Someone as smart as Volk would never make that mistake."

"Unless he wants there to be a paper trail. Do you really think you can trust your friend Mara?"

"You're really trying to ruin all my fun, aren't you?"

"I'd follow Mara closely. You don't know what's going on between her and Volk. Doesn't sound like the healthiest relationship. There's your vulnerability. You need to get between them."

"That's a pretty narrow opening."

"I think it's the only way."

"I'm scared," she said. "I don't want to screw this up." Even as she said it, she knew she was shading the truth. She was about to walk into a dark woods, without a map, a weapon, or maybe even a clue. It wasn't surviving she feared. She always survived. It was what she might do to survive. And how alive it would make her feel.

"I know you can do it," Don said. "But if things go sideways, I'll be right there with you. I've got the whole place wired. If you get caught out, I'll blow the whole fucking place up."

Yuki walked in again, hoping that she would catch Greta and Don doing something other than talking.

"Try this, still Italian silk, slightly higher bodice, the fabric is a bit heavier so it drapes better around your . . . piece. A slightly lighter gray, which I think does more for your eyes. Let's go for elegant, not costumey or jokey. It's your first time in front of the paps, you want to make a refined entrance."

Greta slipped into the dress and a pair of heels and smiled as she spun around, stopping so that her rear end was almost in Don's face, in a way that made it difficult to tell whether she was ignoring him or provoking him.

"It is perfect, I'll take it."

With a mischievous grin, Yuki gave them a ceremonial bow as she left.

"I thought she'd never leave," Greta said. As the door shut, she pushed Don onto the couch and straddled his legs. She needed to exorcise the demons clawing at both of them, and she was tired of waiting.

31

The Metropolitan Museum of Art, New York City

Black limousines lined Fifth Avenue for half a mile north of the main entrance to the Metropolitan Museum at Eighty-Second Street. Founded in 1870 by artists and aesthetes to bring art to the American people, by the twenty-first century, the Met had become a cultural, economic—and social—juggernaut. From a single Roman sarcophagus, it had grown to cover two million square feet and more than two million objects: paintings, drawings, prints, sculpture, architecture, furniture, artifacts, armor, religious art, musical instruments, books, costumes. Among its treasures, the Crown of the Virgin of the Immaculate Conception, snatched from the Inca ruler Atahualpa in 1532, five of the thirty-six Vermeers known to the world, and John Singer Sargent's scandalous portrait of *Madame X*.

On any given day, twenty thousand souls coursed through the museum, but, on the first Monday of May, it closed to all but six hundred personally selected by Anna Wintour, the self-anointed arbiter of contemporary fashion. Ostensibly a charity ball intended to raise money to benefit the Met's costume collection, Wintour's relentlessly commercial instincts had turned it into an orgy of self-promotion for dressmakers, social climbers, pop stars, movie stars, and social media influencers.

Klieg lights raked the sky as Vicker's stretch limo pulled up to the red carpet that ran up the steps to the Met's grand entrance. Burly security guards and New York City police in riot gear manned barricades to hold back a thousand groupies intent on catching a glimpse of Beyoncé, Lady Gaga, Rihanna, Madonna, or their personal mononymous idol of the moment. Sighs and shouts of encouragement and occasional jeering at fashion victims rippled from the crowd. At the edges of the carpet itself, a busy but respectful army of photojournalists and paparazzi snapped photos of Wintour's guests as they alighted, taking their time to smile, pose, and chat, hoping to see themselves the morning after, featured on the websites of *Vanity*

Fair, People, Town & Country, Tatler, the *New York Post,* and, most coveted of all, *Vogue.*

As Greta emerged from the car, two steps behind Vicker, a buzz went up from the crowd: murmured comments, questions. Vicker had few fans in the public square and plenty of detractors, but Piper was always a crowd-pleaser. All Vicker had to do was stand off to the side and let Piper get to work. Sexy, photogenic, perennially one of the ten best-dressed, and uber-connected in the New York social circuit, she made time to chat with and was careful to always remember the names of reporters and photographers, and their dogs, even though she could not have cared less. Piper's absence, and Greta's presence, created a stir.

"Where's Piper?" asked a tall redhead from the *Tatler.*

Vicker ignored her, but motioned to Greta to step closer to him and into the center of the carpet so that the guy from the *Post* and the other paparazzi could get a better angle. Thanks to Pete, Vicker was actually getting better at dealing with the press, smiling, cheerily answering dumb questions, remembering to tuck his chin down and slightly out to hide the beginning of a sagging chin. Within a minute, photos of Vicker and Greta populated social media—Facebook, Twitter, Instagram, Imgur, Pinterest—with captions and questions: *Who is she?* At the *Post,* Page Six editors had already tagged a shot for the next day with the headline: *"Va Va Vicker! McNasty and Mystery Girl at the Met."*

Greta got a thorough once-over at the receiving line: Wintour, Rihanna, Donatella Versace, Amal Clooney. Too bad about Piper, thought Wintour, but this Greta was a find. So stunning that she made the Armani look even more special. Vicker, of course, would be punished for dissing her pal—and for asking to make a late change in his guest list. Probably his last ball, she thought, or maybe next time she would just charge him double the $300,000 donation required to book a table. Sixty tables of ten, at $30,000 a head: a cool $18 million of tax-deductible contributions to the Met's costume department, all to enhance the brands and bankrolls of the already immensely wealthy fashion elite and, of course, Wintour's own.

Pete, who had arrived early to work the room, approached them as they entered the hall. "Moseley would like to chat with you. He owns a company that needs shaking up."

"And he needs a bad guy out front?"

"Something like that," replied Pete, as Vicker loped over to where Leon Moseley, chairman of Tournoire Capital, stood with a small knot of overweight men. With a net worth of more than $20 billion, Moseley was pretty rich, which Vicker respected. But not nearly as rich as Vicker himself.

Pete touched Greta's elbow, hanging back, giving her the once-over.

"Where do you hide the knife?"

Never shy, she placed his hand firmly on her hip, before drawing it across her ass, up to the waistband. Pete could feel the hilt of a superthin switchblade.

"Really, Pete. This is what I got all gussied up for? These people are grotesque."

"For a libertine, you can be remarkably puritanical."

"This has nothing to do with morality. I just can't stand to be around so many rich fools."

As always, Greta had done her homework. She knew how pretty much every one of the six hundred guests had made, inherited, stolen, or married their money. Having seen Wall Street up close, she held no illusion that, as rich as these people were, they deserved any particular respect. Quite the opposite. Where, she wondered, were the writers, scientists, teachers, doctors, artists, musicians, mathematicians, inventors, and soldiers? With the museum given over to grotesque self-indulgence, millions of dollars were being spent not to teach children to think, but to amuse airheaded fashion models, illiterate hip-hop artists, singers who could barely hit a note, puffed up financiers convinced that money made them wise, and fashion industrialists selling T-shirts made in Chinese sweatshops.

Greta looked out over the sea of well-tended heads. In keeping with the evening's theme of honoring sacred vestments, some mocked the very idea of piety by wearing Day-Glo crowns of thorns and rosaries, Christian miters with corporate logos, and scandalous remakes of liturgical robes. Half-naked girls dressed as nuns in sexy habits and buff young men wearing hooded monks' robes slid through the galleries offering glasses of champagne and gluten-free Communion wafers daubed with caviar. Some authentic men of God, invited to thank the Vatican for loaning dozens of sacred vestments from the Sistine Chapel Sacristy—roamed in small groups wearing their finest priestly garb, drinking, laughing, and enjoying the heretical display as much as the secular guests. Patrick Mc-

Mullan, chronicler of uptown society matrons and downtown club freaks, strolled up, camera ready. No self-respecting socialite could rest easy unless she had racked up dozens, if not hundreds, of informal shots on his website.

"Pete, let me grab a shot of you and . . ."

"Greta Webb, meet Patrick McMullan," replied Pete.

"Thanks, Pete, everyone is asking after you, Miss Webb," said McMullan, snapping away. When Pete turned around, he was surprised to find himself face-to-face with Jason Renton. They hadn't talked in over a year, not since Vicker had sicced one of his attack dog lawyers on Renton and *Roundelay.*

"You don't call. You don't write," Renton said.

Renton, usually bluff and confident, seemed like a different man, his rosy face a darker shade, not corpulent, more like burst-blood-vessel red. Clearly, Pete thought, Renton had reverted to his old ways. It made him sad. Pete had admired the way that Renton had once faced down his demons, and he knew how much the man had prized his sobriety.

"Jason, great to see you," Pete said cheerfully, but tentatively. "I don't mean to be unfriendly, but I'm not sure it's such a good idea for us to be seen talking in public, at least not until the suit is settled."

"Why, so you can fuck me even harder?"

"You know that wasn't me. I tried to talk Elias out of it."

"I know, I'm not mad at you. But do you know how fucked I am? I'm almost jealous of all those guys who're getting me-tooed. If the *Times* had me on the front page jerking off onto some intern's face in the company cafeteria, my career would be less shattered than it is now. I tried to get a table at the Waverly Inn the other day. Know what they told me? Booked solid through Christmas. It's May!"

Just then Vicker walked over and put his arm around Renton. Pete was shocked. Vicker never initiated physical contact.

"I saw you two talking and thought I'd say hello."

Pete looked up at Renton and noticed him stiffen.

"Oh, Jason, you're not upset about that lawsuit," Vicker said. "I'm sure we'll work it out like gentlemen, and when we do, we'll go right back to our old fun and games."

"Elias, really, all I want to do is get back to work," Renton said.

"Well, I can't say that we don't make a good team," Vicker said. When he looked up, his expression had changed. "Actually, I was thinking. Why don't we forget this whole thing?"

"That's it. You just walk away, sorry I ruined your life, now we're pals again?"

Vicker turned to Pete.

"Pete, did you hear me apologize to Jason? I don't recall doing so."

To Pete's relief, before Vicker could say anything, Renton jumped in.

"I didn't mean it that way, sorry, sorry, Elias," he said nervously. "Oh Christ, look at me, now I'm the one apologizing."

"I like that." Vicker, taking pleasure in Renton's pain, turned to Pete. "New rule, when anyone who works for me approaches me, they start by apologizing for whatever idiotic mistake they think they've just made."

He paused and looked at Pete, then at Renton, and seemed surprised that neither man was laughing.

"That was a joke," Vicker said. "Why does everyone always lose their sense of humor around me?"

Renton let out an uneasy chuckle.

"That's more like it, my friend," Vicker said. "Now, here's what I am thinking. I'm ready to drop this suit. It's starting to bore me and I can't stand one more second of that suck-up charging me twenty-five hundred bucks an hour. I can get my dick sucked better and more cheaply by anyone in this room."

"Just like that, it's over?" Renton asked. "Thank you, Elias. Thank you."

He held his hand out for a shake. Vicker ignored it.

"Well, I'm sure we'll think of some way you can pay us back," Vicker said. "What do they say in baseball, 'a player to be named later'? I've always loved that. When I was a kid, I thought it meant that we'd be getting Willie Mays or Henry Aaron or something and then you end up with some scrub third-baseman."

He paused and looked Renton in the eye.

"But that's not how my trades work. When I ask for 'a player to be named later,' it better be Willie Mays. I'll be in touch. Now I have to get back to the cardinal. I want to ask him what tastes better, boys or girls."

As Vicker turned on his heel and walked away, Pete saw that Greta had been standing right behind him the entire time. He turned to take her arm.

"And who is this lovely? Piper two point oh?" Renton asked him.

"Jason, you've had a good day, don't push it."

Pete turned to Greta and began guiding her through the galleries, eerily empty of crowds. He paused frequently to exchange pleasantries, impart gossip, collect information. As well as Greta thought she knew Pete and the range of his contacts, she had never before seen him so completely in his element. Knowing and being known. It was, as he put it, his stock-in-trade. He was slippery, but if you wanted to meet someone, he could figure out how to make it happen. Through a kid's school, a pet charity, concert tickets, a frat brother, a business connection, a political fix. Pete pushed and pulled the levers of social and economic interconnections.

"What did our boss do before you came along?"

Pete gave Greta his best sly, calculated, boyish grin.

"Hunkered down in his pariah cave, hands over his ears, taking endless beatings from the press, from politicians. The guy was a bloody mess."

"Now?"

"People still hate him." Pete smirked. "But they pretend they don't."

Greta took Pete's arm as he led her to the main stage for the festivities. They wove through a maze of galleries, parting phalanxes of air-kissing famous-for-being-famous glitterati: Gisele, Yolanda, Taylor, Chelsea, Zendaya, Georgina, Carla, Wendy, Naomi, Diane, Stella, Kate, Bianca, Meghan, Georgia May. But no amount of pretension could subdue the grandeur of the Temple of Dendur as they entered the soaring pavilion that housed it, or quell the pang of awe that Greta felt whenever she saw it. Originally built on the banks of the Nile by a Roman governor, Petronius, more than two thousand years ago, the Temple had been dismantled before its site was flooded by the Aswan High Dam, a gift from Egypt to the United States. Even against the cheesy ecclesiastical props, sixty tables set for ten, a dance floor, and a band playing Cole Porter, the Temple retained its power.

"I wonder what Isis and Osiris would think," said Greta.

Pete gave her arm a squeeze and smiled.

"Why so serious, G? Take it as it is. The evening could be fun, and, just maybe, someone will step out of line and you can beat the shit out of him." Pete grinned.

"Sorry. It *is* the latent puritan—or maybe just the stoic—in me. I cannot help but add it all up. Tickets at thirty thousand dollars a head, probably most of the women in the room spent that much again on shoes and dresses. Then the jewelry. Not to mention whitewashing the Catholic Church."

At the far end of the hall, they found their table. Pete's mood soured.

Greta looked at him quizzically. "This is a wonderful place to sit. So quiet and right up against the Temple."

Pete knew immediately that Piper had put in a fix with Wintour's team. Given the not-so-small fortune that Pete had convinced Vicker to pony up for the privilege, they should have had a table front and center—where they could see and be seen. Instead: social Siberia. Worse, Wintour, who had free rein with seating, had decided to populate their table with a weird agglomeration of leftovers: Bishop Joseph, eyes closed and already drunk, a star-struck teenage gamine who made dresses from bubble-gum comics, sneaking a vape, and one of the original Housewives of Beverly Hills. It was a small blessing that Vicker would not know who any of these people were.

Vicker finally made it to the table and flopped down next to Greta. He wore his mildest, most carefully controlled public face, but, leaning across her to address Pete, he spewed invective. "What the fuck, Pete, if we were sitting any farther away, we would be in Harlem, in the middle of Malcolm Fucking X Boulevard. Not what I paid for."

Pete squirmed. He felt himself to still be on thin ice after the *Hamilton's* debacle, and he really did not want Greta dragged into the middle of the verbal abuse he was about to endure. Oblivious, the morbidly obese bishop walked around the table to introduce himself. Clasping Greta's hand in both of his own, the old letch managed an obvious peek down her cleavage. Vicker ignored him.

"Elias, this was absolutely not the deal," said Pete. "I saw a table map a couple of days ago. We were front and center, and you were next to the cardinal."

Vicker looked up vaguely. Then his face snapped into a sharp frown. Making a beeline for their table was Woody Hamilton, wearing a black silk bow tie, a black velvet dinner jacket, and a broad lopsided grin. He bounded over, extending a hand to Pete and then Vicker. McMullan trailed him, tipped to the photo opportunity.

"Elias, I've been looking everywhere for you. They've really got you in the back row here," he said with a genial smirk. "What did you do to piss off Anna?"

Vicker stood to greet him and mustered a strained grin. Fuck, thought Vicker, the last thing he needed was paparazzi getting a photo of him glaring at Hamilton.

"I've been meaning to call you, Woody. Your conference was a lot of fun, maybe we can do it again next year," said Vicker.

Hamilton laughed. For Vicker, the humiliation of that day still stung. There must, Vicker thought, be some way to get even with this supercilious jerk.

"Super, I'll have my people call your people, let's put it in the calendar," said Hamilton sarcastically.

Before he could sit down, Vicker noticed a mop-haired man weaving toward him unsteadily. Ambassador Cecil Baxter. Old-school State Department. Vicker knew him slightly from Republican circles—Baxter was the genius behind one of the dumbest decisions in history: disbanding Saddam's army, putting four hundred thousand well-trained Iraqi soldiers out of work, and allowing them to run free across the country, thus ensuring that the very fighters the United States needed to maintain the peace after the invasion would become sworn enemies. Word was he was a ski instructor somewhere out West. Sad and pathetic, Vicker thought. He'd heard the stories, how Baxter would show up here and there and start peddling conspiracy theories to anyone who would listen.

Before Vicker could get away, Baxter slid up next to him and slipped his arm around his shoulders like they were old friends.

"Those pricks," Baxter whispered in Vicker's ear, so close Vicker could smell scotch and garlic on his breath. "Those arrogant boy scout bastards. Two billion dollars. They fucking stole it. No one believes me, but I know what happened. They used to talk about it all the time in Baghdad. They finally found their chance in Syria. I spent thirty years in the Middle East. I know everyone, I still hear things. You can't let them get away with it."

Vicker stiffened and tried to pull away.

"I know you think Ben Corn is your new best friend," Baxter hissed, tightening his grip. "I know all about that crew. You have no idea what they're capable of."

Almost as if he'd picked up a telepathic signal, Pete materialized at Vicker's side and smoothly inserted himself between Vicker and the interloper.

"Cecil, so great to see you again," he said, pulling Baxter toward him. "Look, let's go get you a cup of coffee."

As Pete led him away, Baxter slipped loose from his grip. But he lost his footing and fell to the floor. In an instant two security guards scooped him up and escorted him out of the hall.

"Sad story," said Pete. "Thought he was gonna be secretary of state, but after Iraq, they wouldn't even make him ambassador to Burkina Faso. And now look at him. My heart goes out to his family. I hope he gets the help he needs."

Vicker shook his head in disgust, but something registered.

"You're supposed to protect me from crackpots," he said. "I better not see a picture of that juicehead with his arm around me in the *Post* tomorrow."

Without another word, Vicker sat down again and pulled out his phone to scroll through emails and stock prices in Asia, where the markets had just opened. Greta raised an eyebrow at Pete, until she saw Gonzaga approaching. Though he was a youthful seventy, she noticed a slight limp. The only aspect of his appearance that suggested his age. Pete stood to exchange friendly greetings with Gonzaga, and the bishop got a big hug. Vicker looked up briefly and gave Gonzaga a neutral nod before returning to his phone.

"Miss Webb, it is a pleasure to see you again. I can see you are being ignored." Gonzaga looked at Vicker, who seemed not to hear. "May I invite you to dance?"

Greta gave him her hand. "With pleasure, but is your left leg okay? You seem to be favoring it."

"Yes, it's fine. A self-inflicted injury—it hurts like the devil sometimes, but reminds me that I am but an ordinary sinner."

Strange, she thought, wondering whether that was some kind of weird false modesty as Gonzaga guided her to the other end of the pavilion. He reached his hand gently around her waist. Centered in front of the entrance to the Temple, the dance floor, empty except for a few persistent waltzers, suggested an ancient rite. It was a cautious crowd, everyone watching everyone else. Doing mental sums, toting up where they fit in the food chain and the social order. Gonzaga kept up a steady patter as he twirled Greta. He had charm and old-school manners, not fussy, but mindful of his partner and, in his own way, honest. He was willing to discuss his thoughts and to reveal himself—up to a point.

"Your first one of these?"

Greta nodded.

"*Nekulturny*," he said, making her laugh. Surprised by his choice of a Russian slur. Uncultured, uncouth.

"It is all about money, power, how they look, and nearly everyone is worried. Most of the people here are having a perfectly awful time. They are desperate to be here, to be part of it. But, except for a few, it is terrifying. Not fun."

"And you come . . ."

"Because I *do* enjoy it. I almost always meet someone who I want to know better, and it gives me a chance to roam about the museum to see old friends and family, undisturbed."

"Friends and family?"

He took her arm and led her away from the dance floor, out of the first-floor galleries, and up the main staircase. A few guards watched, unconcerned. Gonzaga, descended from both the de' Medici and Gonzaga clans, found ancestors staring at him from the walls of museums everywhere he went. He loved them all: the illustrious, the industrious, the cultured, the conniving, the cruel. One forebear, Lorenzo, had commissioned *The Prince*, from Niccolò Machiavelli. Another, Eleanor of Toledo, had acquired the family's ancestral home, the Pitti Palace and expanded it to create the remarkable building it is today. So much history, honor. They had ruled a large part of Italy as princes and popes long before there was an Italy. On one branch, Cosimo I de' Medici. On another, Lodovico I Gonzaga. He stopped in front of a sixteenth-century portrait of Cosimo I, attributed to Bronzino's workshop.

"Every person on earth has an inheritance and lineage as long as mine. We are all descended from *Australopithecus* and the Neanderthals. But I have the good fortune to come from a family that was better organized, perhaps more ruthless, than most. They conspired, fought wars, kept records, and commissioned thousands of portraits, sculptures, drawings, engravings."

Clever, thought Greta. On one level, he is trying to seem like just another guy, but, at the same time, reminding me that his forebears had been shaping Western civilization for more than eight hundred years. She tried to recall her medieval history. The Medicis and the Gonzagas were pitiless, implacable, and insatiable. Brilliant tacticians, warriors, and politicians. This, she thought—this man—is the culmination of those lines. They stood for a moment, appreciating Cosimo I.

"It is coming back to me," said Greta. "He created the Boboli Gardens behind the Pitti, and founded the Knights of Saint Stephen." She omitted her recollection that Cosimo I—the bastard son of Cosimo senior—was a greedy and authoritarian ruler. He had maintained a personal guard of Swiss mercenaries and thought nothing of assassinating anyone who might threaten his rule, especially blood relatives.

Gonzaga smiled.

"Precisely. Refined, brutal, a man of his times, a man who made things happen."

"Someone to be proud of, then."

Gonzaga took a step back, as if to get a better look at her.

"He did what needed to be done. Organized some fractious tribes. Advanced our family's interests. For that, we thank him."

"Rape, pillage, plunder, but to the victors, the spoils. The family scrapbook must be a lot of fun: Here's a portrait of Zio Giuseppe—throat slit on June eleventh for using the wrong fork. Village of *Che Importa* sacked for a bag of salt?"

"I didn't take you for the squeamish type. Have I gotten that wrong?"

"Just a girl sensitive to injustice, sir." She batted her eyes, gently mocking.

"Ah. A longer conversation, then. But I promised to introduce you to some old friends. Two in particular I would like you to meet."

He led Greta off in a different direction, passing just a few other guests, to Gallery 800. Jules Bastien-Lepage's painting *Joan of Arc*, nearly eight feet square, dominated the room. Gonzaga gazed lovingly at Joan, who stared into the distance while gauzy images of Saints Michael, Margaret, and Catherine hovered over her, in the background, entreating a peasant girl to lead France against the English. Gonzaga stepped back to watch Greta studying the painting intently.

"You look a bit like Joan, or, I should say, like Bastien-Lepage's cousin Marie-Adèle Robert, who posed for him. Joan was caught between two worlds, the earthbound and the spiritual. Do you ever feel that way?"

Greta tried to recall if she had ever been courted so subtly. They were taking stock of each other. Circling. She his target, he hers. Still, she found him charming, maybe even attractive, if a bit too fine-boned for her tastes.

"*Quando mai no, Dottore?*" replied Greta. When have I not, Dottore? "Is it not the natural state of a woman?"

Gonzaga clapped his hands together—with delight. Her Italian is beautiful, he thought. What a thrill.

"It is rare these days that men and women can converse about differences between the sexes. Come with me, just one more and then we can go back to the dancing."

Offering his arm, Gonzaga asked her to close her eyes as he slowly led her to Gallery 637. With a gentle hand on her hip, he guided Greta to a space in front of a mythological scene painted by Artemisia Gentileschi.

"*Esther before Ahasuerus*," said Greta, opening her eyes. "Artemisia was one of the most brilliant painters of her time—after Caravaggio."

Gonzaga beamed.

"She painted for Cosimo the First; many remain in our family." He moved nearer, to inspect the canvas more closely.

"Look at those faces, how she used color. I collect the women painters. In every generation, they faced greater challenges. Few artists today have these skills and this kind of knowledge of history, of art. But, of course, none can claim a father who studied with Caravaggio."

Greta moved closer as well, studying Esther. "I can never look at one of her paintings without thinking about how she was tortured—with thumbscrews—to verify her testimony against Agostino Tassi, who had raped her." Convicted, but never punished. The wrong time to have been a talented woman, or, perhaps, a woman.

"Now, let me show *you* something," said Greta. She reached out to close his eyelids, gently took his hand, led him through cavernous hallways to Gallery 964, and stopped in front of *A Vase of Flowers*, painted by Margareta Haverman, in 1716.

"Open your eyes."

Gonzaga did as she asked. He seemed puzzled.

"It's lovely, but hardly spectacular."

"I could not agree more," said Greta. "That's the point. It's sad that this is the only work in the Met by an early Dutch woman painter. And they don't have a single painting by my favorite, the greatest of her time."

"And who would that be?"

"Rachel Ruysch, of course," Greta replied with an impish grin.

Gonzaga smiled. Was she teasing him?

"Perhaps we can remedy that some day," said Gonzaga, smiling. "I agree with you. It's a serious gap in their collection."

"One of my dreams." Greta tilted her head briefly, resting it on his shoulder. "To have one of her bouquets hanging over my mantel. But, maybe first, to have a mantel."

He linked his arm through hers and led her down the main staircase and left, toward the ball. They could feel the thump of the music. Alcohol and coke were doing their job, the crowd had become louder. Greta turned toward Vicker's table to see if he or Pete was still there, and then turned to give Gonzaga her hand.

"You saved my evening, sir. Thank you."

"In that case, may I invite you to lunch?"

Greta hesitated, giving it four beats. Too easy, she thought, but, then, he was just a man, even if he was almost twice her age. And he found himself to be irresistible. Finally, she nodded.

"With pleasure."

"Tomorrow?"

She smiled her assent, pleased that he was doing exactly as she wanted, but pleasantly surprised at how much she enjoyed it.

32

The Carlyle, New York City

The Carlyle hovered over Madison Avenue like an Art Deco dragon, ready to unfurl massive wings to protect its brood. For nearly a hundred years, the world's elite had nested in its hotel suites and apartments. Only at the Carlyle could Michael Jackson, Steve Jobs, and Princess Diana have randomly shared the same elevator. Jackie, Caroline, and John-John called the Carlyle home after Jack was assassinated. Before that, the rabbit warren of tunnels beneath the building allowed Jack to sneak Marilyn Monroe and his parade of paramours into the family apartment while the rest of the clan cracked lobster shells in Hyannis Port.

The Gonzaga clan had called the Carlyle home ever since it was built, even during World War II, when some of them got stranded in New York. For upper-crust Europeans, particularly aloof, self-described royalty, the Carlyle provided shelter from the undignified maelstrom of New York City. They took comfort that change came slowly. Staff stayed forever, barricading guests from intrusion. A hotel seamstress embroidered the linens with their initials. The pillows were always exactly right, and the monogrammed silverware gleamed. The younger generation might party at raves in Bed-Stuy warehouses, but even they sought the Carlyle's sober comfort, finding it a safe place to crash after a long night of uppers, downers, mushrooms, and booze, with no worry that the staff would tattle to grandmother or to Page Six.

Gonzaga roosted at his regular table in the Carlyle Restaurant, flipping through the *New York Post*. From a corner banquette, he could see everyone and everyone could see him. Surveying the elegant room, watching the cream of international society savor Alba truffles at $500 an ounce, he thought that nearly everything was as it should be. He was not wrong to imagine that when the world watched him back, they saw a wealthy, rakishly handsome man, esteemed counselor to CEOs and an international Mr. Fix-It in his element. None of them had any idea how close his family had come to losing everything. And how hard he'd fought to build that fortune back, by any means necessary.

But, of late, Gonzaga was hardly feeling sanguine. The months since Cyprus had been among the best in the history of IS. That pleased him of course. But Vicker had stopped speaking to him. For more than twenty-five years, they'd spoken daily. Now silence. Last night at the Met, when Gonzaga trekked to the party's outer reaches to say hello, Vicker didn't even pretend to make nice. On a personal level, Gonzaga didn't mind. Small talk with Vicker was hardly his idea of an absorbing conversation, but the cold shoulder was getting in the way. Access to Vicker was the key to smooth dealings with Wennerström. If Vicker was not there to promptly execute SEF trades, Wennerström became impatient. Gonzaga feared that Vicker didn't understand that for the ancient, many-tentacled stichting, Industrial Strategies was just one piece of the puzzle. The trades they gave to Gonzaga, for execution by Vicker, fit into a bigger picture. If Vicker did not give his SEF patrons what they needed, they would soon stop asking nicely.

He could probably handle SEF, Gonzaga figured, because SEF remained Vicker's largest single investor—and took a healthy share of the profits generated by Parsifal events. But the profits themselves were also becoming a problem. Vicker was making too much money, too quickly. Wall Street was a village, and no matter how many different brokers and fronts IS used to execute and disguise the details and scale of its trading, people were going to figure out what Vicker was up to. Brokers talked to bankers, bankers to lawyers, and lawyers to one another. If Vicker kept on, sooner rather than later, some wise guy looking for a plea bargain or a whistleblower award would tip off the U.S. Attorney's office or make a referral to the SEC. Someone needed to tell Vicker to slow down. If it wasn't Gonzaga, Gonzaga had no idea who that could be.

A hush settled over an already quiet room as all eyes followed the sylph gliding toward Gonzaga's table. It was a crowd used to seeing beautiful women, but even they took note of the tall slender woman moving toward him. He rose to greet Greta, pecked her on each cheek, as a white-gloved waiter moved the table so that she could slip onto the banquette. Greta could practically feel the curiosity, jealousy, and disapproval that vibrated through the room, as fellow diners snuck their phones out to snap discreet pictures of the mysterious woman who'd come from nowhere and moved in on two of the richest men in New York, without, from the looks of things, waiting for the sheets to dry in between.

"Miss Webb, thank you for joining me. You look lovely. More Armani? Your signature?"

Greta glanced down at the table. Gonzaga had that morning's *Post* open to Page Six. Two pages had been devoted exclusively to photos of the gala, including one of Greta with Vicker on the red carpet and another dancing with Gonzaga.

"You could go a long way after a debut like that, my dear."

Greta flashed a smile, closed the paper, and pushed it to the far side of the table. The front page showed photos of a pipeline explosion in Canada. Both of them knew, for different reasons, that it had been no accident.

It was a tricky lunch. Gonzaga seeking to bed her, and likely playing other games as well. She, gaming him, and playing for control of IS. Greta had long since made peace with being objectified by men—and pigeonholed by women. The advantages of having been born a rare beauty more than compensated for the superficial insults of being treated as a thing that could be acquired. Just another tool, she thought, to draw men in. With Gonzaga, it would be fun. Lead him on a little, make him work for it. He gestured at the story about the inferno raging in Canada.

"That pipeline has been keeping me busy all morning. The bank has underwritten TransBorder Energy stock and bonds to the tune of fifty billion dollars. The stock is plummeting as we speak, down forty percent."

Greta frowned, wondering what a tender-hearted woman might say in a moment like that. She knew all there was to know about moving gas, oil, and wielding market power from her days on Wall Street and serving in the Middle East, and not least the networked market impact that a broken pipeline would engender. She also knew that, less than a week ago, Vicker had suddenly begun placing massive bets against both TBEC bonds and stock and had also gone long on natural gas. IS showed nearly $6 billion in profit as of that morning.

"I read that five people have died so far, and that several hundred elk and caribou were burned. Apparently, animals are attracted by the heat given off by the pipeline," Greta said tenderly.

"One feels pity for the creatures," Gonzaga said, matching Greta's girlish concern with paternal sympathy. "We have been mobilizing relief efforts. The bank has lots of relationships on both sides of the border. We do what we can."

Greta watched his face intently. Reading microexpressions in real time consumed more cognitive bandwidth than she could safely dedicate to it while working a target. But the high-level take was obvious. Had she seen the flash of a scornful grin? The man was clearly lying about helping the relief efforts, and even beyond an absence of empathy for people and animals, he seemed to take some perverse pleasure in that suffering. He really must think I am a bimbo, thought Greta. If that's what he wanted, that's what he'd get.

"That is amazing," she said. "It seems that most of corporate America just ignores these disasters. You must be proud to be part of an organization like that."

Greta smiled at him, making Gonzaga marvel, yet again, at how the trappings of power drew even the most magnificent young women into his web. A fancy room, expensive champagne, a big title, a little attention, so predictable. Seemingly out of nowhere Greta noticed a sneer flick across Gonzaga's face: the tricky part coming up.

"So, tell me about Greta Webb, and your work at Industrial Strategies. Are you enjoying it?"

"Being inside a huge hedge fund has been a steep learning curve, but—and I know this sounds geeky—I love data. Ever since college. Compiling it, organizing it, analyzing it, protecting it. This is my dream job." Greta wondered if she was laying it on a bit thick, but she had to play her part.

"Where did you do your degree?"

"At MIT. I majored in math—matrices, matrix string theory, gauge theory—and after that I was able to study for a year with Robbert Dijkgraaf and Luboš Motl. But I *really* would put you to sleep with all that. Please tell me about you, sir, how did you come to be at Allard Frères?"

"Ah, now that is a very long story, perhaps we should order lunch first. May I order for you?"

For hours, over smoked salmon, Dover sole, and Egly-Ouriet Blanc de Noirs, Gonzaga regaled her with his earliest memories. How the Germans had used the Tempio Maggiore—the Great Synagogue—on Via Farinias as a stable. How, unbeknownst to his family, he had listened while they recounted the horrors of witnessing public executions of resistance fighters by Nazi firing squads in the Piazza Santo Spirito. How, as a young man, studying at Cambridge, he raced home after the Arno flooded Florence to spend the next year comforting his people and rescuing books and art. How repairing Florence had become his lifelong project—an expensive passion. When, finally, they were the last people in the restaurant, Gonzaga turned back to the conversation they had begun at the museum, about his love of women painters, and his collection, conveniently hung in his apartment on the forty-second floor. Greta saw the bait and took it.

"I would love to see your 'women' sometime."

"Perhaps now? They're just upstairs. Though I suppose that an old goat showing a beautiful young woman his 'etchings' means that he will wake up without a kidney."

"Something like that," Greta replied, with her most enigmatic smile.

Greta gave Gonzaga a rush, stumbling into him artfully, rubbing her breasts against his arm during their elevator ride to his top-floor apartment. The chambermaid who answered the double door had clearly been expecting them: fresh flowers everywhere, a bottle of champagne resting in a cooler, petits fours on a silver tray. Dismissing the maid, Gonzaga gestured toward the windows that faced north and west, bright and clear. He vastly preferred the view before developers began puncturing the skyline with hundred-story towers, but in New York, as in most cities, real estate drove the economy and real estate magnates made a habit of lining the pockets of politicians and police. No matter who ran things, they got what they wanted.

"Taller and taller. Going the way of China and Dubai," said Gonzaga, standing next to Greta at a window, holding two glasses of champagne.

"At this rate, ten years from now, midtown will be in constant shadow."

She turned toward him, too quickly, upending the wine onto his shirt and the Persian carpet.

"Oh, I am soooo sorry," said Greta, seemingly flustered, patting at his shirt. She grabbed the empty glasses from his hands.

"Let me take those," she said. "At least I can pour refills and try not to drench you again."

Greta bustled off to the bar and poured more Egly-Ouriet for them both. When she returned, he had taken off his jacket and was sitting on a couch. He patted the couch, gesturing for her to sit. Greta handed him a glass, kicked off her shoes, and sat just out of his reach on the couch, feet up, her legs tucked under her. Holding her glass out to him, she offered a toast.

"*Za nashu druzjbu*, to our friendship. Please toast the Russian way: we clink glasses and look each other in the eye while downing our drinks."

How lovely, thought Gonzaga as he downed his champagne, this pretty girl wants to play drinking games. Greta turned the conversation to the room. It might have been anywhere in Europe—Paris, London, Rome. Comfortable, French and English antiques, but oddly stripped down, a Zen-like palette. Art, everywhere. Greta was dying to wander around, in stocking feet, but it would have spoiled the moment. He clearly enjoyed the seduction, sitting as they were, just a few feet apart. She got up only to take their glasses back to the bar for more wine.

"Greta, I cannot begin to tell you how much I have enjoyed our lunch. It is rare that I even think about my childhood anymore, but you brought it out of me."

"I am fascinated to hear. You have seen so much of the world, of history."

Just at that moment, Gonzaga began to have difficulty seeing much at all. With a glimmer of recognition, his eyes closed. Greta caught his glass before it spilled and set it down on a nearby table as his head lolled to his chest. Standing, she walked over to lean his head back, propped up by a pillow, and lifted his legs so that, for all the world, he seemed to be taking a midday nap. She loosened his tie, took his pulse, and put her ear to his face, listening for his breathing. Reaching for her cell phone, she texted Don.

Five minutes later, Greta answered the service door to admit Don, a man in a suit carrying a doctor's bag, and four men dressed unobtrusively in business casual, all pulling on rubber gloves as they entered. The four fanned out into the apartment as Don and the doctor followed Greta into the drawing room. Listening to Gonzaga's chest through a stethoscope, the doctor nodded. Greta pushed up a jacket sleeve and undid the French cuff, and the doctor found a vein. He injected enough juice to wake Gonzaga slightly, so that they would not be carrying a completely dead weight on the way downstairs. With one arm over Don's shoulder and the doctor supporting his waist, they followed Greta into the service elevator. For the moment, the elevator operator was one of theirs. Carrying their sleep-walking charge, the three of them made their way through subterranean tunnels into the basement of the hotel garage and piled into a Suburban fitted as an ambulance. As the vehicle sped down East Seventy-Sixth Street toward the FDR, they cinched Gonzaga onto a gurney, put an oxygen mask over his face, and put him into a deep sleep.

33

Millbrook, New York

Gonzaga awoke to find himself in an unfamiliar bed wearing his own pajamas. For decades he'd had them custom-made by Turnbull & Asser: pale blue Sea Island cotton with black piping and the Medici family crest discreetly embroidered on the pocket—five red balls and one blue on a gold shield. Light streamed into the room through large six-over-six windows. Outside, he saw Arabian horses grazing in fenced pastures, rolling hills, and, in the distance, a hump-backed peak that he recognized from hunting trips. Slide Mountain, at 4,200 feet, the Catskills' highest peak. Slowly, his mind began to clear. He recalled lunch, watching Greta kick her shoes off and tuck her legs under her. And, now, waking up on a horse farm somewhere, he presumed, in Dutchess County, two hours north of Manhattan. The champagne. His head ached. Gonzaga prided himself on considering and anticipating, but he'd never seen this coming. Quite a girl, he thought, but not the easy roll in the hay he was playing for.

He wondered what she was after. His mind began to sort through scenarios. Whatever it was—whoever she was—she was part of a big-budget operation, well organized. He wondered who was behind it—the Russians, Wennerström, the Americans? No fool like an old fool, he thought. Greta slid into the room carrying a silver tray with a bottle of sparkling water, a pot of green tea, and macarons from Ladurée. She sat down on the bed next to him, the tray beside her, and held out her hand, offering two capsules in her palm.

"Just ibuprofen this time." She smiled.

Gonzaga swallowed the pills. What a magnificent jailer, he thought. Greta wore her signature outfit: Armani skirt, white silk shirt unbuttoned just enough to command attention, hair pulled back into a dancer's bun. He noticed the gun holstered at the back of her skirt, thinking that she had probably always carried one. He had missed it completely—just as he had completely misjudged this woman. As he nibbled on the macarons and sipped tea, he felt himself beginning to revive and focus. They had snatched him from his safe place, but they were treating him with respect, which meant that they wanted something from him. He started thinking, making connections. If Greta was a mole, certainly Don Carter, who'd brought her into IS, was too. And Carter, of course, had been supplied to IS by Ben Corn. As had Pete Stryker. These clever Americans had Vicker surrounded. He began to relax. The field was taking shape. Vicker. Volk. And now this crew. Bankers, mercenaries, soldiers. And him: What part would he play? The same part that his ancestors had played for centuries: survivor.

"You went to a great deal of trouble. You might simply have invited me to visit. I miss riding, and this seems like lovely country to hack out."

"First, let's have lunch on the terrace. If you'd like to dress, we collected a few things from your flat."

She gestured toward the closet, but what Gonzaga saw first was his cilice, draped over a nearby chair. He had worn the spiked garter favored by ascetics and penitents for most of his adult life. It was a constant reminder of his imperfection, and his penance for doing what he had needed to do in his life for family and for country. He wondered who had undressed him and put him in his pajamas. Greta, seeing his glance, shrugged.

"I recall what you said at the museum about being a sinner. You did not strike me as an ascetic, perhaps you will explain it to me later."

"A habit," said Gonzaga. "But, strangely, the pain has become a pleasure, and I feel naked without it."

Greta withdrew, but the house was riddled with hidden cameras. From the terrace, Don watched Gonzaga shower and utter a small grunt while cinching his cilice before scanning the closet. Looking outside, at the bright spring day, Gonzaga chose navy chinos, Belgian loafers without socks, a white polo, and a seafoam green Cucinelli sweater, which he slung around his shoulders. Outside the door to his bedroom, he encountered one of Don's security squad, wearing an earpiece and a pistol in a well-worn holster at his hip. Following the guard's open-palmed gesture, he followed the hall to a large terrace overlooking paddocks in which four Arabian foals frolicked around their mothers. Two members of the security team, at a discreet distance, stood at each end. Don and Greta spoke quietly, sitting at a table for five, set for an elegant country lunch. Chip, nearby, spoke into an earpiece while typing on a tablet. They rose to welcome him.

"Mr. Carter, we meet again." Gonzaga looked at Greta. Don offered his hand.

Gonzaga considered feigning outrage. But to what purpose? These people intrigued him. They played the game with brio. Somehow, and he did not understand precisely how, they had embedded themselves in Vicker's world, inside Industrial Strategies. Had they surfaced before, he might have handled the introduction to Volk differently. He had no idea as to their objectives, much less who was behind them. Better, he thought, to draw them out, if he could.

"Magnificent horses, Greta. Yours?"

None of them was surprised at Gonzaga's resilience. From what they had pieced together of his personal history, the man had been involved in—and may have been an architect of—some of the biggest financial crimes of the last thirty years.

Their approach to Gonzaga would not rely on threats or brute force, those were implicit. They would appeal to his vanity and pride, and, finally, to avarice and fear. Their assessment was that Gonzaga needed, if not to win, at least to not lose. Their focus was to develop a partnership, not to make an acquisition. They would never own this man. At best, they would, for a time, share his relationships with presidents, princes, and gangsters.

"I enjoy riding them, and we'll find you some jodhpurs and boots."

As Gonzaga joined them at the table, a double espresso arrived, hot milk on the side, as he liked.

"Now then, may I ask who you are?" Gonzaga looked from Don to Greta, and back.

"Let's just say that we, like you, have an interest in Industrial Strategies, although ours is not quite as tangible as yours," said Don. "Seeing that you and some of your friends are Vicker's largest investors."

Gonzaga racked his brain to figure out how they came by that information. Like all wealthy Europeans, he held nothing in his own name. That, simply, was not how he organized his affairs. Not that the superrich in the United States—or anywhere else—were any different. But protecting assets through secrecy and flexibility was part of European DNA. They'd been doing it for centuries. Countless wars, internecine rivalries, expropriations, confiscatory tax regimes, and political upheavals had taught them that, when it came to wealth, it was best to be opaque, stateless. No expense was spared: the right London solicitors, the cleverest bent bankers, malleable government officials in sketchy jurisdictions. In Gonzaga's case, any attempt to trace his assets should have gotten lost in a daisy chain of generically named LLCs, companies and trusts that looped through the Seychelles, Liechtenstein, Monaco, Nevada, Panama, and the Cook Islands before they dead-ended in the black hole of the most opaque and corrupt financial institution on earth: the Istituto per le Opere di Religione, the Institute for the Works of Religion, also known as the Vatican Bank.

Gonzaga deduced that Greta and her crew were likely CIA, and that this estate belonged to the Agency. Good for them, he thought, perhaps there are some pockets in Langley where they still did things the old way, face-to-face, on American soil, taking risks. If so, he was confident that he was among his kind of people.

"Ah, well, Mr. Carter—if that is your name. You are quite mistaken. I am a banker. I make a good living, but I do not have that kind of wealth."

"Lorenzo," said Greta, "in another context, I'd love to spend the day playing cat and mouse with you. But we don't have the time for it."

Chip propped up a tablet on the table so that Gonzaga could see it. The screen showed an elaborate family tree of companies displayed, with dotted lines connecting banking relationships, current balances, and service providers like trust companies and lawyers. Gonzaga studied it. At the bottom of the tree, Via del Corso Capital SrL, named, perhaps, for Via del Corso in Florence, appeared as the investment adviser for a single account at IS worth well over $5 billion. At the top of the chart, a dozen layers away, was a stichting domiciled in Liechtenstein. Gonzaga was impressed. These Americans had gone to considerable trouble.

He clapped his hands slowly. "Nicely done! Did your president send you here to arrest me for the crime of being rich?"

Chip, ignoring the question, displayed the summary pages to Gonzaga's most recent income tax return. Not too shabby: eight million in income. A mix of salary and bonus from Allard Frères et Cie, dividends from a stock portfolio, some tax-exempt income from municipal bonds, capital gains from the exercise of stock options.

"Funny thing," said Chip. "No indication that you're the beneficial owner of so many foreign bank accounts, and no sign of the roughly one billion dollars of income that flowed through Via del Corso Capital on just this one account at Industrial Strategies. That's just last year, would you care to discuss your 1040s for the past four? The statute of limitations is still open."

Gonzaga held out his wrists, miming that they should handcuff him. He would be a prize. For years the IRS had been cracking down on Americans— and permanent residents like him—with undisclosed foreign bank accounts. Given his high profile and the amount of the income he had failed to disclose, they would not only want back taxes and penalties, they would want him to do time. Every year, the IRS made an example of a few big fish to scare the minnows. And, on the fish scale, Gonzaga was a whale shark.

"Please, is that all you've managed to find?"

Greta hung back, lounging in one of the chairs, sipping sencha tea, allowing Chip and Don to be the heavies. Gonzaga was playing it well, drawing them out, trying to get them to show their cards first. "Isn't this quite enough?" she asked.

"I'm guessing that you really don't want to disgorge your ill-gotten billions," said Don. "Or exchange your cashmere-plated lifestyle for prison polyester, seven-to-twelve with a few months off for good behavior? Even if the judge sends you to a minimum-security prison, like Allenwood, it's no fun."

Gonzaga sat back in his chair, taking their measure. Americans were, generally, unsubtle. He decided that he had a bead on the two guys. The one with the computer screen: Ivy League arrogant, mid-Atlantic drawl, a self-possessed hardass, born to privilege. The other guy, Don: formidable, rougher, moved like a boxer, something to prove. But the girl: she was hard to pin down. English was not her first language. Nor was Italian. But he could not put his finger on the trace of whatever accent she had clearly worked hard to eliminate. Whoever she was, Greta Webb was not the name she was born with.

"Mr. Carter, is that how you think a little tax problem will play out? Even if what you describe is accurate and a court accepts your criminally obtained information, no judge will keep me locked away for years while the case drags on. And, if I decide to visit my ancient aunt in Verona, there will be no extradition." He paused. "You must do better."

It was a decent bluff, Don thought, but Gonzaga was overplaying his hand. Most prosecutors would argue that Gonzaga, with his billions in undeclared income at stake, was a flight risk. And most judges would agree. But if the old buzzard feared spending a couple of years in a federal lockup while his trial dragged on, it didn't show.

On cue, Chip displayed a list of names culled from a compilation of 962 members of Italy's clandestine masonic lodge, Propaganda Due—P2: Licio Gelli, Mussolini's fascist financier and liaison to Hitler; Roberto Calvi, "God's banker." Senior members of the Cosa Nostra and the 'Ndrangheta, some alive, some dead. Few, these days, remembered P2, which some said had acted—and others would say still acted—as a right-wing shadow government led by journalists, members of parliament, mobsters, financiers, military leaders, and the heads of all three Italian intelligence services.

"I haven't thought of them for years," said Gonzaga. "But . . . so what? So I didn't pay some taxes. Maybe I made some poor choices in friends as a younger man." The coffee had worn off. His head throbbed. His leg ached. He held up his cup, like a beggar. But he was also growing irritated: whatever they were after, he was ready for them to stop being obscure.

"If you're making a list of my ill-chosen friends, don't forget Flavio Carboni, Bishop Marcinkus, and Pippo Calò." Gonzaga spat out the names in derision. Calvi had been found hanging by his neck under Blackfriars Bridge, in London. Carboni and Calò were accused of murdering him to cover up Mafia involvement, but were acquitted and then became prominent in Italian business and politics. "I thought of myself as a patriot. They were crooks."

Greta stood up and stretched conspicuously.

"Dottore, we found you some riding clothes. If you like, please change and we can ride out before it gets dark."

Coffee had appeared at his elbow, and Gonzaga downed it, like a shot of adrenaline. He wondered if he had the strength to get on a horse, but decided that it would energize him. His hosts clearly wanted to draw this out, but he could hardly complain about the company.

———

Gonzaga made his way down to the paddock, where Greta was breezily warming up a gray Arabian mare with a sequence of technically difficult gymnastic exercises. The groom at the paddock gate held another Arabian, black, also a mare. Handing Gonzaga a riding helmet, he gave him a leg up and Gonzaga swung into a well-seasoned Devoucoux saddle. He wondered, briefly, if Greta knew how much he loved horses, and that, in his youth, he had represented Italy in the Olympics. But, then, he realized, of course she did. These people did their homework.

"Have you ridden Arabians much?" Greta asked. "How were you mounted for the Olympics?"

They hacked out into rolling pastureland, flushing the occasional pheasant or chukar that had escaped local hunters. Even if he was being handled by people who seemed happy to see him behind bars, it felt good to be on the back of a spirited and beautiful animal, feeling the midafternoon Hudson River Valley sun on his chest, and riding abreast this mysterious brunette who looked even more dazzling in well-fitted jodhpurs than she did in a $30,000 evening gown.

"My most joyous days have been spent on horseback. Many of those galloping across the desert. Arabians have such endurance."

"Shall we give them a run?" Greta clicked her tongue softly, and her mare picked up a trot. Another click, and a gentle squeeze with her leg, and they were cantering side by side. Gonzaga sensed her exhilaration and watched her hips, anchored deep in the saddle, rock rhythmically, effortlessly, following the Arabian's gait. He pictured those hips rotating on top of him, not just riding him, but challenging him to keep up. I am a filthy old man, he thought, but that was how he had ended up here. Things could be far worse.

After a few miles, Greta stopped on a ridgeline overlooking a wooded valley, their horses barely winded. Greta swung her leg forward over the English saddle, cowboy style, and slid to the ground, hitching her mare to a tree branch that was low enough to allow the horse to rest and graze. She raised her arm and pointed south.

"If you want to escape, follow that trail for five miles. You'll find a county road. Just tie Shâdî somewhere with grass. She's been freeze branded; we'll find her. If we lost her, Ziba would never forgive me."

Gonzaga dismounted, tethering his mount next to Greta's. Shâdî and Ziba. Iranian names. That explains the trace of an accent he could not identify. And also the girl's linguistic prowess. Upper-crust Iranians of what he assumed to be her parents' generation—particularly in an era when they were isolated from the West—gave their children classical homeschooling. Languages, science, math, and literature, the Western canon—and the Persian.

They sat on the grass, she cross-legged, he with legs stretched out, propped up by his hands behind him. The shape of his cilice was visible under his riding britches

"م‌ن اوتحم همستس‌م," he replied. I am totally content.

Greta laughed.

"Such clever Persian! How did you come by it?"

Gonzaga gave her his best man-of-mystery grin.

"I once helped the Shah out of a tight spot." Heady days, thought Gonzaga. The Shah had been a big spender, had half of the American Congress in his pocket. Gonzaga had helped arrange so many contracts: food, machinery, F-14s, oil. Such an undignified ending. Fading by the day, traveling the world looking for a place to die in peace, dragging around that bag of Iranian soil that he kept under his bed.

"I spent some time in Tajrish as a kid," said Greta, not yet willing to expose her history. "I'm guessing you helped the Pahlavi family move their money around?"

There was no point in being coy. He had to assume that, even if they had not plumbed all the secrets of Vicker's firm, they knew enough that if he lied to them, they would know it and punish him for it. Not that he felt the need to bare all, but he wanted to invest in credibility and the truth cost him nothing.

"I was a young man in a hurry. I needed to make money. A great deal of money. It is no small burden that Castiglione and Machiavelli both offered their advice to one's own ancestors. Good advice at that. After so many generations, what kind of man would I be, were I to have neglected my legacy?"

"Noblesse oblige, generation after generation?" Greta gave him a sarcastic look. "And you end up as what, Elias Vicker's finishing-school teacher? That must be odious."

She ran a finger over the ridge of the cilice beneath his pants. "Is that what this is about? Penance?"

Gonzaga sighed. "Sometimes our creations take on lives of their own," said Gonzaga. "I detest clichés. But they describe essential truths. The vast sums we generate have rendered an insecure and needful man arrogant and cruel."

Greta let the silence resonate. He seemed to sincerely believe that he was different from Elias Vicker, as if Vicker's apparent crimes weren't laws that he broke or chaos that he caused, that his depredations might be excused because he hid them behind a scrim of impeccable manners and urbane chitchat. She had seen that sort of self-deceiving, suave veneer too many times. In too many of the Wall Street crowd: slick and false. In politicians: guileful and scheming. A near-desperate thought popped into her head: As much as she believed that Ben would be the singular exception, what if he was no different than all the other great men who'd entered politics and found it impossible not to succumb to the venal circumstances and temptations?

"If Vicker has changed so terribly, why give him tools he cannot comprehend?"

Gonzaga seemed to not understand.

"Fyodor Volk," said Greta. "I believe you introduced them. Only a few months ago."

Gonzaga nodded. The only way this woman could know of his connection to Volk was if she had been read into the cable traffic from the ambassador in Cyprus who had seen them in Fyodor's company. And that likely would have been a top-secret communication, given that Volk was involved. So, whoever this Greta was, she breathed rarefied air.

"I wouldn't suppose you've been in touch with my dear friend Kathy Harper?" asked Gonzaga.

Greta offered him no sign of recognition, but felt a rush, making progress in reeling in a target. By dropping the ambassador's name, Gonzaga was signaling that he suspected that she knew much more than she was revealing. But Greta wasn't ready to open her robe any further. She was the one asking questions.

"Why bring Volk into the game? You might as well introduce Vicker directly to Putin."

"I'm flattered you think I am so well-connected," said Gonzaga, lightly, before turning serious. "My advice regarding Volk. Never get crosswise with him. The only reason I've enjoyed productive relations is that I am careful to always be on his side. Since I have no side of my own, that is relatively easy. You, I would guess, don't have that luxury."

Again, Greta brushed him off, and pressed. "Did Volk force you to introduce him to Vicker?"

"I had expected to remain the go-between. But, yes, Fyodor insisted. And he and Elias got on much better than I had anticipated."

"It should have been easy to anticipate the possibility that a self-serving mediocrity like Vicker could become dangerously full of himself."

"I kick myself for it." Nothing to be lost here, he thought, sharing views on Vicker with someone who already seemed to know quite a lot about him. About both of them. "But now I seem to have lost my hold on Elias. I can't even get him to return a phone call."

Once more, Greta let an absence of words settle between them. She detected a note of self-pity in his voice. Was it real? Or was he feigning vulnerability to draw her in?

"If you're looking to regain your influence over IS, we have some ideas."

Gonzaga felt a twinge of optimism—and arousal—as he looked at Greta, sitting cross-legged, back strong and straight, shoulders pulled back slightly so that the sheer fabric of her blouse traced the shape of her breasts.

"What do you have in mind?"

"Vicker has outlived his usefulness to all of us. We can discuss it over lunch."

On the ride back, Greta fed him a slow, steady drip of information, sharing with Gonzaga what they had learned from their deep dive into Vicker's psyche. None of it came as a surprise to Gonzaga. After all, he had arranged two murders on behalf of his protégé, but Gonzaga was disconcerted by what all of it implied about her view of him, and her assessment of his culpability, morality, and his place in what he was coming to think was a rather grand scheme. What struck him, though, was the sheer amount of effort this mysterious team of spooks had expended on figuring out what made Elias Vicker tick. They could have saved themselves a lot of trouble by coming to him sooner. But the important thing was that they were here, and that they needed him. Being needed by people who had nowhere else to go was his greatest talent.

———————

As they dismounted, a groom took the mares and they joined Don and Chip around a table where a tray of tuna salad sandwiches, still in their deli wrappers, and bags of BBQ potato chips, Don's favorite food, waited. Don noticed immediately that Greta and Gonzaga were relaxed, almost friendly. Not at all like before the ride, when Greta had been tense, like she was going into battle, and Gonzaga had seemed unsteady, barely able to swing his leg over the horse.

"When the fancy guests show up, Don really goes all out." Greta handed Gonzaga a bag of chips, which he daintily put aside. "Don, I think it's safe to say that Lorenzo is open to hearing our proposal." She turned to Gonzaga. "Am I right?"

"Anything for a tuna sandwich," Gonzaga said conspiratorially.

Don winced. He had handled many prisoners and had never once made small talk with one. Maybe that was the difference between Delta Force and the CIA.

"Before we get to business terms," Chip said, "could we ask you about some of Vicker's trading of late? We have a few questions."

He handed Gonzaga a tablet that displayed a spreadsheet analyzing Vicker's trading patterns since he returned from Cyprus. Black swans had filled the sky over Industrial Strategies—and Vicker had anticipated every one. Gonzaga gave it a once-over and handed the tablet back to Chip.

"Looks like Fyodor. That's his style. Innocent bystanders don't bother him."

"We're well aware of that," Greta said. "That isn't my question. What we have not been able to figure out is how they coordinate. We see all the email traffic and phone calls. There's nothing there. We assumed you were the conduit."

"I suggest you take a look at a fellow named Vadim Ivanov," Gonzaga said. A fateful decision, giving up Ivanov. But he had no choice. Ivanov, he figured, could protect himself. "I've met him only a couple of times. Went to one of your Ivies—Princeton, I think. Very close to Volk, and increasingly so after Anatoly was killed in Syria. He was with us in Cyprus. An all-American Russian spy."

Chip froze at the mention of Ivanov. They had been classmates at Princeton. Chip had always known that there were many sides to Ivanov's personality—and that there was much he kept hidden—but FSB? Indeed, there had been whispers inside the halls of Tiger Inn about the handsome, athletic Russian who spoke perfect English and seemed almost too polished, but Chip always dismissed such talk as preposterous: When Vadim spoke of any aspect of the Communist Party or any of its organs, it was with venom and unbridled hatred toward the dark forces that he blamed for destroying the homeland of his forefathers. They had once been close, mostly lost touch after college, but in the last few years, Ivanov had made it a point to rekindle their friendship as business frequently brought him to New York. His relationship with Ivanov had been documented, in detail, in his personnel file, although Chip always played it down, describing Ivanov as little more than a campus acquaintance.

"You okay, Chip?" Don asked.

"Yes . . . No, it's just weird. I mean, you think you know someone. I thought he was just looking for investors for palladium mines in Siberia."

Greta was surprised that Chip was surprised. They had run across Vadim Ivanov in a war zone. And here he was, popping up again. Why couldn't Chip see the obvious: that his friend was more than likely an FSB plant, and had been reporting back to Moscow as long as Chip had known him. The Russians played a long game. Their favorite gambit was to send their top students to America's best universities to major in the most competitive disciplines: math, computer science, biotech, engineering. Yale, Princeton, Columbia, MIT, CalTech, or whoever would give the kids a free ride, and spending money. Myopic, the schools could not resist the bait. Uber-qualified and, best of all, these students filled self-imagined quotas for international diversity. By the time they graduated, every last one of those deep cover agents had developed wide-ranging networks within the current—and future—economic, social, and political elites. Among the old-line intelligence chiefs, and, it was said, with Putin himself, there were few sacrifices that earned greater respect than a young trainee making a lifetime commitment to an undercover life in a foreign country.

"Mental note," said Don. "We have to find that fucker."

"I'll see what I can do," said Chip.

"There is something else we wanted to run by you," said Greta, turning to Gonzaga while Chip handed him a tablet.

"It's a press release," said Chip, "announcing the formation of Industrial Deconstruction, 'an international demolition conglomerate that will service both civilian and military clients.' One of the biggest roll-ups in history. Seems like a strange business for Vicker to get into."

"Diversification?" Gonzaga said, as if it were a matter of no importance. "I don't know. I was not consulted."

This was disquieting news. Gonzaga had not realized how far the demolition scheme had progressed, or how completely Volk might be manipulating Vicker. By gathering dozens of regionally dominant companies based all over the world under an American corporate umbrella, Industrial Deconstruction, Volk would be able to move demolition experts, engineers, and tightly regulated explosives across borders without having to answer too many difficult questions. There was no way the Treasury Department would ever have allowed the Parsifal Group, or any other outfit with links to the Russian government, to operate any company in the United States, let alone one that specialized in blowing things up. But Washington would be pleased to see a powerful American firm like Industrial Strategies take a dominant position in a large international business. Vicker would not even have to ask for approval. Of course, he would have had to conveniently forget to mention the connection to Volk—a crime in itself. But no one would pick that up before the acquisitions had been completed. Or after, for that matter, with the right lawyers.

"It is concerning," Gonzaga said. "One thing I've noticed about people like Elias Vicker, who are suspicious of almost everyone, is that they sometimes, inexplicably, defer to the exact wrong person."

Gonzaga's weary, man-of-the-world act stirred a sharp feeling in Don.

"*Concerning?*" There was an undisguised edge in Don's voice. "Is that what you call it when a Russian mercenary who runs off-the-books operations for the Kremlin and should be on a U.S. sanctions list has just bamboozled the richest man on Wall Street into buying him cover to move a private army anywhere in the world he wants? Does that *concern* you too?"

Gonzaga was pleased by Don's flash of anger. The Americans were scared, perhaps a little desperate. But he wasn't going to get into a philosophical debate with Don Carter. "Miss Webb mentioned an arrangement," he said, sidestepping Don's challenge. "What do you have in mind?"

"At some point, in the not too distant future, Industrial Strategies will undergo a change in management," Greta said. "We'll need help understanding IS, its historical relationships, and, generally, smoothing the transition."

Gonzaga considered how that might be accomplished, what the challenges might be. There was, of course, Vicker to consider, and he could only imagine what this crew had planned for him. If they needed more material, he knew more than enough to compromise Vicker, push him aside, and help to wrest control from him. That would give him enormous satisfaction. Dealing with Volk would be a more delicate matter, but that was just the sort of negotiation he excelled at.

"I can be helpful with a transition. Reassuring prime brokers, introducing you to the fund administrators, setting up meetings with accountants and valuation experts. Making it clear that the bank remains fully behind 'new management,' so that none of the IS trading relationships are disrupted. And making introductions to important legacy investors."

"Any in particular?" asked Don.

"Only one that really deserves attention. You will not find them on the share register. But you may know them as Stichting Eskandarfond. Or you may not know them at all."

"Makes sense." Greta tented her hands, almost prayerful, not letting on whether she knew of SEF or not. "And there's another layer to this onion that we would like your help to peel back."

"We're curious how Volk funds all these accidents. Some disasters are cheap, others are expensive, and he is making a lot of them," said Don.

"I'm not Fyodor's only banker, and he's got lots of business interests. The simplest way for IS to get him money would be for Vicker to provide him with a special allocation of profits. But . . . well . . . I've heard stories."

"Such as?" Greta asked.

"That one reason Fyodor enjoys owning a bank—and likes managing money for the clients of his bank—is that it gives him access to his clients' money, as well as his own."

"How would that work?" asked Greta, perfectly aware that Gonzaga was about to confirm her most dreaded suspicion, that their stolen dollars were providing Volk the liquidity to fund his murderous schemes.

Gonzaga took a deep breath. "One gets the impression that Fyodor has no qualms about dipping into client accounts to fund his own projects. If a client notices, Fyodor might blame an accounting error and put the money back. I had a similar problem with a protégé, Tony, years back. He liked to punt with client money, but he made bad bets. A complete mess. I'm sure you know all about it."

"You skated away from that one pretty nicely," Don said.

"As I was saying to Miss Webb earlier, life would be simpler if our creations did not take on lives of their own. Of course, with Fyodor, there's a difference. Most of the money he manages for his clients these days arises from ill-gotten gains. If some goes missing, most don't have much leverage to complain."

"I'm not following," said Chip. "Why would you even think about doing business with Volk—much less introducing Volk and Vicker?"

They would need to know more than a little of his personal history to understand the answer to that question, thought Gonzaga. How, for many years, when Russia wanted to do business in the West, it worked through Moscow Narodny Bank and Vnesheconombank, both of which, because they were difficult for most Western bankers to understand, became Gonzaga's clients— and he became one of their few reliable connections to the international financial system. It had been lucrative business, which the Russians knew and, as part of the bargain, knew that they could insist that he occasionally support transactions—particularly after the Berlin Wall fell—that enabled senior KGB officers to, in their parlance, "adopt" orphan assets. How he had been there at the beginning of the wholesale looting of the Russia patrimony, even pioneering what he had dubbed the "bicycle": buying commodities domestically at artificially low prices set by the Russian state, exporting and selling them at vastly higher free market prices in the West—and using the proceeds to repeat the process. And how, on one of his many trips to Moscow, a young KGB officer, Fyodor Volk, showed up with wire instructions to move funds for his betters. Then kept showing up, carrying instructions for many others, and, eventually, for the Butler—and for himself.

"I've known Fyodor for many years. I'm his banker, helped him at the start of the Parsifal Group. And, once he had enough money to need to worry about other ambitious men trying to take it from him, helped him protect it. And if he needs an introduction, information—whatever—I try to be useful."

"Just so," said Greta, feeling uneasy, slightly sick.

Don leaned forward on his elbows. Greta knew something was coming, but not what. He had been playing along too politely. Not his style, and, for certain, not his mind-set toward the project.

"So—no offense—this all seems a little too easy. Too cozy."

Gonzaga leaned back and crossed his legs, but otherwise showed no outward sign of concern.

"How so?"

"You put Vicker in business. You financed Volk. And, suddenly, you want to switch sides?"

"Then what would you recommend, now that I seem to have been tossed out on my ear? That I pretend to put up a fight? I hadn't anticipated you, but, now that you're here, I realize that I've been waiting for you for years. So . . . welcome."

Slippery, thought Don. Even admirable. At least the man was a realist.

"Now, I am curious. What will you do with IS? With the many tens of billions that Vicker has accumulated there?"

Greta glanced at Don and Chip.

"Special projects."

"Perhaps I can help there too?"

Greta studied him, bemused. If he only knew, she thought.

34

Industrial Strategies, New York City

After months of being ignored, Gonzaga found himself summoned to Vicker's office, following a beleaguered Alison. Apparently, after decades of intimate association, he was no longer trusted to roam the halls by himself. As he entered Vicker's glass-walled lair, he noticed that Vicker had not bothered to fog the windows. He sat down across from Vicker, who stared at his screen and pecked at his keyboard for longer than good manners permitted. When he finally looked up, rather than offering his hand, as had been their custom, Vicker stared at him blankly.

"You've had quite a run lately, Elias."

Vicker still showed nothing.

"And congratulations on your new listing on the Nasdaq. First time that an international demolitions contractor has ever gone public, is it not?"

Vicker looked at him with unconcealed hostility.

"Is it not?" said Vicker, mocking. "Yes. It *is*."

Vicker started to say something, but stopped himself, and then seemed to change his mind.

"Lorenzo, I've had it with your arrogance. Your pseudo-royalty bullshit and pretension. I should have known that your many 'brilliant' ideas over the years were cadged from someone else. My 'friend,' the great genius."

Gonzaga mulled how—whether—to engage. He had seen that expression many times before. But, for the first time, Elias Vicker's murderous look was directed at him.

"Elias, I have always been a conduit, and a filter. Good ideas are good ideas; it does not matter where we find them."

"Right. A filter. Adult supervision. Isn't that how you explained me to Fyodor? The pathetic failure you rebuilt . . . from nothing."

Gonzaga could feel his heart pounding in his chest.

"Perhaps you have reason to be annoyed, but please consider. We have played a rough game over the years, but it has been a game of rules. These Russians—they don't play that way."

Vicker shook his head. *No.* He had put up with the condescension, the barely concealed disdain, for years. Volk was right. Not only did Gonzaga no longer add value, he was a parasite, leaching off his billions while looking down on everyone else with that air of unmerited superiority. Gonzaga had patronized him for the last time.

"Maybe so, Lorenzo, maybe so, but that's the past. Fyodor and I are operating on a different scale, and we are just beginning. What we have planned is really quite . . . amazing."

"What would you like me to tell Wennerström? SEF is happy with the way things have been organized. Any changes you have planned, I could help manage them. Especially after that unpleasantness with Oscar."

"Funny you bring that up," Vicker said. "It took me a while to put two and two together. Wennerström never would have sicced those thugs on me without your sign-off. Do you think I've forgotten? Do you think you can kidnap Elias Vicker and not pay a price?"

"My dear man, had I not intervened, I dare say that evening might have turned into a far more unpleasant experience than it did."

"That's exactly what I thought you'd say. You fuck me in the ass, and then act like you did me a favor," said Vicker.

Vicker leaned back with a smug smile.

"We're changing the structure of IS and that means reducing the number of investors," he said, pausing for effect. "Starting with you. Which is why I agreed to meet with you today. I thought that after all we've been through, you deserved to hear it from me personally."

"I appreciate the courtesy," Gonzaga said. "If nothing else, perhaps I taught you the value of being a gentleman."

"You also taught me not to let sentiment guide a business decision. The truth is, I just wanted to see the look on your face when I kicked you out. Goodbye, old friend. Shall I call security or can you show yourself out?"

Part Four:

Fall

35

Saint Barts

Vicker directed Don toward a chair as he tossed computer printouts, a laptop, manila folders, cold medicine, Band-Aids, and hand sanitizer into a canvas bag.

"Mr. Carter, I'm taking a short trip, to get some sun. I don't want your whole army in tow, but two, maybe three, of your guys to watch the plane, run some errands."

Since Vicker returned from Cyprus, Don had seen little of him; Vicker came into the office rarely, usually just before Volk was about to make something happen. After each event, the trading activity became frenetic as pipelines ruptured, valleys flooded, and fires raged. On those occasions, Vicker sat at his desk, which hovered over the trading floor on a glass platform, following the price movements of his portfolios in real time. Like an admiral on the bridge of a battleship, he shouted orders to buy and sell, stamped his feet, pumped his arms, and clapped his hands with glee.

"When and where to, sir?"

"Leaving now for Saint Barts, via Saint Martin."

"Will you need transport after Saint Martin? The Boeing is too big to land at Saint-Jean."

"No need. Staying on a boat."

Twenty minutes later, Vicker was in his Maybach on the way to Newark, and Don sat with Greta and Chip, trying to make sense of his sudden jaunt. Saint Barthélemy, named after Christopher Columbus's brother Bartolomeo, is a spectacularly rugged and beautiful French territory in the Caribbean that attracts the rich and the very rich with unspoiled beaches, great food, and doting service. It was an unusual destination for Vicker, and not likely that he'd want to curl up with a book or dance on the tables at Le Ti. Greta had scoured Vicker's travel records and flight logs. As far as she could tell, the trip to Saint Barts—or any beach resort—was a first, although Piper occasionally used his plane to hop down to Mustique.

The French reverence for money and fascination with intrigue made the island an oasis for rich Russians in a world that had become increasingly hostile toward them. No matter that their unfathomably gargantuan pirate fortunes had been amassed by plundering and pillaging the now-stagnating Russian state, in Saint Barts, well-heeled Slavic parvenus were treated as royalty. In turn, they spared no expense in taking care of the locals, and cosseting the international jet set. Invitations to Gennady Bogdanov's New Years' Eve party had become a hot ticket. Paul McCartney, Demi Moore, Martha Stewart, Wendi Murdoch, George Lucas, Bella Hadid, Emmanuel Macron, Mick, Gagosian, Perry, Diddy: they all showed up.

"My bet is a meeting with Volk," said Greta. "They have a lot to talk about. We have to get eyes on the meeting, ears if we can."

"On it," said Chip.

———

Vicker's 747 taxied to a remote corner of the Princess Juliana International Airport on Saint Martin, where an Airbus H175 helicopter waited, its main rotor turning slowly, ready to take off in an instant. Don's lead minder, Gunner Nuzine, carried Vicker's canvas bag and suitcase down the mobile stairway, but stopped at the bottom of the steps. Three beefy guys with shaved heads and reflective sunglasses—clearly, to Gunner's eyes, Special Forces alumni like himself—made it abundantly clear that they would take it from there. From a window of the plane, Don's security team photographed the handoff, discreetly, streaming it in real time to New York. Tan chinos and Lacoste polos embroidered with a lemniscate, the symbol of infinity, projected a smoothly suntanned nonchalance belied by the sidearms holstered on their hips. The very fact that they had license to carry openly—or did not care about legal niceties—suggested not merely their willingness to use their weapons but also a solid understanding that no official record would be kept if they were.

The chopper lifted off the instant the doors closed, military style, and cruised low across the water. Half a mile away, a yacht the size of a small cruise ship lay waiting, barely moving in the choppy seas, a helipad jutting from the stern.

"You know whose boat that is, right?" Chip said.

"Gennady Bogdanov, *Zemblanity*. Second biggest private yacht in the world," Greta replied.

"Hope no one told Vicker. He wouldn't even get on that thing if he knew there was a bigger one out there."

Built by Blohm+Voss, shipbuilders to the Third Reich, *Zemblanity* spanned 650 feet and came equipped with all the necessary tools and toys of an oligarch on the go: a helipad, twenty-six guest cabins, swimming pools, a disco hall, two high-speed launch boats, bulletproof glass, a minisubmarine capable of submerging to two hundred feet, a missile detection system, a laser shield to zap paparazzi, a complete arsenal, and bunks for the crew of seventy-five mercenaries, sailors, and staff needed to operate the yacht and protect and serve the guests.

As the chopper powered down, they watched two men walk across the deck to greet Vicker; just behind them, a stylishly dressed, but wizened, woman *d'un certain age* followed, in an electric wheelchair.

"Okay, we got Volk and Ivanov." Nuzine kept the scope trained on them. "Who's the lady?"

"Vicker wants to know the same thing. Look at him."

Ivanov met Vicker first, shaking his hand politely before Volk rushed in and wrapped his visitor in a tight and purposeful hug. But Vicker barely seemed to notice. He was staring at the third member of the party with a look that hovered between surprise and anger.

"Now *this* is interesting," Greta said. "Wennerström sightings are rare these days, since what was rumored to have been a very bad accident. A spinal injury while heli-skiing in Kamchatka."

"Wennerström . . . Let me see," Chip said, logging into one of the—many—private, unindexed databases he maintained, for his own use, in the deep web. "Oh, there are two of them."

"Marius and Marina. Brother and sister, fraternal twins, Swedish royalty," Greta said. "Marius heads the family shipping empire. Swings for the fences every day. One day the family is worth tens of billions, the next day, almost kaput. Typical shipowners, cannot help themselves."

"And Marina?"

"Super socialite, on all the right charity boards, like her brother, but murky, lots of rumors in our world connecting her to SEF."

Greta could barely contain herself.

"It has to be Marina," she continued. "You can't believe what a big deal this is. Remember those astronomers who photographed a black hole in space? That's what we've got here, a look into one of the deepest pools of dark money on the planet. They're the perfect package. Marius can deploy the family fleet to move small packages—or entire armies. And Marina can finance anything."

Don whistled. "Not to mention the information that they're privy to about their clients' businesses."

"A meeting of the families." Chip barely looked up from whatever data he was searching.

Don ignored him.

"What's your read, Greta?"

"I just want to know if Vicker has any idea that he's become the front man for two of the biggest criminal enterprises on earth."

"With us riding shotgun."

Don paused. That sardonic smile. Kidding. But not.

"Doesn't get much better 'n this."

He turned back to the screen, but the foursome on *Zemblanity* had already entered the ship.

———————

Zemblanity began moving, its motion, dampened by a rotor-based stabilization system, nearly imperceptible, the waves beneath might as well not have been there. They settled into plush sofas in a room festooned with an indigestible collection of contemporary art that Bogdanov and his wife had snapped up by the—hugely expensive—yard. Their effort to use art to buy their way into Western high society, a common technique of arrivistes, had succeeded. Money, of course, would have been quite sufficient, but the art added a veneer of taste and erudition. The symbolism of meeting on a ship owned by one of Putin's closest friends was not lost on Vicker.

"Gennady regrets not being here to meet you," said Volk, pleased to be on the cusp of joining that elite club of show-offs who lent one another their yachts. "Another time, but we have much to discuss, so perhaps it is best." Movie-star beautiful Russian boys and girls, some armed, served coffee, appearing out of nowhere and then dematerializing. Spooks in training.

Volk turned to the woman in the wheelchair. "Marina tells me that, until now, you two have not formally met. Allow me to introduce you: Marina Wennerström, Elias Vicker."

Vicker reeled, as if he had been slapped. Wennerström? His Wennerström? Marina? It had never occurred to him that the secretive boss of SEF—that the person Gonzaga had always carefully referred to simply as "Wennerström"—might be a woman, and a cripple, no less. This was his biggest investor? The bitch who had manipulated Oscar into financing terrorist car thieves and then had me kidnapped? *Goddamn, Gonzaga.* Vicker began wondering what else he did not know about that traitor Gonzaga, about his investors, perhaps even about IS itself.

His chest tightened. That familiar toxic rush of rage and shame.

"You seem surprised," said Wennerström, her English extremely proper, with the faintest lilt of a Scandinavian accent.

"It is natural," she said. "I prize my privacy. It seems that Lorenzo really did keep his own counsel, which is what we pay him for. Is it not?"

"Used to pay him for," Vicker said. "No need for a middleman anymore, just principals."

"Oh yes, of course." Wennerström eyed him coolly, the way a strict governess might regard an entitled charge who had stepped out of line. "Lorenzo always told me the time would come when you'd decide that he had taught you all you needed to know. He must be very proud of you."

Feeling the lash of Wennerström's tongue, Vicker's face flushed with anger. That snide comment alone will cost Gonzaga a billion, he thought. "Lorenzo has a talent for exaggerating his importance."

Volk allowed himself a tight smile, one that hid contempt. Even though he had engineered their schism, he knew enough about Gonzaga, and the history of IS, to be disgusted by the way Vicker so casually dismissed the man who'd made him. So like an American. Taking everything so personally, making everything about himself.

"I've always greatly enjoyed Lorenzo's company," Volk said with a reassuring smile.

"But I agree with Elias. Lorenzo might lack the vision, or perhaps the stomach, to see how much our partnership could accomplish."

These people are becoming annoying, thought Vicker. How much *our* partnership could accomplish? Industrial Strategies is already the biggest privately managed fund on earth. As big as Norway's sovereign wealth fund—and, well, give it another year or two, they would eclipse even that.

"I couldn't agree more," he said.

Ivanov, sensing that this first meeting of tribal chieftains was not going smoothly, jumped in.

"We've been keeping an eye on Lorenzo recently. The other week, he went up to his suite at the Carlyle with your computer girl, Greta Webb. They didn't leave for three days."

Trying to think on his feet—sorting through multivariable decision trees in real time—had never been his strong suit, but Vicker knew, viscerally, that it was not a good sign that his new partner was spying on his security team and tailing Gonzaga. Looking at them, he couldn't help but feel outnumbered: three to one. He needed to buy time.

"The Webb girl? She's gone. I don't even know what she does. Lorenzo can have her." He reached for his phone. "And I'll make her sign an NDA so tight she won't even be able to send an email to her grandmother without my permission."

"No need to make hasty changes," said Ivanov. "Just flagging the need for caution. Your security is our security. It affects us all."

Wennerström was surprised to catch Volk shooting Ivanov a venomous glare, for no obvious reason, but then raise his wine glass, as if to offer a toast. As he was about to speak, a look of distaste appeared on his face.

"This is the wrong glass for pinot noir." As the steward was about to take it from him, Volk crushed the glass in his own hand, spraying wine and splinters of broken glass on the table, the deck. Opening his empty palm, blood seeping from several cuts, he picked out half a dozen shards, poured water over it, and peered at it, with detached curiosity—as if it wasn't his hand at all. Then, calmly, he wrapped it tightly with his napkin.

Catching Wennerström's eye, Volk nodded, ever so slightly, as if nothing had happened. Marina tried to remain expressionless, but looked toward Vicker, who turned away. She had already begun to get a strong sense that something was off with Volk. And now this. Maybe the rumors were true. Grief had twisted Fyodor.

Vicker did his best to remain oblivious, barely taking in Volk's tantrum, still focused on the suggestion that he ditch Carter Logistics, which was the last thing he wanted to do. Wennerström was, after all, the reason he had to hire them in the first place. And here she was, the bitch who had ordered him kidnapped—from the comfort of her glorified go-kart.

"If you think Ms. Webb poses a security issue, it's best to leave her where she is, where we can keep an eye on her," said Volk, "but at the same time, and—I'm sure I speak for Marina here when I say this—I'd sleep easier if I knew for sure this vaunted security team of yours is as good as you say it is."

Vicker started to chuckle. "I have a feeling I'm going to like this."

"I think you will be pleased. But let's leave it at that. All you need to know is that we'll be out there planning something. But put it out of your mind. The operation will be precise and delicate." Volk turned to Wennerström and put a hand on her forearm.

"Marina, please excuse us for a few minutes? I want to give Elias a quick tour." What was that smug look on her face? thought Vicker. The *Achille Lauro* hijacking came to mind, and how easy it would be to dump her right over the side.

Volk put his arm around Vicker's shoulders, but something in the hardness of Volk's manner gave him pause. Vicker was accustomed to life in a bubble, where no one treated him with anything but complete obeisance. And now, here he was, out in the open, by himself. Among the sharks. Where Gonzaga had abandoned him. That was Gonzaga's deepest and most cutting betrayal—leaving him alone to fend for himself with this crazy Russian, who until recently he'd known only as the shadowy apparition who'd quietly solved problems for him that he preferred not to face himself.

"Gennady made me promise to show you around *Zemblanity*. He's anxious to hear what you think."

Volk guided Vicker through the main salons, a formal dining room with seating for thirty, an informal chef's kitchen, the game room, a gym, the club room lined with floor-to-ceiling climate-controlled humidors, stateroom after stateroom, and a bridge so jammed with state-of-the-art electronics that it made the cockpit of his 747 look like an antique.

Vicker felt admiration mixed with envy. Why hadn't he thought of this? A plane was one thing, but a ship like this, a vessel that made its way around the world, following Gennady and the weather, was a symbol not merely of wealth and extravagance but of an ancient level of refinement reaching back to the solar barge built for King Cheops to cruise with the sun god across the heavens. And what could it cost? A billion? Two at most?

"I'm saving the best for last."

Volk led Vicker down three flights of stairs, through passages paneled in African pink ivory wood and lined with plush carpeting. So quiet, soothing. Deep inside the hull of the ship, at the end of a long hallway, they came to a set of massive doors that swung open automatically as they approached.

"This is perhaps the finest room on any ship anywhere in the world."

Volk held Vicker's arm to keep him from being disoriented as they entered a pitch-black room under the bow of the ship, what might, on a freighter, have been a massive cargo hold below the water's surface. Volk snapped his fingers and, with a faint hum, the outer hull of the ship retracted to reveal floor-to-ceiling glass panels, eight inches thick, running for fifty feet on each side and coming to a point at the apex of *Zemblanity*. Sea turtles floated in front of them, lobsters crawled on the seabed. Vicker was pretty sure he caught the silvery flash of a barracuda off in the distance.

"Please try these seats. Gennady had Christian Liaigre design them just for this space."

Vicker sank into a cocoon of deep, bloodred mohair velvet and let himself be enveloped by the sexiest chair he had ever experienced. He lay back, absorbed by the light that shimmered on the surface and the teeming blue-green waters that surrounded them, feeling as if he were floating. He could not remember the last time he'd been in awe of anything, much less anything natural. Almost, he imagined, as if he were in a womb, or coming home, or had found a new home, a place to be reborn. So this was it. If you were open to it, this is what money could buy, a place of quiet, of peacefulness, and sheer childlike wonder. He smiled. Maybe Volk wasn't so bad after all. And he did want to meet Gennady.

Standing over him, Volk raised his arm high and twirled a finger decisively over his head. The steel plates slid back into place, obscuring the underwater view, and with a pleasing mechanical whoosh, thick, carbon fiber shades unfurled, seamlessly covering three sides of the room.

"It's also a screening room. Like everything else, state-of-the-art. Spielberg loves this place, says there's no better place to watch his work. I was here for an early cut of *Bridge of Spies*."

Suddenly, the room went pitch-dark. Bottomlessly dark. At first, only sound: the shrieks and squeals of Russian girls blasted from hundreds of perfectly spaced speakers mounted in the walls and ceiling. When Vicker looked up, he was staring into himself. Right in front of his eyes, slightly larger than life-size, his face, blown up, like a hideously detailed and revealing Chuck Close painting. His own face, filling the walls, himself, glaring at himself from screens on three sides. Surrounding him, inescapable, and in all the savage clarity of 4K resolution. His face frightened him: unveiled, savage, fearful, threatened. Where had that been taken? As if in response, the camera pulled back to show the larger frame: his pants unzipped, shirt wet with sweat and champagne, drunkenly unbuttoned, he was sitting stiffly on a leather chair while three mostly naked ballerinas pawed at him, and others cavorted together behind them. But he couldn't stop looking at his own anxious stare. And then the Vicker on the screen, the guy always looking for the exit, jumped up and began shouting at them. *Stop. Just stop.* He shouted. It made him cringe to hear his own shrill, pathetic voice echoing in the screening room. And, as he remembered all too well, they did not stop. They kept touching him, pawing at him, trying to strip him, grabbing at his balls, his ass. Until he drew his arm back and, with full force, began striking them, unseeing, maniacal, deranged, grabbing them by their long, braided ballerina hair, tossing them brutally across the room. A wonder that they weren't hurt badly. Or perhaps they had been hurt. Perhaps that was the point of Volk's vile surprise.

Those coked-out little sluts, he thought. Of course they were filming me. Volk was filming me. Should have realized that *kompromat* wasn't just a gambit that Russians played on foreign businessmen and politicians in Moscow hotels. Clearly, they could deploy it anywhere.

Moments later, the lights came back up.

"No need to see any more. I think you know how it ends." Volk gestured toward the screen. "Unless, that is, you were enjoying the program."

A shakedown. Of course. That must be how the Russians do it. It was foreplay to them. They needed to feel like they had you by the balls, so that when they offered you a way out, they could act like they owned you. Doing you a big favor by selling it back to you. All just an elaborate ritual, he figured: Volk would tell him that Svetlana and her friends would all be willing to see the tape destroyed for, say $5 million. He'd haggle it down to two. Volk would probably keep half for himself. The ballerinas would each pocket more than they'd earn in two or three years. Much more than they'd ever get from any of those New York ballet companies that Piper and her friends supported.

Vicker smiled and threw up his hands, but he jerked his arm a little too quickly, too hard, and knocked over a crystal glass of ice water that had been set out for him.

"First thing I thought when I saw myself all sprawled out on that sofa was that I'm a total lightweight when it comes to booze."

He leaned down, weirdly preoccupied with trying to aggressively sop up the spilled water with his napkin.

"And water too, it appears—I hope you don't have that on tape. That would be really embarrassing. If people saw me spaz out and drench myself like that."

He lifted his head up to see Volk looking at him. No expression that he could read. Not judgmental, not mocking. Just . . . blank.

"So how much will it take?"

"Oh, Elias, please. That is not how I do business. That is not how a gentleman does business."

"So, you'll destroy it yourself?"

"You overestimate my powers. Showing you this was simply . . . a courtesy. One friend giving another the lay of the land." Volk waved his arm again. The screens whirred back up into the ceiling and the panels opened again to the ocean beyond.

"I can't see that this matters, so many people hate me." Vicker felt strangely in control, the way he always did when he was negotiating. "I mean, personally, I don't care. So what if I had a little rough fun with some hookers? Like you haven't. Like Marina Wennerström hasn't, for all I know."

"I think the atmosphere has changed in your country. This might not be so easy to walk away from."

"Oh, you mean like Harvey Weinstein? Once Disney showed him the door, people weren't afraid of him anymore. That's the only reason they got him. It was only a matter of time. No one would do that to me."

His bravado was genuine but so was the slowly dawning fear that there would be no way to easily shrug this off. It wasn't merely that he would be the object of ridicule, having fallen for the oldest Russian trick—girls and cameras in a hotel room. Piper would dump him, get out while the getting was good and shimmy off with her prenup settlement, invoking the morals clause to triple it. Fair-weather political friends would stop taking his calls. The big banks might be forced to pull his prime brokerage lines. *Disaster.* People would begin comparing him to Weinstein, or worse, Jeffrey Epstein. Every bit of respect and recognition that he had fought so hard for, everything he valued—the proof of his value as a human being—stripped away. Not just taken out for a public beating, but *canceled.* He knew how that worked: he had seen to it that so many others were canceled, but only now did he realize what it meant. Reviled. Banished from polite society. *Erased.*

"If you burn me, where does that leave you? You can't afford to have me out of the picture."

Just then, Vicker felt a presence at his side. An almost freakishly handsome attendant, but with hard eyes and high cheekbones like blades, had appeared to set down a fresh glass of ice water on his armrest table.

"Thank you, Lev." As Lev walked away, Volk started chuckling.

"Everybody's so jealous of Gennady. Not only is Lev an alum of Shayetet 13 . . ."

Vicker looked puzzled.

"Probably the most secretive unit in the IDF. They can do everything: sea-to-land incursions, counterterrorism, sabotage, maritime intelligence gathering, maritime hostage rescue. Gennady recruits from their ranks exclusively. And Lev can also tell a soup spoon from a dessert spoon. Not easy to find. Everybody who comes on board wants a Lev of their own."

Lev exited as stealthily as he had entered.

"Elias, my friend. I hope you understand me. This was done out of friendship . . . And the videos that your late friend Dr. Kerry took? Also safe with me."

Volk watched Vicker's face, trying to imagine the thought process he was going through, trying to sort through so many pieces of information. He wondered if Vicker was even capable of doing a differential analysis of risk assessment: which other videos might Volk possess, and what might they mean for his future. It shouldn't take him long to realize that his risk was not merely social ostracism, but criminal. Certain ruin faced him unless he played his part in whatever game Volk chose—by whatever rules Volk dictated.

"Elias, what this means to me is that you will always be my friend. That you will look out for me like I will look out for you. It's quite a solemn bond, is it not?"

Volk got up and walked out of the small theater. As the door shut behind him, he heard first the hum of the curtains followed by the fine, high-pitched crack of crystal, as a glass shattered against a glass wall.

36

Council on Foreign Relations, Park Avenue, New York City

Mara glanced, discreetly but pointedly, at her simple Patek Philippe, making certain that Richard Haass, her interlocutor at the Council on Foreign Relations, got the message. She had barely fit in the session, part of CFR's program of conversations with leaders in international finance, fifty precious minutes squeezed from a whirlwind tour: Tokyo, Berlin, London, Washington, and, now, New York. Meetings with central bankers, secretaries of state, finance ministers, and editors in chief, and endless, tedious, dinners with confounding members of the chattering class. Projecting the image, however false, of a new generation of central bankers. With scripted misdirection, and help from fawning journalists and naive pundits, Mara had positioned herself as a leading light of a new generation of financial technocrats, a cadre of well-educated, disciplined central bankers, economists, and policy-makers who had emerged from the dung heap of the former Soviet Union. Mara, trading on her training in higher math, studies of game theory, and degrees from Oxford and Harvard, had become the voice of orthodoxy, articulate in espousing the vapid platitudes of the Washington Consensus, and disparaging of the horror and waste of communist central planning as an historic misallocation of resources that inflicted fifty years of economic ruin on tens of millions.

"Dr. Bērziņš has been incredibly generous with her time," Haass intoned, as he looked out over a sea of raised hands in the standing-room-only crowd that filled the council's largest auditorium. "We have time for just one more question." He gestured toward an elegantly dressed man sitting in the front row who had been waiting impatiently to be recognized, sighing loudly in exasperation.

"Thanks, Dick." Elias Vicker stood, his tone rising imperiously. "Dr. Bērziņš, it's all very well and good that you say you, or your friend Vladimir

Putin, I should say, will treat our money well if we invest in your country. I don't doubt your intentions—those intentions probably get you invited to a lot of nice places. But foreign investors are getting well and truly screwed throughout the entire Eastern Bloc. There's no transparency in how your government makes decisions, and your courts are . . . well, biased at best. Why would I think my money would be safe in any of your sparkling little kleptocracies?"

"Mr. Vicker, I'd like to remind you that respect goes both ways. It is darkly humorous to me that Americans kicked the Russians out of the G-8 and have since quashed any effort to bring them back in. Russia is a permanent member of the UN Security Council, yet you treat it as a pariah. Mexico, a nation run by drug cartels, is treated with kid gloves. You label Russia's most respected businessmen as criminals and sanction them. Meanwhile, no such opprobrium is leveled at China, which farms human beings and slaughters Uighurs and political prisoners for their organs. If the liberal world order is to succeed, it will do so only on a *truly* level playing field. Not a field on which transparently parochial politics—and American bullying—defines a precarious, relativistic morality."

Greta, standing in the back of the auditorium, loved watching Mara in action. Not only had she not been rattled by Vicker, she had sidestepped his sharp question gracefully. Anyone aware of Mara's real business would know there was no good answer to Vicker's concerns. She was, she had to admit, nervous about seeing Mara. She had not seen her since she'd had to beat a hasty retreat from Jūrmala the previous summer. Though they talked all the time, they stuck to business and pleasantries. They'd never discussed that weekend, or anything about their relationship for that matter. As Mara chatted up a knot of well-wishers by the podium, so poised, serious, and buttoned-down, but also radiant, Greta had to admit that she felt a little lost, not sure if she was looking at an adversary or a lover, or both.

She was distracted from her reverie by a burly, florid-faced man in a bow tie and double-breasted blazer striding purposefully down a side aisle, toward Elias Vicker, who was trying to slip out a side exit. When the man caught up with Vicker, he took Vicker by the arm. Vicker looked annoyed, but as the man whispered something in his ear, Vicker began to smile and looked interested, his predatory neurons engaged. The man handed Vicker a fat envelope, which Vicker immediately folded and stuffed into the side pocket of his jacket. Before walking away, he patted the man on the shoulder in a way that was grateful yet condescending. The man seemed disappointed, like he had been hoping Vicker would take him out for a steak dinner.

Once Mara was free, she dashed up the aisle, wrapped her arms around Greta, and placed affectionate air kisses on her cheeks. Warm but business-like. A big beautiful Hermès scarf framing her angular face. Something about her seemed far away.

"Mara, who's the red-faced guy in the blazer over there?" Greta asked without thinking, as she saw Vicker's acquaintance starting to drift out the door.

"That's how you say hello? After a year?"

"Oh, hello, lover. Now tell me who that man is."

Mara turned to look. "Cecil Baxter? A retired diplomat. He's a respected Arabist. Back in the day, he solved some big problems. Now I think he just floats from one open bar to the next, talking about the old days. He's harmless though. Well connected. You don't want me to introduce you, do you? Doesn't seem like your type."

"Oh, God no. You kidding?"

Mara held out a crooked elbow.

"I have a suite at the Four Seasons. Let's walk."

They made eleven blocks' worth of small talk, sometimes holding hands, sometimes drifting apart. Mara updated Greta on mutual friends and acquaintances back in Riga and wanted to know which SoHo boutiques to hit in the hour of free time she had the next morning.

When they got to the Four Seasons, a chilled bottle of wine was waiting for them. The first signal of real interest from Mara, it seemed to Greta. She opened the bottle, poured two glasses, and sat down next to Mara on the couch.

"That scarf you're wearing, it's the most beautiful thing I've ever seen." Greta reached out to touch it. Mara batted her hand away, more forcefully than she meant to.

"Is everything okay?" Greta asked, confused and a little hurt.

"No, no. I'm sorry," Mara said and took a gulp of wine. The confident, snarky, aggressive central banker had disappeared, replaced by a frightened girl.

She started to unwrap her scarf, her face flushing red, tears welling.

"I haven't had anyone to show this to. Please don't judge me."

She unwrapped the scarf. The base of her neck was covered in angry purple bruises, four finger-shaped marks on one side, a thumb on the other.

"Oh, honey," Greta said.

"It started after Anatoly was killed." She touched her neck again. "There are times Fyodor can barely control himself. He always comes by later, begs forgiveness, says he's losing control and is starting to become afraid of himself. You can't tell him I told you this. You have to swear on it. I don't know what he'd do."

Mara took Greta's hands and gripped them tightly.

"Or . . . No forget it. It's a stupid idea."

She wiped away her tears and took a sip of wine.

"I mean, what are we doing? We should just get out. What's stopping us? We could go somewhere. Start over. Now's the time, while I'm in charge of your accounts. We could take as much as we want. Before he loses control completely and kills me."

"Now? You know that I can't."

"You mean you *won't*." Mara's face became a fierce mask. "I know what you think about me and Fyodor. But I see what I do for Fyodor—and what he does for me—very clearly. You, you think you're part of some big plan that your guru—Tommy Taylor—has for you all. But that's *all* you are to him, a cog in some crazy scheme of his. The second you've outlived your usefulness, it'll be like you never existed. Come with me now." She tightened her grip on Greta's hands. There was desperation in Mara's clutch, but Greta felt something else—a hardness to Mara's pleas. She was begging, to be sure, but also delivering what seemed like a threat: *Come with me or not, either way, I'm taking your money.*

———

As Vicker walked in, Vinnie heard him humming a tune. "You're in a good mood today, Elvis. Did I hear you singing?"

Vicker pursed his lips as he handed Vinnie his jacket. "Funny how a song just pops into your head and you can't help yourself." He dropped his head in an Elvis pose and started singing and shaking his rear end like the most embarrassing guest at a wedding. "Remember that song—'Hound Dog'? '*Well, you ain't never caught a rabbit / And you ain't no friend of mine.*'"

Vinnie nodded, flicking a gown over him. "Yeah, I never got the bit about the rabbit. Do you?"

"I let some hound dogs into the house, Vinnie. But they ain't no friends of mine, and they ain't gonna catch this bunny."

Vinnie lathered Vicker's face. "You're too deep for me, Elvis. Whoever it is, I hope you get 'em, and, no matter what, I've got your back."

"I know that, Vinnie." Vicker relaxed into the chair. "There's an envelope in my jacket pocket. Cost me five million dollars, supplied by some Jordanian spooks, if you can believe it. Intelligence reports tying Ben Corn and his GI Joe pals to behavior unbecoming of an American president and his best friends. I had a feeling it might be worth it. Insurance. That's part of the industrial approach. Never forget that. And, Vinnie?"

"Yes, Elvis?"

"Keep it somewhere safe."

37

Nice, France

From Saint Martin, Volk and Ivanov Gulfstreamed to Nice, where a helicopter waited to whisk them to Cannes. The *Better Place* was waiting, fully crewed and moored half a mile off the Boulevard de la Croisette. Unlike other members of Putin's inner circle, whose movements were restricted under American sanctions, Volk could travel more or less freely across borders. In part, this was because he had not yet committed a sufficiently notorious crime. Like the one that inspired the Magnitsky Act, in which a couple of oligarchs got nailed for diverting corporate tax revenue owed to the Russian treasury through a chain of dummy corporations and using the money left over (after taking their cut) to pay for the sarin gas Syrian president Assad dropped on the people of Aleppo in 2013. But mainly because he wanted to try out the Canadian passport—a welcome addition to his collection—that he had recently acquired as part of a deal to invest in a Canadian gold mine.

"A working vacation," he had told the customs official—running his modest business during the day, making the most of the film festival and its various activities by night.

As they boarded, a crewman handed Ivanov a large FedEx envelope.

"This arrived for you yesterday, sir."

Without breaking his stride, Volk grabbed the package and motioned Ivanov to sit next to him at a gleaming glass-topped table. Volk elegantly filleted the envelope using a gold pen knife his great-grandfather had received as a colonel in the Okhrana, Tsar Alexander III's secret police. Inside was a bound report titled *Hudson River PATH Tunnels: Threat Assessment*, pilfered with a surprisingly high degree of expense and complication from a Port Authority archive, and a brittle, faded print edition of the *New York Times* from December 22, 2006.

"This will make an amazing souvenir. Here it is, right on the front page." Volk held up the newspaper so Ivanov could read the headline: *PATH TUNNELS SEEN AS FRAGILE IN BOMB ATTACK.*

"The Americans and their first amendment. They make our job too easy."

The story detailed how the Port Authority of New York and New Jersey had paid a small fortune to two top civil-engineering research labs—Lawrence Livermore National Laboratory and Rensselaer Polytechnic Institute—to analyze the condition of its aging Hudson River rail tunnels. In the wake of 9/11, much was made of bomb-proofing vulnerabilities in New York's infrastructure. Prominent among these concerns was the Port Authority's PATH train, which ferried 250,000 people between New Jersey and lower Manhattan and midtown every day. But the report hadn't been made public or provided to top state or federal officials or to law enforcement—perhaps because the price tag for hardening the tunnels would break the Authority's budget—or maybe to hide the decades of criminal-level incompetence that had allowed an invaluable asset to rot in the muddy bed of the Hudson River. No one would have been the wiser, but for the fact that a whistle-blower, whose children probably rode the PATH every day, leaked it to the press.

Drawing on his Behike cigar, he gave Ivanov a mirthless grin.

"Here's my favorite bit." Ivanov flattened out the newspaper on the table, under the warm Mediterranean sun. "This is a direct quote: 'If we believed in any way that passengers were in danger, we'd close the system. That would happen immediately.'"

Volk had begun to take an interest in the transit systems, because, every year, dozens of "normal accidents" occurred on commuter rail, as trains barreled under, over, and through cities and rivers across the world, often on bridges or in tunnels, that were old and patched together, perennially awaiting budget-busting improvements and staving off decay with duct tape and Band-Aids. Every accident brought cities, sometimes entire regions, to a standstill and provided a perfect, and generally small scale, example of Perrow's hypotheses about how complex systems fail. Tunnel mishaps routinely caused mass fatalities and sowed widespread fear. At Kitzsteinhorn, Austria, a hundred and seventy skiers died in a funicular tunnel when a small fan caught fire, melting thin plastic pipes that carried highly flammable hydraulic fluid. In San Francisco, a faulty circuit breaker triggered a massive tunnel fire that crippled the city's BART system. Dozens died from the detonation of backpack bombs in the Moscow metro.

Some tunnels were stronger and safer than others, but the four PATH tunnels counted as the most notoriously decrepit and vulnerable underwater tubes in the world. The other two crossings beneath the Hudson River—the Holland and Lincoln tunnels—had been bored through bedrock. The PATH tunnels lay atop the soft riverbed, because the owners of what was then the Hudson & Manhattan Railroad thought it would be too expensive and take too long to dig through rock. Three-quarters of the tubes' total length consisted of unlined cast iron—the same antique cast iron that Charles Jacobs, their chief engineer, used to build the tunnels in 1904. Over more than a century, those iron tubes had rusted from the outside. Repeated flooding caused the iron to corrode from the inside as well.

"What does the report say?" Volk spooned delicate *fraises de bois* into his mouth; it was a pity that wild strawberries had such a short season.

In the interest of protecting its readers from the specific and frightening details of the threat, the *Times* had not published the actual report.

"That a relatively small amount of high explosives could punch a fifty-foot hole, flooding a tube in minutes." Ivanov paused. "At rush hour, there are two ten-car trains in each tunnel at all times, roughly two thousand five hundred people per tunnel."

Volk made a mental calculation. Two hundred of his best men murdered in Syria by the American air strike. Each worth the lives of at least ten fat, complacent New Jersey commuters. One tube would even the score. But he wasn't playing for a tie. Two tubes would settle the beef. Definitively. Three tubes would make a nice statement, and it would be wise to build in redundancy. Explosives were, by their nature, volatile, and they would not easily get a second chance.

"Some other interesting bits as well." Ivanov raised his cup, signaling for another espresso. "The Port Authority engineers think they've come up with a solution that will be much cheaper than rebuilding the tunnels—laying geotextile concrete mats over them will prevent them from flooding so quickly if they're breached."

Volk took a long draw on his cigar.

"Not a bad idea—if you're just trying to protect the pipes from an explosion on the inside."

He laughed.

"It shouldn't be too difficult to get the contract to lay those concrete mats, right?"

"We're already on it, boss. And we are the low bidder."

The merger and acquisition program that Volk and Vicker had devised to roll-up small specialist companies into a conglomerate of demolition and remediation outfits had been neither elegant nor subtle. They had overpaid nearly every time, becoming something of an industry joke: the hedge fund fool who had more money than brains. But they achieved their goal: Industrial Deconstruction had acquired the track record and engineering know-how required to bid on major contracts anywhere in the world—in war zones and in wealthy cities, on land, underwater, or underground. Some of the most lucrative contracts arose in Vicker's own backyard. New York State and New York City had been the malificiaries of industrial pollution on a vast scale. Industrial Deconstruction dredging ships, bulldozers, barges, and trucks had become a constant presence on the Hudson River, in Newtown Creek, the Gowanus Canal. The few competitors who refused to sell out grumbled that if Industrial Deconstruction wanted to win a contract, it could afford to underbid everyone else.

Which was why Volk's men, veteran aquatic soldiers who'd worked some of the world's most hostile waters, were currently performing what was basically a plumbing job beneath the silty, sludgy waters of the Hudson River.

"One more thing, and this is something that should go without saying," Volk said. "Don't discuss this contract with anyone. If Vicker asks about it, just play dumb."

"Are you sure he has the stomach for this?" Ivanov carefully refolded the *Times* and slid it back into the envelope.

"It's not really about his stomach anymore. Before we left yesterday, I arranged a screening for him. While you were kissing up to Marina Wennerström—it was like you were auditioning to be her son-in-law."

Ivanov laughed, but carefully. When Fyodor got bitchy, it usually meant he was jealous.

"Always a good idea when you're talking to a queen—some of them have daughters."

"I applaud the long-term thinking. But, still, it's better to concentrate on locking down our new business partner."

38

The Carlyle, New York City

"Let's give them something to look at, shall we?" Gonzaga swiveled his stool to face the willowy blonde sitting next to him at the Carlyle bar. He tilted his head toward three large men dressed in ill-fitting suits sitting across the room.

"Courtesy of my new American friends," Gonzaga said. "A nuisance sometimes, but also quite flattering. Nothing makes a man feel more highly valued than being the object of a round-the-clock surveillance team."

Klara gave him a chaste peck squarely on his lips. "Like that, Daddy?" She smiled at the bartender. If she hadn't grown up at the Carlyle, he might have taken her for a high-end hooker, or a Barnard girl out to make some pocket money.

"How long will you be in New York?"

"Mummy has asked me to stay for a while. Something is afoot." Klara glanced at the steel Rolex on her slim wrist. "She won't say what though. She says you'd know all about that—whatever it is you're both keeping from me. Anyway, she should be home by now, shall we go upstairs?"

They let themselves into Marina Wennerström's apartment, a full floor located immediately below his own, reachable, since Marina's accident, by its own private elevator. Klara's mother looked up from her chair as Gonzaga folded her into a long embrace, followed by a loving kiss. He had known her since she was a child, but, for him, even in her early fifties, and even wheelchair bound, Marina became more beautiful every year. Klara ignored them and settled into her spot at the end—*her* end—of her mother's living room sofa, looking west at the fading light. Growing up, she had caressed the dark brown leather so often, absentmindedly, while doing homework or laughing with friends from Chapin, that it had taken on a patina all her own. Now, as she was being initiated, gradually drawn into the web of the family enterprises, she did as her mother said, and listened.

"Lorenzo, I am not casting blame. You and I agreed that we needed Fyodor, or at least someone with his resources, but . . . it was a mistake." Marina looked worried. "We're losing control. I should have seen it. Especially since Anatoly was killed, he's a different man. His tantrum in Saint Barts was completely out of character, appalling. Used to be that he only wanted people to think he was crazy. But he doesn't seem to be faking it anymore."

Gonzaga poured himself a tumbler of eighteen-year old Caol Ila and took a chair opposite Klara.

"Magnificently twisted psyches, both of them," she said. "And you, for that matter—leading Vicker to think I was a man, and keeping it up for so long, you must have loved that, Lorenzo."

Klara looked up. "You never told him? For how long?"

Marina put a hand on Gonzaga's knee.

"Thirty years, if you can believe it."

"Since before I was born?"

"It began as our little joke. We started off thinking that the less Vicker knew about our world, the better. Then it became a fetish."

"And he never pressed it?"

"For a man who prides himself on being a rational thinker, Elias has a weakness for superstition. Not uncommon among those who hail from such places as Queens, I understand. He was afraid that he'd jinx his good fortune if he asked too many questions"—he gently stroked Marina's cheek—"about my best—unfailingly reliable—source of information."

"And now that he knows?" Klara asked.

"He wants to start kicking out investors who aren't otherwise useful," her mother said. "Starting with Lorenzo. Volk seems to agree. I'm trying to stall them."

"How far out?" he asked.

"In your case, dear, *all* the way out, I'm afraid." Wennerström rubbed his shoulder warmly, as if trying to buck him up. "And you know how Fyodor can be . . . I'm so sorry."

Klara started, as if she had been slapped, but Gonzaga merely sighed. What troubled the three of them wasn't that Vicker wished Gonzaga dead. He could take care of himself. But finding—or, more likely, creating—another Vicker, and another Industrial Strategies, would not be easy. Without the truly meaningful returns Industrial Strategies had been delivering for more than a quarter century—profits that had compounded at 30, 50, 100 percent every year—within a generation or two they would be merely wealthy.

Gustav—Marina's grandfather and Klara's great-grandfather—had had a philosopher's grasp of the vagaries of the world, and the precariousness of great fortunes, no matter how vast or diversified they were. Great wealth needed protection—from war, from peace; from booms and busts. It needed mechanisms to move it around, as close to invisibly as possible. It needed to find ways to grow, to get to new ideas, new technologies, new industries, before anyone else, and to be able to crush competition. And, of course, to be able to disinvest—to get out—before anyone knew they had been there. SEF had been born of that wisdom, a stateless, intergenerational legal fiction. A quietly powerful investment vehicle, unconstrained by law, that could exist alongside the family's legitimate enterprises, whatever those might evolve to be over time.

Gustav's insight had been nothing short of visionary. His shipping and mining conglomerates, which became powerful in their own right, operated in the open. Some years they delivered staggering profits, in others they flirted with bankruptcy. But those ups and downs could be evened out by the rivers of capital they sent into the mostly hidden tributaries of the world economy. The two enterprises supported each other—the dark enterprises financed the ones operating in the light. Whenever possible, the light diverted profits to the dark side, shielding both from taxes.

"So you're warning me to be careful?"

"Even more so after your little sojourn upstate. Seems that everyone wants a piece of you."

Just like Marina, he thought, to conveniently forget why they were having this difficult conversation—because she had decided, against Lorenzo's advice, to put a scare into Vicker by ordering her goons to snatch him from his own party. To rattle Vicker, she said, and make it easier to convince him to let Volk in, to expand their range of action.

Gonzaga scratched at the edge of his cilice, slightly irritating, under his trouser leg. "Too much has been upended by Vicker going rogue, but this invasion by our new American friends—"

"What are they like?" Klara put down her phone, smoothed her skirt.

"Clever. Hard. But I don't fully have their measure yet, or even what to call them. Special Forces, for certain, but also some sort of intelligence service, current or former. CIA, NSA."

"Their agenda?" Marina asked.

"Complicated. Money, of course. But they don't seem conventionally greedy. They remind me of the KGB generals who plundered their nation while the Soviet Union was on life support. For strictly patriotic reasons, at least that's what they told us as we helped them build the secret financial networks that allowed them to hide their first billions. If they didn't rob the country blind, the wrong people might."

Marina laughed: melodious, refined. A laugh he dearly loved to hear, from a woman he had adored as long as he had known her.

"Klara honey, here's a lesson for you," Marina said. "People who think they have a moral claim to money are always more dangerous than people who just steal it for ordinary, venal reasons. Thieves, I can work with. They are predictable. It's the idealists who terrify me. They'll stop at nothing."

Marina and her family had possessed vast wealth for so long that they could pretend that money barely mattered to them. Except that it mattered more than anything. More than it mattered even to Elias Vicker. Money wasn't what they had or the immense capabilities it afforded them. It was the only way she knew herself. She hadn't so much been born as capitalized into existence. Money mattered so much that even if she had been destined to operate in the light, like her brother, she would have chosen not to. She had become addicted to the nearly mystical power not merely of controlling vast sums, but doing so from a position of anonymity. Known to only a few outside of her family, in secrecy.

"And what are our prospects for détente with these righteous spooks?"

"Very good, I would say. Functionally, they're in already, and they may be better partners than either Vicker or Volk. Ferocious, but thoughtful. Dare I say, rational? But we need to solve Vicker first."

"Vicker is the least of it," said Marina. "I know I just acknowledged that bringing Fyodor in was a mistake, but, now that he is inside, none of us—and you in particular—should try to interfere with him. He is so changed, more dangerous than ever."

As close as Marina and Lorenzo were, they still weren't family. They shared a child and great affection for each other, but they still kept their most private agendas to themselves. That way, if they ended up on different sides of a transaction, it was never personal or complicated. But it also meant that certain details of their affairs had to remain unspoken. Like Volk. Gonzaga had no idea how deep that relationship went. It was none of his business. But he knew that SEF had been active in the new Russia, as it had been in the old, financing KGB generals, supporting budding oligarchs, fronting commodity deals. He would hate to put Marina in a position where she had to choose between him and her financial interests. He had no doubt that she would choose the latter. And he was enough of a gentleman to want to spare her from having to make that choice.

"What do you suggest?"

"Caution, Enzo. We can rehabilitate you in time. In the meantime, keep Klara nearby, in case."

39

Rockefeller Center, New York City

It was one of Pete's inviolable rules: when you're doing a live broadcast, always show up in the studio, and get there early. No remote connections, no split screens. Let the viewers see you interacting with the host. Let them experience, if only vicariously, what it's like when Ben Corn focuses on you and you alone—the way he makes you feel seen and heard. But most of all, the way you feel strangely safe in his presence.

Ben was booked for the seven fifteen a.m. slot—prime time for *Morning Joe*, still more than a half hour away. He'd been up for hours, early enough to get in a full workout and make the five a.m. shuttle, careful not to wake Peggy, who'd come home late after her week in Seattle. Maybe that's how you know it's time to call it quits, he thought. Once you stop caring whether your spouse wakes up or keeps sleeping when you leave early or come home late.

After he won his seat, Peggy had wanted to stay in Omaha with the kids. But he'd insisted they move to D.C. He didn't want people back home questioning how Nebraska's most perfect family could really be perfect if Dad was never around. So, after some delicate negotiations and sessions with a very expensive marriage counselor, they worked out a new arrangement. Less forsaking-all-others, more let's-promise-not-to-embarrass-each-other.

Still, he was looking forward to seeing Peggy that evening at The Striped Pony, the fashionably down-at-the-heels gastropub where Vicker would be hosting twenty of the nation's richest men and women in the "secret" prohibition-era upstairs dining room. When Pete described it as "somewhere between an investiture and a coronation," Peggy had gotten interested—and having her aboard and engaged was crucial. She would sidle up to every donor in the room and give Ben an astute read on exactly how to handle each one. She would be the one to ascertain Vicker's commitment to the cause. Was he a true believer or did he just want in on the action? Would he take the lead in fundraising? How much would he commit? Beyond that, she would chat with each of the other guests as well, to judge whether they were all in on Ben or just kicking tires. Peggy had a sixth sense about people's intentions and motives.

It's part of why he had fallen in love with her, and a big part of why their marriage had not worked. Ben's training was in covert operations, in moving with stealth and cunning, creating diversions—and never getting too close, too emotionally involved, or offering any more information than was strictly necessary. Once you got good at operating in the shadows, it became easy to apply those skills to the parts of your life where they have no business. The fact was that they made a better team than a couple. As long they were focused on the future, on accomplishing something, getting somewhere, they got along well enough. Day-to-day was where things got difficult. Especially these days, with Maggie Hoguet hovering in the background.

It was no accident that Ben's *Morning Joe* appearances often fell on Tuesdays. That was the day Maggie did her weekly hit. Five minutes of green eyes, white teeth, and Acela corridor gossip, starting at 6:53. Joe loved her. Mika looked at her with slitted eyes. Which only made Joe flirt with her more.

Ben strode into the green room at six fifty, a little earlier than necessary, but he wanted to say hi to Maggie. She was locked into a conversation with Janan Avin Ramirez—JAR for short—a twenty-nine-year-old first-term Iranian-Cuban congresswoman whose oversize tortoiseshell glasses, tight Chanel skirt, and low-cut silk blouse belied her claim to a conservative upbringing. She cheekily identified herself as a "common-sense Marxist." Though Ben agreed with her on exactly nothing and would happily go to war to defeat what he dismissed as her "pernicious brand of feel-good socialism," he happily accepted the invitation to debate the young phenom on air. Pete thought it would be good for Ben's image to establish a sort-of opposites-attract public camaraderie with her in *Morning Joe*'s coveted 7:03 slot, almost like a rom-com.

"Senator Corn." JAR gave him a big smile and held out her hand, as if to be kissed rather than shaken.

"Janie," he said, using the anglicized nickname she had grown up with in Brooklyn, before she became a mononymous celebrity, known by a single name, like her idols: Fidel, Che, Kobe, Beyoncé.

JAR was there to discuss her proposal to set up a federal agency that would audit—and tax—"excessive privilege" in much the same way that the IRS audited tax returns. To Ben's astonishment, the notion was being taken seriously on college campuses and among the progressive elite in New York, Boston, and Los Angeles, while his calls to slash Pentagon spending and refashion the military as an agile force primed to respond aggressively to twenty-first-century asymmetric threats were somehow viewed at once as recklessly hawkish and a naive giveaway to our adversaries.

"Hmmm, what do we have here," the congresswoman purred, as he took her hand. "A long tall drink of the patriarchy."

Ben blushed. He'd always blushed easily, and it had embarrassed him until he'd realized that an unconscious display of emotion and vulnerability was actually very useful in establishing a quick bond of trust. Especially with women voters.

"Pleased to meet you, Congresswoman," Ben said with his trademark courtliness that no one could ever quite tell was ironic or sincere. "And Ms. Hoguet, it's been a while."

"Congress*person*," JAR said, with the combination of coquetry and self-righteousness that had made her a political star overnight. "And, for the record, my pronouns are she, her, hers."

A page came in to tell Maggie it was time for her spot. She jumped to her feet, slightly annoyed at how long JAR had held on to Ben's hand, and moved in to give him a polite hug, subtly grinding against his hips, lips up against his ear. "I want you to put this on me as soon as you get there," she whispered and discreetly slipped a Lilly Pulitzer print silk blindfold into his jacket pocket. "They gave me an upgrade. Presidential Suite. See you in a bit, Mr. President."

Ben ran his fingers over the silk blindfold in his pocket like he had already drawn it over her eyes and waited a few seconds until his heartbeat returned to its normal fifty-two beats per minute. He'd hoped to have a few minutes alone with the congresswoman, but as word got around the *Morning Joe* studio that Senator Corn was in the house, the green room started to fill up with curious members of the *Morning Joe* staff. Electricians, cameramen, sound techs, people who watch celebrities traipse in and out every day and take professional pride in not being impressed—they all wanted to shake Ben's hand, take selfies with him, or just bask in his self-confident smile. It would have been fatuous—and unfair to Ben—to compare him with Bill Clinton, who was said to make people feel as if they were the only ones on the planet when he looked them straight in the eyes and gripped their hands in his big paws. But Clinton was a narcissist who fed on the adulation of strangers, a man with a vast ache in his psyche that could be salved only by constant affirmation. Ben was different from most politicians in that there was nothing he seemed to want. He was real. Curious about other people. Eager to connect. Not to please or pander, but to engage.

Clearly knowing that this was a big day for Ben, and wanting to apply some pressure to his wayward protégé, Senator Frank Conway had told the *Wall Street Journal* that morning that, no doubt about it, everyone in his caucus would be voting yes on the Enterprise bill when it came to the floor next week. "Foregone conclusion," he'd said, "our party is united in the desire to show brave men and women of the armed forces that we have their backs. With this new aircraft carrier, we will be instrumental in defending American interests against global threats deep into the twenty-first century."

Maggie knew that Joe and Mika would want to know how the senator intended to wrestle Ben Corn, the carrier's most prominent critic, in line. When she'd checked with Conway's flack, usually one of her best sources, the flack had been uncharacteristically tight-lipped, saying, off the record, that it was a delicate matter and he might know more later. She hated going on air with so little. The first time Joe asked her, she managed to dodge the question. But Joe smelled blood. Frank Conway was making a public move against one of the party's presidential hopefuls. How could Maggie Hoguet not know the real story? She always had the best dirt.

"Looks like Conway's throwing the high hard one right at Corn's head," Joe said.

"Very mysterious," Maggie said. "One of my sources implied that they're talking, but that's all we know—"

Joe cut her off. He already seemed bored. "A good-old fashioned surprise," Joe said. "I love surprises." The monitor was on in the green room, but Ben was so immersed in his man of the people routine, he wasn't paying attention. Nor had he read the *Journal* story that Joe would soon be asking him about. He made a point of not obsessively reading newspapers and getting drawn into the between-the-lines drama.

As soon as the red light over the camera went on, Joe jumped right in. And Ben was on his own.

"Good morning, Senator Corn. Here's what I don't get. Senator Conway said he has his party's entire caucus behind this new aircraft carrier. You've said the USS *Enterprise* should be killed—and let me make sure to get this right—'like a hog with swine fever.'"

"Yes, and tossed in a fire. Can't forget that." Ben smiled. "Only way to kill the virus."

"It doesn't sound like Conway has your vote."

"Well, to be honest, I haven't made up my mind. And I haven't talked to the majority leader either." He flashed what *The Atlantic* had described as "the most complicated smile in American politics." Open and disarming, guileless, but at the same time the opposite, closed off and sardonic, as if to suggest that the entire enterprise of politics was ridiculous and somehow not worth the attention of a serious person.

"But that's really not the issue." The first rule of media training: when a TV host asks a difficult question, change the subject. "U.S. military spending is completely out of control and too many of my colleagues are too afraid of the Pentagon and the defense industry to say anything about it."

Joe was about to interrupt. Mika put her hand over his.

"But it's not just the Pentagon," Ben continued. "You know I'm not against the military. I bleed army. The problem is not just military spending, that's just the obvious place to start. This boat the admirals want to buy will cost twenty, maybe thirty, billion dollars and it will be underwater in about twenty minutes if the Chinese decide to point one of their hypersonic missiles in its direction. Those things travel at Mach seven, that's seven thousand miles an hour, two miles every second. Joe, I don't want it on my head that six thousand sailors and airmen drown in the South China Sea because we put them on a sitting duck. But, again, here's the thing: the problem is the entire federal budget, every single line item."

Mika looked startled. "Wow. Don't hear that from a first-term senator every day."

"Or you hear it only from a first-term senator," Joe said, smirking.

"What's next, dismantling Social Security?" Mika asking, practically whooping at her own grand joke.

"Thank you, Mika. I was hoping you'd ask about Social Security. Let me be clear: we can and will provide retirement security for our retirees. They've worked long and hard, they've earned it. And I'll take this point beyond Social Security. We can and should take care of our most vulnerable. Not just our retirees. But we can afford to do this only if we cut out the waste and inefficiency that has crept into the federal system since the New Deal."

Mika looked up from her laptop. "Was the New Deal a mistake?"

"Nope. Not for a minute. But what was right in the 1930s isn't what's right for today. And what *has* been a mistake is the endless, reckless expansion of federal spending over the last seventy years. We were once the envy of the world. What's happened to us?"

"This might seem like a stupid question, Senator Corn," Joe spoke slowly, like he was talking to a child. "But have you ever been to Washington, D.C.?"

Ben put his forearms on the table, leaning forward. "Joe, it won't be easy. But we've run out of time—we've actually run out of money. Except for the fact that most people haven't noticed and are still willing to let us run the printing presses, we'd be in deep trouble."

Ben paused to refocus on the camera. "And not only are we spending ourselves into oblivion, we're spending it on crap. China is building high-speed trains and crisscrossing their nation with million-volt electrical transmission lines. What happens when we try to do things like that? We hold hearings.

"For the past few decades, we've shipped the greatest military machine the world has ever seen halfway across the world to fight two futile wars. Trillions of dollars. Thousands of lives. And then, think of the opportunity costs—what we could have built with all that money and ingenuity and all those strong backs, think of what we could achieve if our dreams weren't shackled to a corrupt and decadent political culture."

He turned to Mika.

"In those years, the Chinese have built state-of-the-art fiber-optic networks, thousands of miles of superhighway, dozens of ports, new airports—entire new cities. I have a question for you. Name one national building project in the last twenty years that Americans can look at and take pride in."

He paused to allow Joe and Mika to rack their brains, scrambling to think of one. But they couldn't.

=====

On Monday nights, the network put Maggie up at the Berryman on East Sixty-Fourth Street, usually in one of the cheap rooms in the back, which was fine with her. But last night, when she checked in, they offered her the Presidential Suite—a reward for being a regular, she figured. She didn't question it. Maggie was used to being treated well.

Even with a late checkout, they never had enough time to explore their sexual fantasies. For a few tightly compartmentalized hours at a time, the three or four times a month when their schedules meshed, they gave themselves to each other. But neither could afford to, or wanted to, give more than that. Their encounters were a mutual folly, a fantasy that seemed to exist outside of their daily lives. It was pure hunger, almost impersonal, the way they gnawed and scraped each other like they did not even know the other's name, blindly feeding on a common primal need for sexual frenzy and adventure.

"That was a wild ride. Thank you." Maggie snuggled into his arm, dozing as Ben dealt with the dozens of emails that had piled up during the two hours they had spent working their way through most of the *Kama Sutra* positions before coming up for air, collapsing in exhaustion and giddy laughter.

Suddenly, she sat up, cross-legged.

"Did you hear that?"

Ben was too wrapped up in his phone to pay attention.

"I think there's someone out there."

Ben pulled on a pair of boxers, grabbed the Glock 42 that he always wore, holstered, on his hip, and walked barefoot into the living room of the suite. Maggie, scrambling to follow him, wrapped herself in a Frette robe.

Majority Leader Frank Conway, corpulent and pink, hair stylishly shaggy at the nape of his neck, sat comfortably—much too comfortably—on a pale green sofa, sipping a glass of Pellegrino. Next to the senator, sitting cross-legged and barefoot, on a Louis XV fauteuil covered in creamy brocade, was a scraggly twentysomething guy with a neat beard, hair drawn back into a man bun, wearing a hoodie and jeans, beat-up sneakers on the floor in front of him. The young man pecked at a computer open in his lap, barely aware that a mostly naked man, an extremely famous one at that, had just burst into the room, with a pistol in his hand.

Conway, with some effort, pushed himself up out of the deep sofa.

"There you are, muh boy! You can put that pistol down. This is one ambush you can't shoot your way out of."

Conway looked at his watch.

"Eleven forty-nine. You two really cuttin' it close to checkout."

Conway gave them his most lascivious grin, eyes on Maggie, who made a show of smoothing her robe over her breasts and cinching it tight.

"But this shouldn't take too long. Then y'all can go back to whatever you were doing. I went ahead and reserved the room for a couple more hours—case you've got any unfinished business."

"Frank, you know I always have time for you." Ben placed his Glock on the coffee table. "I practically think of you as family. But"—Ben pointed at the kid, who still hadn't looked up from his laptop—"maybe you could ask your guy to leave. This seems like a principals-only situation."

Ben poured himself a cup of coffee and stirred in a wad of butter. Carrying it over to a chair, he scratched his crotch absentmindedly, sat down, and waited for Conway to say something.

Conway took a long drink and set the glass down delicately on the table next to the couch. "Yuh know, before we put folks up for the highest office in the land, we like to be sure there're no skeletons. Don't want any Eagleton, Hart, Kennedy problems, stuff like that." Scandals around undisclosed peccadillos—electroshock therapy for Thomas Eagleton, girl problems for Gary Hart, and Chappaquiddick issues for Ted Kennedy—had made it de rigueur for party leaders to make sure that candidates didn't start down the path, much less get the nomination, only to find out that they had dark secrets that would queer the pitch to the American people. Conway, typically, gave himself too much credit. Party politics were far from foolproof, and graybeards didn't have the final say over voters who rebelled, went haywire.

Ben walked over to the window, looking out over the Upper East Side of Manhattan, wondering what Conway had found—or thought he had found. People got used to living this well all too quickly, he thought. Here's Frank Conway, the son of a coal miner, wearing a gold pinky ring, sipping Italian water from French crystal, sitting on a thirty-thousand-dollar couch in a room that rents for ten thousand dollars a night. And here, for that matter, am I, with my fancy haircut, balling a gorgeous super connector who's not my wife. Hard to say who the sluts were in this room, except, maybe, for that kid—but that was just because he hadn't opened his mouth yet.

Ben turned back to Conway, while Maggie's eyes darted nervously between the two of them. Conway looked like he was enjoying himself. "Frank, much appreciated. If someone is out there talking trash about me, better to know it now. What've you got?"

Conway gave him a self-satisfied grin.

"Last couple'a years, Jasper here and his pals been doin' what they do. I don't pretend to understand it, but these boys got some way of exploring internet stuff that you and I can't see. Jasper?"

The young guy with the man bun finally looked up.

"Senator, what we do is to scour both the deep web and the dark web. Looking for associations. We don't need much—really just a name, a fragment of a photo, and, ideally, one of two identifying details—Social Security number, email addresses, driver's license, a credit card. All that makes our algorithm more efficient at eliminating false positives."

Ben wasn't in the mood for a lecture, but he appreciated the distinctions that Jasper Bewick was making. People used the terms "dark web" and "deep web" interchangeably, when they were two very different things. The deep web, also known as the invisible web, simply referred to data that was not indexed and, for that reason, not readily located by the standard search engines. Deep web protocols ensured that sensitive information—like email metadata, online banking information, services behind paywalls—remained secure. The dark web—like the deep web—wasn't indexed either, but referred to data that had been intentionally hidden, completely inaccessible through standard browsers and often cloaking illicit business: drugs, guns, stolen credit card numbers.

"You've heard of Ahmia, Tor, DeepPeep, Scirus—popular off-the-shelf deep web search programs. What we use is kind of like those, but we kick it up a few notches. We use Clearview AI and build our own tools, put out our own crawlers. You might have read about us in *Wired*. They called us the Libertarian Rage."

Too bad Chip and Greta aren't here, thought Ben. Jasper seemed pretty impressive. He wondered if they knew who he was. Or if they should.

"Jasper here can go on for a while. If I don't tell him to get on with it, we all might fall asleep." Conway interrupted. "Son, give the senator here a look at what you've come up with."

Jasper drew up a chair next to Ben. While the boy wore the uniform of all hackers—sneakers, jeans, hoodie—Ben noticed Jasper's artfully torn sweatshirt was made from cashmere, his jeans were French, and the sneakers were Japanese—all no doubt very expensive. It struck Ben that there appeared to be nothing libertarian or raging about this kid.

Jasper clicked on a file. In the second before a video popped up, he noticed the filename: CORNPORN.WAR.jpeg.

"One cool thing about the war on terror, it's the first conflict in history in which soldiers filmed their own movies. There's video of almost everyone who ever served in Iraq or Afghanistan. Those were the early days of social media. People had no idea this stuff would live forever on the web. A lot of it's really grisly. I mean, shocking—not that I judge anyone for what happened in a war zone. I mean, sir, this should go without saying, but, seriously, thank you for your service. Our freedom depends on the sacrifices of heroes like you. I just needed to say that."

"Why thank you, son." Thank you, indeed, for five mindless, meaningless words. Words that I detest, thought Ben.

"Lucky for a lot of those people, most of this stuff is really hard to find. Old LiveJournal entries, blogs that lived on long-dead web 1.0 hosting platforms. It's just digital debris, the cyber equivalent of dead satellites floating in deep space. There are unquantifiable googols of it. Not indexed, not tagged, or the metadata got stripped. Whenever I do a dive on someone who served, that's where I start.

"Now, you were tricky." Jasper looked up at Ben. "Nothing was coming up. I gather that you didn't exactly operate in the daylight. Whoever does your scrubbing did a very good job. My hat's off to them. But it just didn't seem possible there wasn't a photo of you somewhere from that time. I've developed a proprietary AI-based facial recognition web spiderbot—even better than Clearview. I thought if I ran it, I'd get some sort of a hit."

Jasper flashed a photo on the screen. "Oh, that's a bingo," he said.

Ben's nervous smile quickly faded. In front of a garish tropical sunset were him, Don, and Chip. Arms around one another, bleary-eyed. But none of them at ease. Ben in the middle with a forced smile. Don glaring at the camera. Chip looking away. Underneath it were a few lines of text in Cyrillic. He remembered the exact moment: Goa. They'd gone there for a ten-day R&R after Wardak. Chip said girls from all over the world flocked to Goa for drugs, sex, and dancing until sunrise. Don said it was near one of his favorite surf breaks. Tommy had insisted on it. They'd needed to go away, have some fun, work out their differences. At a time when none of them agreed on anything, it had been an easy decision.

Right before that picture had been taken, they'd been sitting at a beachside bar, doing shots, when Don had lost it. "It's me or you," he'd yelled at Chip. "I don't trust you anymore." And then, in the middle of it, these three beautiful Russian girls showed up. Boy, did they ever come along at the right time. It turned out, some kind of small-world, totally random thing, that they knew a friend of Chip's from Princeton, a Russian guy who'd moved back to Moscow. The girls had insisted on the picture. They wanted to show their friend. That had been some night. Yulia. He wondered what ever happened to her.

"I found this on an extinct Russian social media site—it was, like, the Russian Friendster. Wasn't around all that long. The girl was a student at the top ballet school in Moscow. In one of her posts, she said a guy from the government showed up at school, asked her and two friends if they wanted to spend a week in paradise—leaving tomorrow. She posted a ton of pictures, including this one. The caption says наши американские друзья—in case you don't read Russian, 'Our American friends.'

"But I thought there had to be more, so I tweaked my bot, and ran my program again, a few weeks ago. I don't know how I missed this the first time."

Jasper clicked a key, and Ben was back in Afghanistan. The light was dim, early evening, but against the jagged moonscape he could clearly see the back of someone's head, covered by a black and brown keffiyeh. When he watched the head turn, he saw himself facing the camera. Chip was beside him, his head covered. At first, he couldn't figure out what he was looking at. Then another memory. A few months before that, he and Don had been on a surfing expedition in Indonesia, where they met a crazy Australian who was developing a tiny camera you could strap anywhere on your body. He insisted on giving them a few samples. You guys can be my beta-testers, he'd said. A few years later, when it went public, someone remembered to set aside some shares for them. That had been a nice surprise. Ben never understood why, but Don began wearing that camera constantly, and always turned it on when bullets started to fly.

He had no idea this recording existed. He thought Don had erased anything that might one day get them in trouble.

He held up his hand. He knew how it ended.

He didn't need to see any more.

Jasper stopped it and looked up at Conway.

"You sure? I went to a lot of trouble to cobble this together."

"That's okay son, we don't want to make this any more unpleasant for our friend Ben than it has to be."

Conway turned to Ben, who sat in a wing chair across from him.

"Or for me either. Thought I was going to puke the first time I saw it. Couldn't make it halfway through."

"No, run it." Ben changed his mind, eyeing the senator coolly. "The senator needs to see the whole thing. I want to be sure he understands who he's dealing with here."

Over the next 698 seconds, Ben relived his own My Lai. It had begun as just another routine JSOC operation, Tommy sending him out with Chip and Don to deliver a backpack of cash to a local warlord who in return kept a few miles of dirt road clear of IEDs and Taliban fighters so U.S. convoys could pass through. That day, someone, most likely the warlord himself, had tipped off the Taliban—probably with the idea of offering up a few American officers as hostages. Why not get paid twice?

Jasper's footage began just after Ben, Don, and Chip had repulsed the Taliban attack, killing a dozen fighters, sending dozens more scurrying:

Chip jerks his thumb over his shoulder. *"Time to get out of here."*

Wartime Ben, face caked in dust, eyes him coolly. Almost posing for the camera.

"Easy, Chip, get a grip. We're not done, yet," Ben says.

"What say, boss?" Unmistakably Don, speaking from behind the camera.

"The guy we just 'saved,' the guy who probably tried to sell us out, is the kingpin of bacha bazi. He keeps a harem of boys as sex slaves. Chained to their beds. Supplies them to half the commanders in the Afghan army."

"That pig deserves to get slaughtered," says Don.

"No." Chip, horrified, pushes his face right up to Ben's. *"We don't do this. Not our job to impose our version of morality—or reality. Just leave it."*

Don snorts, the camera catches his spit flying in Chip's direction, a narrow miss.

"*The whole village is in on it,*" says Ben. "*Mothers, fathers, offering up their children for a few dollars. They're worse than the Taliban.*"

He looks at Don, then Chip. "*I say we take out the entire damn village,*" he says, and starts walking away, gun pointing forward, finger on the trigger.

Chip seems rooted to his spot. "*I'm as disgusted as you are, but this isn't who we are. You'll regret this.*"

"*If you can't handle it, wait here.*" Don brushes past Chip.

It hadn't taken them long, as the video documented. Thirty-four men, murdered where they stood, walked, slept, ate, defecated. Bodies cut to ribbons by hundreds of rounds, barely recognizable as human, more like bloody chunks of meat. Only women and children remained, more than forty boys between nine and fifteen, milling about, in tears or in shock, hiding behind their mothers.

Afterward, the army press office downplayed the attack, blaming it on the Taliban. It barely made the news. Savages mowing down savages. The Taliban responded by releasing photos of the .223 Remington cartridges that littered the scene. No American news outlet picked up that story. That was the real fog of war, Ben thought.

"Jasper's one clever boy," said Conway. "Jasper, how many guys do you think could have pulled this thing off? Found that tidbit—that single atom in the ocean—driftin' along the floor of the internet?"

Jasper shrugged, smug. "Maybe half a dozen, but, of course, someone would have to be looking. And it takes a fuck-all huge amount of expensive computing power—and, well, my crawlers are pretty special. Supersmart, little AI bitches, teach themselves while they're working."

What now? Ben wondered, waiting for Conway's reveal.

"Do you think you've been able to scoop it all up—so as no one else finds it?" Conway asked.

Jasper looked just the least bit uncertain. "Still working on it. And we'll never be absolutely sure—kind of like sucking PCBs out of the Hudson River. It may be better to lay down more mud, not stir it up. We can mess with the metadata, make it harder to find. Much harder." He turned to look at Ben. "Your cameraman was prolific. Mostly sniper shots. Kind of fun—heads popping, some cool audio in the background—you guys yucking it up. But nothing else quite like this one. You didn't make too many appearances."

Ben didn't react. Conway made ready to haul his bulk off the deeply cushioned couch.

"Son, I'm gonna let you sit with your feelings a bit right now. But I just want to let you know, everything's going to be all right. For now, this'll be our little secret. All you gotta do is stand up at your little party tonight and explain to us all how you changed your mind about those aircraft carriers."

He paused.

"It'll be good for you. If you want to be president, you gotta know how to pull a one-eighty. I call it the D.C. dipsy-doo." He did a little dance with his pudgy index and middle fingers. "All the great ones, they can do it natural as breathing: look voters in the eye and tell 'em the exact opposite of what they told 'em yesterday."

As Jasper opened the door for him, Conway abruptly stopped and turned around. Ben was sitting on the couch, staring straight ahead, completely still. An unreadable expression on his face. Was he meditating? Seething? Plotting? Or all three?

"Think of tonight as your audition. I know you ain't gonna disappoint Uncle Frank. I'll see you later, boy."

40

Greenwich Village, New York City

In any society, coronation by acclamation requires skillful engineering. For months, Pete had been organizing intimate dinners across the country to introduce Ben to men and women who could not only write large checks but, by throwing their financial and social weight behind Ben, smother potential contenders for the nomination. No one wanted to see a bloody primary battle, and if anyone could pull off a fait accompli, it was Ben Corn, under Pete's guiding hand. A discreetly high-profile event in New York, ahead of the early primaries, to draw in all of Ben's biggest supporters and a couple of carefully chosen pundits. That was how you built the momentum needed to transform a well-regarded hopeful into a likely nominee, creating so much distance between him and the other contenders that he could focus all his energy on destroying his opponent in the general election.

But that was only one of the messages Pete intended to send. The other, more of a dog whistle to the elites in media and government, was just as important. In front of the nation's most powerful and exclusive audience, the presumed next president of the United States would be seen kissing the ring of the evening's host. The kingmaker: Elias Vicker.

An hour out from the most important event of Ben's political career, Don paced the hot sidewalk in front of The Striped Pony for the umpteenth time, trying to get a handle on an impossible security problem. The blocks adjacent to the hip gastropub on West Eleventh Street in Greenwich Village had been cleared of parked cars to accommodate the stretch limousines that soon would be dropping off a covey of billionaires and their hangers-on. But the cow paths that passed for Village streets were comically narrow, and the potential targets extremely high value. The only saving grace, from a security perspective, was that the location and details of the event had been handled like a matter of national security, which it was. None of the guests knew exactly where it would be held until ninety minutes before, and, except for a few pampered plutocrats, they were told to arrive on foot.

With any luck, the wider world would only read about the event on Politico, the next day.

Ben Corn's previously undeclared—but much anticipated—entry into the presidential sweepstakes had made him a person of intense interest to the pundit class: darling of the right, yet not a devil to the left. Pete's choice of a hipster hangout to anoint Ben was, like everything Pete did, intended to convey a message to Ben's base and beyond. Ben was the next generation—not old, not gray, not tainted by decades of backroom corruption. Shiny, quick-witted, a war hero who knew the horrors of war, and who vowed to never send young Americans off to be slaughtered senselessly. A child of the frontier, who could hold his own at a Greenwich Village hangout. All things to all people, but also a man of principle. A paradox. It was right there in his face, which was somehow both unlined and grizzled at the same time—a face that had both seen it all and was yet full of innocence. So much so that people's anxieties evaporated when he was around them. Whatever happened, he could handle it. Slow and fast. The explosive reflexes of a sprinter, the loneliness of a man who could go the distance, alone.

=====

Don looked over the guest list, again. Very like Pete to corral so many vast egos in one place: a Koch, the Mercers, Lauder, Langone, Peter Thiel, Betsy DeVos, and a dozen more. At the epicenter of right-wing stealth politics, Ben was about to become inevitable. Without bloviating think-tank hacks, politicians, or deep state sherpas who had never held a real job, more policy would be made at the Pony in two hours than the entire U.S. Congress could manage in a decade. Billionaires talking to billionaires, and talking to their latest boy.

Staffers and lesser lights, wearing holographic badges that could be scanned only once, began arriving at precise five-minute intervals. Anyone who missed their slot would be refused admission, but no one did. Don had organized security around ten men, in five two-man teams. Two pairs on the street, one pair at the door, one manning the stairs to the second floor, and one upstairs. Ten men, plus Don, Chip, and, in a pinch, Greta, who had her own delicate assignment that evening: arm candy for Lorenzo Gonzaga.

Greta and Gonzaga showed up last. Don pulled them along to the second floor, where the donors and their wives and husbands had gathered for cocktails. As Gonzaga drifted into the scrum, Don and Greta found Chip and Pete by the bar.

"You picked a doozie. This place is undefendable, so let's hope no pass-ersby notice who's walking in." Don put a pinch in his cheek and looked at Pete. "I can't wait for this to be over."

"Hate to break this to you, buddy, but this is just the beginning."

"Wasn't the whole idea to keep all these assholes at arm's length?"

"Even if we never need a dime of their money, we can't let anyone think that," Pete said. "They've got to believe that they own Ben, or at least a pretty good chunk of him."

Almost everyone coming tonight knew Ben already. Maybe they'd given him a ride on their jet or sat next to him at some free-market think tank's high-roller fundraising dinner. They didn't need to hear any more. They came tonight because they wanted to see him on his feet, working a crowd. Not just to size him up, but to watch everyone else in the room size him up. One of the many paradoxes of great wealth that Pete had observed in his years of cultivating the billionaire class: People got rich by not caring whose feathers they ruffled. But once they'd bought their way into the world of private clubs, Ivy League boards, and log cabins in Jackson Hole the size of a suburban high school, they were loath to do anything that might reduce their standing among their mega-wealthy peers. This early in the process, you didn't want to be separated from the herd you'd fought so hard to join.

Pete felt a firm hand pulling his shoulder. As he spun around, he was face-to-face with Vicker. "What the fuck is he doing here?"

Gonzaga was standing at the bar, chatting up a mining magnate about financing his exploration projects, looking for rare earths in Greenland and Namibia.

"Elias . . ."

"That slimy wop. It makes me sick to even say his name."

"Elias, we discussed this," Pete said, as if talking to a child on the verge of a tantrum. "We need Lorenzo. Ben needs Lorenzo. To everyone in this room, he's the embodiment of smart money. If he's here, it sends the signal they need to be here."

Vicker pointed at Don. "Okay, just so soldier-boy here makes sure Gonzaga doesn't get anywhere near me."

As Vicker stormed off, Don's earpiece crackled with chatter from the teams on the street: Ben and Peggy Corn had arrived, along with an unannounced guest, despite strict orders that no one whose name wasn't on the list, no one whose background hadn't been checked, would be admitted. No exceptions.

Don raced downstairs. First out of the car was Peggy, all cheekbones and wide smiles. Two people never looked like they belonged together more than Ben and Peggy Corn. Too bad they could barely stand to be in the same room. Next was Ben. Boy, could he ever play the part, Don thought. When Ben wore a suit, it clung to his lean, muscular body like an athletic uniform, one specially designed for a sport he'd invented for himself.

They both turned around to help a rumpled man who was struggling to get out of the car.

Jack Kunze. Brilliant move, thought Don. Bringing his broken, homeless buddy into a room full of billionaires, as if to remind them, "This is who I work for, not for you." No one was better at delivering a subtle fuck-you than Ben Corn.

Once they were upstairs, Peggy peeled off to work the room, but not before Don was surprised to notice her reach under his jacket and give Ben's ass what she thought was a discreet squeeze. He would never figure those two out.

Ben kept a firm, comforting hand under Jack's arm, holding him close, knowing that it wasn't easy for Jack to be indoors, in a group. With his other hand he pulled Pete aside, whispering into his ear.

"Did you talk to Conway's guy?"

"It's all taken care of. Remember the party Vicker threw the night he got kidnapped, the one I am always very careful to tell you to stay away from? Frank Conway was there."

"Of course he was." Ben smiled.

"The senator was so wasted that night he'd forgotten everything. Now that he, um, 'remembers' a little more clearly he asked me to send along the message that he has nothing but admiration for your heroic actions on the battlefield."

"So quiet, for the moment."

"Yup. But just the same, I wouldn't even mention aircraft carriers tonight. No need to rub it in. Conway's pretty fragile right now. He's never had one of his shakedowns backfire like this."

Ben moved away, working the room, chatting easily with each one he met, making it a point to introduce Jack, even though Jack could barely make eye contact and smelled the way he looked: like a homeless man someone had dragged in off the street.

On the dot, Pete flashed a high sign, a cue for Elias Vicker to introduce the evening's guest of honor. As Vicker threaded his way through the crowd to an open spot on the other side of the crowded bar, Jack Kunze blocked his way. Pete noticed Vicker reach into his pocket for a handkerchief and wrap it carefully around his hand before tapping Kunze on the shoulder. Otherwise, Vicker felt very much in control, in his element, shining with anticipation, erect and elegant, in what he imagined to be his Great Man Mode.

"Thank you all for coming. I won't say that Ben Corn needs no introduction, but I will say that we have never had the opportunity to support a man of Ben's quality, his potential." Vicker turned to Ben. "The proof is in this room right now. Ben has not made any official announcements and already, you all have pledged over a billion dollars to his, well, I guess I can't call it a campaign yet. Let's just say that Ben is Microsoft in 1983 and you are all angel investors.

"When we all look back on our lives, we'll think of this as the best money we ever spent. And this is coming from a guy who has a Picasso sketch hanging in the powder room of his own 747."

He paused and smiled at his own joke, as if waiting for laughter from the audience. But the room was silent. Stick to the script, thought Pete.

"So, without further ado, let me introduce the next president of the United States. Ben Corn."

The game was finally beginning, Don thought, watching from the back of the room. What had started out as the musings of four disaffected soldiers smoking bowls full of Black Kush in rugged mountains half a world away was coming into sharper focus. They'd survived countless secret missions— in Afghanistan, Iraq, and many other countries few Americans even knew were battlegrounds, from Burkina Faso to Mindanao. They'd negotiated the briar patch of domestic politics and risen to prominent positions—some official, some not—in the national security establishment, along the way liberating a nice chunk of the Syrian patrimony. Soon they would see if all their sacrifices, not to mention all the bootlicking and brownnosing they'd done to get to this point, had been worth it.

The message that Ben intended to bring to the American people was forthright, but brutal. Since 9/11, Americans had been fighting all the wrong wars, in all the wrong ways, while ignoring the real threats. And now, our beloved country—our kind, decent, and trusting country—was encircled from without and infiltrated from within by hostile forces. The Russians, the Chinese, the Cubans, the North Koreans, the Iranians. The tactics were all-encompassing yet often invisible: cyberattacks, social media manipulation, industrial espionage, covert military operations, economic war. All-out conflict waged by a large cast of enemies intent not only on compromising America's economic interests, but upon rending the fabric of American society.

Ben, a natural showman, nonetheless left nothing to chance. He had been practicing his stump speech in front of family, friends, and staff for months. Honing, tuning, adjusting. Testing ideas, intonation, framing. Getting it to the point where, even though he was speaking in complete paragraphs, it seemed like he was just thinking out loud.

"My friends, and I say that sincerely, because I do not claim friendship glibly, you have heard some of my thoughts before, and I will try to put some order to them in a minute. But, first, I would like to introduce a very dear friend. A sergeant of the U.S. Army: John—we call him Jack—Quincy Kunze. You may have seen his artwork, his stunningly detailed pencil drawings of the Capitol, because they decorate my conference room. And, if you've ever visited me, you'll have seen him—or at least he's seen you. Ever since I arrived in Washington, Jack has lived in a tent. On the street. Always pitched in front of whatever building I happen to be working in at the time, currently the Hart Senate Office Building. This remarkable man has been my self-appointed guardian angel, and from that vantage point, advises me on the state of the union, and on the state of the world. I don't know how he gets his information, but I've learned that, if I ignore him, it's at my peril. Before I go on, I'd like to ask him up here to say a few words."

The room squirmed. For most of them, instructing the chauffeur to drive them to a semi-hip restaurant south of Fourteenth Street in Manhattan was an adventure in itself. Having money meant not having to experience anything outside the thick bubble that money, inevitably, seemed to create. Dinner at Majorelle, Nello, Doubles, Daniel. Lunch at the Union, the Century, the Knick, or the Brook. Summer in the Hamptons. Winter on

Mustique. Bodyguards, pilots, butlers, personal assistants, doormen, chefs, financial advisers, lawyers, housekeepers, nannies, gardeners. Money meant shelter from having to think about—much less see—the world outside the bubble. Even those who could still recall how that world looked—and how it felt to be outside the bubble—could really only see shadows and reflections of its true shape. Like blind men describing an elephant, they peered through blurred, distorted lenses. Few within the bubble even bothered to acknowledge its existence. Of course, they cared for the poor, the less fortunate, the downtrodden—even if poverty was their own fault. Didn't Harvard offer scholarships to the truly worthy? Weren't those the problems that they solved by buying $5,000-a-seat tables at charity galas?

Bringing Jack Kunze inside this bubble—bringing the rank smell of him right under their noses—was precisely what Ben intended. To give them a taste of the kind of campaign that Ben, Pete, and Tommy intended to run. Ben didn't care who you were, where you were from, or what party you identified with. Everyone was invited to step up, to accept responsibility for themselves, for their families, and, this was crucial, for their neighbors. To forswear the politics of parochial personal identity, and to reject the gambit of playing the victim card—no matter whether their ancestors had been slaves, coal miners, or plutocrats. Jack was a piece of it: of the unseen. An important piece.

Jack Kunze stood up straight and proud. If anyone in the room bothered to look, they'd see a man with military bearing. Not the broken man he had appeared to have become. Jack Kunze's story was remarkably similar to Ben's, but the bad-luck inverse. A high school valedictorian and all-state wide receiver from Eastern Oregon, he'd given up a full ride to the University of Oregon just as Nike was turning the OU football program into a machine for producing first-round draft picks, especially small, fast, fearless guys who could get open in the middle. Jack didn't care about that. He'd wanted to be the guy who took out Osama bin Laden. One day, he was leading a three-man raid on a suspected Taliban safe house in Fazel Baig on the outskirts of Kabul. They had gotten there too late. The house was empty. As they were sweeping the simple mud abode, one of them tripped a bomb hidden in a stuffed animal under a little girl's bed. Somehow Jack survived the blast in one piece. The young army surgeon who'd saved his leg was a miracle worker. But Jack lost a part of himself for which there was no prosthetic. He had barely been able to enter a building since. The diagnosis was cleithrophobia, the fear of being trapped. Ben and Tommy had seen to it that Jack Kunze was first in line for any potential treatment—MDMA, vagal nerve injections, even stellate ganglion therapy, which generally had good results with intractable PTSD cases like Kunze's. But nothing had succeeded in loosening the grip of his trauma. Kunze had finally given up—though he did tell Ben that the MDMA helped. When Ben and Peggy had picked him up from his hotel earlier, Ben had slipped Kunze a 30-milligram tab, as he often did, a low therapeutic dose, supplied on the down-low by a sympathetic researcher at Walter Reed.

"I've got the best seat in town," Kunze began, sounding more confident than he felt, thanks to the chemicals flowing through his bloodstream. "Sooner or later, almost everyone who thinks they matter walks by. Congressmen, senators, lobbyists, staffers, lawyers, public relations people, military brass, foreign ambassadors, journalists, tourists, cops, firemen, janitors, bus drivers, farmers. Most of them are headed inside, to ask for favors, plead special interests. To them, I'm not even there. They stop, they chat, they laugh. I listen."

Ben gave him a supportive nod: Jack could still hold a crowd, the way he had in every mess tent, in every bivouac.

"Yup. That's me. The modern-day invisible man." He extended his arms, as if modeling an outfit. "You've all dreamed of it. Right? Wrapping yourselves in a cloak of invisibility? To hear what people are *really* saying. Well, you're looking at it: this is how you do it. Beaten-up boots, a ratty parka. Oh, don't forget a scraggly beard. And try to master this, a little nervous head shake, a downcast eye."

He stood taller and breathed deeply.

"I've fought in a lot of places. I'm not gonna say that every warrior is as cynical as I've become. But I didn't do what I did for you, or for God, or for country. So don't patronize me with any 'thank you for your service crap.'" Jack rolled his shoulders, still looking at Ben. "I did it for my brothers, the guys—even some girls—I fought with. Guys like Ben Corn, the finest man I know. The camaraderie." He paused. "I know, everyone says that. It's a total cliché. But here's another thing about war. Something we don't really say to civilians. Especially fancy ones like you."

He stopped abruptly and looked at Ben. Was he going too far? Ben nodded back. *Keep going.* One of the things Jack liked about MDMA, especially in smaller doses, was that it didn't make him lose control like he did with some of the psychedelic compounds the researchers had experimented on him with.

"Okay, fuck it, I'll just say it. You people should know what makes a guy like Ben Corn tick. And, anyway, you can't really be any more canceled than living on the street."

The room was utterly quiet. Pete had no idea what was coming next, but he guessed that Ben did. This had Peggy written all over it. Right down to not cleaning Jack up first. Pete would have insisted they hose Jack down and buy him some nice new clothes. Surprising, even shocking, moments like this were her specialty. She knew the exact statement they needed to make here tonight.

"Three days after George Washington led men into battle for the first time, in 1754, at the beginning of French and Indian War, he wrote his brother a letter from the Pennsylvania frontier. His men had just cut down twelve French soldiers. The French killed one of his. It was over in fifteen minutes. Here's what he said about his first brush with combat: 'I heard the bullets whistle—and, believe me, there is something charming in the sound.' He was twenty-two years old. Thirteen men lay dying around him. Blood, entrails, young men writhing on the ground, screaming for their mothers. And what's his takeaway? The 'charming' sounds of bullets. And that was a couple of centuries ago. There's nothing charming about a musket. But I know exactly what Washington was talking about. That feeling you get when you decide you're fighting to win, and you're not going to let anything stand in your way. That conviction. That certainty. That's what you get with Ben Corn."

Ben put his hand on Jack's arm. A comfort, but also a gentle prod. Jack smiled, placing his own hand on top of Ben's, giving it a firm, affectionate squeeze.

"I know, Ben. I'll get to the point." Jack began looking more directly, picking out people in the crowd. No one would hold his glance. Too much authenticity, or, maybe, just too much wildness. Too much other.

"So, I'm living this life. Maybe, someday, I'll be able to choose another. For now, I can't. What keeps me sane—so to speak—is that I can listen. And you should too. You might think you can ignore people like me. But there are a lot of us. It's in your interest to hear what we're saying."

Jack inhaled deeply.

"I'm not trying to soften you up for handouts to veterans, or to the poor—or anyone else, Black, brown, Native American, man, woman, or transgender. We've had way too many handouts in this country. I don't mean just to poor people, I mean to people like you—whether it's special tax treatment for producing oil or letting tech giants park their profits overseas. I have nothing to lose by saying this, I'm not interested in showing up at your off-sites at Pebble Beach to provide motivational talks to your twentysomething analysts. No matter how much Pete Stryker tells me I could make. All I'm saying is that everyone has to take responsibility for themselves."

Jack drew Ben toward him, a broad, grimy hand around his biceps.

"Just another minute, then I'll shut up. Pretty much everybody in this country is trying to pick the other guy's pockets. We're always yelling at one another, but the bigger problem is that we're all trying to rip one another off all the time. No one trusts anyone else. Everyone is certain that everyone else has a hostile agenda. And we're sitting on a powder keg. The best chance we have to keep it from blowing is standing right here next to me. I came here to ask all of you not just to write my friend Ben a check. But to actually listen. You won't like everything he has to say. That's the point."

No one seemed quite sure if Jack had finished speaking. Unsure whether to clap. Ben let that uncertainty ride, until, finally, he broke the silence by raising his hands and clapping loudly.

"Jack, thank you." Ben gave him a long hug. The crowd went quiet, again.

"There's just one problem with having you open for me. How do I follow that? Anyway, I'll try to put an order to my thoughts. In the interest of full disclosure, I've been influenced by and crib freely from my conversations with and writings by a wide range of people. Jack Q. Kunze is one. Others include Robert Kagan, Charles Perrow, Irving Kristol, retired Lieutenant General Mike Nagata, Adrian Karatnycky. They're all deep thinkers on issues of social policy, geopolitics, and national security, but I take full responsibility for my synthesis of their ideas.

"To start, let me pick up on an idea that Jack just voiced." As he began, he noticed Pete, out of the corner of his eye, putting two fingers to his temple. Their sign: this is a crowd of entitled billionaires, not the Harvard sociology department, keep it light.

Ben nodded to him, but, as Pete knew too well, he was not about to dumb it down. Ben believed, and Tommy encouraged this, that if people understood him to be guided by principle rather than short-term self-interest, they would be more willing to transcend their habitual pursuit of personal gain—at least at times when it became critical to the survival of the nation.

"You may wonder what soldiers talk about while they're trekking in hostile territory, on missions to target and destroy the enemy of the moment." He thought back to their interminable rap sessions, typically accompanied by dog-eared books and articles from academic journals. "Well, my crew read books, mostly about democracy, about government. Trust me, this wasn't by choice. The leader of our squad, General Tommy Taylor, insisted on it. Now, I may not be the smartest guy in this room, far from it. But I'm smart enough to know one thing. When Tommy Taylor tells you to do something, you do it. Of all the books and articles he had us read, the one we kept coming back to was 'Urban Civilization and Its Discontents' by Irving Kristol. From 1970. It's about the two pillars of democracy: the machinery of self-government and civic virtue, otherwise known as republican morality—with a small r, that is."

He paused, smiled.

"As in, you know, putting the interests of the republic before your own."

Don scanned the room. That line would get a huge reaction on the campaign trail. Here, you could hear the ice cubes clinking in glasses. These people, he thought, didn't come to listen to Ben Corn or anyone. He was sure most of them had already forgotten Jack Kunze's pleas. He wondered if even one of them realized that Ben, in his charming and folksy way, was essentially declaring war on them.

"Kristol says we got the first one right thanks to the Founding Fathers. He considered the Constitution to be one of the most remarkable political inventions of Western man: a beautifully designed machine of representative and limited government, separation of powers, a diffusion of political and economic power."

Knowing nods from the crowd, a few finger snaps of approval.

"It's the second pillar that has been elusive—not set forth in the Constitution, and impossible to legislate. Democracy doesn't require that we agree on everything but it nonetheless depends on the recognition of shared values and virtues, across race and class, religion and, um, orientation. This elusive quality is not found in today's culture of canceling people whose viewpoints you don't agree with. It is founded on steadiness of character, a deliberative state of mind, and a willingness to subordinate our own parochial, tribal, interests to the public good.

"In this day and age—in the culture of 'why not?'— conventional morality and traditional manners are viewed with scorn. When demands for 'justice' and 'equity'—which are too often just other words for unlimited self-interest—supersede the need for principle and order. As if justice precedes freedom and order, rather than the reverse. But I'm not going to discuss my ideas for how we might engender confidence in a new social order. For today, I'd like to talk about threats from without.

"For half a century, we Americans had it all, but world orders do not last forever, and when they begin to crumble, the most primitive elements of our natures take over. Order turns to chaos quickly, to the law of the jungle. As Kagan puts it, the jungle grows back.

"Since 9/11, the U.S. military has deployed more than two point seven million American women and men to fight terrorism in foreign theaters. Thousands have died. Trillions of dollars have disappeared. And where are we? Nowhere. Terrorism is more widespread, virulent, and complex than when we began trying to combat it. New movements, like Salafi-jihadism, have infected Yemen, Sudan, Afghanistan, Pakistan, and a dozen other countries in the Middle East. Terrorists can raise revenue, control vast territories and natural resources, communicate freely and securely using the internet, and recruit operatives using social networks to sow radical ideas in every Western country. The FBI is trying to keep the lid on more than a thousand violent, homegrown extremists in all fifty states, and those are just the ones they know about. All those lives. All that treasure.

"Then, there is rampant adventurism by nation-states: Russia, China, North Korea, Iran, and Cuba, among others. On our eastern flank, the Russians continually probe Europe and NATO. Private armies, proxies, unmarked forces, world-class hackers, deep cover agents. Ukraine serves as their laboratory for hybrid warfare and tests of Western resolve. Make no mistake, those forays are just the coming attractions. When Russia annexed Crimea and occupied the Donbass, Western leaders looked the other way. The Europeans can barely bring themselves to even consider canceling the Nord Stream 2 pipeline projects that would give Russia a knife at their throats—an even tighter stranglehold on Europe's energy supplies. As Britain's army chief, General Mark Carleton-Smith, has said, Russia is prepared to use military force to secure and expand its national interests. They are. They will. Unless something is done.

"But what is to be done? What should we care about? What can we do to secure our interests without spending the lives of our children? Without wasting our hard-won treasure? The first thing we will do—we must do—is to embrace the new ways of warfare. We must become a threat that will make our enemies reconsider their own evil intentions.

"But that's not enough. Not nearly enough. It is past time for all nations of the world to be held to a higher standard, to be the guarantors of anyone who operates within their borders. No one should be given a free pass based on excuses that they don't control the hackers or terrorists who operate from their territory. A word to those enemies, or putative friends, who are listening. Bulgarian hackers, Romanian data thieves, North Korean cyber trolls, Nigerian fraudsters. Just one word: enough. We will hold you accountable. You are not safe, your electrical grids are not safe, your pipelines are not safe, your leaders are not safe. We are rich, but we are not your prey.

"I am dreadfully tired. Tired of reading about how the Chinese are developing anti-satellite lasers and hypersonic missiles. Tired of hearing about their Belt and Road Initiative. Tired of reading about how teenage gamers in Tehran are toying with our social media networks. We must absorb the lessons that our enemies teach us. We must—we will—become the masters, not the paralyzed victims, of asymmetric warfare. My America, your America, must become the big bad wolf of cyber threats, anti-satellite lasers, hypersonic missiles, drones, robots, artificial intelligence. We must become a twenty-first-century power, not a nineteenth-century dinosaur lumbering along and bound for extinction.

"Again, I say to our foes: be afraid. Be afraid because we will make mistakes. And . . . we . . . don't . . . care. No longer will we fear making mistakes. To the pseudo-ethicists and self-styled social philosophers who preach forbearance and proportionality: you will not be welcome in my White House. A hair on the head of one of our children shall, henceforth, be valued more highly than an adversary's entire parliament. Industrial espionage conducted against one of our national champions shall come at a fearsome cost, which we shall mete out in our own time.

"Before I take your questions, let me say just a few more words," Ben said, smiling. "Because you all know I'm a talker. Just a word about the dangerous course that our current president, Rachel Bridges, has chosen. I know many of you object to the fact that I refer to her as 'our' president. But she is, at least until we do something about that at the ballot box. But her latest forays—launching still more random strikes by weaponized drones in Syria and Georgia—bode ill. By making us new enemies at every turn, she makes us unsafe. I know that a lot of people adore President Bridges. But this nation doesn't need a sprightly grandma, no matter if she still has a great forehand. In fact, that's the problem. By not getting tough with anyone, she makes us weaker at every turn."

In Ben's world order, Europe would cease to matter as a geopolitical player. A great place to take the wife, or whoever, shopping, but far from a trusted or major ally. The continent would become a chip, something to add to or take out of the pot. Just like how the Europeans had treated the Russians, the Chinese, the Arab oil states, and, to a lesser extent, the Americans, when they set the rules of the great game in the nineteenth and early twentieth centuries. President Corn would rethink American defense posture. The military establishment, as they knew it, would disappear. The very idea of a slow, vulnerable, blue water navy was ludicrous. The sad agglomeration of admirals and generals and commandants preparing feverishly for the last war would have to adapt to a new vision and break their terminal addiction to high-dollar weapon programs and ponderous procurement systems. They needed to disappear. Ben's military would look more like MIT and CalTech than General Patton's army.

Ben paused. He took a sip of water and looked down, stock-still but still relaxed, like he was off somewhere no one could reach. The moment stretched into an uncomfortable silence as Ben deliberately gathered his thoughts. No one in the room was accustomed to waiting for anything. About twenty long seconds later, Ben raised his head almost imperceptibly and looked back at his audience, seeming to make eye contact with everyone in the room.

"Let me ask you something. Where were you when you heard that awful news about the Cardinal?" The Cardinal was the name of Amtrak's New York to Chicago route. Six weeks earlier, twenty-six people had died when the Cardinal collided with a commuter train coming into Cincinnati's Union Station. Seconds later, a breakaway faction of the Proud Boys, tweeting from a K-Pop superfan account, took credit for the accident and said ten more bombs would soon go off in ten other cities, injecting panic into the nation's arteries for the next thirty-seven minutes, until the cause of the crash was identified as a transformer fire that disabled the station's antiquated switching system. Ben paused. "Right. You don't remember, do you. Having a cup of coffee, thinking about your morning conference call? Just another morning when things felt like they were spinning out of control.

"How much longer can we live this way? That's what this campaign is about. Over the next few months, all of you are going to be in a lot of rooms like this one, listening to people who want to be president. Everyone will tell you they are the one who can unite the country, whether it's by expanding entitlements, cracking down on free speech, raising taxes or cutting taxes. There's really nothing else to say if you're running for this job. Right? But you know something? I'm not going to make that promise. It's not my job. I can't make it happen by myself, and anyone who thinks they can is too emotionally disordered to be president. But I'll tell you what I will do, I'll set an example and I'll follow through on it. I will pledge to do my part. I'll expect everyone else to pledge to do theirs."

He paused, the emphasis unmistakable.

"When I'm president, I won't rule by fiat, issuing executive orders willy-nilly. I don't intend to let Congress off that easy. I expect Congress to do its job, and I'll veto any bill that comes across my desk that doesn't have opposite party co-sponsors and significant support from across the aisle. Plain and simple. Work together or not at all. At the same time, we have to be humble and we have to hold ourselves and each other accountable. You can be up on the dais all you want, making grand sweeping claims and patting yourself on the back. The media will love you. You'll raise tons of money. But did your plan work? Did you stay on top of it? Probably not. In our current system, our dysfunctional, degraded system, all the electoral benefits are front-loaded. There's no mechanism to hold elected leaders accountable, aside from the occasional audit or subcommittee report that gets buried under thousands of other subcommittee reports. The political incentives are way out of step with the governing incentives. We need to bring them into alignment. There are plenty of external threats. We have to stop wasting time and energy fighting each other. That will be my message to the whole country.

"I will also make it clear from the start that the Corn administration will not tolerate violence and disorder. Yes, there have been many injustices over our history. Many grievances that we need to answer for and remediate. But we will not be ruled by mobs—of violent protestors or self-proclaimed cultural commissars. Protest? Fine. Demonstration? Great. Policing speech on college campuses, carving "autonomous zones" out of big city neighborhoods? Intolerable, not to mention selfish and undemocratic. As is so called cancel culture. It might feel good in the short term to see your adversaries driven away or de-platformed. But does anyone realize what this is doing to our idea of being a citizen in a democracy? If big tech doesn't like your politics, kicking you off social media is just the beginning. Today, they don't let you Tweet. Tomorrow they'll refuse to process your online cash transfers, or lock you out of their payment systems. With no due process other than thinking that it will look good on a press release.

"I don't know what the answer is. But I know that we have to fix it in a way that doesn't violate the norms of free speech and free enterprise. The CEOs of Twitter and Facebook can't have the unrestrained, unelected, and unregulated power to decide which voices get amplified and which get silenced. Am I sure how to proceed? No, I'm not. But my door's open. If someone has a good idea, I'll listen, no matter where they're from or what party they belong to."

Watching from the back of the room, Greta felt a thrill. Finally, someone saying what needed to be said. Don's reaction was more complicated. Just that morning, Ben had been on television railing against Senator Conway's pet aircraft carrier. Tonight, not a word. Don would reserve judgment until he learned why. But the crowd seemed happy; they'd listened and were now applauding enthusiastically. Of course, what Ben did not say was that most of the people in that room would, in time, have little choice but to hop on his bandwagon. If Ben's urgent call for national renewal wasn't enough, Ben and Tommy had other ways to convince them. Greta had been handling the cash transfers—well over a hundred million dollars so far—to develop proprietary software tools that would allow them to harvest the secrets of a vast array of the nation's players and potentates.

Out of the corner of her eye, Greta saw something discordant and nudged Don. A wisp of a blond twentysomething, hair drawn into a dancer's bun, had appeared at the door to the back staircase leading up from the Pony's kitchen. Dressed in black, a Valextra cross-body bag slung across her shoulder. She looked naggingly familiar, but Greta could not quite place her. They watched as the girl looked around until, finally, spying Gonzaga, she sidled over to him and began whispering in his ear. A second later, in a hurry, they disappeared back down the way she had come. Greta mouthed: *That's wrong.* Don began speaking into his earpiece to the security team.

"Look sharp," he said. "Gonzaga just bolted down the service stair with a young blond woman. Someone get me a picture of the girl and tell me where they're headed."

"I've got them," came an answer. "They turned right, down West Eleventh Street, not quite running, but walking pretty fast. Didn't take his car."

"Heads up," barked Don. "Could be trouble."

All the while, Ben continued his peroration to a spellbound audience.

"On our western flank, we find the Chinese. Not only do the Chinese threaten Asian stability by disrupting sea lanes and asserting bogus territorial claims in the South China Sea, they are the most aggressive and dedicated military and industrial spies in history. Not a week goes by that the U.S. Department of Justice doesn't indict Chinese cyber hackers and intelligence officers for stealing military technology and industrial intellectual property. Every single one of the three hundred fifty thousand Chinese students, professors, and scientists enrolled in U.S. universities—*every one*—reports to the Ministry of State Security, China's primary espionage directorate. China's 'Made in China 2025' program has a goal of becoming the world's leader in robotics, aviation, and high-tech manufacturing in just a few short years. How? By stealing as much know-how as possible. From whom? Just take a look around this room. I'm sure more than a few of you know what I'm talking about.

"Circling back to the recruitment, training and arming of terrorists: the Iranians attack all our flanks. Iran, on its own and in cahoots with the Chinese, seeks the destruction of the Great Satan. Iran provides funding for all comers: ISIS, the Salafi, sleeper agents in the United States, Europe, and Latin America. Iranians with a nuclear bomb would be a horror, but, even without it, they keep us back-footed and distracted with terrorist threats, real and potential, draining our resources and sapping our resolve . . ."

The roar from motorcycles penetrated the windows of the Pony. At the same time, Don heard a double-tap as the glass of two second-floor windows shattered. His earpiece crackled.

"Under attack. Two bikes. Four men. PP-2000s. Balaclavas."

More shots sounded. Sharp cracks from the 9mm sidearms that Don's men carried, and rat-a-tat from at least two submachine guns carried by an assault team just outside the building.

"Two men down, one of ours, one of theirs. One of theirs taking the back stairs, two more through the front door. *NOW,* front stairs."

Ben drew a pistol holstered in the small of his back and shouted: "*DOWN. EVERYONE. NOW.*"

Without a second's hesitation, Jack was everywhere, pushing, pulling, dragging people to the floor, barking orders to stay down, cover their heads. The only ones who remained standing were Jack, Ben, Greta, Don, and his security team. And Peggy. What the hell is she doing? Greta thought. Actually, the one thing none of them had thought of—directing traffic, pushing people to the floor, making sure they didn't all block one another in a rush to the stairs. Oblivious, and nervy, as a clatter of billionaires, some shitting themselves, huddled on the floor.

Greta was nearest the back door and Don motioned for her to take it. Two more of their team took the front stairs. Don, Ben, and two others crouched over the tangle of prone bodies, weapons extended, in defensive positions. Glass shattered behind them, and then a crash: one of the attackers, repelling off the roof, tumbled through a window and rose to his feet. In the instant before Jack tackled him, the attacker managed to fire a single burst, which tore through Peggy's left arm. Jack subdued the attacker with such a violent blow to his trachea that Don could hear the cartilage snap from across the room.

Their team at the front stairs entered the breach, firing down the stairwell, stopping, wounding, and perhaps killing two intruders. At the back door, a single gunman, his momentum carrying him to the top landing, was met with Greta's foot in his groin and her right elbow under his chin, snapping his neck as he fell. She grabbed the PP-2000 with her left hand and brought it down on his skull for good measure before tossing the submachine gun to Jack, who checked to see that the safety was off. She looked at Don and tilted her head toward the stairwell door. Don barked into his earpiece.

"Four enemy down on the second floor. Am I clear?"

"All clear," came the answer. Jack pointed to the doorway and then to himself.

"We're coming down the back stairs, Jack leading. Greta to follow."

Greta slid into Jack's slipstream, following him down to the street, as Don grabbed Vicker by the collar of his coat, yanking him to his feet. They raced down the stairs behind Jack and Greta, Don instructing Vicker all the way.

"Stay right behind me, we're taking the bike. Got it?"

Vicker nodded, mute. On the street, Don jumped on his Ducati, Vicker fairly leapt on behind him, grabbing Don's waist as they sped down West Eleventh Street, heading for the Negroni house on West Tenth. Don continued listening to the chatter back at the Pony. One of the attackers was dead and three were alive but badly damaged, saved by body armor. One of Don's guys in bad shape, two others wounded. Peggy Corn, the only civilian to have been injured, was losing a lot of blood. Police sirens and ambulances sounded in the background.

Vicker babbled in his other ear.

"What just happened?"

Don ignored him, concentrating on the streets ahead, mindful of the possibility that there could be an ambush between the Pony and the safe house on West Tenth Street and trying to process what had just happened. At the very least, he had done his job, extracting Vicker and leaving the scene. But at what cost? he wondered. His team had been brilliant, and Jack, unexpectedly, seemed to have lost none of his speed and strength. Ben, taking charge of the scene, was the perfect guy to deal with the cops and medics, assorted tycoons, and the press. Greta, doing what she did, had disappeared before any authorities arrived, following her instincts and her own agenda.

On the face of it, the attack made no sense. Unless the marauders had not expected the event to be defended, it was a suicide mission. Yet these attackers were professionals. They had clearly been briefed to avoid random casualties and hadn't even tried to take out the security team, usually the first target in a raid like that. Even more, they hadn't tried to snatch anyone. Had they intended to massacre a bunch of billionaires, there were better ways. A grenade through a window would have been more efficient, incinerating the entire building and everyone in it. Or they could have accomplished the same thing with one rocket round from a lightweight bazooka at a distance of a hundred yards down West Eleventh Street or at two hundred yards from the uptown side on Greenwich Street.

Given that they had managed to deploy PP-2000s, the weapon of choice for the Russian Ministry of Internal Affairs, smuggling a couple of grenades or rocket rounds into New York City would not have been a problem.

Perhaps it was a suicide-strike of some sort. Any number of terrorist organizations would have been proud to take control of a room filled with some of the highest-value Western capitalist pigs imaginable. The spectacle of humiliating a dozen plutocrats, watching them beg for their lives before being beaten, tortured, and killed would have provided the ultimate recruiting video. But a terrorist cell would have blasted its way into the building, maximizing collateral damage. No lives would have been spared on the way to their primary objective. It had to be that whoever was behind it had one target. Odds were that target was the only person who, to their knowledge, had been the victim of a mysterious, unsolved kidnapping only a few months ago.

Elias Vicker.

He hoped this meant the battle was coming to them.

He was ready.

The crew at the Negroni house was waiting for them. The garage door popped open and shut so quickly that all Don had to do was let go of the throttle and glide right into the garage. As he came to a stop inside, Don still felt the adrenaline rush, but Vicker seemed strangely unperturbed. Even calm. They settled into a quiet, comfortable internal room. Vicker asked for coffee from a burly ex-Delta serving as the duty officer. Don was curious to see whether Vicker would try to bully his guys, but suspected that, like most bullies, he preferred to prey on the weak.

"Mr. Carter, what just happened back there?" asked Vicker, as if it were just another day at the office, curious and detached, not even pulling on his knuckles. Strange.

"Still trying to sort it out, and right now there are cops all over the place. Sooner or later they will want to talk to you, and we would like to understand it all better beforehand."

"Anybody hurt, killed?" asked Vicker.

"One of my guys lost a lot of blood. And Peggy Corn, pretty shot up, no word on her condition. One of theirs dead, one wounded, two waking up from concussions."

"I meant any of my guests," said Vicker, slightly testy. "Because, if you think about it—not terrible for Corn. Wife shot by terrorists. 'I won't sleep until I track them down.' Cue 'Hail to the Chief.'"

Don wondered if Vicker would try to get out of paying the catering bill, since the attack happened before the entrees had been served.

"I don't think so. Only one of the gunmen made it upstairs, and so far, no reports of injuries in the downstairs crowd. A lot of extremely frightened people, EMTs dealing with shock."

"Gonzaga? Is he okay?"

"No word, sir. Likely he is fine."

Vicker gave the briefest snarl, and then turned to his phone. And like almost everyone in the world holding a cell phone at the moment, he was looking at a photograph that would become instantly iconic. Ben Corn, standing tall and tailored in a room full of cowering bodies and shattered glass, holding a gun and shooting back from an action-hero crouch.

"Well, well, well, will you look at our boy. Someday he'll thank me for this."

Don slipped out of the room to call Greta, but she didn't pick up. Where the hell was she?

41

The Carlyle, New York City

As soon as they had control of the scene, Greta had slipped away, intent on finding Gonzaga—and the yet-to-be-identified Scandinavian blonde who had helped him to narrowly miss the attack. She had decided that, more than likely, Gonzaga had retreated to the comforts of his apartment at the Carlyle. With its old-world airs and layers of high-tech security, that was his safe place, both physically and psychologically. She took a cab, not wanting to risk losing contact in the subway, and by the time she made it up to Seventy-Sixth Street, Gonzaga had already settled in. Without hesitation, he instructed the concierge to send her up.

The young woman had kicked off her shoes and was lounging, legs tucked under her, on the sofa. They eyed each other with a cold scrutiny. Each trying to understand how the other fit into the universe, generally, and how each of them fit into Gonzaga's microcosm, in particular. Greta observed the woman watching Gonzaga with an indefinable intensity. Adoration, perhaps, or ownership. She could not place the emotion, but it became clear immediately that she played a very important role in this drama and didn't think there was room in it for another woman with an agenda.

"Greta, I'd like you to meet my daughter, Klara Wennerström."

Klara briefly acknowledged Greta and turned to Gonzaga.

"You know what that was all about, don't you?" Klara said. "You were being tested. At least that's part of it."

Klara dipped her finger into a bowl of Beluga and licked it clean before taking a sip of champagne.

"Go on, dear." Gonzaga motioned for Greta to sit.

"It's part of Fyodor's plan to take over IS. He doesn't understand why he should share his profits with Vicker. He'd much rather be in business with Mummy. After tonight, Fyodor was hoping to make a convincing case that Vicker needs a new security team, a Parsifal team."

"Exactly. But he also had another goal, didn't he, dear?"

"I don't like to think about that, Daddy." Klara draped an arm around Gonzaga and cupped his chin and cheeks in her hand, as if he were a small child.

"Well, thank you for saving my life. I could think of no worse way to die—in a restaurant, surrounded by people I barely know."

"Mummy told me I had to make sure nothing happened to Lorenzo. As soon as I heard those motorcycles coming down the street, I knew we had to get out of there. He was going to kill Daddy, as a favor to Vicker. And I stopped it."

Klara scooped another fingerful of caviar and elegantly fed it to Gonzaga. What's with these people, Greta thought, they can make something as creepy as an old man slurping caviar off a young woman's finger look like the height of refinement.

"Marina went along with this?"

"She had to." Klara seemed almost wounded that anyone would question the difficult business decisions her mother had to make. "Otherwise, Fyodor might kick *us* out. Or worse."

"She sent you to get Gonzaga out of there?"

A butler showed up with a fresh bottle of champagne. Klara held out her glass.

"We weren't sure if we could trust you."

Greta was starting to be impressed with the young woman, who, with minutes to spare, had slipped into a potential kill zone, exfiltrated her target, and gotten him away safely. All while seeming to be little more than a spoiled debutante.

"Mummy says, Fyodor doesn't bark. He just bites. And it hurts. But you fended him off. I'm sure you've earned his respect."

"What does that buy us?"

"He probably won't come after you again, not with guns anyway."

Greta turned to Gonzaga.

"And Lorenzo here. How do you know he's safe?"

"Oh, Mummy will just tell Fyodor to pipe down. There's no point now."

"Can 'Mummy' really tell Fyodor what to do?"

"He knows how much Mummy cares for Lorenzo. They'll both let it go. They can't afford to be enemies. They've got too much invested together."

Greta had wondered why they were even listening to this girl, except that as she spoke Gonzaga took in everything she said without interrupting or asking questions.

"Dear girl," Gonzaga said, amused, stroking Klara's hair as if she were a prized Arabian. "I'm beginning to think you understand the game better than me or your mother. And that's more about Fyodor than she's ever told me. Whenever I ask, she tells me I'm being nosy. So, thank you for that."

"That's what I love about you, Lorenzo." Klara looked up at him. "Your best friends try to kill you, and you don't take it personally."

"What I've learned, and what your mother and I have tried to teach you—quite successfully I might add—is that once you take out the feelings, everything is just information. You can choose to be afraid. Or you can choose to be fully informed."

Gonzaga paused, to see how Greta was reacting.

"So now, Miss Webb. You don't miss a trick. Can you tell me what else we might have learned today?"

"That, as big as Industrial Strategies is, it isn't big enough for Elias Vicker, Fyodor Volk, and Marina Wennerström."

"Very good," Gonzaga said. "Triangles—they look good on paper. In reality, they get messy." Gonzaga picked up the champagne bottle to refill Greta's glass. "Oh my, what a terrible host, out of champagne. I'll call for another."

While he went off to find his butler, Greta reached into her purse and snuck a look at her phone. She had turned the ringer off earlier in the evening. Don had called half a dozen times in the last ten minutes.

Excusing herself, she went into a bedroom and closed the door. Don answered on the first ring.

"Jesus Christ, where have you—"

Greta cut him off.

"I am having the loveliest time at the Carlyle. Champagne and caviar with Lorenzo. And Klara Wennerström. Marina's daughter, her spitting image, thirty years removed. Seems that whatever Swiss finishing school she went to teaches a little tradecraft on the side."

As quickly as she could, she filled Don in on what she had learned from Klara and Gonzaga. How the attack had been planned in Saint Barts to test them and, ideally, to kill Gonzaga. Don could barely contain his rage—one of his guys shot, maybe maimed for life, all for this sick little game.

"So Vicker knew?"

"Just the broad outline it seems. But not the when and where."

"I knew something weird was going on. I've seen Vicker more upset when his coffee isn't hot enough than he was tonight."

"Well, I don't think he's going to be so happy when he learns what else they told me. They want Vicker out."

"Who?"

"Volk. The Wennerströms. Guess what young Klara calls Gonzaga. You might want to be sitting down for this."

"Daddy?"

"How'd you know?"

"You know, Europeans."

"Are they going to turn the guns on Elias now?"

"Too messy, is the sense I get. Reading between the lines, they seem to hope we'll solve Vicker for them."

Greta returned to the living room. An open bottle of champagne sat in the ice bucket, and her glass had been refilled. But Klara and Gonzaga were gone.

42

West Tenth Street, New York City

Don returned to the other room, where Vicker sat alone in front of a bank of screens, each tuned to a different cable news network, each replaying loops of the same sequence of photos and video, over and over, while grave anchors tried to make sense of the evening's shocking news. Vicker raised an iPad. The *Post* already had its story up: "*INDUSTRIAL BLOODBATH*," comparing Vicker to Crazy Joe Gallo, a mobster who had been gunned down in Umberto's Clam House by a rival gang in 1972. The *Post* story assumed, of course, that he was the intended victim, because who had a longer list of enemies than Elias Vicker?

"'Crazy Joe Vicker . . . not bad. I'll take it. Every now and then, the *Post* gets it right."

Don ignored him and peered at the video screens. Reporters at Bellevue, New York's trauma center, were following the progress of people injured in the attack. His phone rang again, on Signal: Tommy.

"Don't speak, just listen. The guys that broke up your party were *vory*, full-body tattoos, daggers through the neck. One is on life support, the others are dead. Subcutaneous cyanide capsules. Undetectable, a quick smack was all it took." Tommy clicked off.

Private military companies, like Parsifal, made extensive use of soldiers acquired from Russian organized crime families. So many *vory* were dying of hepatitis C, AIDS, and syphilis, contracted in prison from infected tattoo needles, that risky missions were a godsend: if things went well, they got paid, if things went wrong, money went to their families. He wondered if Vicker had any idea what kind of people he had let inside his world.

Vicker looked up.

"Who was that? One of your super spooks, I'm guessing," Vicker said. "Must be quite embarrassing for you guys, caught with your pants down with the whole world watching."

"Sir, all that matters is that you're okay," Don said stiffly. Years of training had taught him how to focus on the mission and hide his frustration.

"Who would possibly want to kill me?" Vicker asked, almost gleefully. "I mean, what would the papers write about if I was gone?"

"We know they were Russians," Don said.

"How?" Vicker asked.

"Tattoos of daggers across their necks, typical of Russian organized crime syndicates. Indicates they committed murder while in prison."

"Sounds like they sent the best. I'm almost flattered."

"Three are dead, committed suicide using cyanide. The fourth is still in an ICU," Don paused. "We have no idea as to their objective," Don lied.

"Well, I'm sure you'll figure it out," Vicker said, standing up and getting ready to leave. "Oh, by the way," he said. "Didn't you think it was pathetic that Lorenzo showed up? He just can't stand not being part of the action. Well, I hope he had fun."

"I wouldn't know, sir. You should get some sleep."

"Have you got a car ready? I'd like to get back to my apartment, sleep in my own bed."

"Not a good idea, sir. NYPD and ATF are looking to interview you; we need to know what they know before we let that happen. So we're going to keep you here for the moment. More important, there could be more Russian thugs out there. No way to guarantee your safety right now. Tomorrow you'll have to come forward. I recommend you get your lawyer on the phone."

Don gestured toward an adjoining room, almost a replica of Vicker's bedroom at 432 Park. Vicker looked as if he was about to argue, but, then, out of character, decided not to.

———

Don barely slept, anticipating a busy day. Just how frantic would depend on who showed up first. A coven of deep-state apparatchiks would be looking for Vicker—for starters, the NYPD, the FBI's Joint Terrorism Task Force, the ATF, and, in its own circumspect way, the CIA. It would be good sport watching the grandees of the national security establishment jostle for the lead. After all, what could be juicier: a sitting senator attacked, his wife injured, a passel of politically connected billionaires threatened, shots fired from untraceable Russian submachine guns less than two miles from Ground Zero, and three Russian hoodlums suiciding at Bellevue.

For those with the right clearances, the focus would be on the now well-documented link between Vicker and Fyodor Volk. Kathleen Harper's cable to the mothership had not exactly been gathering dust after she filed it from Cyprus. Volk remained a leading light on the U.S. Treasury list for possible sanction, and that alone put Vicker in Treasury's peripheral vision. Now, their sights would be trained on Vicker, and it would not be long before NSA began mapping his recent trading activity.

For all that, Don had a feeling that the NYC Department of Buildings would beat them all to it, likely with a squad from FDNY Company 18 in tow. In what would soon be explained to Vicker as a bizarre coincidence, a battery of alarms, signaling that something was seriously wrong with the foundation of the Negroni house, had broken the predawn quiet. Building out the former town house into the fortress that it had become had required digging a hole so deep that the building code required the installation of a collection of geotechnical sensors to monitor even the most minute structural shifts: accelerometers, tilt levels, piezometers, inclinometers, extensometers, settlement plates, strain sensors, erosion probes. Even a slight deflection or subsidence could send an alarm signal directly to the Department of Buildings, an early warning of possible building collapse, which risked broken water mains, gas lines, fire, explosion, and general mayhem. And all it took to kick off the alarms was a single sledge hammer blow, in the right place.

At 6:32 a.m., the doorbell rang, and Don, already dressed and showered, answered the door, flanked by two of his men. On the stoop stood a tired-looking, short Pakistani man with a New York City Department of Buildings badge hanging around his neck, Inspector Faisal Dar. Behind him, lights flashing, was a fire truck, and half a dozen firemen in full regalia, holding Halligan bars and flat head axes, ready to barge in and mark their passage by poking holes and smashing doors, for good reasons, and for no reason at all.

"Can I help you?" asked Don, mildly, but turning his hips slightly so that they could all see the sidearm holstered at his back.

Taking his cue, the men behind him did the same. Don wondered how quickly the confrontation would escalate. Unlike cops, who more or less required search warrants to enter private property, the rules were more malleable for firemen when public safety was in question. Inspector Dar took a step back, nearly tripping over the fireman standing directly behind him. It was not every day that building inspectors met armed men on New York City doorsteps.

"Sir," said Dar. "We received an alarm from a structural shift sensor on these premises. We need to come inside to inspect, to make certain nothing threatens gas or water mains or the stability of your premises."

"Everything is fine here, Mr. . . . Dar. I'm sure it is a false alarm," said Don, closing the door in his face. A few seconds later the buzzer rang, aggressively, again. Don took his time opening it, but this time with a menacing look.

"Sir, we need to enter and inspect," said Dar. "It is the law." A fireman behind Dar swung a Halligan bar over his shoulder.

"Look, Inspector," said Don, no longer polite. "I don't know what your problem is, but there is nothing amiss here. This is private property, and, last I looked, in the US of A, the Fourth Amendment bars government officials from barging into a person's house for no reason."

Don slammed the door, knowing that the issue had now been joined. Once the firemen saw sidearms, a call would go out to the NYPD to send the fire marshals, cops in fireman's clothing. Within minutes, sirens were blaring and half a dozen police cars from the Sixth Precinct rolled into West Tenth Street from either end of the block. A dozen jaded heavies got out, hands on their hips, waddling under the weight of their equipment belts, jaws set, looking for trouble. A Sergeant Lopez walked to the door and held up a hand to stop the babble; Dar and the firemen had been talking over one another. A small crowd of neighbors and passersby, dogs on leashes, coffee cups from the Grey Dog, had begun to gather. Given the size of the official contingent, typical NYPD overkill, it would not be long before the press showed up, poking their noses in other people's business.

"One at a time," said Sergeant Lopez. "Inspector Dar?"

"Some structural alarms tripped. We just want to walk through the building, look for subsidence, look at the gas lines. Standard stuff, but after all the recent building collapses, we take no chances. Three guys answered the door, and they're all armed."

"Who is the owner?" barked Lopez at an officer standing nearby with an iPad providing access to pretty much every database on the planet.

"EV1 LLC, a limited liability company, but the mailing address is in care of Industrial Strategies Management Corp. That company is owned by Elias Vicker."

"Any permits?" asked Lopez.

"Yes," the answer came back. "Vicker has a pistol permit, concealed carry."

Lopez let out a long breath. He knew precisely who Vicker was, like everyone else who read the *Post*, but also because Vicker gave generously to the NYC Police Foundation, the Patrolmen's Benevolent Association, the Sergeants Benevolent Association, and the Police Athletic League. Not least, there had been an all-points bulletin out for Vicker since late the night before. Not a warrant, exactly, more for his own protection.

As the crowd of onlookers grew, a metro-beat reporter from the *Post* showed up and began nosing around. An array of big swinging dicks kept arriving, lights on, unmarked cars spilling out onto Sixth Avenue and all the way to Fifth. The biggest thing that had happened in the Sixth Precinct since, well, since the night before at the Pony.

The sea of bodies parted for Captain Magdelena Gorzynski, a sturdy, no bullshit, New Yorker from Little Ukraine on East Seventh Street, as she waded to the front door.

"Sergeant, clear the street. We don't need ten cruisers. And move these people back." She recognized some of the guys in suits, the Secret Service Special Agent in Charge and the others FBI.

"Thanks guys, we'll let you know if we need help," she said, flicking them away.

Gorzynski rang the bell. Don, who had been watching from the second floor, walked downstairs and opened the door. So far, the morning was progressing as expected.

"Can I help you . . . Captain?"

"May I see some ID please, and carry permits, if you have them." She placed a hand on her holster, looking at their sidearms.

Don and his two guys, careful to avoid seeming to reach for their guns, handed her their LEOSA ID cards. Under the Federal Law Enforcement Officers Safety Act, law enforcement officers can carry concealed weapons even after they separate from official service. She took a look and passed them to Lopez to run background checks.

"We need access for the DOB, some sort of structural alarm."

"You've got a warrant?"

"Look, Mr. Carter. I don't know where you're from, but let me explain something to you. This is New York City. We live in close quarters, any threat of building collapse is a public safety issue. We don't need a warrant. Is the owner home?"

As she asked the question, Vicker, having heard the commotion, sauntered into view, with just the wrong attitude.

"Officer, do you know who I am?"

Gorzynski shook her head. Cops faced off with assholes every day, but it was the ones who treated her like she was the help that really ticked her off.

"I do, sir. Lucky coincidence, because half of the NYPD, the FBI, the ATF, and the Secret Service have been looking for you all night."

Vicker snorted. It had not occurred to him that he would have to talk to anyone about anything, not even after a shoot-out.

"Then do me a favor and leave us the fuck alone. I give a ton of money to the PBA, the PAL, police this, police that. We don't need you here. Don't make me call the commissioner."

Lopez passed the ID cards back, with a nod to Gorzynski: no problem with those guys.

"Mr. Vicker, we've wasted enough time. We can do this the easy way, in which case I need entry for an inspector and a couple of firemen. Or we can arrest you for obstruction of justice, let them in anyway, and you and I can finish our little chat down the street at the precinct."

Don whispered in Vicker's ear: no way to win it. Vicker backed away, and Gorzynski stood back while the inspector and firemen filed in. Don knew the inspector would insist on seeing the entire building, and he knew how it would end from the moment he opened the armory door. The fireman, ex-military, did a double take and hightailed it back to the front door, with Inspector Dar and Don not far behind. Gorzynski was still holding court. After a breathless description from Dar, she gestured to Lopez to start moving in, followed by the FBI and the Secret Service contingent.

"Mr. Carter, we are coming in. I need you and those two to stay here and out of the way. Mr. Vicker, come with us please."

The fireman led them down the internal stairs to the armory.

"Mr. Vicker, I'm curious why you think it is okay to pack this kind of ordnance into a Manhattan town house, but, for the moment, I'll just say this: you have the right to remain silent, anything you say can and will be used against you, you have a right to an attorney, and, if you cannot afford one, one will be appointed for you. Got it?"

"No." Vicker sneered. "I don't 'got it.' And you don't get it. This is all completely legal, and none of your fucking business. I want you out of my house. Now."

Vicker began to walk away, but was blocked by a patrolman.

"Mr. Vicker, you are under arrest for illegal possession of firearms under Article 265 of the New York Penal Code." Then, to Lopez, "Cuff him, seal the house. Let's go."

On the street, Vicker, Don, and his entire crew were loaded into patrol cars, but not before the paparazzi and the *Post* got shots of a bedraggled Vicker being led away in handcuffs, wearing sweatpants, a T-shirt, and his velvet skull-and-crossbones slippers.

Perfect, Don thought, exactly right.

43

Department of Sanitation Salt Shed, Manhattan

A jagged block of cement squatted at the corner of Spring and West Streets in lower Manhattan, sandwiched between the Hudson River and a ventilation tower for the Holland Tunnel. Faceted to suggest the shape of a salt crystal, the building appeared on the tax rolls as a Department of Sanitation shed for road salt. But, like so many elements of the U.S. government's massive, cloaked, anti-terrorist infrastructure, the salt shed hid in plain sight, a way station on an underground railroad of detention and interrogation centers built in secret and at great cost. In the event of terrorist arrests in the city, it would be to the shed, or to a dozen other nondescript but super-secure structures like it, that detainees would be secretly delivered.

It was here, three levels below the busy Manhattan streets, that Elias Vicker sat in a stark, cement-walled room, feet manacled to the floor, hands cuffed to a table. In contrast to the bright orange jumpsuit he had been given to throw over his sweatpants, his already sallow skin had taken on a skim-milk pallor. He stared ahead impassively, trying to maintain his composure, desperate not to seem rattled to whoever was staring at him through a one-way mirror. Still, he couldn't resist pulling at the chains on his wrists, desperate to crack his knuckles.

On the other side of the mirror, Tommy, Don, Greta, and Chip sat, drinking coffee, staring at their quarry, and waiting for Elizabeth to show up so they could start their interrogation.

"Always wondered what was under here," Don said. "Never believed it was just salt."

"You should have seen the rig he arrived in," said Chip. "A tricked-out garbage truck made for secretly transporting terror suspects."

"Man, we get all the best toys," said Don.

"Even better," said Tommy. "We know how to use them."

Tommy had laid the groundwork for Don's quick release and, in theory, the equally fast turnover of Vicker, but that didn't stop the Manhattan

District Attorney's Office, the United States Attorney, and half a dozen federal agencies from squabbling over Elias Vicker's scalp. Whoever got credit for putting Vicker away would be a national hero. This was the kind of case that made a career. The laundry list of possible crimes was endless: hundreds of separate felonies for illegal possession of weapons, racketeering, money laundering, and securities fraud. Maybe, after they had actually dug in, kidnapping, conspiracy to murder a sitting senator, aiding and abetting a terrorist organization, violating economic sanctions.

But it was Tommy Taylor, a well-connected but little-known general, who'd been able to cut through the interagency clusterfuck and claim the prize. Whether or not Elias Vicker was a brazen criminal was, for the moment, immaterial. This was General Taylor's operation, and, after Vicker's meeting in Cyprus with Volk, any connection between those two men was a matter of national security, and he was not about to let it go. He had people deeply embedded inside Vicker's organization, he was able to argue, and was on the verge of penetrating the vast web of corruption that surrounded Vladimir Putin. Besides, he made the case that Vicker's high-priced attorneys would argue that many of the charges against the tycoon resulted from illicit surveillance and legally questionable entrapment. The cloak of national security was the surest way to keep the prize on ice.

Liz Leonard slipped into the room, having been whisked from Washington to the West Thirtieth Street heliport and then to the shed, in one of Vicker's own Sprinter vans.

"What should we expect?" Tommy asked Elizabeth.

"A typical prisoner, looking at the kind of time he faces, would be bereft, anguished. His world destroyed. He would likely believe that he has lost, permanently, everything he cares about. As a framework, the stages of grief—denial, rage, bargaining, depression, and acceptance—would be a good reference point."

"I take it you think Vicker is atypical."

"There may be some similarities, but different rules apply to psychopaths. Anger, rage, for sure. Some level of denial. But they don't get depressed. Expect a rapid reversion to type. We know he's a bully, manipulative. Really, he is capable of doing whatever it takes to get what he wants. Fostering an armed attack on his own event to test Don? Perhaps to disguise the murder of Gonzaga? Take it as a given that he will never accept that he might lose."

Tommy paced. Don tipped back, balancing, precariously, on two legs of his chair, chewing, spitting, contemplative. Ideally, they would have had another six to twelve months to develop a complete plan to take over Industrial Strategies, working closely with Gonzaga. But Volk, and perhaps Vicker, appeared to have their own calendars. And, with the attack on The Striped Pony, they had just proved how dangerous they could be. Don wondered if that was just a preview. He needed insight into what else Vicker and Volk might be planning.

They had spent the better part of the day discussing interrogation strategies and objectives. For Vicker, Liz advised a pride-and-ego-down approach, demeaning and insulting Vicker in the hope that, eventually, he would attempt to salvage his sense of self-worth. The last issue they had to settle was who would take the lead and whether they should fill a second seat. None of them had more experience with field interrogations than Greta.

"I say we send in Greta, solo," said Don.

"Liz? Chip?" asked Tommy.

"He is not expecting Greta. He's a misogynist, a bully. Greta might unnerve him," Liz said.

"Chip?"

"Agreed. She knows the drill. Cool under fire." Chip grinned at Greta.

"Greta, I know you've done this fifty times, but rarely with someone this damaged," said Liz. "Don't expect a linear progression. Vicker will bounce around, negotiating one minute, perhaps ingratiating, then angry, disbelieving. Always trying to find a way to control the situation."

"Do I get to waterboard him?"

Liz looked worried.

"You're so serious," Greta said. "I was just kidding." Sort of kidding.

Don watched her walk into the room carrying a loose-leaf binder—fierce, resolute, like a boxer entering the ring. He had seen that look before. At Abu Ghraib, black sites in Poland: the professional—and, he sometimes thought, perversely intimate—pleasure she took in breaking men she despised. He almost felt sorry for Vicker. Sitting down, across from her quarry, Greta said nothing, but began pulling out photographs, making a pile. Vicker sneered at her and rattled his chains like a caged animal. Angry, defiant, aggressive. Disheveled, unshaven. Starting to reek.

"Ms. Webb," he said, looking in Don's direction, on the other side of the mirror, like he was trying very hard to hide his surprise. "Is this all because I didn't ask you out for a second date?"

"This is interesting," Liz said from behind the two-way mirror. "I'm reading shock, fear. It's like we're seeing the vulnerability that he's spent his adult life learning how to hide."

"And Greta can smell it," Don said. "That's what makes her so good."

Greta remained silent, but continued pulling photos, which only further agitated Vicker.

"What's supposed to happen, Webb? Giving me the cold shoulder. You think you're gonna break me? You? What are you? NSA? FBI? ATF? IRS? Who the fuck are you, and *get me the fuck out of here!*" Vicker screamed.

Greta looked up, calmly, as if she had noticed him for the first time.

"Elias, I need you to focus. I am on this side of the table for a reason. And I'm the only reason you are not in a city jail."

Greta paused to let it sink in.

She looked at him, unperturbed, expressionless. "You are on that side of the table, trussed like a game bird, for what reason? How did this happen?"

"This is *not* happening, bitch. I don't know what your fucking game is. *Get . . . me . . . the . . . fuck . . . out . . . of . . . here.*"

Vicker shook his chains, straining at them, glaring at her. But she remained silent. When he stopped, she stood, for leverage, and coiled her right arm around her shoulder and gave him a backhanded slap, full force, across the face. His head snapped back. That felt good, she thought.

"Elias. Focus. How did that happen? How did the great genius, the guy worth, what, a couple of hundred billion, end up in handcuffs, prison jumpsuit, smelling . . . rather . . . awful. Being slapped around by a . . . girl?"

"*Rather awwwwful,*" he mocked. "What do you want? You want money? What? How much?"

Greta drew back her arm and hit him again, much harder, cutting his lower lip.

"What I want right now is for you to focus. Why are you here?"

Vicker said nothing, did not strain his shackles, but gave her a hard stare. Later, reviewing the footage, there would be no doubt that he would have killed her, had he been able.

"Maybe these will help."

Greta fanned the photos, like a Las Vegas dealer, and began flipping them over and laying them, one by one, on the table, facing his direction: Vicker in his arsenal on West Tenth Street holding a machine pistol, a photo of wire transfers for stolen cars, Vicker on a hotel terrace in Cyprus next to Fyodor, Vicker at the door of the Geneva Freeport, shaking hands with the art dealer Hervé Charlier.

"Tell me where these were taken, and who was with you."

"I don't have to tell you a goddamn thing." Vicker licked his split lip. "Just get me my lawyer."

He glanced at the photos. In a futile attempt to regain some autonomy, he swept the ones he could reach to the floor, looking at Greta with contempt. Unfazed, Greta left them there, closed the binder, stood, and left the room.

"This is going perfectly," Liz said. "It'll take some time for him to adjust to his new station, but Greta showed him he has no choice but to deal with her."

Through the one-way mirror they watched him crane his neck to study the photos that he could see.

"He needs to sit there for a while. Send one of the guards in to pick up the photos. I don't want him looking at them," said Greta. "I'm hungry. Isn't Odeon right down the street?"

―――――――

"Once again, then." Greta sat across from Vicker. He was still in his chair, but looking more relaxed, playing nonchalant. She thought of what Elizabeth had said: how he would try to devise a strategy to get the upper hand. Scaring her had failed. Now he would try something else. She laid out the photos, again. They would keep playing the same scene until he capitulated.

"Okay, okay, Ms. Webb. Let's play. That's Fyodor Volk."

Without looking up, she laid down another photo.

"That's Hervé Charlier."

And another.

"That's not my best side, but that's me with my favorite gun." Vicker, almost smiling, seemingly back to his old controlled, arrogant self. "You've got me. So let's get moving. Now what? Are we going to make a deal?"

On the other side of the glass, Elizabeth raised a hand to Don and Tommy, signaling her alarm.

"This shift is pretty fast." She spoke into a microphone that connected to Greta's earpiece. "Take care. He would never give up just like that. He's trying to play you."

"It seems you've had quite the epiphany, Elias."

"I'm a realist, Ms. Webb. Here I am, in irons, and you've concocted enough 'evidence' to put me away forever. But at the same time, you've pulled me out of the clink and nailed me to this table, beyond the reach of any prosecutors, which suggests to me that you want something that only I can give you. Tell me what it is, and what's in it for me."

Liz drew a diagonal line through a page in her notebook: so much for analogies to the grieving process. The adaptability of psychopaths fascinated her. You could strip them naked and rip their lives to shreds, but the neurons in their lizard brains would re-form to take advantage of the opportunities of the moment.

"What's in it for you is not doing ten life sentences in a super-max lockup on terrorism charges."

A slow-motion review of Vicker's microexpressions would show exactly what he thought of that, but, even in real time, it was clear that Greta had made a permanent enemy.

"Come now, Ms. Webb." Vicker, unctuous. "Paint me a picture of what my life might be like under the thumbs of you and your buddies?"

Greta looked up and met his eyes for the first time. She spoke softly but with steel in her voice.

"From the outside, nothing much changes. The district attorney will announce that you've resolved your little dispute with the Department of Buildings. And he'll thank you for coming in to answer a few questions about the assault on your life at The Striped Pony."

"And I just walk?"

Greta decided not to laugh in his face. Things were going too well to spoil it.

"That's how it will appear. The unsinkable Elias Vicker. Bigger, richer, more invincible than ever. You might even get the *Post* to go easy on you for a little while."

"Miss Webb, whatever road you think you're going down, you're making the biggest mistake of—"

She cut him off.

"Of course, you forfeit your assets. All your assets, Industrial Strategies and your stake in it. That is a small price to pay considering the nature of the crimes you've committed, but, officially, you will not ever answer for them. To the outside world, you'll still be the richest and most powerful man on Wall Street."

It would require some elegant footwork, she thought, on the part of clever lawyers to place the beneficial ownership of Vicker's stakes under their control. But that, after all, was what lawyers did and, in the end, all it would take to move several hundred billion from one side of the ledger to another would be a few sheets of paper, and perhaps not even Vicker's signature. Everything he owned was held through nominee companies managed by lawyers, and those lawyers had nothing to gain through obstruction.

"But you'll be under our wing."

"And whose wing might that be?"

"If you pay attention, you might figure it out in time. You won't do any jail time, but you'll be under house arrest. You will wear an electronic ankle bracelet. We give you an allowance. You continue to report to work every day. You can still give your blustery interviews, eat at Bilboquet. But every phone call you make, we'll be listening in. We'll read every text you send."

Vicker grimaced involuntarily. He shook his head.

"It won't work. With all of you floating around, word will get out. My investors won't buy it."

"Who's to say you'll have outside investors? For public consumption, IS will become a family office. With your money—and money from a few family friends—it will still top half a trillion. We don't need, or want, outside money."

It finally dawned on Vicker how tightly the noose was being drawn, and how ruthlessly he had been set up.

"It was Pete wasn't it? And that fucking hayseed Ben Corn. It was all a setup. And Volk, Gonzaga, they were in on it the whole time. Why else would Lorenzo just drop me like he did?"

She gathered the photos on the table and put them back in her notebook.

"You guys are in bed with Volk too, aren't you?"

Greta ignored the question, amazed by Vicker's astounding claim that Gonzaga had abandoned *him*.

"You had a good run, Elias, but you got caught." Greta got up to leave. "If you behave, we pension you off in a couple of years. Enough money to keep you comfortable. Someplace we can keep you safe—and keep track of you. Argentina, Dominican Republic, Panama."

Greta asked a guard to unshackle him and left him to think things over. Vicker stared off into space, measuring his prospects and assessing the hand he had to play, whether there even was a play, other than capitulation. He had relied on Gonzaga to sort through the multivariable decisions. It was clear to him that his life was worth something in the near term, but, at some point, before too long, he knew he would become a liability, a traffic statistic, just like Oscar. That's what he'd do if he was in their shoes.

He had no doubt they were capable of it. He was quickly getting the notion that these people were much colder than he was. This all had to go back to Corn somehow, and the morning he showed up at the senator's house. It was as if Ben Corn had stepped in from another dimension, a secret one that operated on a constantly changing set of rules or, really, no rules at all. It disgusted him. Securities laws were barely even laws, they were obstacles, designed by limp-dick SEC lawyers, who then went into private practice and charged you $2,000 an hour to sweep those obstacles out of the way. Everyone did some version of what I do, he thought. I just do it better—or I did it better. But these people. They'd done a lot more than break laws. They were messing with the very order of things. They weren't just blurring the boundaries, they were annihilating them. But why?

Objectively things did not look good for Elias Vicker. There was no way around that. Except Vicker had taken the precaution of buying insurance. Part of the industrial process. It cost only five million to get Cecil Baxter to root through his contacts in the Middle East for evidence that connected these people to the theft of $2.4 billion. They'd certainly figure out what he had on them before too long. All they had to do was buy Cecil Baxter a drink—or six. They would move heaven and earth trying to find the document Baxter had dug up for him. He was confident they never would. The longer and more their futile search, the more desperate they would become. What if Ben Corn were already in the White House by the time they started negotiations? He was fine with waiting.

Watching through their looking glass, Chip was puzzled by the almost beatific smile on Vicker's face. What could he possibly be thinking? A life's work, reduced to utter humiliation. Chip tried to imagine the architecture of Vicker's psyche. He thought back to the videos of Vicker recalling his mother's rejection of him as a child. His career of inflicting remorseless, vengeful carnage on the world at large. And now, after they had stripped Vicker of everything that had given him dimension—money, power, dignity, and autonomy—there he was, seemingly unshaken, unflappable. Completely disconnected from reality and likely to stop at nothing to recover what he had lost.

"On the assumption that we reach an agreement and let him out of here, how are we going to manage him?" Chip asked. "An ankle bracelet won't do it. He'll need guards around the clock."

He shot a look at Don.

"That'll be a couple million bucks a year in billings for Carter Logistics. Nice work. But he's going to need a more or less full-time minder as well. I wouldn't leave him alone for one second."

"You sure that's necessary?" Greta asked. "We have him in a box. We'll have cameras in every room of his home and at the office, we'll listen to every phone call, read every text."

"And he won't be allowed to use email, except what we prescreen," Don said.

"Why take the chance?" Chip said. "We know what this guy's capable of. When shit goes sideways, I don't want to be the one explaining to Tommy and Ben that we weren't on him twenty-four/seven."

"You volunteering?" asked Don.

"Let's see what happens after we debrief him," Chip said, not wanting to look overeager. "But short term? I'd do it. I hear the private dining room at 432 Park has a great crème brûlée."

———————

When Greta finally returned to the interrogation room, it became clear that Vicker had decided on a different approach. If not cooperation, at least something that he thought would look like cooperation to his jailers.

"Ms. Webb, I'd like you to consider something other than a master-slave relationship. Notwithstanding my current circumstances, you will find me to be a good partner. I did build this thing. Lorenzo and I worked well together for many years. More recently, IS has had good relations with SEF and the Parsifal Group. I could perhaps help you understand how it is that we operate, the. . . industrial side of things."

Greta reflected on Vicker's capacity for self-regard. From the trading history she had been able to piece together, going back several decades, Vicker had rarely earned an honest dollar. Every single moneymaker was linked to an information advantage put at his disposal by Gonzaga, and, more recently, by Volk. Strategies devised by his massive teams of analysts—and his own supposedly brilliant ideas—demonstrated an almost uncanny ability to lose money.

And yet, for the first time in the interrogation, she felt like they were making progress: Vicker was offering to give up his secrets.

In her earpiece, Chip whispered: "Volk is probably all he really has to offer—but that's still a massive win for us." Greta agreed. Finding out exactly how the enterprise worked would save them a lot of time; it would be useful to play it out.

"We have noticed your extremely profitable recent trading based on not so random events," she said. "We assume Fyodor Volk is supplying you with information. But we can't find any record of communication between the two of you—either through our own surveillance or external sources. He is not a guy you can ring up without Carnivore and Echelon noticing."

Vicker seemed proud of himself.

"Ms. Webb, really, kiss and tell on our first date?"

Greta, ignoring his feeble attempt at humor, closed her notebook and stood up.

"Elias, I was hopeful that we'd be able to build a mutually beneficial relationship. The way it works is very simple: You answer my questions—and then some. You hold nothing back. You talk to me like I'm Dr. Kerry, and you're some self-hating loser desperately clawing for self-respect. Interrogation isn't so different from therapy. It works only if you're completely honest. It might even make you feel better—there have to be a lot of demons wrapped up in those billions. It will be good to get them out. And, if your information proves to be accurate and useful, that creates good will. Absent good will . . ." Greta began to leave the room.

"A courier," said Vicker. "Old school, in person."

"Tell me more. Spoken or on paper? Coded?"

"Let's just say a trusted go-between. You probably know him."

44

The Carlyle, New York City

Klara gave Greta a hug that was just a little too long to be interpreted as merely friendly. It gave her a thrill to feel the small of Greta's back for the pistol that she knew would be there. Don and Chip got nothing more than polite nods as she gestured for them to follow Greta into the living room of Gonzaga's apartment. Following the attack at The Striped Pony, and the ongoing house arrest of Elias Vicker, the Carlyle had become the nerve center of Industrial Strategies, and the five of them its management committee. The real Carlyle Group, Chip said.

Not wanting to trust telephonic or electronic communications, the entire apartment was swept for bugs daily. They had settled into a comfortable routine, meeting every Tuesday and Thursday afternoon, sometimes joined by Pete, sometimes not. Nothing formal, but an easy, efficient, collegial camaraderie, with Gonzaga, the grand old man, setting the tone and providing wisdom.

There had been endless matters to sort out. First, the attack. The truth was too ugly, far-fetched even: New York mega-billionaire orders his business partner, with whom he schemes to manipulate stock prices through violence, to mount a terror attack on his own bazillion-dollar fundraiser in order to wipe out one of their other partners. The challenge had been to construct a new narrative with new villains—preferably foreign—motivated by some terrifying ideology and hailing from a country few had heard of. Pete came up with Dagestani Islamo-Communists targeting the "foreign oligarchs" (among them Vicker and at least two other guests that evening) who controlled mining interests in their nation.

The message was clear, and it fed right into the central narrative of Ben's campaign: the Pony attack was yet more proof that no one is really safe anymore, that Americans needed protection from a world brimming with chaos and violence. Ben Corn would provide that protection, just as he had that night at The Striped Pony.

That was the easy part. PsyOps like these, controlling perceptions, disseminating cover stories, were already in their skill set. The bigger challenge had been imposing a new management structure on Industrial Strategies while simultaneously learning a massive and complicated business and launching a presidential campaign, which, once it cranked up, would consume virtually limitless funds.

Luckily, because of the Citizens United decision, funneling money in would not be a problem. Nonetheless, Greta and Chip, working closely with Mara and Volk, needed to create sophisticated mechanisms for making funds available, where and when needed, shuttling millions of dollars through various corporate shells and into an array of dark money super PACs that would appear to have no direct connection to Ben's official campaign.

Greta took a particular interest in making sure that Peggy received the best possible medical care. It had become clear that she'd never regain full use of that arm, and had begun sporting so many fashionable variations of her sling that Gonzaga wondered how long it would take for every chic American woman to want one.

But most of their energies were devoted to managing the flow of information about new investable events that had begun coming at them fast from both SEF and Parsifal. It had become almost a competition, Volk and Wennerström each vying to outdo the other. Decisions as to the size of each investment and the allocation of profits popped up almost daily.

Volk was so pleased with the new arrangement that, at least for the moment, he had assented to Marina Wennerström's request and rescinded his order to kill Gonzaga. With Gonzaga's guidance, they were all making more money than ever. Ivanov had even delivered grudging congratulations from his boss, not merely on the reorganization of IS, how it was being managed, and the profits, but on their handling of the attack on the Pony. No hard feelings.

With all that needed doing, Vicker had become something of an afterthought. To their surprise, he settled peaceably into captivity. All it took to keep him in check was an occasional reminder that house arrest at 432 Park Avenue offered amenities that Florence ADMAX did not. Shrinking his bubble seemed to suit Vicker. Not exactly a hardship post: he had freedom to roam through the apartment's sixteen thousand square feet, even if his bedroom door was locked from the outside every night and cameras covered every square inch of the apartment. If anything, his calmness was eerie. No more worries about whether someone else's plane had more speakers hidden in the walls of its screening room or if he made a billion more or a billion less on a trade. Many afternoons and evenings he just sat in his living room listening to Mets games on a cheap, battery-powered, Heathkit GR-151RS AM/FM transistor radio that he'd had since he was a kid, in a tattered faux leather case with his name scrawled in a childish hand along the bottom edge.

They'd told him that Piper had to go—there was no room inside his bubble for another person. Too much of a risk. A lawyer took care of it. They offered her a silence-buying multiple of her original prenup and no further explanation. Though none was needed, Piper had developed sincere affection for Elias—she had to admit they'd had some interesting and unusual times together—but she drew the line at getting shot at by thugs sprung from Siberian penal colonies. In the end, she put up nothing more than token resistance, and once they agreed to throw in a $2 million, fifteen-carat, emerald-cut, D-color flawless Graff diamond solitaire, she'd agreed to a deal, joking: *Let freedom ring.* The girl had style and a wicked sense of humor, thought Greta, making a mental note to get to know her better, at some later date.

In short order, Piper remade herself as a sort of nonprofit mogul and social-circuit thought-leader, infusing millions into hot charities and acquiring a famous but little-read magazine and financing its reinvention as a torrent of conventional wisdom. She decided that if she was going to go it alone, she needed some gravitas. Just like Laurene Jobs did with *The Atlantic*—it seemed like a great way to meet interesting men. She also signed on with MacKenzie Scott's trainer. That was how she wanted her postseparation biceps to look.

The team let Vicker out for regular lunches and dinners with carefully vetted companions, mostly because it would not be easy to explain Vicker's sudden, complete exit from the New York scene. The jet, of course, was off-limits. As were high-profile social events. The story was, Elias Vicker is lying low, taking some time to reflect after the twin shocks of the Striped Pony attack and the failure of his marriage. He adopted the imperiled oceans as his cause, with Pete arranging large donations to conservation organizations and an exclusive sit-down interview with Jason Renton, who was invited up to 432 to hear Vicker distractedly dispense a few quickly digested white papers' worth of facts about ocean acidification and rising sea levels, coming alive only when he got to the worst-case scenarios about the coming collapse of the marine ecosystem.

Chip, far from protesting that the caretaker role was beneath him, reveled in it. He was no longer just the cyber guy. Suddenly, he was in the middle of it all, spending all his time at 432 Park, managing Vicker, communicating Vicker's thoughts about structuring their trades, and executing them. Everything went through him. For the first time in years, he didn't have to be read into anything about an operation because he was right at its nerve center.

Where he belonged. Where he should have been all along. Or close to it. Ever since Wardak, they'd treated him like a sideman. As long as their pallets of money sat in a secret cave in the French countryside, he could live with that. But with all that cash—and Vicker's massive stake in IS—now in play, he had become even more anxious to get control of his share: his *full* share. He deserved it, and, to ensure they didn't try to short him, he needed an operational role. He was done being the guy in the truck, as Don once called him derisively.

Once they dealt him in, his next big move would be only a few blocks north of here, to the baronial splendor of a 740 Park or 834 Fifth. One of those grand old buildings protected by gargoyles, platoons of staff, and co-op boards that had been constructed to keep out not only the likes of Fyodor Volk and Elias Vicker, but also their children—and maybe even their children's children.

For the time being, though, he really couldn't complain about his current quarters. While not his dream, it was undeniably magnificent. Thirteen hundred feet above the sidewalk. Glass everywhere, 360-degree helicopter views—on a clear day you see could Newark, Chip cracked. Every footfall cushioned by carpets so thick you could turn an ankle on them, hobbling around after a few too many vodkas.

The only thing he did complain about was that Vicker treated him like the help, demanding printouts of IS statements and reports. When he was through with any piece of paper you put in front of him, Vicker would absentmindedly tear it to pieces, letting the scraps fall to the floor for someone else to pick up. Not long before Chip moved in, Vicker had replaced most of the wall between his living room and dining room with a two-thousand-gal-lon, floor-to-ceiling saltwater fish tank. Inside it, dozens of species of gaudy, striped, and spotted exotics darted around a huge branch of living coral that a marine biologist whose explorations Vicker underwrote had "rescued" from one of the remaining healthy sections of the Great Barrier Reef. Vicker had insisted on a special allocation of his allowance to charter a cargo plane to transport it from Australia.

"I've seen only one private aquarium that's bigger," he bragged to Chip. "On Bogdanov's yacht. And that was the whole fucking ocean. I don't know, it calms me down."

Every night, he asked Chip to wheel a ladder up to the back of the tank and sprinkle shiny flakes of fish food on the water's surface. On the other side of the tank, in the living room, Vicker would sit on the edge of his couch and watch the fish fight for their dinner, while narrating the un-folding action like he was a play-by-play announcer. He had given the fish names, personalities, and complicated backstories. The fish feuds went back years. He had two different sportscaster voices. The sportscasters were al-ways bickering.

At first Chip was annoyed, but after a while he started to like it. Besides, there wasn't much else to do. One night, Vicker even let him join the broad-cast team. They were funny together. They actually sort of clicked. Vicker loved it. For a couple of minutes. Then he just clammed up. It hadn't hap-pened again.

Ben and Tommy were well aware of how risky it was to put one of their own that close to Vicker. As it was, there was little enough room for deni-ability, but they didn't see that they had a choice. They needed complete control of Vicker's environment. They needed someone seeing everyone he saw, hearing everything he heard, reading everything he read.

"How often does Vadim pass through New York?" Gonzaga took a pull on his scotch.

"As needed," said Chip, "but at least every three weeks. It depends on the timing of Parsifal events."

"And he stays with you?" They all knew the answer, but Klara always seemed curious about how others managed sleeping arrangements. Her im-perious directness annoyed Chip. She was a kid; she hadn't earned her seat at the table, and he wondered what she was getting at.

"Usually he stops by for an hour or two, sometimes he stays in a guest room overnight. Comes up through the garage, which, now that I think of it, is how you and Vicker escaped to Cyprus that time." Chip cast a knowing look at Gonzaga.

"Are Vicker and Ivanov ever alone together?" asked Gonzaga.

"Absolutely not. If Vadim is there, so am I, and 432 is monitored by us twenty-four/seven."

Ready access to Ivanov meant that they had direct advance information as to exactly what Volk had on tap, and Industrial Strategies could organize its trading in ways that made the events seem less obvious, more difficult to connect to IS, if anyone decided to look, although no less brutal. Greta and Don had planned to develop a more subtle approach to making normal accidents happen, but, for the time being, they depended upon Volk, not only to generate profits, but to feed money into their campaign coffers, through Mara. Greta, conflicted as ever, had no choice but to watch as Volk became more and more blasé about whether people lived or died, or how many died. People just as innocent as the soldiers that Ben wanted to stop sending to far corners of the earth to get slaughtered.

Her mood could swing wildly: sometimes depressed at what Volk was doing, sometimes exhilarated by making and controlling massive amounts of money. As with so many in the upper echelons of finance, the relentless focus on abstractions—doing deals, making money, then more, then much more money—became a compulsion, addictive. Neurologists had long known that acquiring massive amounts of money had observable epigenetic effects, changing the wiring of the brain by causing the right supramarginal gyrus—the part of the brain that recognizes a lack of empathy and autocorrects—to shrink: vestigial and unnecessary. But, no matter what the root of her emotional lability, in the near term, she and Don agreed that they were making so many changes at IS, so quickly, that reining in Volk and implementing a new regime of more subtle, but equally normal, accidents had to wait.

Of late, the Russians had become increasingly infatuated with accidental death as a driver of value, because it required little in the way of infrastructure. Mechanical failure was their specialty: helicopters in particular. Choppers were ideal because they were a preferred means of transport for top executives, and were rarely maintained under conditions of strict security. It took only two minutes for a semi-skilled mechanic wielding a hand wrench to ensure a crash within ten minutes of takeoff. Since choppers were the way rich people died in the best of times, the fact that eponymous founders of tech unicorns bit the dust by flying too close to the sun raised no special alarm. But the stock prices would still crater—even more so if they managed to take down an entire executive team. Heart attacks were another favorite. Pharmacies were completely insecure, and the sudden death of crucial corporate executives could be engineered by adjusting prescription medications: the wrong dose or the wrong pill compounded to look just like what the doctor had ordered. Under Greta's increasingly skilled hand, their trading involved so many different securities that there was little chance that IS would receive unwanted attention when one of their portfolio companies crashed and burned. As before, they made outsize profits from being short the right stocks, at the right time.

"What progress are you making in transitioning IS into a family office?" asked Gonzaga.

Don looked at Greta; he had been surprised. It should have been an easy thing to return $200 billion of cash to outside investors, but the decision to give people their money back ran into angry protest. IS had produced such stunning returns on the back of Volk's normal accidents that the European pension funds and university endowments that made up the bulk of Vicker's outside money screamed, whined, and cried to be allowed to continue investing. Some offered to lock up their money indefinitely—usually attractive to hedge fund managers. Others suggested fee arrangements that would give Industrial Strategies 50 percent of the profits, rather than the usual 20 percent. More effective was the pressure that the biggest investors exerted indirectly, through the Wall Street firms—Goldman Sachs, Morgan Stanley, and their ilk—that IS needed to execute their trades in stock, bonds, and commodities. In order to buy peace, and to reduce the attention being paid to Industrial Strategies and quell speculation about the increasingly elusive Mr. Vicker, they agreed to redeem most investors over time, and to require that they pay vastly higher fees in the interim.

"We're almost there," said Don, turning to Gonzaga. "At the end of the month, we will be down to four investors: what used to be Vicker's stake— which is now held by a Nevis-based trust that we control—you, SEF, and Volk's account, held through an obscure bank in Liechtenstein."

"And staff?" he asked.

"Down by ninety percent," said Greta. "Not only don't we need them, we couldn't even figure out what most of them did. And, now that we're private, we no longer need fifty people handling compliance. We're paying everyone two years of severance, with no complaints so far, as long as they sign an extremely restrictive nondisclosure agreement."

"Not that an NDA will keep the world from knowing the broad outlines of what is happening," said Gonzaga. "As we have had to keep the investment bankers and other counterparties fully informed in order to maintain trading lines."

"And Pete suggests that sooner, rather than later, we should have a communications strategy. Introduce Greta to a few friendly journalists as the new chief investment officer. Taking the lead with the press should help us maintain some control over the rumors," Chip added.

Gonzaga nodded. These people were turning out to be his best partners yet. Professional, decisive, hard-working, smart—and tolerant of moral ambiguity. Of course, they were still on their honeymoon and absorbed by the process of a transition from Vicker. He still had no idea of their endgame, but it had become increasingly clear that there was another member of the team, perhaps more than one, who had a say in major decisions.

Beyond that, even though they intimated that their takeover was meant to serve some higher purpose, they had yet to tip their hand as to precisely what their goals were, beyond confiscating several hundred billion from Vicker. He was struck by their solidarity, and that no one broke ranks to gossip. Their communications with him were cordial, but disciplined. Try as he might, they were not sharing any broader objectives, except to say that, if he did not like how Industrial Strategies was being run, they would return his money too.

A few days a month, they let Vicker come to the office, where he seemed just as disconnected as he did at home, padding around the largely empty IS trading floor in a dark blue cardigan and his velvet skull-and-crossbone slippers. He seemed content to fade into retirement, happy to introduce the new team to senior bankers at the trading firms and to soothe the few investors who were allowed to come calling, begging to be readmitted to the club.

Chip got most of the credit for Vicker's quiescence. His presence seemed to work some kind of magic with Vicker. Perhaps it was as simple as their shared love of baseball, as long as Chip, a diehard Yankee fan, kept his outer-borough disdain for the Mets to himself. At times, Vicker even got somewhere in the range of likable. In a first, Alison broke down in tears, not because he had berated her, but because he remembered her birthday, sent her an enormous arrangement of flowers, and personally brought her a two-pound box of champagne truffles.

Tommy and Ben worried that it had all become too smooth, too easy, that Vicker was being too cooperative, and that he might yet have something up his sleeve. Liz's analysis fell between that skepticism and equanimity. She monitored Vicker continually and made it her ongoing project to analyze his demeanor. There was no doubt in her mind that he was hiding something, but she would have been surprised otherwise, given the speed of his descent from a seat of such vast power. Had she not seen the evidence against him and the uncompromising, if comfortable, prison his life had become, she might have agreed that he seemed to be far too relaxed, almost as if he was biding his time, waiting for the right moment to play another hand.

During his last several visits, Ivanov had been telling Vicker and Chip, with steadily increasing confidence, that Parsifal had developed an event that would become what he called the trade of the century. Volk, indirectly, through Ivanov, was insisting that Industrial Strategies position itself for an event of geopolitical significance: one that would rock markets around the world. But, uncharacteristically, he had refused to provide specifics. Before most events, Ivanov provided granular detail about Parsifal's timing, location, and method—essential details when the target was a single company, a currency, or a commodity. This time, when they'd pressed for details, Chip said, Ivanov shut down. The broad idea was all anyone needed to know. Parsifal had figured out a way to make the world's major exchanges all drop, sharply and in unison.

When they pressed him, or expressed doubts about Volk's judgment, he suggested they simply look at the record of enormous, consistent profits that the Parsifal Group had produced for them all. There was also, he reminded them, a very limited downside. This was a fat-tail trade. The cost of betting on it was low, a very small percentage of recent profits. When Chip informed Ivanov that his Carlyle friends remained uncomfortable, he told them that Volk had authorized him to agree that the Parsifal Group would absorb any losses, in exchange for a larger share of any profits. It seemed to them all that there had to be more to this play than spreading $500 million around the markets and waiting for something to happen. But, in the face of Volk's implacable insistence, they relented.

Even though they had eyes in Vicker's apartment, Chip was their only connection into how those scenes played out among three men in a room. They worried that the cameras were imperfect or that Chip was somehow being played. Whenever they pressed Chip about what Ivanov had said about the nature of the event, his body language, Chip merely suggested that they review the video together. Again.

Don couldn't let it go. They had to be missing something. Was it possible that Vicker and Ivanov had some kind of protocol that enabled them to deceive the cameras and to avoid Chip?

Don bore in on Chip. In any interrogation—and that was how Chip experienced it—Don was always the bad cop.

"Once more. What, exactly, has Ivanov said?"

For the twentieth time, Chip recounted his conversations with Ivanov.

"Look, you've got the videos." Chip was peeved. "But I'll say it again: he wants us to build a trade on the premise that, when a black swan with geopolitical dimensions appears, major markets tend to fall in unison. They may not all fall to the same extent, but investors seek liquidity until uncertainties are resolved."

"Did he mention specific sectors?" asked Greta.

"Property and casualty insurers, both the primary underwriters and the reinsurers. He also suggested financial services firms, with a focus on money center banks. Maybe an unexpected debt default from a major borrower. But, basically, to anticipate a broad market falloff—at least until the Fed steps in."

The entire scheme seemed to galvanize Vicker, who appeared to have accepted the premise wholeheartedly: he was back to his old self. Even though he was no longer permitted to enter trades directly, he peppered Greta with all manner of ideas.

"Your roommate keeps barraging me with trades in stocks, market indices, commodities, but I'm puzzled," said Greta. "Every single one is significantly—very significantly—out of the money. Vicker seems to think whatever Volk is up to will cause prices to drop far and fast. With the trades he is suggesting, that's the only way we would make money. Not a conservative strategy."

"Anyone care to speculate on what we're looking at?" asked Don.

"Too long a list," said Greta. "Could be a cyberattack on major financial institutions, a political crisis in an EU member state. The possibilities are endless. He could bring down an electric grid, snip an undersea communications cable, disrupt oil supplies."

"Or stage a series of simultaneous terrorist drone attacks on crowds in one or more of the G-7. There is no way to protect against that, and they no longer need suicide bombers," Chip suggested.

Greta held up her palms. "Let your imagination run wild. Whatever it is, afterward, we'll wonder why we didn't see it coming."

The room went quiet. None of them was squeamish, but Volk was capable of anything. Whatever Volk was planning, the scale of the promised impact suggested an event that would take place in a developed country—in Western Europe or, perhaps, the United States. One-off murders, however unpalatable, had become acceptable costs in their relativistic universe. The business of national security, like any business, required a fluid assessment of costs and benefits measured against a projected rate of return. But the prospect of a single large-scale event, perhaps on American soil, shifted the balance to a nearly irreconcilable level of cognitive dissonance—particularly because they had lost control.

Without telling Chip, Greta and Don had alerted Tommy. And gotten his approval. His reasoning was that, since Volk was moving, no matter what, there was no obvious conflict in positioning IS to profit. But their first loyalty was clear: each of them had sworn an oath to defend against all enemies, foreign and domestic, and both Greta and Tommy remained in active service. Tommy had alerted the CIA, the NSA, and the FBI, and then their anglophone intelligence alliance, the Five Eyes. If Volk was really planning something big, it would likely show up in the chatter.

"Chip, do you have *any* sense of the timing?" Greta pressed.

"I gather that it could happen anytime. He knows that we're positioned."

"Then how will you trade it?" Gonzaga, nonplussed, looked at Greta.

As a model, the nearest analog that Greta had been able to conjure was the economic impact of the September 11 attacks on the World Trade Center in New York. Not that they had any reason to believe New York was the target, but, in terms of broad market impact and international linkages, 9/11 was really the only parallel. The low-hanging fruit would be gold prices—after 9/11 they spiked from $215 to $287 an ounce. Ditto for oil, which could double. Insurance stocks—Berkshire Hathaway, Swiss Re, Munich Re—would take a major hit. So would indices on the major stock exchanges, the London Stock Exchange, the NYSE, Euronext, Canada's TSX, Nasdaq. Emerging markets could be expected to dive, making Mexico, Argentina, and Brazil good shorts. And, on the flip side, defense stocks and defense contractors would skyrocket. Economic chaos would become a smorgasbord for them, as traders, not least because fat tails were never priced into the thinking of investors, and that made it cheap to bet against that complacency.

Tommy was right. As a purely financial matter, it made sense to play along with Volk, thought Greta, since the risks were easily managed. But the prospect of making huge profits from an international crisis of unknown origin made her deeply uncomfortable. They were flying blind, just following orders issued from Cyprus, maybe even Moscow. She could be Vladimir Putin's stooge and not even know it.

"This is a major shift for us," said Greta. "We do not work for Parsifal. We sometimes work with them. Remember, our goal is to wean ourselves off them completely, at some point."

Both Don and Gonzaga shared her concern, but, as Gonzaga pointed out, repeatedly, if the trade went bust, at the very worst, they stood to lose four to five hundred million, which they could easily handle. "Besides," Gonzaga added. "As galling as it is to imagine losing that amount of money, it might not send a terrible message to Volk, if he gets something wrong—that he's not omnipotent."

"I don't like it," Don said. "By blindly following his instructions, Volk puts us in a bind. We either go along with him and make tons of money. Or we push back and piss him off. Do we really want to make an enemy of him?"

"That would not be advisable," said Gonzaga. "If we are going to lessen our reliance on his ideas—and I agree that we should—we need to do it gradually. And we need to generate our own, better, ideas."

"And let's not forget that he's told us that the event will happen no matter what," said Chip.

"Weighing it all, I don't see how we can back away from this one," said Don. "The only thing worse than having a maniac like Volk inside our tent is having him out there on the loose, where we don't have any visibility on him."

Gonzaga drew on his, nowadays, ever-present cigar.

"I agree with most of that, but I take exception to your characterization of Fyodor. His methods can be distasteful, I'll admit that. And I know that Marina thinks that he's unbalanced these days, but, from my experience, he is anything but a maniac. He is a supremely rational player, and he's in an unenviable, delicate spot. Us on one side, his patrons in the Kremlin on the other. He can ill afford to alienate either side. I am quite confident that whatever he has up his sleeve, he'll be careful. Fyodor knows how to thread a needle."

Part Five

45

Hoboken, New Jersey

Fyodor Volk sat, comfortably, on the balcony of the Electric Circus Suite on the forty-fourth floor of the Spark Hoboken Hotel, sipping a double espresso. He held up one hand to protect his eyes from the brilliant morning sun rising in the east. On a side table just inside the sliding glass door leading into the suite, a small tray held a single shot glass and a silver ice bucket with an unopened bottle of Belenkaya vodka. Beads of water condensed on the neck of the bottle, and he admired the way that the rays of sunlight caused them to sparkle, bringing to mind Kim Tschang-yeul's photorealistic paintings of water drops. Not his favorite vodka, he thought, but the only Russian vodka that the hotel's room service had to offer.

Looking down, he reflected on the urban legend that, with foreknowledge, Muslims had gathered on nearby rooftops in Hoboken and Jersey City to admire the collapse of the World Trade Center. It was not far fetched to imagine that the 9/11 planners would plant spotters on the Jersey side to create a record for posterity. It's certainly something that anyone who took pride in their work would have done. The idea of seeing events through the eyes of people who were there—people who had made them happen— aroused him.

Volk breathed deeply, delighting in the color of the sky and wondering how Constable or Turner might have painted the dazzling edges of the few high clouds. He finished his espresso and moved inside. A pair of Oberwerk long-range observation binoculars, mounted on a tripod standing just inside the room, would give him a granular view of the river and the streets of Manhattan. Oberwerks might be overkill, considering the short distance across the Hudson, but they would produce crystal-clear images and record them through a digitizer attached to his iPad. Peering through the Carl Zeiss–designed lenses, Volk could easily read license plates and maybe even badge numbers on the shields of New York City cops. The sublime optics made it feel as if you were across the river, standing on the streets of

Manhattan. Swiveling north, Volk picked out the tower that housed Industrial Strategies.

He turned his Oberwerks toward 432 Park. Amazing. He hadn't believed it when Vadim first told him that, after his visit to *Zemblanity*, Vicker had built his own, enormous aquarium. But there they were—exotic fish swimming for their master high above the city streets. He had been wrong to dismiss Elias Vicker as an arrogant fool. He had grown to appreciate the strange man's malleability and lack of any moral compass. What Volk was about to accomplish would have been impossible without Vicker—a pity Elias would never enjoy the fruits. Perhaps an anonymous plaque honoring Vicker, somewhere in the Kremlin. If Putin was pleased, he might agree to that—it would appeal to his dark sense of humor.

But for himself and Anatoly, VVP should bestow the Order of Saint George, the highest military decoration of the Russian Federation. If I succeed, I will have earned it, he thought, able to script my own future. Not, of course, a very Russian idea. Not even Vladimir Putin could do that. VVP: prisoner of the Kremlin, beholden to his longtime FSB and GRU masters, his entire presidency an unending series of plots and counterplots, stealing from any and all, always recruiting more thieves to steal on his behalf. The rule of kleptocracy: not the license to steal but that stealing is the only way you survive. He remembered Putin's chilly smile as they walked through the empty city that afternoon in Saint Petersburg. Acknowledging Anatoly, Putin's admission of the price he himself had paid—continued to pay—to become a modern-day tsar. Every step toward absolute power further enmeshed him in a world he could never escape.

That would not happen to Fyodor Volk. He was about to open a new door.

At precisely 8:16 a.m., during the height of rush hour, Volk pressed a virtual button on his iPad to detonate all nine charges. He wondered whether anyone, other than a Japanese historian, would appreciate the symmetry. On August 6, 1945, at precisely 8:16 a.m. Japanese time, an atomic bomb dropped by an American B-29 bomber detonated over Hiroshima, killing eighty thousand people.

Through his binoculars, Volk watched as the river began to boil. Before Industrial Deconstruction divers had dropped geotextile mats over the PATH tubes, Volk had brought in some frogmen of his own to adhere nine sheets of M118 block demolition charges directly to the cast iron. The mats only offered protection from bombs placed inside the pipes. Lodging explosives under the mats intensified the compressive force by a factor of four. The primary explosions blew the tops off each tunnel, tearing jagged, gaping holes thirty feet long and shredding the track. Secondary explosions sent shards of hundred-year-old cast iron fifty feet into the sunny sky over the Hudson, piercing the hulls of a passing barge and two tugboats. A shock wave roiled the water for miles north and south as bubbling air escaped from the tube and the vacuum created by the explosion sucked water into the tunnel. The tube, and everything in it, flooded in three minutes. On his laptop, he could see his demolition engineers, by now relaxing, beachside, at a Russian military compound on the Venezuelan island of La Orchila, as they whooped and hollered over an encrypted video. High fives all around. For them, the exercise had been a complete success. An intriguing physics project, as well as an opportunity to serve the motherland. They had debated, at length, the size and positioning of each charge. Some, being artists of destruction, argued for elegance and wanted to see what could be accomplished with minimal amounts of explosive material. In the end, they opted for overkill: their client wanted absolute certainty.

Volk tuned the radio to 1010 WINS. Nothing at 8:20. Still nothing at 8:22. Then, at 8:23, report of a brownout in lower Manhattan and flooding at a PATH station. He watched fire trucks, ambulances, police cars, and ConEd emergency vehicles racing down the West Side Highway. Volk popped the cap of the vodka, poured himself a glass, and toasted Manhattan. Still wearing latex gloves, he packed the Oberwerks and iPad; slipped on a New Jersey Devils jersey, sunglasses, and a baseball cap; and took an elevator down to the basement garage, which backed onto a side street lined with redbrick condos inhabited by people who put on their best faces every morning and sullenly rode the PATH train to jobs in Manhattan. An exfiltration team based at Russia's mission to the United Nations bundled him into a Suburban with diplomatic plates for the forty-mile ride to a safe house in Rockland County, one of dozens that the Russian government maintained around the United States, around the world.

By his own conservative estimate, fifteen hundred to two thousand commuters would die. Some from the percussive force. Others from shrapnel wounds as the cast-iron tubes were shredded, impaling hundreds with shards of metal. But most would suffocate. They would drown as brackish river water flooded their lungs, interrupting the ability of their bodies to absorb oxygen, leading to cardiac arrest caused by hypoxia and acidosis. Not a quick or painless death; they would take three to four minutes to die. The entire Eastern seaboard—maybe the entire country—would be paralyzed. Roads closed, airports shut down, troops mobilized. Chaos. Richly deserved chaos. If one bad death deserved another, Volk had exceeded even his own monstrous expectations.

Just a short distance away, beneath the river, Alison Winger sat on a PATH train for the short trip from her home in Jersey City to Industrial Strategies in the West Fifties. Tucked into a corner seat with the hood of an oversize Uniqlo sweatshirt draped over her head, she managed to block out most of the morning crush. The Beats headphones covering her ears shut out the rest. She cradled a Tupperware container of cupcakes on her lap. She'd spent hours the previous evening bent over a pastry funnel, drawing a skull and crossbones on each one, just like those funny slippers Mr. Vicker wore around the office. He'd insisted she take the day off today, all but ordering her not to come in. But it was his birthday. The poor man's wife had just left him and he would be making a rare appearance at the office today. If she didn't throw a party, no one would.

She was watching a segment from *The View* that was trending on Twitter, about the upcoming Illinois primary, just a few days away. Senator Ben Corn was cruising to the nomination. His two top rivals had dropped out in as many days: one because her campaign fell apart after a top aide was caught taking secret payments from a Chinese telecom billionaire; the other brought down by a leaked dick-pic he'd sent to his pregnant daughter-in-law. But, rather than speculate on the sources of this compromising material, the women gabbed for two minutes about a photo of a shirtless Ben out for a jog; the way the sweat beading on his chest made Whoopi want to take a cold shower. Such a nice man, Alison thought, that Senator Corn. Every time he came to see Mr. Vicker, he always remembered my cat's name.

Just then, she felt an ear-shattering pop. She grabbed the side of her head, shrieking as the pressure wave burst her eardrums and excruciating pain radiated through her skull. Unable to hear, she looked down. A torrent of blood spurted from her nose. Looking up, she saw shock and abject fear on the faces around her. She tried to stand, but the train, blown off its tracks, had begun to skid, bouncing off one wall of the narrow tunnel and then the other. Alison was thrown ten feet forward into a writhing scrum of bodies, each person trying to regain their footing, stepping on one another, breaking heads, arms, necks, legs, and hands in the process. Gasping for breath under the weight of tumbling strangers, falling on top of one another, struggling desperately to stand as the train came to a screeching stop and toppled on its side, its metal skin shredded.

Hitting her head, she passed out briefly. Coming to, she found herself lying on the side of the toppled car as cold water rose around her, the lights flickered into darkness as the power shorted out, leaving only weak emergency lights to illuminate the ghastly scene. She struggled to lift herself above the swirling, murky pool, stepping on bodies, some already dead, others writhing and gasping for one final breath. Managing to grab a strap and balance precariously, she experienced an odd detachment. Alison scanned the train. The cupcakes. Where are the cupcakes? Mr. Vicker will be so sad. Brackish, greasy, icy, dark water shot up around her hips, waist, breasts, neck. As the weight of her clothes dragged her beneath the water's surface, a soggy cupcake, skull-and-crossbones icing intact, floated past her. Her heart beating furiously, Alison sank into the water, swam a few strokes, held her breath until she could no longer, and then the river filled her lungs.

46

Industrial Strategies, New York City

Through the glass walls of Greta's office, she and Don watched Vicker amble down the hall. He stopped, stood at the end of the trading floor, which was more than two-thirds empty as a result of Greta's cuts, and glanced, almost expectantly, at the enormous monitors hanging from the ceiling, silently streaming news. One was tuned to CNBC, another to Fox, still another to Bloomberg. He cracked his knuckles absentmindedly and bounced from foot to foot, checking his watch. Since his return from the salt shed, he had, at their insistence, kept a low profile at the office, spending his days watching the trading screens, talking to no one other than the two of them and Chip. He still occasionally tormented Alison, who had little to do other than bring him snacks and coffee. One of their crew, usually Chip, monitored him continually, observing what he was looking at on his computer terminals.

As he had for weeks, Vicker compulsively followed price movements in the large portfolio of financial instruments that Industrial Strategies had assembled to make the black-swan bet that Volk had insisted upon. As a percentage of the firm's assets, the size of those positions was modest, but, in absolute terms, huge. More than $5 billion was at risk, and the skew was massive: the ultimate asymmetrical investment. If no event transpired, there would be some decay in the value of those positions—IS would lose 25 basis points, roughly $12.5 million every month. The asymmetry arose on the other side, since they were betting on an event that no one in the market—in the world—anticipated. If IS was on the winning side of the trade, the investment was skewed to return twenty to fifty times the original $5 billion that had been invested. By purchasing deep out-of-the-money puts on the major market indices, baskets of stocks, and calls on gold, Greta created a portfolio that no one would ever be able to connect to the anticipated event, whatever it turned out to be. The combination of instruments that she acquired would look—and function—like precisely the kinds of hedging transactions that a prudent fund manager would implement to protect a portfolio from catastrophic losses. It just so happened that, depending on how far markets moved, Greta's models predicted that IS would earn, conservatively, between $100 and $200 billion. Under some scenarios, earn as much as $500 billion. Or more.

The anticipation was wearing her down. She was on edge every time she scanned the headlines. One day, when a magnitude 6.9 earthquake destroyed a section of downtown Jakarta, she felt the beginning of a panic attack. She knew it was irrational, but Volk's powers had grown to such outsize proportions in her mind that, for a moment, she wondered how he might have made it happen.

At 8:26 a.m., the three news channels being streamed on the trading floor interrupted their morning shows, cutting off market pundits, talking heads, and endless nattering about video game fads and the prospects for cannabis stocks. In their place, images of chaos, mostly forwarded from iPhones, filled the screens. The streets of lower Manhattan had become gridlocked with emergency vehicles. Moving aimlessly, cops, EMTs, and firemen milled around the entrances to PATH stations on both sides of the Hudson. Befuddled. Initially, there was nothing to be done on the surface. Whatever had happened, it had happened underwater in a now twisted and buckled tube of century-old iron. The accident site was accessible only by scuba divers and, eventually, salvage crews. The Twitter universe erupted with speculation. Traders across the globe—a twitchy bunch in the best of times—began dumping stocks and corporate bonds and buying gold. The prices of financial assets moved slowly at first, and then, as automated, algorithmic trading kicked in, at an accelerating pace. Gold and oil prices spiked, up 30 percent.

By 8:30 a.m., the Department of Homeland Security had asked the air force to scramble fighter jets, observing 9/11 protocols, to give the appearance of action. F-22 Raptors buzzed the skies above New York City like mad hornets, pointlessly skimming loops at a thousand feet. Police choppers took to the air, adding noise, confusion. Trucks from local news stations burrowed as close as they were allowed, pointing parabolic antennas skyward. On-air talent and their camera crews hoofed it to the PATH station on West Ninth Street, not knowing why. Some cameras cut to the Hudson. At the Pier 25 Marina in Tribeca, powerboats, sailboats—and kayaks with kayakers still in them—had been overwhelmed by a tsunami-like wave that lifted them fifteen feet into the air above West Street before slamming some into

Hudson River Park and shattering others against the facade of the Borough of Manhattan Community College like so many matchsticks. Prices on stock exchanges in the United States and Europe continued to plummet. As Greta watched, real-time calculations of the value of Industrial Strategies' portfolio ratcheted upward like the National Debt clock. Already they were up $50 billion. A home run. A grand slam.

At 8:32 a.m., sixteen minutes after ignition, as the Russian mission car ferrying Volk passed the Paramus exit on the Garden State Parkway, fragments of a story began to emerge. Live video on NY1 showed firemen half dragging, half carrying a few people out of the PATH stations. Reporters caught bits and pieces, collecting scraps from overheard conversations among cops and firefighters. The NYPD SCUBA Team arrived and disappeared into a PATH station. At least one, and perhaps more than one, of the PATH tunnels had flooded, but no one knew how or why. A shell-shocked survivor, hands against her ears, chuntered about a crashing sound from what might have been a blast, her train derailing, a mad scramble to exit the front of the train, running on the tracks until a column of water, rushing from behind, swept her through the tunnel and into the station, where she was yanked onto the platform by strangers.

Greta and Don hotfooted it to join Vicker on the trading floor, fifty feet down the hall, Chip trailing in their wake. Someone had turned up the sound on the bank of monitors. Everyone watched in silence, slack-jawed. Some remembered the destruction of the World Trade Center. This was vastly different and somehow even more disquieting: no low-flying planes, no smoke, no visuals at all. Wearing an indecipherable expression, Vicker alternated between watching news feeds and peering at his computer terminal, following the performance of the portfolio he'd so avidly helped to construct in recent months. The graph of its performance marked a line sharply upward to the right, like a hockey stick. The tally clicked higher: $58 billion, $62 billion, $69 billion in profits.

Greta felt sick. Don, enraged. Both believed that, in some way, they were responsible. How could they have missed it? Had they exhausted every investigative and forensic path trying to figure out what Volk might be up to? They *had* briefed Tommy, with as much detail as they could. Tommy knew that an event of consequence was coming, and he had sounded an international alarm that the CIA had credible intelligence that an event was in the offing. Had they wanted to indulge in denial, they could have fallen back on the facts—true enough—that they had no idea what might happen, or when, or where. But, in the moment, none of that helped. They had been too close to it, and, perhaps, a source of their uneasiness was the fear that they had willfully, if unconsciously, ignored the signs. If they had anticipated anything, it had been the expectation that an event would occur somewhere else. Anywhere else. An event at a geographic remove might have upset them, but it would have been in the abstract, isn't-that-awful kind of way that distance permits. A foreign war. A bombing in Berlin. Westminster Abbey. A mine explosion in Australia. A short-circuit on a string of GPS satellites. It could have been anything, anywhere. They all knew that something was coming. But not where. Anywhere but home.

"Let's take some profits, get some cash off the table," said Vicker. "Any minute now they'll close the stock exchange. These things never follow a straight line."

"What things?" Don asked.

"You're the know-it-alls. You tell me."

$72 billion . . . $76 billion.

"We should listen to Elias," said Chip. Don let it pass. It had been years since he let Chip get to him, but Greta was furious. Was this how they taught Park Avenue rich boys to handle a crisis? Get your money off the table, let someone else clean up the mess.

$78 billion . . . $82 billion.

The feeling in the pit of her stomach had given way to an adrenaline rush. Watching Vicker's face, the live videos, the trading screen. A chyron crawled across the bottom of the big screens quoting a terse statement issued by the police commissioner: *A PATH tunnel has been breached and flooded, no more information is available at this time.* Talking heads on network news had already dredged up reports about the incompetence of the Port Authority, a litany of misfeasance, confusion, deferred maintenance, and engineering failures that led to this unimaginable horror. Greta looked at Chip, searching his face, trying to resist her suspicions. The guy could be a jerk at times, but, unlike Don, she had always trusted Chip. It was impossible to imagine he was part of this. But he practically lived with Vicker and he was their link to Ivanov. If he was aware of something, he would have mentioned it. She wondered if Don was jumping to the same conclusion. Chip looked back at her. He seemed unusually quiet, an odd version of anxious. Somehow slightly off.

$88 billion . . . $92 billion.

Don's phone rang: Tommy, using Signal. Don picked up, glanced at Greta, and tilted his head toward her office. In her office, he put the phone down and placed it on speaker.

"Who's with you?"

"Just Greta."

"Gonna make this quick. They blew up one of the PATH tunnels, and so far, we've found explosives on two of the other tunnels, but they didn't ignite. Intentionally not detonated, from the looks of it."

"How—" Don began, before Tommy cut him off.

"No, just listen. Until we know any better, this is just a horrible accident. We think it's best that way."

In shorthand, Tommy laid out what they knew already and ran through the security and anti-terrorism protocols for a major urban disaster. Most of those measures were useless and backward-looking, the products of decades of bureaucratic turf battles and inertia. Thousands of skittish, wet-behind-the-ears National Guard troops would be deployed in force, to wander aimlessly—more likely to shoot one another or random civilians than to provide protection. Hundreds of agents assigned to a dozen specialized task forces at the DHS and FBI were already on their way to New York. The city was on the way to being locked down: no one in, no one out. At best, a show of awesome force and dramatic activity might give the press something positive to report—and mollify a frightened and angry populace. If the truth were known, people might wake up to how pitifully vulnerable they remained, notwithstanding $3 trillion spent on endless wars since 9/11. Or, more likely, as Tommy predicted, people would mourn but breathe a collective sigh of relief that the entire sad episode wasn't a terrorist act after all, but could be blamed on the incompetence—or criminal misfeasance—of Port Authority bureaucrats and managers.

"Don, get Vicker out of the city right away. Just take him somewhere. Greta, you stay put. I'll need you." Tommy clicked off.

"Get Vicker," Don commanded Greta, as he dragged two enormous duffel bags from the corner of his office. "And meet me on the roof."

Greta sped back to the trading floor. As before, Vicker was following prices on different stock, bond, and commodity markets, concentrating only on the numbers, seemingly unaware of the catastrophe—what might have caused it, how many people might have died—unfolding on the ubiquitous screens.

$96 billion.

"Come with me," Greta barked, grabbing Vicker by the arm. "Chip, help me."

"Really, Ms. Webb, this is important." Vicker gripped the arms of his chair, refusing to budge. "We still have profits to take. Another ten or fifteen billion. Maybe cover some of the bank stocks we shorted; whatever else you're doing can wait."

"I will deal with that. Right now, we have to get you out of town. Don is waiting for us on the roof."

Vicker frowned and scrunched down farther in his chair.

"No thanks. I'm having too much fun right here." Vicker, snide. "Watching telly and making money." He gripped the armrests, trying to hang on even tighter, like a petulant child.

Greta stifled the urge to snap his neck. But before she could speak, Chip laid a hand on Vicker's forearm, leaned down to whisper something in his ear, and motioned with his head for Vicker to follow them. Without a word, Vicker got up from his chair, almost obediently. Greta wondered what that was about. Maybe she should be suspicious.

When they reached the roof, Don was already zipped into his wingsuit and was strapping on the latest addition to the Industrial Strategies air fleet, an experimental BMW jetpack. He tossed a tandem rig to Chip, who snapped the harness into place around Vicker's torso, cinched it tight, and attached Vicker to Don's back. With Chip's help, Don and Vicker got in position on the building's ledge. Vicker seemed strangely calm, given the circumstances, quietly grinning and moving right out to the edge with assurance. Don never would have guessed it. A Zodiac was already in position in the Hudson, just off a grassy stretch of Riverside Park South at Sixty-Fifth Street. Don put on his helmet and called for the skipper over the radio: the Hudson was choppy, but nothing he couldn't handle. Don looked at his watch. "I'll be there in three minutes." Don hoped that the short, strange flight of two men in black helmets and goggles would be one of those peculiar sightings, an urban legend that, in the general mayhem, no one could be certain they remembered or had imagined. Don flapped his wings to get the feel of the wind. Vicker hadn't stopped grinning, as if at some incredible joke that only he got.

"Ready?"

Don stepped off the parapet, felt the air filling the suit's wings, powered up the jetpack's two 7.5 kW engines, and they began to accelerate, gaining altitude and flying toward the Hudson River, high above standstill traffic on West Fifty-Seventh Street. Don felt something wet and warm leaking into his suit. Vicker wasn't that different from most other first-time passengers. Most pissed themselves before they even jumped.

At the river, Don banked north. The city was gridlocked, a cacophony of angry horns and sirens. They had plenty of lift, and not a lot of ground to cover. He slowed the engines and glided down to a grassy riverbank park near Sixty-Sixth Street. Don unhitched Vicker, and they scrambled over a low breakwater, where Don practically tossed Vicker to a crewman in the waiting Zodiac. Seconds later, they were strapped in and skimming up the Hudson, twin Mercury diesel outboard engines, 175 horsepower each, at full throttle.

"Where to? Teterboro?" Vicker asked.

That would be his first choice, Don thought, but it would be impossible today. With DHS protocols for a terrorist event, every airport within a hundred miles would be shut down. Up the Hudson seemed like the only way out of town. All the cops, joined by boats from any state or federal agency that had any reason to be on the water, would be massed in lower Manhattan. If they were to get stopped, his skipper was ex-NYPD, with a badge to prove it.

They could barely hear each other over the roar of the outboards as Don shouted into Vicker's ear. "We're going upstate."

"Where?" Vicker asked. "I have a house in Bedford. Only been there once. We could go there."

Don ignored him. Vicker didn't seem to mind. He remained freakishly nonplussed. A preoccupied grin on his face, humming an indecipherable tune. Don struggled to retain his focus as feelings of anger and guilt crowded his mind, mixed with a continual stream of commentary and questions pouring through his earpiece from Greta, Chip, and, indirectly, Tommy. They peppered him with speculation and questions for Vicker, even though they knew it would be impossible to interrogate him at least until they made landfall at Poughkeepsie and began the drive to the Millbrook safe house where they had previously detained Gonzaga.

Fifty minutes later, they cruised into the Shadows Marina, where two of Don's crew met them in a Sprinter van. A bag of clothes for Vicker, who cleaned himself and changed in the clubhouse. He and Vicker had not exchanged more than a dozen words during the entire trip. As they got into the Sprinter, Don tied a blindfold over Vicker's eyes and cinched it tight.

"Mr. Carter," Vicker said, in a sarcastic tone. "Really? Is this necessary?"

Don dialed Greta and Chip, put the call on the van's speakers so they could hear, and turned to Vicker.

"You're not surprised by what happened?"

"How can I be surprised, Mr. Carter, if no one will tell me what happened."

Don stared at him impatiently.

"Okay, Mr. Carter, I'll play. A wild guess: a dilapidated metal tube has been lying on the bottom of the Hudson for a century. It sprang a leak this morning. How'm I doing?"

"Sprang a leak? Is that what you call multiple explosive devices?"

For an instant, Vicker looked genuinely surprised, almost amazed. Maybe he was acting, maybe he had not known precisely what Volk had planned, Don thought. But, either way, Vicker did not care.

"Early estimates are that as many as two thousand people may have drowned."

Vicker put on a fake-pouty frown.

"Bad things happen all the time. Who d'ya think they'll blame it on? I'm saying the bloated, inefficient, and corrupt government agency that let those tunnels rot. Don't you think that's what Ben Corn should say? Good issue for him. Rebuild this country. Might put him over the top in Illinois."

They drove up the long dirt drive to the safe house, and once inside planted Vicker, none too gently, in a wing chair in the grand living room, shades drawn and darkened, and removed his blindfold. A squad of six men, led by Gunner Nuzine, lurked in the background, not all of them visible in the shadows.

"This will do, comfortable enough."

"Enjoy it while you can. It might be the last comfortable chair you ever sit in."

Vicker lowered an eyebrow in feigned consternation. Greta and Chip, able to view the entire house on a video stream, could see and hear everything.

"I doubt that, Mr. Carter. Why pick on me? I didn't do anything."

"Really? Aiding and abetting a terrorist attack on American soil. Let's add that to the list of charges still pending against you."

"I'd say that all those crimes fit you much better than they do me, Carter." Vicker seemed genuinely unconcerned. "You're the one who stole Industrial Strategies out from under me. You broke it, you own it. Now it's all on you . . . buddy." Vicker cackled. "You are well and truly . . . fucked."

Vicker lifted his leg to better see the ankle monitor.

"It will be nice to get rid of this thing."

Don motioned to the two burly minders standing on the far side of the room.

"We're not getting anywhere. Show our guest to his new room."

They took his arms roughly and dragged him down to the basement and into a crude cell—a bed, toilet with no seat, shackles and rings attached to the walls and suspended from the ceiling. Had curious neighbors or a tradesman stumbled on it, they would, more likely than not, have seen it as a dominatrix's lair, rather than an actual jail. Vicker accepted it without protest, flopping down on the cot, ignoring his jailers. Humming to himself, nodding to his guard.

"Tell the chef I don't eat sea urchin, and I like my steak well done."

———————

At 11:22 a.m., Tommy, typically cryptic, texted Greta: *Roundelay just posted something you need to see. Call me.*

She took a deep breath and pulled up the magazine's website on her phone.

A picture of Don filled the screen over a headline that read:

AMERICAN OSAMA: THE ROGUE SOLDIER WHO MASTERMINDED THE TUNNEL PLOT

The story, written by Jason Renton, and based on a dossier purportedly leaked to him by a "brave anonymous whistleblower, a true American patriot" identified Don Carter as the "greatest mass murderer in American history." With only a tepid disclaimer that the public had a right to know what he knew—even if he hadn't yet had time to verify all the details—Renton portrayed Don as a disgruntled ex-army sniper who had crossed over into the shadowy world of military contracting. In Renton's telling, Don capitalized on his national security credentials and relationships, and, working for Elias Vicker, had been the driving force behind the creation of the world's largest demolition contractor: Industrial Deconstruction, Inc. In the world according to Renton, it had been Don Carter who negotiated each acquisition, and Don Carter, personally, had tendered an almost impossibly low bid to become the preferred security contractor to the Port Authority. The contract to protect the PATH tunnels with concrete mats had been IDI's biggest to date.

Even though the attacks had occurred barely three hours earlier, it hardly occurred to a credulous press—much less the retweeting wizards of the blogosphere—that no one, much less Renton, would have had the time to write, much less research, a story with the kind of detail, documentation, and background that Renton had produced. Whoever had written it knew all about Don's scrapes with the law growing up as an army brat, his service record, his multiple tours in Iraq and Afghanistan, his court-martial (acquitted), his more recent business running a security outfit. Where the article stopped short was describing his relationship with Tommy and Ben.

With Chip reading over her shoulder, Greta quickly scanned through page after page; she could not believe that anyone would take it seriously, much less republish it. The entire package presented a story that was too neat, and complete, too pat and perfect to be true. But, the internet being what it was, and the agony of the possibility that there had been another monstrous attack on New York being an open wound, she knew it would take on a life of its own.

Greta admired the craftsmanship—likely Russian handiwork—that had gone into the frame-up. Volk certainly knew what he was doing. In addition to the main narrative, Renton had provided hundreds of pages of leaked documents: certificates of incorporation, reams of correspondence, trust agreements, powers of attorney and management contracts, all ostensibly created by some of the finest white-shoe law firms in New York, Hong Kong, and London, skeins of shell companies in a dozen jurisdictions. A spiderweb of cross-holdings had the look—superficially—of an effort to disguise the ultimate ownership by using companies in Nevis, Cyprus, Anguilla, South Africa, Seychelles, Cook Islands, Malta, Grand Cayman, Nevada, and Morocco. At the very bottom of the chain sat a Delaware company by the name of Industrial Deconstruction, Inc. Every company had its own bank accounts, and *Roundelay* managed to include what were, ostensibly, copies of wire transfers and bank statements showing the movement of tens of millions of dollars north, south, east, and west. At the top of the chain, a Liechtenstein trust, governed by letters of instruction drafted by a prominent Geneva-based legal boutique, named Donald P. Carter Jr. as the beneficial owner of the entire, elaborate charade.

"Just so you know, there is an APB out for Don," Tommy said.

Of course, Greta thought, expressionless. The FBI had no choice, really. Everyone in law enforcement or national security had to at least appear to take a story like this at face value—until proven otherwise. No matter how strenuously the law firms that had been mentioned in the report denied their involvement, she knew the press would cover those denials as ass-covering prevarication. In the popular mind, lying was what law firms did in exchange for their four-figure-per-hour fees. Double ditto for the banks, which the public has viewed as crooked since the Medici Bank failed in 1494.

"What would they want with Don?" asked Chip. "It's a hoax. It should be easy to see that this dossier is bullshit. A classically baroque lie, disinformation, too much random detail strung together."

Tommy said nothing for a moment.

"And why just Don?" Greta asked. "Why didn't the story mention Industrial Strategies, Don's biggest client? Why aren't all our names, especially Ben's, in those documents? It would have been just as easy to frame all of us."

"Volk's toying with us," Chip said. "I'm sure he's got another set of phony documents ready to leak to Renton if we don't do exactly what he tells us."

"He's letting us know that he could do a lot more damage to the country and to us," Tommy said. "He wants us to think we're lucky that he only killed two thousand people."

"What about Don in the meantime?" Chip asked.

Greta felt certain that given a week, two at most, she could figure out how the dossier had made its way to Renton and discredit it as pure fabrication. She was certain Volk knew this too and assumed that they would realize the cover story he provided them—Don as a rogue soldier—was in their interest as well.

"Is Volk assuming that we'll be willing to sacrifice Don?" Greta asked.

"Very smart play on his part," said Chip. "Ties up a lot of loose ends."

Greta stared at him, angry and perplexed.

"Except that it's the kind of a witch hunt that would never end. Until we clear Don, we're all at risk." Her voice tightened.

"Hey, I was just gaming out the situation," Chip said. "Isn't that what we do?"

"Only those of us who see everything as a game," Greta said coldly.

"Just stop," Tommy said, sharply. "Every law enforcement organization in the country—state, federal, and local—has a raging hard-on for Don Carter right now. I'm doing what I can, but I may not be able to protect him."

"Have you reminded them that it was Don who sounded the alarm that a major attack was imminent?"

"They don't care. They just want a scalp. Public humiliation makes them defensive and aggressive. Every second they don't find someone to blame is another second they get blamed."

"What do you need from us?" Greta asked.

"I'll tell you what I don't need: Don being paraded around in handcuffs on CNN. Clear your heads. Get to work. Solve it."

47

Millbrook, New York

Don sat quietly on the safe house porch, anguished and disconnected, watching the news on his laptop. An endless loop of photos of him scowling during his court-martial hearing alternated with images of bodies being pulled from the river. He could not believe that not one of the dozens of retired generals, political analysts, and former spooks jabbering away on CNN, Fox, and NBC saw through the obvious frame-up. The director of the FBI had announced the launch of the biggest manhunt in American history. The president was saying that no one in government would rest until that certain person of interest had been detained and questioned. It sickened him to think that, in the event he was caught and prosecuted, that sanctimonious, corrupt phony in the White House would probably sail to reelection, vilifying Don Carter, the ultimate toxic white man, and all he stood for.

He had to hand it to Volk and Ivanov. They were industrious, well organized, and clever, but, to his mind, it was a ham-handed deflection. No one who knew anything about anything would believe the frame-up for more than a second, because it was completely false. But truth was not the standard as long as he was the *only* person of interest—and they had a prima facie case. And a great narrative: an angry ex-soldier fragged a senior officer, carried a grudge, and had access to the tools. Capacity and motive.

His dark reverie was interrupted by the ringing of his cell phone. It was Greta, calling from her office at IS, Chip sitting across from her.

"The fact that I am not already in custody tells me that at least you and Tommy have my back," Don said wryly.

"*We* do," she said. "Not that it's doing much good right now."

"Vicker knew everything. Right up to the last moment. Pretty sure I know how."

"Got it," Greta replied. "Good travels, Yogi."

"Yogi, out," said Don.

Don pulled the SIM card out of his phone and destroyed it before smashing the phone processor under his heel. He slung his survival pack over his shoulder, not that he needed it where he was going, but extra knives, fresh ammo, snares, and a half dozen fully charged burner phones might prove useful. Don motioned for Gunner to follow him.

"Bear cave. Bring in enough support to manage this place, then come find me. We might be there for a few days." Don paused. "I don't need to say this, but don't believe everything you read."

"Reading is overrated," said Gunner, patting the pistol on his hip.

Trotting to the garage, Don pulled on a helmet, flipped the visor down, and mounted his Ducati Testastretta DVT 1262. A fine bike on highways, but a truly superb off-road machine, skipping over roots and rocks like a white-tailed deer. He cruised down the three-quarters of a mile of gravel driveway and turned right on Route 5. Staying just below the speed limit, he made his way to Route 44, then followed back roads: Route 55 to Route 216 to Route 52.

Twenty-eight miles from the safe house, he turned left onto Lime Kiln Road and then bumped along East Mountain Road until it met the northern boundary of Fahnestock State Park, just south of Wiccopee. Don turned south off the road, into the park, and began a careful climb through dense woods in full leaf. With fourteen thousand acres of near wilderness, barely penetrated by roads and trails, Fahnestock had long been Don's personal refuge. He had hiked most of it, sometimes living there, off the land, for weeks at a time, in all seasons. Two miles from the park boundary he came to his secret spot, a remote ridge with a naturally occurring cave formed by granite outcroppings. Before Don discovered and renovated it years before, the cave had been a comfortable lair for a family of black bears. But, after Don had carved it deeper into the side of the hill, he closed the entrance off with a dozen small boulders that no ordinary bear would likely be able to move. Yogi's sanctuary.

Don had told himself, and Greta, that he needed this elaborate hideout for the same reasons she needed her stash in Geneva: just in case things— exactly what things he never said—became too hot. She did not buy it. Inevitably, that led to one of their longest-running rows. How could he expect her to truly give herself to someone who spent his spare time planning his escape? *Sure got that one wrong, babe*, he thought.

Over time, Don had equipped the cave with everything he might need to survive in the woods, indefinitely, without being detected. It hid a dozen large military transit cases fitted with combination locks and booby traps. Extra passports, several hundred thousand dollars in cash, a pouch of Canadian maple leaf gold coins, small arms and ammunition sufficient to fight a short war, tarps, cold weather gear, extra boots, flints, matches, MREs, water purification canisters, propane tanks, concertina wire, snares, rope, batteries with hand-crank chargers, more burner phones, an encrypted Chromebook, Jetpack MiFi mobile hotspot, a ham radio, and six subcompact Mission crossbows with Hawke scopes, for silent hunting.

After camouflaging the Ducati, Don opened, unpacked, inspected, and repacked his gear, leaving one crossbow within easy reach. He ate an MRE; packed the trash; and disassembled, oiled, and reassembled his Glock. As the sun began to set, he sat down on a rock to wait. And think.

Don was accustomed to moral ambiguity, and nothing he had ever done in the course of following orders had given him pause. Death and destruction were the objectives of combat. He had killed dozens—no, hundreds— of people. Many innocents. Civilians. He never saw himself as a murderer. The endless war might be illegitimate and immoral, but he was a soldier in that war, licensed to kill by, and for, the United States of America. But he had never before watched America's enemies kill American civilians at close range. Mental pictures of human carnage and twisted metal on the riverbed crowded his mind. He told himself they had done what they had to do— after all, they had a mission to consider. But there was one crucial difference between this operation and hundreds of others he'd been a part of: This time, they were not following orders. Nor were they ignoring them. There was no directive, no orders passed down through a chain of command; they had not been sanctioned by any committee, commission, panel, or agency. Six independent, self-appointed actors. For months, they had watched Volk make things happen in other places—things that had taken lives and destroyed billions of dollars of property, all with the goal of making money. For the first time, the event was not merely close to home, but in their home. All six of them were actors, unprotected even by the transparent trope of just following orders. Not guilty, exactly, but complicit. An unaccustomed, discomfiting weight of responsibility.

What was his next move? What cards did he have left to play? If the authorities caught up to him before his name was cleared, which Greta said would take at least a week, he was most certainly a dead man. They would shoot first and try to make sure that as few questions as possible were asked later. Or ever. An opaque cloak of national security would be drawn over this day's messy events and the Pentagon, CIA, FBI—not to mention the alphabet soup of secret and semi-secret agencies—would happily go along with it.

He racked his mind trying to come up with a way forward. He had survived, literally and metaphorically, by always knowing where the exit was. Now, at least for the moment, he was out of moves.

His wristwatch vibrated: five minutes to the appointed hour, his cue to listen for Greta. Don extended the high-gain antenna and flicked a knob on the HF ham radio, already tuned to the 40-meter band that Greta would expect. They could speak, if absolutely essential, but, more likely, and to reduce the risk of being tracked to his location, he would simply be ready to monitor her transmissions at regular intervals. Greta could signal him with any of a hundred codes that could be used individually or in combination, an elaborate system of their own design and known only to them. Their failsafe was a passive alarm. If Greta did not check in on a pre-agreed schedule designated at the end of each transmission, he would know that something had gone wrong. Most likely, badly wrong.

48

Tuxedo Park, New York

Greta ran her fingers through her hair and pulled her arms across her chest, stretching: forty-eight hours at her desk with only a couple of short naps, and not enough progress. Every investigation starts with a loose thread, and Greta had begun this one by reading everything that the so-called journalist who bylined the Don dossier story had ever written. Jason Renton. As soon as she pulled up his picture, she realized that she had seen him before. That loudmouth from the party Vicker had taken her to at the Met.

She remembered the story he had written for the *Guardian* about the U.S. Army paying the Taliban millions of dollars—in cash—to secure supply routes for military convoys. She had ridden some of those routes and knew foreign military trucks survived only by paying off the enemy they were supposed to be eradicating. But from what she could tell by tracking Renton's passport entries and exits and poring over his credit card statements, he had never been to Afghanistan. Same with an exposé he'd written about Charles Taylor's secret blood diamond empire, claiming to have camped out in Monrovia for months, but Liberia was another country that he'd never set foot in.

Chip watched international financial markets, some of which reopened the next day. They followed Vicker's advice and took their profits. Predictably, after plummeting, prices had rallied once the market discounted the possibility of further events—and they had made as much again by anticipating that bounce. Eighty billion dollars on the down leg. Fifty billion dollars on the upswing. Pete had been monitoring every news source and maintained open channels, swapping stories, with his stable of journalists and elected officials and their staffs, culling what he could, making certain that he knew everything that anyone was saying, or hearing. He ran point with Tommy, who, as before, urged them to keep digging and to lie low. Strangely, as detailed as the dossier purported to be, neither Renton nor anyone else had flagged Don as Vicker's director of security. Odd on one level, but not on another. Volk had a big investment in IS. Why would he take the risk of tarnishing the brand?

"Why was Renton willing to run with something completely bogus?" Greta asked Pete.

"Money? Fame?" said Pete. "It's starting to fall apart bit by bit, though the press won't really start reporting that until the news cycle runs its course and their traffic starts to dip. It'll be another few days, then they'll want a new narrative."

Of course, they had the benefit of knowing that the accusations against Don were false and that the analysts at Langley and in the FBI would not be fooled. The G-men also had the benefit of being able to rummage through the law firms' files and accounts and would have been the first to know that their flat denials were true, and their threats to sue *Roundelay* were real. The general public might not understand the distinction, but the outfits named in the dossier were high-toned and had much too much to lose by setting up strings of opaque offshore companies designed to disguise ownership and camouflage flows of money—at least without making efforts to conceal it. Pretending that blue chip lawyers were the architects of Don's sordid scheme meant that whoever prepared the file wanted it to crumble.

"It makes no sense," Pete said. "Jason is corrupt, but he's not sloppy. And he has to know this will end his career."

"Unless someone paid him fuck-you money to run with it, and he doesn't care."

"That, or whoever fed him the dossier has something on him," Pete said. "It couldn't have been Vicker. It's too professional a job."

"But maybe Vicker made an introduction?"

"Exactly what I was thinking," Pete said, remembering the night at the Met ball when Vicker collected a favor from Renton for dropping his lawsuit.

"The obvious conclusion is Volk."

Pete's phone rang.

"Just a second, I have to get this."

Pete listened intently. He held an index figure to his lips, asking for quiet, and began taking notes. Greta turned to look out the window, at a tower being built across the river, not trusting herself to look directly at Chip. A minute later, Pete rang off and slowly laid his phone on the desk.

"That was my friend at *Roundelay*. The place has been crawling with cops and spooks for the last twenty-four hours. Apparently, about twenty minutes after the tunnel blast, Jason Renton showed up at the office saying someone, a few weeks earlier, had dropped off a laptop with his doorman. It was impossible to determine where it had come from, but the laptop appeared to belong to Don Carter. Renton had given his editors a stark choice. Publish the dossier immediately—or he would take it elsewhere and they would be scooped on a huge story. The editors decided that, even though they couldn't definitively prove the laptop's authenticity, public interest would be served by publishing the story. What if this terrorist was planning another attack?

"My friend there said Renton bolted as soon as it was uploaded. Threw the computer and his phone into a backpack and ran. No one can find him."

There seemed little doubt that Russia's GRU or FSB had commissioned the phony story and coordinated its release through Volk, who, most likely, had compromised Renton. The blizzard of disinformation that had erupted, beginning almost the instant that the PATH tunnel was blown, resembled in every way the character, quality, and volume of noise that flooded the internet and social media platforms after the botched assassination of Sergei Skripal and his daughter, Yulia, in Salisbury, England. Classic Kremlin. A playbook that had lately been part of the Butler's portfolio, implemented through hundreds of managed data streams, fake Twitter accounts, Facebook groups, Reddit threads, phony news sites, message board comments, and compromised cable news pundits. The Russian fog machine absorbed bandwidth, captured the popular imagination, and sowed massive confusion. They could only begin to estimate the extent of the resources that had been dedicated to that effort. Hundreds of operatives and accomplices, some conscious, most unwitting. They moved to the SCIF and rang Tommy.

"We know that the reporter, Jason Renton, is bent," Pete said. "Someone fed him the dossier, and he maneuvered *Roundelay* into running it. He took off the second it was uploaded."

"Volk's friend: the Butler," said Greta.

"Tell me something I don't know," Tommy said. "His phone and his MiFi went dead at the same time, two blocks from the office."

"How long before someone tells *Roundelay* to pull it down and issue a denial?" Pete asked.

"Don't hold your breath," said Tommy. No one in government had a strong interest in seeing Don cleared right away—if at all. The FBI and the DOJ liked simple, straightforward cases, even if they were built on sand; convicting innocent people was all in a day's work. Maybe Don was guilty, maybe not. Maybe he had been framed, maybe not. No one cared. They needed a perp and, until someone came up with a better one, Don was it. The CIA was a more delicate issue. Its ultimate plans for the takeover of Industrial Strategies were sub rosa and not, exactly, an agency mission, but Greta's infiltration of IS was on the books—as Tommy kept reminding them. Even if Don was not officially Agency, he was close enough to be an embarrassment. And he had been introduced to Vicker by Ben Corn. No way any agency—including the FBI—wanted to risk pissing off Ben.

"So Don remains in the wilderness," Greta said.

"For now, while we play this out. Besides, Don loves survivalist shit. He'll be fine."

Just as Tommy disconnected, Greta's watch vibrated. It was time for her to signal Don, not with news, but with a code signifying that there was nothing new. Chip watched as she stood and left the SCIF at a brisk pace. Every two hours, like clockwork, Greta disappeared, reappearing ten minutes later. Clearly she was in touch with Don. He wasn't sure how, but given their training, they had to have worked out some kind of blind communication system. As he expected, Greta reappeared ten minutes later.

Chip tried to hide a yawn. "Anything you need me to do?"

Greta stretched. "No. I'm hitting a wall. I'm going to head home for a few hours."

"Let me give you a lift," said Chip.

They rode the elevator down in silence, each absorbed in their own thoughts. Greta knew that being as tired as she was put her in a physical danger zone. For the most part, because of her training and natural resilience, she could push herself, keep going for days without more than a nap here and there. On a rock ledge, a hard floor, a park bench. Sitting, prone, even standing. But the previous forty-eight hours of mental and emotional load had drained her reserves. The chaos had arrived. She didn't see how it would ever end.

The city was still in partial lockdown; you could only get out. Fifty-Seventh Street was pandemic quiet under the city-wide canopy of helicopters and scrambling jets. Greta drew in all the air her lungs could hold. As she exhaled, she felt she might drift off to sleep standing up. She looked up, through the branches of a stand of blossoming gingko trees. Spring had arrived, a season had changed, but she hadn't noticed.

Would she ever notice things like seasons changing again?

Chip had organized a Suburban, windows tinted dead black. A bit much for a trip to the Upper East Side, she thought, pausing to take one last breath of the fragrant spring air. Chip jumped in front of her and opened the door with his mechanically perfect manners.

And then, leaping out of the back seat and wrapping her arms around her, inviting her to sink into her long lean frame, was Mara.

"Fyodor thought it would be a good idea if I fetched you."

Greta pushed her away, hard enough that Mara would have fallen to the sidewalk if Chip hadn't been there to catch her.

"You need to come with us," Mara said. "Jason Renton's next story is about you, and unlike his last story, a lot of it will be true."

"No thanks," Greta said. "I'll walk."

"At least come talk to us. While you still can."

"What about him?" She pointed at Chip. "The whole time?"

"It's the only way, Greta," Chip said. "Just get in."

Russian diplomatic plates meant that they sailed through checkpoints with no more than a cursory look inside. Three guys and two girls, one sound asleep. In any event, roadblocks ended after they crossed the Henry Hudson Bridge. From the bridge, they took the Saw Mill River Parkway to the Tappan Zee Bridge and headed west along Route 17, finally passing through elaborate iron gates embedded in massive stone pillars: Tuxedo Park, an insular enclave of three hundred mansions, stopped in time. Former home to the likes of J. P. Morgan, the Duchess of Manchester, Emily Post, and Chip's grandfather, the fading years of the twentieth century had led to a generational—and cultural—rotation.

Before the Berlin Wall fell, Russians had been watched closely and most were forbidden to travel more than twenty miles outside of Washington, D.C., or New York without permission from the State Department. But since then, they had descended, with a vengeance, on the sanctuaries of the wealthy and well-connected. The more isolated, protected, parochial, and exclusive the better. At Tuxedo Park, Fishers Island, Dark Harbor, Conyers Farm, and a dozen others, the Russians snapped up hundreds of properties, providing their diplomats, business elites, and visiting dignitaries with opportunities to mingle, on equal terms, with people of influence. This archipelago of well-secured and remote mansions served a darker purpose as well, creating a sort of underground railroad of safe houses, hidden in plain sight, convenient harbors for people and things that needed to move undetected.

Volk and Ivanov were waiting, in a forty-room cottage that Volk was beginning to think of as his own. It had been a tense couple of days. The Butler had sent word that the boss was pleased. Though he would not be happy if he discovered that Volk had exceeded his remit by wiring two other tunnels with charges, deciding to stick to the plan only at the last possible moment. For once, Volk had listened to Ivanov, who had pointed out that, if there was blowback, there was no question who would take the fall. The entire point of the operation, from the perspective of the Kremlin, had been to send another clear, but deniable, warning to the obtuse, short-sighted Americans and, of course, to permit Volk a measure of recompense for his losses in Syria. The option value of a strike on a single tunnel was obvious. It could easily be attributed to ailing infrastructure. They knew Rachel Bridges would accept it, just another mind-boggling tragedy, an opportunity for the grief counselor in chief to soothe the nation with empty platitudes. Mara led Greta into a small parlor, nearly empty but for an elegant table on a very old Kirman carpet, set for five. Volk and Ivanov rose as she entered.

"Greta, so delightful to see you again."

Volk held out his hands, gently holding her arms as he kissed her on both cheeks.

"You could have texted."

Volk merely held her hands. "Well . . . this seemed simpler. There's so much noise at the moment."

He gestured toward Chip but held eye contact with Greta.

"Of course, you know Mr. Beekman here, though probably not as well as you thought."

Greta ignored the comment. Volk looked almost gaunt, leaner than the last time she'd seen him. In Riga, he had projected a placid coolness, an almost regal distance. Now it seemed like a different current ran through him. Not anxious. But agitated, all his nerve endings exposed. Though he was dressed in the requisite billionaire loungewear—a white polo shirt, black linen blazer, and boat shoes without socks—he looked like he was playing dress-up. Clothes made for standing still didn't suit him. She felt numb, off-kilter, and confused, but, still, she managed to give him her warmest smile and shook hands cordially with Ivanov. Buying time. For Chip, using all her mental reserves, she offered nothing more than a blank look.

"Greta, look, I'm really, *really* sorry about all this," Chip said. "I wanted to talk to you first, but there was just never the right moment."

She was amazed that he would actually say something so moronic. *Really, really sorry?*

"Fyodor, you have my attention, but I really need to sit down and have a cup of tea."

Volk gestured for her to take a chair. Mara poured sencha tea for them all, and lunch materialized, almost out of nowhere. All so civilized, she thought, but wasn't that the nature of civilization? A thin veneer of refinement and restraint that men who were mad for power—and whatever wealth or control power bought—adhered to themselves? And now this brutally, frighteningly polite conversation. *How will you take your tea, dear? Another helping of chicken salad? What's your favorite color for body bags?*

"Greta, I would like to thank you for the superb job you're doing at Industrial Strategies. Personally and on behalf of the Parsifal Group. The returns have been spectacular. Of course, if I may say so, we have not been unhelpful." Volk, smug, pleased with his understatement.

"Oh, did I forget to thank you? Is that why you just killed two thousand people?"

Volk bristled, slightly. Perhaps she didn't know enough Russian history. Or, at least, not enough of his personal history.

"You couldn't be more wrong, Greta. Far from pointless; in fact, the experience has been liberating, freeing . . . fair—an act of recompense."

Revenge. Of course. How deeply prideful, quintessentially Russian. Violence and vengeance under the guise of Old Testament righteousness but, really, she thought, there was nothing righteous about it. It was grandiosity. Volk had put his son at risk on the battlefield, but, somehow, thinks *he's* the victim.

Ivanov, in a preppy-pink polo under a lime-green cashmere V-neck, sleeves pushed up his forearms, leaned in, putting down his knife and fork.

She read him as the closer. A chameleon. The seducer.

"Done is done," Ivanov said. "Now we are even. And moving on."

Chip began to say something, but Ivanov silenced him with the barest flick of his fingers, dismissive.

"But why risk what you have built with Vicker and, now, with us?" Greta asked.

Ivanov feigned confusion. "What risk? *Our* money won't disappear; we just have to decide who runs it. And if we want our partnership to survive, it will."

"And do you?"

Ivanov looked to Volk, leaving it for him to respond.

"I see you yawning, let's discuss this over dinner. We're just getting started."

"By the way, we dress for dinner here," Ivanov said. "Mara can help. See you at seven thirty."

Mara escorted Greta to a bedroom. A rack of clothes hung in the closet. "I think I made Yuki's month," said Mara. "I wanted you to be comfortable."

Greta sat on the bed, head in her hands, too tired to think or to sort out her emotions.

"Come lie down," said Mara.

"What happened to getting away from Fyodor?"

"It was too dangerous."

"You had an open runway."

"Fyodor would have blamed you. I couldn't do that to you."

"But blackmail's okay."

"It was the only way. Now, come here." Greta leaned back on the bed. Mara undressed her gently, with great care. She took Greta in her arms, and climbed under the covers next to her, holding her tightly. Greta was too exhausted to push her away. Just before Greta fell asleep, Mara whispered in her ear, barely audible, even being so close.

"There's a Latvian proverb my grandfather used to say. '*The woods have ears and the fields have eyes.*' I never really understood it. Until I met Fyodor. Now I do. If they can't see you, they can hear you. If they can't hear you, they can see you." She hugged Greta tightly. "You can survive for a long time that way. But once they touch you, it's all over."

She buried tear-stained cheeks in Greta's shoulder.

"I'm scared. You have to take care of Fyodor. Neither of us is safe. *Please kill him.*"

In the formal dining room, silver and crystal table settings sparkled under three enormous Murano chandeliers. A Regency table that could seat twenty comfortably had been set for just five at one end. Volk, Ivanov, and Chip wore white tie and tails, and, as Greta and Mara entered, Volk began pouring Bollinger La Grande Année champagne into Baccarat flutes. The house deserved that kind of formality, Greta thought, but on so many other levels, the pretension was completely absurd. Dressing for dinner? White tie? Who does Volk think he is? But she'd heard stories about how the crooks who had grown rich and fat under Putin's kleptocratic rule styled themselves as tsarist aristocrats, throwing elaborate parties, dressing in imperialist regalia. Previously invisible, white-gloved staff, their eyes downcast, circulated, offering foie gras on toast and delicate salmon canapés. From a different time, fin de siècle, thought Greta, as Volk offered a toast: to their guest, to fallen comrades, to the future. He made eye contact, in the Russian manner, as he clinked glasses with each of them, but, just perhaps, he held Mara's gaze a second longer.

Over warm blinis slathered with Iranian Almas caviar from the southern Caspian, courtesy of the Russian diplomatic pouch, Volk barely mentioned events unfolding fifty miles southeast of them, in lower Manhattan. Tallies of body bags, heart-wrenching stories of lives lost, loved ones left behind, endless speculation about the whereabouts of Don Carter, held no interest for him. But he was intensely curious about how the CIA viewed whistleblowers and hackers like Julian Assange, Edward Snowden, Chelsea Manning, and Daniel Ellsberg. Volk became even more animated on the topic of outright traitors, double agents like Robert Hanssen and Aldrich Ames.

"Greta, please help me to understand," said Volk. "Why is it that your CIA and FBI are so vulnerable? At all times, we have moles in your service. For sure, now, we have moles. And what do you have? Zip?"

Tiresome, thought Greta. "You must have a theory. Why are you so much better at penetrating our networks than we are at yours?"

"Consistency. Focus. It would be one thing if we were better only during times of diametric choices, like the depths of the Cold War, when we were selling the idea of a more righteous form of government. Even if the

Soviet system was rotten at its core, we attracted ideologues—idealists—who hoped to make a better world."

"But our successes did not end with the Cold War," said Ivanov. "If anything, in the internet age, we are even more successful."

"Okay. Let's just stipulate that Russians are geniuses at espionage," said Greta, annoyed. "None of this explains why you blew a tunnel and murdered two thousand people."

Volk shrugged again.

"Making a statement. One tunnel, four tunnels. Really, Greta, who cares? As long as it's in the service of the state—or at least our own exalted view of it—anything can be justified." He cracked a gaudy smile. "Otherwise, how could anyone of us live with ourselves."

Greta felt an icy quiver of recognition. Everything that they had ever contemplated doing was in the name of a greater good—their notion of the greater good, that is.

"How does that cut with the likes of Polyakov, Hanssen, and Ames?" asked Greta. "Traitors to their own state, loyal to another? Justified?"

Volk leaned back and laughed, almost joyous. Mara's right, she thought. Volk had come unhinged. Greta looked around the room, the table. Was there time? What could she use? A fork, a knife? A very high degree of difficulty. And not enough time. Volk's men would be all over her before she could do serious damage. And she'd never make it out alive.

"So much fun, like being back in KGB school. I'm reminded of Goethe, didn't he say 'you must either conquer and rule, or serve and lose, suffer or triumph, be the anvil or the hammer.' I prefer to be the hammer. And you do too."

Animated by the wine, everyone seemed, nearly, to be joined in fun, even Chip, who had earlier seemed morose. Mara, reticent, said little, but every time Greta opened her mouth, she seemed to listen with her whole body.

For their second course, Volk had chosen a Meursault from Domaine d'Auvenay to accompany white asparagus and Dover sole, filleted at table, served with a beurre blanc sauce.

"You'd like Snowden," Volk said, looking at Greta. "He's a very intelligent young man, well spoken, and a patriot. He loves America." Volk compressed his lips, and smiled at Greta. "I don't believe that there is a Russian citizen who loves America more."

Despite ambivalence about his methods, Snowden was, perversely, one of Greta's heroes. Like them, Snowden knew the American system was deeply broken and, like them, he was willing to make huge sacrifices to push the country into a reckoning with its moral, legal, and political sins. Ben and Don both largely agreed with her. Tommy could not forgive the sheer quantity of Snowden's rule-breaking but admired the young man's conviction and commitment to a higher ideal. As for Chip, she never really cared what Chip thought.

"Have you spent much time with him?" Greta asked.

"Not as much as Vadim, but that's a generational thing. They pal around."

"Come to Moscow," Vadim said. "Hang out with us. We'll go to one of his broadcasts. Ed's a little bit of a know-it-all and he takes himself very seriously. But once you get to know him, he's a lot of fun."

A tempting offer, thought Greta, but, in reality, a cruel joke. No matter how powerful and connected Volk and Ivanov might think they were, they could never protect her inside Russia. Nor would they try. The FSB would not pass up an opportunity to detain an American NOC indefinitely, to squeeze her for operational details, to extract information on sources and methods, and, eventually, if her body survived, to trade her for a few of their own. She would bring a good price. In the statistical pantheon of villainy, Volk and Ivanov were in the top decile. Yet, as much as she knew about psychopathy and manipulation, she found herself taking pleasure in their attempts to engage and flatter her. She also had to admit that the charm offensive was working, even with Mara's warning caroming through her mind. These two defined realpolitik, and as much as she hated to admit it, she knew that she and her team could work with them. That they had to, in fact. If they wanted to escape blame for the tunnel plot and retain Industrial Strategies as their fiefdom, there was no alternative. At least for the moment. At some point, she hoped soon, prospects might be reversed.

Volk interrupted his peroration on Snowden's brilliance as a champion of free speech and personal privacy to allow the final course to be served: a dacquoise, a dessert invented by Fernand Point, the father of modern French cuisine. Three airy disks of almond and hazelnut meringue nestled between layers of chocolate ganache and buttercream.

"I hope you enjoy the sweet, Greta. Irina, our chef, will take a bow later. She apprenticed with Troisgros. But the wine, my favorite vintage . . . something worth thinking about."

He uncorked a 1917 Barbeito Sercial Madeira. As he poured, candlelight filtered through the amber liquid. He reverently handed them each a glass before raising his own, in something like a toast.

"I suspect you are upset about what happened to those trains. To those people." He shrugged. "You've seen worse, and I would like to put it in perspective."

He took a sip of wine, encouraging them to taste it.

"Does it taste slightly bitter to you? A hint of ash? Animal? Vegetal? Chemical?" Volk swirled it in his glass. "Extraordinary how wine tastes of terroir. Not just what is in the ground—the limestone, the silt—but what was in the air, the fog rolling in from the sea. The rain that fell. What particulates settled on the grapes while they were growing, during harvest."

He put the glass down, saying nothing, letting it sink in. The island of Madeira, except for a few ships scuttled in Funchal harbor and three hours of bombardment from German U-boats two miles offshore, had escaped the worst devastations of the First World War. But 1.7 million soldiers, and uncounted civilians, died not far away, in Ypres, Passchendaele, Lys, and Wijtschate, where then-corporal Adolf Hitler won an Iron Cross for bravery. Months of shelling vaporized flesh, bones, boots, gunpowder, hair, urine, and the sweat of men dying in fear, terror, and privation high into the atmosphere. Air currents, wind, and rain spread that fine dust for thousands of miles, covering every inch of Europe, the Mediterranean, North Africa, and the Purple Islands. On Madeira, they breathed it, ate it, bathed in it. But their precious grapes, otherwise undisturbed, grew fat and rich, absorbing the detritus of war. The Madeirans, living in a world apart, reaped a bounteous harvest in the fall of 1917, and made their sumptuous wine, a wine characteristically capable of living for decades. Perhaps centuries.

"It was a very bad year for Europe, but an excellent year for Madeiras. It's why I like old-world wines, they taste of life and death. American wine is much too simple. Like your adoptive compatriots."

Greta suddenly grew weary and wondered how much longer she would have to endure his pseudo-intellectual philosophizing.

"Ypres was utterly pointless." Greta agreed quietly. "Two sides swapping a hundred yards of mud back and forth. Month after month. Achieving exactly nothing, other than spending hundreds of thousands of lives."

"Like our war. Pointless," Ivanov said.

"Are we at war?" Greta asked.

"Aren't we?" he replied.

"Oh, Greta," Volk interrupted, sounding slightly exasperated and nodding at Chip, his mole. "We've been fighting an endless war. A war that I know frustrates you as much as it frustrates me. Spending men and money to move our flags a few feet in one direction or another, to no purpose, other than feeding the egos of politicians. And giving the Chinese space to maneuver."

She had no idea whether Volk believed what he was saying or was pandering to her, knowing, from Chip, how she, Don, and the others saw the world. "Shall we make peace, then?" she asked.

Volk's eyes lit up.

"I thought you would never ask. Yes."

"And what does that look like to you?"

His eyes sparkled.

"For one thing, and I know you already know this, it is the only way for you to continue to have access to your 'trust fund.' We'll keep shoveling money your way, doing our best to ensure that Ben Corn is elected. Don Carter might want to talk to us as well. We can clear his name. We created this mess, and we can clean it up. I assume you know how to find him."

Volk, she figured, had a narrow range of options. Find Don and make a deal. Find Don and kill them both. Or, worse by far, bundle them up to the Maine coast and onto a Russian submarine en route to a dimly lit cell somewhere deep in the forests of Arkhangelsk. She would not make a pretense of enduring ultimately pointless resistance, possibly torture. She had seen too much and interrogated too many. Only fictional spies held their secrets. In real life, everyone broke. Whatever Fyodor extracted from them in return for their lives, it was difficult to imagine it would leave them in a worse situation than they were in now. Besides, by now, Don would know they were coming—that someone was coming. She had not signaled him for nearly eighteen hours. He would be concerned. He would have a plan. She just hoped it wasn't a stupid one.

"Let me sleep on it?" she asked respectfully. But she already knew her answer. She had no choice.

"Of course, let us know in the morning," Volk said.

Volk stood, clearly dismissing them, and watched as she and Mara left, making their way through the house to the bedroom wing.

"That's it?" Greta asked. "All that show, that elaborate seduction—and he just sends us off?"

Mara stopped and turned to face Greta, before circling her arms around her waist and kissing her. "That feeling . . . it catches you by surprise, doesn't it? You decide that he's completely mad, hate the way he backs you into a corner with no obvious way out—and all either of us can think about is why he doesn't want to fuck us?"

Greta nibbled at Mara's ear lobe. "The night's young. And I've got you." She took Mara's hand, leading her to the bedroom. Volk's invisible gremlins had turned down the sheets and decorated them with red rose petals. A bottle of champagne, on ice, sat on the sideboard: with three glasses. And, at the end of the bed, lengths of elaborate, deep red ropes.

"Looks like someone has been thinking of us, after all," said Mara, pouring three glasses.

As if on cue, Volk walked in, held out a hand, and accepted a glass.

"I've been looking forward to getting the band back together."

Without saying anything more, Volk slowly undressed each of them, tossing their clothes behind him. He caressed them, gently, kissing their breasts, their bellies. Still fully clothed, he knelt in front of them, where each stood, licking them, tenderly. Mara moaned. In that moment, they were his, willing to do whatever he asked. He gestured to the bed.

"Tie Mara down. Nothing gives her more pleasure. Tightly, with her legs spread—the way she likes it."

Greta took her time, watching Mara, who appeared to be in some ecstatic state, and watching Volk. Carefully, but thoroughly, she bound Mara's hands together and then lifted them over her head, tying them to a bedpost. Without being asked, Mara opened her legs so that Greta could lash them securely to the legs of the bed. She stood back, admiring her handiwork. Volk had watched patiently. Sipping champagne, still fully dressed in his formal attire.

"It's all about trust, isn't it?" He asked. "You always have to trust someone. In that leap, you know you're alive."

Greta responded by offering him her wrists in a gesture of complete submission. He kissed them, ever so softly, before binding them. He led her to the bed, next to Mara, and tied her hands and legs to the frame, their arms and legs touching, before blindfolding them both.

He caressed each of them, slowly. Kissed them, brought each of them nearly to orgasm before backing off, bringing them back, again and again to the brink, to places beyond pleasure, nearly a torture. Until he stopped, and they heard him undressing. He entered Mara first, but just to excite her, then Greta. One after another, nothing rushed. He savored each of them, both of them, his sweat mixing theirs, theirs with each other's, writhing beneath him.

Finally, he entered Greta, moving more purposefully, ready to allow her to reach a climax. Sensing her excitement, he removed her blindfold, she could see Mara, eyes still covered, his hand on her neck, squeezing her throat.

Moving rhythmically on top of her, Volk brought his lips to Greta's ear, whispering so softly that Mara could hear nothing. His words for Greta alone: "Your deepest secret is that you know this truth: you were put on earth to find me. Your life led you to me—and mine to you. That day in the desert, we conjured each other out of the sand."

Her heart was pounding too hard for her to speak, but she found herself nodding involuntarily as she tried to regain control of her breath. Even as he moved inside her, Volk studied her, his hand still on Mara's neck, his grip tightening; Mara struggled to breathe, gasping, wrenching her torso, trying to speak, pulling the ropes harder with her arms, her legs. Consumed by her own frenzy, a half-formed thought flashed through Greta's mind: that Mara and Volk played a very rough game—at every turn, in business, in life, in bed. At last, Volk let her come. And, in that moment, she saw Volk's hand clamp down even harder on Mara's throat. A final wheeze escaped Mara's lips. She had nearly stopped moving, but Volk didn't let go until Mara was completely still. Greta began to shake, to shout, to try to buck him off. But the ropes held firm, becoming even tighter as she struggled.

"Tell me it's your game!" Greta screamed. "Mara!"

Volk rolled off of her, and walked around the bed. Looking down at Mara, now completely quiet, eyes rolled up into her head, eyelids open, purple bruises forming in the shape of his hand and fingers around her neck. Ever so gently, Volk slid his hand down her face, closing her eyelids. He kissed her slightly open lips, gently. Lingering.

Tears streamed down Greta's face, but she had no words.

"I could never have handled both of you," Volk said, turning away. "Now she has nothing to worry about."

49

Fahnestock State Park, New York

Greta woke at sunrise, her head aching as if she'd been drugged. Shafts of light spilled through velvet curtains. For an instant, she wondered if she had dreamed it all. Reaching her climax as Volk murdered Mara—watching Mara die. She clamped her eyes shut, hoping to return, even for a second to a place where last night had never happened, and she'd hear Mara's voice, see her padding across the room and sliding under the sheets next to her. But, except for Mara's scent on the pillow and a strand of her hair under it, it was as if nothing had happened, as if Mara had never happened, as if she had simply vanished off to the distant tropical beach of her dreams. At least, Greta thought darkly, she won't always be looking over her shoulder, dreading Volk's vengeance.

She sat up and pushed those thoughts out of her mind. There would be time for grief when this was over, as if it would ever be. The room had been restored to its natural state: tidied, elegant, impersonal—lifeless. Right now she needed clothes. She looked in the closet, nothing to suggest Mara had ever been there. But the bureau drawers were full of clothing— all in her size—ready to dress her for anything. Jeans, shirts, jackets, hiking boots, flats, sneakers—tags still attached. Someone, she guessed Mara, had planned ahead. As she tossed a pile of clothing onto the bed to sort through it, a small sealed envelope fell out. Inside, she found a note in Mara's hand:

> *My Love,*
> > *One last Latvian proverb:*
> > *It is better to die than to live dishonestly.*
> > > *Yours for eternity,*
> > > *M.*

Sunlight streamed into the ornate orangerie, where breakfast had already begun. Half-eaten croissants, bowls of berries, plates of bacon, and pots of coffee and tea littered the table. One empty seat. Mara: erased. On seeing Greta dressed for an outing, Volk gave a small clap of pleasure. Volk, Ivanov, and Chip had been poring over the morning papers. The headlines reported more of the same. No conclusions. Still counting the dead—1,252 confirmed, more than a thousand still not accounted for. Page after page profiling the fallen. The search to understand more about Don, and whoever else was involved in planning and executing the biggest attack since 9/11. The *New York Times* led with a long piece about the fragility of the New York City infrastructure, the first inkling in the press that Don Carter might not have been the villain, after all. Many subway tunnels had been built at the same time as the PATH, using the same technology, and were equally vulnerable. Reports that had been written after 9/11 had begun leaking out, and no one in city or state government, the Port Authority, or the MTA looked good. It was not a counternarrative, exactly, but someone—maybe Tommy or his NatSec minions—had clearly been working the press corps. *Be careful what you write. Be sure you have facts.*

"What a delight to see you dressed for travel. Are we going for a hike?" Volk asked.

A fresh pot of tea appeared at her elbow.

"Where is he?" Ivanov asked.

"Fahnestock Park, in Dutchess County. He likes to go there when he needs time to himself."

Chip, taking a sip of coffee, started coughing. Coffee dribbled down his chin. "Really? He went camping? And we all thought Ben was the boy scout." Chip turned to Volk. "Fyodor, I'd be careful. He'll be expecting company."

"You think so?" Greta feigned irritation, addressing only Volk and Ivanov.

Volk looked at her over his cup, savoring the bitterness of the espresso. Of course Don would be prepared. He grew excited. "A Russian would go down shooting, but I am afraid that we fight with more passion. Your men with more intelligence."

"I can't predict how a meeting will go," Greta said. "But I'm sure I can convince him to listen to what you have in mind." Not completely sure, she thought. It could all go very badly. But what's the worst that could happen? All of us die. None of us die. Something in between.

Greta piled into the back of a Suburban with four facing seats in the center for Volk, Ivanov, Chip, and herself. Next to a driver, another soldier rode shotgun and two more took a rear-facing jump seat, tending a small armory. That made seven.

━━━━━━━

As they drove briskly through Tuxedo Park's winding, wooded streets, no one spoke. Greta knew the feeling. Getting into the moment. Connecting with your gut, clearing the space in your mind and soul to forgive yourself for whatever might happen next. The Zen warrior bullshit, as Don liked to call it.

A few miles from their compound, at the on-ramp to Route 87, the local cops had set up a roadblock. The driver turned around and gave Fyodor an anxious, how-do-we-play-this-boss look. Fyodor, calmly staring out his backseat window, smiled wryly.

"Gently, Ivan. Very gently. We're not in Aleppo anymore."

As Ivan slowed to a stop and rolled down his window, the Russian soldiers in the van sprang, almost imperceptibly, to attention. After glancing at the license plate, the cop walked up to the window, peering inside. "Man, you guys have a full boat today," the cop said.

Ivan stared at him blankly, saying nothing, simply handing him his diplomatic passport.

"You're good to go, man. Orders are to let you guys through."

They drove off. The tension broke. Chip, sitting across from Ivanov, looked around, trying to make eye contact with anyone who would engage.

"Really, the local cops?"

Volk didn't take his eyes off whatever he was staring at.

"Let's just say we have a mutually beneficial relationship with the local constabulary."

He paused. "You and your friends should be so lucky."

For the rest of the forty-minute drive, Volk did not say another word. There was no traffic on the Taconic, save for state police cruisers roaring down the empty parkway at 100 miles per hour, light bars flashing, their sirens screaming pointlessly. Country cousins trying to act like they had something to do with the catastrophe a few counties to the south.

While the bad guys sailed right by them going in the other direction.

Greta wondered whether she should interrupt Volk's reverie. Going against Don Carter was a dangerous business. If a small platoon came upon him the wrong way, Don might feel the need to take them all out. She thought it would be better for them all if Volk left his men in the truck and they went in alone.

But she kept her own counsel. Volk was a soldier. He had been there, in the Syrian wasteland, when Don lit up those trucks full of Assad's special forces. Volk had watched Don coolly pick off *vory* gunmen at The Striped Pony. He knew how Don Carter dealt with threats. If Volk felt that a few goons with automatic weapons gave him an advantage, so be it. Greta decided that it was better to let him have whatever false sense of security she could encourage.

————

At the parking lot, Volk's crew assembled their kit: SR-3 Vikhrs, the compact assault rifles favored by the Spetsnaz, fitted with suppressors. On their hips: 9mm GSh-18 pistols with eighteen-round magazines, likely loaded with bullets that could pierce body armor. Once they were ready, Volk shot Greta a cross look, as if she were the one holding them up.

"We'll follow you." He looked at his men and gestured for them to train their rifles on Greta. "Just in case." He smiled, almost apologetically. "My mother raised me to never to point a gun at a woman. But she never met a woman like you."

Greta knew that there was no way they could sneak up on Don. She had tried, and failed, too many times. One of their games. The three-mile trek from the lot was lined with hidden tripwires, cameras, and snares. He would not be found unless he wanted to be. It would not matter if they sent a master tracker, a pack of hounds, or an army.

Even though there were well-marked trails leading up the ridge to Don's lair, she avoided them. She led them on a circuitous route, scaling boulders and hacking through brush. Anything to shrink the attack surface, to give Don whatever edge she could.

After ninety minutes, they reached a small clearing. There were unmistakable signs of recent habitation, but Don was nowhere to be seen. A good sign. He wanted Volk to find him.

She carefully shifted her body out of Volk's sightline, to give Don or whoever was hiding in the brush a clear shot. Just in case. Volk looked around in the cautious way of a tracker considering the direction of his prey. As he pondered his next move, a series of faint pops pierced the air and his four-man posse collapsed like puppets whose strings had been cut. Carbon fiber arrows stuck out of their necks at impossible angles, targeted, precisely, at their carotid arteries, spurting blood. Four more pops, severing the femoral arteries in their thighs. More arrows flew, a fusillade that made Volk's troops look like pincushions, puncturing their body armor. But not killing them quickly.

Don's archers could have, mercifully, cut them dead before they hit the ground. Direct hits would have shredded their hearts. The spring-loaded razor blades built into each of the Razorcut SS mechanical broadheads had been designed to take down serious weight—an elk, a wild boar, a six-point buck. And even more lethal against smaller targets. The four *vory* writhed on the ground, barely conscious as the few remaining tremors of their hearts exsanguinated them, rapidly pumping their blood out of their bodies into the dirt.

Volk stood slowly and looked around. Crossbows. Impressive. Where there had been seven, now there were three. Himself, Chip, and Ivanov. He had misjudged Don's level of preparation; he should have anticipated that, even while on the run, Don would be able to field a squad of assassins. Of course he'd take out my guards, he thought. Simplify the battlefield, and he wants me scared. But perhaps it was better this way, to allow him to feel that he's in control.

Volk glanced at his fallen men, watching them twitch, nearly done, and then looked up, holding his arms out, palms up. He roared with laughter.

"Magnificent!" he shouted. "We send drones halfway across the world to do our fighting for us. But when you get down to it, here you are running through the woods shooting at me with a medieval weapon."

Volk reached, slowly, for his pistol and carefully laid it on the ground, kicking it to Greta. He gestured for Chip and Ivanov to do the same.

While maintaining eye contact with Volk, Greta collected the handguns and then rolled the dead men over with her foot to search the bodies, removing additional weapons, ammunition, and knives. She emptied the magazines, cleared the chambers, and pocketed all the ammo, before tossing the guns into a pile, out of reach.

A minute later, taking his time, Don ambled out of the woods, gripping a pistol at his side. But Gunner and his marksmen remained where they were, hidden. Behind bushes, in the trees.

"I was wondering who'd show up," Don said. "These two, I was expecting."

Don gestured at Volk and Ivanov, who stared back impassively.

"But what the fuck is he doing here?" Don turned to face Chip. "I didn't think you liked getting your hands dirty."

"Believe me, I didn't want him here either." Greta waved her gun at Volk and Ivanov. "These guys invited him. They go way back."

Don raised his gun, taking aim at Chip, but Greta pushed his arm down firmly.

"Wait."

"Oh Jesus, Don. Grow up." Chip scowled. "We don't need anymore of your psycho shit."

Don stared at Chip as if he had never seen him before. "I guess you can't see the bodies floating up to the surface of the Hudson River from Park Avenue."

"I know how this looks," Chip said. "I'm pissed too. But I'm also a prag-matist."

"Save it." Don said, sharply, and turned to Greta. "So, sweetheart, you're the ringmaster. Speak."

Greta nodded and walked over to him, to speak privately, whispering in his ear. "Trust me. We need to hear him out."

"There are deeper currents here," Chip said.

Don began to raise his gun toward Chip. "Just shut the fuck up."

"You cannot live here forever," Greta whispered. "You cannot run. Just listen to Fyodor."

Don gestured for them to join him and sat cross-legged on the ground. Greta, watchful, remained standing.

"Start with the 'why.'" Don addressed Volk. "We had a good thing. You were part of it. Why this. Why here."

Volk leaned forward, his hands on his knees.

"We needed to get your attention. We have been trying to find common ground for years, since the Berlin Wall fell. But we couldn't. So I guess you could say that we decided to build the common ground ourselves, to our own standards and specifications."

"Who is the 'we', and who are 'our' people that you're trying to connect with?"

"You and your merry band. Our true allies. 'We?' We is VVP—and his emissary, yours truly, a man who is, at least for the moment, trusted. A man who can make things happen," Volk said, pointing to his chest with both index fingers. He leaned back, arms behind him and stretched out.

It began not as a lecture, exactly, but a sober, calm, detailed exegesis of relations between the United States and Russia. Volk wanted to describe, in sorry detail, how the potential for alliance was soured when American cold warriors had refused to draw Russia fully into the Western alliance and to trust Russia even after the Soviet system had crumbled.

"You rebuilt Japan and Germany after you defeated them. But us? Russia? We were treated with nothing but mistrust, as just a continuation of the USSR."

"I know the argument," said Greta. "That we compounded the insult by aggressively expanding NATO. Absorbing the Czechs, the Poles, and the Hungarians, further isolating Russia. Implicitly, threatening Russia."

Volk nodded.

"While we did not stand in the way while you pursued your interest. We backed both of your invasions of Iraq. But our goodwill predated that. The START treaties were a gift to America," Volk said. "It was not enough for you. Never enough."

"We allied with you against Saddam Hussein," said Ivanov. "Primakov told that Sunni scoundrel that you would invade and that you wouldn't back down. We tried our best to help you avoid a war."

Yevgeny Primakov, Boris Yeltsin's prime minister and, at the time, Putin's special envoy, had delivered a stark message to the Baathist dictator: resign, agree to a six-point peace plan, and Russia will guarantee your safety. Primakov, who had known Saddam for decades, shuttled between Moscow and Baghdad, but he had been unable to overcome Saddam's misunderstanding of Western resolve. Not his fault, thought Don. Primakov was the A-team, he tried and failed. That had been the first olive branch. Then, Russia had gone a step further and voted with the United States at the Security Council to legitimize the Iraq war.

Don sat, impassive, reflecting on the irony of having what might have passed as a civilized conversation with a mass murderer, while sitting cross-legged ten feet away from four corpses—and agreeing with pretty much everything he said. START I, signed in 1991 by Gorbachev and George H. W. Bush, had been the most complicated arms control treaty in world history. Russia and the United States agreed to eliminate over 80 percent of all strategic nuclear weapons then in existence. A stunning diplomatic achievement, and undeniably an act of good faith on the part of Russia. Lots of blame to go around among the graybeards who came after, not rewarding Russia by helping it to reindustrialize, trying to maintain it as a beggar, a poor cousin—a vassal state.

"How did you repay our goodwill? Inch by inch, you invaded our space, our security perimeter," Volk continued, speaking without rancor. "Why did NATO need to annex Bulgaria, Estonia, Latvia, Lithuania, Romania, Slovakia, Slovenia, Albania, Croatia, and Montenegro? They were—they are—weak no-account countries, if you can even call them countries. What was the point? Except to poke at us or, worse, find new markets for your sneakers and soft drinks and weapons systems."

Volk made the point that Putin had every reason to fear the expansion of NATO. Relatively defenseless, as it then was, all Russia sought was a definitive line that the West would not cross. An arc of neutral countries assembled from the territories of the former Soviet republics. But American policy makers—mostly unreconstructed cold warriors—had insisted on pushing NATO right up to the Russian border. To what purpose? Don always wondered. Were the motivations strategic? Or was it just business—to create new customers for the American defense industry? The point was arguable, Don thought, and Russia had the better side. Perhaps the Europeans couldn't be blamed for wanting to draw former Soviet satellites into their economic orbit, but sucking them into NATO was very different, because NATO was a military alliance.

"That's how you justify taking Crimea, occupying the Ukraine, and messing with the Middle East?" Don probed, genuinely curious.

"Why shouldn't we have a buffer zone? You didn't like us putting our rockets in Cuba, or abetting Chavez and Maduro in Venezuela. We don't want you militarizing our near abroad."

No doubt, Chip had prepped Volk for his tutorial. Volk had barely strayed from Ben Corn's own talking points—that squaring off as adversaries had corrupted the foreign policy agendas of both the United States and Russia, to the detriment of each.

"Assuming we agree with your view of how relations between Russia and America have become toxic, and, mostly, we do," Greta said, "I'm not clear exactly what you want to achieve, or what you're offering."

"Really?" Volk gave them a tight, almost pained, grin. "I do go on, don't I? Vadim always tells me, too much with the lecturing, but I get excited. Can't stop. You'll get used to it." Volk twisted his torso, loosening his back. "We want the United States to leave us alone in our backyard. Let the Europeans fend for themselves. Stop blocking the pipelines we want to build into the continent and into Turkey. Cut Europe loose. Leave Turkey to us. Then we go after our real enemies. Together."

"And those are?" Don asked.

"As if you don't know. The Chinese. Iran's mullahs." Volk curled forward, stretching. "Sorry, an old injury, sitting too long. Where was I? Oh yes, the Chinese."

He straightened up, placing his palms on his thighs. "I worry that Americans don't get it. Even you, some of the most intelligent people I've ever met. Take the coronavirus. Maybe some Chinese grandma ate a bad bat. Maybe she bought that bat at a wet market. Maybe that bat was stored in the wrong fridge in the Wuhan lab, and it just wasn't disposed of properly. Or maybe they let it out on purpose. We'll never know. But the Chinese People's Liberation Army has been collecting viruses for years. A novel biological weapon was coming from China sooner or later. So what if it happened earlier than planned or got out by accident?

"They make no secret of what they're up to. Selling the sweat of their people—nothing more than slaves to the Chinese Communist Party, really—to amass enormous profits. They've turned cheap Chinese labor into Western hard assets. Look at Italy. They've taken control of huge swathes of Italian infrastructure. I don't just mean sending in workers from Wenzhou to Prato to make leather handbags and label them 'Made in Italy.' They've got big stakes in Fiat, Telecom Italia, Generali, Eni. And the ports? Venice, Naples, Genoa, Trieste: all owned by the Chinese."

It was a good line, and even if the Russians and the Chinese were friendly for the moment, Kremlin strategists were convinced that a future conflict with China was inevitable. The Chinese old guard remembered Stalin's belligerence in Manchuria, Zhenbao Island, and Xinjiang like it was yesterday. But now China, not Russia, was the military and economic superpower, no longer the weak sister. Vladivostok was five times closer to Beijing than Moscow. Were the Chinese to seize Russia's sole major ocean port, it would render Russia virtually landlocked. The same DF-ZF hypersonic glide vehicles that gave Pentagon planners nightmares would make short work of the Russian Pacific Fleet, clearing the way for a Chinese ground invasion—infantry battalions swarming off 071 and 081 amphibious landing platforms and into Russia's exposed eastern flank.

"I see what's in it for you," Greta said. "NATO goes away, you develop a stranglehold on natural gas supplies to Western Europe, and you enlist us to protect you from the Arabs and the Chinese. But what do you bring to the table? Russia is corrupt and underdeveloped, with a GDP less than a quarter of ours. All we do is help the FSB stay in power and amass more money."

"Really, Greta. Really? You need me to explain this to you? The Chinese want to cripple you—they want to eliminate any possibility that America can threaten them in any way: militarily, culturally, or economically. Forever. They don't care about the rules—they mock your Washington Consensus. That means undermining Taiwan, stealing your most sensitive technology and intellectual property. It means launching cyberattacks on utilities, stock exchanges, and ports, and hooking your underclass—whose jobs they stole—on cheap fentanyl they ship into your country by the ton. It means keeping North Korea in business, violating the WTO, suborning the WHO, and never supporting you on UN sanctions. The list goes on. I know you see that. How could you not? You know how you stop them: with an ally, a real ally. One a president can sell to voters. White and Christian, has a seat on the UN Security Council, isn't shy about killing extremist Muslims, and lies above the world's largest proven oil reserves. Really, could it be any more obvious?"

Volk wasn't finished.

"Kissinger was a fool for opening the door to the Chinese. They are eating your children"—Volk paused for emphasis—"stealing their jobs, taking their places in your schools."

Volk clapped his hands, wanting to keep their attention. "Not to mention subtly fueling your country's economic and racial tensions. The Chinese are good at that—"

"I thought that was your specialty?" Greta said.

"Thank you for noticing. All your social disorder—occupy this, occupy that. Who's behind it? We send in our Cuban friends. Handy that they're black and brown, speak Spanish—natural camouflage. With a little coke, some weed, bags of hamburgers, they can build an encampment of hippies, petty criminals, Antifa, kids, addicts, mental cases, and homeless to occupy anything, pull down your monuments, burn down police stations. Easy. Did you notice what we did in Chile in 2019? We shut down the country, brought a prosperous, stable democracy to its knees with just a dozen subway bombs and a platoon of Cubans. We can start there. Or with your political system. It doesn't matter whether our disinformation campaigns affect the outcome of your elections. Americans think they might. We've won already. It looks like we're that powerful."

"Didn't really work for Saddam Hussein, did it?'

Volk seemed surprised.

"Pardon me, Mr. Carter, but I don't follow."

"Overplaying your hand. Saddam just wanted everyone to think he had chemical weapons—and was crazy enough to use them. But you know what: we don't care if you're just trying to scare us, we're still going to come after you if you come at us."

Ivanov, who'd been nodding approval all along, jumped in. "I'm not sure you understand the level of resources we have deployed against you. The U.S. is on borrowed time," he said. "We have been coming at you for a decade, cranking up domestic tensions, turning races, social classes, even neighbors, against each other. 'Heightening the contradictions,' Lenin called it. We can turn it down anytime. Maybe we stop funding the immigrant car-avans that funnel tens of thousands of empty stomachs to your border every year. Maybe we pull back the dozens of agents we have working in the upper levels of media, finance, Hollywood, and Silicon Valley. Oh—you'll like this: maybe we tell you how to find the Iranian sleepers before the mullahs make PATH tunnels look like a pillow fight. Or maybe we help you break the cycle of endless, pointless wars, mostly started or intensified by us—particularly in the Middle East."

Volk paused. "Maybe we even stop paying bounties for American scalps in Afghanistan and elsewhere." He paused again. "It's like what Mao said, about his guerrillas. 'The guerrilla must move against the people as a fish swims in the sea.' We are the fish. Everywhere you swim, we've stocked your sea with renegade fish. Dangerous fish."

"That's just the old-fashioned, low-tech stuff, working the streets," Ivanov said. "We're five generations ahead of you in cyber—and undetectable. Six generations in hypersonics—and unstoppable. You may as well sink your own navy and save the lives of your sailors, because between us and the Chinese, the U.S. fleet is just target practice."

Ivanov shifted, clearly uncomfortable, sitting cross-legged on the ground. Volk looked pleased at the way Ivanov was taking the floor.

"You guys may understand this, but your 'people'—your academics and politicians—don't. You know what none of them seem to realize: With the flick of a switch, we—or the Chinese or maybe even the Iranians—could launch a cyberattack that would fry a couple of nuclear power plants. With a little more effort, we could drop the Golden Gate Bridge into San Francisco Bay. Look at what Fyodor did two days ago, how easy it was."

He looked at Don and Greta, straight in the eyes.

"I know you both agree. Chip has been telling me for years how brilliant the two of you are. He's very proud of that."

Volk nodded and patted Chip on the knee. "A real find, Charles Francis Rittenhouse Beekman. We sent Vadim to Princeton to meet young men exactly like you. The angry scion of a grand fallen family. He locked onto you his very first week. It's rare to find such instincts in a young agent. Very well done, Vadim."

"I started by searching the campus directory for students with more than one middle name." Ivanov chuckled cynically. "That and studying the *Official Preppy Handbook*."

Volk turned back to the group.

"It's clear to us what you are up to. The White House, your own Quds Force. And I applaud you. The audacity. I thought your country had lost that spirit. But you have two big problems. First, you're not operational. Second, I've got your money. Once Ben Corn becomes president, both of those become bigger challenges. We would like to help."

Volk was not insane. Nor was Ivanov. But Greta could not help but think about what Nietzsche, in *Beyond Good and Evil* wrote: "In individuals, insanity is rare; but in groups, parties, nations and epochs, it is the rule."

"From your silence, I can only assume you see the logic." Volk's voice sounded warm, inviting. "At the risk of stating the obvious, we were made for each other."

Suddenly his demeanor changed. Don glared at him.

"Go ahead, shoot," Volk said calmly. "Vadim too. It'll feel good. Cathartic."

Don stared at the ground stonily, barely able to look at the three of them. Volk turned to him full-face.

"You're just like me," Volk said. "A man of tactics. Not emotion. A rare quality. That's why we are so lucky to have found each other."

Don't push it, thought Greta. If there was ever a man consumed by unexplored emotion, it was Don. Goading him was not a good idea.

"You're lucky, Chip, to have a friend like Vadim. Few of us do. He would do anything for you. It's a responsibility he takes very seriously."

Greta noticed Ivanov cast his eyes downward as Chip bit his lip.

"Who else would drop everything and fly from Moscow to Goa to counsel a friend having a moral crisis. It sounded like quite the bacchanal, by the way. We told the girls not to get attached, but they were lovesick for months afterward."

Volk looked at Don, then Ivanov.

"Vadim told me that Ben Corn sat by the pool one morning playing those videos, over and over, on that tiny screen, watching himself shoot unarmed men, casually, efficiently, like he was sweeping the sidewalk. Quite an image. Like George Washington chopping down the cherry tree."

Chip practically exploded. "You guys were losing your minds." Desperation choked his words. "Something had come undone in the two of you. If you were going down, I needed to protect myself. Vadim was the only person I could trust. I had no idea."

"Vadim, why don't you take over? I'm sure Mr. Beekman will enjoy hearing the rest of the story from you."

Volk nodded at Ivanov. "A few months ago, I heard that Senator Conway had hired Jasper Bewick, who we'd been keeping an eye on for years, ever since he won the Hackers Cup when he was fourteen. That caught my interest. I assumed it had to be about your friend Ben, given that Frank Conway saw Ben's opposition as a personal betrayal. According to Conway's FSB file, that's what he does when his feelings get hurt, digs up dirt on his friends. So, just for fun, we hung a couple of goodies out on the dark web. But we made them very difficult to find. I wanted to see if Jasper was as good as people say. And Fyodor wanted to see how Senator Corn would act when faced with a difficult choice."

"How'd they do?" Don's voice dripped with sarcasm.

"Senator Corn proved himself to be a very sensible politician. And Jasper, we wouldn't mind having him on our side. Snowden needs someone to push him a little."

Chip, who'd been silently stewing through Volk's seminar, turned to Don.

"That Rambo shit of yours was going to destroy us. Destroy Ben. I wasn't going to let that happen."

"So you called up your, I don't know, your wingman here?" Don pointed his gun at Ivanov. "Who was strangely willing to drop everything and show up in Goa with three insanely gorgeous nymphomaniac ballerinas when you needed a shoulder to cry on. And it never occurred to you that he wasn't who he said he was?"

Don let out a bitter laugh. "You don't know anything about Ben. None of you do. You see only what you want to see. What's on those videos? I hate to ruin your savior fantasies, but that was all Ben. I couldn't talk him out of it. I went along only to keep him from getting killed. What a joke—that you think you're protecting Ben Corn from me.

"Everyone thinks I'm the angry loner, but Ben might be the most broken one of us all. You know how he deals with trauma. By thinking he can save the world. I sometimes wonder if we're making it worse for him by fueling his delusions."

Don stopped abruptly. Why go on? he thought. No one was listening.

"Sorry for interrupting, Mr. Volk. I'm still not sure what the point of this is. And why I shouldn't just pop you all and be done with it."

Volk looked at Greta, trying to determine where she stood. Unclear.

"I'll be dead. You'll be in jail." Volk spoke through a tight jaw. "Pointless. My people, your people, they'll have died in vain. And let's not forget, four more years of your pleasant but ineffectual President Bridges. While, of course, we continue to step up active measures."

"Or, everybody wins," Ivanov said.

"What about you, Fyodor?" Greta asked. "What's in it for comrade-citizens Volk and Ivanov, other than a pat on the head and another medal?"

For the past two days, one thing in particular had bothered her. Kremlin strategists were very careful when it came to assessing risk. They ran infinite numbers of scenarios before embarking on even as modest a venture as poisoning traitors in a British park. So why, if they were just trying to get our attention, would they sanction an attack as bold and deadly as Volk's tunnel plot? With an attack of this size, Volk would have needed state support, or at least tacit approval. But was it possible that he had gone beyond his remit? Killing a thousand Americans, on American soil, surely fell outside the Kremlin's tolerance for risk. But not beyond Volk's.

"For now, we just need things to proceed as they've been," Volk said. He turned to Don. "I told her this last night, she's doing a splendid job managing our account. We might want to open accounts for some friends. The beneficiaries will have to remain anonymous, but you would recognize their names."

Indeed, thought Greta. Even Vladimir Putin himself needed an exit strategy, in case his billion-dollar armed compound on the Black Sea wasn't enough to protect him from the anger of a nation that he had swindled. Putin's fortune was said to approach a trillion dollars. Someone had to manage it and know how to hide it. It would make sense that Volk would try to cement his relationships by generating high returns for Putin and others in the Kremlin power structure.

"Same goes for the presidential campaign," Volk said. "No changes. I'm not a micromanager. Whatever you need, we're here to help."

"That's it?" Don asked facetiously.

"Not exactly," Volk said. "Someday we may need new . . . personas. Names, faces, life stories. Somewhere out of the way. A ranch in Arizona, maybe. Or a small vineyard in the Willamette Valley—I've heard it's marvelous country, as long as you don't have to drink the wine."

"A custom-made witness protection program. You know who needs one of those?" Don asked. "Criminals."

What Volk was saying made some sense, Don had to admit. But he'd studied his Russian history. For centuries, the abiding interest of Russian autocrats, be they tsars, party leaders, or "democratically" elected presidents, was to weaken the West and undermine Western values—rule of law, free markets, democracy—in order to prevent their spread into Russia's vast territories. In the twentieth century, they used Communism as their cudgel against the West, exporting a criminally defective Leninist ideology as a counter to American free enterprise. When that failed, Vladimir Putin and his cronies came up with a more insidiously effective export: corruption. After taking control of their own country with a state-sponsored, gangsterized smash-and-grab version of capitalism, they were spreading their tentacles of coercion and corruption outward. They had made serious inroads in Europe, flushing the plunder they'd looted from their own country through the continent's banks, stock exchanges, and real estate markets. Now they had the White House itself in their sights. Ben and Tommy would think they could handle the Russians. Don wasn't sure they could. He wasn't sure anyone could.

Don stood up, went over to Greta, who had been standing the entire time and led her a few yards away, just over a small rise, knowing that Gunner and his crew had sharp eyes on Volk, Ivanov, and Chip.

"What do you think?" he asked, softly.

"What choice do we have?"

"Is that why we did this? So we could sell out to the Russians? Is that what we're about?"

He kept looking past her, into the distance, not merely into the woods. Into their future. For the first time in his life, he was in a fight he didn't see a way out of.

"Since the moment we blew up those Syrian troop transports," Greta said, "Fyodor's been running this whole game. He found us. He needs us. We have leverage: we can give him the one thing in the world he'll never be able to buy for himself, no matter how much money he makes: a magic doorway out of the Kremlin."

Don looked at her blankly. She knew that look. She had seen it often enough in the field, the combat officer zeroing in, assessing, making decisions. Going down every path before saying anything.

"And, if he's as smart as we think he is," Greta said, "Fyodor hasn't told his bosses much about us. He'd never give up that trump card."

"I get the pitch, Greta," Don said. "But that's all that this is. A pitch. An appeal to our ambition. We walk out of here, arm in arm, singing folk songs, but really with knives at each other's throats. And the tunnel? Not to mention them paying terrorists to knock off our guys? We just move on? A game of Risk? All's fair? Sorry about those two thousand people we killed. Why can't we all be friends?"

Then he stopped and said, almost gently, "No, Greta. Not okay."

"Just keep them talking."

Don turned around and they walked back to where the others sat on the ground. "Let's say we agree," Don said. "What then?"

Volk extended his hands expansively, suggesting that the sky was the limit. "First off, we make you a hero. I'll give you all the 'terrorists' you need." He motioned toward the corpses on the ground. "Here are your first four, right here. I have four more sunning themselves on a Venezuelan beach right now. Jason Renton makes nine. And, of course, the ringleader himself—the evil, corrupt, and venal Elias Vicker, a fanatical fundamentalist fueled by the world's most dangerous ideology: free-market capitalism. The perfect villain for the age of what your president likes to call systemic inequality. No one will ever ask another question."

Don smiled. "I don't think ten's enough."

In a single smooth motion, he drew his Sig .45 caliber, took aim, and shot Chip between his eyes, at a downward angle. It happened so quickly that none of them—least of all Chip—had time to react. The load entered at the middle of his forehead and took off the back half of his skull as it exited. He fell backward, still cross-legged, like an extreme yoga pose, blood and brain seeping out into the soil.

"Thank you," Ivanov said softly. "He was starting to get on my nerves."

"You both got on mine," said Don as he shifted his aim to Ivanov. "I should've done this in Syria."

In one fluid motion, he shot Ivanov through the temple. As he fell, all that remained of his head was the surprised expression on his face.

Volk barely reacted to the shots, not even bothering to wipe away the blood that spattered his face, hair, and neck. Instead, he looked up, serenely, at the great canopy of foliage surrounding them. Dead bodies in dappled springtime sunlight, trillium, lilies of the valley, and violas poking up through the forest cover.

Don gave a low whistle and Gunner, seeming to appear out of nowhere, stepped into the clearing.

"Gunner, Greta and I need to have a private conversation with our friend Mr. Volk. Take your crew and clean up this mess." Don gestured toward the six bodies strewn before them, broken dolls.

"You're sure?" Gunner asked.

"We've got this." Don put a few more steps between himself, Volk. Continuing to hold his pistol, he nodded toward Greta, never taking his eyes off Volk.

With a hand signal from Gunner, five more men materialized, crossbows hanging casually from their utility belts, and quietly slung the dead men over their shoulders like sacks of rice. Making barely a sound, they set off into the woods, in a direction opposite from the one from which Greta had led Volk to them.

"Now then. Where were we?" Don looked at Greta. "Right. Greta doesn't think that we have much of a choice."

Volk, still sitting, cross-legged, watched them closely. Greta dropped her voice and stood close to Don. "Of course we do. One direction, we have a lot of optionality. The other way, we'll be fighting for our lives—forever—against long odds."

"Always the same with you, isn't it, Greta?" Don said with quiet fury. "Wall Street talk—optionality, playing the odds, game theory. Your clinical, unemotional, dispassionate analysis. Oh, I forgot that concept you love so much—'sunk costs.' We don't need to think about what's behind us, not the soldiers they've assassinated or justice for the hundreds they murdered, because they're already dead. 'Sunk' in the Hudson. Just a line on a balance sheet. Right?"

"Be a prick if you want to, but we've always made those kinds of decisions. When do we ever have two good choices?"

"Maybe I'd rather die or at least go down having exposed what really happened."

Greta's eyes narrowed. "You can't make that decision. This isn't just about you."

"Ben will become just as corrupt as the rest of them. It's already started happening. Have you noticed he's stopped talking about that aircraft carrier he swore to kill? And what about you? Remember how you used to cry on my shoulder about all the arms dealers and drug lords who never paid a price for all the death and suffering they caused? You're going to give those bastards a pass? You're the biggest fucking sellout of all."

Don began to raise his arm, about to take aim at Volk.

She had always been fast—and, in that moment, much faster than Don. Almost unconsciously, all brainstem and adrenaline, she struck him, right hand full force to his solar plexus, left elbow to the side of his head, right knee crushing his testicles, the most efficient way, they taught at the Farm, to disable an attacker, provided they weren't expecting it. Two seconds: to subdue, not maim. Don crumpled to the ground. She kicked his gun away, raising her own—with no solid purpose in mind. It would only occur to her later, reliving those seconds, endlessly, that she had no clear intention. Would she actually have shot Don?

In an almost acrobatic display, Volk dove for Don's gun, grabbed it, and rolled back up to his feet. Tap tap tap. He shot Don once in the abdomen, then in the face, and once more in the chest. In an instant, Don had become almost unrecognizable, his face blown apart, an open, gaping wound where his jaw and nose had been. Only the eyes remained: the light fading, but, to the end, focused on her. Glaring at her. That beautiful face. Gone, a muddle of blood and bone.

She fell to her knees and gathered him up. Cradling his head, holding what was left of his face against her own, then looking at him, feeling him try to breathe, until he couldn't, and his body stopped. She put her hands on his still chest, the lifeless body of her friend, her partner, her lover, her brother. I did this, she thought.

She felt Volk's hand on her shoulder.

"I had hoped it would be otherwise. There was no other way. He died a hero."

She looked up at him, tried to push him away. But he wouldn't let her go. Holding her arm, he brushed her cheek with the back of his other hand. Volk drew her to him, enfolding her body. Her chest heaving, her face painted with Don's still warm blood, she fell into him without thinking, needing to be held, letting herself be held.

50

Guantánamo Bay, Cuba

Peering through a one-way glass window in the door to Vicker's six-by-eight-foot cell at Echo Special, Liz almost felt sorry for the man huddled on the metal cot, rocking back and forth, nuzzling a filthy pillow, his only comfort. Elias Vicker, it occurred to her, might go down in the annals of abnormal psychology as one of the most closely observed psychopaths in history. First, the thousands of hours of Dr. Kerry's videotapes and, now, the continuation of that extraordinary documentary record through constant surveillance and frequent questioning by one of the CIA's most sophisticated interrogators.

Known to his guards and his inquisitors simply as Detainee 807, Vicker had spent the months following the tunnel attack in this heavily fortified corner of Guantánamo Bay Naval Base in complete isolation. Due to the nature of his alleged crimes, there had been little public outcry over the fact that Vicker, an American citizen, was being held, with no official charges against him, in a prison designed for enemy combatants. Americans, like most people everywhere, yearn for simple stories, not least when fear and grief demand closure. And closure requires a straightforward narrative, whether it is a matter of seeing the dead body of a spouse or being told that a smudge of cremated ash contained their child's DNA. Not since 9/11 had an attack of such ineffable horror occurred on American soil, and not since 9/11—when the roles of various Middle Eastern actors had been ignored in favor of blaming bin Laden alone—had such an expedient official explanation been adopted so quickly, and repeated so assiduously: that one evil mastermind, who had already amassed an unspeakably large fortune by systematically breaking the law, decade upon decade, had murdered more than two thousand Americans as part of a stock trade and had conceived the plan on his own, in contravention of the practical reality that an attack of such magnitude and complexity had required the assistance of dozens of witting, and unwitting, accomplices.

The secret, single-occupancy units at Echo Special were designed to eliminate outside stimuli. No light. No sound. No conversation, except for episodic interrogations, for which Vicker was hooded and led, in manacles and leg irons, to another, equally stark, windowless room. The only light in the interrogation cell emanated from a dim bulb overhead.

Since being taken into custody the morning after the Striped Pony massacre six months earlier, Vicker had spent virtually every second under Tommy's invisible thumb. He'd had no unapproved contacts with anyone outside his bubble, not even a lawyer. In addition to the salt shed and now Camp Delta, he'd been a guest of more black sites—in Washington, Miami, and another one in Virginia near CIA headquarters—than any other individual American citizen. Since he had never been charged with any crime, technically he had no right to counsel. The Constitution was written in large part to prevent such flagrant abuses of a citizen's rights, but few were sticking up for Vicker beyond a couple of ACLU fussbudgets and a bad-boy Silicon Valley libertarian famous for an ability to recite large tracts of *Atlas Shrugged* from memory.

Vicker was beginning to fray around the edges. Solitary is not easy. But the finest interrogators in the FBI and the CIA had been unable to break through what they viewed as his outlandish conspiracy theories. He still refused to tell the truth about the unspeakable crimes he had committed. He stonewalled every question, saying only that once they allowed him to speak to a lawyer, he would be able to prove that he was the victim of the greatest crime of the century.

Recently, Liz Leonard had been making monthly field trips to Camp Delta. She had a deep understanding of the psychological theories behind the manner in which Vicker was being detained, and broken. She had pioneered their design and objective: to achieve omnipotence through the imposition of psychological stressors. Prisoners were broken not merely through degradation and debilitation, but by the monopolization of perception. Some prisoners, of course, quickly became pliable witnesses, willingly revealing operational details of whatever plots against America they had fostered. Others cracked under the pressure—their minds reduced to mush, sometimes permanently. But Vicker had, characteristically, followed his own path. His rage and sense of entitlement seemed undiminished. Even at Echo, robbed of agency and any control over his environment, he labored under the delusion that he could yet steer his own destiny. If Liz could not loosen the grip of those delusions, Tommy would use her report to argue that he was mentally unfit to face whatever charges might eventually be filed against him.

Liz turned to a petite, twentysomething blonde in tight jean shorts and a low-cut shirt. If the CIA had learned anything over the course of eighteen years of endless war, it was that the most unlikely interrogators were often the most successful. None more so than Ginny Hall, a bubbly surfer girl from San Diego.

"Any changes from last month?"

Ginny shrugged.

"He's not swearing and kicking the walls anymore. He's in that straitjacket twenty-four/seven because he won't stop pulling at his knuckles."

In addition to his incessant knuckle cracking, Vicker had taken to scratching his cuticles compulsively, causing serious infections in several fingers and in one of his hands. Army doctors had amputated a pinkie, but no one wanted to see him lose a hand or an arm. Or die. At least not just yet.

"Is he still talking to himself all the time?"

"You've seen my notes. He's completely committed to that crazy story. He sits on his bed, looks in the mirror, and repeats it to whoever he thinks is listening: that he was set up by Putin's cronies and that Ben Corn stole billions in Syria to pay for his presidential campaign. With most detainees we'd have gotten past the elaborate conspiracies and closer to the truth by now."

"Have you been employing all the protocols?"

"Same as what you saw when you were here last month. Every time he starts confabulating, I rub my breasts up against him like you taught me. With the Muslim guys, that sends them into a frenzy of prayer. With Vicker, touching or threatening to touch him sexually shuts him down. Anything sexual seems almost painful to him. But he still doesn't break. Nothing in my training prepared me for a guy like this. This whole conspiracy of his. He claims he has proof and the government knows it. He wants them to pay. He swears he won't stop until he gets justice for someone named Alison Winger. That's why he says they won't let him talk to a lawyer. He claims it's the only reason he's still alive—because if anything happens to him, this proof of his is going straight to that Politico reporter who's always on TV. The pretty one. Maggie something."

"Not my department. But if he had this so-called proof, don't you think we would have found it by now? We've left no stone unturned," Liz said. That part was true. Greta had tracked down Cecil Baxter, who confirmed that he'd supplied Vicker with an eyewitness account, compiled by Jordanian intelligence from interviews with Syrian and Jordanian soldiers, tying Don and Greta to the desert heist. They'd searched for it madly. "We know what the truth is. He just has to accept that. It may not set him free, but it might earn him a few privileges. Just stay with it, he can't hold out forever."

"I'm so relieved to hear you say that. I was worried I was messing this whole thing up."

"He's had no contact with anyone since I was here last month, right? Let's see if a little alone time has brought him any closer to reality."

"Sure, no prob," said Ginny, turning to Private First Class Sam Paxton, the soldier on guard duty. "Sammy, take 807 to Room 2, please."

A few minutes later, in a room down the hall, Liz watched through another two-way mirror as two guards undid the straitjacket and clipped Vicker's hands and feet to bolts set into the floor and the table. A gray stubble had grown back on his shaved head and hollow cheeks, he was emaciated. Ginny walked into the room and, from behind Vicker, she gently rubbed his head. He flinched.

"How goes it, Elias?"

Vicker tried to shake her hand off, reacting as if he had been hit.

"I need my pillow," he said.

"Your pillow is fine, Elias. If you help me out, I might even be able to find you a blanket."

"My pillow. *My pillow!*" he shouted.

Ginny reached down and took a firm grip on his crotch.

"No, no, no, no, no. Stop."

She took her hand away.

"Let's pick up where we left off yesterday," Ginny said. "That meeting in Saint Barts you were telling me about last time. I've read through all your files. I know how you spent every day for the past year. It never happened. You never went to Saint Barts. There weren't any Russians. There weren't any fancy billionaire Swedish ladies in wheelchairs."

Vicker looked up at her. Despite his unshaven pallor, his eyes came alive and a sly smile lit up his face.

"Let's make a deal, Miss . . . I don't know your name."

"Elias, if you want your pillow, you've got to start being more helpful. I might even be able to find your Heathkit radio . . . and a Mets game."

Vicker's eyes widened. "Miss . . . I can make you rich. What would it take to change your life? A million dollars? Five million? Ten million? You help me. I'll help you." He looked down at his hands. "Could I see my radio?"

Ginny pulled out her phone and showed him a picture. "I don't understand what the big deal is about this radio, but if you behave, I'll let you have it."

The irony, of course, was that for all the money and manpower Dr. Elizabeth Leonard and her team of postdocs and behavioral specialists had burned through collecting enough data about Elias Vicker's psyche to model it in three dimensions, they'd never bothered to spot the one human connection in Vicker's life, his friendship with Vinnie Pantangelo. Anyone who met Vinnie naturally assumed that the slightly dim, kindly barber had a job at Industrial Strategies only because Vicker felt an obligation to support the neighborhood halfwit who grew up down the street from him. Some even saw Vinnie as proof that Vicker had at least one redeeming quality. But if Elizabeth had clued in on Vinnie, she might have better understood the fear and shame of a man plagued by profound deficits of impulse control. Vicker had stolen the radio from Vinnie, and Vinnie had simply said, "If you want it that bad, you can have it." That was the only time anyone had ever forgiven Elias Vicker. For anything. Vinnie had been scorched by the flame of Vicker's raging appetites and hadn't run away. Vicker trusted no one. But he trusted Vinnie. And now, when the time was right, Vinnie would save him.

"It's almost impressive, isn't it?" said Liz from the other side of the glass. "He still thinks he holds all the cards."

PFC Paxton, sitting next to her, nodded.

"You don't think that stuff about Senator Corn is true, do you? I'd sure be disappointed if it was. He's the guy—"

Liz, impatient, cut him off.

"Soldier, let's stay focused here. This is what he does. If you let this guy get under your skin, he'll eat you alive."

Back in the room, Ginny stared at Vicker expressionlessly and stood up as if to leave, but then took a step toward him and cuffed him on the head.

"Let's hit the reset button here, Elias. If you tell me what I need to know, I could be your best friend."

"What you don't understand, my dear, is that I have never had a friend. Why would I start now? I don't believe in friends. I believe in people whose interests align."

"Elias, I am just trying to show you a way to get out of this box."

He slammed his hand on the table. His face flushed red.

"Shut up, you stupid bitch. Keep your tits to yourself, and listen to me. If you weren't such an idiot, you'd realize that I have much more to offer you than you have to offer me."

"For the sake of argument, I'm going to let you talk." She stood up and leaned in close to him. "But if you start spouting nonsense," she said, cupping her breasts, "I'm going to have to take these out again."

Ginny stroked his arm, causing Vicker to stiffen. But he proceeded with his story.

"The whole truth . . . It all began at my annual spring bash—I call it the Fire Rites of Beltane. Legendary. That's the night when I get all the people I need to do things for me drunk and laid. I was minding my own business when this impudent Swede in a twenty-thousand-dollar suit tells me I need to come with him, like, right then and there . . ."

On the other side of the two-way mirror, a look of irritation flashed across Elizabeth's face.

"Turn off the video recorder, right now," she said, turning to PFC Paxton. Then she flicked on the button connecting her to Ginny's headset.

"I'm pulling the plug. We'll try again next month. I can't fucking believe I'm going to have to come back down here again."

Moments later, Ginny came back into the observation room.

"How'd I do? I felt like I was getting somewhere."

"We're never going to get anything useful out of him. Just keep showing him the picture of that dumb Heathkit radio from time to time. See if that softens him up. Seems to be all he really cares about. I'm going to recommend that he's not mentally fit to stand trial."

Liz watched Vicker for another few seconds while the guards retied the straitjacket. As they prepared to slip the hood over his head, he turned to the window and, unmistakably, blew her a kiss.

Epilogue

They'd just hit cruising altitude in the 747, en route from Jackson Hole to Jacksonville, where, the next evening, Ben would accept the Republican nomination. The seat belt sign was off. Ben, tired and a little distracted, stared at his phone.

"Pete, you have to talk to the messaging staff. This action hero president business is going too far. It's embarrassing."

Pete shook his head. "Ben, no one told you to pull out a gun in the middle of Manhattan and shoot terrorists with the paparazzi watching. Besides, look at those small donor numbers. They keep going up."

"I thought that was your funny stuff?"

"We might have primed the pump a little. But a lot of what's happening now is real."

Ben had more or less waltzed to the nomination. He reached beyond his party's base to the millions of voters in the middle, tired of the same stale choices and pissing matches. He listened to everyone. He appealed to the nation's sense of purpose. Every idea was a moonshot: He wanted to reinvigorate democracy by increasing the size of the House and Senate tenfold, making it nearly impossible for special interests to control Congress. He wanted to strip the military down to its core, abandon its outmoded doctrines, and rebuild it as a unified force against a new array of threats—not just military but financial, cyber, and climate. He wanted to cut corporate subsidies across the board, and turn the federal bureaucracy into a true meritocracy, creating a culture of excellence, not tenure, by annually sloughing off its lowest performing workers—like Goldman Sachs and Netflix did. On immigration he wanted to expand skills-based visas, tighten borders, and deport new illegals while offering broad amnesties for those already in. He thought Congress wouldn't solve healthcare until all elected representatives and senior government employees were forced to go on Medicare. On any given night, both Rachel Maddow and Sean Hannity might attack him viciously. Those were Ben's favorite evenings.

America was swooning. The proof was in the fundraising numbers, more than $700 million collected in amounts of $200 or less—three million separate donations. For the record, Pete credited his algorithms. Awestruck reporters wrote about the campaign's wizardlike ability to target potential voters and predict their behavior. But even if Ben Corn was the man America was looking for, they weren't taking any chances. Greta had been mainlining their profits, through Volk, to a maze of banks and shell companies managed from a windowless concrete building in Bangalore where eighty Russian and Indian computer scientists sliced and diced those cash flows until they emerged as countless $199 donations to bencornforpresident.com, untraceable and just below the Federal Election Commission's $200 reporting threshold. Tens of millions more flowed into the coffers of political action committees, and more still was spent on Volk's surreptitious program of active measures, to both influence voters and to sow dissension. Ben didn't need—or want—to know the details.

"Okay, what's next?"

"Elizabeth Leonard," Tommy said.

Ben perked up a little. "Is Vicker still making threats about the Baxter envelope?"

"About a hundred and fifty times a day, usually in a dull monotone," Tommy said. "We're just going to wait it out until Elizabeth can make the case that he's lost his mind. Then we make him go away, indefinitely, without trial. Not a lot of sympathy for the man these days."

Ben rubbed his eyes. "I'm spent." He leaned out the conference room door. "Peggy, you guys done?"

Peggy Corn came in from the next cabin with her new best friend, Lorenzo Gonzaga. They had been working out the seating for a dinner she and Frank Conway were hosting for Ben that evening. The fact that Peggy had taken a bullet that had been meant for him brought out the noblest side of Gonzaga's character. Surgeons had to reconstruct Peggy's shattered arm. The rehab was excruciating, and Gonzaga spent days with her in the hospital, sometimes just holding her hand, helping her weather the pain. He listened to her, doted on her, kept her up to date on court gossip, and, if Peggy had strong views on something, he made certain that Ben knew. The courtier: shuttling between the king and queen, trusted by both, where Gonzaga did his best work.

"When we got on the plane tonight, we discovered that Tommy left one of these on every seat." Ben held up a memo, three pages of bullet points labeled "agenda for flight." He flipped to the last page. "Heading three, item eleven: 'cocktail, time permitting.' I'm not president yet. You guys don't have to listen to me. But I'm going straight to item eleven. Pete, where's that bottle?"

Pete fetched a bottle of Hillrock bourbon and handed glasses around.

"Just take a moment here." He stood up and put his arm around his wife. "We're doing something no one's ever done before. We've taken some hits. Huge hits. What we lost. What we almost lost." He squeezed Peggy and stopped for a moment to regain his composure. "Don Carter was the eyes in the back of my head. Half the time I wanted to slug him. But I trusted him, not just with my life, but with all of your lives too. And Peggy, love. All you did was love me. It's all you ever did."

Peggy had become the most talked about woman in America. In just a few months, her sling had become as iconic as MAGA hats had been way back in 2016. Millions of people, across the political spectrum, wore their arms in slings, in any color as long as it contained no slogan, partly in solidarity with Peggy Corn, but more to say "enough" to the real and rhetorical violence that was driving the country toward an armed standoff with itself. A recent article in the *New Yorker* had detailed the extraordinary life of Don Carter, the now great American hero who had prevented two other PATH tunnels from exploding—while being the target of the most intensive manhunt in history. There were already three competing Don Carter movies and TV shows in development; a TikTok influencer gained millions of followers after he had Don Carter's face tattooed on his own. Even though the honor guard burial at Arlington National Cemetery was simulcast on every news channel and republished endlessly on YouTube, sightings of Don Carter were reported almost daily on Twitter and Instagram: a man with a beard and shaggy hair popping up in an astonishing number of places.

Ben, making a conscious effort, settled himself.

"A reporter asked me the other day if I'm out for revenge. I said no. I mean it. I'm mad. But not vengeful. But I'm more determined than ever. One way or another, Fyodor Volk was coming. I'm glad he found us.

"And I'm glad Lorenzo did too," he said as he put his arm around Gonzaga's shoulders. "I would not be here without the five of you. We look out for one another. We listen to one another. If you stop telling me when I'm messing up, you're failing me. You're failing the country . . . I could really use a joint right now."

"Whiskey will have to do—at least until you're elected and can pardon yourself," said Tommy.

"Not so fast." Greta pulled a tin of Copenhagen, Don's favorite dip, from her purse. Inside were half a dozen joints. "I found these when I was going through Don's desk. I think he'd like to know they were being smoked right now. Anyone have a lighter?"

Pete pulled out a well-worn solid gold Dunhill lighter. Everyone looked at him in surprise. "It was Saddam's. Don found it. He gave it to me. And he didn't even like me yet."

Greta took a reefer from the tin, perfectly rolled, like a tiny dirigible.

"*That* is a thing of beauty," Pete said.

"It was one of the things he was proudest of. He said he rolled the best joint in Hermosa Beach, it's how he got in with the surfer crowd." Greta started to weep.

"I so wish he was here." Ben closed his eyes and inhaled.

Tommy raised a glass. "He'd be so proud of you." Pete and Gonzaga did the same.

As the smoke spread into their thoughts, a somber mood fell over them. Chip was in the room too, a ghost in life and death. Chip, always so reserved and inner-directed, had slipped under Tommy's radar. With everyone else, Tommy pushed and pulled, told them how to live their lives. But Chip never showed a rough edge or a loose end. He never seemed to need anything. Perhaps that was what Tommy had missed, a side of privilege that he would never understand.

"Don would hate it here," Greta said. "Imagine if he'd had to hand his gun over to the Secret Service to get on this plane? He'd just as soon give it to a meter reader."

They all laughed, until her smile trailed off into more tears.

Tommy wrapped an arm around her and drew her close.

"You couldn't have saved him. None of us could."

"That's not why I'm crying. I'm crying because I don't know who is going to save us."

ACKNOWLEDGMENTS

It took a village to feed the fantasy that I might have something to say—much less something that anyone else might want to read. But . . . well . . . those villagers made this possible: they gave me the courage to try.

First, foremost, my *very* patient and incredibly supportive wife, Elissa Lipcon Kramer. She was my first reader and has remained my biggest booster, sticking with me through so many months of distraction.

In those early days, my sons David (naming rights for *Undermoney*) and Daniel also encouraged me to persevere, as did many other early readers who took the time to react to my pages, and help keep me on track. Brian Miller, my oldest and best friend from the hedge fund world, thought I was onto something. NG, for her trenchant insights. Scooter Libby, schoolmate and novelist, helped hone the plot and develop the characters. Charles Jaskel, for his close reading—and for sharing his reflections on war. José-Luis Manzano provided inimitable insights into how the world really works. Willem de Vogel gave me the benefit of his astute, relentless focus on the China threat. Jamie Marshall, a talented writer, was there, reading from the very start. Robert Cohen and Rich Sokolow: for their wisdom. My thanks to Rebecca Swanberg, as well, for sharing her thoughts on narration. My friend, the photographer Phil Balshi, very kindly took the photo that graces this book jacket. Alvin Schecter, thank you for turning your eagle eye to these pages.

In particular, I owe a deep debt to two men who have lived at least part of the lives of my military characters. Don Carmel a soldier/scholar in the finest tradition of our military—and an astute observer of risk, and of the world. And Ed Luzine, who has seen the connections between finance and war up close and is one of the best-read men I know.

Then began the daisy chain: villagers speaking to villagers, passing me along, introducing me around, as from house to house.

Knowing nothing about how to move from tatty pages to an editor, an agent, much less a publisher, I called Brandon del Pozo. We met when he commanded my then neighborhood police precinct—the Sixth—in

Greenwich Village. Brandon, who seems to know everyone, introduced me to Lorin Stein, and through Lorin I met Will Dana.

I remember, vividly, sitting on the raised platform at the back of the Gotham Bar & Grill. Will told me that, before he read my pages, he was pretty sure that he'd brush me off, politely. But, that day, he said he'd be willing to edit me. If books have midwives and life coaches, that has been Will. This book would not be what it is without his energy, wisdom, and talent.

Finally, when the pages began to take shape, Will said that he knew someone, a literary agent, who might take a look. I have no illusion that, absent Will making the call, Sloan Harris would *not* have taken a look. That's how I met Sloan Harris, éminence grise at International Creative Management, and not just *any* superagent—but the guy who represented one of the contemporary writers of thrillers I admire most, Jason Matthews. Sloan's editorial advice, fierce advocacy, and constant encouragement are what put everything in motion. Seriously, pinch me.

Under Sloan's guidance, my team got even dreamier. Sloan said there was only one guy to publish this: the guy who had edited Matthews. A subtle man with a wry smile and a dark sense of humor: Colin Harrison. Colin understood what *Undermoney* is about, sometimes better than I did. And he wasn't shy: cut it by 25 percent, said Colin. Cut it hard. Of course, he was right.

By now, it's no longer a village, but a small town. I owe thanks to Chuck Googe and Nicole Albano, of Paul, Weiss, and to Julie Flanagan of ICM. And I offer my humble, ongoing appreciation to the amazing team at Scribner—extraordinarily talented, dedicated, and creative: Nan Graham, Brian Belfiglio, Sarah Goldberg, Roz Lippel, Brianna Yamashita, Ashley Gilliam, Jennifer Weidman, Dan Cuddy, Emily Polson, and Jaya Miceli. Thanks to you all, it has been an amazing journey.

Jay Newman
Vero Beach, Florida

ABOUT THE AUTHOR

Jay Newman has worked in the field of international finance as a trader, investment banker, and investor for forty years. During most of that time, he focused on investments in the defaulted debt of sovereign nations in Latin America, Eastern Europe, Africa, and Asia. *Undermoney* is his first novel.